THE DUSK WATCHMAN

Also by Tom Lloyd

The Stormcaller

Book One of the Twilight Reign

The Twilight Herald

Book Two of the Twilight Reign

The Grave Thief

Book Three of the Twilight Reign

The Ragged Man

Book Four of the Twilight Reign

Lloyd, Tom, 1979-
The dusk watchman /

2012
33305[illegible]536
gi 09/27/13

THE DUSK WATCHMAN

BOOK FIVE OF THE TWILIGHT REIGN

TOM LLOYD

an imprint of Prometheus Books
Amherst, NY

Published 2012 by Pyr®, an imprint of Prometheus Books

The Dusk Watchman. Copyright © 2012 by Tom Lloyd. All rights reserved. No part of this publication may be reproduced, stored in a retrieval system, or transmitted in any form or by any means, digital, electronic, mechanical, photocopying, recording, or otherwise, or conveyed via the Internet or a Web site without prior written permission of the publisher, except in the case of brief quotations embodied in critical articles and reviews.

The right of Tom Lloyd to be identified as the author of this work has been asserted by him in accordance with the UK Copyright, Designs and Patents Act of 1988.

Cover illustration © 2012 Todd Lockwood
Cover design by Grace M. Conti-Zilsberger

Inquiries should be addressed to
Pyr
59 John Glenn Drive
Amherst, New York 14228–2119
VOICE: 716–691–0133, ext. 210
FAX: 716–691–0137
WWW.PYRSF.COM

16 15 14 13 12 5 4 3 2 1

Library of Congress Cataloging-in-Publication Data

Lloyd, Tom, 1979–
The dusk watchman / by Tom Lloyd.
p. cm. — (Twilight reign ; bk. 5)
Originally published: London : Gollancz, an imprint of the Orion Publishing Group, 2012.
ISBN 978–1–61614–630–6 (pbk. : acid free paper)
1. Fantasy fiction. I. Title.

PR6112.L697D87 2012
823'.92—dc23

2012036661

Printed in the United States on acid-free paper

For Ella Louise Wright

DRAMATIS PERSONÆ

Abay, General Hym—general of the Knights of the Temples and member of its ruling council
Aels, Counsel Mirani—Vanach Commissar of the Fourth Enlightenment
Afasin—White-eye general of the Knights of the Temples, ruler of Mustet and member of its ruling council
Alterr—Goddess of the Night Sky and Greater Moon, member of the Upper Circle of the Pantheon
Amah, Suzerain Duril—Deceased Farlan nobleman, died at battle of Chir Plains
Amah, Suzerain Koshir—Farlan nobleman, uncle of Duril Amah
Amavoq—Goddess of the Forest, patron of the Yeetatchen, member of the Upper Circle of the Pantheon
Amber—A Menin major in the Cheme Third Legion
Antern, Count Opess—Narkang nobleman and advisor to King Emin
Anyar, Duke Heyl—ruler of Sautin
Aracnan—Deceased Demi-God, first son of Death
Ardela—Farlan devotee of the Lady, Legana's companion
Arek, General Kontor—Menin general, commander of the Fourth Army
Aryn Bwr—Battle name of the last Elven king, who led their rebellion against the Gods. His true name has been excised from history
Ashain, Coternin—Narkang mage
Azaer—A shadow
Bahl—Deceased Lord of the Farlan; Chosen of Nartis before Lord Isak
Belarannar—Goddess of the Earth, member of the Upper Circle of the Pantheon, once patron of the Vukotic tribe
Bessarei, General Saraventole—General of the Narkang Kingsguard
Beyn, Ignas—Deceased member of the Brotherhood
Bissen—Mage in the employ of Natai Escral, Duchess of Byora
Carasay, Sir Cerse—Colonel of the Tirah Palace Guard Legions
Carel (Carelfolden), Marshal Betyn—Farlan nobleman, mentor, friend and former commander of Lord Isak's Personal Guard
Cedei, Herred—Member of the Brotherhood

Celao, Lord—Litse white-eye, Chosen of Ilit and ruler of the Ismess quarter of the Circle City

Cerrat, Jeco—Legion Chaplain of the Ghosts, raised directly from novitiacy by the posthumous order of Lord Bahl

Certinse, Knight-Cardinal Horel—Commander of the Knights of the Temples, younger brother of Suzerain Tildek, Farlan by birth

Certinse, High Cardinal Varn—Deceased Farlan cleric. Third son of the Tildek Suzerainty, younger brother of Suzerain Tildek, Knight-Cardinal Certinse and Duchess Lomin

Certinse, Duke Karlat—Deceased Farlan nobleman, former ruler of Lomin, nephew of Suzerain Tildek

Cetarn, Shile—Deceased mage from Narkang

Chaist, Duke—Ruler of Embere, Member of the Knights of the Temples

Coran—Deceased white-eye bodyguard of King Emin Thonal of Narkang

Cotterin, Suzerain Piranei—Narkang nobleman

Dacan, Priesan—Vanach Commissar of the Fifth Enlightenment and member of the ruling Sanctum

Daima—A witch of Llehden

Daken, General (the Mad Axe)—White-eye from Canar Fell, a General of the Narkang Army and Marshal of Inchets, aligned to the Litania the Trickster, an Aspect of Larat

Danva, Suzerain Woral—Deceased Farlan nobleman, suzerain-in-regent for his infant nephew

Danva, Suzerain Wattan—Farlan nobleman, son of Woral Danva

Darass, Prefect Shor—Vanach Commissar of the Fifth Enlightenment and, Overseer of Toristern Settlement

Dashain (Dash)—Second-in-command of the Brotherhood

Dass—Carastar mercenary

Dassai, Marshal Canerin—Narkang nobleman and colonel of the Green Scarves

Death—Chief of the Gods and head of the Upper Circle of the Pantheon

Dechem—Chetse champion from the Eastern Desert

Dedessen—A minor daemon

Derager, Gavai—Wife of a Byoran wine merchant, a Farlan agent

Derager, Lell—Wine merchant from Byora and Farlan agent

Derenin, Suzerain—Narkang nobleman, lord of Moorview Castle

Derral, Captain Kinen—Soldier from the Circle City, member of the Knights of the Temples

Dev, General Chate—Chetse general and Commander of the Ten Thousand
Doranei, Ashin—A member of the Brotherhood
Dorom, Colonel—A Menin officer
Ebarn, Fei—A battle-mage from Narkang
Echer, High Cardinal—Deceased Farlan cleric and leader of the cardinal branch of the Cult of Nartis
Ehla—The name Lord Isak is permitted to use for the witch of Llehden
Eleil, Cardinal Luth—Deceased priest of Ilit from Ismess, member of the Knights of the Temples, former head of the Serian in the Circle City, then deputy of the Devout Congress
Endine, Tomal—Narkang mage in the employ of King Emin
Escral, Duchess Natai—Ruler of the Byora quarter of the Circle City
Escral, Duke Ganas—Deceased husband of Natai Escral
Etesia—Goddess of Lust, one of the three linked Goddesses—with Triena, Goddess of Romantic Love, and Kantay, Goddess of Longing—who together cover all the aspects of love
Farlan, Prince Kasi—Farlan prince during the Great War, in whose image white-eyes were created and after whom the lesser moon was named
Farray, Sepesian—Vanach Commissar of the Fourth Enlightenment
Fate—Deceased Goddess of Luck, also known as the Lady, killed by Aracnan
Fernal—a Demi-God living in Llehden, son of Nartis and nominated by Isak to be his successor as Lord of the Farlan
Fershin, Horman—Farlan wagon-driver, father to Lord Isak
Firnin, Camba—Specialist mage from Narkang
Firrin—A member of the Brotherhood
Fordan, Suzerain Leren—Farlan nobleman, died at the Battle of Chir Plains
Fordan, Suzerain Karad—Farlan nobleman, son of Leren Fordan
Forrow, Ame—A member of the Brotherhood and Coran's replacement as King Emin's bodyguard
Frost—Nickname of a Menin nobleman
Fynner, Chaplain—Priest of Nartis from Lomin and chaplain of the Knights of the Temples
Galasara—Elven poet from before the Great War
Garalden, Sergeant—Soldier in charge of a squad in King Emin's Narkang Army.
Garash, High Priest Kel—Priest of Belarannar from Narkang, member of the Knights of the Temples and head of the Devout Congress
Gaur, General—Beastman warrior from the Waste, former commander of the Third Army and most trusted aide of the former Menin lord

Genedel—A dragon

Gesh—Litse white-eye, Chosen of Ilit and Krann to Lord Celao, First Guardian of the Library of Seasons

Gittin, Colonel—Officer of the Knights of the Temples from Mustet

Gort, General Jebehl—Deceased general of the Knights of the Temples and member of its ruling council

Govin, Keyt—Menin mage, adept of Larat and part of Larim's coterie

Grast, Deverk—Infamous former Lord of the Menin

Grisat—Mercenary-turned-penitent of Ushull in the Circle City

Haysh (The Steel Dancer)—Aspect of Karkarn, one of several Aspects linked to a specific style of fighting taught in training temples prevalent among the Menin

Hesh, Isalail—Litse boy, son of a carpenter in Byora

Hirta—Female member of the Brotherhood

Holtai, Tasseran—Narkang mage and scryer

Horotain, Priesan—Vanach Commissar of the Fifth Enlightenment and member of the Sanctum

Horshen, Commissar—Vanach commissar of the Second Enlightenment

Hulf—Dog belonging to Isak

Ifarana—Goddess of Life and once member of the Upper Circle of the Pantheon until falling at the Last Battle

Ileil, Child Soisa—Litse inhabitant of Byora and follower of Ruhen

Ilit—God of the Wind, patron of the Litse tribe and member of the Upper Circle of the Pantheon

Ilumene—A former member of the Brotherhood, now disciple of Azaer

Introl, Tila—Deceased Farlan political advisor to the Lords Isak and Fernal; fiancée of Count Vesna

Isak—~~Deceased~~ white-eye, former Lord of the Farlan, Duke of Tirah and Chosen of Nartis

Istelian, Child—Byoran member of Ruhen's Children

Jachen, (Major Jachen Ansayl)—Commander of Lord Isak's personal guard, former mercenary

Jackdaw (Prior Corci)—Former monk of Vellern

Jailer of the Dark—Dragon that fought the Gods during the Age of Myths and lost. Too powerful for them to completely kill, it was chained to the doorway to Death's throne room on the lower slope of Ghain

Jeil—Farlan ranger assigned to Lord Isak's Personal Guard

Jesters, the—Four brothers, sons of Death, all Demi-Gods and Raylin mercenaries

Kadin, Major Sessero—Officer of the Knights of the Temples

Kantay—Goddess of Longing, one of the linked Goddesses—with Etesia, Goddess of Lust and Triena, Goddess of Romantic Love—who together cover all the aspects of love, sometimes referred to as Queen of the Unrequited

Kao—Berserker Aspect of Karkarn

Karkarn—God of War, patron of the Menin tribe and member of the Upper Circle of the Pantheon

Kayel, Sergeant Hener—The alias used by Ilumene in the Circle City

Kervar, Quartermaster-General Pelay—Farlan Quartermaster-General of the Farlan Army

Kestis, Commissar—Vanach Commissar of the Third Enlightenment

Kirl, Horsemistress Lay—Deceased Menin auxiliary, attached to the Cheme Third Legion

Kitar—Goddess of Harvest and Fertility, member of the Upper Circle of the Pantheon

Kosotern, Captain—Member of the Knights of the Temples from Mustet

Koteer—Demi-God and eldest brother of the Jesters, a son of Death

Lahk, General—Farlan white-eye, commander of the forces in Tirah and a marshal of the Tirah-Tebran border district

Larassa—Deceased Farlan caravan driver, mother of Isak Stormcaller

Larat—God of Magic & Manipulation, member of the Upper Circle of the Pantheon

Larim, Lord Shotein—Menin white-eye mage, Lord of the Hidden Tower and Chosen of Larat

Legana—Farlan Mortal-Aspect of the Lady, formerly a devotee and former agent of Chief Steward Lesarl

Lehm, Suzerain Preter—Farlan nobleman

Lesarl, Chief Steward Fordan—Principal advisor to the Lord of the Farlan

Leshi—Farlan Ascetite soldier, attached to Lord Isak's Personal Guard

Litania (the Trickster)—Aspect of Larat

Lomin, Duchess Feya—Deceased Farlan noblewoman, wife of Koren Lomin, mother to Duke Karlat Certinse, sister to Cardinal Certinse, Knight-Cardinal Certinse and Suzerain Tildek

Lomin, Duke Koren—Deceased Farlan nobleman and former ruler of Lomin

Lomin, Duke Belir Ankremer—Farlan nobleman and ruler of Lomin, bastard of the previous duke

Lopir, General—Narkang general

Luerce—Byoran, first among Ruhen's Children

Macove, Count Perel—Farlan nobleman and member of the Brethren of the Sacred Teachings

Malich, Cheliss—Deceased mage from Embere who led the expedition to Castle Keriabral, father of Cordein Malich and tutor to Morghien

Malich, Cordein—Deceased necromancer from Embere

Maram Boatman—The mysterious entity that patrols the River Maram between Ghain and the home of daemons, Ghenna

Marn (ab Codor ab Veir)—A Harlequin

Mekir, Count Terman—Farlan nobleman from Lomin

Menax, Sergeant—Menin sergeant commanding Amber's guards

Mihn (ab Netren ab Felith)—Failed Harlequin, now Lord Isak's bodyguard and dubbed "The Grave Thief" by the witch of Llehden

Morghien—A drifter of Embere descent, known as the man of many spirits

Nai—Former acolyte to the deceased necromancer Isherin Purn

Nartis—God of the Night, Storms and Hunters. Patron of the Farlan tribe and member of the Upper Circle of the Pantheon

Nostil, Prince Velere—Aryn Bwr's heir, first owner of the Skull of Ruling, assassinated during the Great War

Nyphal—Goddess of Travellers

Osir, High Priest Beras—High Priest of Death and member of the Ruling Council of the Knights of the Temples

Ozhern—Undead mercenary, leader of the Legion of the Damned

Peness—Mage from the Byora quarter of the Circle City

Perforren, Captain Halier—Farlan officer of the Knights of the Temples, aide to the Knight-Cardinal

Pettir, Swordmaster Korpel—Farlan soldier who succeeded Swordmaster Kerin as Commander of the Swordmasters and Knight-Defender of Tirah

Purn, Isherin—Deceased Menin necromancer, once apprenticed to Cordein Malich

Rojak—Deceased minstrel originally from Embere who died in Scree only to reappear in Venn's shadow, first among Azaer's disciples

Ruhen—The name taken by Azaer as a mortal

Saranay—Agent of Ilumene's and servant of Azaer

Saroc, Suzerain Fir—Farlan nobleman and member of the Brethren of the Sacred Teachings

Saroc, Scion Intonay—Farlan nobleman, teenage heir of Suzerain Saroc

Sebe (Sebetin)—Deceased member of the Brotherhood, also the name Isak uses when in Vanach

Sechach, High Priest Usech—High Priest of Tsatach and member of the Ruling Council of the Knights of the Temples

Seliasei—Minor Aspect of Vasle that now inhabits Morghien

Shanas—Young devotee of the Lady from south of Aroth

Shanatin, Witchfinder Otei—Member of the Knights of the Temples from Akell and servant of Azaer

Shinir—Farlan Ascetite agent attached to Lord Isak's Personal Guard

Shotir—God of Healing and Forgiveness.

Soldier, the—One of the five Aspects of Death known as the Reapers

Sorolis, Priesan Estess—Vanach Commissar of the Fifth Enlightenment, Anointed First of the Sanctum and effective ruler of Vanach

Sourl, Cardinal—Ruler of the Akell quarter of the Circle City and member of Ruling Council the Knights of the Temples

—, Scion Kohrad—Deceased Menin white-eye, son of the former lord

—, Duke—Menin white-eye, former Lord of the Menin

—, Marsay—stillborn younger sister of Major Amber

Tachan, Captain Choes—Member of the Knights of the Temples originally from Lochet

Tebran, Suzerain Kehed—Deceased Farlan nobleman

Tebran, Scion Pannar—Farlan nobleman, son of Kehed Tebran

Thonal, King Emin—King of Narkang and the Three Cities

Thonal, Gennay—Deceased elder sister of King Emin

Thonal, Queen Oterness—Queen of Narkang and the Three Cities

Thonal, Prince Sebetin—Son of King Emin and Queen Oterness

Tillen, Captain—Officer of the Knights of the Temples

Timonas, Sergeant—Witchfinder of the Knights of the Temples from Akell

Tiniq—Farlan ranger and General Lahk's twin brother, member of Lord Isak's personal guard

Torl, Suzerain Karn—Farlan nobleman and member of the Brethren of the Sacred Teachings

Tremal, Harlo—Member of the Brotherhood

Triena—Goddess of Romantic Love and Fidelity, one of the three linked Goddesses—with Etesia, Goddess of Lust and Kantay, Goddess of Longing—who together cover all the aspects of love

Tsatach—God of Fire and the Sun, patron of the Chetse tribe and member of the Upper Circle of the Pantheon

Vasle—God of Rivers and Inland Seas

Veil, Arin—Member of the Brotherhood

Vener, General Telith—Member of the Knights of the Temples and ruler of Raland

Venn (ab Teier ab Pirc)—Former Harlequin, now disciple of Azaer

Verliq, Arasay—Celebrated mage and academic, killed by the last Menin lord

Vesna, Evanelial—Farlan soldier and Mortal-Aspect of Karkarn called the Iron General, once Count of Anvee

Vrerr, Duke Sarole—Ruler of Tor Milist

Vres, Heser—Village headman in Tarafain

Vrest—God of the Beasts and member of the Upper Circle of the Pantheon, formerly an Aspect of Veren before Veren's death

Vrill, Duke Anote—Menin white-eye general

Vukotic, Princess Araia—Second of the Vukotic children, cursed with vampirism after the Last Battle

Vukotic, Price Feneyaz—Third of the Vukotic children, cursed with vampirism after the Last Battle

Vukotic, Prince Koezh—Ruler of the Vukotic tribe, cursed with vampirism after the Last Battle

Vukotic, King Manayaz—Former ruler of the Vukotic tribe and ally of Aryn Bwr who died during the Great War

Vukotic, Prince Vorizh—Fourth of the Vukotic children, cursed with vampirism after the Last Battle and subsequently driven insane

Vukotic, Princess Zhia—Youngest of the Vukotic family, cursed with vampirism after the Last Battle

Wentersorn, Edelay—Mercenary battle-mage from Akell

Wither Queen, the—One of the five Aspects of Death known as the Reapers

Xeliath—Deceased Yeetatchen white-eye intended to be Isak's queen, who had the Skull of Dreams fused to her hand

Yokar, Commissar—Vanach Commissar of the First Enlightenment

Acknowledgments

Screw everyone else, this one was all down to me.

THE LAND
Xomejx
Merlat
Perlir
White Isle
Canar Thrit
Vanach
Tirah
Lomin
Tor Milist
ELVEN WASTE
Scree
Helrect
Mantil
Narkang
Raland
Canar Fell
Aroth
The Circle City
Embere
Tor Salan
Denei
Ter Nol
Castle Keriabral
Mustet
Thotel
Sautin
Vijgen
ELVEN WASTE
Lochet
Mekray
Verech
Cholos
Tserol
TioHe
Lenei
N
DS'05

What Has Gone Before

As the Farlan retreated from the battle of the Byoran Fens, Lord Isak chose to face his proscribed fate and stay to cover their retreat. He died at the hands of the Menin lord, who had been driven half-mad with grief after Isak killed his son, having goaded the Menin lord into sending him directly to Ghenna.

In the wake of Isak's death, the Chief of the Gods, Death himself, incarnates on the battleground to gather those Aspects Isak had inadvertently torn from His control—the five minor Gods known as the Reapers—only to discover one, the Wither Queen, remains beyond His control. After her bargain with Isak, the Wither Queen has become too strong to be recalled. Fulfilling her bargain with Isak, she is far to the north, hunting Elves in the forests beyond Lomin, where she find the Elves are enslaving local spirits there to use as weapons. The Wither Queen subsumes these spirits and uses their power to bolster her strength as she looks to remain a Goddess in her own right, separate from her former master, Death.

In Byora, Doranei mourns his best friend, Sebe, in the company of Zhia Vukotic. Sebe died at the start of the battle as he tried to assassinate Aracnan on a Byoran street. He managed only to wound the Demi-God, but the poison he used is now slowly killing Aracnan.

In Llehden, Mihn, Xeliath and the witch of Llehden set Isak's desperate last plan in motion: Mihn travels into the underworld to attempt to break Isak out of Ghenna. The Chief of the Gods permits him to pass through onto the slopes of Ghain, the great mountain at the heart of which is the Dark Place, the home of daemons. Mihn ascends to the ivory gates of Ghenna, crosses the fiery river Maram and enters the lowest domain of Ghenna, where Isak's dreams have told him the soul of Aryn Bwr, captive in Isak's mind, would end up. He is successful, but for them to escape back to the lands of the living, Xeliath, Isak's love, is forced to fight the Jailer of the Dark, an ancient dragon bound there by the Gods, and is killed in the battle.

Meanwhile in the Circle City, Zhia Vukotic and her brother Koezh take the sword Aenaris to a temporary hiding-place out in the spirit-haunted fens beyond Byora, since the Menin lord disturbed its long-standing rest in the Library of Seasons and woke the maddened dragon they had set there as the sword's guardian. The Menin lord himself, lost in his grief over his dead son, is ignoring the ravages of the enraged dragon, which is laying waste to each quarter of the Circle City. The Duchess of Byora and her ward Ruhen—a young boy who is in fact the vessel Azaer has taken as his mortal form—come to petition him, and only then is the badly injured Major Amber able to succeed in waking his lord from his all-consuming grief. The Menin lord agrees to free his newest subjects from the dragon, and Ruhen uses the opportunity to forge a link between himself and the man grieving for his lost son.

Azaer's disciple within the Harlequin clans realises it's time to lead them south, to add legitimacy to Ruhen's burgeoning power.

In Llehden, Mihn and the witch bury Xeliath and try to coax the traumatised Isak back to his senses. Isak has been left broken and horribly scarred by the tortures inflicted on him in Ghenna; in the days after his escape he is a catatonic wreck.

Elsewhere, in Narkang territory, the Mortal-Aspect Legana has escaped the Circle City in search of King Emin, and she finds him at last as he is gathering an élite strike-team to send to Byora and kill Ruhen. The king believes Ruhen to be a vehicle of Azaer's control over the Duchess of Byora, rather than the mortal form of Azaer he actually is. She and the king come to an agreement: he will provide sanctuary for her and her former sisters, the Daughters of Fate, and in return they will help his over-stretched élite assassinate Harlequins across the Land before Ruhen can twist them all to his service.

In the Circle City, the Menin lord discusses the next step of his plan to ascend to Godhood with General Gaur. They start a programme of murdering priests of Karkarn, and send an Elven assassin to kill Count Vesna, now the Mortal-Aspect of Karkarn, in order to weaken the God of War and ultimately allow the Menin lord to replace him. Once that is in play, the Menin lord very publically kills the dragon plaguing the city as a way to demonstrate his strength to the powerbrokers there. Elsewhere in the Circle City, Luerce—the principal disciple of Ruhen's rabble of followers—meets with Knight-Cardinal Certinse, the leader of the Devoted, to offer them a solution to their crippling problem of a fanatical priesthood taking control of their martial Order.

As the Farlan army retreats home and Count Vesna begins to appreciate the full implications of becoming Karkarn's Mortal-Aspect, he discovers Isak had left orders to make Fernal, a Demi-God and companion of the witch of Llehden, next Lord of the Farlan. Isak's order includes a deal with High Cardinal Certinse, the newly established head of the cults in Tirah, but before Fernal can profit from this collusion the fanatics within the cults have the High Cardinal murdered, forcing Fernal to do a deal with the nobility instead, to shore up his uncertain position and avoid the tribe descending into civil war.

When Count Vesna does get back to Tirah at last, it is to a city almost under siege, as the religious factions are all struggling to control it. His first meeting on his return with Carel, Isak's surrogate father, is fraught, but Vesna begins to realise Isak might have had a plan in dying the way he did; that he might not have thrown his life away as they currently believe.

In Narkang, King Emin is visited by the God Larat, who warns him that the Menin will soon invade and he must not face them in battle, so powerful has the Menin lord now become.

Not far away, in the sanctuary of Llehden, Isak's sanity is slowly returning, helped in part by the gift of a puppy, Hulf, and the witch removing those portions of his memory that are too horrific to remain. However, with the loss of those memories go some remembrances of his life before his imprisonment in Ghenna, including his knowledge of Carel, and the damage this has caused to Isak's mind becomes increasingly clear. Meanwhile Mihn hears the legend of the Ragged Man from a local girl, who presumes Isak is that figure out of folklore.

King Emin's strike-force reaches the Circle City and attacks the Ruby Tower of Byora. Though they fail to find Ruhen, they do manage to kill the failing Demi-God Aracnan. Doranei is then given a journal by his lover, Zhia Vukotic; the prize Azaer's followers were hunting in Scree, for which they sacrificed the Skull of Ruling to possess. The journal belonged to Zhia's mad brother, Vorizh Vukotic, who stole Termin Mystt, Death's own sword, a weapon equalled in power only by Aenaris.

After the attack on the Ruby Tower, the Menin focus entirely on invading Narkang. Following Isak's last decree, his troop of personal guards is sent to King Emin and a few travel on to Llehden, where they discover their lord reborn. King Emin makes his final preparations for invasion with

Legana, while desperately searching for a way to defeat a man born to be invincible in battle. When the Menin do invade, they are savage in their assault. Frustrated by the Narkang armies' refusal to meet them in battle, they decimate the eastern half of the nation, culminating in the wholesale destruction of Aroth, one of the nation's biggest cities.

Azaer's followers, Venn and the spirit of the minstrel Rojak caught in Venn's shadow, make a deal with the Wither Queen for her support. In return, they break the bargain she made with Isak that constricts her. Luerce and a Witchfinder within the Devoted engineer the death of a high-ranking priest who had been containing the worst excesses of the fanatics within the Devoted. As the Devoted suffer increased oppression from their own priests, they start to remember their Order's original doctrine: they were created as an army for a coming saviour. All the while, Walls of Intercession appear across Byora as the desperate and mad begin to see Ruhen as a saviour sent by the Gods in the place of a corrupt priesthood.

In Tirah, while Fernal agrees to break his mutual defence treaties with Narkang in return for the support of the Farlan nobility, Vesna and Tila's wedding day finally comes—but before the ceremony can be completed, the assassin sent by the Menin lord strikes. Vesna survives, but the rest of the wedding party is killed before the assassin dies. In the aftermath he discovers there is a larger plot afoot as priests of Karkarn are also murdered. Now apart from the usual structure of Farlan society, not bound by the agreements made between Fernal and the nobility, he is free to continue the war Isak sacrificed himself for. Grieving deeply, he leaves to aid Narkang.

Isak is now partially recovered, and when he discovers he has the means to defeat the Menin lord, he tells King Emin. He halts the Narkang retreat and together Isak and Emin stand their ground at Moorview Castle. The battle sees terrible losses on both sides, almost shattering the allies, even as Vesna, accompanied by the Palace Guard of Tirah, arrives and forces the Menin lord into desperate actions. The Narkang mage Cetarn sacrifices himself to bait the trap, and Emin's white-eye bodyguard, Coran, dies leading the charge to close it.

Isak summons the Gods of the Upper Circle and compels them to curse the Menin lord and strip his name from history, just as they once did to Aryn Bwr. He is not killed, but entirely crippled. Once divested of his Crystal Skulls, the Menin lord is transported to Llehden to take Isak's place as the Ragged Man, leaving his army in disarray—some to fight to the death, others to flee.

CHAPTER 1

HE FELT IT AS A DISTANT CRY; an eagle's shriek swooping down from the heavens. In his bones he heard it, rumbling up from the dark places underground to shake the very stones of the city. He stared up at the overcast sky, then all around at the courtyard. The veteran soldier found himself suddenly and unaccountably afraid. He reached behind his back and drew one scimitar, but the reassurance of it in his hand was eclipsed by a mounting sense of foreboding.

There was a clatter from the street outside and he struck blindly as he turned, but there was no one behind him. Voices broke through the soft patter of rain on stone, sounding confused and angry, but not like men ready to kill. Then the whispers started, running around the courtyard, and he turned a full circle, his scimitar ready, but saw nothing but empty ground and bare high walls.

The voices in the street grew in number; he heard broken sentences that tailed off into nothing. He felt suddenly weak and though he still circled, his movements were more hesitant as his knees threatened to collapse. The whispers were so close now, in his shadow. Cold fingers probed at the recesses of his mind. Instinctively he shook his head, trying to clear the sensation, but it had no effect.

A moment later the claws came.

He gasped and dropped his sword, clutching his head in both hands as tiny teeth started to tear at his mind. Their chill touch dug deeper and he fell to one knee. For a moment he was paralysed by shock and pain. He didn't notice his own nails tearing into his skin, nor feel the blood running down his fingers. The greater pain was inside his skull: an icy fire that spread through his mind leaving a scorched trail of memories.

Now he screamed. Oblivious to the impact of stone, he toppled over. He convulsed, writhing on the ground as the claws rooted in every forgotten corner, rending with swift, dispassionate precision. Words from his past were ripped away. A memory of his proud parents flashed past his eyes, then their voices were empty sounds. He felt a name torn out and scattered to the winds. Eventually the pain receded, to be replaced then by a numbing cold; one that made him gasp for breath and shake uncontrollably. He lay on the ground, knees drawn up to his chest and arms wrapped around his head. Stars burst across his vision before the cold took him. Darkness wrapped itself around him and he sank willingly into its embrace.

He felt himself shaken awake and rolled onto his back. A hushed voice was speaking urgently above him. It sounded familiar. When he opened his eyes a whip-crack of pain flashed through his head.

The voice spoke again, a word he thought he recognised, but his mind was a mire. He tried to speak, but it came out only as a feeble moan.

"Amber," the voice hissed, "Amber, you must wake up!"

He felt himself pulled into a seating position, but as soon as the pressure lessened he flopped back to the ground. The Land swam and blurred around him as he was hauled up again.

The voice didn't give up. "Listen to me, Amber: you must *listen*."

He was held steady, and now dim shapes slowly started forming before his eyes: a blank courtyard wall and a weathered face with light hair and a smear of mud on one cheek—a man he thought he'd once known.

The man crouched before him, maintaining a firm grip on his arms and staring hard into his eyes. "Amber, I need you on your feet."

He didn't move. He could not fathom the words washing over him, nor command his limbs to move.

In frustration the man shook him like a doll and clouted his boot to try and attract his attention. "On your feet, Amber—if you don't get up now, you're dead."

He looked down at the boot the man had struck, then at the man's own bare feet: they were mismatched. One was normal, the other a squat lump with fat little toes. The sight sparked something in his mind, causing him to flinch even as he said a name: "Nai."

"Yes, that's right," the man said encouragingly. He cast a nervous glance to one side before returning his attention to the stricken man. "Now you, your name is Amber—remember? Say it, say 'Amber.'"

His first attempt came out as garbled nonsense as panic filled his mind. *Name? My name . . .*

His head snapped back as Nai slapped him hard across the face. "Say it, Amber. *Say it.*"

"Ahh— Amber," he gasped as tears spilled from his eyes and without knowing why he started to keen softly until Nai struck him again, then grabbed his head to keep his attention focused.

"There's no time for that. Don't think, just do as I say, soldier! Your name is Amber, do you understand me? Your name is Amber and you need to get on your feet." Without waiting for a response Nai arranged Amber's feet so they were flat on the ground, then stood on them and hauled on the big soldier's arms.

Amber felt himself lurch forward, but he was unable to do anything to help, instead concentrating on the one word he understood, the name he clung to with the desperation of a drowning man. He nearly toppled onto Nai, but the smaller man caught him in time and held him balanced.

"A little help would be useful right about now," Nai muttered as he manoeuvred himself around and underneath Amber's right arm. Before he tried to stand he grabbed Amber's lost scimitar and slid it back into the scabbard on his back, then gave him a pat on the shoulder.

"Now, push upwards," he said. "I can't carry you all the way."

Nai forced himself upright, and Amber felt his legs respond to the movement and straighten. For a moment he was standing tall before he slumped back down onto Nai.

"Good," Nai puffed, "but we'd better try that again. I can't carry you out of the city."

"I— I've lost—"

"You've lost a name, yes, I know," Nai said in a softer tone. "It was stolen from you—it was stolen from us all, but you felt it worse than anyone."

"Wh . . . ?" Amber tailed off, defeated by the effort of thinking as a swirl of unformed questions clouded his mind.

"Now's really not the time for that conversation. Come on, try to take a step forward." He leaned forward, trying to make Amber move his feet and take his own weight. The right drifted a little and caught on the ground until Nai knocked it with his instep and got his boot flat on the ground again. This time Amber moved forward on instinct and the weight across Nai's shoulder's lessened a touch.

"That's good, now one more," he said encouragingly, and the pair began to make painfully slow progress across the courtyard.

Once they reached the gate Nai stopped and looked up at Amber. "You're not strong enough yet, but I need you moving quicker than that or we're both dead." He edged Amber to the wall and leaned him against it to take some of the weight off his shoulders, but a moment later a second voice broke the quiet.

"Hey, who're you?"

Nai turned to see a man with long blond hair standing inside the half-open gate to the courtyard: a Byoran labourer, by the way he was dressed, holding a cudgel in his hands. The man peered forward, his eyes slowly widening as he looked at Amber.

"That's a damned . . ." The man didn't bother finishing his sentence but raised his weapon and headed towards them.

Nai saw a flicker of surprise in the man's face as he advanced with his own empty hands outstretched.

The Byoran got ready to smash Nai in the face with his cudgel, but before he had fully raised his weapon, a flash of light erupted from Nai's palms into the man's face. The smell of scorched flesh filled the air and the man reeled, dropping the cudgel and clapping his hands to his cheeks.

Nai kept moving, drawing a dagger from his belt and punching the tip into the man's stomach, then tilting it upwards and driving it towards his heart. Then he withdrew it and ran the blade across his throat, just to make sure. The Byoran fell without a further sound and lay spasming on the ground.

Nai bent and wiped the blade clean on the man's shirt before he sheathed the weapon and eased the courtyard door shut again. Amber hadn't moved throughout the brief struggle, and when Nai returned to him he didn't seem to have even noticed it. He stood a little taller now, holding one hand on the wall to steady himself, but Nai could see he was still in no condition to walk down the street yet, let alone run.

"Another turn about the grounds then?" He asked as he slipped under Amber's arm and turned the soldier around. He spared a look at the corpse on the ground, a small trail of blood making its way towards the courtyard wall. "Let's just hope you prove useful enough to make this worthwhile."

Struck by a thought, Nai stopped and passed a hand across Amber's face, muttering arcane words under his breath as he did so. After half a minute he stopped. "At least the link's still there," he muttered to himself. "Not sure who will be glad to see a Menin soldier after today, but King Emin might be able to use you to track down his turncoat, Ilumene. It isn't much of a choice, but it's the best one you're likely to get, and a man in my profession could always use a king owing him a favour."

Amber still didn't respond and Nai's expression turned pitying. "Gods, your parents wouldn't have expected this when they named you for your lordly, albeit distant, relation—who could have? That was one of the odder sensations in my life, I think, having a name plucked from my mind—and it didn't even involve necromancy! This life's full of surprises, but let's just be glad no one's used your real name since you joined the army, otherwise I think you'd be on the ground, and undoubtedly crippled."

He paused a moment, wincing, and had to blink away a sudden unpleasant sense of disjointed loss. "How curious: it's uncomfortable to even try and remember—very uncomfortable. Well, no matter; he must be dead by now, and I can think of him as the Menin lord easily enough."

He patted Amber on the shoulder again and directed him back across the courtyard. "And you, my friend; you're still Major Amber, so not much has changed there really—except you're a major in an army currently being obliterated, and you're as fragile as a baby. Just as well I can think of a use for you, and a certain king who might pay rather well for that use."

They started walking, short, shuffling steps away from the courtyard gate. "Don't worry," Nai added with forced brightness, "you can thank me for saving your life later. Once I've sold you to the enemy."

CHAPTER 2

DORANEI AWOKE WITH A WHIMPER from dreams of sapphire eyes. Lost in dark corridors, exhausted and afraid, he'd followed the faint scent of her perfume for an age and more—walking deep in the bowels of some unknown castle, through bloodless corpses and shit while dead Menin soldiers reached at him from the shadows.

Somehow he'd kept himself upright, prising cold grasping fingers from his flesh and beating them away. They'd decayed before his eyes but more rose in their place until his limbs screamed with pain and he could scarcely breathe. When Doranei woke the ache of exertion intensified and he lay there for a long while, barely able to move, every shallow breath feeling like a knife slashing down his ribcage.

"Don't complain! At least you're alive."

With a groan he rolled himself onto one side to face the speaker. Veil sat slumped in an armchair, a handful of other members of the Brotherhood asleep on the ground nearby.

"Did you hear me complain?" Doranei said, wincing as he spoke. He'd survived the battle virtually unscathed, just four or five minor nicks and a whole ton of bruises.

"You were about to." There was no humour in Veil's voice, no space for anything more than weariness. He wore a fresh shirt and a blanket wrapped around his shoulders, but neither hid the bandage encasing the stump where his hand had once been.

Thank the Gods it was his left, Doranei thought again, his eyes lingering on the injured limb until Veil tugged the blanket over it. Veil had tied his dark hair neatly back, but like the rest of them he'd had no chance yet to wash out the blood and mud.

"How is it?"

"Hurts like a bastard." Veil tried to smile, or maybe he grimaced, Doranei couldn't tell which. "Hopefully not for much longer. Tremal said he smelled opium in the night—went to steal it for me."

Doranei nodded absently. He struggled to rise, using the wall to steady himself, and stood staring down at his feet until he decided he could trust them. Diffused sunlight shining through a window on the right told him he'd clearly slept long past dawn, however little actual rest he'd managed. His stinking, sweat- and blood-stiffened tunic was still lying on the floor, where he'd dropped it with his armour. He picked it up and inspected the stains. "Heard one o' the king's clerks say it'd be quicker to count the living than the dead." He looked up. "A sour kind of victory, this. I ain't one for praying much, but I'll kiss the feet o' any God can see to it I never witness that again."

"Aye, nor lose so many Brothers again," Veil added. "Ain't many of us left to make good on the bet."

"Bet? Who won?" Doranei shook his head as sadness filled his heart. The Brotherhood would bet on almost anything—it was one way to cope with the strange, dangerous life they led; one way to remember those they lost along the way. After yesterday's slaughter, even a veteran of the Brotherhood found it hard to believe anyone cared to collect on the wager.

"That fucking loud-mouth white-eye," Veil said.

"Isak? He didn't kill—" Doranei scowled as the ache behind his eyes increased. "He didn't kill the Menin lord, whatever we're telling the Land."

"Not Isak, the Mad Axe—that bastard was dragged out o' the north ditch just before sundown, half-dead and brains scrambled but still claiming his win. Turns out he killed the general attacking that flank, Vrill, Duke Anote Vrill."

Doranei sighed and slipped his complaining arms through the sleeves of his tunic. He left the armour on the floor but buckled on his weapons-belt, now holding only the ancient sword he'd taken from Aracnan's corpse. Then he stood still for a moment, letting Veil's words filter into his exhausted mind. "Wonderful," he said finally, stirring himself to hunt through his pack for the cigars he thought he'd left there. "So now I get to live the rest o' my life with some fucking white-eye's name tattooed on my arse."

He lit one from the coals and headed outside.

He squinted at the weak sun as he gingerly wove a path through the makeshift camp in the grounds of Moorview Castle. He stopped outside the walls on the slope that led down to the moor, brought up short by the chaos of the previous day.

There were three great pits, one still being dug. The first was already filled with bodies and wood from the forest and a column of dirty smoke was rising high in the windless sky. Images from the battle flashed before his eyes:

friends falling as the Menin threw themselves forward with frenzied abandon. The Brotherhood had lost half their number, a shocking proportion that was matched or exceeded by at least a dozen legions.

"Brother Doranei." Suzerain Derenin sat on the sloping grass to Doranei's left, his back against the wall of his castle. His right arm was in a sling and he winced as he gestured to the ground beside him with the spherical bottle he held in his left. "Join me."

"Got any food?" Doranei asked as he eased himself down beside the Lord of Moorview. Whatever was in the bottle smelled more potent than wine.

Suzerain Derenin shook his head. "Couldn't stomach it." He was muscular, both bigger and younger than Doranei, his long limbs and broad shoulders well-suited to battle, but he'd still been so exhausted he'd almost crawled out of the fort once the last Menin had fallen.

"Your first real battle, right? You sure can pick 'em."

Doranei received only a grunt in reply, and when he took the bottle from Derenin he saw tears glisten in the man's eyes. "Don't matter who tells you what to expect, nothing prepares a man for what he sees on a battlefield, and that . . ." He tailed off. None of the Narkang men had seen anything like it, experienced or not. Scree had been a place of horror and slaughter, sure enough, but it was the Farlan and Devoted troops who'd seen the worst of it. And they'd got off lightly, he now realised.

There were tens of thousands of men lying dead out there on the moor. Someone had guessed at fifty thousand, but others thought the figure higher. And a great many of those who survived the battle would have died in the night of their wounds. Bodies were lying everywhere, despite the efforts of the gangs working to drag the dead into those great pits. The earth was stained rusty-red, and the stink of death was rising with the clouds of flies.

"Can't get the taste out the back of my mouth," Suzerain Derenin muttered. "No matter what I try to wash it away with."

"Try this." Doranei proffered his cigar. "Covers up most stinks that can be covered."

He watched Derenin puff away at it, grimacing at the unfamiliar taste but drawing all the harder on it for that. "You fought well," Doranei said. "There's not much to feel proud about when you're treading on the faces of the dead and sticky with their blood, but you were a hero yesterday. Never forget that."

"I won't," he murmured. "It's right there with the screams of men I've known my whole life—men who were only in that hellpit because of me."

"I've got no answers for you," Doranei replied wearily. "There's no justice in war, no consolation. My best friend died before the battle of the Byoran Fens—you know why? Because we tossed a coin and he got unlucky. Much as I hate myself for it, that's all there is, and no amount of blame'll change that."

"And life goes on," the nobleman said bitterly, wincing as he shifted slightly. "I've heard men say that half-a-dozen times already this morning."

"It's the only truth we know. You got the luck o' the draw, others didn't. I ain't claiming to have worked this out myself, but all you can do is mourn and keep on living." Doranei paused and looked at the battlefield. When he spoke again it was with a firm nod of the head, as though he was still having to remind himself that what he said was true. "If I meet Sebe on the slopes of Ghain and he asks me how I lived the life won on that toss of a coin, I better have a good answer for him. Hard as it might be, we got to try."

He hauled himself up again and started on down the stepped gardens into the small forest of tents pitched on the moor's edge. To the right was a second, smaller camp where the worst-injured of the prisoners were; anyone able to walk was out on the moor dragging bodies into the pits. The prisoners were a mixed lot, mainly Menin as most of their allies had fled when they felt the Menin lord's name ripped from their minds. Some, unable to escape, had surrendered; only the Menin élite had fought to the death, but it did mean there was no chance of pursuit.

He walked forward, drawn without thinking towards the fort where he'd made his stand at the king's side. He was still not sure how they'd survived that crazed assault. He felt his hands start to shake as he neared it. When he reached the mound where Cetarn had sacrificed himself, his legs gave way and he sank to his knees, feeling the anguish build up inside him, but the tears would not come; no matter how much he craved the release, the outpouring of grief, it wouldn't come.

At a sound behind him Doranei gave a cry of alarm and tried to turn and draw his sword, but his body betrayed him and he staggered sideways, waving the weapon drunkenly until he used it to steady himself on the uneven ground. The group of soldiers behind him were enlisted men, wearing the Narkang legion's uniform.

"My apologies, sir," said the nearest, tugging frantically at his greasy curls of hair, "din't mean to disturb you, sir."

Doranei wavered and his vision blurred for a moment before he was able to pull himself together. "I— Ah, no, it doesn't matter. What do you want?"

The man glanced back at his comrades. The lot of them were caked in mud and blood, and several were very obviously injured. "Well, sir, we was hopin' you'd tell us what happened."

Doranei tried to grin. "We won, didn't you hear? Can't you smell the glory?"

The soldier winced and bobbed his head again. "Aye, sir, we all felt his name taken, but no one knows what happened—some said the Gods themselves must've—"

Doranei stopped him. "Cetarn," he said, "Shile Cetarn, Narkang's greatest mage: you want someone to thank in your prayers, he's the one. Him and Coran, they both sacrificed themselves."

"The king's bodyguard?"

"Aye, him, the one and only, stubborn, stupid, vicious white-eye motherless shit that he was." Doranei felt his lips tremble, but suddenly he couldn't stop talking. "A man with no friends and lots of enemies, who liked his whores bloodied and bruised and never had a good word for any living man. The sort o' fearless bastard you wanted at your side when it got down to the bone, one who never backed down from a fight in his life and enjoyed pain more than any fucker I ever met."

He took a long, shuddering breath and glanced back at the mound of earth where Cetarn had died. The earth was scorched and ripped open by the terrible magic unleashed there, the fury of an earthquake visited upon that small scrap of moorland.

"And Cetarn was the best of men; 'cept for his size he had nothing in common with Coran before this. But neither one hesitated, or took a step back when the time came—they marched into Death's bony arms, glad they were doing their duty and never a backwards glance from either of them."

Doranei turned his back on the soldiers' stunned silence and looked at the killing ground between the fort and the mound. There too the grass was scorched black, the earth furrowed and seamed with white as though burnt to ashes. Crows and ravens hopped across the brutalised ground, their calls cruel and callous to Doranei's ears. The faint smell of smoke carried on the wind and for a moment he felt his soul tug free to drift on the breeze with the voices of the dead and carrion birds.

There were still many hundreds of bodies there on the killing ground, still lying where they had fallen. Not all could be identified, not even from one side or another, but there were enough green and gold Kingsguard uniforms to show Doranei where Coran had likely fallen. He hadn't seen the body himself, but someone had said it bore terrible injuries—more than would be needed to kill a normal human or most white-eyes.

Stubborn even to death, Doranei thought before muttering a prayer to the dead. *I've no doubt you were a bastard to kill—you'd have had it no other way.*

Out of the corner of his eye he saw a group of people heading his way and his heart sank. Isak and Vesna, with Mihn in close attendance. The broken white-eye was entirely hidden by a long patchwork cloak, as though trying to hide his identity, but it was hard to mistake a shuffling seven-foot monster of a man, no matter how stooped he now was. The harsh voice of a crow swooping above them made Isak look up and follow its movement with wary intensity.

By contrast Vesna, the Mortal-Aspect of Karkarn, looked pristine and regal. His title had been taken from him; Vesna was no longer a nobleman of the Farlan but had been dubbed Iron General by the God of War. Unlike Isak he still looked the part: his clothes were spotless, his hair neat and oiled, even the strange armoured arm Vesna now sported was clean and undamaged.

Doranei sheathed his sword and turned to wait for them as the soldiers fled. He couldn't blame them for being unwilling to loiter when Karkarn's own approached them across a battlefield. Isak's identity remained a secret. Even if his death hadn't been widely reported, the horrific mass of scars on his face and body rendered him unrecognisable to anyone who might have known him.

The King's Man nodded as the group of Farlan reached him, not caring to do more even if they still expected it after giving up their noble titles. Seeing them here and now, he realised it meant as little to both men as it did to him. "Didn't get a chance to thank you yesterday," he said to Vesna.

The handsome Farlan looked startled at the idea. "Because we charged the Menin?"

"Aye, well, some of us appreciated it."

Vesna's face darkened. "Not too many left to do so, by the time we got there. Not sure even our final stand in Scree compared to what I saw there. How many of you survived? Maybe a hundred all told, around the king?"

"Easy to look heroic when there's nowhere to run," Doranei said awkwardly.

"No," Isak interrupted, "it would have been easy to give up—none of you did that."

Doranei scowled at the furrowed ground at his feet. "Yeah, well, sure I'll find a knighthood in my morning porridge. What're you doing out here?"

"Walking."

Doranei cocked his head and looked inside the drooping hood Isak wore.

The dead man's face was twisted strangely, but whether he was trying to make a joke Doranei couldn't tell. Isak's expressions were forever ambiguous now: the daemons of Ghenna had seen to that.

But there was something different about the young white-eye. Though permanently stooped, thanks to the abuse he'd received in Ghenna, Isak definitely stood a fraction taller today; it made Doranei think a weight had been lifted from those scarred shoulders. He had been born to be the Menin lord's adversary, in more forms than one, so Isak could truly feel his purpose in life had been fulfilled.

"Just out for a walk? Picked a funny spot for it."

"As have you. Maybe we're doing the same thing, though: remembering the dead."

"Lost many friends yesterday, did you?"

Isak's head bowed for a moment, then tilted towards Vesna. "Some. Others I just heard about."

Doranei hesitated. Just before he'd crashed out yesterday, someone had mentioned an assassination attempt on Vesna, one that had left Lady Tila dead—on her wedding day. It hadn't surprised him at the time, not after the horrors he'd just witnessed, but now it seemed sick and unreal—that beautiful young woman no different to the brutalised corpses all around him. He shook his head as if to clear the image from his thoughts.

"What now for you?" he asked.

"Now? Now we've a war to win." Vesna's black-iron fingers flexed disconcertingly. "The worst may be yet to come."

"You make it sound like all this was nothing!"

Mihn stepped around Isak and placed a hand on Doranei's shoulder. "This was far from nothing, my friend. The man created by the Gods to defeat Aryn Bwr was beaten, and that in itself will be remembered as one of the great feats in history. But your war was not always with the Menin lord."

"Azaer," Doranei said, finally getting it. "Do you have a plan?"

Mihn gave an apologetic little smile. "Nothing quite so simple, I'm afraid, but there is much work to be done."

"Where do we start?"

"The king wants you to interrogate the Byoran prisoners—there are men of the Ruby Tower Guard claiming they have information for the king, if he is the one who sent men to assault the tower."

"I better get to it then. There aren't many of the Brotherhood left who know what questions to ask."

Mihn stopped him as he turned to leave. "Afterwards, come and find us at the Ghosts' camp," he said, pointing to where the Farlan tents stood in neat blocks. "We have something else you might be interested in, you and all your Brothers. If you would gather them and anyone else you consider bound to the Brotherhood?"

"Why?"

The small man glanced back at Isak. "I do not want to promise too much in advance, but there is a common saying: 'a burden shared is a burden halved.'" He scratched at his chest where the witch of Llehden had burned the heart rune into his flesh. "I am hoping the same does not go for gifts."

There were three of them, two captains and a major, filthy and bedraggled in their torn uniforms. Buttons and braiding had been ripped away, most likely removed when they were disarmed, and they'd been relieved of any money they might have had. One of the captains was in a bad way, his right arm as poorly splinted as the gash in his shoulder was stitched.

Only one looked up when Doranei approached, but it was enough for him to see the misery of a cowed dog.

Ignoring the Ruby Tower Guardsmen surrounding him, Doranei advanced on the officers and squatted beside them. There were two Brothers behind him, Cedei and Firrin; neither were close enough to save him if the mob went for him, but they all knew the remaining regiments would be butchered if they did any such thing.

"The Menin's dead," he started in a quiet voice."You came here as allies of his, against your will, I'm sure."

The battered captain nodded briefly, and returned his gaze to the ground.

"So we don't care much about you right now—no one wants the effort of imprisoning or slaughtering you all—but you're soldiers and you know how easily that can turn. You all killed a lot of our countrymen getting here." He waited a few moments to give them time to think about that, then continued, "So this is me asking nicely so I don't have to bother showing you how nasty I can get: tell me everything you know about Sergeant Kayel and the child, Ruhen."

The captain's fear fell away for a moment. "That scar-handed bastard?

Gladly—the kid too. There' somethin' unnatural about the pair of 'em; the duchess is my liege, but when that Ruhen's around she ain't all there."

Without warning a soldier leaped from the huddled mass, a short knife in his hand. For a moment Doranei didn't react to the sudden movement, his exhausted body failing him, then he saw the knife-tip pass him by and something went *click* in his head as he saw the man reaching for the captain. Doranei launched into the slimmer man and knocked him sideways, then scrabbled to get his fingers around the man's wrist. They crashed together into the injured captain, who cried out as they flattened him.

The Byoran twisted underneath Doranei, trying to kick him off, but the King's Man hooked one leg under him and let his greater size do the work for him. Once he had a good grip on the man's wrist he pushed forward, lying nose-to-nose on top of the attacker while stretching his arm up away from his body. The Byoran wrenched around and managed to turn onto his front, trying to bite Doranei's arm until he smashed an elbow into the back of his head.

The blow seemed to drive the frenzy from the Byoran and gave Doranei time to bend his knife-hand back behind his shoulder. A quick twist and the man's fingers opened, releasing the knife with a yelp that turned into an agonised howl as Doranei increased the pressure and felt the man's shoulder pop out of its socket. That done, he pushed himself upright again, leaving the wailing man on the ground as he drew his black broadsword.

"Anyone else fancy being a martyr to a false god?" he demanded, raising the sword. His ragged voice was thick with hatred and the crowd of soldiers shrank further back, some falling over each other to get away. He saw the fight was gone out of them. Not even the brutal treatment of one of their own could make them raise a hand against him. Doranei turned and found Firrin right behind him, sword drawn, with Cedei two paces behind.

"Take this one—I'm sure the king'll be interested to meet a fanatic," he said, giving the prone Byoran soldier a nudge in the ribs. As Firrin hauled the man up Doranei saw the fear in the captain's eyes. He realised the man was watching his own men, expecting another attack to follow as soon as he was left alone. "You're coming with me," he announced, and grabbed the man's arm, pulling him away until they were clear of the mob. There he released the Byoran officer and gestured for him to keep walking with him as he sheathed his sword again.

"There'll be more of them, waiting for me," the officer whimpered.

"Don't you worry about that. Tell me the truth and if it checks against our intelligence, you won't be going back to them—not until we win this war."

"What? But—? I'd look like a traitor, selling out the whole Circle City!"

"Bit late now," Doranei said, grabbing the man by the arm and stopping him short. "Your only other choice is me beating the fuck out of you 'til you tell me what I want to know. Don't be surprised if I kill you, I ain't in the best o' moods and I can always ask the same of your major afterwards."

The Byoran's head drooped. "What is it you want to know?"

"Like I said: Kayel and the child—how do they act, how do they speak, how old is the child now. And how did you mean 'ain't all there'?'"

"That's it?"

Doranei laughed. "We just battered the best of your army and the Circle City ain't got many special defences to speak of—got any secrets our spies don't already know?"

The Byoran just looked blank at that and Doranei started walking again. "Exactly. Either you're a better liar than I am, or you don't know anything else of use. So tell me about Kayel."

"I don't understand him myself," the Byoran said with a miserable shake of the head. "He's mad, vicious to the bone, that one—"

"I've met the bastard; tell me something I don't know."

"Well that's just it," he captain insisted, "it doesn't make sense—Kayel's not one to take orders; he's not one to take shit or even leave alone anyone who looks at him in a way he doesn't like. But he follows that weird brat's every word like he really is the saviour they're saying."

Doranei stopped short. "Kayel's taking *his* orders? You mean he's taking the duchess' orders when Ruhen's near her?"

"No, not just then; it's whether or not the duchess is around. That's what has half the quarter persuaded Ruhen's everything those white-cloaks, Ruhen's Children, claim he is. He's growing faster than any normal child, could only be by magic, but Kayel don't look ensorcelled. That man'd rather cut out his own eyes than think any man's his better, but he jumps when that shadow-eyed bastard says, just as quick as any of the rest of us."

Doranei gave a cough of surprise which turned into a painful wheeze as the aching muscles in his back reminded him of their presence. "'Shadow-eyed'?"

"Aye, that child's got shadows in his eyes, drifting like clouds on the breeze." The Byoran shivered at the memory.

"Shadows in his eyes," Doranei whispered hoarsely, "and Ilumene's his errand-boy. Fires of Ghenna, the boy's no instrument—"

"Nope," the Byoran agreed, puzzled by the name he didn't know but eager to be helpful, "the little bastard's in charge sure enough, and by now I'd guess half the Circle City's willing to accept him as their saviour."

Doranei had started running blindly until his brain caught up with him and he tried to work out where King Emin would be at this hour. The Byoran captain followed him like a lost puppy until they came upon a nobleman, who wisely decided not to object when Doranei left the Byoran in his charge. He directed the King's Man to where he'd seen the king's party last. Unnoticed by Doranei, more than a few Narkang soldiers had grabbed weapons in his wake, looking in vain for the danger as they followed him, but he jolted to a stop as he passed another Brother, the thief Tremal.

"The king, you seen him?"

Tremal nodded, his mouth full of the honey-cake he'd procured from somewhere. "Heading to the Farlan camp with most o' the remaining Brotherhood—I just been sent to round up the last few."

Doranei had to walk to the Farlan camp. It was on the other side of the battlefield, half a mile away and beyond the long defensive ditch now half-filled with corpses. Long before he got there his body was protesting violently. Tremal and the remaining two members of the Brotherhood caught up, but none of them bothered with questions; they recognised Doranei's expression well enough.

At the Farlan camp it was easy to find King Emin amidst the duller liveries of the Tirah Palace Guard and Suzerain Torl's Dark Monks. Doranei was so focused on the king that he almost barged the suzerain out of the way, checking himself just in time as he glimpsed a hurscal's sword leaving its scabbard. The white-haired Farlan was one of a crowd around a large fire and as he made space for Doranei to pass, the King's Man realised they were all watching a small group sitting inside the circle.

The figure closest was Isak Stormcaller; still clad in his tattered cloak. The white-eye was looking into the flames, paying no regard to those around him. The heat would have been uncomfortable, save, perhaps, for those who'd felt the flames of Ghenna. Close behind him, the Witch of Llehden had one hand tight on the cord around the neck of Hulf, Isak's dog. She was staring at Mihn and the Mortal-Aspect Legana. The witch noted his presence with a flicker of the eyes, but clearly she wouldn't be distracted from whatever she was watching between Legana and Mihn.

He didn't even bother trying to work out what she was seeing around those two; they could have been wearing Harlequin's masks for all he could make out in their faces. Legana had a shawl shading her eyes from the morning sun as usual, while Mihn was shirtless, for reasons Doranei couldn't fathom, with a blanket loosely draped around him to cover the leaf-pattern tattoos running from wrist to shoulder. The pair sat silent and still, as close as young lovers.

"Doranei," the king said from the other side of the fire, "I've not seen you look so glum since you told me you were in love."

The King's Man tried to smile at the gentle needling, but he failed as completely as those around him. Their losses had been too great. Instead he ducked his head in acknowledgement and looked around at their allies to check he could speak freely.

"News, your Majesty," he started, "from the Byoran prisoners."

"Speak it then."

Doranei hesitated, in case he'd misheard or misunderstood, but he knew it wasn't so "You'll want to hear it yourself, but I think we judged it wrong in Byora," he said. "The child, Ruhen, isn't a vessel or tool; he's the one giving orders. Ilumene jumps on his command—the command of a child with shadows in his eyes."

There was a cold silence, every remaining member of the Brotherhood digesting the information as they remembered their failed assault on Byora's Ruby Tower.

"Azaer has taken mortal form," King Emin said at last. "A mortal body, an immortal soul—but why?"

"The greatest magic always involves sacrifice," Isak said abruptly, looking up from the fire at last, "the change from life to death."

"And the potential for catastrophe," the witch added. "Azaer does not intend some basic working of magic, but something to unpick the fabric of the Land so it can weave the tapestry anew. Even the Gods are weakened by grand undertakings; whatever power the shadow can bring to bear, it must risk everything in the act."

She pointed to Isak who flinched slightly at the gesture. "Isak knew he would die at the Menin's hands, their destinies had been entwined long before he was Chosen by Nartis. He would never have managed what he did yesterday without first gambling all he had."

"And now Azaer gambles," Emin finished, an edge of hunger in his voice. "Now the shadow has allowed itself to be vulnerable. If *we* can choose the time of its passing rather than allowing it to do so, we might yet win this war."

"Speaking of gambles," broke in a young devotee of the Lady called Shanas standing nearby, a woman barely old enough to be part of this fight, "Legana says it's time to raise the stakes in Vesna's own effort."

All eyes turned to Shanas, then to Legana who beamed unexpectedly at the assembled men. With a surprised cough Shanas continued, "Ahem, she also wants to say you all look fucking stupid with your mouths open—she's part-Goddess! Are you surprised she can speak into a devotee's mind?"

Emin's laugh broke the hush. "A fair comment. But what's this about Vesna?"

The big Farlan soldier stepped forward. He matched the strangeness of emerald-eyed Legana with a ruby teardrop on his cheek and his left arm permanently encased in black-iron armour.

"I think she's talking about the Ghosts," he explained. "Life back home in Tirah remains fraught, but I knew there was a greater fight coming. Lord Fernal was forced by his nobles to sign a peace treaty with the Menin, so to pursue the war further, the officers of the Ghosts took holy orders so that they would have to be released from their military positions or prosecuted. Following the assassination of Karkarn's priests in the city, presumably to weaken the God's powerbase in advance of a challenge by the Menin lord, the soldiers of the Ghosts were only too willing to join us."

"You have an army of ordained priests?" Emin replied, doing his best not to look surprised. "All dedicated to the God of War?"

"A third of the Ghosts," Vesna said quickly. "The rest are priests of Death or Nartis, so as not to unbalance the Upper Circle of the Pantheon. General Lahk and I reasoned that it would at least buy us time to halt the Menin's plans."

Emin turned back to Legana and Shanas. "So where do you fit in here, Legana? One Mortal-Aspect helping out another?"

"Something like that," Shanas said, looking nervous as she voiced Legana's words. "They are no longer the Palace Guard of Tirah, but they still call themselves Ghosts." The Farlan soldiers in attendance nodded at that and Legana, her green eyes flashing with divine mischief, patted Mihn on the head as though the failed Harlequin was a dog. "A precedent has been set: a man bound to service even as he was imbued with powers."

Legana gestured towards all those present, picking out specific groups in turn while Shanas continued, "Those who live in the shadows. "—Legana jabbed a thumb back at Doranei—"these dark soldiers. "—as Torl's Brethren of the Sacred Teachings were indicated—"these steel-clad ghosts." Legana's gaze fell on Vesna and General Lahk as the leaders of the Palace Guard.

The unnaturally beautiful woman kept her eyes on those two while she jerked the blanket from Mihn's bare shoulders and turned his palms upwards so all present could see the owl tattoos there.

"Those who choose to serve, let them be as ghosts," Shanas repeated for Legana, louder than before. "Let their skin be marked with silence and service. It is time to take this war to the shadow."

King Emin wasted no time. The entire company was ordered to sit, the order rippling back through the ranks outside, and Doranei found a place at his king's side, placing himself between Emin and the white-eye, General Daken. Morghien sat grumbling on Emin's other side, while behind him the ranger Tiniq crouched in the shade of the king's war standard and squinted down at the churned ground below.

Daken's grin was barely visible behind the swelling and split lips, but the man still managed to express his amusement at the whole proceeding. Doranei tried to forget the bet Daken had won against the Brotherhood, instead looking at the assembled soldiers and trying to estimate how many they were.

The Farlan had been least hurt during the battle, arriving late to catch the Menin unawares, but anyone meeting the grief-maddened Menin heavy infantry had taken losses. He guessed one and a half thousand remained in total; the double-legion of the Ghosts wouldn't have been quite at full strength, not after the major engagements of the last year, and some had to have remained to man the walls of Tirah Palace. Veil was nearby, looking exhausted, but in less pain now. He gave his Brother a prod with his boot and was rewarded by an obscene gesture with Veil's remaining hand.

"You two, swap places," said the witch, Ehla, as she assessed the crowd of soldiers. Doranei looked up and realised she was pointing to him and Daken. The white-eye heaved himself up and Doranei reluctantly let him take his place at King Emin's side.

"Want the best up front, eh?" Daken wheezed as he thumped heavily down onto his backside, tipping backwards until Veil shoved him upright again with his boot.

"Not quite—the last thing we need is that bitch on your chest getting involved and marking any more soldiers."

Daken lifted his shirt as best he could, exposing part of his tattoo of Litania the Trickster. For once, the blue lines on his skin were perfectly still. "Don't you worry about that. Like most women lyin' on my chest she's all tired out. She won't be movin' any time soon."

"Perhaps," the witch said dismissively, "but I prefer not to trust her. The power will flow outwards from Mihn. With Doranei as a buffer there she'll not let herself be carried on it into him."

"Why? The boy smells, but so do most've us."

Her eyes narrowed on Doranei. "It's who he smells of Litania will be wary of—yes boy, her. There's a perfume on the wind that isn't coming from the Farlan nobles."

Doranei looked away from them both and the witch moved on, raising her voice so she could be heard by all.

"All of you—put your palm against the chest of the man behind you, over his heart. You must all be linked; you must all choose to give yourself to this service."

Doranei felt Daken's meaty paw thump him on the chest, almost knocking him backwards, and he grabbed it with his left hand and held it over his sternum, where he knew the heart rune had been burned into Mihn's and Isak's flesh. Reaching back he felt Veil push forward against his hand and all around them men and women copied them, or followed the king's example and reached out with both arms.

It took a long while for everyone to link themselves, but the witch—unable to have her own magic turned back on her, Doranei guessed—continued on out through the ranks, neatly picking her way over the outstretched arms towards the back. Finally he saw the witch waving from the far end of the seated soldiers, indicating Legana could start.

As Shanas passed on the message—Legana's eyesight was too poor to see so far in daylight—Daken clicked the fingers of his free hand towards Isak. "Here doggy," he whispered as Legana took her place between Mihn and King Emin.

"What are you doing?" Doranei said as Hulf pricked up his ears and Isak slowly looked over. The young dog was sitting on Isak's feet, watching events suspiciously.

"Come to Uncle Daken," the white-eye called, clicking his fingers again. Eventually Isak focused on the man and stared at the gestures he was making. He watched the man a moment, then removed his hand from around Hulf's shoulder. "That's it, boy, come here," Daken called again.

"Leave the bloody dog alone," Doranei whispered. The palm on his chest briefly became a claw as Daken dug his fingers in to shut Doranei up.

"It's for the best," he said, nodding encouragingly to Isak. "That dog was with him on the battlefield—they might not've been part o' the fighting, but it ain't leaving his side any time soon. You ever seen a dog fight an armed man? It's gonna need all the protection it can get."

From behind him Doranei heard a snort. "Don't be so surprised," Veil said softly, "if a dog can't eat or fight something, it's only got one use for it—remind you of anyone?"

Isak pushed Hulf towards Daken, and at last the dog padded warily over. The white-eye mercenary let Hulf sniff his fingers before he made to stroke him, but once that was done Hulf went easily enough and Daken hooked an arm over the grey-black dog to hug him close.

"Now don't you bite my face, you little bugger," Daken whispered as Legana reached out, a Crystal Skull in each hand. One she pressed against Mihn's chest, the other against King Emin's. After a moment Doranei heard the king gasp and braced himself.

Mihn had told him acquiring the scar had hurt enough to make him pass out. Legana hadn't mentioned anything like that, but the erstwhile Farlan assassin had a strange sense of humour at the best of times. If it wasn't for the fact that she'd grown close to King Emin and he was to be the first recipient of the markings, Doranei thought it an even bet she'd gladly have knocked out more than a thousand men in one go.

Daken's fingers tightened on Doranei's tunic and he pulled it against his chest, a moment later feeling Veil follow suit as best he could. Hulf gave a short bark, more puzzlement than alarm, but Doranei couldn't look to see if Isak had reacted. Instead he closed his eyes and focused on the warm tingle that was building on his chest. His heart began to beat faster as the warmth spread around his chest like a belt, slowly tightening on his ribs.

A furious itch began on his palms and down his arms, the skitter of a thousand tiny spiders on his skin. Carefully he opened his eyes, wincing slightly as the pressure on his chest increased with every second, and turned his free hand over to look at the palm. A white speck of light was dancing madly over his skin, leaving a trail of ink behind it. All around him he heard gasps as others discovered the same sensation, but he only looked up when he heard a gasp of pain from Mihn.

The Crystal Skulls in Legana's hands shone with a fierce, bright white light, and it looked like the shafts of light had impaled Mihn. His arms and head hung limply behind him; his lips were moving, but whatever he was saying Doranei couldn't hear.

Then Mihn's whole body shuddered as though Legana had shaked him like a toy and he moaned, "It is given." His voice was hoarse from the pressure being exerted. Doranei felt a renewed surge of power wrap around his body and Mihn's words echoed through his bones. Then the power increased again and Mihn's words became lost in the storm that filled Doranei's head. "Whatever asked . . . in darkness a path. . . ."

Doranei howled as the pressure abruptly focused into a burning pain, as though Daken's hand was a white-hot brand. Distantly he heard others cry out, and Hulf whimpered, but the sounds were lost amidst the stars of pain bursting before his eyes. Though reeling from the agony, he felt impaled by Daken's hand, nor could he wrench his own hand from Veil's chest.

A cool gust of wind swept across his face, whipped into life by the magic running through his body. It carried the stink of scorched flesh and Doranei realised with a flash of fear that the smell was him. The itch on his hands, feet and arms intensified. Unable to see through the pain he had to picture the tattoos unfolding on his skin, spun like silk and burned onto his body: circles within circles to keep him hidden and silent, leaves of rowan and hazel on his arms to shield him from magic.

With one final surge the searing magic drove deep into his chest, then went racing down his arm and on into Veil. He heard his Brother cry out even as Daken's hand fell away and the pain receded. When the magic was gone and through Veil the pair sagged, flopping sideways and clinging desperately to each other for support.

Doranei gasped for air, his heart racing as fast as it had the previous evening. Almost drunkenly he inspected his arms: there was a perfect replica of Mihn's tattoos, and on his palms too, running unbroken over the various scars he'd acquired over the years in service to his king. The charms of silence and magic to hide him from both men and daemons were now indelibly imbued into his skin.

"Do you reckon—" Daken wheezed from nearby, one arm still around a distraught Hulf, "—do you reckon this means we'll never find Veil's hand out here?"

He gasped for breath and cackled at his own joke while Veil, too drained to do anything more, muttered insults. Doranei forced himself upright and looked around: the magic was still working its way outwards. It resembled a ripple of wind sweeping over a field of wheat as the magic flowed from one man to the next, leaving them toppled and exhausted in its wake.

Legana sank to her knees, spilling the Crystal Skulls on the ground. Mihn and Shanas caught her befoe she fell flat on her face.

"It's done," King Emin groaned, fumbling at his tunic a while before he managed to open it and look at the rune burned into his chest. Doranei did the same. He could just make out the symbol. It was strange to see it there; since the age of sixteen he'd worn the tiny heart rune on his ear, the mark of the Brotherhood, but this enlarged version looked oddly out of place. The skin was red and blistered and painful to the touch, just as any burn would be.

Isak began to laugh, awkwardly at first, as though only slowly remembering exactly how to do it. The big white-eye stood up as Hulf ran to his side and jumped up, his front paws resting on Isak's thigh. Still laughing, Isak ran the fingers of his right hand through the dog's thick fur while with his left he pushed back the hood of his cloak and let the garment fall open.

"Isak?" Mihn said quietly.

The white-eye turned to him with a broad smile that had been entirely absent since even before his death. "Think of it as a tradition," Isak explained, and Mihn gave a cough that was akin to amusement.

Doranei frowned, a shadow of memory stirring. Had he heard something about this, when Mihn first linked himself to Isak? There was something about the connection it made between them—hadn't Mihn, while his scar was still raw and sensitive, been able to feel something of Isak's pain?

"My grave thieves and ghosts," Isak announced to the moor at large, turning as he spoke, "welcome." And before anyone could respond, he jammed his thumbnail hard enough into his own scar to draw blood. All around him men howled, but it only made Isak and Mihn laugh all the harder.

CHAPTER 3

RUHEN STOOD AT THE WINDOW and looked down over Byora. Smoke drifted on the breeze from the armoury where the Menin garrison had been stationed. Even from his high position the boy could sense the activity and turmoil going on below. He could smell the sour tang of fear like a perfume on the wind, but this morning it couldn't stir pleasure in his ancient, immortal soul.

As the shadows of his true self raced over the whites of his eyes, Ruhen let his thoughts slowly settle into order. It had been a shock, to be surprised like that. Such a thing happened only rarely in thousands of years. Even rarer, he had underestimated his enemy. Azaer had always been a being of weakness, avoiding direct conflict and keeping to the dark, lonely places where it had been born.

The King of Narkang possessed a rare mind: still beautifully human, and yet surpassing most Azaer had ever encountered. They had both found the enmity between them, the decades of something approaching intimacy and fascination, had driven them and spurred them to heights they would never have reached alone. Exactly how King Emin had managed this latest feat, this commanding of Gods and crippling of a warrior without equal, Azaer could not guess—but what mattered was the price he had paid.

Was that Emin's desperate last move? If so, he would come to regret it. Whatever strength he might have left, he had only improved Azaer's hand for when the final cards were played.

The door opened behind him, but Ruhen didn't turn. He knew it was Ilumene returning.

"Looks like you were right; ain't a Menin alive left in Byora."

"With so much fear, they needed someone to blame."

Ilumene settled into a chair behind Ruhen and dumped his boots heavily on a delicate table that promptly splintered under the force. "Fucking insects that they are: something surprises or unsettles 'em and all they want is someone to hurt."

As though highlighting his point the big soldier drew a thin dagger from his boot and began to deftly slide it over the scars on his left hand, just breaking the skin enough to make the runic shapes well bloodily up.

"I've sent every man we got onto the streets to break some heads—most of the Byoran Guard are as bewildered as the rest of the quarter, so they're glad to have orders to follow. Means they don't think about having a name stolen out their heads."

"That has always fascinated me," Ruhen said, turning to Ilumene, "the need to be busy, the desperation for purpose. I have done nothing but watch a tomb for decades at a time. Humans would prefer to spend that time in slavery. It is astonishing, the chaos one can cause with just a man seeking a purpose."

Ilumene regarded the little boy, the twitch of a smile at the corners of his mouth. "You saying I should get off my fat arse and get busy?"

Ruhen matched the stare for a while, unblinking, before turning away. "You are a man of action."

"Oh, I don't know, I'm getting the hang of giving orders and watching someone else do the dull bits. I've been busy already—time to watch my geese come home to roost, or some such other stupid rural saying. I'll send a messenger to the Narkang network today; every cell will be active and ready to move in time."

"Venn arrives today."

"And I'm ready for him too," Ilumene said, reaching for his boot again. He drew out a piece of folded paper and raised it, but Ruhen didn't bother to look. "Two lists and instructions simple enough even Jackdaw couldn't screw them up." Ilumene heaved himself up and headed for the door. "I'll go and check in with Luerce, make sure everything is arranged at his end—Knight-Cardinal Certinse is already primed to move. There've already been enough deaths in Akell to change the minds of many."

"Good. Time to put on a show and welcome our players back."

Nai moved slowly down the alley, listening for movement up ahead. Hearing nothing he glanced back at Amber, who stood at the corner, his eyes on the ground, desperately clutching the staff Nai had found him. Nai had changed the colour of their clothes with a simple glamour, but there was no disguising

Amber's height and bulk. Only the listless bewilderment of the population had allowed them to get so far, but he knew they shouldn't attempt to head out of the industrial district of Wheel.

The city walls were intended for defence rather than containment, but once the search for Menin soldiers got organised someone would send out cavalry patrols. The Menin hadn't mistreated the population of Byora, but Nai certainly didn't want to be standing next to a high-ranking officer when they decided what to do with their conquerors.

He beckoned Amber over, but he didn't seem to notice.

"Amber," Nai hissed, "Amber, come here." As always he was careful to use his name as much as possible, the only name the Menin had left now. For his entire career the soldier had answered to "Amber. " rather than his birth-name, and that detail was likely all that had saved Amber's mind.

Nai shook his head in irritation and went to fetch him, pulling him down the alley by the arm until he started following. When they came to a fork, Nai stopped the big man and fumbled in one pocket for a small silver-backed mirror.

"This takes me back," he muttered under his breath as he used the mirror to check around the corner that it was clear. "For an erudite man, I think my former master rather enjoyed running from a mob every few years."

He gave Amber a smile, but it was lost on the man—perhaps just as well since Nai's former master, the necromancer Isherin Purn, hadn't exactly endeared himself to Amber the one time they met.

"Bet you never thought you'd have to rely on my skills at evading a witch-hunt, eh, Amber?"

Satisfied the way was clear, Nai looked to see what buildings were in view. "Right, we're not far from the city wall now. If they intend searching every house they'll start at the wall and head back in, so we'll stay here."

Behind one wall of the alley he heard sounds of activity, a hammer and chisel at work. With luck whoever was in there was alone and there would be no need for spilled blood, but Nai was a necromancer. He didn't see the point in killing without a purpose, but his survival instinct was as strong as any white-eye's. He pushed Amber out of view of the door and reached into his pocket again.

The last time he'd seen Amber, they'd fought in a tavern in Breakale. Since then Nai had been lying low, trying to decide upon his next course of action, but he was never without the few essentials any good necromancer needed to escape self-righteous persecution. He withdrew one of these now and held it lightly between thumb and forefinger, ready for use as he rapped on the door and waited for it to be answered.

With his sometime benefactor, the vampire Zhia Vukotic, off to the West, Nai's thoughts had been turning towards stepping away from the conflict entirely. It wasn't his fight, after all, and he owed no one much, but a necromancer knew the value of earning favour. Some instinct told him Azaer would prefer the term *master* to *benefactor*, and that could prove lethal to a mage of Nai's minor skills, but King Emin was sufficiently amoral to be a good alternative.

The King of Narkang was unburdened by piety and ever the champion of pragmatic business. He would almost certainly be happy to buy Amber, and consequently the magical link he bore to Ilumene, off Nai. He didn't expect much negotiation to be possible, but anything would be better than staying here. He glanced at Amber. The big soldier was near-insensate.

Though they'd parted on bad terms and Amber was a man who lived by the sword, Nai had enough respect for him to think he deserved better than a club to the head or a hangman's noose. He had no idea what sort of life King Emin would offer him, but it couldn't be any worse: they both had to rely on that.

The workshop door jerked open and a slender Litse poked his head out, pushing back long wisps of blond hair as he peered down at Nai.

The necromancer gave him his best smile and raised what he was holding to show the man. It was a peach stone, cleaned and smoothed, with three symbols carved into each side. "I was asked to give you this," he said.

The man looked from the stone to Nai and back, his mouth opening to speak, but confusion made him hesitate and quick as a snake Nai shoved the stone into the man's mouth. The Litse recoiled, closing his mouth reflexively as he did. He took a frightened step back and then stopped, his expression of fright fading into glass-eyed blankness. Without waiting, Nai dragged Amber inside with him, nudging the Litse aside and closing the door behind him.

When a voice quavered, "Who are you?" he turned and saw a young boy frozen in the act of rising, a chisel in his hand as though he was ready to attack Nai. The boy took a second look at Amber and opened his mouth to shout, but Nai already had his knife to the unresisting man's throat.

"Don't scream or I kill him," he commanded, and ushered the man, clearly the boy's father, forward. He moved willingly, staring vacantly ahead at the space between them.

"What have you done to him?" the boy asked quietly, trembling as he spoke.

"I've put a spell on him," Nai admitted. "He's entirely under my control now. If you don't want me to order him to put his head in the fire, you'll not cry out or try to escape, understand?"

"A *spell*?"

The necromancer nodded and lowered his knife, pointedly turning his back on the man. "Go and stand by the door," he ordered. The peach stone was a popular necromancer's tool, but it was only useful for short periods, unless one had an inexhaustible supply of people: the spell would last until the stone was taken out of his mouth, but the victim could neither do it themselves, nor eat or drink with it in.

"What do you want?" The boy was no more than eleven or twelve winters, Nai guessed, old enough to be learn a trade but still just a skinny child when it came to intruders.

"Somewhere to spend the day quietly. We'll leave once nightfall comes."

"He's a Menin." He pointed at Amber.

"One the enemies of his people are keen to capture, so I cannot allow the duchess' men to hang him before then, do you understand?"

The boy nodded and Nai helped Amber into a chair, where the big man slumped wearily down.

"What's your name, boy?"

"Isalail, Isalail Hesh."

"Well Isalail, can you tell me if anyone's likely to come visiting today?" The boy shook his head and Nai looked around the small workshop, then walked over to a doorway in the far wall, watching Isalail out of the corner of his eye as he did so. The boy was staring at his father, clearly unable to understand why he was just standing there rather than grabbing a log and hitting Amber over the head with it.

Then Amber grunted and jerked up in his seat, as though waking from a bad dream. One of his scimitars was out of its scabbard before he was even aware of it, and that action seemed to end any thoughts Isalail might have had of escape.

The door led to a store rather than family quarters. "Your father is safe," Nai said. "Where's your mother?"

"Dead, sir."

"Brothers, sisters?"

"Also dead. It's just me and Da."

"Good." Nai returned and said to the man, "You, tie your son to the chair—not tight enough to hurt him, mind."

The man at once moved to obey, fetching a coil of rope from a nail on the wall while his son shrank back in his seat.

"Don't worry, Isalail," Nai added, "you won't be harmed, but I don't want to have to put the same spell on you. It is not without its risks."

Tears spilled from the boy's face. "You said he was safe!"

"And he is. There is, however, an unfortunate side-effect of the spell—he is perfectly safe until I break it, but afterwards he will be vulnerable to ah . . . outside influences. Before we leave I'll show you what to do, but you will have to make sure you don't leave him alone, or in the dark, until dawn—that's very important."

"Why?" Isalail asked miserably.

"You really don't want to know," Nai said firmly as he watched the father secure the first knot. "Is that too tight? Does it hurt?"

Isalail shook his head and looked away.

"Good. Look at me: we'll get through the day and then we'll be gone, and come the dawn your life will be back to normal." He paused and walked over to Amber. Finding the Menin's purse he pulled out two silver levels and dropped them on the worktable. "Back to normal," Nai repeated, "but best you fetch a priest and pay for an exorcism after, just in case. Now, do you have any food?"

Ardela scratched at her belly for the fiftieth time that day and tried not to swear. The dress was filthy and stank like a cavalryman's crotch, but that was her own fault for getting one so rancid. The fact that it came with fleas was a delight too far, but there was little she could do about it now. She had sat on the fringes of the crowd outside the Ruby Tower for three days, fading into the background alongside a hundred other broken souls in dirty-white capes or scarves. Brutally cropped hair coupled with fading bruises and a haunted look in her eye had been all the explanation she'd needed to be there; folk knew what that indicated in the wake of invasion. They'd seen she belonged with the rest of the broken.

The truth was she'd chopped off her own hair, and for the second, she'd had no trouble talking some off-duty soldier into doing that. Though she had encouraged him to vent his petty frustrations on her, the man had been too practised at beating an unresisting woman for her liking.

No different to dogs, when they're worked up, Ardela thought as she walked through the market in Burn's main square, idly begging for food. *The beating I'd asked for, sure enough, but more fool him for not stopping when I said.*

A woman held out a hunk of bread to her and Ardela accepted it like a votive offering, tears of thanks in her eyes. The woman looked embarrassed at that and gestured for Ardela to move along, but she was far from the only one to have taken pity on Ruhen's Children. They were a symbol now: the woes of Byora given form.

The mood in this quarter of the Circle City was strange, a rare mix of pent-up frustration and ill-defined optimism. The priests had been displaced from their district of Hale, and now the Menin were gone too, murdered or chased away as the priests had been.

In their place stood the white-cloaked followers of the child Ruhen, now divided into three distinct groups: the broken and wretched beggars were Ruhen's legitimacy, the proof that the priests had betrayed the people of Byora and their Gods had spurned them; the soldiers who bolstered the numbers of Byoran and Ruby Tower guards, Ruhen's burgeoning power, and the preachers, who were his voice in the Land.

Ardela tore hungrily at the bread as she made her way back to the highway that ran down one side of the square. It was the main route between the looming dagger-shapes of the district of Eight Towers and the outer wall. She didn't know why they were here yet: Luerce, first among these filthy disciples, had led his ragged flock there early that morning, and she'd known in her bones something significant was coming. As she reached the crowd a collective moan rose up on the air and Ardela turned to see the Duchess of Byora's carriage approaching. She joined the rest of the crowd on their knees, reaching out as though for alms, droning their nonsensical prayer for intercession.

Ardela was furthest from the carriage when it stopped, but then the object of their worship stepped down and advanced towards them, his big bodyguard close behind. Ruhen wore a long white tunic and a single pearl at his throat. He looked to be ten or eleven winters, but Ardela knew from King Emin's intelligence that he was far younger—and yet he surveyed the people of Byora with a king's distant composure rather than a child's curiosity.

Right then Ardela saw why they all believed, or hoped to believe: Ruhen looked both ethereal and immortal, a child apart from the rest of humanity, and he commanded their attention as easily as the grey-skinned Demi-God Koteer, who formed part of his retinue.

Let's see how lasting their belief is, she thought cynically.

As the six- or seven-score beggars started forward towards Ruhen, the child's bodyguard raised a hand before they could reach him and called, "Clear the road!" One hand rested on his sword-hilt. "Make way!"

He wore a Ruby Tower uniform, but to Ardela's practised eye it had been modified for combat, despite the gaudy gold buttons. While he wore a beautifully worked bastard sword on his hip there was another secured on his back, wrapped entirely in cloth.

Instinctively the beggars shrank back and retreated off the road. Ardela pushed her way to the front of the group and sank to her knees, ignoring those who tried to jostle her out of position. Ruhen approached them with a small, indulgent smile that had no place on a child's face. Ardela felt her hand twitch as he came less than a dozen yards from her, but she made no other move. The renegade man of the Brotherhood, Ilumene, was too close for her liking, so she did nothing but mimic the others as they basked in his attention.

Somewhere off to her right she became aware of voices, breaking this moment of calm. Further down the road people on foot were heading towards them. The voices grew in number and volume while she strained to see past those with her at the roadside. Folk started to drift over from the market in the square, obscuring her view further, but Ardela couldn't be seen to be impatient, so instead she watched those around her, the slack-faced addicts and haggard survivors of a region at war.

On the other side of the road was a group of labourers and shopboys. Most were looking down the road at whoever was coming, but a few stared at Ruhen still, and Ardela felt a prickle run down her neck. Once a devotee of the Lady and now confidante of her Mortal-Aspect, Legana, Ardela knew in an instant something was coming, some twist of chance she might yet be able to exploit.

She turned her attention back to the newcomers as folk began to gasp and exclaim, her hand automatically tightening when she saw who was approaching. A group of eighty or ninety people had entered the square and were marching towards Ruhen, not quite in military order, but still in three distinct columns. At their head was a man in black, but the bulk of the rest were far more colourful and instantly recognisable, dressed identically to the man and woman she'd personally murdered in Tirah on Mid-summer's Day.

In a crowd the Harlequins would have looked almost comical, dressed as they were head to foot in diamond-patchwork clothes, but for the blank expressions on their white masks, each with a bloody teardrop under the right eye and slender swords crossed on their backs. They walked with an effortless gait that made their companions look awkward by comparison, but even they had an athletic aspect to them that suggested they were also of the Harlequin clans.

Ardela slowly forced herself to unclench her fist. Here at last was evidence that the murders King Emin had arranged on Mid-summer's Day had not been senseless. It made little difference to the weight on her soul, but any small comfort was not to be rejected.

Ruhen started forward to personally greet the Harlequins' leader, the man in black, who Ardela remembered was named Venn. He dropped to one knee, head bowed low before his master. In the next instant the rest of the Harlequins did the same and a collective gasp ran through the crowd: the Harlequins, who served no master and bowed to no authority bar Lord Death himself knelt to *Ruhen*.

The power of that symbol was clear for all to see. They knelt to a child whose followers preached a new way of worship, free of the burdens and strictures of power-maddened clerics. They made obeisance to the promise of peace in a Land beset by war, and in that moment the watching people of Byora felt the blessing of the Gods upon them all.

"Heretic!" came a sudden cry from across the road, and a man started running towards Ruhen, who had moved ahead of Ilumene and was momentarily out of reach of his bodyguard. A second man started forward in the next instant, a knife in his hand, and two more broke from left and right to cover their fellows. Screams rang out from the beggars and Ardela wasn't alone in starting forward, but before any of them could reach Ruhen Ilumene was there.

Ardela watched Ilumene explode into movement, thin knives appearing in each hand. Unable to get in front of Ruhen in time, he barged forward at the first ambusher and kicked him in the side. The man was knocked sideways by the blow and before he'd hit the ground Ilumene was turning away the second's blade, then in the next instant swinging around to stab him in the kidney. He whipped his other knife up across the man's throat and slashed it open before returning to the first.

Ilumene's kick had knocked the man right over, but he found himself on his hands and knees only a yard or two from where Ruhen stood motionless. He lunged forward at the child, but Ruhen finally moved, stepping neatly away from the reaching weapon and into the protective lee of the Harlequin Venn. Ilumene pounced on the man and stabbed him in the neck, even as the crowd of beggars had started rushing forward, intent on reaching the remaining two attackers following close behind. Ardela's hand was inside her cape, her fingers closing around a dart tucked into the waistband of her dress, before she'd even thought.

She gave a practised flick of the wrist as she passed Ruhen and threw the dart. There wasn't time to watch it strike; her attention was already on the remaining ambushers, but amidst the chaos of voices and running feet she thought she heard a yelp from the boy. Ardela continued on, side by side with a thin man whose arm was covered in weeping sores.

She let him reach the last of the ambushers first. The man did not check his pace as he shrieked with rage and clawed at the man's eyes. The first knife-blow to his stomach he appeared not to notice; the second was hard enough to drive the wind from his lungs, but then Ardela leapt on the ambusher.

With one strong hand she gripped the man's wrist to keep his knife clear as she used her own bodyweight to bear him to the ground. She sank her teeth into his cheek for good measure, biting deep and shaking her head like a terrier, tearing a chunk of flesh from his face. The man shrieked as she pulled back. By now others had arrived and were kicking and stamping at them both in their frenzy. She felt him release his grip on his knife and she deftly scooped it up, and stabbed down furiously.

It was a killing blow, she knew that, but she kept going, artlessly slashing and stabbing until she was dragged off the brutalised corpse. She fell to the ground and let the knife fall from her hand as she looked around. There was fear and anger on the faces of the beggars around her, but more than a few looked back at Ruhen with concern. No one looked at all concerned with Ardela's savage killing of the man and she breathed a sigh of relief. She'd just been quicker than the rest—they would all have done the same for their saviour.

She kept on her knees, fighting the urge to run before her assassination attempt was discovered. No venom was instantaneous, and once he saw the dart Ilumene would be on the lookout. All around them the Harlequins were spreading out, their swords drawn, and the crowd withdrew.

Then Ardela saw Ruhen hold something up to his bodyguard. Ilumene took it and inspected the dart quickly. "Wait," he called angrily, "check them all! One of them has a blowpipe!"

Ardela was careful to look around in bewilderment with the rest of Ruhen's Children as the Harlequins converged upon the crowd. She knew it wouldn't be long until they started to check the beggars too, and in the meantime anything suspicious could mean her death, but the longer the confusion took, the longer the venom would have to work.

After Aracnan's poisoning had been exacerbated by his attempts to heal himself with magic, they would hesitate before running to the nearest mage. Ruhen was a little boy, and ice cobra venom was fast-acting. It could be as little as five minutes before his throat closed up and the little saviour of Byora breathed his last.

A pair of Harlequins started directing the disordered crowd, and at last Ardela stood up and joined them as they began to stumble away from Ruhen. She saw Venn kneel, concern abruptly flourishing on his tattooed face.

Never send a man to do a woman's job, Ardela thought to herself, recalling the Brotherhood's failed assault on the Ruby Tower a few months before.

She watched Ruhen put his hand to his temple and felt a cruel sense of satisfaction rise inside her. The venom was already starting to act. Dizziness was the first sign. She just had to hope that it was also a symptom of sea-diamond venom, the poison that had almost killed Aracnan. If even half of what the Brotherhood said about Illumene was true, he would know all the vicious little details; she didn't need him to realise too soon a mage could be used.

Venn raised a hand towards Ruhen, but Ilumene grabbed it and shook his head. Ardela was too far away to hear their words, but she could imagine the debate easily enough: how long would they have? How long before the venom could not be purged and they would need a healer instead? How lethal was seadiamond venom when amplified by magical energy?

Ardela was fifty yards away when she saw Ilumene come to a decision. He wrenched the wrapped sword from his back and began to unroll it.

What in the name of Death's bony cock is going on there? Ardela started to struggle against the bodies pushing her away, fighting to maintain her view. Another prickle went down her spine, this time one of foreboding. A sixth sense told her the glory of her success was about to be stolen, though she had no idea how Ilumene's spare sword could help.

The last fold of cloth was removed just as a bulky man moved in front of her, shielding her view. Ardela bit back a curse and battered the man aside just in time to see a glitter of light emanate from the wrapped weapon. Ruhen put his hand around the shining sword and cried out in pain, his high voice clear against the scuffle of feet and muttered protests from the crowd. Ardela gasped in astonishment and stopped resisting the press of bodies around her, allowing herself to be carried away by the crowd.

What just happened? What the fuck just happened? she wanted to scream, knowing that if she did her death was assured.

What was that shining sword? How can a sword counteract ice cobra venom, for Fate's sake? What just happened to my victory?

The prickle down her neck became a cold shard of ice.

Ardela took the long route to the Deragers' wine shop, then spent an hour watching the Beristole, the dead-end street where it was located, as well as the surrounding tangle of alleys. A less paranoid agent might have missed the signs, but Ardela had survived this long only by assuming everyone was trying to kill her.

The busy dead-end street was a street market during the day. Normally that meant a dearth of city guardsmen around the Beristole—the merchants had licence to police the area themselves—but not today. *And they're not useless amateurs either*, Ardela noted as she watched a thin prostitute briefly catch the eye of a man at a window over the road. *There are altogether too many innocent little gestures going on in this street—they might still be a bit green and lacking subtlety, but whoever trained them knows what they're about.*

She'd stopped for a hurried scrub in the cracked basin at the inn where she'd left her belongings and a change of clothes. That turned out to be all for the better; if it was her they were looking for and she'd managed to get here first, she'd have not been getting out of the wine shop any time soon.

The prostitute loitered within the shelter of a tavern's side door, keeping a low profile in a dress modest enough not to induce the ire of the local matrons. She could have been a merchant's young wife herself easily enough, but for the symbols of Etesia, Goddess of Lust, incorporated into the posy of flowers on her bodice. At the front window was a barman who was paying too much attention to the mug he was drying, while over the street a pair of drivers lounged on their empty cart rather too obviously to be in the employ of anyone nearby.

Add that to the face at the window, a pair of labourers waiting for work on the corner and complaining about their feet, and a beggar near Ardela whose patter lacked the usual mix of resignation and hope, and she was pretty sure she had marked out each assigned section of the street.

Eight at least and almost certainly more on the Beristole itself. That's a lot of bodies for one foreign agent.

She slipped away from the main highway and into a side street and waited by a street vendor's stall to watch for anyone following. A scarf covered the uneven mess of her scalp, but there was little she could do about the bruising on her face and she saw a spark of something other than pity in his eyes as he turned to her.

"Over from Burn today?" he inquired in a soft accent, looking her up and down as he continued rolling out flatbreads with the ball of one hand. He was more than a head taller than Ardela, and white wispy tufts of beard that made a man of middle years look past his prime.

"You think men round here don't beat their wives?" she murmured softly. She kept her eyes fixed on his cart as she spoke; he was a Litse; he would take her staring him down as more of an insult than her actual words.

The man shrugged and gestured to the small iron stove that comprised a third of his stall. Ardela nodded and he tossed on a handful of thin meat strips, so heavily spiced they were dark red. With a practised hand he kept the strips turning until they were starting to blacken then scooped them all up into a cooked flatbread. She dropped two copper houses into the dish behind his stove and accepted the small parcel of food, using the time to think on her predicament.

So what's suddenly so interesting about the Farlan's agent in Byora? And how was Derager's cover blown in the first place?

She started eating, barely registering the strong flavour of the meat until her stomach reminded how hungry she'd been the last few days.

Well, why did I come here? Because Legana told me King Emin had a communication slate here. She paused mid-mouthful as realisation dawned: *Damn, he must know. The Brotherhood adopted Derager as their agent here and moved the slate to his shop to coordinate their assault on the Ruby Tower. So somehow Ilumene must have found that out. Clearly he's set up a separate intelligence network here—that couldn't have taxed him too greatly, not when he knows the Brotherhood's faces and their methods.*

But this isn't the usual surveillance; they're ready to pinch someone—which means he's willing to risk revealing what he's found out—that taking me is worth the loss. But is it to find out what poison I used, or to prevent King Emin hearing what I saw after?

She finished the flatbread and turned away. She was certain now she'd not been spotted by the watchers, and even more certain she wanted to be clear of them as swiftly as possible.

Time to start the long walk home, Ardela realised, heading for her lodgings to collect her remaining belongings and plan a quiet exit from the Circle City.

Whichever's true, there's a reason I've forced their hand and that's something King Emin'll want to know. Might not be the glorious return I was hoping for, but it'll have to do.

CHAPTER 4

THEY STOPPED ONLY WHEN THE GHOST-HOUR CAME, not speaking except to quarrel and even then fatigue and hunger meant those quickly petered to nothing. General Gaur was the last to dismount. While his men flopped from their saddles and sprawled on the crushed moorland grass, Gaur stared off into the distance. His furred face was matted with blood, his right arm bound in a filthy sling, but he made no sign of noticing his injuries beyond the deeper hurt he bore.

"Gaur?"

There was no response, though a few soldiers glanced up at him nervously. The beastman had already demonstrated the murderous rage within him that day, and none of them believed it had subsided. Gaur had only ever cared for two living beings, Kohrad and— and the lord they could no longer name. The lord who'd been stolen from them by some monstrous magic of King Emin's devising, the lord they would have gladly followed to the ivory gates and beyond. They still could not believe he was gone so entirely.

"Gaur!" The speaker towered over the Menin soldiers who scrambled to clear his path. Even Larim's robes were torn and dirty and marked with blood, his own and that of many others. That the Chosen of Larat had survived at all was a testament to his white-eye heritage as much as magery. Of the troops he'd led to attack the south flank of King Emin's fort, only the Byoran allies at the rear had survived, by abandoning their comrades.

Slowly Gaur turned, aware he was being addressed. "Lord Larim," he said, his heavy tone even more of a growl than usual.

"We've plans to make."

Gaur regarded the Chosen of Larat. "Why?"

"Why? Because our current options are death or slavery, and I would prefer to find another." Larim gestured to the soldiers with them, perhaps two legions' worth, now that their former allies had left and headed back towards their home states. "I suspect most of them would agree with me."

There was no reply; Gaur just stared at Larim with an unreadable expression, his tusked jaw still for once, his face empty of emotion.

"Well? Do you want to live to return home?"

"Home? What home?"

Larim walked closer. "The Ring of Fire is their home, and they look to you to take them there, General."

The white-eye was bald, his smooth face ageless. He wore a brightly coloured patchwork robe of predominantly yellow and blue, within which were set half-a-dozen glowing magical charms. Though young, Larim had the reptilian air about him that all Larat's Chosen seemed to possess: an unblinking dispassion that was far from human.

"Then they will be disappointed," Gaur said. "My plans are only for revenge."

"Revenge?" Larim laughed. "And how do you propose to manage that? There is no revenge to be had here, only more death. Can you not accept that we've lost?"

"I *will* have revenge for my lord's death," Gaur insisted. He looked away, not interested in listening to any more of Larim's scorn, but the white-eye walked around Gaur's horse until he was once more in the general's field of view.

"Gaur, you will only die," Larim said. He cocked his head at the beastman, puzzled by Gaur's blind determination. "Do you think the Gods will care that your lord's faithful hound followed him even unto death? Do you think the families of these men will appreciate this sacrifice?"

Larim shook his head when he received no answer and turned to the broken troops surrounding them. "Soldiers of the Menin, it's time for you to decide! Do you want to live and one day, perhaps, return home, or do you wish to follow General Gaur to a pointless death?"

The faces were all turned towards him, but no one spoke. If that perturbed Larim he didn't show it. "You have the night to make your decision. Helrect is the nearest city we have not waged war upon. You can go there, or head south and attempt to meet up with the Fourth Army, but either way you don't have the numbers to cut a path through. The injured will not make it, but the rest of you can. You may live as mercenaries or die as fools. That is your choice."

"And your choice?" Gaur growled.

Larim turned. "Mine? My choice is to survive, of course, to return to what is now mine in the Menin homeland."

"To run like a coward and abandon us here?"

"You are only looking for death," Larim said with contempt, "and you'll find it without my help. The Ring of Fire is a long way from here, but Govin and I alone can travel faster than any army might." He looked to the side, where his one remaining coterie member stood. The small man with a large head shrank under Gaur's gaze.

"The troops of the Hidden Tower were slaughtered in Thotel; I have no allegiance to these men." Larim opened his mouth to say something more but then he stopped, an expression of surprise appearing on his face.

A moment later his acolyte reacted in the same way, and both men turned to look west over the moor. Those soldiers who followed their gaze saw nothing, just the advancing gloom of dusk as the sun vanished below the eastern horizon for another day.

"It seems you don't need to go looking," Larim muttered, reaching inside his robe for a silver pendant that bore the rune of his God, Larat. "Death has come to find you."

At last Gaur looked, but there remained nothing to see, just his exhausted soldiers trying to summon the energy to make camp for the night. And then there was something else: though indistinct in the waning light he could just make out something moving beyond the disordered clumps of troops.

Shouts of alarm erupted from the nearest soldiers; men scrambled to their feet and drew their weapons even as they retreated. Gaur turned to Larim but the mage clearly wasn't the cause of the disruption: the white-eye appeared apprehensive at whatever was happening out there, and his acolyte, Govin, was clearly terrified.

Gaur mounted again and pulled his axe from his saddle. He urged his horse towards the disruption, ignoring Larim as the mage began to say something in protest. The beastman was too exhausted with grief to feel fear any longer—if this was Death come to claim him, so be it.

Overhead the sky darkened steadily as dusk marched on towards night. Gaur tasted the sharp tang of fear on the wind as his soldiers fell back from whatever it was that had found them. Before long his horse stopped too, tossing its head with anxiety as it smelled something amiss. He spurred the beast hard, but it had no effect, so Gaur dismounted and advanced on foot as Menin soldiers streamed forward and his horse fled.

Some animal sense danced down Gaur's spine, like the raised hackles of a dog faced with the unnatural. He tightened his grip on the axe even as he started to make out the figure waiting for him: standing still with eyes fixed on Gaur as the gloom shimmered and danced on either side of it. Thick plates of chitin armour glowed a whitish-amber in the waning light, broad shoulders tapered into slender arms, each carrying a long javelin.

He walked on and at last the figure moved, advancing towards him with a few swift, delicate steps. He saw it more clearly now, a reddened body with pale limbs—four legs like a spider's, jointed up at the height of its waist, and a segmented thorax twitching behind it like a grossly fat tail. The daemon peered at him with two slanted pairs of eyes formed in an X shape about a slit Gaur guessed was a mouth. Its torso was criss-crossed with burnished gold chains, each bearing shifting, arcane symbols that made Gaur's eyes water to behold.

He came within ten yards of the monster and stopped, spending a long moment observing it before looking to its left and right as the shimmering air started to coalesce into shadows, hinting at fresh horrors arrayed around what the Menin had intended to call their camp. There were dozens of them, no, *scores*—far more, Gaur realised, than even Larim could have called into existence.

"Unsummoned by man, yet here you are incarnate," Gaur called, unafraid.

"The breeze sings a song of pain and fear," the daemon said in a soft, rasping voice. "Drawn to the horrors of your doing we find a Land altered." It gestured expansively, at its comrades and its own body. "The powers are weakened and we come out to drink the fear of mortals." It paused and cocked its head at Gaur. "But not you. Your scent is one of hatred alone. Tell me, little mortal, tell me why this is before my kin come to rend your flesh from your bones."

"My lord is dead. There is nothing within me but a thirst for revenge now." Gaur hefted his axe. "If you want my flesh, try to take it."

The daemon didn't move, but there came a whisper Gaur realised was laughter. "Revenge? How sweet a flavour! Tell me, little mortal, what would you give for your *revenge*?"

Gaur looked back at the broken army behind him, shrouded in the veil of dusk. "All I possess."

The daemon laughed again, quietly joyful at the prospect of more than just mortal flesh now. It raised itself up high and brandished one javelin at the shadows on its right. The shapes drew back a shade while one was dragged forward and slowly coalesced into a grey lizard-like daemon—six-limbed and sinuous, with a frill of barbs to protect its head. The new daemon crawled up to its master, head low to the ground, subservient.

"You have the grave thief's scent still?"

The smaller daemon hissed and clawed furiously at the ground, carving deep furrows in the moorland. "I smell him," it replied, "even among the dead of the battlefield."

The greater daemon stood up on its hind legs and snuffled at the evening air. Gaur could sense its delight, but he remained impassive. Their agenda was their own. He didn't care what that might be, or who this grave thief was. If they could deliver the destruction he wished upon King Emin and the Narkang armies, that would be enough.

"Revenge," the daemon repeated. It shivered with pleasure and edged closer.

CHAPTER 5

IN THE GROUNDS OF MOORVIEW CASTLE every possible lantern and torch had been lit to banish the shadows of evening. Ghosts patrolled the walls, barefoot and silent as they savoured the witch of Llehden's magic upon their bodies. The sky was cloudless and the deepest of blues, punctured by the brightest stars and the lesser moon, Kasi, which lined the stone walls with silver.

"Not a vessel," King Emin whispered to himself. Such was the hush his voice carried to all of the forty or so people there. "Not a tool or lamb for the sacrifice, but shadow incarnate."

"Still a vessel," Isak said, reluctantly looking up from the fire. "Azaer's just a shadow, nothing more."

"So how do you kill a shadow?" Emin asked bitterly. Recalling a conversation he'd had with Legana on the subject, he added, "Preferably by giving it everything it wants, then twisting that against it."

"What sort of a question's that?" Vesna interjected. The Mortal-Aspect flexed his black-iron fingers restlessly and reached for a jug of wine. Just as he touched it he changed his mind and withdrew. "A shadow can't be harder to kill than a God, and we have power enough to do that."

Karkarn's Iron General raised his armour-clad hand to emphasise his point. When he'd tried to return the Skull of Hunting to Isak, the white-eye had shaken his head sadly and pushed the artefact back, pressing it against Vesna's vambrace until it moulded itself around the armour as a clear crystal band. Now, unbidden by its new owner, the band around his wrist shone with an inner light that made the Mortal-Aspect stand out even more amidst his mortal companions.

"Azaer has taken a mortal form," the witch of Llehden said from Isak's side where she sat close with Legana and Mihn, "stolen from its owner while still in the womb, most likely, but that does not make the shadow mortal. More likely it possesses the body in the same way a daemon would, and can give it up with ease."

"So what, then? It's weaker than a God, so how can it be so hard to kill?"

"Not hard to kill," Emin said, "hard to find, hard to get to, hard to pin down. How do you catch a shadow that can fade from sight?" He tossed the remains of his cigar into the fire and reached into his brigandine, from which he extricated a slim grey book bound in tarnished metal. Beside him Doranei watched the book warily, as though expecting it to bite him, while continuing to pour liquor down his throat.

"However," Emin continued, raising the book, "we may not have to. There is a final arbiter that no daemon or shadow could run from, that extends beyond the physical. Kill a boy with Termin Mystt and no soul inside will be able to escape its power."

Vesna regarded him incredulously. "Your recklessness with the balance of the Land astonishes me. Coming from Isak I can understand it; he was born to upset the order of things and he's a headstrong white-eye! But you—don't you know any restraint or caution?"

"Can you think of another solution?"

"Yes! Kill the child and his disciples, set their plans back a decade at least and give ourselves time to prepare properly."

"It is too late for that," Mihn said unexpectedly from Isak's lee. His voice carried a strange authority that stopped the argument dead. He stood and looked around at the tired, surprised faces around him. Mihn was normally like a ghost at Isak's side; silent and observing. It was why the witch of Llehden had tattooed him the way she had, to make greatest use of the man he was. As Emin watched him capture their attention by his stance alone, he reminded himself that Mihn had been trained as a Harlequin; shy and unassuming he might be by nature, but addressing an audience was in his blood.

"The Gods are weakened, the cults undermined. We cannot allow it to continue this way or we serve Azaer's purpose. In Tirah the cults almost sparked civil war. From all directions we hear that priests have been murdered—how many other cities will be like Scree and try to drive out the Gods? Reports from Byora say that is the case there; consider how many prayers the Gods would receive if we let this play out for five years more."

"But to bring into play the Key of Magic too?" Vesna protested. "The weapon eclipses even a Crystal Skull for power—and it isn't just Death's own weapon; it's a part of the Land's very fabric."

He appealed to Isak directly, knowing the decision was ultimately his. "Isak, the part of me that's a God fears Termin Mystt being used by either side in this war—fears it being merely present. It's a fundamental piece of the Land, older than mortal life, old when the Age of Myths was still young!"

Isak shook his head. "That doesn't matter now; we're too far gone down the path. This Land will be remade; it only remains to decide who'll do so and how."

"How could we even use it?" Vesna continued, refusing to give up so easily. "Who could wield it, me? You? No mortal can touch it without having their sanity stripped away."

"No living man," Isak corrected with a mad, crooked smile, "but what about one who is only half-alive?"

"And only half-sane!" Vesna snapped.

His words made Isak smile, and General Daken laughed out loud from the sofa that had been carried out for him. The white-eye's injuries had opened up again under the strain of the ritual, but he had refused to be left inside when there was drinking to be done.

"Half-sane too," Mihn agreed, "but most importantly, carrying the Crystal Skull aligned to Death. We know already they act as buffers for the mind, and of all the Skulls, Ruling should be best able to protect Isak."

"This is all still conjecture surely? Gambles and guesswork with the most powerful object in creation—you're mad! You have no concept of the power you propose to use as a plaything."

"It's educated conjecture," King Emin argued, speaking louder than before. "Shile Cetarn and Tomal Endine working together had few rivals in the West. Their work has surpassed anything I've ever read bar Verliq's own writings. Couple that with the power of the witch of Llehden, perhaps the greatest of her kind alive today, the insight of a demi-God and Isak—a man who's passed through death and was born to be the Gods' own catalyst of change . . ."

Vesna hesitated and looked round at the faces of those who'd clearly been party to the plan's formulation. Morghien, the man of many spirits, was swigging brandy from a bottle he was sharing with Doranei; Legana and Ehla were both as impassive as ever, while Endine himself was still unconscious after his efforts during the battle.

"So what's there to worry about then?" he asked bitterly.

"Catastrophic failure and death," the rather-drunk Doranei supplied helpfully, raising his bottle in toast of the notion. "And half-vampire children, maybe."

Only the men of the Brotherhood and Daken managed to find that funny; to Vesna it was a knife to the gut. He rose to leave, visions of Tila and the life they had planned together filling his mind. Without bothering to bow to the king he headed for the lower gate, suddenly desperate to be outside the confining, crowded walls of Moorview. His chest felt tight and constrained. Just as he passed beyond the lit area of grounds his vision blurred and he stumbled forward on the cut-up ground, barely catching himself in time. When a soldier reached out automatically, the Mortal-Aspect lurched away, unable to bear the touch of another person, even if it meant falling flat on his face.

He walked on and ducked through the sally-port to the grounds beyond. There were Kingsguard camped all around. As he marched on through them towards the lower meadow, planning to cross the ditch to reach the moor proper, he heard a horn sound from one of the pickets. His divine-touched eyes caught movement in the darkness beyond the ditch: not fighting, but confusion of some sort.

At the sounding of the horn, half-a-dozen squads converged on the forward picket, weapons at the ready. Vesna tasted the air and knew in his bones there was no army out there, even as he recalled the king's scryer, Holtai, tell them exactly that earlier. He stopped. No army, but something strange on the wind; something he didn't recognise and muted by the enduring stink of the battlefield, but even for a man aligned to the God of War it overrode the shed blood and spilled bowels.

Vesna advanced towards the disruption, barely aware of the complaining voices coming from the Kingsguard's tents as the horn sounded again. It wasn't an attack alarm so no one raced from their beds, but it signalled that strangers had been sighted, and it was loud and persistent enough to wake the soldiers who'd turned in at sunset. As he got nearer Vesna saw a party of soldiers was advancing towards him, marching up the path to the castle and escorted by squads of Narkang troops. A larger group corralled by the picket out on the moor itself appeared to be doing nothing but waiting, so Vesna returned his attention to the party in front of him.

When they were some twenty yards off he realised with a start they were Menin officers, judging by their size and uniforms; what was more, they were led by a dark-furred figure who was surely no human.

"So General Gaur leads his men back," Vesna mused. "Better than starving on the moor, I suppose."

The elusive scent on the wind grew momentarily stronger and Vesna took a startled step back as the smell of hot, bitter ashes filled his nose before the breeze carried it away. Underlying it all was the stink of rot that came swiftly after any battle in the hot sun, but it was the first aroma that set Vesna's fingers itching for his sword. The divine thread inside him recoiled at it, sensing something evil in the air.

He looked back at the castle. It was still peaceful and quiet. The sounded horn had attracted a few guards to watch from the battlements, but there was no frantic activity.

"You, soldier," Vesna called, pointing at the nearest man to him. "Go to the king, tell him I think there's something strange coming."

The soldier turned and Vesna saw sweeping curves of blue on his cheek, marking him as one of General Daken's troops. Litania the Trickster had marked all the officers of his cavalry strike-force and, according to Daken, the Aspect of Larat would be working her way through the enlisted soon enough. The man was clearly no officer, though he had a fine sword hanging from his belt, a sabre with Menin markings on the scabbard.

"Aye, sir. Strange, sir?"

"Just run, tell them to be on guard."

The cavalryman bobbed his head and sprinted off, his plundered sabre flapping at his heels. Vesna returned his attention to the approaching Menin. General Gaur was accompanied by six men, all officers, though their uniforms were torn and filthy and they walked like men beaten—unlike the beastman, who held himself proudly.

Vesna reminded himself that the heavy infantry had been the élite of the Menin troops; Gaur had been in command of the cavalry or he'd never have escaped the field. The rest might be officers, but they commanded the weakest units in the army.

When they were twenty yards off Vesna put his hand on his pommel and called out to the group and their escort, "That's far enough. Stop there!"

The squads flanking the Menin stopped dead, but when their charges failed to halt they hurried to make up the ground and get in front. Even then, and with spears half-levelled, the troops had difficulty persuading Gaur to stop. The beastman walked right up to the point of one soldier's weapon and in imperfect Farlan called out, "I speak to your king. I offer surrender." Up close the beastman's fur looked lighter, black brushed with white, but not through age; rather, it looked like Arian, the Land's third moon, was shining down on Gaur on Silvernight.

"You can offer it to me instead," Vesna replied in Menin, the dialect coming easily to the Gods-blessed soldier. "Is there a mage among you?"

"You are the Mortal-Aspect?" Gaur said, ignoring the question.

"I am." Vesna took a step forward. "And you are most likely one of those responsible for the death of my bride, so do not test my patience or you'll not live to see the king."

As though to emphasise his point the faint light of the Skull glowed bright as a flicker of anger raced through Vesna's body. His words seemed to terrify the officers behind Gaur, but the beastman regarded him with what appeared to be a complete lack of interest, though it was hard to make out the emotions of a creature he'd never seen before, the thick fur and tusks hiding most expression. The beastman still wore his battle-dress. Blood matted his fur and streaked his breastplate, and the vambrace and gauntlet of his left arm were missing entirely.

"There is no mage among us," Gaur said. "Menin do not send mages to offer surrender."

"But you're not Menin," Vesna said sharply, his hand tightening on his sword. "You're some sort of hybrid race the Menin keep as pets."

He stared straight into Gaur's bronze-speckled eyes, hoping the beastman would rise to the insult, but he didn't appear to notice. His eyes were vacant, as dulled as an addict who'd given up on life.

"My heart is Menin; my master, Lord—" Gaur faltered.

Vesna saw Gaur's eyes flicker, and he felt a similar ache as he also sought the Menin lord's name in his mind, but for Gaur it intensified and became waves of pain. The weight of grief struck with the force of a blow and the beastman shuddered and sagged under it all.

Insults he fails to note, but he still feels, Vesna realised. *His mind is occupied by one thing alone. I could spit on his mother's grave right now and he would hardly care.*

"I am a general of the Menin armies," Gaur said eventually, his rasping voice quieter than before. "I conduct myself accordingly."

"You act as any Menin-trained dog would," Vesna said contemptuously, "the chosen tribe of the War God, who prefer to win victory by trickery, who employ enemies of the Gods to assassinate your rivals. Your conduct might be as expected of a Menin officer, but that means little of value."

Gaur again ignored the barb. "Am I to be prevented from meeting King Emin?" he asked. "Does your king fear to face me?"

"Not my king," Vesna growled, stepping closer, "and I couldn't give a shit what he thinks of you. There's some stink in the air that I don't like. You move another step further without my permission and I'll kill the lot of you where you stand."

While the Menin officers cringed, the beastman looked at Vesna as though he'd not even heard the threat, let alone was unafraid of it. But before he could speak again, a voice called from the direction of the castle, and Mihn appeared, alone, come to investigate anything so strange that a Mortal-Aspect would send a vague warning before meeting it.

Vesna was watching Gaur's eyes and he saw them twitch Mihn's way, just for a moment, but it was enough to alter the beast-man's demeanour completely. Vesna stepped back and looked at Mihn. The small man was carrying his steel-capped staff as always, but he was barefoot, and wearing only a cropped shirt that displayed his tattoos.

"The thief," hissed a voice from behind Gaur.

Vesna felt time slow as the scent of hot ashes filled his nose once more, and at last he recognised it as the memory of a winter's day in Irienn Square in Tirah flashed across his mind: the day of Duke Certinse's trial, and the daemon the duke's mother had released.

"Back to your lord!" Vesna roared, drawing his sword, and his voice spurred Mihn into movement. The dormant spirit of the War God swelled inside the Mortal-Aspect, raising his voice beyond a shout as he called to the whole camp: "To arms!"

A slim shape darted from the shadow of one Menin officer, off to Vesna's left, but he had no time to follow it for two huge fig ures were unfolding from the darkness. The Crystal Skull on his fist blazed with light as he retreated a few steps, but in the next instant four more had appeared: strange, angular bodies erupting from thin air as the officers fell to the floor.

The largest two advanced on Vesna, their crooked jaws hanging open with anticipation. Each bigger than a bear, their hides were covered in twisted overlapping plates of some green-tinted metal. Each forelimb ended in a pair of two-foot-long hooked talons. One dropped to the ground, preparing to spring, even as a dozen more daemons appeared from the shadows surrounding the Menin.

Gaur stepped forward. His eyes had changed, now slanting sharply and entirely bronze in colour. He shook his body and some of his thick fur fell from his body, revealing pale plates of chitin covering his broad shoulders. Gaur—or the daemon that had once been Gaur—moved forward awkwardly, leaning at an unnatural angle to peer at Vesna. His arm reached jerkily behind his back and tugged his axe free, while a javelin coalesced from the night air into the other hand.

"An Aspect of a weakened God," the creature rasped. "Kill him!"

The two bear-like daemons started to circle Vesna, moving in opposite directions, while the rest spread left and right, to get around him and head up to the castle. Gaur gave Vesna a baleful look, then followed his minions, but Vesna didn't see him go; he was already moving to attack.

The crouching daemon reared back in surprise as Vesna made up the ground in one leap, striking as he landed. His slash opened the beast's belly and it howled and raked down with its huge talons. Vesna raised his armoured arm and caught the blow on the Skull in an explosion of white sparks.

The daemon shrieked at the contact, but its cries were cut short as Vesna went right and hacked up through its elbow, then, in the blink of an eye, thrust overhand with all his strength, driving the point of his broadsword into the daemon's throat. The enchanted blade tore right through; there was a great gout of ichor, and the daemon was dead before it hit the ground.

Its comrade dropped to all fours to leap and use its greater size. Vesna was preparing to jump aside, but he hesitated as the power of the Crystal Skull screamed to be used: the image of a white ball of fire appeared in his mind, and in the next moment the night air was split by raging energies.

Before the daemon could move it was consumed by flames so bright even Vesna had to turn away. As it died away one of the squads of guards was running forward, their spears lowered. He left them to finish it off and turned to face the more dangerous enemy.

"Gaur!" he roared, running after the pale daemon, obvious amidst the darker bodies of its kin. A gust of chill wind swept down over him, momentarily washing away the stink of daemon from the air, but then the Gaur daemon stopped and faced him, leaving the rest of the daemons scampering on towards the castle.

As the demon stood up straight and regarded Vesna, the shining bronze of its eyes burned through the night and Vesna felt a sudden, overpowering sense of loathing. His divine side recoiled from the creature's stench even as his hand tightened on his sword, aching to strike.

As the two closed the ground between them with quick, careful steps, Vesna recognised the challenge for what it was, and knew that none of the soldiers would dare interfere in this.

"So the Gods have found themselves another champion," the daemon said contemptuously. "How long before they cast you aside too?"

"Long enough."

"So you say now, but your Gods are easily bored; soon you will find their promises empty, and you will see that their strength is spent in this Land."

"And yet you fear to incarnate fully as you come seeking your revenge. You wear a mortal's form—that is who will die when I slay you—yet you send your minions without any such protection." Vesna laughed. "Spare me your coward's words; my soul is not for sale, daemon."

"Are you so sure?" It stopped and cocked its head at Vesna, tasting the air with its long tongue. "You wear grief like a mantle, a loss most raw."

"Enough!" Vesna yelled, feeling the daemon's words like a punch to the gut. He took a breath, knowing it was feeding off his pain and sensing his vulnerabilities, but unable to suppress his feelings.

"Would you like to see her face again?" the daemon continued, its voice husky with laden promise. "Hold her in your arms?"

"Such a thing is beyond your power," Vesna growled. "It is beyond all power: Death is the final arbiter."

"Are you so sure? Her death was recent: I can tell that from the scent of your grief." The daemon edged closer and lowered its voice. "What if her soul still walks Ghain's slope? My hunters can find her and bring her to me. That *is* within my power."

Vesna shook his head, unable to speak as the memory of Tila appeared in his mind, her beautiful face marked by a single spot of blood, the smile that lit up rooms twisted into a grimace of agony.

"She is dead. She is gone," he said quietly.

"Her body perhaps, but another can be found," the daemon insisted, edging ever closer. It was barely three yards from him now, its weapons held low. "She might be wearing some other beautiful face perhaps, but it would be her voice, her laughter still. There are many who pledge their souls to my kind: spurned lovers, vengeful mothers—many beautiful women whose bonds could be broken in exchange for their mortal form."

"It would not be *her*," Vesna insisted.

"Her beauty exists in your mind," it continued. "You could share your bed with her double every night of your life—that too is within my power."

Vesna didn't speak. He could hear the music of her laughter in his mind but then it faded, to be replaced with the crash of glass on stone. His stomach tightened, desperate to retch up the black grief within him, but he smothered the feeling, all too aware that the emptiness was not so easily expelled.

"No," he whispered, and struck without warning: two quick steps with a God's speed, his sword rising even as he extended into a duellist's lunge. The weapon pierced the Gaur-daemon's chest, sliding neatly in with barely a sound. The daemon never even managed to raise its weapons in defense; it simply stared at the weapon transfixing it as a strange laugh bubbled up from its ruined chest.

"Pledge myself to a daemon?" Vesna whispered, his arm still outstretched. "What would she think of me then?"

He whipped the sword out and stepped smartly aside as daemonic ichor spurted from the wound. The daemon staggered, drunkenly trying to raise its weapons, but Vesna spun and struck off its head with one great blow. A distant shriek of rage echoed across the moor and he sensed the daemon vanish on the breeze. He didn't wait, but turned to Moorview Castle as screams cut through the night.

Isak was on his feet before Mihn had entered the castle grounds. Legana recoiled in alarm as Eolis blazed with light right in front of her face, but her rasp of shock was drowned out by Isak's own anguished howl.

That was enough for King Emin and the assembled company—before Mihn's cries had echoed around the castle walls they were up and armed, watching for whatever had set Isak off. The air became hot and heavy around them, and a dry, dead taste coated the back of their throats as they looked frantically around.

Doranei saw Legana reel and frantically pulled at his boots. Veil saw him and nodded understanding, dropping his axe to draw a dagger and slice through his own laces. A smile crossed his face as his bare feet touched the grass and he reached for his axe again. Doranei watched in wonder as Veil receded into the gloom as the magic of his tattoos activated. Then he did the same, and felt the intoxicating sensation rush over his body as the darkness drew in to envelop him in shadows.

All around others were following suit, fading like candles extinguished by a sudden gust of wind until Isak, Hulf and Legana were the only ones illuminated by the firelight.

Mihn reached Isak's side. He put a hand on the white-eye's arm, and as he spoke, the single word, *daemons*, sent a chill through them all.

Isak, realising they would be there for him and Mihn, shrank inwards before catching himself and shaking his head violently. His abused lips twitched as he mentally steeled himself. He shrugged off his cloak and straightened his damaged body as best he could, holding Eolis with more purpose than he'd managed before the battle of Moorview. His pale skin shone bright under the light of Kasi, the lesser moon, highlighting the thick shaded lines of scarring that covered his bare chest, as though the man he'd been named after mocked what he had become.

Doranei looked over at Daken and saw the white-eye had thrown off his blankets to expose his own tattooed feet, but he was struggling to rise. "Veil, help Daken," he ordered, and drew his sword.

The clatter of hooves or something similar came from the lower gate, and as everyone turned to the sound, Doranei forced his way to the king's side. For a moment everyone was still, listening intently for whatever was coming, then a man's death-cry broke the air and the Brotherhood all rushed to defend their king while the Ghosts and Kingsguard manning the walls descended on the attackers.

Dark shapes poured through the gate and Isak felt another surge of fear drain his body of strength. Deliberately he bit down hard on his own lip and felt one jagged tooth tear through the flesh like a knife. The pain reached beyond his blind fear of Ghenna's denizens and found something deeper inside him, something he could use. He leaped forward as the daemons headed straight for them, oblivious of the surrounding soldiers. A shout of fury burst its way out as Isak closed on the lead daemon with inhuman speed and hacked down at its head. The daemon raised a spine-clad arm to defend the blow, but Eolis chopped right through the limb, and the head behind.

Another daemon presented itself for Isak's blade, and he moved left and struck again, barely registering a flail crashing down where he'd just been standing. Eolis parted the daemon's outstretched arm with ease, carving arcs of moonlight as it danced almost of its own volition. Moving too fast for the daemons to match, Isak cleaved left and right, hewing a path through the enemy as shadows pounced on them from every side.

One tall, long-limbed daemon reached for him with sickle-claws and Isak ducked under, ignoring their fleeting scrape down his shoulders as he chopped through the daemon's knee. It toppled with a howl and he slammed his shoulder into its gut to knock it backwards. Hot blood spurted across his shoulders as he battered the daemon to the ground and stamped on it, already seeking the next one to kill, until a sudden rush of wind from above caused him to check and turn.

He slashed upwards wildly as something swooped down. The creature screeched and reeled, but Isak grabbed at its bony legs and hauled the flying daemon from the sky. One leathery wing smashed against the side of Isak's head, but he refused to let go and cut it again. This time Eolis tore through the wing and the daemon lurched downwards, coming close enough for Isak to hook an arm over it and drag it to the ground. Snarling furiously, he punched and stamped at the flailing nightmare beneath him, tearing the flesh from his knuckles on its scaly hide, until he remembered about the sword in his hand. He reversed Eolis, then stabbed down with it, impaling the daemon and pinning it to the ground as its screams filled the air and drowned out the battle going on around him.

A rush of movement on the left caught his eye. He ripped Eolis from the dying daemon just as something slammed into his side and gleaming teeth closed around his arm as it knocked him down. Though Isak stabbed blindly upwards as he was thrown to the ground, the teeth tightened on his arm and the pain intensified. The daemon's hot stinking breath washed over him as it scrabbled clawed feet on his belly and released his arm, instead seeking his throat. Isak howled with pain and rage, unable to get his sword around in time as he watched the blood-coated fangs lunge forward—

—as a steel-shod staff lanced out of the night, driven right into the daemon's open mouth and down its throat. The daemon reared as Mihn put his full weight behind the thrust and managed to drive the creature off Isak, quickly withdrawing the staff before it could bite down again. He stepped closer and swung the other end around, smashing it into one high, bulging eye that burst under the impact and sprayed orange fluid over them.

The daemon shook itself, growling like a hunting dog, but before it could pounce again Hulf threw himself fearlessly at it. The powerful dog grabbed the daemon's hind leg and dragged it around, hauling the larger creature off-balance as Isak stood. Though blood was pouring from his arm and torso, Isak didn't appear to notice his injuries as he chopped the daemon in half with one brutal blow and sought the next enemy.

When he found it, Isak hesitated for the first time, the raging fire in his veins dimming as he recognised that one, even in the weak half-light. The lizard-like daemon was scuttling low to the ground, circling around Mihn while trying to keep out of the reach of Eolis. Isak hurled the weapon through the air and it embedded itself deep into the daemon's scaled tail. The white-eye screamed, as much with fear as hatred, as he ran forward and dived on top of the daemon. It twisted around to meet him, snapping at his face, but Isak caught it under the frill of spines around its neck and forced its head away.

The daemon tried to curl up instinctively, bringing up two pairs of legs to rake Isak and drive him away, but he ignored the assault and grabbed the nearest limb. With a great roar he summoned his unnatural strength and hauled back on its leg, the muscles of his huge shoulders bulging almost to bursting point as he pulled as hard as he could, until at last something gave.

The daemon shrieked in agony as Isak snarled and roared at his victory. Ichor came fountaining up over them both as he ripped the leg clean from its socket.

Lost in blood-lust, Isak tossed the limb aside and reached down, grabbing the next leg and tearing that off the screeching daemon too. It convulsed and went quiet, too weak to scream now, but he didn't stop, snapping off the next with savage ease. The daemon went limp, dead by now, but Isak continued relentlessly, placed one foot on its scaled torso and tearing the fourth leg from the daemon.

This time Isak realised there was no more gushing ichor, and he registered it was dead. He retrieved Eolis and, soaked in his own blood and the many hues of daemon ichor, he sank to his knees atop the corpse of his erstwhile jailer. The humans were beginning to take their toll now, Isak's furious assault having blunted the onrushing daemons long enough for the tattooed warriors to use their arcane advantage.

As Isak gasped for air, the last two daemons were cut down by a dozen blades and the castle grounds went quiet. He looked down at his arm, only now seeing the terrible damage the daemon's teeth had done to it. The pain was excruciating, but after Ghenna it felt like nothing to him.

Isak let Eolis fall from his fingers and banished the sensation to the back of his mind. His belly and chest were burning and Isak looked down to see a dozen or more cuts overlaying the scars there. With one finger he traced an unsteady path over them, smearing the blood that ran from his skin. The daemon-script that had been cut into his flesh was obscured in several parts now, overlaid by new and random abuse from daemon-claws. He smiled despite the pain, and let Mihn lift his injured arm with the care of a fussing mother. Somewhere a shout went up for healers, and then was lost in the clamour of voices that became mere jagged sounds to accompany his pain.

Mihn was speaking to him, but Isak couldn't make out the words. The small man was reaching for something to wrap around the injury, but Isak pushed him away gently and looked inside himself, trying to recall the time when the magic had rushed through his body as easily as breathing.

Reluctantly the energies came to his call and he felt a sense of calm descend as a pale light began to play over his skin. Mihn stepped back in surprise, but Isak continued to smile, even as the brightness and pain intensified. Holding his arm up to inspect it, Isak saw Doranei and King Emin, just past Mihn, both standing with mouths open as the light traced every open wound on his body, wrapping his arm in a garland of light.

The stink of daemons was suddenly overlaid by burning flesh and pain enveloped his entire body, searing through everything, and at last he cried out, briefly, before succumbing. Isak felt the Land lurch underneath him and fall away, and in its place came darkness. There, blessedly, the pain was only a memory lost among many.

CHAPTER 6

WITCHFINDER SHANATIN GLANCED BACK at his companions and felt a renewed flush of fear. His hand went to his mouth and without even realising he started to gnaw again at the raw mark on one knuckle. His mind remained entirely on the soldiers behind him. He told himself *they* were the ones who should be afraid, but it did no good; his own fear only burgeoned. Luerce had reassured him when he gave the fat witchfinder his orders, but now he was alone in the depths of night surrounded by armed fanatics.

No, not alone: never alone in the shadows.

As Shanatin turned back to the deserted street ahead he accidentally scuffed his foot on the cobbles. The sound echoed off the surrounding buildings before he managed to catch his balance again. His heart chilled as he peered timorously behind himself and caught Chaplain Fynner's thunderous expression; he only just managed to stop himself bursting into a torrent of apologies, which would have enraged the chaplain even more.

Behind the white-haired chaplain were three full squads of troops, two of regular infantry in heavy armour and one of witch-finders. Shanatin wasn't marching amongst his fellows because he had no spark of ability himself. Those discovered among the rank and file—there were always a few—were transferred to the witch-finders, and the regular troops considered the regiment to be full of misfits and madmen under the command of spies, reporting as they did to the Serian, the Order's intelligence branch.

The Knights of the Temples would not use magic in battle, but they knew its power full well, and pooled the limited power of its witchfinders to deflect their enemies' efforts. As they were about to arrest one of their own for being a secret mage, they needed all the defences they could muster.

Fynner caught him up and grabbed Shanatin by the arm. "Keep yourself together, man," the chaplain hissed. "There's no place for cowards in the Devout Congress—not that it will matter, if your information about Captain Perforren proves inaccurate."

Fynner was two decades older than Shanatin, but he was more than his match physically. It was clear the priest was comfortable in armour and knew how to use the sword on his hip, while the closest Shanatin had come to battle was the regular beatings he took from anyone who took exception to his face.

"Sorry, Father," Shanatin whispered meekly, and cringed until Fynner let go.

They were marching down a backstreet in the eastern district of Akell, the quarter of the Circle City ruled by the Knights of the Temples. Considering the Devout Congress now dominated Akell there should have been no need for stealth, but their numbers remained few; those who had not been disarmed by the Menin had been conscripted into the invasion of Narkang or lost their weapons when the armoury burned.

"Just don't make any more noise," Fynner said as he waved over the captain commanding the troops. "We're almost at the meeting point, and we've still the best part of an hour to wait. Captain, position your squads out of sight—that warehouse, I think, and have some on the other side of the main road so they can cut off any escape. Remember, hiding his abilities as a mage while being promoted to his position of trust is a capital offence under the Codex of Ordinance. We want to capture Captain Perforren alive for him to face trial, but he'll be desperate to escape, so use whatever force is necessary. As for Sergeant Timonas, I don't give a damn about one corrupt witchfinder. Taking him alive for interrogation is preferable, but it's unlikely he'll have any useful information for us."

Shanatin had to stifle a smile at the idea of Sergeant Timonas under questioning. Fortunately the gloom of night hid his reaction and Fynner only paused at the movement, not bothering to waste any more time on him.

"You'll stick beside me," Fynner ordered. "You'll only get in the way otherwise. If Timonas arrives first I will want you to confirm his identity."

The witchfinder bobbed his head in acknowledgement and followed Fynner to a dark stone house at the corner of the street. The chaplain produced a key and let himself in, then led Shanatin up to a room on the first floor that smelled of mould and rotten wood. They gingerly settled themselves down on the broken furniture, positioned so they could watch both directions from behind the tattered curtains covering the windows.

Shanatin took care to test a rickety stool before easing himself down onto it. The last thing he needed was to further incur Fynner's wrath—the chaplain's plans were going to go sufficiently awry already.

Captain Perforren slipped out of the tavern's rear door and walked slowly through the yard. It was lit by a single lamp in the window of the back room, barely enough for anything other than to make out the lines of the privy. Perforren checked inside the shed for drinkers relieving themselves, and after confirming it was empty he headed for the gate beyond it, slipping the bolts as silently as he could and making his way into the street outside.

He waited a long while in the shadows for a tail to appear, but after five minutes he concluded there was no one watching him that night. Head down, the collar of his coat turned up, Perforren hurried across the street and turned east. The message had been too short for explanations, and the messenger was as nondescript as the coat he'd handed over, but the man had certainly played the part of a fervent follower of Ruhen to Perforren's satisfaction.

Drinking companion has urgent information. Meet at small bridge in Yatter. Bring only those trust completely.

At any other time Perforren would have laughed in the man's face and knocked him down, but times were far from normal. Ruhen's Children remained a limited presence in Akell, enough to annoy the Devout Congress but not distract their enthusiasm from the violence they inflicted on their own Order. Sergeant Kayel—Ruhen's bodyguard, who'd visited Perforren and Knight-Cardinal Certinse one night for a drink—had promised them help to take back control of the Order. They had been waiting patiently for weeks now, enduring the insults and iniquities the fanatics of the Devout Congress regularly imposed upon the Order's secular majority.

It was a half-hour journey to Yatter, a small, poor district in the east of the quarter where foreigners comprised most of the inhabitants. It had fewer inhabitants since the Menin conquest, but night patrols still walked the streets and Perforren was forced several times to hide from soldiers whose allegiance would not be apparent until too late. Eventually he found himself at a stone arch behind which, during the day, a smallholders' market took place.

It was a secure vantage point from which he could see the bridge he'd been directed towards, but when he arrived the streets on both sides of the river were empty. The bridge was only five yards across, and no taller than waist-high; there was nowhere to hide aside from crouching under the bridge itself. He waited and watched, listening intently for sounds in the street beyond, but aside from the distant, regular tramp of a patrol he heard nothing. Above the building ahead he saw a sliver of Kasi, well on its way to the horizon: that meant midnight was not far off and the darkest part of the night had begun. As though to confirm that thought, a cloud drifted over the greater moon, Alterr, and what little he'd been able to see in the street faded.

"Seen anyone?" came a whisper in his ear, and Perforren's heart jumped into his throat. He was reaching for his sword even as he realised it was Kayel who'd spoken. The big mercenary grinned, hands resting easily on the knives in his belt.

"No one," Perforren said once he'd recovered himself. "Unless you were followed, we're alone."

"Good. I've got something to show you." Kayel indicated the bridge ahead of them and started off, not waiting to make sure Perforren was moving. The captain took one look behind, wondering how Kayel had come through the market so silently, then hurried to catch up. It sounded like his light footsteps were the only ones in the street: Kayel's moved without sound and Perforren guessed the soles of his boots were covered with something to muffle the noise. For once he wasn't wearing his long white cape, preferring instead a dark jacket covered with black-painted steel links. In the spirit of stealth he wore a peasant's cloth cap to shade the pale skin of his face, and Perforren noticed the man was serious enough about secrecy to eschew his usual gaudy, jewel-hilted bastard sword. Instead he wore only his daggers and a plain short-sword like any nightwatchman in Yatter might carry.

At the bridge Kayel paused and looked around. They were alone as far as Perforren could see, and Kayel seemed similarly satisfied.

"So?" Perforren whispered.

Kayel's smirk returned as he pointed down the largest of the streets ahead of them. "Look."

Perforren did so. "I don't—"

Something whipped across his throat and Perforren felt a rush of cool night air on his skin, then something warm spilling over his skin. He tried to speak, but the Land tilted underneath him and a sharp flood of pain stuck him so hard his knees buckled. He staggered, and felt his thigh strike the bridge. The impact twisted him around and he saw Sergeant Kayel watching him, eyes glittering with infernal delight.

Perforren put a hand to his throat and felt something wet there as the chill of night enveloped him. His knees crumpled underneath him and he sank slowly down, his back against the bridge, transfixed by the sight of

Kayel. In moments the pain started to fade and his mind grew heavy. The Land started to recede as his limbs grew cold and his vision darkened, drifting further and further until, with the softest of sighs, Captain Perforren of the Knights of the Temples went still.

Ilumene gestured behind him and wiped his dagger clean. Looking down he saw the late captain's blood slipping closer to his boots. He deliberately lifted one boot then the other, slipping off the cloth coverings from the sole of each and stepping squarely into the widening pool of blood. Footsteps came from behind him and he turned to see a small man scamper over, barefoot and dressed like a tramp in ragged clothes.

The man was of a similar age to Ilumene, but there the similarity ended. He had a fleshy face that looked too big for his slim body, and a tangled thicket of hair dark enough to be Farlan or Menin.

"Find yourself a nice spot down Balap Street," Ilumene ordered as he carefully trod bloody footprints across the bridge to the other side. "You saw men in witchfinder uniforms run that way, get it?"

"Aye, sir."

"Good. Got me some arson to do now."

The agent recognised that as a dismissal and raced off, careful to keep his feet away from the bloody trail Ilumene was leaving so carefully. The renegade Brotherhood man followed until the blood was nearly used up, then he slipped the coverings back onto his shoes again and checked around once more. There were no shocked faces in sight, nor vengeful troops, but that would change soon enough.

A distant voice broke the quiet: the long, low cry of a dying animal or a person whose mind was broken. Ilumene felt a *frisson* at the sound. It was followed by voices, so quiet he could barely hear them: it could have been monks chanting a prayer, it could have been the whisper of witnesses to his latest crime, but he knew it was neither. There was a sour taste in the air that made him tighten his grip on his knife and looked up into the sky. The clouds were thin and drifting slowly, but against them he saw movement as though dark coils of shadow were overlaying them.

"Right again, Master," he said with a tight smile. "The boundaries are weakened; the sound and scents of the other lands touch us now."

He disappeared silently into a side-street and took an indirect route west, skirting the streets used by the patrols. Before he was halfway to his destination the first human calls went up, and he allowed himself a smile of satisfaction. They were as attracted by the spilled blood as the Dark Place had been.

"He's taking his time, witchfinder," Chaplain Fynner muttered. "If you're wasting mine, it will go hard on you."

"This is what the message said!" Shanatin protested, a hot flush of fear in his cheeks as he spoke. When the chaplain rounded on him Shanatin didn't need to feign his emotions.

"I hope so, for your sake."

The Devout Congress had appropriated the long arcade of shops in the northeast of the quarter that for centuries had sold temple offerings to the faithful. In these troubled times it now resembled a conveyor belt of tribunals. In the cold stores below they obtained their evidence, while magistrates heard the accusations and passed sentence above. The sentences weren't carried out on site, but Shanatin guessed that was simply because it lacked the public arena High Priest Garash preferred.

Anything could lead to an arrest—and when you did the work of the Gods, those you arrested were never innocent, otherwise those guided by the spirits of the Gods had made an error, and how could that ever be? Shanatin recognised the looks in the eyes of the fanatics and their followers: some believed, some saw an opportunity. But the much-abused fat fool of the witchfinders was an expert on bullies. With no fear of retribution, the worst of humanity was brought to the surface. Shanatin wasn't so certain of his standing with Azaer that he dared test the shadow's loyalty to its followers, but he knew he was on the right side if he opposed such men.

"Timonas'll be here," he insisted, "and Perforren too."

The chaplain returned to his vigil at the window and Shanatin relaxed a touch. The street was empty and quiet outside, and the strong stink of mud rose in the warm summer air. He squirmed as a trickle of sweat ran down his back, but stopped at a look from Fynner, flinched and edged closer to the window, realising Fynner would have struck him had they not been trying to keep quiet. Before a threat followed however, there came the sound of feet in the street below.

Glad of the distraction, Shanatin peered between the half-dozen remaining shutter slats. They had seen a few false alarms, but now the witchfinder felt a flicker of fear in his stomach as he recognised the brass-plated cuirass and red sash that denoted a low-ranking officer of the Order.

The man walked without haste, remaining as unobtrusive as possible, but his polished armour caught Alterr's pale light and seemed to flash a warning to Shanatin.

"A captain of the Order," Fynner whispered, voice laden with anticipation. "It must be Perforren—our prey is most obliging."

"Unless his dose has worn off," Shanatin muttered, to himself as much as anything, but Fynner was in an obliging mood and took the bait.

"Worn off? I thought you said he'd have plenty from last time."

"Sure, if he's only buying for hisself. If he's got himself a friend in the same situation, they'll both be needing their next dose soon. Message did say it was urgent, might be he needs more before he can pass any test."

Fynner released Shanatin's arm and thought hurriedly. They were waiting to catch Captain Perforren in the act of buying a potion that would suppress dormant magical abilities. Any officer hiding a capability for magery, as they believed their quarry was, would be in serious breach of the Order's Codex of Ordinance, quite aside from the stricter regulations imposed by High Priest Garash's Piety Congress. That Perforren was aide to Knight-Cardinal Certinse, supreme commander of the Knights of the Temples, made him a prize worth waiting for.

"That's why you brought the squad of witchfinders, ain't it?" Shanatin asked, not giving Fynner too long to think.

"I brought them because this is under their jurisdiction," Fynner said angrily. "You implied Perforren would have no magic to command when we arrested him."

"Probably he doesn't! He's been hiding who he is all these years, not practising . . . I'm just sayin', wouldn't want to be the one to arrest a mage with nothing to lose."

Chaplain Fynner stared at Shanatin's fat, guileless face for a few seconds before realising the witchfinder was making sense; the troops could restrain Perforren and Timonas well enough themselves, so no need for him to be at the forefront if he resisted.

"Well, then, where's your man Timonas?" he muttered, returning to the window.

Down below they saw the man they assumed to be Perforren stop at a corner and check around it before he secreted himself into the shadow of a doorway. All fell silent again, and it was five minutes or more before any other sound broke the night. Rather than a second set of footsteps, Shanatin heard more distant noises, distorted into nothing recognisable by the city streets.

He didn't know what sort of disturbance had caused it, but Luerce, first disciple of Ruhen's Children, had been very clear in his instructions. Shanatin glanced at Fynner and was relieved to see the chaplain wasn't looking to be in any hurry to leave their vantage point. They needed a witness to report back, and with any luck Fynner's testimony would heat up Garash's hair-trigger temper and push this internal struggle over the edge.

It wasn't long before Sergeant Timonas of the witchfinders appeared from the other direction, in time to play his small part in matters. Shanatin watched the man anxiously; he knew Timonas was innocent in this, but the bastard deserved everything he got. He found himself holding his breath as Timonas approached the corner with far more caution than Perforren had, looking in all directions as though bewildered he was there at all.

"Well?"

Shanatin looked over and realised Fynner was staring expectantly at him. Timonas wasn't wearing his black and white uniform, of course; the man had more sense than that, having received an anonymous note that his life was in danger.

He nodded and gestured at the newcomer. "It's him, for certain."

Fynner reached up and, checking neither of the men was looking his way, drew the curtain away from the shuttered window. The lieutenant in charge of the squads was watching for his signal and in the next moment a door burst open a short way down the street Timonas had just walked along. The two men panicked at the crash, but in the next instant a second clatter came from down the next street and then a third from somewhere below where Shanatin stood.

"Drop your weapons!" someone yelled as Shanatin hunkered down at the window and watched events. Timonas was standing like an idiot—Shanatin could see his stupid thick jaw hanging open in astonishment as he turned, first one way, then the other, to watch the onrushing troops. By contrast Perforren was already moving with purpose, drawing a pair of swords.

Shanatin jammed his knuckle in his mouth as he tried to suppress a gasp of surprise, but the sound was echoed by Fynner anyway as Perforren broke into a sprint from a standing start, covering the ground to the nearest squad before the last man had even made it out of the building. One slender sword slashed open the first soldier's throat, even as the second was piercing the side of another. Perforren kept moving, slipping between the spears of the next two, hopping left and right, almost with the grace of a Harlequin.

Both soldiers reeled away, to be immediately replaced by a fifth and sixth, but those too were no match for Perforren's speed. He deflected one thrust and darted right around the shield of the other, kicking high into the man's shoulder and knocking him into his comrade even as he chopped up into the elbow of a third soldier.

Gods, a Harlequin—dressed up and made to look like Perforren?

The remaining men of the squad, thrown back by the force of his attack, now fanned out to surround him, but Perforren stood his ground. He stopped a moment and his voice cut through the confusion, but he was not speaking any words Shanatin could recognise. Abruptly he slashed through the air between himself and the last troops and a blinding white light tore in an arc after the tip of his sword. The light whipped across each of the men and ripped through their armour like paper. They fell without a sound, a gaping wound stretching across the chest of each from which Shanatin glimpsed the white stubs of ribs.

Shanatin felt a hand drop onto his shoulder and almost shrieked before he realised it was Fynner, stunned by what was happening.

"Merciful Gods, it's true and more," Fynner mumbled in shock. "He's a trained battle-mage!"

Loud, angry voices came suddenly from a side-street, and in the next moment another squad of Devoted troops burst into view. Fynner gasped: these men weren't under his command. In the moonlight their unit markings were clear on their shoulders. He could easily make out the designation: C11, Knight-Cardinal Certinse's own élite troops, the Tildek mounted infantry. Most had been co-opted into service by the Menin, but Certinse had been allowed a regiment of personal guards to remain with him.

"It's an ambush," Fynner gasped, leaning heavily on Shanatin as though all the strength had gone out of him. "They're here to kill us all."

The Tildek infantry charged straight for the witchfinders, howling furiously and giving them no time to steady themselves. The squad of witchfinders were not front-line troops and they quickly collapsed under the assault, half of them dropping in the initial rush. The élite troops swamped their foes, battering through them with rare savagery so that in seconds they were all on the ground, dead or dying.

"Sergeant!" yelled Perforren, striding towards them with blood trailing from his swords, "those men too!" He pointed to the remaining squad who'd surrounded the terrified Sergeant Timonas and then found themselves frozen to the spot as they watched the unexpected onslaught. "They're murdering officers loyal to the Knight-Cardinal!"

Invoking their commander's name seemed to be enough and with a roar they charged at the last remaining men who fled, only to be run down before they'd gone twenty yards. They were butchered to a man.

Shanatin grabbed Fynner and pulled the chaplain slowly to the ground, frantically gesturing for the man to be silent, but though Fynner didn't seem to notice he was too aghast to make a sound. Shanatin tried to control the panic surging through his own heart. At least thirty men had been killed in less than a minute. He felt his hands start to shake at the idea that the loyalist troops might start to check the surrounding buildings, but he knew he couldn't risk the slightest noise, not yet.

He took a slow breath and the musty smell of the floorboards calmed him: it contained a faint old strain of decay that put him in mind of Rojak, first of Azaer's disciples. Luerce had said he was dead, but at that moment Shanatin knew the malevolent minstrel's spirit was with him there, and if anyone could hide him in the shadows, it was Rojak. He tightened his grip on Chaplain Fynner, clutching the man as close as a lover as he listened to the soldiers in the street below and waited for his chance to escape.

Knight-Cardinal Certinse opened the door to his study and stopped dead. Despite the guards posted all round the house the study wasn't empty. He sighed and closed the door behind him. "I don't suppose there's any point asking how you got in here?"

Ilumene smiled. "Not a whole lot," he agreed, "but we've got rather more pressing concerns today."

Certinse grunted in agreement. He was wearing battle-armour, a rare occurrence when most of the last few decades had been spent in a formal uniform. He wore a broadsword and thick-hilted dagger on his belt, with gauntlets stuffed untidily in behind the dagger. "You heard the news then?"

"About your aide? Aye, strange that." The big soldier, looking quite comfortable in Certinse's favourite armchair, was also dressed for a fight, in a white brigandine and breeches, with his big bastard sword nestled in the crook of his arm. The man Certinse knew as Hener Kayel couldn't have stood out more on the streets of Akell. White was now the colour of Ruhen's Children, so if any cleric had seen him they would have arrested him on sight—

or tried to, at least. That he was ready for a fight was good news to Certinse though; a small ray of light amidst the deluge.

"Strange?" Certinse sat at his desk and pulled out a sheaf of paper. "Not the word I'd use."

He knew his guest didn't stand on ceremony and he had orders to write after the crimes of the previous night. He gave Ilumene a hard look before picking up his pen and starting the first letter.

"Strange, because I'd heard Perforren was going to be arrested—as an unregistered mage," Ilumene explained. "If you've got that planned, why go and murder him instead?"

Certinse abandoned his letter. "You heard what? *A mage?* That's bloody ridiculous!" He hesitated. "Even Garash must have realised how stupid and contrived that would look. Must be he changed his mind, but still wanted Perforren out of the way. I'd thought the murders of the last few days had been building up to an assassination attempt on me, not this. But Perforren's the man I trusted most to carry my orders, so by killing him they limit the speed I can react to whatever they're up to."

"Aye, today's the day," Ilumene agreed. "I heard there was a fire at a barracks too?"

Certinse nodded briefly. "Fifteen dead, all good and loyal men. From the report it looks like it was a botched job—the bastard was trying to fire the officers' quarters next door, but the thatch in the barracks caught first. It's worked against them now; the men are ready to storm the armoury and march on the temple district."

"Well, you can't trust a fanatic to think before he acts." Ilumene declared as he stood and straightened his weapons. "Which is why I'm here."

"Your vague promises to me shall finally bear fruit? And speaking of such—Harlequins? Gods, man, remarkable followers of Ruhen, I think you described them as!"

"Weren't lying now, was I?" Ilumene said with a grin.

"Far from it—indeed, I hadn't expected the term to be so accurate. I don't suppose you'd care to tell me how you persuaded the Harlequin clans to join you?"

"Nope."

Certinse watched Ilumene as the man scratched the ragged edge of his left ear. A small part of the lobe was missing, no doubt bitten off in some squalid bar fight. They had yet to set the terms of their agreement, if agreement was in fact the term for the flirtation of suggestion and vague assertion each had made. Now the crucial time had come, and there was bargaining to be done.

"I can't help but wonder if I need your help now. My greatest problem was the piety and obedience of my men, and High Priest Garash seems to have solved that for me."

"Far from your only problem though," the other commented with a yawn, "and no one likes a tease. In case you've forgotten, the Menin dragooned most of your troops. Garash might still be outnumbered, but not by armed soldiers, and he still controls the armoury."

"So you offer me the armoury today?"

Ilumene gestured expansively. "If that's your heart's desire, certainly. I'll even throw in a little confusion within the enemy's ranks too. If we come to an agreement you'll have full military control of Akell by the end of the day, with the clerics of the Knights of the Temples more than aware you're no longer their bitch."

The Knight-Cardinal sat back, puzzled at Ilumene's bluntness. He'd expected more dancing around than that, whether or not time was of the essence.

"And the price?" he enquired, noting his guest's complete lack of reaction at the question. It boded well; Ilumene might be more than the simple thug he appeared, but he was still a bully and a brawler. Once he had the advantage of a man he'd want to lord it over them.

"Friendship."

"Perhaps you should define that a little more clearly for me."

Ilumene shrugged. "He asks for stricter terms. Some people, eh?"

As he spoke, Certinse felt the faintest breath of wind and saw Ilumene's eyes flick briefly to the dark corner of the room beside his desk, but which happened first he couldn't be certain of. For a moment though, he had the sense that Ilumene wasn't just being theatrical.

"I want clearer terms, not more severe," Certinse said carefully, trying to shake off the impression he was negotiating with two people rather than just one.

Ilumene didn't help that impression by cocking his head to one side as he thought, almost as though listening to a whispered voice, but Certinse could hear nothing during the short pause that followed his words.

"Clarity then," Ilumene said with a flourish of the hands, "a throwing back of the shadows we shall have. Ruhen wants the right to take his message to all corners of the Land, but he's not looking to build an army. We'll leave any recruiting up to you, but I'm sure if you do so in Byora there'll be no complaints from our corner. If the Knights of the Temples would be so generous as to provide escorts for Ruhen's preachers where necessary, the problem of security would be solved."

"Easily granted, so long as you recognise the Order is in no fit state to invade any city-state."

Ilumene inclined his head to accept the point. "Both of us also need greater ties between Ruhen's Children and the Order—I'm not suggesting you cut the holy orders out of your structure, but some recognition of Ruhen's message would serve us both."

"Certainly," Certinse said thoughtfully, "a message of peace is a complicated one to sell to a martial order, but until the fanaticism in the Land runs its course, Ruhen remains a better guiding light."

The big soldier leaned abruptly forward. "Tell me, Knight-Cardinal: do you believe in the Order's central tenet these days?"

"The Army of the Devoted?" Certinse asked, unable to conceal his surprise at the question. "I—we were founded to protect the majesty of the Gods. Certainly I believe in this charge."

"And providing an army for the saviour, when he comes?" There was a slight smile on Ilumene's face.

Certinse couldn't tell whether the man found the entire subject ridiculous or was setting himself up for some sort of rehearsed argument or joke.

"I fail to see how the two would be exclusive of each other," he said carefully, "but I am told by the Serian that many mages, scholars and other heretics consider the point moot. They say that destiny has been twisted awry and the question of whether the Order will have a saviour to follow is now moot."

"So that's a no," Ilumene said, looking satisfied. "You're a politician and a man of power after all. You can't spend your time dreaming about such things—most likely you reckon if it does turn out that way the best thing you could've done was build the Order's strength anyway."

When Certinse didn't comment Ilumene smiled and reached into his pocket. "There is one other thing," he said, almost apologetically. "Many of Ruhen's followers have taken to wearing a symbol of their devotion. We ask you wear this—not openly if you prefer—in acknowledgement of our alliance."

He held up a thin chain on which hung a small silver coin. Certinse took the coin from Ilumene's open palm and inspected it. He guessed it had once been a silver level from Byora, but someone had done a good job of erasing what had been stamped into the metal. Now it bore only a circle on one face and a cross on the other, and each groove had then been painted in.

"A charm?"

Ilumene shook his head. "A symbol only—feel free to have a mage investigate." He watched Certinse examine the coin, not speaking, but when the man continued to look sceptical Ilumene reached into his collar and pulled out a second coin, identical to the one he'd given Certinse. "You can have mine if you prefer? For a man in your position wariness is never a wasted effort, but this one's certainly done me no harm."

Certinse agreed and they swapped. Ilumene wasted no time in hanging the first chain around his neck and tucking it back under his tunic. Feeling foolish, Certinse did the same, gingerly slipping the chain over his head and letting it rest on his armour for a few heartbeats. Nothing at all happened, and when he slipped it underneath the only result was a slight cold touch as the metal came into contact with his skin.

For his visitor, that seemed to be enough. Ilumene rose and slipped his sword onto his back. "Consider your wishes come true then."

"What, now? Already?"

"Come with me and you'll see. Your men will get no resistance at the armoury; you can mop up the Penitents and the rest easily enough—they're all waiting for orders that aren't likely to come unless the remaining clerics are less argumentative than either of us believes."

"And you'll be alongside me why exactly?"

"Solidarity," Ilumene said brightly, "and in case there's a fanatic within your own men you don't know about. Don't worry, the victory'll be yours; I'm just there to be seen on your side. You can even give me some orders publicly if you like."

"So this was already in play? But what if I'd refused your terms, struck my own bargain?"

The big man in white shrugged and opened the door, holding it for Certinse to go first. "Some priests I don't care about would have been dead. Maybe your guilty conscience would have kept you up at nights, but you strike me as a man who prefers his nights restful."

He gave the Knight-Cardinal a gentle pat on the shoulder as he urged him out the door. "Jumping at every shadow or strange noise grows tiring, so I'm told."

CHAPTER 7

"WHAT ARE YOU DOING, NECROMANCER?"

Nai paused in his gestures and glanced over at Amber. The Menin soldier sat in a slouched heap beside their small fire, looking as exhausted as he sounded. Small sparks smouldered on his boot, orange pinpricks against the black leather. When Nai pointed to them Amber frowned at the fading glows for a long while before eventually dropping a heavy hand on them to extinguish them. The only other movement he could bring himself to make was to scratch the scabs of a graze on his cheek, where Nai had scraped a temporary rune into his skin.

"I'm going to summon a spirit," Nai replied at last, "something that can scout the path for us. There's likely to be all sorts roaming in the wake of an army, but none friendly to us."

"Spirit or daemon?"

Nai ignored the question and returned to his preparations. He'd drawn a circle in the bare earth beneath a yew tree and scattered a handful of bones within it around a small, blackened bowl into which he'd put a pinch of herbs soaked in blood.

He spoke a long mantra over it before igniting the herbs. "Dedessen, I summon you," he intoned, bowing towards the bowl, "Dedessen, receive my praise; Dedessen, accept my sacrifice."

Behind him was a young rabbit, feet bound together and magically subdued but still alive. Nai bowed again to the bowl and drew a knife across the rabbit's throat. Blood spurted out over the circle as the rabbit convulsed twice, then died. The air around him seemed to thicken, becoming hot and close as a bitter stink filled the fitful evening breeze.

Nai bowed his head again and was about to repeat the mantra when a whispery voice cut through the night.

"Ever faithful to the old covenants," the daemon said from somewhere nearby, "your sacrifice is welcomed, Nai."

The necromancer bowed again before sitting up straight and looking all around, trying to work out where the voice had come from. It had emanated from several directions at once, but he knew it would incarnate soon.

"I am glad it pleases you, mighty one."

"What do you seek of me? Wisdom or wrath; concealment or craft?"

In front of Nai the deep blue evening sky shimmered, folded back on itself and tore to reveal a slender-limbed figure draped in black cloth. The cloth hung down over its body in long strips a hand-span wide, each weighted at the bottom by a writhing iron charm. The daemon itself had parchment-pale skin and thin eyes that glowed red as they moved between Nai and Amber. Despite its long hooked claws and a pair of massive fangs, its speech was refined, its gestures neat and elegant.

"You have found a protector, at least? But no, it does not reach for its swords—it cannot be much of a guard dog."

"More of a commodity," Nai said with a smile and a twitch of the finger that caused the scabbed rune on Amber's cheek to glow briefly. The big soldier flinched and looked away. He knew the fate Nai had in mind for him, but he believed Nai when he said the rune's spell would make doing anything about it a dangerous prospect.

"I beg for assistance, some creature of yours to scout the way for me and provide a safe path towards Narkang."

"You seek Narkang, or its king?"

"Its king—why—is he dead? I raised shades both within the Herald's Hall and on Ghain itself, and no word of King Emin was mentioned there."

"Perhaps he lives, perhaps he has fallen." The daemon edged closer, as though wary of being overheard. "The borders are weakened between this and the other lands and many of my kind can cross freely. King Emin chooses dangerous company."

"'Cross freely'? The Gods weakened themselves that much?"

Dedessen hissed like a snake, but Nai knew the threatening sound was more an expression of pleasure than anything else.

"They have broken their errant Chosen, but so high, so high the price. Now they reach into the mind of every mortal, every immortal, and tear out what they cannot stand, then retire across the seas. Now has come another Age of Darkness, now daemons hunt freely, and some they hunt with a rage never before seen."

"Do any hunt here?"

"Certainly," the daemon said as it gestured to the east, "they gather even now. Byora has cast out the Gods from their hearts. There is space only for fear there now, and my kind will be drawn to feed."

"But not you." It wasn't a question; not all daemons were the same and those bloodthirsty monsters descending upon Byora were of a lower breed. Age brought wisdom of a sort to daemons, a diminished hunger for violence and savagery when better sources of power were available. Dedessen would be naturally wary of Byora, given recent events there. The Devil's Stairs—direct paths between the Land and Ghenna—made it an enticing hunting ground, but either Stair's creation suggested great power was present there, and Dedessen lacked the strength of a daemon-prince.

"The entire Land is a hunting ground now. I will eat the dead souls of man and daemon alike once the slaughter is done, but I do not go to war on mortals—there will be plenty enough eager for that."

"And King Emin is their first target?"

The hissing came again, but this time Dedessen flexed and clenched its clawed hands too.

Pleasure and anger together, or have I misread it all these years? Nai wondered.

"The princes of Jaishen cry for vengeance, this much I hear in Coroshen. Some great offence was done and only blood will quench the flames of their wrath."

"Should I not seek him out then? I would not offend any prince of Ghenna."

"Now is a time for feeding and growing strong on the blood of others. Those who seek vengeance will overlook new rivals and become prey themselves. Go to King Emin and earn your coin for this one's soul—but once you have your reward, you must sacrifice a child to me in return."

Nai bowed again. "As you command."

The daemon approached the circle Nai had drawn and reached into it, digging its long fingers into the dirt while a haze of bloody light reflected off the scattered white bones. Nai sensed magic fill the air and run down into the ground, but the daemon's workings were a language separate from the spells Nai understood.

Dedessen withdrew its hand and stepped back as the earth wriggled and heaved. "Your guide."

Nai watched in fascination as a small shape pushed its way to the surface, claws tearing away at the earth until it had cut itself free like a corpse rising from the dead. It was small with a squat, furred body and leathery wings furled tight to its body. The creature turned its eyeless, whiskered snout up towards Nai and he realised it had once been a mole, now twisted by the daemon's magic to suit his purpose.

The daemon-creature opened its wings and gave them an experimental flap before beating them hard and rising up in the air just in front of Nai.

He looked for Dedessen but the daemon had already receded into the night and faded from view.

"My guide," Nai repeated softly. He held out his palm and the daemon settled on it, using a hooked thumb on its wings for balance like a bat would.

"Go, scout the Land all around us; return to me if you see danger."

The creature dropped from his palm and darted off with surprising swiftness, disappearing from view in two rapid wing-beats. Nai stared after it for a long while, puzzling over the daemon's words: a new Age of Darkness? Even he, a necromancer, felt trepidation at the notion.

He shook his head and returned to the fire where Amber was staring at the branches of a dead tree. In the uppermost branches sat a pair of large black birds, ravens, Nai guessed from the size. Both were watching them. Perhaps they had been wary of the daemon, but now that it was gone their scrutiny did not waver. Amber matched their unwavering stare without moving or speaking, apparently captivated by the birds.

What are ravens to the Menin, death omens? In Embere they were the souls of the dead come to speak to the living. I remember leaving out scraps for them as a child on feast days—payment for whatever words they might speak at twilight.

Nai realised he'd been holding the dead rabbit all the time. Now he held it up to his companion. "Dinner? Or shall I leave it for the ravens—a gift for lost souls?"

Amber blinked at him. "Lost souls?" He shook his head. "Ravens take all the payment they need."

The child walked alone through the streets of Wheel, Byora's largest district, towards the long city wall. The evening sun painted his dark hair golden, and he paused in the middle of the street, eyes closed, as he savoured the warmth on his skin. All around him the life of the city continued, and the boy was barely noticed by those passing by. Those not busy with work or thoughts of heading home had another sight to linger on: a man trailing well behind who looked far less comfortable on Byora's meaner streets.

A grey sprinkling in his hair and beard was the only hint to his true age. The silver charms on his robe were a greater clue to his profession. The mage looked nervous, cowed even, repeatedly checking the nearby alleys, but his attention always returned to the child before too long. The locals gave him a wide berth, but they were used to seeing mages walking tall and fearless, so they took the opportunity to inspect him more thoroughly.

He was far from impressive-looking: just a thin man of average height, with the pale skin of a scholar. But for the charms and pendants hanging around his neck more than one watcher might have tried to relieve him of his fine opal and firegem rings.

Just as some started to follow his gaze and wonder at the child in fine clothing standing before the open gate, another figure came down the street behind him and joined the mage. The watchers immediately looked away, as though the scent of wild roses accompanying the newcomer on the breeze was Death's own perfume. Here was one who appeared to own all he surveyed, and none of Wheel's residents were keen to argue the matter.

At last they realised who the child was, and the newcomer grinned as he heard gasps and whispers from all directions. He was dressed like a hero from some tale, shining breastplate and helm over a white tunic and breeches, while the hilt of his sword glittered in the light. All he lacked was a knightly crest on his shield.

"What's wrong, Peness? Not looking forward to this?"

"Of course I'm not—" Mage Peness hesitated. "What are we even doing here? Why is the gate still open?"

Ilumene laughed. "You think a gate will stop them?"

"Surely some defence is better than none? Summon the guard, man; do something!"

"And who're you to give me orders?" Ilumene demanded. Peness didn't reply so Ilumene rested a heavy arm on the smaller man's shoulders. "Why'd you want to panic the good folk of Wheel, then?"

"Why?" Peness lowered his voice to a whisper. "Sergeant, there are daemons waiting out there, just waiting for sunset before they come to kill us all!"

"No need to get excited about it, these things happen." Ilumene ushered Peness forward, keeping a tight grip on the man's shoulder.

"Wait! I can't go out there!" Peness gasped, struggling against Ilumene's greater strength with increasing panic. "Every one of them will be after me; my soul's a greater prize than any other in the entire city!"

"Oh I doubt that," Ilumene said darkly and continued to shove Peness forward.

At last the mage stopped panicking enough to think, and a crackle of light burst over his body, darting over the silver threads of his robe and singing Ilumene's fingers. The big man backed hurriedly off, hissing and cursing.

"Touch me again and I'll tear your limbs from your body!" Peness snarled as the locals scattered in all directions to leave the two men facing each other.

"Reckon so, do you? Fucking try it then."

The mage didn't hesitate. A nimbus of energy played briefly around his head as Peness summoned his strength, then he made a grabbing motion towards Ilumene's legs and the soldier was thrown from his feet. Though he crashed heavily to the ground, somehow he managed to draw and hurl a knife—but a bright cloud of smoke enveloped it before it hit the mage, slowing it enough for Peness to pluck the weapon from the air.

In his hand the dagger spun violently about its axis while a long shaft of crimson light appeared behind it. Peness stabbed the new-formed spear down, under Ilumene's breastplate, and felt it bite. The big soldier curled up under the force of the impact, then twisted violently away as a burst of ruby light illuminated them and the spear-shaft vanished. Ilumene rolled on the ground, his hands clasped to his chest, his face contorted with pain.

The soldier flopped in the dirt like a fish, barely a yard from Peness, who did nothing but watch. Suddenly Ilumene's leg flashed out and caught the mage in the side of the knee. Even as he was knocked over Peness saw Ilumene scrabbling forward, not bothering to get off his knees. He pounced on the mage and punched him with his steel-backed glove, and Peness felt his nose pop and blood squirt across his cheek. The hot burst of pain took hold of him and he howled, momentarily blinded, while Ilumene crashed his fist into the mage's ear and rolled off him, directing a kick into the man's ribs for good measure before backing off.

Peness gasped, the breath driven from his lungs, and whimpered. Raising one hand above his head to ward off any further blows, he kicked feebly against the ground as though trying to run. Out of instinct he reached for his magic again and sparks crackled into life all down the silver thread of his robe and cast a ruby light from his blood-spattered fingertips.

He felt a hand on his shoulder and whipped round with a fistful of raging energies, but even as he cast the magic at his assailant he felt a shadow fall over him and the magic fell apart, withering to nothing. A sudden chill ran though his bones and the mage stopped dead at the sight of the small, smiling face of Ruhen rather than Ilumene's weathered scowl.

"Peace, brother," Ruhen said softly. "No more fighting."

Peness stared up at the child in wonder, his mouth dropping open and hanging slack as the shadows in Ruhen's eyes washed cool and soothing through his soul. The pain of his injuries faded, numbed by the sweep of shadow. He tried to speak, but he could only wheeze after Ilumene's kick.

"Peace," Ruhen repeated. "Forget your pain and breathe in the beauty around you."

Peness blinked in surprise and looked around. There were frightened faces at windows and the mouth of a nearby alley, pinched with poverty or scarred by disease. Stinking grey water slopped over an abandoned rag in the gutter near his feet. The uneven cobbles on the ground were stained and dozens were missing—

A flitter of movement caught his eye: up on a windowsill the tiny form of a bird peered down at him, then returned its attention to the grey bricks of the wall beside it. Its wings were a bright green, its head was marked with a long golden stripe. The bird hopped forward along the sill and Peness saw at the end a bowl-shaped blue flower growing in the gap between bricks and a beetle the colour of finest amethyst. In a sudden burst of movement the bird darted forward and plucked the beetle from the wall, then carried it up to the slate roof of the house where wild roses were nodding in the breeze. There it sat and stared defiantly at Peness, beetle in its beak, before vanishing away over the houses.

"Peace," Peness croaked, shakily trying to get to his feet.

Ilumene came forward and hauled him up. "Peace," he agreed, less than impressed with the idea, but unwilling to argue with Ruhen.

The pristine white of Ilumene's clothes were now spotting with blood—his blood, Peness realised belatedly. He tried to find the anger inside him, but nothing came though the stiffness and returning pain.

"How?"

"Got my ways," Ilumene said with a half-smile. "Don't think I'd go up against a mage without a little protection, did you?"

Peness stared at the man. He couldn't see a charm or anything on Ilumene's armour, but there was a silver chain peeking out from behind his tunic. "I suppose not," he admitted.

Surreptitiously he opened his senses and tried to discover what it was the man was wearing. He detected some small presence of energy in the air around Ilumene, but the weave of magic was too subtle for him to unpick further. That alone told Peness something, however: he was the most skilled mage in Byora, and if he could not discern the shape of the magics Ilumene wore, that meant it was of the highest quality, most likely ancient, and Elven-made.

"Nah, I'd have already cut your throat by now if that was the case." Ilumene made a show of dusting the mage down as he spoke. "Best you remember in future, though: whatever you throw at me, I'll get a shot in before I go down." He paused and grinned evilly at Peness. "And I only need one."

Before the mage could reply Ilumene had sauntered past him and taken Ruhen's offered hand. Incongruously the burly soldier allowed himself to be led by the child out through the gate without even a glance back. Once they were through it, he jabbed a thumb in Peness' direction. On the other side Peness saw the tall shape of Koteer, the Demi-God, with his two remaining brother Jesters. Koteer beckoned for Peness to join them and, still wincing at the stinging rib, he did as bidden.

Ruhen continued walking into the fading sunshine of the open ground beyond the wall. Peness couldn't hear any conversation between them, but after a while Ilumene left abruptly and with a minimum of fuss he rounded up the traders and labourers who were working just beyond the gate and ushered them all inside the wall.

"And now we wait?" the mage complained. "This is madness."

"Now we wait," confirmed Koteer in an expressionless voice.

Koteer was significantly taller than Ilumene, and he too was dressed for war, in strange armour of curved scales. But what four warriors thought they could do here was a mystery to Peness. He'd been the one to send the warning to Duchess Escral in the first place, when, for once, his daemon-guide had been unambiguous: there were scores of daemons, perhaps as many as a hundred, marching on Byora.

The boundaries of the Land, like the Gods, had been weakened. Daemons still shunned the daylight, but dusk was fast approaching. The people of Byora had rejected their Gods, and consequently the border was weakest here. Byora would see a feeding of daemons not witnessed since the end of the Great War, when the Gods' strength had been taxed almost to extinction.

"What did he do?" Peness whispered, then cringed as he realised he'd spoken the words aloud.

Koteer turned to face him, his expression hidden behind his white mask. "Who?"

"The, ah, the Menin lord. The Gods must remember how weak they were left after striking Aryn Bwr's name from history—what could have made them do so again?"

Koteer regarded him for a long while, then turned his attention back to Ruhen without replying. Peness stared at the grey-skinned son of Death and wondered at his motivations too, but this time he managed not to speak them aloud. The Jesters had lived as Raylin mercenaries for centuries now; violence would always be their first recourse.

At last Ilumene returned to Ruhen's side and the pair stood on the road out of Byora, looking towards the treacherous, spirit-haunted fens in the distance. The sun had dropped behind the montain called Blackfang now and Byora was in shadow again. Even in summer the ghost-hour started early there. The evening gloom was still further advanced over the watery fens, where solitary ghost-willows lurked on the banks of ponds and lakes, and copses of marsh-alder hid the deepest parts from sight. Still waters were gateways to the other lands and it would be through the fens that any daemons came to Byora—the people's innate fear of that place would ensure it.

"Not long now," Ilumene commented to Ruhen as Peness watched them from a safe distance. "How many do you bet there'll be?"

"You are not a King's Man now," the child said. "A wager serves no purpose here."

"Keeps me from getting bored."

"There is enough to consider already."

Ilumene sniffed and inspected the bloodstain on his gauntlet. "The fabric of existence ain't really my department. What the Gods have done to the Land I'll leave to greater minds."

"Flattery is one lie that does not come easily to your tongue. Tell me your thoughts."

"On the weakening of boundaries? Not much to tell. I've no idea how Emin managed to force the Gods into that position—he must have known the result. Most likely the only God walking the Land right now is the Wither Queen and that's only with Jackdaw's help."

"Perhaps the Gods did not fear it. Their enemy was Aryn Bwr; the Menin lord was their potential rival. We do not figure by comparison, not in a way that threatens the divine. The Menin lord defied them, turned from the path they had prophesied, so he appeared a threat, but they do not care to involve themselves in the power-struggles of nations and men, and with both threats defeated they had no reason to hold back."

"Well, whatever the reason, it speeds up our plans another notch. It wouldn't surprise me to hear the Farlan boy was the one who started it off somehow, gave Emin the means or something."

Ruhen stopped dead and laughed, high and innocent, as realisation struck him. "We gave him the means," the child said. "We sacrificed it for the journal—the Skull of Ruling, the prize we dangled before Emin so he would kill the abbot in Scree for us. How else would he compel the Gods to expend such power?"

"That's what did it? Worked out better than we'd planned, then."

"Indeed. Your king has embraced its chaotic nature with greater relish than anyone could have anticipated. Now he just needs to bring the Key of Magic into play and every piece will finally be on the board—more than we even need, now the Gods are so weakened." He raised a hand to stop any reply from Ilumene, and took a deep breath of the evening air. He glanced back at Blackfang and saw the halo of evening sun dimming around the broken mountain's ragged brow. "I smell them," he murmured.

"Here?"

"In the air. They're waiting, watching and waiting."

"No doubt. Not much beats a daemon for looking forward to a bit of slaughter." Ilumene fitted his round shield properly onto his arm and loosened the ties around his sword-hilt. "We'll make 'em think twice about it, though."

The pair walked slowly down the road beside one of the many streams that ran from Byora to the fens. The evening grew around them, a steady, stealthy creeping darkness accompanied by the whisper of wind, and faint voices. Ruhen and his protector faced the stiffening breeze in silence until they were fifty yards from the gate and the only visible souls there, all the more obvious for their bright white clothes. A scent of age came to Ilumene on the breeze, the dry and musty chill of a tomb, the silence and patience that was Azaer, reaching out into the twilight and luxuriating in the precarious balance between one moment and the next.

Ilumene smiled as he felt Azaer's presence surround them both: tiny, delicate touches down his neck—the lightest imprint of a spider footstep, the brush of a fly's wing—while the twisting threads of shadow in his soul blossomed into dark buds.

In the distance shapes as yet unformed advanced towards them, discernable only as wisps of movement. With each advancing second of evening, the daemons came closer to the Land, and in their wake the howls of the damned echoed. The deepening blue sky was overlaid with a bloody red haze and the shadows of roiling smoke-clouds. Ilumene drew his sword as Ruhen stood and stared, transfixed by the sight of figures coalescing out of the evening air.

Already they could make out individuals, coming on two feet or four, clothed in bright cloth, or plates of bone and chitin, armed with claws and teeth or rusted, hook-edged axes and swords. They marched not with threats or shouts but with a near-silent intensity of purpose and halted when they were no more than forty yards away from Ruhen and Ilumene.

The leader of the pack was a tall beast that stood on a dog's hind legs and carried a pair of ornate axes. Its muzzle was drawn back into a permanent snarl by iron chains set into its cheeks, shaping its skull into a blunt wedge.

"Leave this place," Ruhen called to them, his child's voice carrying clearly through the evening air, but it seemed to be followed by strange whispers that raced in all directions like zephyrs through long grass.

The daemon regarded Ruhen for a long while as its fellows hissed and gnashed their teeth. "Give us tribute and worship and we will let you live." Its voice was a threatening growl, and sounded like random noises that just happened to form human words.

"No tribute," Ruhen said plainly, "no worship. This is a place of peace. Your kind are not welcome here."

"What are you to make such demands?" the daemon barked, the anger in its voice echoed by the dozens at its side.

The clamour of their howls hammered at Ilumene's ears so intensely that for a moment he wondered if he'd missed Ruhen's reply. Then he realised the child had said nothing; he was waiting patiently for the chance to speak. Inexplicably, the daemons stayed where they were, and eventually they quietened. Peness' daemon-guide had claimed the warband was thirsty for flesh and blood, that nothing would stop or slow them until they were sated, yet not only had they failed to attack, but they stood well back of the little boy and his single protector.

"My name is Ruhen," he said, "and your death stands in my shadow."

To emphasise the point Ilumene raised his sword, but he was one against dozens.

The daemons started to advance on them, their jaws open and weapons held ready.

"The Circle City is under my protection," Ruhen continued, as if oblivious to the danger closing on him. "I will not allow you to harm its people."

When the leader of the daemons only snarled and increased its pace, Ruhen made a small, dismissive gesture with his hands. "So be it," he murmured.

From their hiding-places the Harlequins burst up to attack, their white masks shockingly bright in the deepening gloom. They moved as one, converging on the daemons in seconds, weapons already moving for the kill. Ilumene charged the dog-legged daemon with a yell, reaching it at the same moment as a young warrior whose slender sword caught the daemon's raised left arm.

Ilumene ignored a blow from the daemon's axe on his shield, instead pushing inside its guard and smashing up at its dog-muzzle with the pommel of his sword. The blow snapped its head back and Ilumene wasted no time in chopping down into the daemon's arm. He followed it up with a thrust into its gut and the daemon vanished just as the blow struck. The Harlequin had already passed onto the next daemon, striking with blinding speed. The Harlequins moved in a complex dance, each one aware of where the others were, each one constantly in motion.

Ilumene held back, aware his own style, however effective on a battlefield, could not fit into that dance. He marvelled at the bloody ballet being executed before him as eighty Harlequins, a slim sword in each hand, slashed and pirouetted their way through the mass of lumbering beasts in concentrated silence, always moving, each step fluidly transforming into the next lethal strike. Some fell, unable to avoid the wild sweeps of the huge daemonic weapons, but the majority continued in their silent dance. The daemons were now striking out in wild, uncontrolled frenzy. Blows were coming from all quarters, but none of the Harlequins stayed still long enough for the daemons to focus: it was impossible to find one foe to face before that was replaced by another, identical and just as deadly, moving in from a completely different direction.

One monster raised itself up on its hind legs and flexed great talons, ready to swipe down at whatever stood before it, only to have a dozen long cuts appear, circling its belly. A black-clad Harlequin appeared quite suddenly before it, momentarily stepping out of the main dance and into a solo.

The daemon roared like a bear, but even before it smashed its taloned paws down on Venn, half a dozen more cuts had been torn through its shaggy hide. Venn dodged the claws with ease and slashed again at the daemon's flank, each strike cutting to the bone amidst a shower of ichor, then he rammed the point of one sword into the leg-joint and sliced it away entirely.

That done, Venn returned to the dance and vanished into the storm of swords, even as another Harlequin appeared in front of the daemon and sheared through the bony protrusion under its eyes. A third exposed its teeth with a deft cut to the cheek, then another came, and another and another. The daemon howled and tried to protect its face, but the Harlequins had already switched focus to its supporting leg, and cut after cut flashed into that knee-joint until, within a matter of seconds, that too was sheered through and the daemon flopped to the ground, helpless.

One, a lithe daemon with reptilian eyes and a grey spiny coat, tried to batter its way through to Ruhen. It moved with abrupt, darting steps, avoiding the worst of the blows, but it found Ilumene moving to intercept instead as it dodged free of the Harlequins.

The daemon tried to feint one way and nip past, but Ilumene, seeing its intention, threw his shield towards where it was heading, then brought his sword around behind his body and hacked cross-wise at the space he'd just left. Even with a spiny claw outstretched for protection, the daemon was smashed off course by Ilumene's heavy sword. It staggered a step or two, its arm shattered by the blow, by which time Ilumene had made up the ground and with a great roar of triumph chopped through its neck.

Ilumene looked up to see Ruhen with a small smile on his face and the shadows in his eyes racing with delight. His lips were slightly parted, and Ilumene saw him breathe in the stink of the dying daemon's blood with relish, but before the soldier could return to the fight a sound came from behind the boy and he raised his sword again as they both turned—

—and wonder fell across Ruhen's face. Scores of people were streaming out of the city, then the stream became a flood of men and women, soldiers and shopkeepers and labourers, all barrelling towards the mass of daemons, shouting with outrage, crying "Byora!" and "Ruhen!"

They brandished whatever they had been able to find: spears and swords, cleavers, knives and clubs: a poor army, but in seconds it was two hundred people, then three, all racing towards the battle without a thought for their own safety. They threw themselves on the remaining daemons even as the Harlequins continued their own lethal dance.

Ilumene gaped at the unexpected turn of events, nearly dropping his own sword in surprise. The population of Wheel had been watching them from the walls—he had expected that—but their love of Ruhen ran so deep that they would attack a horde of daemons? He laughed, long and loud, as more and more of Byora's poorest ran into the fray.

Ruhen was staring in thrilled silence; his delight at the daemon's death had paled into insignificance compared with what was plain on his face now. As the people of Byora stabbed and battered and pulled down the last of the daemons, the shadows all around them deepened until there was nothing left to kill and darkness shrouded the victors.

Chapter 8

Nai looked in the direction from which the winged daemon had come. The awkward little thing was warm, but entirely motionless; it felt odd sitting on his hand. Its wings hung limply over the sides as though it were dead.

Images blossomed in Nai's mind: dark snapshots of the Land around them and the creatures that walked it. Here and there he saw distortions, uncomfortable blurs of darkness he guessed were daemon-spirits on the border between realms. Further in the distance were pinpricks of light, farmsteads and villages, all hiding behind a haze of enchantments thrown up by witches and minor mages, hastily done and of varying degrees of effectiveness.

Beside him Nai sensed the large presence of Amber. The big Menin didn't speak; he knew to let Nai finish before questioning him. It wasn't clear whether Amber fully comprehended his new situation, but Nai saw no reason to press the matter. Amber understood the journey, the simple purpose of travelling, and he appeared content to take refuge in that while his mind recovered. Taking Nai's orders was easier than remembering what he'd lost, whether or not they were headed towards the man who had nearly broken Amber's mind.

"Amber," Nai said eventually, "the daemon has seen another traveller."

"Menin?"

"I doubt it; it's a woman, and a strange one at that."

"How?"

"There is some trace of the Gods on her, but a daemon too. But she's safe from what we're keen to avoid: her soul is owned already, and nothing out here intends to compete."

"Necromancer?"

"No, Amber, I don't think so, but you never know your luck," Nai said, at last turning to face him.

A thick growth of white-streaked stubble highlighted the biggest of the scars on Amber's cheek, a sword-cut. His expression was taut, the face of a man anticipating pain. His loss of both of his life's purpose as well as his name loomed large, always poised to descend on him again.

"Let's go and find out," Nai said at last.

Alterr was bright, and they were travelling through open pastureland for the main. With the small daemon to guide them the pair moved quickly.

"She's near," Nai said less than an hour later, pointing to a humped rise studded with boulders. They followed a rabbit run, the closest thing they had seen to a path all day, and on the other side Nai motioned for them to move more cautiously.

Amber instinctively reached for his sword, but Nai grabbed his arm before he could draw it. "We're not here to fight," he whispered. "You might provoke her into shooting you if she's got a bow."

Fifty yards past the rise they smelled smoke on the breeze: a small fire was burning somewhere nearby, though it was currently hidden from view somewhere in the small copses of silver-leaved ash and young oaks that dotted the ground. They could see nothing in the shadows, but anyone who was surviving out here on their own was more than likely aware of their presence already, Nai mused. They moved slowly, carefully, until at last they spotted an orange glow reflecting off the surrounding tree-trunks, though Nai rightly guessed the fireside would be empty.

He motioned for Amber to wait for him and went on ahead. After a dozen more paces a voice called out from the darkness off to his right, "That's far enough. Who are you?"

Nai froze as he turned to face the blank shadows: she'd spoken in Farlan, and something about her voice was familiar. A woman out in the wilds alone, smelling of Gods, most likely indicated a devotee of the Lady, but the daemon's touch narrowed the field hugely.

"A traveller, like yourself," he ventured.

"You don't look much like me."

"But maybe you recognise me all the same?" He explained, "I'm a mage, I did a bit of scouting the ground and found you out here, wearing the perfume of Gods and—ah, something else. If you are Farlan and were once a devotee of the Lady, it might be that once we met."

"Go on," she prompted as he paused.

"Were you once employed by the Certinse family, or perhaps the Tenash?" he asked.

A shape appeared from the darkness: a muscular young woman with short hair, wearing a scowl of contempt. "Fucking necromancers," she said at last, "you really are like cockroaches." She did have a crossbow to hand, but she pointed the weapon at the ground.

Nai gave a little bow. He was used to the scorn; it came with the territory, and he'd found a little self-directed humour worked far better than his former master's disdain. "We are an adaptive breed, I like to think. Am I right in thinking we've met before, then?"

"Aye, you were Isherin Purn's servant—the one with the weird feet, right? I remember some about you too. Your name's Nai?"

"Indeed. I trust everything you heard was delightful and complimentary?" Nai said with a grin, easily falling back into his obsequious, *I am harmless* routine.

"Cockroach summed it up pretty well actually." She looked past him to where Amber was standing. "Who's this one?"

"My companion's name is Amber. Might I know your name?" He wasn't positive, but he thought perhaps the woman's grip on her crossbow had tightened at the mention of the Menin major's name.

"My name's Ardela, and as it happens, I've heard of both of you. Seems we're both heading out of Byora at the same time, and probably for the same reason."

"The regrettable change in leadership?"

Ardela snorted. "Not my reason, but your friend's Menin so I'm guessing there are people in Byora who'd be keen to kill us both—perhaps all three of us, since your lot are rarely welcome anywhere, necromancer."

"Need I point out the circumstances of our first meeting? I don't think you should get so comfortable up there on your moral high ground."

For a moment a look of pure, savage anger crossed her face and in that instant Nai imagined the thump of a quarrel hitting his stomach. He actually took a pace back before he caught himself.

"Don't push me."

A brief crackle of energy danced across Nai's callused knuckles. "Good advice for us all," he said coldly, before pointedly dismissing the magic at his command.

Ardela stared at him for a long while, then nodded. "Aye, maybe. So in the spirit of sharing, how about you tell me why you're heading west when, if there's anything left of the Menin armies, they'll be retreating in the other direction."

"First things first," Nai said. He moved a little closer and lowered his voice. "My companion isn't quite the man he used to be. I would appreciate it if you didn't mention whatever happened out west, or any effects of a spell that might have been done."

Ardela said thoughtfully, "Grieving his lord?"

"It is rather more than that," he said, wincing. "In that army men are allowed to use an alternative name if theirs might be associated with some family shame, or if it might attract attention because of being named after *some distant relation*."

Ardela's eyes widened. "Damn," she said eventually, "that must have hurt." She stared at Amber, who was just far enough away not to be able to hear their words.

"The Gods themselves reaching into your mind and tearing out your name? Yes, I suspect it might have. In any case, his mind is still fragile. I have worked hard to salvage it, and I would prefer that not to be undone." Nai hesitated and glanced at her cross-bow a moment before continuing, "In answer to your question, I'm taking him west to King Emin, whom I hope is your ally."

"And if he had turned out to be something different?" Ardela asked. "You risked a bolt in the belly there."

"If your allegiance had lain elsewhere, your bow-string would have snapped before you could aim it; trust me on that." Nai smiled unpleasantly at her. "As it is, I'm guessing the delightful Legana told you about us. She's met us both, and whatever your past—ah, *exploits*, they still took place within the Farlan sphere. If there were other walkers in the dark involved in events, I'd know about it—indeed, I'd most likely be on their side."

Ardela frowned. "You're selling him like a piece of meat? Can't say I'm surprised, but I don't see why the king will care enough to buy."

"I'll just have to take my chances on that. Does my story buy us a place at your fire though?"

"I suppose so. If Ruhen sent someone I know after me it's not to hunt me down, and they're a suspicious bunch back in Narkang. I'll let them figure out any ruse you might come out with and in the meantime just be glad of the extra swords. You wouldn't believe what I saw out walking last night." She sniffed. "Well, *you* might, I suppose."

"Indeed I might," Nai beamed, "and if you've got any booze I'll even tell you why it's happening, too."

He beckoned for Amber to join them and the big man trudged forward without comment. Nai watched as Ardela waited for Amber to reach them first, sized up the soldier and then turned her back on him just as he came within arm's reach. Ardela was particularly muscular for a Farlan woman, but she was still the better part of a foot shorter than the heavily built soldier. For his part Amber didn't appear to have noticed anything.

Soon they were settled around the small fire, with Nai watching Ardela and Ardela scrutinising Amber, who stared blankly into the flames, snapping out of it only when Nai shoved a chunk of bread into his hands. The big soldier grunted and tore at it with his teeth, not even bothering to pull out his waterskin to soften it, as most people would do.

"So the heavily armed soldier is a prisoner," Ardela commented, ignoring Nai's wince.

Amber grunted, but that was more confirmation of their circumstances than Nai had seen from the man thus far.

"You wearing a dead man's bag round your neck, or some other sort of enchantment to stop him slitting your throat?"

Nai nodded as Amber swallowed down the rest of his bread.

"Maybe I'm just waiting," Amber announced abruptly, his Menin accent making the Farlan words sound thick and heavy. "Maybe there's someone else I want to kill more."

To Nai's surprise Ardela agreed. "I can see why you would. You won't find me standing in your way, but others will."

He turned to face Ardela. "I've got nothing else," he said, and Nai caught a glimpse of kinship on her face.

"Legana's got a few things to say on that subject," she said. "Go and speak to her first. Necromancer, the first watch's yours." She pulled her cloak over her and settled down, her head on her pack, to sleep.

Isak eased his head up off the bed and tried to look around. There was pain, but it felt distant, as though he were feeling someone else's injuries rather than his own. The room beyond the carved bedposts was dim and blurry. For a while he could make out nothing more than he was alone, then a faint huff of breath from somewhere over the edge of the bed reassured him of Hulf's presence. A chill settled on his skin, a memory of his dreams that had again been of the lakeside in Llehden.

But now it's someone else's dream, he thought, too tired for relief or satisfaction at the notion. *I've cursed another with my nightmare. He's the one who wakes up in the cold house beside the lake now, unable to remember who he is.*

He tugged away the blankets wrapped tightly across his chest. Even now the fingers of his right hand looked strange, as if they belonged to another man; these awkward, uneven hands weren't his; they were just what he had to put up with now. There were stubby ridges where his fingernails had been torn out in Ghenna. They were growing back, but who knew if they would eventually hide the runes carved into the skin underneath? Isak hoped the daemon-script and incantations might yet be put to service: he felt their presence constantly, a warm, insidious tug on his soul that was for ever urging it away from the mortal shell he inhabited.

On the far wall a door opened. Isak's hand quested unbidden across the wide bed and closed around the grip of Eolis. He blinked hard to try and clear his eyes, but he succeeded only in sparking a wave of dizziness and nausea that forced his head back down onto the pillow.

"Awake at last," Mihn said, appearing at his bedside. He placed a hand on Isak's chest to stop him trying to rise. "How is your arm?"

While Isak screwed his face up in thought, Hulf jerked awake and pounced on Mihn, driving him back in his enthusiastic greeting. Eventually Mihn managed to work his way around the powerful dog, tugging his sleeve from Hulf's teeth with a chiding tap on the nose.

The white-eye raised his arm and saw Mihn lean back from Eolis' lethal edge, then realised he meant his other hand. With Mihn's help he freed himself from the blanket and as he raised it he realised where the greater part of the pain in his body was coming from.

"It hurts," he mumbled, looking at the clean white bandage that covered his entire forearm, elbow to thumb. In the weak light it blended neatly with the lightning-bleached skin of the rest of his arm.

Mihn smiled. "It would. You really are a bloody fool sometimes."

He took Isak's hand to support the arm and gently removed the pin holding the bandage tight. After carefully unwrapping it part-way, he inspected the skin of Isak's wrist, then continued to expose the greater part of the wound. Isak caught a glimpse of red, blistered lines and blackened skin, then the memory rushed back hard enough to make him moan with pain.

"Cauterising your own wounds, having let a daemon-hound chew on your arm?" Mihn said with a disbelieving shake of the head. "So at least some of the madman I knew remains."

Hulf, determined not to be left out of proceedings, hopped up onto the bed and clambered across Isak's legs until he reached the far side. Isak twitched, and watched Hulf's forward-flopped ears prick up. The dog had patches of pure white on his belly and running down the inside of each leg since the ritual: hidden under the thick fur were the same tattoos the Brotherhood and the Ghosts now sported. The dog was completely unperturbed by the magic bound to his skin; he was adapting already, using his new skills to hunt in the forest, and gleefully stealing from soldiers's tents.

He moved his foot under the blanket again and Hulf pounced, slamming his front paws together, then wrapping his jaws around the prominent hump that was Isak's blanket-covered toes.

Isak smiled weakly. "It seemed like a good idea at the time."

Now Mihn laughed out loud. "It always does, my friend, no matter how many times we tell you to leave the thinking to the rest of us. At least you heal quickly—all you white-eyes do. Daken is demanding to be helped to the nearest whorehouse to check everything still works, and he was as near as dead after the attack."

"Couldn't the whores go to him?"

"One would think," Mihn agreed. "Perhaps it is a matter of pride for the man? Or pethaps he just has not thought of that yet."

Isak focused on Mihn's face: there was something different about it. Eventually he realised there was a long, shallow cut down the side of Mihn's head. He tried to remember the last time he'd seen Mihn actually injured, but could not think of a single instance. "One got you," he said at last, pointing as best he could.

"The dangers of your company, my Lord."

"Don't remember seeing that ever, you catching more than a bruise."

"You have not been present for most of my fights," Mihn said. "This is far from my first injury."

"Less than your fair share, though. They must have been desperate for revenge if one got that close."

"You flatter me." Mihn said with a smile.

Isak sat in silence for a while, then raised Eolis again. "Take it. They'll come again."

"No. You killed your jailer, the one who had my scent and carried my bond."

"Please." Isak sighed and closed his eyes. "I'm so tired—tired of this all. I don't have the strength to carry Eolis any longer. But you, you're worthy of it. They'll not get so close again, not if you were wielding Eolis."

"I want that burden even less than you," Mihn said gently, pushing Isak's hand away, "and I shall not break my vow again. Whatever claim you have on my soul, you cannot order me to do that. There are others more worthy than me, soldiers who will see it more properly used."

"Who? It's tied to my soul—who else could I trust with it?"

"Vesna, Lahk—there are many here you can trust, and now there are hundreds who wear my tattoos and are just as bound to you as I am."

Isak felt sadness wash over him. "No, none are as bound as you," he said, feeling tears of shame threatening in his eyes. "None whose soul I'll spend again and again."

"Enough of that," Mihn said firmly. "I never wanted to go down in history, but if that is the price of success I will pay it gladly."

"You will pay it, Grave Thief," Isak muttered, "and for that I'm sorry."

"Isak, enough! Your share is more than any man or woman should ever have to bear. There are no apologies to make, all right? Now, can you get up? King Emin is leaving soon."

Isak nodded and sat up on the bed, wincing. "Where's he going?"

"South; there is one Menin army undefeated on Narkang lands. His intelligence says they have occupied a town and are holding position—they have no plan, but they are showing no interest in surrender, and none of the local forces are strong enough to dislodge ten thousand Menin veterans."

"While we go north," Isak commented, easing his bare toes onto the rug below his bed. He was in Moorview Castle's royal suite, a grand bedchamber reserved for the king, but Emin had insisted Isak take the room. There was a second smaller bed for Mihn in the far corner, and an enormous wardrobe covering most of the right-hand wall, but all Isak cared about was the enormous oak bed that looked as if it had been built for a white-eye of his size and weight.

As soon as his feet were on the ground Hulf jumped to the ground and gave each foot a cursory lick before darting towards the door.

"I'll dress myself," Isak said, watching the dog. "Go and let him out before he ruins any more of this rug." He pointed to a tasselled corner that was now well chewed.

Mihn encouraged Hulf out after him and left Isak in peace. The white-eye dressed slowly, wincing as he slipped on his tunic. He was fumbling ineffectively at his boots when Mihn returned to help.

Once dressed he belted Eolis around his waist, alongside the leather bag containing the Skull of Ruling, and headed out into the bustle of the main part of the castle. Isak was forced to acknowledge two dozen salutes and bows, from men of the Kings-guard and Brotherhood for the main, before he reached the half-moon-shaped hall where the king was directing proceedings.

"Isak," King Emin called, coming to greet the stooped white-eye with a warm smile. "Your powers of recovery never cease to amaze me. It's good to see you upright, my friend—although I will suggest you don't cauterise your own wounds in future."

The king was dressed for travel in uncertain times, but unsurprisingly, his green-and gold brigandine was covered with the finest, most intricate stitching that portrayed branches of oak leaves with beehives hanging from them, as well as his usual bee device.

Isak took the king's arm and muttered his thanks as he looked around the assembled company. Doranei and Veil were in their king's lee as usual, while Legana and the witch of Llehden were presiding over a group of ten or so people sitting at a long table that occupied one half of the room. Vesna, Lahk and Tiniq were among them.

But Isak barely noticed these details. There was one figure, standing just inside the doorway, who instantly dominated his attention, and if he had looked around at the other faces in the room it would have been clear he wasn't alone there.

Hulf stood out on the terrace at a wary distance, his ears flat against his head as he edged forward, torn between keeping away and running to Isak's side.

"Just as well not all men stare so. Someone might get jealous."

Isak took a step forward, and Hulf darted past the newcomer, determinedly placing himself in front of Isak, but so close to his feet the white-eye had to stop dead.

"Your puppy's better trained than mine," Isak said at last, one eye on Doranei. The grim King's Man hadn't moved. He kept his arms folded, making the point that he was at his king's command here.

"Yet they share the same adorable eyes," Zhia said with a smile that showed her small, bright teeth. "I've discovered mine is not averse to having his tummy tickled either. Is that how you got the tattoos on him? I'm glad to see reports of your untimely death have proved inaccurate—in the long run at least." Sapphire eyes flashed darkly in the shadow of the dark grey shawl she wore pulled right over her head to protect her skin from the dull morning light outside, but there was a drawn look to her face that even Isak could see. She had on a strange combination of clothes: long strips of cloth decorated with small blue flowers that combined to form a long skirt but would not restrict movement if she needed to fight, over a more functional pair of trousers and long boots. She wore a plain fitted jacket, with blue silk gloves that extended from elbow to fingertip and mirrored the pattern on her skirt.

"You're hurt," Isak said at last, finding he had no response to her comment.

Zhia inclined her head. "Fortunately I heal even quicker than you do, and there are a still a few meals wandering lost on the moor."

"Zhia and her brother attempted to stop the battle before it began," Emin explained, watching Isak's reaction carefully. "My mages sensed something violent was taking place within the Menin lines. Now we have an explanation for what that was."

"You will, of course, note the slight scepticism in the king's voice," Zhia said. As she shifted the weight on her feet slightly Isak could see the discomfort it caused her. The vampire drew her right arm closer in to her body. She wore her long-handled sword on her belt, but she didn't look like she was in much condition to draw it. "I had forgotten what a suspicious man he is; even with my brother's Crystal Skull in his possession, he wonders. However, here I am at your mercy, ready to scratch Doranei behind the ears and help you in your endeavours."

"Help?"

She inclined her head. "You managed to defeat a man created to be peerless, one who twice cut my brother down in single combat. If that does not indicate you are capable of ending this all, I don't know what does. King Emin remains cautious, but he understands my argument."

"You will forgive me a few misgivings," Emin interjected, "when you have spent this long *not* helping our cause, whether or not you've hindered it."

"And they are forgiven," she replied with a sudden, dazzling smile that Isak felt like the heat of a fire on his skin. From their reactions, Doranei and Emin did too: the king drew back slightly while his agent had to fight to avoid taking a step towards her. "All the same, here I am at your disposal and, I suspect, still likely to be useful."

"What makes you so sure of that?" Isak asked.

"You have Vorizh's journal. I assume by now you've translated it."

King Emin glanced at Doranei. "I had heard you and Koezh didn't know what was within it."

"That's true enough," Zhia said with a snort, "but one doesn't have to be seven millennia old and the brother of the author to guess what aspect of my utterly deranged sibling's life you're interested in. It could be his exploits during the Great War or his experiments on wyverns—or perhaps Doranei is looking for a living male relative of mine from whom to ask permission." She blew Doranei a kiss that only made his cheeks colour more.

Then she continued, "However, I'm guessing it's because he stole the most terrible weapon in existence from the Chief of the Gods." Zhia shrugged. "It's just a guess, mind."

"And you choose your side," Isak stated.

"I knew the time was coming," Zhia said, "and now I've chosen. Any objections about the time I took to decide are really not of concern."

From King Emin's expression it was clear he had no intention of taking the debate any further. "On that note, I'll take my leave. The Kingsguard and the bulk of the army will be travelling south with me, to negotiate the surrender of the last remaining Menin army group, and make ourselves obvious on the border so General Afasin down in Mustet doesn't get any ideas. The Ghosts have their orders. Half of them are leaving with me, the rest will act as escort for you, Isak. I leave it up to you to decide how much of our plans you reveal, however much she's guessed thus far."

Emin reached for Isak's arm again and grasped it tightly. "Look after yourself, my friend. I will see you soon."

Isak nodded in response. Clearly the king's farewells to the rest had already been made, for he wasted no time in leaving, soldiers and generals clustered at his heels. Doranei spared one final look in Zhia's direction before following, despite the fact he would be travelling with Isak rather than his king. Isak saw her gaze soften for a moment, but in that look there was no hint whether she was a true ally or something less. A moment later the inscrutable expression she normally wore returned.

Isak sighed, gesturing for her to join the people sitting at the long table.

What assurances could we trust anyway? Logic and instinct are as good reasons as any to trust her, and we will certainly need the help.

"So, are you planning a trip?" Zhia asked brightly, sapphire eyes carefully noting all the faces of the group they were joining. "Somewhere nice, I hope?"

She made a particular point to embrace Legana, casting her eyes over the remarkable changes that had taken place since they last met. Though physical contact with the woman she'd taken under her wing in Scree discomforted Zhia now—Legana's divine spirit was anathema to the vampire—it was not enough to stop her running tender fingers down Legana's cheek. The fierce Mortal-Aspect seemed to soften at the gesture, the emerald glow of her eyes lessening as she smiled in welcome.

The Farlan men had all risen as Zhia joined them. "Does it sound likely?" growled Vesna as he retook his seat. The Mortal-Aspect of Karkarn scratched the ruby teardrop on his cheek irritably, as though the War God objected to her presence. "We're following a trail left by your mad monster of a younger brother; it's a long way from nice."

"Which is to be expected really," Mihn said. "There is reasoning behind it, if you think like an insane heretic."

Zhia turned to scrutinise the unassuming man. She had not realised his status among the Farlan nobles was high enough to permit him to freely join the conversation. She was a great politician, and she knew the Land's customs well, especially those of the Farlan, for they had endured for centuries.

"Vanach," Vesna said sourly, "that happy little hole of religious fanaticism and brutal tyranny. According to your brother's journal, all that misery is his way of hiding Termin Mystt until the time comes for some saviour to claim it."

Isak grinned at the group in general, the broken lines of his face serving only to enhance his dark humour. "So you've got to pick your saviour then: me or Ruhen?" He shared a look with Mihn, but the man didn't join his mirth. "I've said it before: you lot need to be more careful when you hand out jobs."

When no one responded, the witch of Llehden took that as her cue and rose. She was swiftly followed by all the Farlan men but Isak, though she ignored them as she made her way around the table. She gave Legana's hand a squeeze in passing before beckoning to Isak. The white-eye left his seat without a word and fell in beside her, with Mihn and Hulf close behind. They went into the next room, the lord of Moorview's study in more peaceful times.

The air was redolent with the scents of old, polished wood and leather and pipe smoke. Over a small fireplace was a tall gilt-framed mirror that dominated the room, and for a while the witch faced it, as if subjecting herself to the same exacting scrutiny everyone else received.

"I must leave too," the witch said once the door was closed behind them. "Llehden needs me, now more than ever, and Zhia's presence is not one I relish."

Isak ducked his head in acknowledgement. "Someone has to clear up after me," he said, apologetically. "Will you— Will you be safe?"

Her face was unreadable. From somewhere she had found an old silk shawl of faded green and brown. He guessed it was a cast-off of Countess Derenin's, but suited her: autumnal colours on a cool summer's day.

Isak suspected he knew the woman as well as any man now, but still she remained a mystery to him. Even on the journey to Moorview she had shared little of her opinions and nothing of her history. Mihn said that was the way of witches; part of their power was in being apart from the rest of humanity.

Isak didn't envy her having to make that effort. Having had it thrust upon him, he knew how heavy a burden that could be.

"There is no way of knowing," she said eventually. "Daima will be well clear of the lake; only the gentry will go near it now. They know he is dangerous, but I suspect they have much in common with each other now, the Ragged Man and the gentry."

He lowered his head, both an acknowledgement of her point and a pang of shame that she was handling the fallout of his actions. "Thank you," he whispered.

"For what? I share in the responsibility for what we did to him, Isak. And my task will be easier than yours."

Isak leaned heavily on the back of a chair, drained by the memory of what they had done. "Not just for this, for all you've done. My home is Llehden, but I give it up to another. I don't know if I'll ever see you again, and I've much to thank you for."

She put a small hand on the twisted scars of his arm. "I am a witch of the Land; it is my place to do what I must, what is right, so there is no need for thanks—but I'll take it gladly, all the same."

Before he could say anything more the door burst open. Mihn and Hulf were already moving towards the intruder before he was even in the room, and he yelped with fear at the sight of both of them. Isak watched with a slight smile as Endine hopped backwards and collided with the wall, ending up in a small heap with Hulf standing over him barking defiantly.

Realising the little mage was no threat, Mihn dropped down and hooked his arm around Hulf's chest in one practised movement. The powerful dog squirmed to get out of his grip, but Mihn managed to manoeuvre him back far enough for Isak to take Hulf by the scruff of the neck, at which he finally quietened.

"My— Ah, my Lord, my apologies!" Endine gabbled, hands still protectively over his head. "I didn't realise the room was in use."

"I was just leaving," the witch said. She inclined her head to both Isak and Mihn and stepped neatly over the floundering mage, taking the opportunity to leave before anything more could be said. Isak watched her go with a strange sense of loss, but he suppressed the feeling and reminded himself of everything he still had to do that day.

"Come in, Master Endine," Mihn said, helping the man up. "You are recovered then?"

It was rare that Mihn physically overshadowed any man, but he looked large and powerful compared to Tomal Endine. Though they were of a similar height, Endine was as frail as a decrepit old man. He reminded Isak of someone back in Tirah, but as the thought struck it was accompanied by a sharp pain in his head and he lurched sideways against the armchair, bandaged arm flailing wildly as the chair scraped across the parquet floor before catching on something.

Mihn grabbed his good hand and hauled on it as hard as he could, fighting to keep the huge white-eye on his feet until he had steadied himself.

Moaning, he sank to his knees, one arm draped over the chair's armrest, as sparks of pain flashed through his head and a cold, empty void opened up in his mind. "It's not there," he gasped, blinking back tears. "His name's darkness, just darkness—!"

"Darkness?" squawked Endine. "What do you mean my name is darkness?"

"Quiet," Mihn ordered before crouching at Isak's side. "Isak, *breathe*, just look at me and breathe. His name is Tomal Endine, you remember?"

Isak shook his head. "Not him, another man, looks like him." He shuddered and screwed up his eyes until he found the strength to take a long heaving breath, then a second. "The holes in my mind—it's not like forgetting," he whispered.

"I know—I wish it were; but some of your memories could not be forgotten—we had to cut them out," Mihn said compassionately.

"Who's the man? The man in Tirah?"

Mihn turned to the bemused Endine. "Who looks like him?"

"A priest? I see his face, a man in robes, and Death's hand on his shoulder."

"A dead priest? High Cardinal Echer, perhaps?"

Isak looked blank at the suggestion, and Mihn decided that was probably correct, if Isak couldn't remember the name of the man who'd performed his investiture as Lord of the Farlan.

"The High Cardinal, yes—there is a superficial similarity between them, though Echer was an older man."

"Ruggedly handsome, I presume?" Endine asked with tentative humour.

Isak shook his head drunkenly and allowed Mihn to help him up into the chair. "A worm," he gasped as he recovered himself, "a madman we had to kill."

"Well, honestly!" Endine bristled, his attempt at wit eclipsed by the white-eye's antagonism.

"Calm yourself, Master Endine," Mihn interrupted, "he was killed by his own. It was the High Priest of Death I murdered, so you are quite safe. Now, you came in here for a reason?"

Endine opened his mouth, then shut it again with a snap. He had been unconscious for days after the battle, drained by his exertions, and then spent another two in complete silence as he mourned his friend, Shile Cetarn, who had died during the battle.

The two had been constant companions, colleagues and magical sparring partners for more than a decade, and without the over-sized Cetarn beside him, Endine looked even less substantial.

Isak found it hard to believe this man was one of the finest battle-mages in Narkang. He'd grown used to using physical strength to contain and channel terrifying levels of magic, and he equated that to power, but it wasn't necessarily so; a mage's mental control and skill was at least as important as his physical capacity. While Endine was a weak man, he was brilliant and deft, almost the opposite to Isak's own raw talent.

"I came to use the mirror," he said in a quiet voice. "The king ordered me to fetch a man who's travelling here from Narkang."

"Help yourself," Isak said. "I'll just sit here if you don't mind. Is it a magic mirror?"

"No—well, yes, sort of. Judging by the quality of workmanship it was clearly made using magic, but I'll be the one performing the spell." He scuttled over to the fireplace and after a wary glance back at Isak, reached into the pocket of his robe. It showed signs of careful repair after the battle; he might not be strong enough to wield a sword effectively, but Endine had been in the fort with King Emin as the Menin infantry launched their final frenzied assault, and without his desperate efforts it was very possible there would have been no survivors of that final stand. In the whole Narkang Army, probably only Cetarn had killed more men.

From his robe Endine reverently withdrew a Crystal Skull. It was too large for him to hold comfortably in one hand so he pressed the artefact to his chest while he drew chalk symbols on the edge of the mantelpiece.

"Snap," Isak muttered, and when Endine turned and looked at him with puzzled irritation he held up the bag containing the Skull of Ruling.

"So you are one of those chosen?" Mihn said gravely.

Endine stopped working a moment and visibly stiffened. "Of course I was chosen," he said in a quiet voice. "Who else is more qualified? And besides, I refuse to allow that fat oaf Cetarn to have all the glory—I cannot have history remember me as some sort of apprentice of his."

Isak saw Mihn smile at that. The squabbling pair of mages had fitted into the Brotherhood perfectly; the competition and abuse between them had matched anything Doranei and his fellows came out with, and it had masked the same fierce loyalty and friendship.

"It will be dangerous," Mihn said quietly.

"I have learned a little of duty in my years, young man," Endine snapped, "and I'm better able than most to deal with the danger."

"Who else has them?"

The Crystal Skulls had been divided up amongst people they could trust—quite apart from the fact that few mages would have the strength to control more than one, the Menin lord had clearly been hunting them all down. King Emin decided it would be far harder for Azaer to steal the greater part if they were not all in one place.

"Camba Firnin has Protection, since you, Lord Isak, did not want it returned, while Tasseran Holtai has accepted Dreams, which should expand the scope of his scrying skills enormously. Morghien will take Joy with him into Byoran territory—more as a Brotherhood joke, I suspect—while Blood has been entrusted to your General Lahk. Unsurprisingly, Fei Ebarn was given Destruction. Knowledge I hold here, and Elements is to go to the man I summon today."

Mihn bit back any further questions and left the mage to complete his preparations. Once the thick front edge of the mantelpiece had runic symbols down its length, Endine wrote with a tall, florid script on each side of the mirror before touching the Skull to the glass. Under his breath he started to chant, and Isak found himself holding his breath as the texture of the air started to thicken and the already dim room grew steadily darker.

The Land contracted around him with the growing gloom and Isak found his hand questing down for Hulf's reassuring warmth as the walls and ceiling started to fade from his perception. There was a tiny sound, on the edge of hearing, but one that made him shiver all the same—it was too close to the far-off wails of the damned in Ghenna for his liking.

"Damn imagination," Mihn muttered, echoing Isak's thoughts.

"You heard that?" Endine said softly. "That wasn't your imagination; the boundaries between worlds are weakened while the Gods are drained. Most normal men wouldn't hear it, but I suppose you would be rather more sensitive to the other side than most, wouldn't you?" He paused and looked back at Mihn. "Some sounds you never forget."

Before Mihn could find a reply Endine had returned to his spell—then the reflection in the mirror moved unexpectedly. Isak blinked, and realised it had become more than just a reflection; the lines of the darkened room had turned into somewhere different entirely, and he could now make out a much larger figure than Endine. Without warning a hand reached forward and pushed through the surface of the mirror, followed swiftly by a man's head. The man blinked at them, as though checking they were in fact real, before he stepped through onto the mantelpiece and dropped down to the ground.

"Master Endine," he said gravely, offering his hand in a perfunctory way, apparently unsurprised when it was ignored.

The man was no older than forty summers, Isak guessed, with a thin, clipped beard and more jewellery than even most Farlan nobleman would think appropriate. His travelling clothes were expensively cut, and he had rubies dangling from his ears, a fat pearl at his throat, and all sorts of gold rings on his fingers. Both the clasp of his cloak and his belt-buckle were golden dragons with displayed wings and rubies for eyes, while the long dagger on his belt was so ornate Isak could scarcely believe anyone could use it in anger.

"Are all your servants so insolent?" the newcomer demanded as Mihn, standing closer than Isak, inspected him with obvious interest. The man's fingers dropped to the garnet pommel of his knife.

"Ah, he is no servant, Master Ashain," Endine said quickly, stepping in between the two. "This is Mihn ab— Ah, well, I forget the rest, but he is a much-respected man by the king."

"I'm also no servant," Isak piped up. Mihn turned and put a hand on the white-eye's shoulder, hearing the antagonistic tone to his voice, but Isak didn't take the hint. "But I am pretty insolent, so if you're planning on pulling that knife, stop teasing and fucking well draw the thing."

To his credit Ashain didn't take a step back, merely withdrew his hands and delicately brushed his fingers. There was no fear on the man's face, just astonishment and disdain as he gazed at the scarred white-eye sitting before him. His eyes were cold and grey, with faint crows-feet at the corners and long dark lashes.

"And you are?"

"Someone who doesn't like your face."

"As someone appears to have taken a dislike to yours."

Endine took another step forward. "Gentlemen, please! Isak, there's no need for that; he is not the enemy."

Now the shock did register on Ashain's face. "Isak? *Lord Isak?*" He looked the white-eye up and down, clearly now registering Isak was bigger than most white-eyes, and so likely to be one of the Chosen. "What— How?"

"My servant here," Isak said, pointing at Mihn, "you can call him Grave Thief if you like."

"Astonishing! Endine, you will take some time later to let me know how it was done?" Ashain said, suddenly alight with academic curiosity.

"I shall, as far as I have gleaned the details," Endine agreed, "but first we have rather more pressing business."

"And what would that be? As much as I enjoy mirror-travel when someone else capable is doing the work for a change, I have had to come a long way on horseback beforehand. Your master had better have a good reason for dragging me out this way without warning."

"My master, but the king of both of us," Endine warned. "That you have a personal dispute with him makes no difference; we are his subjects and he requires your service."

"My service?" spluttered Ashain. "Has he taken leave of his senses? I'm no mere King's Man to come running when he clicks his fingers."

Isak made a face. "Sounds like you are now."

"Isak is, I'm afraid, essentially correct. He requires your contribution to the war effort. You will be rewarded, but he will not accept no for an answer."

"Well, that's all he's going to bloody get, king or not!"

Endine raised a hand. "Master Ashain, we may have had our disputes, but I respect you as a peer of remarkable skill. However, the king is not interested in respect right now. Our losses have been too great. Because of your dispute, you have been under surveillance for a while now."

Ashain narrowed his eyes. "What are you saying?"

"That we are already certain you hold no allegiances that could compromise us, and at such short notice we don't have time to make sure about someone else. Your king requires your services to aid the survival of the nation. To refuse him will be considered treason."

"Treason?" Ashain growled, "this is outrageous—it flouts the very laws the man wrote with his own hand."

"And as such demonstrates the gravity of the situation," Endine said, almost wheezing with the effort of maintaining a calm, diplomatic demeanour. "I would rather not spell out what might happen if you refuse him."

"But it'll start with someone like me cutting your fucking head off," said Isak, who had fewer qualms about that. "Don't know who he'll send after your family and friends, but the Mad Axe has got a strange sense o' fun, and

Zhia Vukotic is just in the next room, so I'm guessing they'll be just as screwed."

Ashain purpled at what he was hearing, but not even Isak displayed the slightest hint of amusement. He watched each twitch with almost detached interest, wondering how many times a subject of King Emin's had been pressed into service this way. While most would surely not have required such threats, Ashain was clearly a rich and powerful man in his own right, and obviously one of the few King Emin couldn't command with a look.

But this is an age of burning bridges, Isak reminded himself sadly. *What else will we sacrifice for this fight? Is there anything we won't do for victory?*

The mage's thoughts were writ clear on his face as anger and astonishment gave way to acceptance with the speed only a self-made man could manage. His accent had already betrayed him as a man not born to the wealth he now displayed, and it was obvious to the men in the room that he was now calculating what profit could be made from such outrage.

"The king's terms?" he asked in a quiet voice.

"To be negotiated when you next see him. He has just left Moorview; you could probably catch him, but your position might be strengthened by proving your worth first."

"And what is this service he requires? To march with his armies?"

Endine withdrew a second Crystal Skull from his robe and held it out. "For the time being: possession of this."

"Merciful Gods," breathed Ashain, "is this a joke? You coerce me into service and then gift me with one of the greatest artefacts in existence?"

"It is not a gift," Endine said firmly, "it is custodianship. You must be able to use the Skull in battle but most importantly you must guard it."

"And the king cannot do this himself?"

"We control nine of the Skulls, perhaps ten now. Our enemies will be seeking them, and it would be madness to keep them all in one place when our goal is to deny them to that enemy. The Skulls cannot be tracked or traced except by the inefficient expenditure of energies, but you will have to be on your guard at all times, even when you are with the army."

Ashain held the Skull up to catch the light and stared at the slight flaws and colours it revealed. Wonder and delight spread across his face. "The king's service is less onerous than I imagined."

"Don't worry, this is as good as it gets," Isak said, gingerly lifting himself out of his seat. "Unless visiting foreign cities is your thing?"

"That would depend on the city, I suppose."

"Vanach?"

"Hah! You'd have to be mad to try that."

Isak gave him a humourless grin. "Daken's coming, so we've got that covered. Fortunately for the rest, we've got inside information that should see us to the Grand Ziggurat itself."

"And you expect me to join you?" Ashain asked, looking pale.

The man's arrogance had its limits, Isak was pleased to note. Ashain wasn't so foolish as to consider infiltrating a repressive religious state lightly, especially given the recent wave of fanaticism that had swept through the Land following the fall of Scree.

What news they did have of the state came from those few Carastar mercenaries who had been given free rein to kill and rob along the Vanach border, effectively hemming in the population. The stories were likely to be inflated, but they described nonsensical laws punishable by death, mass mutilations and murder; the reality would be awful enough.

"No, my twelve are already chosen. You'll come north in our wake, however; your skills with mirror-magic might well be required and Endine's needed with the army."

"Just twelve? Will you even get past the Carastars with so few?"

Isak nodded. "There'll be four Crystal Skulls among us, as well as a vampire and two Mortal-Aspects. However bad the reputation of the Carastars, they're just mercenaries. Whoever gets in our way will regret it. It's the competition we need to watch out for."

"Competition?"

"Our enemy has also seen this information; it's unlikely we'll get a free run at it."

The mage frowned. "What are you looking for there?"

Isak patted the man on the shoulder and headed for the door, snapping his fingers at Hulf as he went. "Think of the stupidest thing I could be hunting; one that could only bring ruin down on us all."

He didn't wait for an answer.

CHAPTER 9

LORD CELAO WENT TO THE BALCONY and looked out over Ismess, Southern quarter of the Circle City, as the last light of evening faded into nothingness. Three great white structures punctuated the view, even more startling at dusk as the dull mud-brick houses below merged with the shadows. To his right was the great snub-nosed obelisk that loomed tall from the centre of Ilit's temple, the tallest structure in Ismess, flanked by the two long arched roofs that marked both halves of the temple proper.

Ahead was Death's own house, the huge open doorway facing directly towards Celao's palace. He could just make out a figure in black at the top of the steps. High above was the great dome that covered half the temple floor, a full, rounded tit that served to remind Celao that the priestesses there were all shrivelled, shrill harridans who plagued his every step. In the lee of that was the house of Belarannar, an altogether more pleasing temple of high walls and lush, shaded gardens that he, as Chosen of Ilit, was unwelcome in.

A gust of wind lifted up from the quarter and Celao's wings, unbidden, half-opened to feel the press of air against his feathers. It had been a long time since he'd flown, since he'd looked down over the city and watched the normals scurry below.

He saw it in the eyes of foreign dignitaries when they saw his size, the wonder and incomprehension that turned swiftly into contempt. More than once Celao had though to cut off his wings, have some surgeon incise just *there* and *there*—to snip the dead weight from his back and relieve him of one small burden. Chosen of the weakest of Gods, lord of a haughty, empty tribe and set apart even from other white-eyes by a freakish body—Celao longed for release from it all. What little emotion he could summon was quietly directed at the God who'd made him thus.

"And yet I do nothing," he said, addressing the squalid misery of his city with a tired voice. "I refrain even from following the child's example. My priests are worthless shits, but they have long ago whipped this tribe into obedience. The only true value of a priest is to provide a different focus for their hatred."

Celao glanced back at the canopied terrace he'd just walked from, lit by ornate, wrought-iron lanterns and a pair of braziers. A vast couch sat at the centre of the sheltered rooftop, big enough for Celao and his two current favourites, currently waiting patiently for his command. He hadn't bothered to learn their names.

One was a Litse, long-limbed and elegant, the very picture of pale, porcelain beauty; the other, the older of the two, was a dark, lithe girl from the north. She was athletic to the point of muscular, and he'd had her worked almost to death when he first acquired her to ensure she was no agent of the Farlan. Her small features and sparkling eyes were a long way from the Litse definition of beautiful; it was why he preferred her, and most often made the Litse girl debase herself. After all, that one had been a nobleman's daughter until Celao bought her. Earning trinkets with a whore's tricks was what she'd been bred to do, whether or not she'd realised it at the time.

"Wine."

The blonde was the first to scramble up and pour him a goblet. Celao smiled as he accepted it; she knew her place and was eager to please him. The fearful eyes and desperate smile caused a stirring in him and once he'd taken the wine Celao caught her arm. A look was all it took and she sank to her knees, fumbling at his trousers. He turned to face the city again, grabbing her by the throat to manoeuvre her around until her back was pressed against the balcony rail and her face obscured by the roll of his belly.

From somewhere in the city below he heard a mournful wail, carried on the wind from the concealed streets. He peered down, unable to make anything out at that distance, unsure even whether it had been a citizen of Ismess or an echo from the Dark Place. That and other, stranger, things had been reported to him of late—voices in the wilderness and great spiralling flocks of bats skirting Blackfang's forbidding slopes.

The whole Circle City was gripped with fervour and fear, but the reports of daemons attacking Byora had only made Celao laugh. At last some misfortunes had taken place outside the stained white walls of Ismess, descending upon some other people than the pathetic remnants of Ilit's chosen. Slum fever gripped the outer districts, while reports of the white plague from the countryside meant he risked bringing the latter in to the city as he tried to alleviate the former.

The sound of wings came from the dark above him. Celao yanked at the girl's hair and she stopped her softly moaning attentions, refastening his trousers with deft fingers just as a dark shape descended. A servant ran forward even before Lord Celao reached out a hand, offering a scimitar-bladed spear that Celao grabbed hard enough to send the man tumbling.

Up above he saw the dark shape of outstretched wings, a white-eye circling slowly. Celao hissed with anger: Gesh had been his Krann for mere weeks, and the impudent worm was already presumptuous. Aware he had betrayed his emotions already, Celao lowered his spear and closed his wings. Another disadvantage of the damn things—the first hint of violence and they would open, for balance as much as flight. Even from high above Gesh would have been able to see the effect of his presence.

"My Lord," Gesh said as he banked with effortless grace and landed on the rooftop, his white formal robes dancing in the darkness like a moth's wings, "I trust your evening has been pleasant."

Celao didn't reply immediately, letting the man wait as he was inspected. He was armed, of course, but with nothing more than his Ilit-granted bow and a dagger. He was without his ceremonial breastplate, a slender and austere sight, but Celao's sharp eyes noticed the pearls at his throat and gold pins in his rich blond hair.

"You forget your place, Krann," Celao said eventually. "You do not land here without an invitation from your lord."

"Under the circumstances, I thought it prudent."

Gesh furled his own wings and let the light of the lamps onto his face. Normally Gesh was impassive to the point of condescension, but tonight the Krann's expression was tense with anticipation.

"Circumstances?" Celao tightened his grip on his spear and checked his guards out of the corner of his eye. Both were alert, their weapons ready. He had taken great pains to ensure their loyalty: they were bonded men and the lives of their families were forfeit if Celao died.

"I heard of a plot to assassinate you," Gesh announced, hands conspicuously empty of weapons. "I thought it best to flout custom."

Celao waddled away from him, edging towards the guards, while Gesh stood still and watched him. "Soldier, summon my guards!" Celao barked nervously.

"I don't think that will do any good." Gesh took a step towards him, and Celao drove unexpectedly forward, his spear outstretched. Fat he might have been, but Celao still had the speed and strength of the Chosen, and he could move faster than a normal man when he needed to.

"Didn't have the guts to try it yourself? I expected as much," Celao spat, pushing the tip of the spear right against Gesh's chest. The enchanted steel neatly sliced through the cloth, but Gesh didn't retreat, nor did he unfurl his wings.

"I'm not here to kill you, nor have I arranged anything of the sort," he said with infuriating patience, "and your spear is pointing in the wrong direction."

"Do you take me for a fool?"

"I think he was trying to help," said a voice behind Celao as a sword-tip pierced his shoulder.

Celao grunted with shock and tried to turn, but a second blade impaled him low in the ribs and held him fast, caught like a stuck pig. His mouth fell open, but the only sound that came out was a faint hiss of expelled air as pain struck him like a hammer. Then the swords were withdrawn and Celao staggered sideways, drunkenly reaching for his two guards. In their place was a single figure in diamond patchwork clothes and a ghostly white mask. Blood trailed from each of its swords, which were held outstretched, as though the figure was awaiting applause after a dance, while the bodies of his guards twitched on the ground either side of it.

"You politicians, always looking for the hidden meaning in what men say."

Celao tried to turn and bring his weapon up, but his arm was a lead weight, his legs treacherous. He lurched around and saw a slim man in black behind him, Harlequin swords in his hands and teardrop tattoos on his cheek. When he spoke, the man's voice seemed to come from elsewhere, as though he was being used as a tool for some far-distant mage.

"It is time for a new ruler in Ismess, do you not agree, Lord Gesh?"

Celao tried to lunge, but he was clumsy and slow; the man in black moved, faster than he could follow through the haze of pain, and battered the blade away. Celao felt the patter of blood on his left foot and wavered, fighting to keep standing.

"A change, yes," said Gesh, his eyes never leaving Celao's bow, still in its sheath, "but one I could have brought about myself."

The assassin looked thoughtful for a moment, then he reached forward. Celao watched the tip of his sword draw close, but his body was unresponsive as the man prodded him gently in the shoulder, once, twice. The motion was so neat and deliberate Celao didn't even feel any pain, but his spear fell from his fingers and his arm flopped dead. He staggered back a step before catching his balance and looked down in disbelief at the now-useless limb hanging at his side.

"You got it on the second," the black-clad assassin said, almost to himself. "It doesn't count—I win." He paused and cocked his head at Gesh. "Certainly you could have done this. I suspect that fine bow was intended for just this task. Lord Ilit would not have chosen a Krann likely to miss such a target."

"In which case, do not consider me in your debt."

"Debt?" The assassin giggled like a girl and Celao blinked. The man's expression hadn't changed from studious concentration, yet the laughter didn't sound forced. "No debt; this is a gesture of friendship."

"No price?"

"None. It serves our purpose that the Litse have a stronger ruler, one less encumbered by alliances and allegiances."

"One easily influenced."

In the firelight the assassin's shadow twitched and moved as though alive. "Influence is best achieved through gain—if Ruhen's friendship aids your purpose, you will continue and further it."

"Friendship," Gesh said, without feeling.

The assassin said, "I realise it does not come easily to your kind, but pragmatism does. You can either ally yourself to us and restore your people's glory, or watch us from the sidelines."

"What do you need?"

"You could usefully turn a blind eye to a series of unfortunate accidents; beyond that I ask only that you allow us to help our friends: your poor need feeding, your borders need protecting. Your lost souls need nurturing."

Gesh said, "Your preachers will minister to my people, feed them and tell them tales of a child sent to intercede with the Gods on their behalf."

"It is not the warrior they expected, perhaps, but that is the difference between what a man wants and what he needs. 'A saviour comes in disguise, for we are tyrants to ourselves' wrote the poet Galasara."

"A heretic and enemy of the Gods."

"Beloved of the Gods in his time; he played no part in the Great War."

Celao, ignored by both men, sank to his knees. The rooftop was slick with blood. A chill was seeping into his limbs, leaving him light-headed and lumbering. He could feel the breeze on his skin, more real than the pain of his injuries and the trickle of blood on his thigh.

"Ah, I almost forgot!" the assassin exclaimed, and kicked Celao onto his back. The vast white-eye flopped back with a gasp, one wing pinned underneath him. The clouds raced above him, calling him up to join them; he could feel the tug of their presence, the freedom of the air he'd rejected all those years ago. His free wing extended weakly, brushing the terrace floor.

"There is one last thing," the assassin said, peering down at Celao with distaste. He held out a silver chain on which had been strung a coin. Celao watched it catch the light with wonder, his jaw working away as though he were trying to ask for it, but no sound came from his throat. "A symbol only, but we ask you to wear this in friendship."

Gesh took it and inspected the coin. "No magic," he commented with surprise. "Something—a blessing? An echo?"

"No magic," the assassin confirmed. "Do you accept Ruhen's gift?"

"I do," the white-eye said, tucking the coin away, "but I will not wear it—the priests will not stand for me to wear the symbol of any other than Ilit."

"As you wish, but keep it safe, and out of sight of prying eyes."

The new Lord of the Litse nodded. "You, girl: what happened here tonight?"

The dark-haired girl approached, shivering with fear but unable to take her eyes off Celao as he wheezed his last on the floor. "The—the guards?"

"No." Gesh glanced at the bodies of Celao's bodyguard, then the assassin. "They were true to their duty. This was me alone, do you understand?"

"'The conqueror's hand holds life and death in the breadth of a palm,'" breathed the assassin, watching her face with a strange expression of delight.

He gave the girl a knife from his belt and gestured to his Harlequin companion to do the same for the other girl.

"A landed fish could not look so pathetic," the assassin said as their knuckles went white around the grips.

Celao's eyes were wide with fury and fear as the pair crept close.

"I think you two have earned the right to finish him as you see fit," the new Litse lord said.

Knight-Cardinal Certinse hesitated at the gate of the gaol as it opened, releasing a gust of festering air from the gaol's depths: sweat, shit and other stenches he couldn't even begin to identify. He shivered and put a perfumed cloth to his nose, but the stink overpowered even that. Although his companion wrinkled his nose, Sergeant Kayel's evil smirk was unwavering.

Certinse gestured for the man to go first, and once Kayel's back was turned, pinched the bridge of his nose in an effort to force away the ache behind his eyes. Somewhere in the street behind them something scraped over stone and Certinse cringed at the sound. For days now he had been jumping at shadows, distracted by the constant throb of sleeplessness ringing through his skull and hearing the distant echo of daemon-song on the wind.

The few minutes of sleep he managed were punctuated by horrific dreams of vengeful priests, of torture and pain that he could still feel in his bones hours later. His newly returned power had done little to calm his nerves. The round-up of zealot priests and their devoted followers had been swift and relatively bloodless: a handful of mysterious deaths had helped Certinse's troops catch them by surprise and the majority of the troublemakers were now crammed into this ageing gaol. A tense peace gripped the streets of Akell, but Certinse found his anxiety only increased with every passing day of quiet.

"How many, gaoler?" Kayel asked up ahead.

The guard was wearing a Devoted sash. He scowled at having to answer an outsider's question, but no one in the company of the Knight-Cardinal was to be denied, so he kept his temper as he replied, "More'n four hundred all told, sir."

"How many officers?" Certinse said.

"About a third, I'd reckon."

"Do you have a ledger of names?"

The soldier ducked his head, looking uncomfortable. "Some, Lord Cardinal. Others refused even after they got a beating for it. I know it's our duty, but there's a good fifty who won't speak."

"Yet only a handful appeal to me for clemency—the rest remain defiant."

Certinse sighed wearily and walked through the narrow gate into the squat block building which was set into a hump of black rock at the eastern end of the city wall, which gave it the impression of being slowly drawn into Blackfang Mountain. There were few windows on the outside walls.

"They're too far gone," Kayel commented as he headed into the guardroom. "Their minds are burned through with rage, and nothing you could do to them here will change that."

Certinse had only two guards with him; the rest waited outside while the gate was locked and bolted behind them, but it was still cramped in the narrow passageway. Beyond the guardroom was a heavy iron grille, within which was a narrow gate that the guard now unlocked under the watchful gaze of a crossbow-armed colleague.

They followed the corridor to a gated stairway and walked up to the second floor where a second, empty guardroom overlooked another corridor with more locked doors. From beyond came the muted sounds of imprisoned men. Shadows around them slunk away from the light; further away they were as thick as the rancid flavour of the air.

"My Lord Cardinal," the guard said with an apologetic look, "the higher-ranked prisoners are up here. This first cell holds the men who're appealing for clemency, but—" He stopped and shifted his feet and stared at the ground, not sure how to continue.

"What is it, man?" the sergeant prompted.

"It's High Priest Garash, my Lord. He's confined and shackled, but he's extremely violent. I—*we*—don't know how to treat him, sir. Usually he'd be sent to the lower dungeon, but being a high priest—"

"You're wary of dropping him down a hole and forgetting him," Kayel finished with a grin.

Certinse stared down the corridor for a while, not speaking. The upper level had been built for prisoners of rank and it was certainly cleaner than the ground floor, but it remained a dank, dismal place. Kayel's lamp illuminated the bare stone. Just as he was about to speak, a flicker of movement caught his eye at the far end of the corridor—just a glimpse, and he wasn't sure it was even real, but it set his skin crawling. He shook off the feeling and asked, "They are all confined?"

"Yes, my Lord, five to a cell up here. No one's free to roam; even below ground they're chained to the wall. We put your seven in leg-irons so you could call 'em out one by one."

Certinse shivered, imagining the cold lower dungeon where the prisoner would be forced to wallow in his own waste. Inmates receiving special punishment would be left there. He blinked owlishly down the corridor, but there was no movement there now and the only sound was the echo of voices. There was no sign of the ragged cloak or skirt he thought he'd seen swish through the gloom, nor any glint of tarnished metal or dead eyes. The more he tried to recall the image, the more he realised it had to have been his imagination. There were no women among the prisoners—there were none at all of any rank in the Knights of the Temples.

"Keep Garash in irons and keep the door locked," he ordered.

The guard bobbed his acknowledgement and pointed to the nearest door. "The officers you came for." At Certinse's nod he opened the door and a weak thread of daylight came through the arrow-slit window and showed him seven terrified faces. The men were all dressed in stained uniforms and shackles.

Only one was of an age with Certinse; it was the younger faces he scrutinised until he found the one he was looking for. "Captain Tillen," he said, "come forward."

The soldier shuffled to the door. Certinse had last seen this promising young soldier from Narkang on the march to the Circle City. The Knights of the Temples were a military order, but their success was down to a combination of rich benefactors and sound financial management. They ran many noble estates—for a price—leaving the owners free to pursue more noble callings, and providing a vital income for the Order. Tillen was a simple, idealistic young man, but he was also the scion of a wealthy family whose father Certinse knew well.

"My Lord," Tillen gasped. He leaned heavily on the wall as he dropped to his knees, moaning with pain. There was a large bruise on his cheek and his lips had been split open, by a fist, Certinse guessed. From the way he carried himself the Knight-Cardinal guessed he had at least one broken rib too.

"You seven are the only members of this mutiny who have shown any repentance," Certinse said, "but you remain complicit."

"I understand, my Lord," Tillen replied, looking at the ground. "We know we must accept punishment for our actions. But sir, I wish to say in our defence that we were coerced. We were given no choice but to obey. You know the fervour of the cults—they were savage to any opposition."

"That I do know," Certinse said wearily, "but I must know the truth of your parts in these events." He pointed to Kayel, looming threateningly with a dagger dangling from his fingers. "This man here is bodyguard to the child Ruhen; he is adept at discovering the truth. You will each be interrogated by him; it is he who will decide your fates."

Kayel leaned forward to scrutinise the faces of each. "You," he said with a grin, pointing at one on the right. "You'll be first."

"My Lord?" Tillen said with dismay, "we're to be tortured?"

"Oh yes," Kayel announced cheerily, "I'm going to cut bits off that one 'till he tells me about all the rest o' you."

"Heretic!" shrieked the man Kayel had picked, "daemon-lover! You'll burn in Ghenna for your treachery against the Gods!"

Kayel laughed. "Bloody fanatics! Even the sneaky ones can't help themselves." He turned to Certinse. "Reckon he's the only one among them though. The rest are just scared at the thought of me cuttin' on 'em."

"How can you be sure?"

"Trust me, I know fear in all its lovely flavours. You starve and shackle a man, then tell him his enemy's got free rein on his body, he's got to be trained well to pretend his hatred is fear enough to fool me. None of this lot are better'n me at lying."

Certinse almost sagged with relief. He'd been imagining Tillen's father reaction to the news that his only son had been hanged for mutiny. "Free the rest," he ordered, and the guard hurried to obey, helping Captain Tillen to stand up and then unlocking his leg-irons. Before long the six were all free, and standing unsteadily in the corridor, rubbing at the skin of their ankles.

The remaining man lingered apprehensively at the back, shifting his feet as best he could and unsure what to do next. Kayel lounged against the doorpost and watched him as the man's gaze darted between them all.

"Try it," he suggested helpfully. "You never know, you might make it."

The knife stayed in Kayel's hand and the fanatic suddenly went very still. He was a jowly sandy-haired man in his early thirties, too young to be the shape he was, in Certinse's opinion, and looking more like an indolent youngest son than a zealot. After a long pause the man sagged.

"Too late!" Kayel announced as he closed the door again and let the guard lock it.

"Gentlemen, please go downstairs and collect your possessions," Certinse said, and they dutifully shuffled off, the gaoler leading the way, leaving Certinse and Kayel standing alone at the cell. Without warning there came a crash against the cell door, making Certinse jump in surprise. The remaining officer had thrown himself against the door and was pounding on it with his fists and screaming obscenities. Before long the clamour died down to sobs and wordless cries, but it had been enough to set off the more desperate or enraged in the other cells and the shouting echoed down the corridor.

"I still don't know what to do with them," Certinse admitted, looking up at the larger man with a near-pleading expression. "There are many well-connected men here besides Captain Tillen—how I can execute the lot of them without fracturing the Order? I'm half-surprised an army from Raland hasn't already appeared to secure their release."

Kayel shrugged. "Worry about 'em after you get a grip on the Order. Might be you don't need to do anything about this lot."

"What are you saying?" Certinse demanded. "How could that happen?"

Kayel paused and stared at something down the corridor, then moved, perhaps nodded?—Certinse only caught the movement out of the corner of his eye and he missed most of whatever it was. "Who knows?" Kayel said, suddenly the picture of innocence. "That's something I'd leave in the hands o' the Gods, but gaol's an unhealthy place, what with all these foul vapours and such."

He put a hand on Certinse's shoulder and the Knight-Cardinal felt the strength drain from his body.

His knees weak, his legs unsteady, he allowed himself to be ushered downstairs to the strong-room where the weapons and valuables of prisoners were kept. His head throbbed with every step, the stench of the gaol filling his mind with sickening clouds.

In the corridor upstairs, unseen by all, grey-blue eyes shone in the darkness and broken fingernails scraped lightly along the walls, unheard even by the prisoners.

Chapter 10

THEY SET OUT AT DAWN, after each had first ascended the high tower of Moorview Castle and surveyed the battlefield one last time. The sky was dark and inauspicious, a steady drizzle falling from sullen clouds. The remaining troops camped on the near edge of the moor were barely stirring, except for a few listless sentries manning the guard-posts. Most of the camp was occupied by the injured who couldn't yet be moved and the garrison that would occupy the castle once Isak had left. Almost half the Ghosts had gone ahead a few days earlier, pushing on towards the Vanach border to establish their camp.

Isak stared for longest at the unhappy ground, rain running down his cheeks like tears as he listened for the cries of the lost. He couldn't hear them, but he did not doubt they were there; too many had died—sixty thousand dead, so the king's clerks now said: sixty thousand souls now arrived in the Herald's Hall. And many of the survivors were so shocked by the savagery of the battle they barely knew what to do with themselves.

"I just watched," he whispered to the wind, trying to summon a sense of shame but feeling nothing; "I watched and I waited while you all died."

His arm began to ache again, a sharp, insistent pain rising up from the bone. He looked down and ran a finger over the unnaturally pale skin of his left hand. The scars from his time in Ghenna were almost familiar to him now; he was having trouble remembering how he'd looked before then. Sometimes in the night the memory of a reflection returned to him, but just as often it was not his face. Sometimes Aryn Bwr appeared in the mirror and sometimes it was a white-haired man with a blank face. The dreams only added to his sense of loneliness, showing up the empty part of his soul where the last king had once resided, and the holes in his mind where much of his childhood had once been.

"Am I still me?" he whispered, though he feared the answer. "Without the memories that made me, am I anything now?"

The dead souls didn't answer. Only the wind noticed him at all, briefly gusting cold over him before ebbing again. Isak tasted blood in the rain, but these days he couldn't tell if it was his imagination or something real.

"Isak, it is time to go," Mihn called from behind him.

He turned. Mihn had barely changed since he'd first met the man. He was neat and efficient in every movement, softly spoken, and so quiet a presence in any room that at time he could have been a ghost. Now, though, Mihn seemed to stand a little taller, as if he was a little more aware of his own worth. He had always acknowledged his own skills, but as if they were nothing of note—something other than humility, though, more bordering on shame. These days, however, there was something a bit more substantial to his company. Now his friend was a man comfortable in any company, not just the quiet and unobserved shadow Isak cast.

And why not? He stole a soul out of the Dark Place itself; in his place even I might manage to be boastful.

"My Lord?"

Isak realised a grin had stolen onto his face. He made a dismissive gesture. "I was just thinking how much of a swaggering braggart you are these days."

"And after all those demonstrations of humility you gave me," Mihn said with a bow. "Now come on, the others are waiting for you to show them how a sack of potatoes really rides."

They went down together to the courtyard at the rear of the castle where horses stood waiting. Twelve of them would cross into Vanach, that specific number one of the many ostensibly pious instructions Vorizh Vukotic had described in his journal. Doranei had gone ahead to arrange fresh horses and supplies, accompanied by the night-dwelling Zhia. Only Isak was taking two horses, Megenn and Toramin, with him; the others would change on the road regularly. The ever-practical General Lahk had looked after Isak's incredible beasts; he had taken the smaller, Megenn, himself and given the other to Swordmaster Pettir, who was a fine horseman and well-capable of handling the fiery, nineteen-hand stallion Toramin. They had been more than happy to return the horses to Isak, and while he hadn't been able to remember the pair, his hands had seemed to know what to do and he found himself grooming them as each preferred.

As Isak exited the tower his companions all mounted up, but for a moment he stood and surveyed the small party willing to follow him into Vanach, a city-state notorious throughout the Land for its savagery towards both outsiders and its own citizens. Daken sat uneasily on Isak's far right; the white-eye was barely recovered enough from his injuries to ride, but he would not be left behind. Legana looked just as uncomfortable, despite her regal detachment.

General Lahk's twin, Tiniq, from Isak's personal guard, stood alongside Leshi, his kindred spirit, and the savage Ascetite agent Shinir, while Mihn, Vesna and Veil, waiting with the Narkang battle-mage Fei Ebarn, formed a more friendly coterie.

"Goin' ta give us a speech?" Daken asked with his usual antagonism.

Isak shook his head slowly. He realised the white-eye would be constantly pushing him over the course of the journey. King Emin had been confident that Daken would follow orders when there was danger nearby, but less sure how he might act during the quieter moments.

"Daken," Vesna called, and when the white-eye ignored him, Vesna nudged his horse forward until he was directly in Daken's line of sight, then moved close enough that the white-eye couldn't help but see it as threatening. "We'll have no white-eye bullshit here, you hear me?" With the spirit of Karkarn inside him, Vesna's voice carried authority and power with every word.

Daken's fingers twitched, aching to go for his axe, but he held out and did not respond to Vesna's challenge—but it was a real effort to tear his eyes off the Mortal-Aspect and turn his horse away.

"No speeches, not from me," Isak said. With an effort he hauled himself up into the saddle and looked around at his companions. "I'll be glad if I manage not to fall off my horse today."

"You better not," said Shinir; "we really don't want to be in Vanach too long after harvest. They're going to want our horses any time of year, but once winter hits they'll eat anything, so strangers get really welcome all of a sudden."

A roughly stitched scar ran back down the side of her head, and that tight, swollen skin added to her usual expression of contempt. The supernaturally-skilled Shinir was, along with the ranger Leshi, one of the few who managed to penetrate the state of Vanach—and return. Neither were keen to try to repeat the performance, let alone travel to the city of Vanach itself.

"Nothing like a bit of incentive," Isak muttered to Mihn.

He paused a moment, then remembered to touch his heels to Toramin's flanks and the huge warhorse started off eagerly, barging a path past Shinir's mount as he had been trained to do. With a click of his fingers Isak summoned Hulf. The dog raced ahead, still nervous of so many horses. Mihn sighed and fell in behind Isak, as Isak'd no doubt intended Hulf to do so. He ignored the muttered comment and sniggering behind him; the journey was going to be long enough already without bickering to start them off. This wasn't the first time he'd travelled in similar company. Isak might not be quite the white-eye he had once been, but there were still more strong personalities here than you'd want in an entire army.

Sorting that out can be Vesna's problem, Mihn decided, watching Isak, who had lost much of the natural balance he'd once possessed and was clearly struggling to match Toramin's natural rhythm.

Most likely Isak will manage to provide me with enough problems to deal with. He usually does.

Knight-Cardinal Certinse held back in the shadows and watched the soldiers eying each other suspiciously. They might all be dressed in the uniform of the Knights of the Temples, but each man displayed subtle differences, declare their allegiances. Their lords sat in Akell's magnificent council chamber, the Hall of Flags, through the pair of grand doors. Certinse had no doubt that the same posturing and sizing-up was taking place within as well as without.

He recognised only one of the faces, the one man who sat with his eyes half-closed and ignored the rest. He was a hatchet-faced knight from Canar Fell, a renowned fighter even among that city of warriors, but wearing the white braiding that indicated he was General Afasin's man, the other half of the Mustet delegation. The rest of the young bucks came from Embere and Raland; they were here as escorts for their lords, and desperate to win names for themselves if the opportunity presented itself.

Certinse sighed, his fingers automatically moving to the old coin hanging around his neck. He briefly ran his fingers over its grooved surface, then tucked it inside his tunic.

The point of no return, he thought, but in his heart he knew it was not; that was long-past. Now he had to come good on the promises he had made. His thoughts returned to the coin. Even when he took it off he could feel it resting against his chest, a reminder of the bargain he had made.

The Knights of the Temples had no mages and Certinse had not met many, but even so he fully understood the acceptance of a bargain with a creature of magic. He hadn't appreciated it at the time, but the more he considered it, the more he realised the significance of taking Ruhen's coin.

"Planning your strategy?" whispered a voice in his ear.

Certinse managed to hide his jolt of surprise. Ilumene moved like a cat, but the big mercenary had crept up on Certinse half a dozen times in the past weeks and the Knight-Cardinal was growing accustomed to soft voices from the shadows.

"Just reflecting," he muttered in reply. "Now I know your true allegiance, it occurs to me my family has not profited from its association with Azaer." Cetinse's broken nights of sleep had culminated in a waking dream where he'd conversed with a figure of shadow and learned much about his family and the future of the Land.

The comment didn't appear to surprise the man he'd known until recently as Sergeant Hener Kayel.

"You don't think so?" Ilumene asked. "High Cardinal of the cult of Nartis in Tirah, the Dukedom of Lomin, Knight-Cardinal and Supreme Commander of the Knights of the Temples—what were you hoping for exactly?"

Certinse faced Ilumene, who wore a white brigandine and trousers; his weapons were barely hidden beneath the long white cloak that was as much of a uniform as Ruhen's Children had. That he was openly dressed that way in Akell spoke volumes, given the violent response Ruhen's followers had received in recent weeks from the fanatics of Akell.

"My father is dead. My brothers are dead. My sister and nephew are dead. It's enough to give the last remaining Certinse pause for thought, don't you think?"

"Mebbe, true, though we all die in the end—it's what happens before most folk care about. Could just mean you're not so rash as some members of your family."

"Or they were sacrificed when their time came?"

"Wasteful of us, then." Ilumene's face went suddenly serious. "More the style of the Gods than Azaer, if you think about it. They like to play with their toys, then throw 'em away, careless of the mess they leave behind."

Certinse frowned in thought. "What does that remind me of? I'm sure I've heard of something similar said before."

"Aryn Bwr's first charge against the Gods," Ilumene said. "I wouldn't mention that to your colleagues, though; he's not so popular in these parts."

"Yet you want me to follow the path the great heretic once trod?"

"The last king wanted to tear down the pantheon," Ilumene corrected, "to break the power of the Gods. Our goal's to redraw the lines, not tear up the map."

Certinse didn't look convinced. "And Azaer had no hand in his rebellion, in the Great War?"

"Azaer is a shadow born of the light of creation, ever weak, ever on the periphery. To get involved in a war of that magnitude—well, Azaer looks that reckless to you?" Ilumene pointed towards the closed doors of the Hall of Flags, where the remaining members of the Council of the Knights of the Temples awaited their leader.

"We want a holy war as little as they do. Azaer doesn't ask for control of your order. You've made a bargain with the shadow, but you have *not* sold your mind; Azaer doesn't demand that of you.

"The majesty of the Gods has been diminished by the actions of priests and our enemies, both Lord Isak and King Emin. Steps must be taken, or humanity faces a second Age of Darkness at best, while the Gods recover their strength. They might not have taken the losses of the Great War, but the cults have done fine work in turning worship away from them."

Certinse raised a hand. "I know, I know."

"Then act: if your troops see Ruhen as the saviour the citizens of Byora do, so be it, but we don't require any declaration of the council."

"And when they ask Ruhen's ultimate goal? It is a question I've refrained from asking, but perhaps I need the answer before I go in there. Whether or not you lie to me, well, that's what men of power do, but allegiance is a mutable thing and we must know the limits of your declared intentions."

"A legacy," Ilumene said without hesitation. "Redress of the imbalance in the Land is, we believe, not incompatible with forming a domain of our own."

"You make it sound like you are an equal partner with this immortal being," Certinse said, a warning in his voice.

Ilumene smiled. "Don't worry, I know my place. I may be favoured son, but disciple I remain. My reward's a bargain already agreed. Your councilmen will be suspicious of anything they don't suggest themselves. Make it clear there's enough of this Land to satisfy the ambitions of all, and they'll be the ones with armies when the dust settles."

Certinse nodded, almost light-headed at the idea of what the Land might look like once this had come to pass. All he knew was that change *was* coming, like stones tumbling down a hillside, and trying to resist was not an option, not now.

All that remains is to see how the hand is played, he realised as he marched through the antechamber. All eyes turned his way and for a moment none of them moved, then the older knight stood and saluted and the others sheepishly followed suit.

Certinse ensured he got a good look at the face of each while he returned the salute. It was enough to see that flicker of anxiety in their eyes. He didn't need anything more.

Once inside the Hall of Flags the Knight-Cardinal shut the doors behind him and took a moment to look over the remaining members of the council. They were much depleted, the traditional eleven members whittled down to him and these four, an elderly sixth member having sent his anticipated letter of resignation in his place.

General Gort had died in some ridiculous last stand to protect the Temple Plaza in Scree, while Cardinal Eleil had suffered a fatal heart attack in his study one evening here in Akell. High Priest Garash had succumbed to red vein fever along with his followers in Akell Gaol, and High Priest Osir had reportedly died in a daemon attack as he travelled up from Tor Salan for this meeting, and High Priest Sechach had apparently not received the summons. Rumour had it the ageing cleric was confined to his own home after killing a serving girl by setting light to the room they were in, all the while gibbering about shadowy figures stalking the house.

No need to ask Ilumene if he knew anything about that one, Certinse reflected, *even if I'm not so sure about Garash or Eleil. I can only hope Azaer considers my life more useful than my death.*

"Gentlemen, honoured council members—I thank you for the speed with which you have all attended my summons." Certinse bowed to the four men, lower than he needed to. He had found over the years that a little excessive respect at the start of council meetings smoothed most feathers nicely. He might be the Commander of the Knights of the Temples, but each of the four here were outright rulers of city-states and unused to obeying any sort of order.

"This all of us then?" General Afasin barked gruffly. The ruler of Mustet, the only white-eye on the council, was a tall, brown-skinned man of middle years. He had travelled the furthest to be here today—indeed Certinse was sure the man must have been much closer to be able to get here so quickly. No doubt his army had been probing the Sautin border again.

"I'm afraid so," Certinse said. "General Abay has resigned, High Priest Garash died recently in custody and I'm sure you've heard about Cardinal Eleil and High Priest Osir."

"And Sechach," Afasin confirmed, nodding towards Duke Chaist opposite him. Chaist was the ruler of Embere, where the high priest lived. He had personally given the order to confine him.

"So few are the representatives of the Gods," Cardinal Sourl croaked. The emaciated man peered around his fellow generals, his recently adopted austere lifestyle clearly taking its toll and advancing the onset of old age. "This Order has indeed lost its way."

"This Order has been driven from its path," Certinse snapped, making Sourl flinch, "hijacked by fanatics whose illegal acts forced me to retaliate. Do *not* remind me of your part in events, Sourl."

"You brought us here for this argument?" Afasin rumbled. "I could have stayed at home and had it there."

"But which side would you have been on, General?" Certinse retorted. "Or is it Cardinal? I confess I am confused as to which title you prefer these days."

The white-eye was very quiet for a dozen heartbeats. His skin was dark enough that Certinse couldn't see if he was flushed with anger, but the set of his jaw suggested Afasin was fighting the urge to draw his sword.

"The Circle City is not only the only place where there have been tensions, but some of us managed to avoid wholesale slaughter while we got over the worst," he said at last.

"Then I congratulate you on such deft handling, *General* Afasin, but we have not all been so fortunate."

There was a creak and a thump as the last man there, General Telith Vener, pushed his chair back and dumped his feet on the table. He folded his arms, making a show of getting comfortable. "Wake me when the pissing contest is over, Chaist," he asked the man next to him, ignoring the hiss of contempt he received from his neighbour. The two had spent the previous summer fighting for control of the city-state of Raland and Duke Chaist was not a man to be gracious in comprehensive defeat, it appeared.

Certinse turned away from Afasin, his point made. General Vener was the biggest problem he had, and the man knew it. He had ducked every request for a private meeting beforehand and had made it clear who held the power right now: the wealth of Raland could sway most decisions in times of war.

"I apologise if we're boring you, Vener—perhaps I could turn the conversation towards a more stimulating subject?"

"That would be nice," Vener said, closing his eyes and not shifting position. "Perhaps we could discuss this saviour I hear you're intent on forcing on us? It's one thing to sell your own men as mercenary escorts to Prince Ruhen, quite another to devote the entire Order to his service."

The general was a lean, fit man whose physical prime seemed to have extended ten years longer than most men's. He was five or six summers younger than the newly decrepit Cardinal Sourl, but Vener hadn't succumbed to greying hair or a thickening waist yet. Certinse guessed Sourl would die within a year, but he had the creeping suspicion Vener would still be leaping from his horse when Certinse himself had need of a cane.

"I intend no such thing," Certinse said calmly, "but I hope you will recognise the Land is at a crossroads and the Order should act decisively?"

"Take advantage of the chaos, you mean?"

Certinse felt his hand tense; Telith Vener taking the moral high ground was enough to make any man choke with disgust.

"Let me get this straight, Vener. You are still a member of the Knights of the Temples, correct?"

"I am."

"Why?"

That made the bastard open his eyes at least. "What sort of a question is that?"

"A fair one," Certinse said. He didn't bother waiting for an answer; he wasn't trying to humiliate the man, just to get his attention. "From what I can gather, you appear to be against the very concept of a saviour. You feel we should not step in to restore order to chaos, even when daemons have free reign over the wild parts of the Land and the Gods are weakened by enemies unconfirmed. Beyond a belief your uniform brings out your eyes, I'm not certain what reason you have for being a member of the Order."

"You of all men accuse me of that?" Vener roared, jumping to his feet. "Given the violence that has gone on between priests and soldiers here, you ask what reason *I* have for being in the Order?" He started towards the door. "The stench of hypocrisy in here has become too much for me, I think—"

"General," Certinse broke in, "please retake your seat. I accuse you of nothing. As for hypocrisy, I am willing to admit I too have forgotten the founding principles of our Order in recent years."

Vener halted and glared at him. "This child, Ruhen, has reminded you?" he asked sceptically.

"The grace of the Gods works in myriad ways," Certinse said by way of reply. "The child has played only a part, I assure you of that. More importantly, this Land cries out for protection and leadership, and we can give it both."

"*We?*" General Afasin echoed, leaning forward in his chair. "An army of the devoted, that's our creed—under command of the saviour. Are you saying the child is the saviour of our prophecies or not?"

"I'm saying that Ruhen holds a unique position in the Land, but his message is one of peace. This child has no desire to lead an army, so why force one upon him? Whatever we do or do not acknowledge publicly, the common folk in every quarter of the Circle City see him as an emissary of the Gods. Given the iniquities the cults have imposed these past few months, his message is perhaps not as heretical as we might normally have believed."

All four men blinked at him: Sourl in disbelief, Vener, Chaist and Afasin each trying to process the implications and to find the benefit for them.

"You would cast out the priesthood?" Sourl demanded at last, "and follow these peasant preachers all the way to the Dark Place instead?"

"No," Certainse said firmly, "the priesthood cannot be cast out. There would be no Order without them. But it is this council, not unelected priests, which rules the Knights of the Temples, and it has always been clear that our soldiers must outnumber the priests."

"Why do we need this child, then?" Vener asked, at last retaking his seat. "Even as a figurehead, the mission of the Order is clear enough, established down the centuries. So why now take direction from some child?"

"A child who willingly faces down daemons," Chaist pointed out. "There our theology coincides."

Theology? A child of that age shouldn't know what the word means, you damn fool! You still think him just a child? Certinse screamed in his head, but he smiled and said, "A wise observation, my friend. The child has set his stall against corrupt priests and daemons—which is entirely consistent with our creed—and if he truly is an emissary of the Gods, his word and followers deserve the protection we can offer."

"And what can the child offer us? The common folk are fickle; their approval of this child might not last through winter."

Certinse nodded and opened his mouth to reply, then paused as though hesitating. He pulled his chair back from the table and sat. At last he started, "Ruhen counts the Harlequins among his followers; I hardly think he'll be so easily forgotten. However, we are men of the Land, men of power and politics." He raised a hand to stay any objections as he continued, "Our obligations have always been to the temporal as well as the spiritual: ours is a Land where both armies and natural disaster have destroyed cities, where priests are murdered and temples lie empty because of the actions of the few.

"Ruhen's Children go to preach to all peoples, to reignite their faith in the Gods. Our military might can ensure that takes place safely. In the process both our reach and his will be extended accordingly. Gentlemen, on such an understanding I have a new member of the council to propose: Lord Gesh, Chosen of Ilit and Lord of the Litse."

Both Afasin and Vener jumped in their seats when they realised the implication.

"Ruhen offers us the entire Circle City?" Vener demanded. "Can he really deliver Lord Gesh?"

Certinse nodded. "The Litse are a pious tribe who share our devotion to the Gods, but they have spent decades constrained by the cults in a way we've only recently been able to appreciate. For anyone—us or Lord Gesh—to take Ruhen as their declared lord is to invite chaos, but to foster understanding between parties . . . Well, that is more palatable for all involved.

"Byora will not object to the sight of our uniforms on its streets, but its free status will help Ruhen, and foster trade with our neighbouring states. Ismess and Fortinn quarters will formally become Knights of the Temples protectorates."

"The trading heart of the West," Vener mused. "Tor Salan was crippled when the Menin conquered it—Ruhen's message might find fertile ground there if we carry it, Helrect and Scree too."

"In Sautin too," Afasin agreed. "Anyar's murderous rule wins him little affection with his people."

Certinse solemnly bowed his head in acknowledgement and pressed his hands together. "And Narkang's eastern lands: the Menin have made that area a lawless, beleaguered place, the people abandoned to their fates by a godless king. Gentlemen, the Land itself cries out for intercession and the Knights of the Temples must answer that call. It is our holy and moral duty."

Chapter 11

TRAVELLING IN THE WAKE OF TIRAH'S GHOSTS, Isak and his companions made good time heading north. Like all travellers in those parts they skirted well clear of Llehden, that strange, isolated shire in the heart of Narkang territory where Isak had recuperated. A sense of longing had Isak again and again turning Toramin in the direction of the cottage by the lake, and each time Mihn corrected the horse's path without comment. He knew the direction Isak's thoughts were taking: Llehden had been a sanctuary for him, a place of quiet and calm. But Isak could not return there now. The people of Llehden avoided the lake where Isak had lived for fear of the Ragged Man, a local myth of a vengeful spirit without a soul. That role had now been filled by another. The Menin lord was even more suited to it than Isak had been, and as a result that lakeshore would now be as perilous as the locals believed it to be.

"Always the wagon-brat," Isak had muttered to himself two days before they reached the Morwhent, the great river that ran all the way west to Narkang.

"A little more than that, my Lord," Mihn responded.

The suggestion prompted a shake of the head from Isak. "Not any more. We're coming full circle now: no longer a lord, no longer a man with a home. Llehden's the last home I'll ever have and I can't go back there now."

"Look around you," Mihn said gently. "How many of us truly have a home? Me? Vesna? Legana? You are far from alone."

Isak laughed unexpectedly. "I didn't mean that as a complaint, my friend. If anything it was the opposite."

"This is your home," Mihn said after a moment's thought, "riding in the wilds, not wearing a ducal circlet and playing statesman."

Isak nodded. "This's all I have ever really known. Here I can think. In Tirah I was as out of place as Bahl—that man was born to be some sort of saviour; it was never me." He smiled. "All those titles and expectations, the armies of men looking to me for guidance . . . Vesna could have been a king, but not me; I was born to tear things down. The best I can hope for is to give someone else the chance to rebuild."

Mihn guided his horse closer and spoke quietly. "Not everyone has found such peace out here."

Isak followed Mihn's eyes to where Vesna rode alone, his head bowed. "What can I say?" he whispered.

"Nothing that will help, but still you must. He is your friend."

He looked up at the sky. "When we stop for the night."

When the light started to fade a few hours after that Isak called a halt and set to attending to his horses' needs. The battle-mage, Fei Ebarn, walked a long circle around their small camp, warding it against daemon incursion. The effort was most likely unnecessary; daemon sightings had been few since they'd left Moorview, and if any still walked Tairen Moor they would keep their distance from power they couldn't match.

At twilight, their brief meal finished, the others settled down. Isak watched Vesna for a few minutes as the Mortal-Aspect sat lost in his thoughts, his eyes fixed on the distant swirls of dark cloud on the horizon. Eventually Isak rose, carefully not to wake the hound lying between him and Mihn, and skirted the fire to reach his friend's side. Only when Isak crossed his field of view did Vesna look up, but he said nothing by way of greeting. Isak looked down at him for a few moments, wondering how best to broach the subject with him, before a thought occurred to him: *I'm no duke now, no landowner or nobleman; I'm just another troublesome white-eye wagon-brat.*

He grabbed Vesna by the man's metal-clad arm and hauled him up. In his surprise Vesna didn't even try to fight him off. Only when he was on his feet did he shake Isak off, an angry look on his face.

"Come on," Isak said, heading for the line of trees on a rise that was protecting the camp from the wind. Trusting Vesna would follow rather than argue with a turned back, Isak walked over the rise and sat down on an exposed root on the other side. He fished out a tobacco pouch and filled the bowl of his pipe and was lighting it with a brush of the thumb as Vesna appeared and sat down opposite. The white-eye looked out into the darkness beyond Ebarn's invisible perimeter line. He still wasn't sure how to proceed, and hoped Vesna would be the first to speak.

"Well?" Vesna demanded at last.

Isak shrugged. "Just looking to share a pipe with my friend." He offered it over and Vesna frowned.

"You know I don't."

"Ain't sure of much these days." Isak tapped the depressions in his recently shaved head. "So much spilled out when this got cracked."

"I'm sorry, my Lord—"

"No, I am," Isak interrupted.

"For what?"

The white-eye turned to face him. "Do I really need to say?"

"No." Vesna's eyes fell. There was a long moment of quiet. "I don't blame you—you know that, I hope?"

Isak nodded. "I do. There's no shame in what you feel, none at all. It's just a simple fact: I'm here and she isn't. Death's hard enough to deal with already."

It's hard enough to lose a friend, but a bride too? That'd break most men, and now he's got to sit with the daemon's plaything he used to call friend, and every moment's a reminder that she ain't coming back.

Vesna's black-iron hand tightened involuntarily. Isak watched the fist form and slowly be forced open again. He freed his own left arm from the folds of his sleeve and held it up in the pale starlight. It didn't look so horrific in this light; the scars and bleached-white skin became more of a dream that belonged to someone else.

"Reckon I'll glow bright white on my birthday, on Silvernight?"

Vesna gave a snort. "If you do, some damn fool will probably try to worship you."

More silence. Isak found his words were caught in his throat, unable to fight their way through to be spoken.

"Why didn't you tell me?" Vesna asked at last. "These plans you made with Mihn and Ehla—why keep them secret from your closest friends?"

"You would have tried to stop me."

"Of course I would! It was *insane*! Look at yourself, Isak, look at what you put yourself through—there had to be a better way!"

"I couldn't find one," he said softly. "And you—you had a life to lead, a family to hope for. Mihn chose to be a weapon in this war and I—well, I was born to be one. It didn't make sense to ask that of anyone else."

"What about your family, your friends? What about the chaos back in Tirah? Lord Fernal is barely holding the Farlan together, and his grip is even more tenuous without the Palace Guard on hand!"

"And if I had stayed in Tirah, fighting a civil war while Narkang falls to the Menin, forever frightened to face them in battle because I know it will mean my death? Who does that serve?"

Vesna gave up, unable to find the strength to argue further. "I only wish you'd told me, not let us mourn your death."

"I didn't know if it would even work," Isak whispered. "Some days I'm still not sure."

"The news of your death—it broke Carel, you know? Aside from when he shook me from my grief, he couldn't look me in the face."

"Who?"

Vesna looked up, remembering too late. Tears were leaking from Isak's eyes, and his faced was screwed up in the pain of lost memories.

"Carel," he said gently, "the father you should have had."

Isak's hand started to shake and he hunched over, his elbows clenched tight to his body as though protecting himself from blows. "Tell me," he croaked, "tell me about him."

"He—" Vesna didn't know where to start. For a while was paralysed by the sight of the shuddering white-eye, but at last he said, "He loved you like his own. He tempered you; you always said Carel helped you be more than just the colour of your eyes. He retired from the Ghosts when you were a child and worked as a wagon-train guard. He was the one who taught an angry boy how to fight, and when not to. He would—ah, he would be amazed you'd bought your own tobacco for a change."

"If he was broken by news of my death," Isak said, "what would it do to him to know I can't even remember him?"

The Mortal-Aspect of Karkarn looked Isak in the face, the ruby tear on his cheek glowing with inner light. "It would kill him."

Isak smiled sadly and rose. "Perhaps it's best he doesn't know, then." He tapped out the pipe and turned to head for his bedroll, but then he hesitated. "I stole this from Sergeant Ralen though," he said, tucking the pipe away. "Maybe there's still hope for us."

The miles passed quickly, thanks to daily changes of horses and the advance supplies secured by the Ghosts. The locals were curious, but they were glad to see the soldiers, for nightfall brought lone daemons prowling the village boundary stones. This was a part of the country that had known peace for a long time, the garrison towns on the Tor Milist border ensuring Duke Vrerr's mercenaries had looked elsewhere for plunder during the civil war there, so even foreign soldiers didn't provoke much fear.

Vesna, Karkarn's Iron General, drew the most curiosity. King Emin had been careful to spread the news that the God of War had favoured them with his Mortal-Aspect. Though he might scowl at the pointing fingers and whispered awe, it was clear Vesna was born to play such a role, willingly or not. The Farlan hero was tall and strong and handsome, and adulation settled naturally on his shoulders.

Behind the tattered shawl he used to shade his face from the afternoon sun, Isak smiled as he watched Vesna chafe under the attention. He didn't need to remind anyone of their last journey together through Narkang lands: Isak Stormcaller, riding like a figure of myth in shining armour of liquid silver, a crowned emerald dragon on his cloak. Now he was anonymous in tattered clothes and a face masked by scars; marked out only by his size, he could be any hired Raylin mercenary.

At the southern border of Tor Milist they found Doranei and Zhia waiting for them at a ferry station with a large barge ready to take them all downriver. They would travel down the River Castir halfway to the sea, then follow the King's Highway to Canar Thritt, around the slow-to-traverse hills south of Vanach and into the crumbling city-state itself. Mage Ashain would be sent here with a mirror, ready to provide them with an escape path, should one be required.

A small village had grown up around the ferry and as Isak's party rode up they spotted the unlikely couple sitting at a table outside the inn, shaded from the evening light, with a bottle of wine between them. The villagers watched them arrive anxiously, not unhappy that the mercenaries would be staying overnight, but wary these days of anything that arrived in the waning light. As far as Isak could tell there had been few actual daemon attacks, but more scares or sightings, and many more rumours.

"Now there are a few faces I could have gone a few months longer without seeing," Doranei called as boys ran out to stable the horses, jostling each other to reach Isak's huge charger first. "But since you're here, you might as well join us."

He gestured expansively to the table while the travellers dismounted and stretched out the stiffness from their bodies.

"Ah, there you are, Mistress," Doranei continued as the innkeeper appeared to survey her new guests. "I think we'll need food and a lot more wine." He wagged a finger in Daken's direction. "And a whole lot of beer for the fat one."

Daken grinned and took up a seat opposite Doranei, his axe slung from one shoulder and saddlebags draped over his thigh. "You still being a sore loser then?" the white-eye replied, taking Zhia's hand to kiss in a fit of chivalry. He winked at the vampire. "Or is his arse just hurting him? How does it look, by the way? Better than before, I'm guessing, with a reminder o' me in nice big letters."

"Oh indeed—how could a nicely-sculpted buttock not be improved by your name and a few roses?"

Doranei spluttered as Daken's eyebrow rose. "Roses, eh?"

"She's joking!" the King's Man protested, "there's no such thing!"

"Oh, come, dear," Zhia purred, "there's no need to be embarrassed about your admiration for the general."

Daken's eyes glittered with delight. "As the nice lady says, it's only natural to feel a bit o' worship for me. You ain't the first, I promise; you should've heard all the lovely things Legana was sayin' to me only last night!"

As if on cue Legana arrived at the table, assisted by Fei Ebarn. Her vision was always poorest at dusk. Ebarn's cheek crinkled as she scowled at the memory and pointed at Daken.

"Your boy here likes to dry off naturally, so to speak. It's not a sight we're quite used to yet."

—I said I'd cut off anything I saw hanging within reach, Legana added, writing quickly on her slate.

"It's all in the delivery," Daken said with mock wistfulness, "as the actor said to Etesia. Makin' your eyes burn with green fire and wavin' a knife around, that's my kind of flirting."

The rest arrived, Isak taking the furthest corner where he could wedge his back against the wall of the tavern and observe the rest. Veil went around behind him, struck his fist against Doranei's before hopping over the bench to sit beside his Brother. Tiniq pointedly inserted himself between Shinir and Daken to prevent anyone getting stabbed while they ate. Leshi took Shinir's other flank and Fei Ebarn followed Veil around to the far side, Mihn and Vesna taking position on either side of Isak.

Perhaps having seen white-eye mercenaries before, the inn-keeper was remarkably quick at sending out half a dozen pots of beer and as many bottles of wine. Daken descended on two of the former with love in his eyes, and the first had been sunk before they'd finished pouring the wine. While the rest were served, Isak watched a pair of stablehands fetch out lamps and hang them off the building. It wasn't dark yet, but given what the ghost-hour heralded these days, they clearly wanted as much light in the village as possible.

"We'll be needin' a whole lot o' food out here," Daken warned the serving girl as he handed her an empty pot. "May be a time before we get decent food again, so you tell your cook if we don't get the best out here soon, I'll go in and give 'em a beatin' before I take over the kitchen."

"Is that why you brought him, Isak?" Zhia asked once the serving girl was out of earshot. "He's your chef?"

"Why, you needin' some domestic service?" Daken asked cheerfully. "Told Doranei he drank too much."

"I brought him," Isak broke in, "because someone needs to carry all your spare clothes—and his is a name the Carastars'll know. Ours might not be so welcome there, after all."

"But mainly it's the clothes," Veil commented, raising his beer to Daken, who took the comment in good spirits. "Does a good turn as a mule, our noble general."

"You all joked enough?" Shinir demanded suddenly. The woman's eyes were suddenly alight as she looked up and down the table. "You better all damn well make sure you get it all out of you before we reach Vanach. They ain't ones for joking or laughter. It's pretty fucking easy to get the Commissar Brigade after you, but opening your mouth without thinking's the fastest, and they won't give a shit if we're following some prophecy or not."

The whole table looked startled. That speech near as much equalled the sum total of what anyone had previously heard Shinir say.

"And that's bad, right?" Daken asked, happily needling a woman considered dangerous even among Chief Steward Lesarl's agents.

Shinir ignored him and continued to address the whole table. "The Commissar Brigade has at least one agent in every village. They enforce the laws and they don't even answer to the cults. They're the ones who control Vanach and they kill anyone who doesn't act like the perfect servants of the Gods."

"The Commissar Brigade," Leshi added, "are independent of the cults—have been so for decades now." He spoke hesitantly, starting too quiet, before loudly clearing his throat. "If they decide you're a threat, they'll kill you. We can take down a lot of them, but their numbers won't run out. Every citizen can be drafted into service, and maybe one in ten is already a brigade agent—they'll make women and children fight, so it'll look like the Temple Plaza in Scree, day after day."

Leshi was a Farlan ranger and Ascetite, just as Tiniq was, and he epitomised the brave, taciturn warriors who haunted the wild forests east of Lomin. They had little use for conversation, and Leshi's obvious unnatural skills had made him something of an outcast even within that élite band. Though he verged on gaunt, he was almost as strong as a white-eye, and incredibly fast—but it was his ability to fade into the shadows that had allowed him to infiltrate Vanach on Lesarl's orders.

He and Shinir were two of a small number ever to get out of Vanach, and their intelligence had satisfied the Chief Steward, so no more had been sent. The population were permanently on the verge of starvation, and rigid controls on travel and interaction between classes meant Vanach barely functioned as a state. Only the fertile northern regions prevented outright calamity, while the labour camps and executioners prevented any opposition to the commissars.

"No glory in that," Daken muttered darkly, looking around at the faces of those who'd been in Scree at the time.

No one responded; most could not find the words to describe what had happened in Scree and even Zhia's face went stony. It was unlikely anything would match the horrors of the Last Battle—the Gods' victory over Aryn Bwr had seen the fabric of the Land permanently frayed—but even the Menin's efforts to wipe Aroth from the map had not been so effective as the madness and subsequent firestorm in Scree.

Isak hunched his shoulders a little more and reached out for a cup of wine. "I've left enough slaughter in my wake," he said. "I don't want that added to my tally too."

"We won't. This is going to go smooth as you like," Doranei replied for the rest of them. "Way I see it, this is a Brotherhood operation, and that means we plan from here to the border, rehearse everything we need and leave nothing to chance. We'll be ready, I promise."

Zhia raised her cup. Isak could taste a shred of magic on the breeze as she spoke, just a tiny fragment that tingled warm down his neck and lifted his spirits a touch. "Here's to not killing everyone we meet," she declared.

The assembled company smiled and joined her toast. "Not killing everyone." Shinir looked to her right and gave Daken a thump on the shoulder. "That means you too." "Aye, 'spose so," he grumbled and raised his pot of beer. "Just you make sure there's some. I'm a man o' appetites, me."

Mihn yawned and set his wine down unfinished. It was late in the night and half of their party had retired to the rooms they'd taken upstairs. He looked around at those who were left. Zhia, bright-eyed and alert, sat curled in Doranei's lee, the lovers talking quietly with Legana. Daken was more or less asleep, waking only to growl whenever someone tried to pluck the clay bottles nestled in the crook of each arm from his grip, while Veil sat in silence and mourned his hand. He plainly didn't want any company beyond the presence of Ebarn, sound asleep on his shoulder, and one of Doranei's cigars.

As for Isak . . . Mihn sat up, suddenly fully awake as he realised Isak was missing. Hulf lifted his head from the old bearskin in front of the fire and sleepily regarded Mihn. Then he too was awake, looking for his master as automatically as Mihn.

Legana raised a hand to catch Mihn's attention.

Outside, he read off her slate and nodded his thanks. He slipped off his boots out of habit and headed for the door. Hulf beat him there and danced about impatiently until Mihn thumbed the latch. They didn't have far to go: Isak was sitting in the cool night air, bathed in moonlight and puffing on his pipe. He didn't turn at the sound of the door opening. He knew who would be looking for him.

Hulf bounded over and forced his nose onto Isak's thigh. The white-eye shifted to scratch the dog behind his ears, but as soon as he moved, Hulf was off with his nose to the ground, following some scent. Mihn watched him move into the shadows and vanish from sight. Thanks to Daken's intervention at the Moorview ritual, he'd not be able to follow Hulf's path.

"Should we not keep him near?" Mihn asked softly.

Isak shook his head. "There are no daemons out there, not tonight. There's only us."

"You wanted to be alone?"

At that he turned and Mihn saw a smile on his abused face. "I like the moonlight," he said simply, "and this tobacco's good."

"I remember once you were not so comfortable in the presence of shadows," Mihn said, taking his usual position at Isak's side.

Isak inclined his head in agreement. "I was many things," he commented. "Some I've lost, some I've learned to live with. I can't decide yet, has all this left me unrecognisable, or put me back to where I began?"

"Which would you prefer?"

A sigh. "Dunno. I've forgotten enough already so I'd hope there was some of me left."

"Then I dub you the brat I first met," Mihn pronounced with laughter in his voice.

The night air was soft on his skin, the packed earth pleasingly cool underfoot. From the trees came the rustle of leaves, like a drawn-out sigh of the Land readying for sleep. The rest of the village were long abed and silent, though he could see lamps still lit and hanging from the eaves of houses. The furthest was just a yellow glow against the dark silhouette of a house on the far bank of the River Castir.

"A waiting soul," Mihn commented, looking past Isak to the distant lamp, "a light that doesn't move through the darkness, just waiting for the living to perform some task."

"Or follow," Isak added. "I know some folklore, and you don't need to coddle me any longer."

"As you say, my Lord."

Isak gave him a shove at the formality. "And enough of that too!" His tone became serious. "You don't need to worry; I'm not haunted by death any more. That burden's been lifted."

"But we are all closer to it, every day closer."

"Now who's being morbid?"

Mihn bowed his head. "There are many souls waiting for us these days, so many lights in the dark."

"Sometimes a light in the dark is a witch, remember? And sometimes it's just a fucking lamp."

"Still I feel them waiting," Mihn said sadly.

"Well, don't worry, you're not dying, not until I let you," Isak declared. "Any soul doesn't like it, they can face me. The daemon that owned your death is gone, and I own your life. My death meant a breaking of the prophecies that had me snared, and all that was tied to me, my title included—but you told me yourself: you don't get off that easy."

"'The ties that bind,'" Mihn whispered to the night, "'are cut by Death's pale hand. The ties that make us whole He does not sever.'"

"Exactly; Eolis remained part of me, just as you are while you still live." He put a hand on Mihn's shoulder. "Come on, we both need sleep." He gave a click of the tongue and in seconds Hulf was bounding from the dark edge of the village and running silently to his side. He followed Mihn inside. The scarred white-eye lingered a moment longer and looked around the empty village as a cool breath of breeze brushed his cheek.

"I am no longer afraid of shadows," he whispered to the dark. "You hear me, shadow? Your turn to be afraid."

A ghost of laughter danced out from the moon-shade of an old yew. Beside it the village's shrine to Nyphal, God of Travellers, looked grainy and insubstantial, and no match for the darkness.

"No longer afraid? Oh my brave, foolish boy. You are enough to make a father proud, and who made you more than I? How you escaped Ghenna I do not know, but I am glad my plaything did not fall so meekly. What use will I put you to now? A daemon perhaps, risen from the Dark Place, against which I can rally the armies of the Devoted? A fool even, serving me without realising? Do you remember the words you spoke once to Morghien? 'Life is for the living,' you said. Will you recall them at the end, I wonder?"

CHAPTER 12

AGAINST A BACKGROUND OF DEEP PINK CURLS OF CLOUD, knife-winged birds danced and swooped on their evening hunt. Larim watched their silent flight with rapt fascination, arrested by their swift, sharp turns and rapacious dives. The birds were as fast as any hawk he'd seen, moving with more haste than any fleeing insect could possibly require.

It's what they are, he realised with a smile. *They are born to fly at such speeds; they revel in their nature.*

"Few appreciate such a quality in a white-eye," he muttered just as Govin, his acolyte, appeared around the edge of the abandoned farmhouse.

"My Lord?" Govin inquired, hearing Larim's voice, but the expression on the white-eye's face made him drop the matter immediately. Govin was a man who looked in a permanent state of worry. He was only thirty summers at most but he was already balding, with just a few strands of hair dragged across his over-sized head, and he had the air of a man beaten down by life. His rather feeble body and prominent ears prone to turn pink at a moment's notice were coupled with no surfeit of intellect, giving him the charisma of something normally found under a rock.

"The village?"

"Ah, not the sleepy hamlet you hoped," Govin said quickly. "A company of soldiers are camped on the common ground there, and sentries are posted on the road."

"What sort of soldiers?" Larim asked wearily. *If you hadn't been the only one of my coterie to survive, I'd have killed you the first night for being dead weight.*

"Ah, the banners say Knights of the Temples. It doesn't look like a raiding party or patrol, though. Most of the soldiers are keeping together, and it looks like they're taking orders from men in white."

"Ruhen's Children?"

Govin bobbed nervously. "Could be; looked enough like them, certainly, and who knows what changes our defeat has brought about in the Circle City?"

"Not you, certainly. So the Devoted and Byora's little saviour have become allies? An interesting turn of events, to be sure."

"Why?"

Larim resisted the urge to slap the man across his uncomprehending face. "The Devoted? Originally founded as an army of the devoted waiting for their saviour to come and lead them in battle against the last king reborn. Men who might, in troubled times, be looking for a saviour to follow? Is this an alliance or have they declared Ruhen the fulfilment of their prophecies and leader of their entirely military order? If so—do they claim Aryn Bwr is reborn, or is there some other enemy of the Gods to crusade against? 'Interesting' barely covers it, and still you ask why?"

"But what is that to us? We're leaving the West aren't we?"

"We are somewhat impoverished of late," Larim pointed out. "Money is no issue, of course; we just need to murder a few people for that, but who knows what sort of trouble might await us at home, our journey notwithstanding? Spending a few months in Byora is unlikely to make much difference to what happens at home, and we might yet profit from the time. Our soldiers will have to become mercenaries if they are to have any chance of returning home, and we might sensibly do the same, if the pay is better than gold. It will make us stronger."

He straightened his robe, tattered and muddy though it was, and indicated the two laden horses tied to a nearby fencepost. "Bring the horses. It's time we sought honest employment—or whatever approximation of it I can be bothered with at any rate."

"And if they attack us?"

Larim's pale lips turned into a thin, lizard-like smile. "Then I'll kill them all, of course."

The farmhouse by which they stood had been recently abandoned, but he saw no signs of violence done there. Perhaps they had fled the Menin advance, perhaps daemons had taken them in the night; Larim didn't care much. This nation meant nothing to him, and the rural eastern parts even less so. Rumour said the city of Narkang was a place of learning and magic, and Larim had hoped to take Narkang for his own private fief once Tor Milist's mages had been slaughtered, but beyond the city there was nothing here to interest him.

Not bothering to wait for his none-too-deft acolyte to bring up the horses, Larim walked around the farmhouse and headed for the village. It was a warm evening and still bright, so the first sentry spotted him well before he had neared the village proper. Before he had even reached shouting distance, a pair of riders had galloped out past the picket on the road and, stopping well short of the white-eye, called out, "Halt! State your name!"

Larim scowled at that. Even though in a less than pristine state, his size and colourful patchwork robe should have made him unmistakable. Since neither of the riders appeared to be carrying a bow he continued walking. He could hear Govin huffing somewhere behind with the horses.

"I said, stay where you are!" roared one of the Devoted, a bearded young man with some insignia of rank on his shoulder.

"I wish to speak to your commander," Larim replied, still walking, "and if I stop, he will have to come to me, surely?"

His Menin accent startled the pair and they backed away. The probable lieutenant barked something at his companion and spurred his horse back towards the village without waiting for a reply.

"Apparently new to the Order," Larim commented over his shoulder, but Govin made no reply.

The other soldier moved to the side of the road as Larim approached. He was as young as the first, but with a harder face, for all his apprehension. He kept his spear-tip high, as though trying to avoid giving offence, but the white-eye ignored him and marched past, heading for the picket. A cart stood at one side, ready to be rolled back across the small bridge that crossed a little brook; he supposed the cart would provide some conceivable barrier to invaders, but the bridge was so small it barely warranted the name. *Of course, the brook may be small enough for me to hop across, but some visitors might be less able to cross running water*, he thought.

"Where's your commander?" he demanded loudly, and right on cue an officer appeared with the bearded lieutenant, now on foot, trailing along behind.

"I'm Captain Derral," the man replied, doing a fair job of not sounding afraid, "and you're under arrest."

The man looked Litse, Larim judged, and his stupidity sealed the deal for him. "I don't think I am," he replied, "but I will travel back to the Circle City with you. I don't intend to negotiate with a mere captain. I have an offer to put to your superiors."

"You'll come with us in leg-irons and dosed," warned the captain, motioning to his soldiers.

The two on the picket levelled their crossbows at Larim and at last he did stop.

"You're Menin, and as such, you're to be arrested or killed on sight."

Larim sighed and was about to release the magic he'd been casually storing when another man appeared in view. This one was not of the Devoted.

"Perhaps I can be of assistance?" the man enquired, putting a hand on the captain's shoulder, and the gesture was enough to make the soldier deferentially fall back and out of the newcomer's way.

"Oracle?" he said in surprise, "my—my orders are clear: I have to arrest him."

The oracle cocked his head at Derral. "In the interests of keeping you and your men from being slaughtered, might I suggest he be put into *my* custody instead?"

Larim watched the exchange with fascination, trying to work out who the oracle was. He wore a Harlequin's patchwork clothes, but dyed black, and instead of a mask he had teardrops tattooed onto his face. That in itself should have been enough to warrant Larim hearing of the man, but it was clear he was a powerful mage too. Larim could taste the swirl of magic spicing the air around them, twisting uneasily on a breeze that failed to touch the grass between them.

"Who are you?" he asked at last.

"Me? Just a simple storyteller," the oracle said with a half-smile. "I have many names, but you may call me Venn." He gestured for Larim to come closer. "Come, you can remain in my custody while we eat."

Larim accepted the invitation and accompanied Venn to the village inn, passing a sloped expanse of common ground currently shared by sheep and soldiers. The inn itself was set on a small rise and flanked by a pair of old spreading oak trees that provided the inn's name. The road ran below it.

The villagers were gathered in small, nervous clumps to watch the Devoted soldiers pitch their tents, but as Larim arrived he saw a party of white-clothed preachers had started to collect each group and usher them to one side. They spoke respectfully but firmly, and the presence of the soldiers ensured there was no argument from the locals.

"Have you experienced the peace Ruhen offers?" Venn inquired as he offered Larim a cup of wine.

"I have had little time for peace recently," Larim said, watching a new group exit the inn to look him over. He counted five Harlequins, a low-ranked Litse white-eye and a variety of armed men wearing various badges of rank and office from Akell and Byora. They all kept a respectful distance, watching him, not the preachers who were asking a similar question of the villagers.

"Few of us have," Venn agreed amiably. "However, the time is coming for men to choose: Ruhen's peace or King Emin's war."

"I've fared badly with one, but now my thoughts turn elsewhere, beyond the problems of the West."

"Even a man with such obligations is well served to embrace peace. Ruhen's message is one of clarity, of simplicity. I see hunger for power in you—a power rightfully yours, perhaps, but your eagerness to claim it eclipses all."

Larim put down his cup. "I am a white-eye and Chosen of Larat," he said quietly. "The Lord of the Hidden Tower *is* power. My thoughts are not clouded; my whole being demands I return to the Ring of Fire and claim my position. Do not think I can be persuaded or turned—my devotion is to my art and no words could change that. Save your message for those for whom it was intended."

"The Hidden Tower is a long way to travel." Venn inclined his head to look past Larim and at the acolyte struggling along behind him. "Certainly in such limited company."

"My means are diminished," Larim confirmed, "and that is why I'm here. I know my worth to any ruler facing war, whether or not they espouse peace."

Venn arched a practised eyebrow. "You seek employment?"

"If you have something of true value to offer in payment."

Venn was silent a while. "Such a thing could be arranged, but you would have to kneel to Ruhen first."

"A mercenary must know whose orders he obeys," Larim acknowledged.

"Good. Your terms will be acceptable to him, I believe, and payment is assured by the fact we have currently have no mages of your skill." He reached into his tunic and pulled a chain from out around his neck, which he offered to Larim.

The Chosen of Larat inspected it carefully before accepting it. The chain and the coin strung on it were made of silver, but he could detect no actual spell on either, nothing beyond an echo of some presence—and even that was eclipsed by the strange swirl of magic surrounding the black Harlequin.

"Wear this—show it to Sergeant Kayel and he will know we have met."

"What is it?" Larim turned the coin over and inspected the scored lines on its surface. "Your runework needs practice."

"It is just a symbol, acceptance of our Lord's peace. You need not wear it publicly, but few know of its use anyway. Not all Ruhen's Children wear it. Kayel will know you have got this from me."

"Might he not think I killed you and took it from your body?"

Venn laughed, his voice unexpectedly high and strange, as though not his at all. His finger tapped his belt, which, Larim now noticed, had been custom-made to include a discreet pouch; he recoiled as a burst of power pulsed out from it.

Somewhere behind, Govin cried out in shock, causing the horses to startle.

"He knows you would find that difficult," Venn said, taking his hand away from the concealed Skull.

Larim nodded. "Now I understand—but what are you doing out here, escorting a handful of preachers—and with Harlequins for company? Haven't you just torn down every temple in Byora? So how are they here with you now?"

"Ruhen is here to intercede with the Gods on our behalf, to perform the role that the greedy, vainglorious priests have failed to do. This is no war on the Gods, only on the dogma and vanity that fallible man has used to shade their light. The Harlequins understand purity of thought and action—that is the art *they* are devoted to—so they have embraced Ruhen's message."

"Impressive, but you didn't answer my first question. What are *you* doing out here?"

Venn inclined his head. "My apologies. I am bound for the West, tasked with something other than spreading Ruhen's word." He paused and looked again at Govin as the acolyte struggled with their horses. "Does he follow you into Ruhen's service?"

"Govin? He lacks the brains to do anything without orders."

"But if he is an acolyte of the Hidden Tower he must be skilled."

Larim curled his lip. "His talents are sufficient to follow orders, but expect no greatness from the man. If I should find another acolyte in the Circle City, or a sufficiently intelligent mule, his worth is greatly diminished."

"I could use him," Venn said, thoughtfully. "Our mages are limited, but an expendable one on my journey could prove useful."

"As you wish." Larim turned and raised his voice to his acolyte. "Govin, you will accompany Master Venn here; obey him as you would me."

He didn't wait for a response but returned his attention to Venn, who refilled their cups and raised one in toast. "Our first bargain," he said with a smile. "Let us drink to many more."

King Emin signalled the halt before they reached the northern-most defensive works and went on ahead, accompanied only by a small body of guards. He looked tall beside his companions, the diminutive Dashain, who was second-in-command of the Brotherhood, and High Mage Endine. Behind them were a messenger and two more Brothers, Endine's favourite thief, Tremal, and a pock-faced young Brother called Ame Forrow who now served as the king's personal bodyguard.

For reasons best known to Forrow, he had foregone the Brotherhood's usual anonymous black and instead wore scarlet sleeves and pauldrons. While he lacked his predecessor's size, he apparently wanted it made clear that he had taken Coran's place in more than just name. Given he shared the man's thuggish lack of humour, no one was inclined to argue. There was a grim air around the young Brother that was a stark contrast to the Land around him.

The sun had remained consistently warm on their faces as they skirted the Blue Hills and travelled southwest through the unspoiled heartland of the Kingdom of Narkang. At the roadside fruit was ripening amidst a bustle of bees and butterflies, and birds chattered constantly around them, filling the air with song, but Forrow took his new position seriously, and he saw nothing but potential dangers.

"Where's Suzerain Cotterin?" the king wondered aloud as he surveyed the ring of defences surrounding the town of Farrister.

All looked peaceful there, just as they'd been told, but he knew the sight of his standard might change that very quickly. The town was surrounded by a wooden fence, more a barrier to stop untaxed goods than attacking forces. This deep into the kingdom there had never been a need for anything more.

The Menin army currently occupying Farrister hadn't had time to be picky about where to make their stand. They had been sent to harry the south of the kingdom and lure troops away from the main invasion, but they had fought only one minor battle before the decisive battle of Moorview. When they had realised their lord was defeated they had taken Farrister and barricaded themselves in while their allies from Thotel and Tor Salan fled home. They'd been there for the last few weeks, sending scouts out in search of news and fortifying their position as much as they could as they realised how far from home and supply-lines they now were.

"Riders, sire," Dashain said, pointing east. She was as serene as a standing stone, and nearly as immovable. It had taken a while for the men to get past her beauty and realise they couldn't dominate her; several had suffered in the process.

While the king waited for the cavalrymen he sent the messenger to order the troops to make camp within the spiked earthworks that protected the besieging army.

"Your Majesty," called Suzerain Cotterin as soon as he came within hailing distance, "I'm relieved to see you fit and well. The reports we've had from Moorview have been most grave."

"Good to see you too, Cotterin," the king replied, adding gravely, "Unfortunately your reports were no exaggeration. The kingdom mourns many heroes."

"Truly? I heard thirty thousand Narkang men marched to the Herald's Hall."

"A shade over," Emin confirmed as Cotterin reined in and dropped from his horse to kneel before the king. "We took as many as we lost. A few Menin regiments escaped, but none surrendered."

Cotterin rose but didn't immediately reply as he looked over to the town he had been besieging. He was a broad man with long fair hair, and only a winter or two older than the king. His accent betrayed the fact he'd not been born into nobility; to many in Narkang that was a sign that he was not a man to trifle with: the king remembered his friends, and many of them greeted the men of the Brotherhood by name.

"That's a poor omen for what this lot will do then, your Majesty."

"We must hope they've had time for their blood to cool. How many do you estimate are in there?"

"Approaching ten legions-worth, now their allies have abandoned them."

"So it's rather cramped in there now."

"Must be. Half the townsfolk had already fled, but the local lord says there's never been more than four thousand living there at the most."

Emin looked around at the fortifications before walking up the earth bank the army had thrown up, the suzerain and the bodyguard following closely behind. A river cut through the city, running southwest off the Blue Hills, and the surrounding ground was parcelled into fields growing a whole range of crops. From what he could see, the Menin had not been able to harvest most of it: Cotterin's troops had arrived too soon for that.

"But we're still not going to starve them out in a hurry," he commented.

"No, your Majesty: the town is the wheat market for the whole area. The grain stores will most likely have enough left to keep them fed a good while longer. They'll be ripe for disease, being confined like that, but there are reports of that from the east anyway, so we might not do much better outside. The common folk are saying a plague followed in their wake. That might not be too far from the truth."

King Emin looked down at the group waiting for him on the ground. "Dashain, go and fetch out an envoy," he called. As she hurried to her horse and started off towards the town, Emin caught his mage's eye. "Endine, if they fire on her or anything else, I want a hole ripped in that fence, understand?"

The scrawny mage bowed, one hand on the Skull at his belt. He knew Emin was keen to avoid a fight, so magic would be the best way to persuade the Menin. They might have nowhere to go, but they were largely heavy infantry, the brutal mainstay of the Menin Army, the troops who'd almost slaughtered Emin and his entire Kingsguard at Moorview. Narkang had to march on Byora; they didn't need to fight any more Menin élite to the death first.

Dashain returned untroubled half an hour later, in the company of two Menin officers. Both were bearded, their long black curls neatly tied back. Most tellingly, Emin decided, their grey uniforms were clean and in good repair. Grief-stricken madmen were unlikely to take pride in their appearance. Though their invasion had been destroyed, these men maintained their military order.

"King Emin," Dashain called, jumping down from her horse, "may I present General Arek and Colonel Dorom?"

"Gentlemen," the king said coolly, inclining his head to the soldiers. With their clipped beards the pair looked similar-enough to be brothers. "May I offer you some wine?"

Aside from dismounting, the officers made no gestures of respect, and they ignored the wine that had been brought out. The discourtesy started Forrow growling, until the king stopped him, as he often had Coran. A twitch of the finger proved sufficient.

"You summoned us, King Emin." Arek said at last. "Do you offer your surrender?"

"Not quite," the king said calmly. "I assume some of your scouts made it back, so you will know of the events at Moorview."

Arek's eyes narrowed. "Every one of us felt our lord's name being torn from our minds. A scout found some retreating Byoran soldiers, who spoke of thousands dead and our army broken."

"They did not lie," Emin said. "Your lord is dead; your conquest of the West is ended. What you felt will also have been experienced throughout all the cities you had taken. Most likely your garrisons are all dead."

"This much we can guess."

"So what now for you? Where does your allegiance now lie?"

Arek looked insulted by the question. "To my tribe and my God, as they always have." The Menin's fingers twitched.

Emin reminded himself how fanatically loyal the Menin soldiers had reportedly been to their lord; no doubt they hated him with a passion for what he had done. "And to your men?" he asked.

"They are Menin, they obey their orders."

Emin shook his head. "No, I did not mean that. Is your loyalty to them, to their survival?"

"Save your threats. We are Menin."

"General Arek, please—put aside your hatred of me for one moment," King Emin commanded. He took a pace forward, to the Menin's surprise, moving within sword's reach. "Do you wish your men to live or not?"

"I do—but you remain our enemy."

"The war is over. You lost."

"Not while we still live. You will not take us as slaves."

Emin exhaled, a long, weary breath. For a while he didn't speak, then at last he gestured to Forrow, standing beside him. "My bodyguard," he explained. "He's hoping you will go too far, say something that will allow him to kill you both. Narkang lost many soldiers at Moorview, far more than any general would like when his war is only just beginning. *All* of my soldiers are hoping you will fight, so they can exact revenge for the comrades buried on Tairen Moor, and the civilians murdered by your armies."

"Then attack. We are not leaving."

Emin raised a hand to stop him. "*All* my soldiers want to fight, but I would prefer not to. I think there is an alternative that serves us both."

"What?" Arek demanded rudely, his patience obviously wearing thin.

"We do not fight—not each other, at least. Your mission in the West is over. There is nothing more for you here, but it's a long way home and you will not make it back without help. I doubt you'd even make it much past Tor Salan, not with the Knights of the Temples consolidating their position there, but if you did get past, I'm damn sure you wouldn't get further than the road approaching Thotel."

"You offer us a way home? Why?"

"Because I need soldiers. The child Ruhen is my enemy, and I believe the Devoted will soon declare him the saviour their doctrine speaks of. The Order controls Mustet in the south and it will likely sway Sautin as well. In addition, the Order has troops in Raland, Embere and the Circle City. This is a war I can ill afford, but I must pursue it. Troops of your calibre would prove crucial to stiffening my armies."

"Mercenaries?" Arek spat. "There is no honour in that life."

"Precious little, perhaps, but without my help you will never even make it to the Waste, of that I'm certain. Discuss it with your officers; see how many of them wish revenge for the death of your lord rather than the chance to see your homeland again."

Endine illustrated the king's point by affording them a glimpse of the Crystal Skull he carried at his waist. The threat was clear.

"I will speak to them," Arek replied, having exchanged a look with Dorom, his tone noticeably less belligerent. "But how can we trust each other? There is too much blood between us."

"Let us not pretend trust is necessary," Emin said dismissively. "If both our purposes are served, that's enough to begin with. As a gesture of goodwill, Dashain here can procure supplies, should you be running low. I would appreciate an answer in the morning. General, Colonel, good day."

Chapter 13

"And here we are," breathed Vesna as they rounded a sprawl of young oaks and spied the lights of a fort two hundred yards away. "Now we're the faithful on pilgrimage to the holy city."

"I can feel the blessing of the Gods upon me already," Zhia commented. She slipped the shawl from her head and shook her hair out loose behind her.

The sun had set behind the hills more than half an hour ago. As twilight lay heavy on the Land they looked an otherworldly collection; the dark gleaming eyes of Zhia and Legana, Isak's shadowed scars and Vesna's ruby teardrop catching the last of the light. One thin cloud reminded Isak of a pike's mouth against the dark sky, but he kept the thought to himself. His companions might not be a superstitious lot, but they were apprehensive about what they would find in Vanach, so no sort of omen would be welcome.

Isak led them to the fort where a regiment of Ghosts was waiting, formed up in two neat company blocks and ready to receive them. The men had been sent on ahead to reinforce the fort's permanent garrison, ready to provide military support should Isak call for it. It was a compact place, one of a string of six along the Vanach border, too small to cope with the additional hundred soldiers and their horses. Isak counted more than a dozen three-man tents pitched behind the fort; a makeshift corral had been set up within a cluster of ash trees beside that.

"My Lord," called a soldier not wearing the Palace Guard livery; Sergeant Ralen, once one of Isak's personal guard, approached them and saluted the white-eye he still considered his commander. "You've made good time. We only got here yesterday."

"Where's Major Jachen?" demanded Vesna as Isak slipped grimacing from his horse.

Ralen's expression wavered a fraction. "Ah, ill, sir."

"Drunk?"

"Sure it's somethin' he ate, sir."

The Mortal-Aspect of Karkarn advanced on Ralen, who had taken a few steps back before he even realised. "I don't care, Sergeant," Vesna said quietly. "Moorview hit Jachen hard; we all saw that before you left."

"Still sure it's somethin' he ate, sir," Ralen insisted. "Major's always been prone to thinkin' too hard, I'll admit, but he'll be right next time you see 'im."

"That's good enough for me," Vesna said. He turned to the rest of the party as the last of them dismounted. "We eat quickly, then we're off again."

"Off?" Ralen echoed in surprise. "But it's dusk. You're travellin' at night?"

"It is part of our pilgrimage," Isak explained, easing his way down to one knee and allowing Hulf to clamber up his thigh. These days he had a permanent frown on his face: partly because of his scars, but also because of a sense of disconnection with the Land around him, one that eased when he felt Hulf's thick fur under his fingers. "If we're to make it to the Grand Ziggurat we're going to have to pass bands of Carastars and Black Swords, and the commissars will be watching everything we do. The first step is to travel only under Alterr's light—to claim the sanctuary of her gaze."

"Sounds like jumpin' through hoops to reach your death," Ralen commented, "but the Menin lord couldn't stop you, so this lot don't have much chance—they're all fuckin' starvin' anyway, so I hear."

Isak couldn't help but look past the man to the empty plain beyond the fort. He knew there would be Carastars watching it—the mercenaries were permitted free rein along the Vanach border to dissuade the population from fleeing—but their camps were not near any potential invasion route. They weren't being paid to defend the state, just to terrorise those parts the commissars didn't.

The Black Swords, Vanach's army, was a less known quality.

The soldiers served as both religious enforcers and police, under the direction of the commissars, but both Leshi and Shinir said they rarely ventured into the borderlands.

"Let's hope they're not too hungry," Isak muttered, raising his still-bandaged left arm. The bite-wounds and burns were much improved, but the scar tissue remained sensitive. "I'm not yet healed from the last time something chewed on me."

Ralen laughed and gestured towards the food being brought out for the party. "Don't worry, sir; all the buggers'll be after Daken first. Plenty of time to get away while they're eatin' him."

Beyond the border, with night fully fallen, seeking the sanctuary of Alterr's light proved more literal than Isak had expected. Several among them had excellent night vision, with Legana and Zhia most obviously unhindered by the dark, but the rest were forced to rely on their comrades to choose a safe path. Trade between Vanach and Narkang had dried up years back, and what had once been a road was no longer anything more than a strip of relatively level ground, so barely a minute went by without someone needing to point out a hazard to those behind.

Vorizh Vukotic's journal stated that only a party of twelve, the number in the Upper Circle of the Pantheon, would be afforded Alterr's sanctuary; the clear implication being that it had to be *exactly* a group of twelve for the commissars to honour that agreement. So they rode two abreast, with Zhia and Doranei in the lead, no one going ahead as forward scouts in case they were attacked on sight.

After a couple of hours of unimpeded travel, Isak began to wonder if there was anyone around at all.

"It's uncharacteristically thoughtful of my brother," Zhia said to the Land in general, "to ensure we can travel only under cover of night. He was never usually one for practicalities."

"Self-interest," Doranei grunted from her side. "He wants someone to find and use Termin Mystt or he wouldn't have left a journal in the first place. So he might as well tailor his directions to the two most likely to do what he wants."

Zhia patted him on the arm affectionately. "That's a little too direct a thought process for him, pretty one."

"It all sounds rational enough," Veil said, riding behind Doranei. "Might be he was having a good day?"

"You don't build a state in a day," Zhia replied, "and that's what Vorizh did in Vanach—rebuilt the whole society according to his needs. That requires more than just one good day. It takes time even with skilled underlings to carry out your orders. The hierarchy of Vanach is a strict one, with every citizen finely graded. Only Black Swords, commissars and priests can travel between provinces at all, let alone head towards Vanach City. Vorizh coopted an entire nation and imposed these rules upon the people, but don't expect all of it to be rational or obvious."

"Well, ain't you just a ray of sunshine?" Daken muttered from further back. "Still, I'm fine with leavin' you to figure out what yer bugshit-crazy brother is about. I'm just looking for something t'kill."

"Then you'll get your wish soon enough," Zhia replied cheerily. "We're being watched."

Isak tore his gaze away from the ground beneath him and sat upright, but couldn't spot anyone. There were trees beyond the fifty yards of open ground on the left, while their path ran beside the tree-line on the right. "Where?" he asked.

"Ahead," Zhia said, "under cover of those tall pines: there's a company of men."

Isak still couldn't make anything out under the trees, but they were still a few hundred yards away from the spot Zhia had indicated. If they continued on their current course they would pass within a dozen yards.

"I can smell them," Zhia confirmed, flashing Isak a quick smile. "One is carrying an injury; his blood is on the wind."

Isak nodded and closed his eyes briefly. With one finger he brushed the Crystal Skull hanging from his belt and opened his mind to its stored energy. A dizzying burst of power fizzed through his mind and he hunched low over Toramin's neck, gripping his saddle tightly until it had passed. After the initial discomfort came a more familiar sensation: the warm metallic tang in his mouth as magic raced through his veins and traced a delicate path over his many scars.

He felt a lurch as his senses caught a breeze and drifted up into the night air. The starlight prickled faintly on his soul as he moved up above the trees; the lesser moon, Kasi, a warm, familiar touch, with Alterr a sharp, clear flavour in his mind. The cool presence of clouds hung above him as he reached out with the dew drifting slowly down and caressed the grass ahead.

The Land was dormant there, with few night creatures anywhere nearby, but Isak could not tell whether that was because of the scent of a vampire, or the distant presence of Ghenna that occasionally appeared on the edge of perception. A breeze shivered through the trees and Isak gave a soft gasp as it seemed to run right through him, but he continued his questing and soon found the waiting soldiers.

Moving outwards, he drifted away from the excited clicks of the bats darting around the treetops and plunged down into the woods on the right. His nose was full of the scents of bracken and bark, but he found no bright human minds shining in the dark there and soon let the wind carry him back to the warmth of his body.

He opened his eyes and blinked down at his huge horse, still walking patiently behind Daken's smaller steed. Beside him, he saw the whites of Mihn's eyes looking up at him. The small man already had his boots off and the magic of his tattoos was gathering the night around him.

"Go—Veil and Leshi, you too. When Alterr next goes behind a cloud, circle around behind them. They'll be expecting to ambush anyone coming this way and we can't be sure there's a commissar among them."

"Did you sense a mage?" Zhia asked as Mihn looked up at the greater moon.

Isak shook his head. "You might see more."

"Certainly, but I'm more interested in gauging the extent of your remaining powers. You're not long returned to the Land, and Vorizh is certain to have some surprises in store for whoever takes Termin Mystt."

"Planning on being elsewhere?"

"No—but he might well test you alone." She returned her attention to the Carastars ahead just as a cloud began to advance across Alterr and the moonlit ground around them began to dim. "What's more, the closer we get to Vanach, the more likely there will be mages, and I doubt any are tolerated outside the Commissar Brigade. If they see how strong we are, they may perceive us as a threat."

"You want to kill every mage we meet?"

Zhia laughed. "No—I'm saying we might have to."

They rode on in silence. Isak tried to follow the three men he'd sent off on foot, but they had disappeared entirely before they had gone twenty yards and he quickly gave up staring out across the still plain. When he looked down, he realised Hulf was also gone, but the dog had vanished just as silently; he had adapted to the witch's tattoos as quickly as any of the Brotherhood or Ghosts. He realised there was nothing he could do about it; he'd have to rely on the fact that Hulf wouldn't attack a man unless he was going for Isak.

No Carastar will see or hear him. Maybe it's better Hulf keeps away; he'll most likely get trampled in a fight.

They covered the remaining ground quickly, the soldiers among them surreptitiously loosening the ties on their weapons as they rode. Half-anticipating the flash of a crossbow bolt at any moment, Isak found himself angling his scarred belly away from the trees where the mercenaries were waiting.

"That's far enough!" called a gravelly voice in the Narkang dialect. "Throw down your weapons and dismount."

Doranei glanced back at Isak, who nodded to him.

"Why?" The King's Man demanded on behalf of them all. "Sounds like a stupid idea with all the dangerous sorts round here."

"Your choice," laughed the Carastar. "Keb!"

Nothing happened. A hail of arrows failed to leap from beneath the trees. In the hush, Isak thought he heard a grunt of puzzled consternation before the speaker gave another shout: "Keb, Dass—shoot him!"

Still nothing happened, and after a minute or two Doranei gestured for the group to keep on moving—at which point two men armed with spears broke from cover and charged towards them. Before anyone else could react, Daken had hurled his axe over-arm; it caught the nearest in the chest and smashed him to the ground in a spray of blood. The second mercenary yelped and threw himself to one side, abandoning his spear in his terror and ending up on his knees with his friend's blood running down his cheeks.

The white-eye slid from his saddle and walked unconcernedly over to him to retrieve his axe. Another Carastar ran to intercept him before he could retrieve his weapon, but Mihn appeared from the lee of a tree, swinging his staff. He caught the man in the gut and sent him wheezing to the ground.

A second appeared, lunging with a spear, but Mihn had already skipped out of the way as though performing some dainty dance and before the mercenary could react he had lifted one leg and slapped his bare sole against the shaft of the spear, sending the head plunging down into the ground. Without pausing, Mihn snapped his leg forward and kicked the Carastar in the face with enough force to knock the man flat.

"Enough!" shouted a new voice from the trees. "No more killing."

Doranei cocked his head at the new speaker: this one wasn't a Narkang mercenary, as the first had been; most likely that was a Vanach accent, which meant he was a commissar.

"We claim the sanctuary of Alterr's light," Doranei announced, hoping it meant something to the man.

There was a pause.

"The first sign?" the commissar asked in a stunned voice, more to himself than any other. The shock of Doranei's claim seemed to have driven the wind from his lungs, and when he emerged into the moonlight the man walked as though dazed. He was a large man with thick limbs, much to Isak's surprise. They were renowned as blackmailers and cruel bullies, using fear and spiteful words to turn men against each other, so Isak had expected some sort of rat-faced weakling who hid behind his authority.

The commissar wore a basic brown tunic and trousers, his lack of armour and the pale scarf around his neck making him stand out from the mercenaries. In the dark it wasn't clear what colour it was, but Doranei guessed at pale yellow, an echo of the greater moon above them, since Alterr was the dominant God here.

"You claim Alterr's sanctuary? I—forgive me, it has been a long time since my days of instruction. I had almost forgotten— And the mysteries of . . ." He tailed off, but then visibly rallied as he remembered what he had learned when first inducted into the ranks of the commissars. "You must number twelve."

Doranei inclined his head to concede the point. "Veil, Leshi."

In complete silence the pair picked their way out from the darkness of the trees and stood with weapons drawn as the commissar counted them again.

"You are twelve," he said eventually, adopting as dignified an air as he could muster. "Lady Alterr blesses you with her light, and so you may travel safely so long as you do so." He turned to the copse. "Captain, you and your men may come out."

"Rather not, if it's all the same ta you," the Carastar replied nervously. "I've heard talk o' the mysteries and the halls o' the ziggurat. Some sort o' saviour or prophecy, right?"

"It is a prophecy," the commissar said, "but one beyond your comprehension—only the most faithful of Alterr's servants are revealed the mysteries, so you should not gossip or speculate."

"Aye, I won't. My point being, we didn't know who you all were, sirs and ladies, before you announced yourselves. Don't mean no disrespect, but given we almost made a terrible mistake there, I'd sooner slip away right now rather than show my face."

The commissar was momentarily speechless, flustered both by the ancient legend standing before him and astonished that his orders had been questioned for once. Even the Carastars were subject to the rule of the Commissar Brigade; the captain knew to defer to him.

"No disrespect will be taken," Doranei interjected before the commissar could recover himself. "We would not object."

"You—? Well, then, as you wish, Captain." The commissar shook his head in puzzlement, but he was not going to countermand Doranei's statement. "Wait for me at the camp—but first send your fastest rider on ahead to Ghale Outpost and inform the ranking commissar there that the first sign has been revealed. He will know what to do and make arrangements for our guests."

He bowed low to Isak's party as the sound of men retreating came from the trees. "My name is Commissar Yokar," he said, peering at Doranei and then Zhia, before scrutinising Isak as the largest among them and Vesna as the most regal. His knowledge of their prophecies would be limited by his rank, but he clearly expected one of them to stand out and show him what the mysteries expected.

"I am at your disposal. Might I—might I ask who is the leader of your group?"

There was a pause before Isak nudged his horse forward. "I am."

"I am honoured to be in your presence. Might I ask my Lord's name?"

"Sebe," he replied as he slid the shawl from his head and saw Yokar visibly flinch when he saw Isak's battered face, but he managed to keep silent. "My name is Sebe."

The commissar was too overawed to notice Doranei's reaction to the name, but it took only the smallest movement from Zhia to keep the King's Man quiet. They all knew the king and Isak had agreed he should not use his own name, to avoid provoking months of religious debate. Isak had said that if their mission was to become famous, it deserved to be in the name of a man whose renown had been missed by the Land at large.

"My Lord Sebe," the commissar said awkwardly, unsure how to address the white-eye, "I cannot offer you an escort according to the lore, but should you need supplies or horses, you have only to command me."

"That will not be necessary." Isak replaced the shawl to keep Alterr's light off his face. "We have a long way to travel before dawn, so you may return to your work."

Seeing the exchange was at an end, Doranei and Zhia started off again across the moonlit grass. The tattooed soldiers leaped back onto their horses and fell in behind their lord, and they all moved off quickly. The commissar was left alone and staring after them. He jumped as Isak turned in his saddle and clicked his tongue, then stumbled backwards when a grey shape broke from the trees opposite.

Hulf trotted out into the open and regarded Yokar. Man and dog watched each other suspiciously for a few moments before Hulf gave an unexpected sneeze and turned after Isak, dismissing the commissar with a swish of his tail. When thick cloud crossed both moons Hulf seemed to disappear entirely and that was enough for Yokar. The commissar fled back into the trees.

An hour before dawn the party reached what appeared to be an abandoned farmstead and Isak called a halt. While the soldiers of the group went on to investigate, Isak eased himself off his charger and watched Legana do the same. Vesna had offered the Mortal-Aspect a hand, knowing her balance was permanently affected by the loss of her Goddess, but she had ignored him. Even when she stumbled and had to grab the saddle to steady herself, she shrugged off any attempts to help.

Isak watched Vesna frown at the display of independence, but he said nothing, just stayed as her side until she had recovered herself and glared at him. Dismissed, Karkarn's Iron General trudged back to his horse and led it to the dilapidated corral where Ebarn and Tiniq were starting to rub down the horses.

Isak followed. He nudged his friend as his horse was taken off him. "You've been quiet."

Vesna's frown deepened. "Not much to say." He headed around the back of the corral, away from their companions to a break in the trees behind, through which he could see the western sky where the sun would soon rise. The colours of night were already bleeding from the sky, but Isak knew Vesna saw none of it. The neat patter of paws behind them told him Hulf had joined them and on instinct Isak knelt down and drew the dog close.

All of a sudden Vesna's head sagged and his legs wavered. Gods-granted strength or not, the famous warrior would have fallen to his hands and knees had Isak not jumped up and reached out to steady the man. He guided Vesna to a wide tree-stump a few yards away, sat him down and sat on the ground himself, while Hulf inveigled his way under Vesna's thigh until he was sitting between the man's legs and looking up, begging for attention.

Vesna gave a bitter, pained laugh and began to scratch the dog behind one ear with his un-armoured hand. Hulf arched appreciatively and tilted his head until he was pressing against the Mortal-Aspect's leg.

"He'll never get too much of that," Isak commented.

"Mihn said Ehla gave him to you?"

"So he tells me. I don't really remember." He winced and pressed his fingers to his temple. One fingernail had refused to grow back after his time in Ghenna and the rest were marked strangely, symbols or some strange script cut into the skin beneath. "The time after my escape . . . I see the cottage by the lake, and figures around me, but they're like ghosts in the mist."

"We all are now," Vesna commented sadly, peering down at Hulf's bright eyes. "I feel like we've slipped out of life, as if we're just shadows hunting for the bodies we once possessed."

"Some of us are," Isak replied with a slight smile. He put a hand on Vesna's shoulder. "But not you—you, my friend, have greatness ahead of you."

"Greatness? All I feel is emptiness like ice."

"That's because you mourn, right down to the bone. Tila's death hurt us all, but your loss was greatest and there's nothing can ease your pain. I'm sorry. But she saw the greatness in you; the strength not only to survive but overcome."

"You speak to *me* of strength?" Vesna asked, astonished, "when it chills me to even imagine what you endured?"

"We white-eyes, we're born to survive, to wade through rivers of blood until we've reached our goal." Isak tried to smile but the effort defeated him. "We're tools to be used; I see that now. Whatever purpose the Gods or Aryn Bwr sought to use me for, I've found my own path—but the white-eyes are the bloody hand of history. We're not equipped for what happens after victory; we must leave that to greater men."

Vesna glanced back at the house behind, where a light now shone through the shutters. It was too bright for a lamp; it had to have been cast by one of the mages. "You're not alone there. Perhaps it would be best for some of us if we did not survive this war."

"Enough of us'll die already; there's no need to seek it out. His hand will reach for us all in due time."

"So we just have to wait our turn?"

Isak shrugged and rose, offering a hand to Vesna. The Mortal-Aspect took it, but he did not rise immediately, instead taking a moment to stare at the strange contrast between the two. Each man had used his left hand: Isak's scarred and white, Vesna's a black metal gauntlet. They interlocked like some esoteric symbol, a curious symmetry that seemed to hearten Vesna.

"Let's hope history doesn't think me a fool, then, wallowing in my personal misery when the fates of every man, woman and child hang in the balance."

"You are far from a fool, my friend," Isak said. He hauled Vesna up and pushed him towards the house. "Only a monster wouldn't feel the pain."

The pair slowly made their way back to the front of the house. It was a large building, considering the remote location, and looked as if it had been abandoned for several seasons. Rampant creeper swarmed over the nearside walls, so thick that when someone inside tried to opened the shutter, the mass hanging off the roof obscured their face entirely. Isak watched as the person hacked away at the worst of it while Hulf stalked the twitching trails at the base of the wall with geat delight.

On the other side of the building was a half-collapsed barn and animal pens, none of which looked safe to enter. Daken was standing beside the barn, surveying it, then he gave the whole thing an almighty kick and hastened its downfall. The groan and snap of timbers seemed to satisfy the destructive little child in him and he turned away with a wide grin.

"Ain't running out o' firewood today," he commented brightly, accompanying them inside. "Piss and daemons; this the best we could do?"

Isak inspected the interior over Vesna's shoulder. It was not so very different from the cottage by the lake where he'd lived so recently. The smell was more the musty scent of slowly rotting wood, but there was no stink of bodies, human or animal, nor mould. There was little furniture beyond a broken table and two benches, but it was an improvement on spending the day out in the open. He knew Zhia at least would agree with him. "It'll do for the day," he said out loud, prompting nods from several others.

Veil had already collected a great armful of kindling which he was unloading into a brick-walled firepit at the back of the room. A rough clay chimney had been incorporated into the wall behind. Isak took the largest pieces of kindling and lit them, holding them just below the chimney; when the smoke rose up freely and he was sure it was clear he dropped the sticks into the pit, let Veil put the rest of the kindling down, then watched as Doranei deposited two logs on top. He lit the lot and watched the flames start to hungrily consume the wood, for a while losing himself in the dancing orange flames.

"I don't understand," Fei Ebarn said as she came in ahead of Tiniq. "This house looks sound enough—so why was it abandoned?"

"Most likely the owner got marched off for some transgression or other," Shinir said darkly as she rooted through her pack, "and out here, there's no one to take the place once it's empty."

"Marched off where?"

"Slave camps, though they're not called that, o' course. No one's allowed to own another human in Vanach, but they say everyone belongs to Alterr, so some—lots—get taken off to serve their Goddess in whichever ways the Commissar Brigade chooses. They don't want anyone but the Carastars within a couple days' ride of the border; makes it simple to work out if you're fleeing the benevolent fellowship."

"So this land's used for nothing?"

Shinir nodded. "You'll see: two days of riding and we'll reach the first town. From there on, nothing's allowed more than one day away from any local administration. You grow crops past that, you're trying to evade the moral guidance of the commissars—and by extension, the priesthood and the Gods themselves—"

"—which means you're a heretic," Vesna finished, "and we've seen enough of that talk in Tirah to guess how they treat heretics here."

"This farm must have been used by a commissar in recent years," Shinir said. "The edict for the protection of souls was issued ten years back, well before this place was abandoned."

Isak crouched down in front of the fire as the flames continued to rise. "'The protection of souls?' Vorizh really is mad."

"If it was he who issued it," Zhia said quietly from behind Isak, "then he has much to answer for here."

Isak turned and saw the dark, angry gleam in her eyes. "You don't think he did?"

"My brother might be mad, but capable of self-delusion? I'm not so sure. We were all cursed to feel the suffering of others, and even now I feel a sickness in my stomach for what we might find around this first town. If he is the one issuing orders from the heart of Vanach, he will be constantly pained by the suffering he is causing."

"I can tell you what we'll find," Shinir growled, unafraid of the expression on Zhia's face, "guarded farms, where slaves must pray all night and work all day, where it must be their fault if the crops fail—it can't be the soil suffering without crop rotation because Alterr's light nourishes all. The women get raped as often as the guards want, and strangled if they become pregnant, because a baby's a divine blessing which no heretic would get. It can't be the rape that gets her that way, so she must have been consorting with daemons instead, and so she'll be carrying a daemon-child."

"Do not think to lecture me, girl," Zhia said, taking a step forward, "and do not think my rage is any less than yours, when the Gods have cursed me with always knowing the pain of others. My point is solely that mortals need no vampire ruler to inflict such horrors on each other. You are all quite capable of it without anyone's help."

Vesna stepped forward and placed himself between them. "Enough, both of you. Let's get some food and sleep; it's been a long-enough day without picking fights amongst ourselves."

"Oh let 'em fight," Daken grinned, "I like that idea."

"Fuck yourself, you white-eye shit," Shinir snapped, drawing her khopesh and pointing the sickle-like weapon at him.

"I said *enough, all of you*!" Vesna demanded, his voice suddenly full of the War God's divine authority. It was enough to make anyone who'd fought in battle stop dead, even a blood-mad white-eye like Daken, who inclined his head and turned away with a small smile on his face.

Vesna realised belatedly that Daken had spoken up to keep Shinir from getting herself killed—she was a vicious woman who didn't know when to back down from anyone, even when she was out of her depth. Luckily, someone so quick to anger was also easily deflected.

"Sleep," Isak echoed as he headed for the corner where Mihn had deposited his baggage. "Save your fights for the morning—I'm sure I heard that once."

"Not from someone who's travelled all night," Zhia pointed out before she headed into the back room, where the shutters were still closed and the dawn light would not disturb her. "Someone wake me when there's food."

Both Veil and Daken opened their mouths as Doranei moved to follow her, but Vesna raised an admonishing finger before either of them could speak. "I said enough. Your jokes can also wait."

Their first day in Vanach was uneventful. Word of their arrival travelled slowly in the empty borderlands of the Carastars, so they all managed to sleep before dusk came and they set out again. That night they encountered a second band of patrolling mercenaries camped across the road: two low-ranking commissars accompanying nearly fifty men. They had met Commissar Yokar's rider and come to investigate for themselves.

They were probably a raiding party, Vesna thought, armed for war. Doranei and Veil had to work hard to control themselves, having seen the results of such raids, but Isak was more interested in the less-deferential attitude of the two commissars leading them. As soon as they had passed on by, the white-eye spurred his horse forward to join Zhia at the front of their column.

"Tell me again about your brother's journal," he asked the vampire.

She gave him a level look. "The answer you're after is no."

"You didn't hear the question yet."

The moon was again bright overhead; Alterr's eye was a day away from waxing full and shone all too clearly on Zhia's exposed teeth as she smiled humourlessly. "I heard it easily enough; one learns to read people after the first few lifetimes."

"And your answer's no?"

She turned away. "No, yes and no. No: there was nothing contained in the journal that specified divisions or branches within the Commissar Brigade; yes, I saw the bone clasp on the scarf was a different colour; no, I do not know the significance."

"But," Doranei supplied from Isak's other side, "considering they claimed the same rank as Commissar Yokar, it's still significant, even if it only tells us they're marked according to what job they're doing. The ones in charge of raids ain't the same as those supervising patrols, and most likely there'll be more differences."

"And yes, it means some commissars don't care so much for the mysteries, so they're probably in this for more simple reasons," Isak finished.

"Good news at last," Zhia concluded with a smile. "If someone tries to kill us before we reach the ziggurat, I might not have to eat the girl before we get there."

On the fourth day they were forced to camp under a canopy of tall pines. Zhia retreated into a double-layered tent to hide from the sun while the others cooked or lay out in the tree-filtered light. Isak and Fei Ebarn managed between them to coax a deer close enough for Leshi to shoot, whereupon half the party set about butchering it and cutting half of the meat into thin strips to dry above the fire while the rest roasted below.

After an hour of activity, they were finished and sat down to eat, tearing apart blackened hunks of venison with their teeth to expose the more succulent meat below. The humour of the group was markedly improved now they had settled into a routine to match the strange nocturnal life Vorizh Vukotic had forced upon them.

After he'd finished eating, Veil lay back against his pack with a satisfied sigh and loosened the adapted vambrace that had been made for him, with its twin prongs extending past his wrist. "So what happens to the people of Vanach once we're done here?" the King's Man asked. "If this place is built around a lie, does the lie collapse?"

"Not if Isak plays it right," Zhia said through the open entrance to her tent, which had been angled away from the sun to keep her from being burned. She watched her lover pull a cigar from inside his brigandine and blew a kiss towards him; a wisp of smoke drifted through the air and settled on the cigar's tip to light it for him. "Only the commissars know what to expect at all, and all they know is what Vorizh has left for them on the inner walls of the ziggurat."

"So we sell them another lie?"

Zhia raised an eyebrow. "Unless you have a spare army hidden about your person? We give them hope, something these people have lacked in a long time. The commissars can hardly argue with their mysteries being fulfilled and their saviour leaving to pursue the work of the Gods—certainly not if it leaves them in charge with an even greater mandate than before."

"How long does hope last?"

"Ten thousand days," Isak mumbled, lost in the lazy glow of the fire's embers, "longer than good intentions."

Mihn reached out and put up a hand on his friend's arm, but only succeeded in startling the white-eye; his flinch prompted Hulf to wake and wriggle up closer, thumping his tail against the ground until Isak reached out to him.

"Long enough for the Land to have changed," Mihn said with finality. "Whether or not we are left to see it, the faith of Vanach will be overturned by what comes. There will be no exceptions."

Before anyone could respond Legana began to click her fingers. With no time to bother with the slate hanging from her neck, the Mortal-Aspect pointed out through the trees with an urgency that needed no words.

Leshi was guarding that flank of the camp; he was already moving silently from tree to tree. He worked his way forward, bow at the ready, but he made no attempt to draw it fully yet. The others went for their weapons. A muffled curse came from Zhia's tent, but Doranei turned to the entrance and motioned for her to stay where she was. If her help was truly needed at this point in the journey they had sorely underestimated the Commissar Brigade; they didn't want to risk her getting burned by sunlight anywhere there were religious fanatics.

Isak closed his eyes and opened himself to the magic in his Crystal Skull, but before he could reach out to the Land around them he realised Zhia was doing the same. With a deftness that astonished him, he felt the vampire's mind sweep past him and catch him in her wake, bringing his thoughts with her as she danced between the trees. Her touch was as cool and smooth as the emerald set in Eolis' hilt, as unyielding, but just below the point of discomfort.

He fought the urge to resist, knowing she was the stronger and posed him no threat, but it proved nearly impossible: her perfume filled his nostrils and grew thick in his throat, but it could not obscure the scent of a vampire that his white-eye soul screamed to kill. It was a faint and ancient odour, the tang of old blood mixed with the more familiar taste of magic, and something else he couldn't identify.

For a moment he managed to block out Zhia's nature, and he glimpsed a party of men in black hoods advancing on them from the left, but then it all became too much and he had to tear himself from her magical grasp. He fell to his knees, gasping and shivering as he tried not to retch.

Zhia returned to her scouting; it took her only a few heartbeats to sweep the whole area; with his senses still open to his Skull Isak could almost follow the slight disturbance of her mind through the afternoon air.

"*Ten coming in on our flank with crossbows*," she said in his mind and pointed Isak towards the group he'd seen, "*and another twenty spearmen moving from the north*."

Isak repeated the words out loud and Vesna pulled his breastplate over his armoured arm and let Doranei strap it around his body. "Daken, Mihn, Tiniq—flank the crossbows; Ebarn, you draw their attention, and Shinir, get up a tree with a bow."

The Farlan woman nodded and grabbed her weapons. She had been born with some natural magical talent, but her tough upbringing had made her an Ascetite rather than a mage, turning the magic inwards and giving her unnatural physical skills instead. With little apparent effort she scampered up the bare trunk of the nearest pine and found herself a good position from which to shoot. Leshi, their other Ascetite, had already half-vanished into the forest; crouching in the lee of a great pine trunk, the ranger's mottled brown cloak blended into the bark, and combined with his preternatural stillness made him easily missed by any scanning eyes.

"Legana, stay here and look helpless in case any slip past," Vesna ordered. She was beautiful enough that they'd most likely want to capture rather than kill her, and anyone coming within reach of those knives was as good as dead.

"Doranei, Veil, keep close behind me; Isak, head away on our right flank. We go as fast as we can. I'll punch through the spearmen and we'll come at them from the back while Isak lights them up."

Nods all round and weapons drawn showed his orders were understood. Each of them looked serious, grim-faced. Without a mage the attackers were never going to win the fight, but that wouldn't be much consolation to anyone who lost a friend in the process.

"Let's move."

Isak watched Vesna lead the way across the needle-carpeted forest floor. The Mortal-Aspect moved as silently as the tattooed King's Men, running at a crouch in the direction Zhia had indicated. Isak went slower, knowing he was less stealthy than the others, but making sure he'd be in position when Vesna attacked. The enemy had split their forces: they no doubt wanted to spread panic with the crossbows first, so the larger group wouldn't be expecting to be attacked themselves.

Behind him Isak sensed Ebarn embrace the energies in her Crystal Skull, her magic unfolding like a flower with its sharp tang overlaying the forest's resinous scent. He stumbled and nearly fell, his mind alive with sudden memories, as Doranei ducked down behind a tree, sword held low at his side. For a moment he was on the south trail, east of Helrect, where he'd first seen Doranei's black sword, where he'd first tasted magic filling his mind.

I'd been hoping for the scent of pine again, the forests of home no different to these. In his mind there was a blank emptiness at the heart of his memories, a picture torn in half where a man he couldn't remember was lost from his memory.

Carel, his name was Carel.

Reminding himself didn't matter, however; the memory was lost from Isak's head no matter how much Vesna or Mihn told him of the veteran Ghost. A dull throb flourished in the back of his head, the numb pain of ice pressed against skin that always came on when he tried to remember things that were lost, as if the holes in his mind opened onto a void where even warmth was dead. A part of him feared the cold would consume him if he tried to look into that void too long.

I'm dead to him; he's dead to me. "Balance in all things," Isak whispered.

The pain fled and he found himself blinking out across the forest floor at the still figure of Vesna, half-armoured, half-God.

"We must find balance," Isak continued as though repeating a charm against sickness, "before hate, before rage or revenge. I'm nothing without control and the Land's a wasteland without balance."

He forced himself to continue, moving sluggishly at first but quickly recovering himself as the white-eye's anticipation of a fight began to sing him his blood. He couldn't tell how close the enemy were now, and tried to gauge it from the three ahead of him. They advanced steadily, covering the ground quickly before the shooting started elsewhere, using anything they could as cover, fallen trees and dips in the ground serving where bushes or bracken did not.

After fifty-odd yards they stopped and Vesna looked back to check on Isak's position. The Farlan hero gestured to let him know that the enemy were approaching and Isak raised Eolis in acknowledgement. Where Leshi was they couldn't tell; the ranger had vanished from sight, but Isak knew he'd be close. He could hear the Vanach soldiers now, the faint brush of bracken betraying their presence not far off. He put his hands down to the Skull at his belt and saw tiny threads of lightning crackle over his scarred fingers. He might be free of his obligations to Nartis, but the spirit of the Storm God lived on inside him and he could feel the magic hungering to be released.

As one, Vesna, Doranei and Veil broke from cover and charged. Isak followed, and saw Vesna reach the enemy first, his armoured fist encased in spitting green energies as he cleaved through the spear of the nearest and spun to shoulder him out of the way. He caught a second shaft with his left arm and it exploded into matches while he chopped through the mail-covered thigh of another.

Before any of the men could react Doranei had arrived with his enchanted blade, his long, graceful sweeps parting shields and men in a single blow. Veil followed his Brother, not looking for the killing blows as he slashed with a longsword, just putting them down: one he winged, another managed to deflect the blow with his spear, but was caught with a punch to the ribs from Veil's spiked arm. The twin spikes were barbless and came away freely as Veil passed. Isak saw a bloody wheeze of air expelled from the man's pierced side: he was no further threat.

As the three pushed on through their enemy, the line folded inwards to follow them. On their left flank a man suddenly staggered drunkenly, and Isak saw an arrow protruding from his neck just as a second shot from Leshi struck the next in the chest and knocked him over. Isak could see their uniforms now, and he launched a coruscating lance of magic at the black longsword stitched onto a pale leather surcoat, which ignited when the bolt struck. The lightning wrenched the first man around and grabbed the next in its teeth too fast to avoid; then another was taken by the spitting energy, striking with the force of a ballista bolt and smashing them to the ground where they convulsed, screaming as their black swords burned yellow on their chests.

Now Vesna turned and attacked from the other side. He stepped between spear-points and cut left and right before the soldiers even saw him. Limbs were severed and bodies dropped away, but he didn't wait to see; he was already moving on to the next. The quickest of the Black Swords dropped their spears and pulled out their own swords out, but Vesna adapted in a heartbeat, turning away their weapons with a duellist's flicking skill, then stepping in for short, lethal thrusts.

Isak did not bother with artistry but trusted to the edge of Eolis and his own supernatural speed. Holding his sword in two hands, he turned an out-thrust spear and stepped in to decapitate the owner. Seeing Isak was inside his guard, another soldier slammed his shield into Isak's side, trying to throw him off-balance. Isak rode the buffeting and slashed back, chopping the wooden shield in two and eliciting a scream of pain.

The Black Swords fell like wheat, unable to meet the skill of their attackers or resist the power of their swords. Isak punched one soldier with a magic-wrapped fist and the man's head snapped back, his face shattered, while another, bewildered and terrified by the storm of blood all around him, stood still and stared aghast at the arrow protruding from his chest. Doranei glided past him as he looked down, caught in a dance of his own and barely noticing as he lopped the soldier's sword-arm off—

And then there was only one.

Vesna struck the last a glancing blow, his armoured fingers whipping across the soldier's face and sending him crashing to the ground, and at last he could be still: his sword outstretched and ready for another blow that was not needed. He looked around at the squirming injured at his feet and peered intently at each, then stalked over to one lying face-down and kicking weakly.

He rolled the soldier on his back and found the yellow scarf around his neck denoting a commissar. One of them had opened the man's belly and the pock-cheeked man was gasping like a fish even as he tried to scream. Vesna ended his pain and moved on to the next, assessing the man's injury before putting him out of his misery.

Isak checked those near him: the closest two were dead, but the man who'd hit him with a shield was still alive. He lay on his back, his face contorted with pain as his life's blood pumped from the stump of his arm, spurting weakly with every panicked breath. The man was little older than

Isak himself, but the white-eye felt nothing inside as he kneeled to inspect the injury.

Mihn said I did this once for Carel, he recalled. The man stared up at him with horror in his eyes, right hand clamped around what remained of his arm. *Did he thank me, I wonder, or was it my fault to begin with?*

He reached down and touched two white fingers to the spurting wound. The soldier shrieked then fainted as searing flame encased the end of his arm, blessedly passing out as his blood steamed and the fat sizzled with the stink of bitter pork.

"That one still alive?" Vesna called. Isak cocked his head, for a moment unsure, before he nodded to Vesna.

"Good, that gives us two—that's enough to find out who among the commissars doesn't want a saviour."

"Two?" Leshi asked with a humourless laugh. "Don't reckon so." The ranger walked to where Vesna stood over the man he'd struck across the face instead of killing him. "You've got something of the white-eye about you now, Iron General." He rolled the soldier over with his foot and pointed. The man's jaw, nose and cheek were shattered and bloody. There wasn't quite the impression of a hand in his head, but the damage was clear. No one needed to check if he was still breathing. "See?"

Vesna stared down at the corpse, then flexed his black-iron fingers with a worried expression. There was blood smeared over the ornate metal.

"Don't worry," Isak called, "you get used to it."

"I barely caught him," Vesna muttered. "It should have just knocked him over."

"Try getting an accidental elbow in bed," Doranei muttered darkly as he bent to wipe his massive sword on a corpse. "Pretty sure Zhia broke my rib once when she rolled over in her sleep."

Isak hauled up the unconscious Black Sword and draped him over his shoulder. Before moving off he turned to view the bodies of the rest. "Not one thought to run."

Leshi said grimly, "Unless their commissar's dead, they don't dare. Better to get massacred than have your name reported back. The Black Swords are faithful soldiers o' the Gods, the first tier o' the Blessed. They're encouraged to have families and raise the next generation of devoted warriors."

"And if the parents are found wanting, the children must be defective too?" Vesna guessed.

"You run from battle, you're defying the word of your God—heresy through cowardice, and that means they make 'em face their death." The stoical, otherworldly ranger shivered and looked down. "Saw a mechanism for it in a core settlement, made just for executing cowards. They strapped every member of a family into the frame and swung down a bar with two spikes—impaled 'em through the eyes, one by one."

With that Leshi turned and headed away from the slaughter to see how their friends had fared. Isak found he couldn't tear his eyes off the dead bodies, it was only when Vesna started to go through the jacket of the commissar that he seemed to jerk awake.

"There's nothing here," Vesna reported after a short while. He fingered the dead commissar's scarf. It was fastened by a white leather band just below the man's throat.

"I'd swear Yokar's wasn't white," Vesna said, looking at Doranei, who had been closest to the man.

Doranei nodded in agreement. "It was darker, hard to tell exactly what colour at night, but certainly not white. Reckon this indicates a faction within the brigade?"

"There are markings on it, a script maybe? It's not Elvish or any I recognise. Some sort of designation I'd guess. Who watches the watchmen, eh?"

The King's Man sheathed his sword and started back towards their camp. "Aye, keeps 'em all in line, then, recruiting the worst for secret internal security. Not so far from my job as I'd like."

Back at the camp they found their comrades all healthy and unharmed. Though Daken was liberally sprayed with blood, the white-eye's cheerful expression told them it wasn't his own.

"You took a prisoner?" Mihn asked, as they approached. He glanced back at Daken. "Somehow we managed to forget that bit."

"Bring him in here," Zhia ordered. "I'll find out what he knows."

Vesna gave a cough of shock. "Hey, hold on now—just what are you proposing to do?"

Isak deposited the unconscious soldier on the ground outside Zhia's tent and looked from one to the other as Zhia, peering through the flap, stared Vesna down. The rest of the party took an imperceptible step back, with the exception of Mihn and Doranei. The King's Man stood his ground, but Isak saw dismay on Doranei's face rather than anything antagonistic. He guessed this was an uncomfortable discussion the lovers had already had.

"You disapprove?" Zhia murmured.

"I'm asking what you're planning on doing."

In the shadows of the thick shawl that shaded her face, Zhia raised an eyebrow. "And yet in a way that makes me think you don't really want an answer. How about this: nothing worse than the murder you've already done and the torture you were likely planning for the boy."

"You'll feed on him?" Vesna persisted. "Turn him with your curse? Gift this place with one more of your kind—most become blood-hungry monsters when they're turned, no?"

She glanced at Legana. "My dear, what lurid stories have you told them about our exploits in Scree?" There was a playful edge to Zhia's voice, but in a way that reminded Isak what parts of a sword were dangerous. "How I live isn't your concern, *Iron General*—be glad I have joined your cause when *your* lord was one of those to flay my soul with this curse!"

"Oh, I've not forgotten you're an enemy of the Gods, be assured of that."

Isak stepped between the pair. "Peace, my friend," he said, putting a hand on Vesna's shoulder.

The Mortal-Aspect tensed and Isak could see him physically resisting the urge to shake it off him and draw his sword again. After a moment the man inside won through and he met Isak's eyes. He gave Isak a slight nod: *I'm fine.*

He turned to Zhia. "My apologies."

Zhia dismissed it with a wave. "There is a God inside you, one that is born to fight. To deny it will take more effort than you could have imagined. I am just glad it is a man of such discipline holding Karkarn back; the War God was ever in need of a controlling hand." She forced a smile. "We are such opposites that I'm sure there will be tawdry romances invented about us, but in the meantime there are things we must know about our enemy. This man will die—I cannot leave him alive to inform on us—but nor do I make others suffer needlessly."

With that, she covered her head again, walked forward and grabbed the soldier under his remaining arm. The petite vampire carried him back to her tent and tossed him effortlessly inside. Looking like a spider with its prey, she ducked in after him, but not so quickly that Isak didn't catch a glimpse of shame on Zhia's shadowed face.

Cursed to be a monster, he recalled, *cursed to always know what a monster she is. A lesson more of us could learn.*

CHAPTER 14

AS THE POACHER'S MOON APPEARED over the treetops and cicadas gave way to the dawn chorus, the group reached the first real sign of civilisation in Vanach. They had been travelling for six nights, and the only people they had encountered were Carastar mercenaries and companies of Black Swords from Ghale Outpost, to which Commissar Yokar had sent word of their arrival.

The outpost itself was little more than a hastily built army camp, protected by four wooden towers that looked down over a defensive wall and ditch. The outpost housed a good thousand troops, Vesna had estimated; it was the base for all the patrols in the region. In the feeble moonlight of the early hours it had looked a dismal place to be stationed, the stink of effluence carrying a long way on the wind.

They had been cordially escorted around the camp by a regiment of Black Swords under the command of two commissars, one of whom, a one-eyed woman with short hair and a white clasp to her scar, didn't bother speaking as her colleague went through the formalities. Their captive had revealed that the white clasp indicated a specialised regiment within the Commissar Brigade. Once a secret within the ranks of the commissars, the Sentinels now wore their authority openly. The normal commissars enforced the law and monitored the Faithful, the common folk of Vanach, while the Sentinels oversaw the Blessed: the priests, commissars and Black Swords; as that gave them significantly more freedom and authority within Vanach's borders, they were used by several councils of high-ranking commissars to enact their commands.

As the one-eyed woman was a Sentinel, it was almost certain she had known of the attack on them; she may even have ordered it herself. Leshi had been able to provide the name of one other faction within the Commissar Brigade; the Star Council was tasked with rooting out spies and revolutionaries. But that was only the largest and best-known of the factions; it was likely some operated as private fiefdoms or cult-aligned armies, and more than one of those would surely see any fulfilment of prophecies as a threat to their position.

Past Ghale Outpost and alone again, the party started to encounter enclosed monasteries and farming communities. Some of the latter looked like traditional villages; others under heavy guard were clearly labour camps. All had graves outside their perimeters, individual ones beyond the villages and pits outside the camps. None of these were hidden from the travellers. Life in Vanach was dangerous and the punishments were harsh, and so entrenched in public consciousness that the commissars and soldiers did not even consider how it might be viewed. Scavengers had dug in many of the pits, dragging out the bones of those deemed unworthy of proper burial; similarly, that didn't appear to warrant action.

The Black Swords patrolling the camps were wary of newcomers and challenged them at every step of the way, but each time a commissar appeared and, with varying degrees of deference, waved them on their way. Taking too much interest in the camps themselves sparked angry shouts and drawn weapons from the guards, but Daken especially was happy to call their bluff and watch the feared soldiers back down at the order of their commanders.

They saw none of the inmates, though they could see easily enough past the corralling fence that surrounded each camp. In each one large, chimneyless buildings were positioned like spokes in a wheel around a mound bearing a square-towered temple, while low guard-towers manned by crossbowmen stood every thirty or forty yards around the fence. The fence itself could be easily scaled or kicked through, but the corpses impaled on high crosses by the gate were still wearing leg-irons that were not removed even after death.

On the sixth night they reached the gates of Toristern Settlement, the hub of all human life for fifty miles in any direction. Isak could see faces in the stone towers that flanked its main gate watching their approach. Compared to the great cities he'd visited, Toristern was an unimpressive, functional place. It was clear ostentation was not for the common man: grandeur in Vanach was reserved for religious structures, even more than in somewhere like Ismess. Anything approaching imposing displays were restricted to the great metal frameworks outside the walls, where several dozen naked or poorly clothed unfortunates slumped in confined cages, while corpses rotted beside them. The well-gnawed bones scattered around the base indicated scavengers were given free reign over the condemned.

The main gate of Toristern opened without any form of challenge; not even the cavalry stationed on the road to the settlement did anything more than watch them pass. Within, however, a reception committee stood to greet them with far greater ceremony than they had met with so far. A full regiment of Black Swords was formed up in the square beyond and ahead of them there were more than a dozen commissars wearing the formal uniforms of their brigade. Squat houses and larger wooden buildings were crammed together on each side of a large avenue; they appeared to have been built according to one template and with little skill.

"Lord Sebe," called the leader of the group, the first portly figure they'd encountered in this starved nation. "You come under the blessing of the great Goddess Alterr and are welcome in our poor settlement."

The commissar had the sloping forehead and wide nose that was so common in Vanach, but he still looked out of place, standing amongst a group of pallid, gaunt religious police. He spoke in the Narkang dialect, and Isak knew it well enough that he didn't need Mihn to translate. He looked around at the small city they'd just ridden into. Unlike Tirah or Narkang, places that had evolved over the years, this had been built to a specific plan. It followed some strict pattern that he guessed would be echoed throughout Vanach.

"I thank you for your welcome," Isak replied at last. Aside from the committee and the guards on the walls there were no signs of life on Toristern's ordered streets, something he found disconcerting. "May I ask your name?"

The man bowed. "I am Commissar Kestis, of the Third Enlightenment. The Prefect of Toristern has instructed me to welcome you and escort your party to your allocated lodgings."

Isak was about to reply when another commissar stepped forward and gestured to the soldiers behind them. "Lord Sebe, Brother-Under-Alterr Kestis—there is first the matter of the Ziggurat Mysteries. You come claiming the sanctuary of Alterr, but that is only the first of the signs that must be revealed."

Isak peered at the man. This one was taller than Kestis, but skinny, and obviously lacking Kestis' good nature. He also had a white band to his scarf, which made Isak's fingers itch for his sword-grip.

Kestis turned in surprise, but checked himself before he said anything to admonish the man. Isak guessed he outranked the Sentinel, but they were challenged only cautiously when they policed their own.

"It is necessary to demonstrate that immediately, Horshen?" Kestis inquired.

"So the Night Council has decreed, Brother-Under-Alterr," Horshen said haughtily. "Before the sanctuary of a settlement is granted the first two signs at least must be revealed."

The soldiers Horshen had gestured to disappeared into a nearby building, fetching out a shackled man. The prisoner was painfully thin and almost naked, with crude tattoos on his hairless chest that were doubtlessly marks of slavery. On his arms and legs Isak could also see long bruises and red welts, the signs of regular, sustained beatings.

"Very well," Kestis muttered. "I had been under the impression the Prefect intended for any such revelations to take place tomorrow, but if the Night Council prefer you to provide a first-hand report . . . The mysteries and signs are their purview." He glanced back at the troops and commissars behind him. "Commissar, dismiss the troops."

The bulk of the Black Swords vanished quickly enough, until only ten remained in position. Three commissars also took their leave. At that distance Isak couldn't see anything to mark them out on their uniforms, but clearly they were of the first rank only, and not privy to the mysteries of the second.

"Horshen? Does the Night Council's decree extend to soldiers witnessing the mysteries?"

The skinny man shot his superior a look of pure venom. "They are servants of the Council, tested by the priests of Karkarn and Alterr and worthy to witness such signs as I deem necessary."

"So you want a demonstration?" Isak said. "Something to report back?"

Horshen looked defiant, but he knew his role enough not to stray beyond the bounds of his orders. "It is the duty of the commissars to question; to test the faithful and ensure they walk with the blessing of the Gods." The commissar turned to his terrified prisoner, standing helpless in the hands of the two soldiers. "The second of the Ziggurat Mysteries speaks of the ability to kill with a single word."

Isak grinned in his unsettling, lopsided way and shrugged.

"Shinir."

The prisoner whimpered and sagged in the restraining grip of his captors, but his captivity had left him so cowed and feeble he did not even try to fight them and the two had no effort in holding him steady. Shinir raised her bow and let fly in one swift movement.

At that distance the arrow tore right into Commissar Horshen's neck, passing a foot out the other side as it threw him to the ground. The man hit the ground, legs kicking in uncontrolled spasms, as the remaining Black Swords immediately drew their weapons.

"Hold!" Kestis croaked at them, visibly shocked at a spray of blood that pattered over his boots. He recoiled a pace even as he spoke, distancing himself from the dead body. "Sheathe your weapons!"

There was a moment of sullen silence before any complied, but even those under the authority of the Night Council were not willing to disobey the direct order of a commissar. Eventually the soldiers stepped back while one of the prisoner's guards inspected Horshen, confirming what they all knew: the commissar was dead. The stand-off lasted only a few moments, then a second Sentinel pushed her way forward through the remaining commissars. Isak felt the hairs on the back of his neck rise. Just from the way she walked he could tell this was not some spiteful, low-ranked fanatic.

Though plain-faced and lacking Zhia's dark presence, the commissar still reminded him of the vampire. This was someone who knew their own power all too well and had no need to adopt the sort of supercilious air Commissar Horshen had.

"Clever," she commented in accented Farlan, which made Isak assume she was from the north, where the two nations met. She sounded disinterested rather than scornful, as though Isak had not yet merited anything further from her. "You kept to the letter of the mystery, at least. But a waste of a loyal servant of the Gods—and for what? A slave?"

She gestured towards the cowering man and one of his guards hauled on his arm to make him stand a little higher. The slave had taken one look at the newcomer and fear took hold of him; urine was trickling pathetically down his bare legs.

"Sister?" Kestis said hesitantly. He too recognised the woman's bearing as that of a superior, but from the way he was peering at her it did not marry with the markings on her scarf band.

"Sister-Sapesien Fesh," she supplied without bothering to look at him. "Secretary to the Night Council and here to observe on their express orders."

Thanks to Zhia's interrogation, they recognised the different ranks of commissar; Kestis was a Tarasien, the third rank. Sapesien was the fourth rank, but few ever got that high. The difference in power was clearly enormous.

Fesh approached the cringing slave and inspected him for a few moments before turning to Isak. "This man is a heretic, condemned to death."

Without any further ceremony she whipped a thin stiletto from her belt and jammed it into the man's belly. He wheezed in shock and clutched feebly at the dagger hilt, a tiny cry of fear escaping his lips.

Fesh swatted the man's hands away from her knife and withdrew it again with deliberate slowness. "Now he will die more slowly."

With a twitch of the fingers she ordered the guards to release the slave and he collapsed to his knees, mewling pathetically. Dark blood trickled out from between his fingers and mingled with the puddle of urine on the ground while his weak cries grew increasingly piteous.

"You want to test my compassion too?" Isak growled, his words thick with restrained anger. The white-eye leaned forward over his horse's head and stared intently at Fesh, while trying not to glance back at Zhia. He could sense a build-up of magic from the vampire; no doubt her Gods-imposed curse was filling her with discomfort at the man's suffering and hunger at the slowly spilling blood.

"I do not test," Fesh declared, meeting his gaze, and apparently completely unafraid, despite the fact Isak was so much larger. "I serve the wishes of the Night Council."

Isak made a dismissive sound and urged his horse towards where Commissar Kestis had earlier gestured they find their lodgings. He caught Zhia's eye as he went and called back over his shoulder, "Goodbye, Commissar."

A muted crack broke the hushed night air as Zhia invisibly hastened the slave's inevitable death, then the rest of the party followed him at a slow pace. Kestis hurried to catch up with his guests and usher them down the wide avenue leading to the heart of the city.

Commissar Fesh did not speak.

They were guided into the centre of Toristern, down a road studded with blockish, functional shrines and onto a tree-lined strip of open ground that formed a ring around a central district. Silver birches had been carefully cultivated to form screens that abruptly hid the slumbering city from view. The ground was covered in some sort of limestone gravel; it was obviously kept scrupulously clear of weeds and it shone in the pre-dawn gloom.

"This ground is restricted to the Blessed," Commissar Kestis announced as he directed the party to walk down the white avenue. "The entire inner circle of Toristern is sacred; you will be the first outsiders to ever view this ziggurat."

"I hadn't realised there was more than one," Isak said.

Kestis inclined his head solemnly, then looked up at the yellowed bulge of

Alterr, high above them. "Every core settlement has a ziggurat now—none as remarkable as the Grand Ziggurat of Vanach Settlement, of course, but fitting places of worship all the same." He turned, his eyes suddenly bright with fervour. "And now you are here, come to fulfil the signs and reveal mysteries beyond those inscribed on the walls of the Grand Ziggurat—perhaps every city in the Land will be blessed with a ziggurat to elevate their worship?"

"Not sure that would be so popular right now," Isak murmured.

"No doubt," Kestis agreed gravely. "The wider Land has been forsaken by the Gods for so many years. We of the Commissar Brigade understand the extent of the task ahead of us; unbelievers will not easily accept the embrace of the Gods again."

"Lucky you've got so many Black Swords, eh?" Isak commented, noticing yet another troop of soldiers watching them silently from under the trees.

"The enemies of the Gods are many and devious," Kestis replied, a sharpness entering his voice. "The faithful must be protected, and more so than ever since the recent rise in daemon attacks."

"Rise?"

Kestis blinked at him. "We have ever been plagued by daemons roaming the wild parts of our nation; it is our lot as most favoured of the Gods. They enter the minds of mages and weak men, sometimes manifesting in their hundreds and slaughtering entire villages." He frowned. "It has always been that way—that is why the Shield Council was forced to redistribute the population and ensure they could be protected as they worked for the glory of the Gods. Surely your own people have the same problems?"

"Oh sure," Isak said quickly, "daemons with the faces of men: always been a problem where I come from. There's one growing with power even now, one that wears the face of a child." His face became suddenly tight. "Don't even ask me what's living in the cottage I used to own."

Kestis went as wide-eyed as a child as Isak confirmed everything he had been told about the Land beyond Vanach's borders. "It is a fight we are ready for, my Lord. The people of Vanach are strong and unflinching; the Commissar Brigade has worked for years to prepare them for what will be required."

Isak said grimly, "It may be you'll find that fight soon." He spoke in Farlan.

"I'm sorry, Lord—I did not understand you. That was Farlan you spoke? Only very few here know that language, I'm afraid. Could you please repeat it?"

Isak waved it away as unimportant and turned to give Zhia a look instead. "Villages 'disappearing' because of daemons? The entire population being 'readied for war'? Remind me to kill your brother if I see him."

The vampire indicated the soldiers they had just passed. "Have a care, my Lord—Commissar Fesh may have colleagues who speak Farlan."

"Oh, right, we wouldn't want anyone to become suspicious of us," Isak snapped. "They might try to kill us if that happened."

"It was a limited effort," Zhia countered, "enough to test whether or not we were just some fools who'd chanced upon a way to travel unmolested in Vanach. I don't doubt we're in danger from this Night Council, but it doesn't look like they are the dominant force in Vanach, so they will be cautious about acting publicly."

Isak scowled and didn't press the matter. He let Commissar Kestis guide them in silence around the outer ring to a second avenue leading into the heart of the city. As they turned onto it they were immediately confronted by a ceremonial procession of priests, looming like phantoms out of the darkness.

Dressed in white habits and shuffling along behind a circular silver standard, it was clear they were from the Cult of Alterr. Mindful of the position priests occupied in Vanach, Isak nudged his horse to one side and slipped respectfully from the saddle until they had passed.

Strangely, the priests paid him no attention at all. The hoods of their habits hung low over their face, but he knew the effect he had on passers-by, so it came as a surprise when there was no apparent reaction at all.

Maybe the mysteries aren't for the cults to know about, he mused. *These commissars do seem to like keeping their power close.*

He watched the procession as it shuffled away along the tree-line avenue, a hushed drone of prayer on the wind. The man at the rear swung a thurible on a long chain, but no smoke was emitted; there was only a deep *thrum* as air passed through its cut sides, a strange and haunting sound that lingered on the night air even as the priests moved away.

"No incense?"

"The Shrine Council removed incense from the list of accepted religious tools," Kestis said, careful not to indicate he had any opinion on the subject himself. "It was deemed a distraction from the majesty of the Gods and a lure for daemons."

"Ah, all that smoke and stink," Isak said. *Thought it reminded me of something.*

"Yes, Lord," Kestis said, in all seriousness, "to echo their home realm is to encourage them into the hearts of men. To cause the faithful to breath smoke is to lower them to the level of a heretic. It is well documented that heretics commonly have disorders of the throat and speech, choking on the evil they spread as it draws the smoke of the Dark Place into their lungs."

"This has been documented by the same folk who report daemons causing whole villages to disappear?" Isak said before he could stop himself.

"Indeed, Lord."

"Oh. And who would that be, then?"

Kestis faltered a little, giving a nervous glance around before he replied, "I— My knowledge of the councils is limited, my Lord. I know little even of the one I serve. It is heresy to question those who preserve the majesty of the Gods."

"Guess," Isak commanded unsympathetically. He took a step towards the commissar and stood a little straighter. "I'm not asking you to reveal state secrets, just the name of whichever council issued those reports."

Kestis stared miserably at Isak's feet for a few heartbeats, then his resolve broke. "It was most likely the Dusk Council—the works of daemons is their purview."

"Friendly lot, are they?"

"I know nothing of them, but they go with the blessing of the Gods," Kestis replied, falling back on doctrine in his anxiety. "Please, I can tell you nothing more."

Isak stared at the quivering man a while longer, then let him off. "Of course. Please, lead on."

Kestis scampered ahead while Isak's party remounted and started down the street. The buildings within the sacred district started out looking as boringly functional as those outside, although more frequently stone-built, but as they penetrated further into the district, Isak saw temples and the ziggurat rising above the rest. Each temple was set in a compound of its own, with an attending network of buildings half the height or less of their corresponding temple.

In the centre was the unmistakable bulk of the ziggurat: four square levels of pale stone topped with a half-dome structure that Isak assumed was the Temple of Alterr. To his surprise the sides of each level bore images, both carved and painted, and ornate statuary stood along the stark edges. The temples too were remarkably grand compared to the rest of the city. High spires and obelisks dominated the view, and the great variety of ornaments and embellishments was in stark contrast to the rest of the settlement's architecture.

They approached the ziggurat under the watchful gaze of yet more Black Swords. It seemed strange to Isak that their escort consisted of only one man, even though it was likely they were never out of sight of at least one unit of soldiers. He hoped it meant they were trying to keep his arrival quiet until the ruling councils decided how to react, but as Kestis had ably demonstrated, nothing in Vanach could ever be assumed to be predictable.

"My Lord Sebe," Kestis declared, his spirit partially returned, "lodgings at the Commissariat await you."

Their path to the ziggurat was blocked by a large fort-like compound, entirely enclosed by a stone wall and overlooked by low guard-towers. They passed through the gate and found themselves in a large courtyard that had been divided into two. The larger part was behind an iron gate, through which Isak could see a gibbet and narrow, barred windows.

"A fucking prison?" he demanded, pointing up at the armed guards peering down at them.

Kestis flapped madly in his haste to correct Isak. "A secure station," he gabbled, pointing to the right, where the buildings were somewhat less brutal in aspect. "Yes, it is next to a prison, but as a result this is our most protected place. The Prefect has decided it best to spare you the curious eyes of the Faithful and Blessed alike; here you may have both privacy and security."

"Security from whom? The Dusk Council? The Night Council?"

Kestis couldn't have shaken his head harder. "Insurrectionists, daemon-worshippers—the Faithful are ever under threat of those who have turned from the Gods."

Isak looked around at his companions. None of them made any comment, but Vesna tapped his wrapped Crystal Skull and urged his horse onwards. The gesture was obvious, and Isak nodded his agreement: *Any trouble and we can carve a path through it.*

"Then it will serve, I suppose." Isak followed Vesna inside. "Tell your Prefect we await his pleasure."

The Prefect's invitation arrived late in the afternoon. Much to the discomfort of their guards, Isak had gone up one of the guard-towers to look out over Toristern Settlement; he saw the messenger approaching with his escort. The guards, unable to speak the same language, had tried making threatening gestures to get him back into the secure quarters, but a determined white-eye was not easily stopped, and Isak was willing to take a chance that their orders didn't include violence—at least not at this stage.

In the light of day Toristern remained unimpressive. The screen of silver birch limited his view of the city beyond, but what he could see was a uniform view of basic, single-storey buildings punctuated with the occasional warehouse. Only the restricted district bore any resemblance to the ancient grandeur of Tirah or even Scree's modest prosperity.

Buildings of any significance or permanence appeared to be strictly limited to the cults and ruling councils. The massive ziggurat was not the only example of skill and endeavour, but even compared to Scree, before the firestorm had destroyed it, Toristern was little more than an overgrown town.

The messenger was another commissar; a man not much older than Isak with short hair and a neat beard. He came on foot with a squad of Black Swords trailing behind, the commissars' feared enforcers echoing Isak's opinion of their city: young and insubstantial when seen in the light of day.

"My Lord Sebe, I bring the greetings of Prefect Darass, overseer of Toristern Settlement and Priesan of the Commissar Brigade."

"Priesan? That's the highest rank, right? You have to walk the labyrinth to be raised to that?"

The man bowed. "That is correct, my Lord. He invites you and your companions to be his guests at the Dusk Ceremony this evening." Despite his youth the commissar was as blank-faced as the most experienced politician. Kestis had come across a devout believer, but this one was either a zealot of the worst order or a willing participant in his state's cruel excesses.

"Away from prying eyes, then," Isak remarked dryly. "You commissars don't trust each other much, do you?"

The young man bowed. "It is the duty of a commissar to question. Those of true faith can endure any test."

Isak grinned nastily, drawing the scars on his face tight as he revealed the missing teeth in his mouth. "You reckon? Give me some pliers and a hot fire and I'm willing to bet otherwise."

"There is no force greater than faith in the Gods," the commissar countered smoothly, "but such a debate might best be continued with Prefect Darass rather than a man of my modest rank."

Isak inclined his head to agree. "I'll go and get ready."

"The Prefect anticipated you might wish to leave some of your companions behind, given that the shrine atop the ziggurat is of modest size."

Isak hesitated. What exactly the Priesan rank would know of Vanach's founding remained unclear, but they would be aware of *some* of the truth in Vorizh Vukotic's schemes.

Is this a ruse to split us up, or a sign that he's aware we might have Zhia or Koezh among us?

"I'll do so then. Three of us will suffice."

Isak returned to their quarters, pausing at the door where Doranei and Daken were standing guard. Though mismatched in size, dress and weapons, the strange pair were united in their hostility as they stared at the newcomers.

"Could you look less like you want to pick a fight?" Isak muttered to them.

"Only face I got," Daken replied softly.

"I'll alter it if I get back and find out you've started something."

Before Daken could utter any reply, Doranei gave him a warning look and the Mad Axe pursed his lips, fighting his natural instincts, and nodded stiffly. He was part of the Brotherhood now, and King Emin had made it clear he needed to follow their rules: the mission was everything, you never let any personal bullshit get in the way.

Inside, Isak dug out a long midnight-blue robe from his pack, similar to the formal ones he'd worn as a lord in Tirah. It looked a little austere compared to the noble silks and lion-embossed cuirass Vesna had, especially when he kept the hood up, but with a white leather belt and stylised golden bee pendant—Death's own symbol—he managed the noble ascetic image he was aiming for. Naturally Mihn wore no finery. He needed only to set aside his staff before setting off with Isak and Vesna, adopting his usual persona of humble manservant.

The walk to the ziggurat was quick and uneventful; Black Swords at every corner ensured even the Blessed of Toristern steered well clear. Once at the heart of the core settlement Isak stopped and took a few moments to appreciate its size, aware he had a while until dusk fell.

Under the commissar's urging, Isak eventually started the long climb up the massive staggered ramp that ran up one side of the ziggurat, pausing at each level to survey the settlement as it was incrementally unveiled. The priests standing on each of the levels kept their distance, withdrawing before he came into view so there was no way Isak could interact with any of them.

Before they reached the upper level, he rounded on the man escorting them. "Commissar, tell me, why is it in a nation of the faithful, your priests keep their distance?"

The commissar blinked in surprise, but it only lasted a moment before the young man recovered himself. "My Lord, as yet your status is uncertain and the purity of our priests is our greatest defence against evil. The priests of these temples live cloistered lives, the better to contemplate the will of our Gods and commune with their servant Aspects. It is the obligation of the Commissar Brigade to conduct all interaction with outside elements and endure the disruption of order this may lead to."

Isak gave Vesna a look, but the veteran soldier was careful not to comment. He could see Vesna's amazement, though: this nation's fanaticism had tied even its own priesthood in knots, making it a prisoner of a political wing gone mad. Every other class in Vanach had been reduced to an irrelevance; even the heads of each cult were probably subordinate to the Commissar Brigade, answering only to some faceless council.

"'There can be no greater tyranny than good intentions left unchecked,'" Mihn said in Farlan. He earned a quizzical look from the commissar, but stared blankly at the man until he gave up and looked away.

"So until all the signs are revealed," Isak concluded, "my existence goes unreported and unexplained to the people?"

"Vigilance is our watchword," the commissar replied firmly.

"We are guardians of the people and entrusted by the Gods to see them safely to the coming Age—even unto keeping them safe from themselves and their own failings."

"Naturally." Isak sighed and trudged on, suddenly keen to be away from the conversation.

As he reached the top of the ziggurat Isak discovered the commissar had discreetly stayed behind where they'd spoken, leaving the three of them to ascend the final stair alone. The shrine of Alterr stood in the very heart of the upper tier; a circular groove was cut into the smooth stone underfoot, marking the sanctified ground. At its centre was a simple round altar covered in a white cloth. The breeze was brisk that high off the ground, and the cloth's edges fluttered madly, but it was held in place by five beautiful silver chalices.

Around the altar were three people, two men and a woman, with a fourth standing back in the recess of the half-dome shrine. He was dressed as an officer of the Black Swords, and was of no importance to proceedings here, even though he'd been summoned to a meeting where ranked commissars had not.

Of the other three, one, truly ancient, was a High Priest of Alterr. The white-haired, white-robed relic stood with his hands clasped and eyes downcast. He had perhaps been instructed to avert his gaze even as he bowed with the other two.

"My Lord, you honour us with your presence," declared the elder of the remaining two, a man past his prime but still strong and fit-looking. "I am Prefect Darass, Overseer of Toristern Settlement, and this is my deputy, Counsel Aels." He indicated the handsome woman of perhaps fifty summers beside him who bowed a second time. Both wore plain brown clothes of good cloth, the yellow scarves of the Commissar Brigade, and identical black coats that hung like academic robes—but there was one crucial difference between them. The deputy, Aels, wore the white clasp of the Sentinels on her scarf, while Darass had a black one.

So Aels, Isak guessed, *must be the Night Council's local commander.* He stopped himself right there, telling himself, *don't be stupid now; it doesn't mean they're the* only *danger, just the most obvious one.*

Isak introduced himself and Vesna briefly before the Prefect turned to face the sinking sun and declared it was time for the dusk rituals. As though restored to life, the high priest jerked into action and began to drone a long, monotone prayer to Alterr. Isak kept silent, though he could hear Vesna reciting the Farlan equivalent under his breath. After five interminable minutes he was bored and restless, but at last the priest took one of the chalices and lifted it to his lips.

The brim was reverentially wiped with a cloth and both chalice and cloth were passed to Darass, who did the same before giving it to Isak. Rather startled, Isak swallowed some of the water it contained, then Vesna reached out to accept it from him, knowing he'd rarely been to temple and barely knew the rituals of Nartis, let alone any other.

When the chalice made its way back round to the High Priest and a second round of incomprehensible droning started up, Isak felt his heart sink. He belatedly realised each chalice must contain a different liquid, no doubt to be sipped in turn, and he gave Mihn a look—but the failed Harlequin had anticipated him. His hands clasped across his stomach, he was already staring fixedly at Isak. The white-eye got the message and returned to his former stance, closing his eyes to let the words slip gently over him with the evening breeze.

After four more rounds the ceremony was over, and after a nod from Prefect Darass, the High Priest bowed to those present before leaving. He didn't make eye-contact with Isak at any point, apparently afraid, even in these circumstances, to risk what a commissar might view as contamination.

"And now, my Lord Sebe," Prefect Dasass announced, advancing with a studied smile of welcome, "may I offer you refreshment?"

The soldier standing in the wings was already moving as the Prefect spoke, heading around behind the half-dome and returning with glasses and a swan-necked glass jug that Isak could see was filled with pale red wine. With each of his guests served, Prefect Darass spoke several toasts—to the moon, the Upper Circle and his guest. Each was recited as if by by rote, the words no doubt set in stone.

"You bring us exciting times, my Lord," Darass said next, the formalities finally completed. "The future of Vanach and all servants of the Gods may now follow your guidance, but I find my thoughts lingering on the past still. Your name is not known to me; might I enquire a little of your background?"

Isak forced himself to keep eye-contact. "There's little to tell. My parents were Farlan. I became a soldier like most white-eyes, then I found a different path."

"Quite a path, my Lord," Aels interjected. She indicated the Roaring Lion emblem on Vesna's cuirass. "Whilst we might be isolated, we do hear a little of the Land beyond our borders. Another white-eye had the renowned Count Vesna as his vassal—"

"Who then died, as I'm sure you also heard," Vesna said, the menace in his voice unmistakeable. "Nor am I a nobleman of the Farlan any longer, the Gods have set a different path before me. The tribe of my birth lies behind me."

Aels inclined her head. "I am reminded of a saying by one of Vanach's founding Priesans: 'Mindful of our past, we walk to the embrace of the Gods with ties of family and honour falling in our wake.' Our future does not lie with the Tribes of Man, nor with the tyranny of kings: so it is written in the Ziggurat Mysteries the messenger of the Gods granted us."

"Everything will change," Isak agreed. "For good or for worse, change has come."

"Surely you do not doubt the power of the Gods?" Aels asked in studied surprise. "No force could overcome their majesty, not even the Great Heretic when he is reborn and summons his daemon army."

Isak blinked. He couldn't see Mihn's face, so he didn't know what dogma or prophecy this daemon army might refer to, but he was not surprised the last King of the Elves, the great heretic Aryn Bwr, was part of these zealots' ultimate calling.

Let's just hope they don't find out in whose body Aryn Bwr tried to be reborn.

"The enemy of the Gods is born," he said carefully, "and my fear is that the power of the Gods has been turned against them. Your priests must have informed you that the Gods are weakened, drained by the effort of striking a faithless servant's name from history. The enemy will act soon, and the faithful must be ready for him."

"The enemy has a name?" Darass demanded before Aels could speak again.

Isak inclined his head. *It seems lies come more easily now I'm not a politician or nobleman.* "It masquerades as a child, a ward of Byora named Ruhen. Under its influence the duchess has already banned the cults there, and its disciples now carry its heresy throughout the Land."

"Troubling news," Aels said with less emotion than Isak would have expected, "but the faithful of Vanach are ready. We walk with the Gods. I pray you share our resolve for the third of the signs requires that be demonstrated unflinchingly."

"You think I lack resolve?"

Aels shook her head. "No, Lord, but I fear you must lose a powerful ally to fulfil the sign. The loss of a servant means little in the eyes of the Gods."

"Loss? I've no intention of losing anyone," Isak said. His fingers itched for the grip of Eolis, currently wrapped in cloth on his hip to avoid it being recognised as the weapon of the great heretic.

The woman looked genuinely apologetic, but there was no such emotion in her voice when she explained, "Lord Sebe, the third of the signs, as described in the Ziggurat Mysteries, is that the one sent by the Gods shall know the true meaning of sacrifice. This has been debated at length by the Councils of the Commissar Brigade, who believe it calls for the sacrifice of one of the twelve. I am here as a member of the Night Council to attest to your constancy.

"The death of a servant cannot be of any true loss to one who will lead the faithful in battle, however, and now the sign is invoked it must be fulfilled properly and under Alterr's watch this night."

Isak nodded towards the Black Swords officer. "That why he's here? To take the place of the one I kill?"

"Your companions must number twelve still, so the mysteries say."

He looked at Vesna and shrugged. The Mortal-Aspect said nothing.

Aels saw the spark in Isak's eyes and drew back a touch as Isak growled, "And who are you, to make such demands of me?" Anger smouldered in his belly. "You demand a sacrifice from me? You demand to see what I have lost—what I'm willing to lose in this war?" He could feel his hand shaking; the weight on his shoulders building. On the distant breeze he could hear the groan and rumble of the Dark Place, voices raised in unholy cries. His nostrils filled with the sulphurous stink of Ghenna's tunnels and something deep inside him began to scream for what he had lost, for the pain he remembered in his bones.

An image of Tila's face flashed before his eyes, her elegant features contorted in death, and looming behind her was the dark shadow of a man whose face he could no longer see. *Carel.*

The word meant little to him, but it sparked a pain like no other and the loss tore through his gut: the nameless, unspeakable pain of a part of him that was gone for ever: his childhood, the foundations of his life, vanished into a murky void. With it mingled the death-scream of Xeliath, and the feel of huge claws tearing through the rune burned onto Isak's chest.

"Pray," Isak ordered, voice tight and rasping with rage, "pray you *never* understand what I have sacrificed."

He took a step towards her without even realising and found himself looming over the woman, his hands clawed and apparently ready to grab her by the throat. Aels was plainly terrified, and frozen to the spot, staring up at the tortured vision now standing before her.

Slowly, with great difficulty, he withdrew his hands, gasping for breath as he realised how close he had come to tearing out her throat with his twisted fingernails. His hands went to his head and he pushed the hood back off his battered scalp.

Mihn had cropped his hair close to the skin to highlight the indentations and claw-marks that defined his head. A lopsided widow's peak indicated where part of his scalp had been torn away; a furrow ran from his ragged ear down to his throat, and it was there Aels' eyes lingered: on the deep, dark regular curves of scarring from the chains that had bound him in Ghenna.

Isak opened his robe to reveal his bare torso. The patterns of scarring continued there, covering so much of his chest and arms that Aels gasped aloud in horror. Chain-marks looped over his shoulders and across his belly. The indentation where the Menin lord had opened his guts was only the largest of the injuries visited upon his body. Runes and daemon-script were carved into his skin: rough, uneven symbols inscribed with savagery, torture beyond anything that could have been inflicted on the living.

His left arm had been burned white by the touch of Nartis in Narkang, and in the fading light of dusk his skin now shone with terrible intensity. Haphazard loops and slashes of shadowy scarring seemed to rise and swarm like traces of dark magic before Aels' eyes.

Eventually she turned away, unable to bear the look on his face as the memories of those injuries returned afresh in his mind. From across the city came the haunting sound of daemon-song, a terrible jubilation ringing across a land of weakened Gods, running its cold claws down the spine of all who heard it.

"I know sacrifice only too well," Isak breathed, "for I am its favourite plaything."

"It was a mistake to try and kill them," said a figure in black, one slim shoulder visible against the open window behind.

Counsel Aels froze, halfway inside the door to her private office. Her hand went to her belt, but the knife wasn't there now. She'd left it behind on her desk; there it was, just visible in the twilight of the darkened room.

"You?" she exclaimed, "how did you get in here?"

The man inclined his head to the open window by way of explanation.

Aels frowned as she pictured the wall outside: twenty feet at least of sheer stone, all while regular patrols walked the path underneath. Only an acrobat could climb that, or a Harlequin. "You take a great risk, invading the office of a member of the Night Council," she muttered as she shut the door behind her.

She jumped as she saw another figure shift slightly in the dark, this one wearing the familiar diamond-pattern clothes and white mask. "Still more so by dictating to us how we should respond to threats to the state."

"You showed him your hand by sending troops to kill him."

She dismissed the comment with a wave of the hand. "An underling overreacted; the council did not sanction the action."

"That is no longer relevant," said the one who'd named himself Venn on his previous visit. He stood perfectly, unnaturally still as he watched her, unnerving her and making her wonder about this new ally of the Night Council, but she suppressed the question. This one claimed to be the enemy of their so-called saviour, the man who would tear down everything they had built here in Vanach. The Night Council's decision was correct, and the price of Venn's information modest.

"There will be no further efforts."

"Good. Have you decided how you will proceed?"

Anger welled inside her. "Who are you to demand answers from me?"

Aels snapped. "I am a Sapesian of the Commissar Brigade and Second of Toristern Settlement, sitting member of the Night Council. Adopt a more respectful manner or my inquisitors will ensure you can never climb again."

If there was any change in Venn's expression it was too minute for Aels to discern. "My apologies, Sapesian Aels."

Again, the man's manner made her hesitate. His words sounded entirely sincere and cowed, but his poise indicated no such correction.

"We will proceed as we see fit," she said at last. "The Night Council does not rule the Sanctum; other ranking councils must have a reason to follow our lead."

"Confirmation of your concerns?"

She narrowed her eyes. "Exactly. Why? Can you arrange this?"

Venn bowed and slipped out of the window. His mocking reply drifted through the night air. "All things are possible for those of faith."

Chapter 15

Major Amber looked down the main street of Kamfer's Ford in a daze, unable to quite believe this wasn't a dream. From some of those passing, civilians and soldiers alike, came a few askance glances, but bizarrely, that was all: no shouts or curses, no drawn weapons . . . Were these people used to such strange sights that an armed enemy in their midst was barely noteworthy? In a Menin camp, a Narkang soldier would have been beaten into the ground or run through, not ignored.

The most suspicious looks came from the groups of women prowling the town—priestesses, he guessed, escorted by armed, scowling women who looked like they had once been Hands of Fate, devotees of the Lady trained as killers. Most were wearing pendants of emerald or green glass, some new symbol of allegiance, most likely.

The early autumn sun casting a low yellow haze over the cloudless sky somehow added to Amber's disjointed sense of bewilderment. The streets of this bustling town were similarly tinted, and even the gloomy mien of Camatayl Castle on the hill was diminished. A squad of troops in Kingsguard uniforms tramped past and Amber turned to watch them go, wondering why his hand was not automatically reaching for a scimitar.

The town was in a sorry state, he realised. The Menin Army had passed near here, destroying much of what was in its path. According to Nai, this town had been the heart of military operations in Narkang, and the people had fled before the Menin arrived.

"They got off lightly," he said, frowning at his own lightheadedness. "I thought most towns were destroyed."

"Most were," the soldier behind him replied, his hand returning to his sword. He couldn't have been more than a year or two in the army; he was too young to hide his fear of the big Menin officer he'd been assigned to guard. "The locals left enough supplies behind that your scouts were more interested in scavenging than burning. Bastards still managed to wreck it, though."

Amber nodded distantly. He had nothing to add to that, and no reaction at all to the soldier's belligerence.

In every direction he looked there were repairs taking place, and new construction too. Two large fields of tents flanked the town, and it looked as though they were planning on wintering here. The major looked back to the castle. His companions had gone there, Nai and Ardela both demanding to see King Emin as soon as they arrived here. He'd felt a jolt in his stomach at the prospect of meeting the man responsible for all that had befallen the Menin, only to be left empty when informed that the king was away.

A cool gust of wind, unexpectedly chilly in the bright sun, woke him from his reverie. Amber sighed and turned to the door nearby. There didn't appear to be much else to do since the king wasn't here, so he went in. Eyes watched warily as he stepped through the door and blinked at the dim interior. There was a fire ahead of him, dividing the room in two, and a bar extended the length of the wall on the right. Amber ignored the looks and not-so-subtle loosening of weapons and headed to the bar.

"Beer," he said to the plump man behind it, a greasy, nervous specimen with a short, scraggly beard, but once Amber spoke, hatred won over fear on the barkeep's face.

"Not for you," the man said with a shake of the head. "Get out."

"Make me," Amber growled.

Aside from the handful of locals there were four soldiers in the tavern. He could feel their eyes on his back, Nai had insisted Amber be allowed to keep his scimitars for some reason, and he was big, even for a Menin. If they wanted him out they'd need to do more than throw punches. After what their king had done Amber didn't have any fear left; pain was an old friend of his and there was nothing more they could take.

"I don't serve Menin here."

"I'll fucking serve myself then."

"Not while I breathe." The barkeep pulled a shortsword from behind the bar, no doubt plundered from some battlefield. He didn't look like he knew how to use it, but he pointed it defiantly enough at Amber. The Menin officer let his baldric slip off his shoulder and the grip of one scimitar fell into his hand. He didn't yet draw it, but turned side-on so the soldiers behind him were in view.

"Doesn't strike me as a problem," Amber said as his left hand moved slowly to the hilt of his other sword.

"Major!" the young soldier called as he moved between the Menin and his comrades, his hand still on his sword. "You are paroled under honour—stow your weapons."

"The only word you've had," Amber said slowly, "is that of some fucking necromancer. I got no honour left."

His escort hesitated; he hadn't been part of the discussion Nai had had with his captain.

Amber began to slip one scimitar from its scabbard, planning his first strike and parry in his mind, when one of the locals at the bar spoke up.

"Give him a damn beer." The speaker was a good decade or two older than Amber, and not from these parts, by his accent. The whole room stared at him in surprise until he lifted his head and looked back at them. Amber saw a weathered face and a white collar to his tunic; there was no fear in the man's eyes, just irritation and weariness. He had his jacket draped over his shoulders and when he shifted round Amber saw the left sleeve of his tunic hung empty.

"You hear me? Put your bloody swords away and give the man a drink. I'll even pay if you children start playin' nice."

Amber glanced at the barkeep and saw him deflate. He lowered his sword and grabbed a mug instead. The Menin nodded and relaxed his own grip, slung the baldric back up on his shoulder and took the nearest stool. He grunted as a mug of beer was dumped in front of him and reached into his jacket, but the older man had already tossed a coin onto the bar.

"I can pay."

"Said I was payin', friend."

Amber took a long drink and turned his head. "I ain't your friend."

The old man snorted. "Reckon I'm the best you got right now. Unless some necromancer counts."

Amber tried to think of a real friend who might still be alive and felt a fresh ache blossom behind his eyes. He put his elbows on the bar and hunched over his beer, running a hand over his tangled hair to cover the pain on his face.

"Aye, as I thought." The old man pulled out a tobacco pouch and set it on the bar, removed a battered wooden pipe from it and tried to fill it one-handed. The pipe slipped from under his hand and scattered shreds of tobacco over the sticky bar top.

"Mind helping an old veteran?" he said, waving the pipe at Amber, who scowled, but took it and quickly filled it. "Thanks, friend." The old man jammed it in the corner of his mouth and lit it with a taper.

"I ain't your friend." Amber finished the beer and gestured for another one. When the barkeep took the mug off him he glanced at his companion's. It was nearly empty, so he pointed to that too.

"I know you're not," the old man said quietly. Amber felt a familiar flicker in his gut, but the old man did nothing more than take a swig of beer before continuing, "Truth be told, I hate you fucking Menin, and if I find my way t'Moorview I'll piss on your lord's grave there."

Amber's hand clenched. "One word more and you'll never make the journey." There was murder in his voice.

The old man recognised it sure enough. He went still, but his demeanor was not that of a frightened man; Amber recognised it only too well: this was a man with nothing more to lose.

"Reckon you're right there," the old man said carefully. "Don't expect me t'sing his praises, though. Man took my boy from me, sent him straight t'the Dark Place."

There was something in the way he said it that made Amber hesitate. Veterans weren't prone to theatricality, but it was a strange expression to use idly.

"Your boy?"

"Aye." The old man's hand shook a little as he drew hard on his pipe, but the smoke seemed to help him recover. "Not by blood, but I raised him."

"White-eye?"

The old man nodded.

Amber shook his head in disbelief. "I heard about that—didn't see it myself; I'd been knocked out by then. Way I heard it, he went defiant to the last, goaded my lord even when he was beaten."

The old man smiled sadly. "Aye, that'd be just like the little bastard. As wilful as the storm he was sometimes, as great as any God at others."

Amber was silent for a while, unable to think of what to say to the man who'd loved Isak Stormcaller as a son. He finished his drink and bought another round, feeling the tension in his head slowly start to ease as alcohol softened the jangle of his thoughts.

"What brings you this way then?" he asked eventually. "I didn't see a Farlan army out here and you're no nobleman. Why'd you travel all the way out here?"

The old man gave a bitter laugh. "There's nothing for me back home. My closest friends are out this way; joined up with King Emin, or dead. Those back home are only interested in keepin' out of any war. I've seen too much to hold my tongue around cowards like that."

"So you've got nothing left," Amber said with empathy.

The old man snorted and raised his mug in mock salute. "Here's to the broken, you and me both. Ain't nothing can help us now, 'cept drinking our way to an early grave, mebbe."

"Aye. Strange that."

"Eh? What's strange?

Amber rubbed a hand over his face, stubble rasping against his palm. "Me, all broken. There's a man back home, got wounded in the head years back. Man was frightened o' his own shadow before that day, but when he came round he was changed. Forgot who he was—" He shuddered, and screwed his eyes up tight shut. It took a while to pass, but the old man waited it out patiently, and when Amber at last blinked away the stars he saw understanding in his eyes.

"He forgot where he'd come from," Amber recommenced hoarsely, "forgot everything about his life 'cos of that injury, and he forgot how to be afraid too. He got called Frost after that—his hair had turned as white as snow. Every time he went to sleep he forgot everything that'd happened to him the previous day—he could remember places and things, but not who he'd met, where he'd been or what he'd done his whole life. He needed a protector, so he got assigned a veteran who'd seen one too many fights.

"Turned out they helped each other, so when the veteran recovered, Frost got another broken protector assigned, and he helped him too. The man's got a quiet way about him, they say. He's almost a myth back home these days. Supposedly you can't lie to Frost; he's so innocent he walks with the blessing o' the Gods."

Amber sighed and shook his head, exhaustion suddenly catching up with him. "Somehow my lord knew I'd end up this way. He trusted me with some o' his most dangerous missions—he thought me strong enough for that—but something told him I'd end up broken, so he said there'd always be a place for me with Frost. If I ever get home, I'll go and find him, maybe. Make sure my lord's promise to him is kept."

The old man stared away into nothing.

Amber concentrated on his beer, but he could see the glowing embers of the veteran's pipe wavering uncertainly in his peripheral vision. Another round was bought, but the old man just stared at his drink, not touching it as Amber raised his in silent toast.

At last the old man turned in his seat and offered his hand. "Name's Carel. Marshal Betyn Carelfolden of Etinn, properly, but that's all just so much piss, between you an' me."

Amber nodded and took the man's arm. "Amber," he said. "Just Amber now."

To Lord Fernal it looked like the stone-walled town had been breeding in the night. A pair of staggered defensive earthworks now stood on either side of Borderkeep, the southernmost of Helrect's major towns, and a small fort at the western end of the town commanded an uninterrupted view of the vast grassy plains to the south and, more importantly, the roads that cut through them. Behind each set of earthworks was a village of tents for the soldiers stationed there, brightly coloured banners marking the territory of each suzerain and count in attendance.

Since the collapse of the White Circle, Helrect had suffered a chaotic struggle for power among the noble families. With many of the most powerful tainted by White Circle associations or weakened by the fall of Scree, those unable to defend their positions had been murdered or cowed into submission and their lands stolen.

While the state hadn't ceased to exist so completely as Scree had, the common folk of Helrect were almost as pleased as their neighbours to hear the Farlan's declaration of annexation. The remaining nobles and their warbands hadn't been so pleased, but there had been little they could do other than submit. Other than a few mass executions of marauding soldiers, the Farlan had effectively conquered two city-states in the name of peace.

"My Lord!" called an approaching nobleman through the clusters of hurscals. He ended up barging soldiers out of the way as he approached, almost knocking one proud young knight to the ground as he went. "There is a delegation to meet you," he announced as he reached Fernal at last. He sank to one knee, unclipped his sword from his belt and offered it to the massive Demi-God.

He was from one of the oldest families in Lomin, Fernal had been told, in a way that made it clear this was important; the count was an experienced soldier and commanded the scouts sweeping the fringes of Helrect territory.

"Rise, Count Mekir," Fernal said, gesturing with one huge taloned hand. "What sort of delegation?"

"Knights of the Temples, my Lord, and a group of preachers wearing white." Mekir stood and pointed back the way he had come. "They follow a mile or so behind me, escorted by some of my men."

Fernal scowled as he followed the man's pointing arm, looking over the heads of his guards. In the distance he could see a large group of riders approaching, still too far for him to make out any banners or formation.

Clearly my instructions were not simple enough.

"Duke Lomin," Fernal said as he turned to the recently raised nobleman, one of those attending their lord, "what instructions did you give your men regarding parties from the south?"

Belir Lomin's face tightened as the eyes of all the men present turned to him. He was barely secure in his position and still learning how to act in the company of his new peers, and he knew they'd take any opportunity for scorn or condescension.

"I relayed your orders exactly, my Lord," he said carefully, taking note of who might be enjoying the implied rebuke. He outranked all of the five suzerains and scions present, but he was equally sure they all considered themselves above him, even if Suzerain Lehm was the only one who showed it.

"My Lord," Count Mekir interjected hesitantly, "they came in greater numbers than my men, and they refused to turn back. When they heard your decree they asked specifically to present themselves to you as a delegation from the Circle City. As I did not have troops enough to forcibly stop them, I had no choice but to accede."

So they did pay attention, Fernal mused. *It's amazing what loyalty these Farlan show once the niceties of rank are agreed and observed and there's profit to be made.* "I understand. Duke Lomin, have your troops make ready."

"My Lord, is the hostility necessary?" asked Suzerain Fordan, gesturing to the soldiers surrounding them: there were five legions of troops, either camped around Borderkeep or patrolling within a day's ride, and a similar number were stationed around Scree and Helrect to maintain order there.

"That can't be more than two regiments approaching; the threat is unnecessary, and it will be considered an insult if they are an official delegation."

Fernal gave Lomin a look, and the duke relayed the order without waiting to hear Fernal's response. Once men were rushing for their horses and forming up, the Demi-God addressed his six high-born companions, who had been granted the greater bulk of Scree's territories between them, each to rule their portion as they would their own suzerainty. Of the six, two were scions, bearing the full authority of their suzerains as Torl and Saroc had marched west with the Palace Guard.

"Let me add to my decree for the benefit of all of you: the territories in Scree you now own were granted because of your loyalty—or your lords'—in the expectation that you will command this first line of defence of the Farlan nation and protect our borders. I do not care what deals you make with your peers to secure troops or boost trade, so long as Farlan law is extended to Scree and Helrect and is equally respected in our protectorate of Tor Milist.

"These laws include bans on the Knights of the Temples and all followers of the child Ruhen, and I mean the laws to be kept to the letter." He took a pace forward, his lupine fangs bright against the dark blue of his fur. "The Farlan like laws; you like your bargains and compromises. This I understand—and I have Chief Steward Lesarl for this—but there will be no compromise where Ruhen's Children are concerned, nor for any other groups that preach his message.

"You will all do well out of me, you who govern the Farlan and gather the wealth of the nation: I will make you even more wealthy and powerful by the time my father chooses a new Duke of Tirah, this I promise. I shall not demand the Farlan make war on Byora, as my predecessor did. That is the price, the bargain that keeps the Farlan from civil war. What I expect in return is no grey areas; no unseen deals or 'interpretations' of my decrees. It is very simple: any man or woman within the Farlan nation who aids or encourages the followers of Ruhen in any way will be deemed a traitor of the nation, and they will be killed."

Fernal plucked at the long shirt he wore, fitted loosely over his powerful furred frame, and gestured to the adapted trousers and boots he had adopted to conform to the strictures of Farlan society. "I wear this to show publicly that I, as Lord of the Farlan, am one of you, but do *not* forget my heritage. If you wish to test me on this, you will see what I have inherited from my father, God of Storms—and you will see how widely and indiscriminately I can destroy."

As the noblemen stared aghast at their lord, Fernal realised just how close to a growl his voice had become.

Lomin was the first to move; he dropped to one knee in acknowledgement of Fernal's words. "Your words are clear, my Lord. Shall I order the delegation to be slaughtered?"

Fernal shook his head, the dark mane of hair flying freely. "I think they also must hear it explained clearly. Let them report my words back to the shadow so there will be no later 'misunderstanding.' I will meet them."

The hurscals spread out to flank the assembled lords. Fernal's company of liveried personal guards formed a narrow avenue, to physically limit the numbers approaching their lord. A tense hush fell over the Farlan soldiers as they watched the newcomers arrive, and Fernal noticed more than one of his men whispering to each other. Even the officers were looking a little uncertain of how to treat the arrivals—until they looked at their lord, and took their cue from him.

Fernal stood with his arms crossed, his axes ready at his belt. He knew to his cost that humans could read little from his face, and that they always assumed a creature his size was capable of nothing but aggression—but in this instance that was precisely what he wanted his subjects to display.

When the Devoted and their white-cloaked companions were within shouting distance, one officer nudged his horse ahead of the rest and called out, "Lord Fernal, I thank you for receiving us. My name is Major Kadin. I am a Knight of the Temples."

His accent placed him as Farlan, no doubt one of those Tildek men who'd followed the Knight-Cardinal into exile when Lord Bahl, Isak's predecessor as Lord of the Farlan, banned their Order. The major dismounted and those behind him followed suit and continued their approach on foot, showing no apparent apprehension. Another Devoted officer, a captain, took up position next to a white-robed woman carrying an oak staff.

"May I present to you Child Ileil, whose preachers we are escorting?" Major Kadin said.

The preacher bowed. She was tall and thin, no doubt once beautiful by Litse standards, though perhaps twenty winters past her prime now. "Your divine blood graces us with its presence," she murmured.

Child? That's the title she uses to bear Ruhen's authority? "Why are you here, Major Kadin?" Fernald asked bluntly. "Did you not understand my decree?"

"We thought official relations between the Circle City and Tirah might yet be possible," he said smoothly, "especially given this mercy mission you have engaged in here."

"You bring them peace," Ileil broke in, her face shining with fervour, "you bring them the justice of the Gods, to save them from lawlessness. The child Ruhen asks us all to do what we can to aid our brothers and sisters in these parts—we carry his message of hope to everyone in these troubled times—"

"Not without breaching the laws of the Farlan," Fernal said loudly, forcing the woman to break off from her rehearsed speech. "This is the only warning you will receive, you and any others sent in your stead: the lands of the Farlan are closed to you all. Any violation of this will be considered an act of war and receive the appropriate response."

Child Ileil looked aghast. "How can you threaten war in such troubled times? The Farlan are assailed by the cruelties and corruption of the cults, just as the Circle City has been. Your people are wearied of war and fear—all we ask is to speak to them of peace!"

"You ask to speak lies!" the Demi-God roared, anger welling up inside him. The fury in his voice forced even the fanatic to move back several paces, fear on her face. He growled, "Your master is a daemon with a child's face, taking advantage of the Land's troubles to further its own power."

"Ruhen is but a child," Ileil gasped, "special only in that his mind is not clouded by the fears and desires suffered by others! Look around you—look at the Land you inhabit and the allies your nation claims." Her voice became shrill as she spoke louder, to reach as many of those nearby as she could. "We are plagued by daemons, all of us. The borders of this world have been weakened by the rash actions of King Emin. Just as the cults have poisoned the message they were entrusted with, so King Emin has weakened the Gods in his desperation for power, for victory—and his madness has opened the very gates of Ghenna!"

Fernal shook his head, unable to find the correct words to dismiss her claims outright. This was a perversion of what King Emin had done, he knew that, but he had always left the verbal diplomacy to the witch of Llehden. Instead he snarled, "Your master is a shadow, one that twists everything to its own advantage. I will not have Ruhen's message inflicted on the Farlan."

"Your people cry out for peace," Ileil begged. "How can you deny them that? How can you deny it to those innocents within Scree's borders after all they have suffered? Outside the walls of Byora the child Ruhen faced down the daemons—he cast them back to the Dark Place; with no army at his back he faced them down, and they could not withstand the power of his message."

"I do not care what bargains he makes with daemons," Fernal snarled, "his message is not welcome here. You have had your warning. Leave now, or die."

The Child lowered her head sadly and started backing away. "Ours is a mission of peace," she replied, her voice still raised. "If you are so clouded by fear and hatred that you will not hear of peace, we will not inflict greater suffering upon this place. The plague of daemons is a punishment upon us all, but if you refuse to be freed of them, if you refuse to hear Ruhen's message, then he cannot force you."

She fixed him with one last, sorrowful look and returned to her horse, her head bowed as though in grief. The entire party left without another word, followed by the Farlan cavalrymen ordered by Duke Lomin to escort the party to the border. Behind him Fernal heard dismissive words from the older nobles and veteran hurscals, but they were not the only mutterings he made out on the wind.

The seeds had been sown. He knew in that moment that the woman had succeeded in her mission; the trouble had only just begun. Fernal watched the preachers leave with sadness in his heart, but those who turned his way saw only the fierce features of a monster and quickly averted their eyes.

CHAPTER 16

ISAK CRESTED THE HILL and a shiver of dread ran down his spine. In the grainy grey light of pre-dawn, Vanach Settlement was slowly unveiled in all its brutal glory. The city on the valley plain below straddled the narrow mouth of a long lake, its arrowhead lines picked out in lanterns along the waterside and on the bridges between the shore and the lake's two small islands.

"Reminds me of Tirah," Vesna commented from his right, "all that old grey stone and dark slate. Just needs a few impossible towers and we're halfway home."

Isak nodded slowly. "And it's dwarfed by the lake, like the forest does for Tirah."

"There were towers once," Mihn said, "maybe not as grand as those of Tirah, but still built tall with the work of many mages."

"The commissars pulled them down?"

Mihn inclined his head. "Before they were called that, yes. It is a common theme of history: people build these monuments, others tear them down. To look down on the Land from upon high . . . well, men must sometimes be reminded they are not Gods."

"Speak for yourself," Daken growled from behind them. "Some of us got ambitions."

Isak turned to look at the irrepressible white-eye, who courteously inclined his head at his commander. The man was a handful, but had mostly accepted his second-tier status in the group in a way most white-eyes wouldn't have. Daken's boasting and lascivious behaviour was mere window-dressing, Isak had realised; a sop to his innate antagonism and stubbornness that demanded some sort of release.

"You don't want to be a God," Isak said eventually. "You'd get bored."

Daken laughed. "Maybe I would at that," he agreed. "Anyways, not sure I'll like the look o' this Land once you an' Ruhen are through with changing it. I'm a creature o' habit, me."

Isak didn't have an answer to that, but when he met Vesna's eyes the

Farlan hero turned away, his lips pursed. The pain of Tila's death remained etched clear in the lines of his face, but Isak could see the man was developing something of Lord Bahl's timeless air.

How many years will you have to live with this loss? Isak wondered.

Vesna drew his arms a little tighter around his body, almost as if Isak had asked the question aloud. If the Mortal Aspect had an answer, it didn't appear to be one he liked.

"My Lord," called a rider in accomplished Farlan: an officer of the Black Swords, coning down the road ahead. "Dawn will be upon us soon. Lodgings have been prepared."

Isak acknowledged him and watched the man ride away. The journey to Vanach had been slow, hampered by the Black Swords accompanying them. For days they had feared an attack; that some rogue part of the Night Council would decide to wipe out the uncertainty of Isak's presence, but nothing had transpired. It had been a cold sort of relief when they'd discovered the truth, pushing their escort to move as fast as possible and coming across soldiers clearing civilians from their path.

Inevitably some word of the saviour prophecies carved into the Grand Ziggurat's walls had reached the general population over the years. For people without hope, oppressed by the very Gods they worshipped, Isak's arrival offered a chance of change, and there were those who were desperate to see if the rumours were true, even as the Commissar Brigade were desperate to prevent any contact that might spark insurrection.

Isak's heart ached for these people. The dismal air of despair infected even the smallest communities under the ever-watchful eye of the commissars, while the labour camps they passed grew incrementally larger. Two days out of Toristern he had tried to get close enough to one to look in the eyes of these so-called heretics—and to test the limits of their escorts' orders. The commissars marching with these Black Swords were of low rank, and no one stopped him when he rode up to the camp's gate, though he had been expecting threats and drawn weapons. When Isak had peered over the gate at the emaciated faces beyond, part of him had hoped it would come to violence; but the result of his action was something he couldn't defend against.

Shouted orders to the camp guards had been obeyed immediately, without even a request for confirmation: one low-ranked commissar's word was enough for the camp guards to instantly butcher every slave within sight. Only Mihn's swift action had stopped Isak from turning on his escort and killing them all.

It was only when he had mastered himself that he realised they too were pushing for a reaction; it appeared that the Night Council was more than willing to sacrifice a few regiments for the chance to muster an army of the Blessed against Isak's group. After that he was more careful with the lives of innocents.

"Come on," Isak muttered eventually, nudging Megenn, the smaller of his two chargers, down the road. "One more day and then we enter Vanach. One way or another, this will all be soon over."

Hulf appeared from the roadside, tongue lolling, after an hour or more out of sight. Isak hadn't been worried; the "heart" rune had been tattooed on Hulf's skin along with Mihn's rowan and hazel leaves. Hulf was a dog bred to hunt, and Isak was certain the connection between them would allow the hound to track him from leagues away.

"That's what's worrying me," Vesna said as he took up his position alongside Isak. "This whole nation has been built with one purpose: for you to enter the Grand Ziggurat unchallenged and unhindered. What comes after that, we've no idea."

Isak nodded, his eyes on the road before him. "Time to find out."

They were shown into what looked like a large hunting lodge surrounded by a long drystone wall, built on the periphery of a village. It was clearly the retreat of some city official, though there was nothing inside to indicate the nature or rank of its owner: it had been picked clean before their arrival, and only food and furniture had been left by its departing servants.

The upper floors of the lodge afforded them a fine view of both Vanach's low city walls and the three shrines that separated the lodge and village. A few dozen Black Swords loitered near the shrines in the shade of a row of yew trees, one of which was dead, but covered by a blooming rambling rose, the pink flowers a stark contrast to the dark needles of the other yews and the dour, unpainted shrines.

"A local tradition?" Mihn wondered as he saw Isak's gaze linger on the unusual sight. "This is not some recent settlement created to feed the monster on its doorstep."

"Maybe. Didn't think traditions were allowed here." Isak shrugged. "It seems power's the same across the Land, always with its own set of rules."

"Not quite," Mihn said. "The commissars have turned their people into tools, or cattle, perhaps. I have no doubt even the rulers spend much of their time looking over their shoulders, but at least they are allowed to be people. That is something denied to most in Vanach. Even the Farlan nobility are not so cruel."

"Maybe they just lack the imagination?" Isak was unable to force a smile at his own joke. "No, not even Lesarl's that much of a bastard."

Mihn stared at the city in the distance, lurking at the bottom of the great valley like a snake waiting in ambush.

"Piety, unquestioned certainty and obedience; they have been distilled into a terrible concoction here. For all his flaws I do not believe the Chief Steward would allow anything he had built to take on a life of its own. He would have not allowed this monstrosity."

"But then, he is not a monster," came a voice from behind them, causing Isak to flinch in surprise.

He turned and saw Zhia at the doorway to a darkened bedroom, still wearing her long shawl over her head.

"The same cannot be said for my brother."

"Is that what you'd call him?" Isak asked.

She regarded him for a long while, her expression betraying no anger, but otherwise unreadable. "My brother's suffering surpasses my own," she said eventually, "and I doubt even you know the lengths I will go to."

"Even I?" Isak echoed.

"Your torment was greater, but was intended to break the soul, to tear it apart and leave nothing but the seeds of daemonhood behind. Mine . . ." Zhia hesitated for a moment. "My punishment was to become a monster and always to know it—the Gods did not want to destroy my soul but to torture it. If we succeed, you know my price, but I add something to that now: vengeance should never be exacted in anger; that is one thing my long years have taught me. You must ensure the Gods also appreciate that lesson. They should not repeat their mistakes."

Isak nodded, feeling the weight of responsibility on him increase a fraction more. He put his hand on Mihn's shoulder and leaned heavily on the small man. Mihn barely moved, despite the effort it took to support a man almost three times his own weight.

The failed Harlequin was transfixed by Zhia's words; only when the vampire turned away did he return to himself. "All these mistakes," Mihn muttered, to himself as much as Isak.

"What's the saying, 'to err is human'?"

Mihn shook his head. "And when the sins are of Gods? Who then forgives?"

"We'll all need to," Isak said in a tired voice. "All this enmity and retribution, it cuts the heart from us all. Hatred poisons even the finest soul and lessens us all."

He straightened up as best he could and headed for the stairs, leaving Mihn alone at the window.

"You're a better man than I," Isak called over his shoulder. "Without you in my shadow, it might be Azaer there."

The road to Vanach followed the path of the river flowing out of the city. Their escorts were two new regiments of Black Swords, dressed in ceremonial uniforms, but with the look of hardened veterans about them. A flotilla kept pace with Isak's party. The river itself was slow and wide for much of the way, but as it narrowed to enter the city, the road became a large avenue lined with statues. It brought them to an enormous peaked gate set in the grey stone wall surrounding Vanach, where what looked like four hundred or more soldiers—approaching a full division—were lined up in formation, awaiting them.

Huge flags hung from the gate bearing symbols of the Upper Circle of the Pantheon. Isak found himself shocked by the grandeur of the whole scene; he had expected a grim, colourless city dominated by the Grand Ziggurat, but Vanach was far older than its current regime and had much architecturally in common with Tirah, the Farlan capital.

Through the great gate Isak could see the ziggurat, framed neatly within the enormous peaked arch. Even in the half-light of evening, the ziggurat's torch-defined lines were clearly visible against the glow of the eastern horizon. Isak couldn't judge the distance to it, but he realised it was as large as any building he'd ever seen, maybe the biggest in the entire Land. Even with many mages involved in its construction, Isak guessed it had been steeped in the blood of slaves long before completion.

Large open shines stood at the foot of each side of the gate, one dedicated to Death and the other to Alterr. As they rode closer, Isak saw a group of men and women clustered about each, kneeling in prayer until he came within fifty yards. From behind they looked like monks of Belarannar, in their voluminous brown robes, but they got to their feet and advanced towards Isak and he saw they were far more richly dressed. The brown robes were edged in some yellow pelt, and they fell open at the front to reveal long white tunics bearing the moon-and-river device of Vanach. Each of them wore a different golden chain. They were ten in total, all Priesans, with fifty or more of lesser rank lingering behind. Some of the ten were old and white-haired, but others looked younger even than Prefect Darass.

As Isak, Zhia and Vesna dismounted and approached them, he noted how the escorting soldiers drew discreetly away. In response a tiny, withered woman started forward to meet him, flanked by two men only a little younger than she, and accompanied by a sudden fanfare from both sides. Isak bowed his head and Vesna offered a more formal greeting. Zhia did absolutely nothing, but the Priesan gave no indication of offence.

"Lord Sebe, the Faithful of Vanach welcome you to our grand settlement," the woman croaked in capable Farlan, continuing to move forward until she was no more than two yards from Isak and could speak without straining her voice. "I am Priesan Sorolis, Anointed First of the Sanctum. I am the voice of the Sanctum and the lesser councils of Vanach. These are Priesans Dacan and Horotain."

She indicated the men on either side of her in turn. Dacan was a bloodless-looking specimen with prominent eyes and lips so thin Isak could barely see them, while Horotain, the tallest of the three, had probably been handsome once, when he was thinner and younger, but that was a long way past. In his effort to maintain his looks the Priesan now looked like the painted eunuchs Isak had seen in Tor Salan years back.

"So you rule Vanach," Isak stated after a long pause. He had tasted the air, and he could tell she was no mage, just a frail old woman with kindly eyes—hardly the tyrant he had expected of Vorizh Vukotic's deranged instrument.

"That, my Lord," she said with the hint of a smile, "may yet depend on what comes to pass this night."

"You ten are the Sanctum?"

"We are—the elders of the Fifth Enlightenment, appointed by our own to act in council for the glory of the Gods and the good of Vanach."

"Any of you also sit on the Night Council?"

Sorolis wheezed as she turned slightly to the scowling figure of Priesan Horotain.

"Holding a grudge, my Lord?" he asked. "We heard of the attack only after it had taken place. It was not ordered by sitting members of the council, I assure you."

"Do you know what I seek?"

"I know what you will find." She gestured to the other members of the Sanctum. "To reach the Fifth Enlightenment is to know the mysteries of the Grand Ziggurat and Vanach itself. We are aware, my Lord, of what lies at the heart of our nation."

"And you're bound to it," Zhia broke in suddenly, "compelled to obey—I can see the threads of magic that bind the throats of each of you."

The old woman's face tightened at that and Horotain purpled, but they could not deny it. "You are of the blood," Priesan Sorolis choked, fighting to get out each word.

Zhia took a step forward and smiled in a predatory way. The bloodless commissar, Dacan, cringed at her closeness, but he was apparently unable to retreat with her eyes fixed upon him. "I am of the blood," she confirmed, "and you chafe under my brother's yoke, it appears."

"We are bound as his protectors," Sorolis confirmed reluctantly, "charged to see his will done." Her face hardened. "It is the sin we bear to see the will of the Gods done."

"And what of after?" Isak demanded. "All your different councils, what will they do afterwards?"

"That depends on your actions," she admitted. "The Night Council is not alone in fearing this new age; even within the Sanctum we have debated what upheaval this will bring, what new course the Gods will set us. The one that sleeps in darkness may be Vanach's dark heart, but we remain true servants of the Gods. We will allow no man to divert us from the path of the Blessed."

Isak bit back his instinctive retort. That she seemed to genuinely mean her words somehow disgusted him more. What little they had seen of Vanach hinted at the nation's dark heart indeed, but that wasn't Vorizh Vukotic, it was the cruelty they were willing to inflict on their own. Denunciation, starvation, sleep deprivation, torture, mass execution—Shinir had provided the details they couldn't see as they rode past labour camps and abandoned villages—and the Commissar Brigade were unrepentant.

If Priesan Sorolis recognised the anger on Isak's scar-twisted cheeks, she gave no indication. Instead she stepped to one side and gestured through the great gate that led into Vanach Settlement. "Come my Lord. The remaining tests await you."

As she gestured, a dozen litters appeared, carried by unarmed soldiers. They were chairs, rather than the beds used in Narkang, but as with Isak's visit to King Emin's city, the lead litter was borne by eight large men, twice the usual number of porters, to account for his great weight. The chairs were all intricately decorated; when Isak saw the one intended for him bore stylised black bees of Death, he realised each displayed the totem animal of one of the Gods of the Upper Circle. He matched them in his mind, taking a moment to recognise the seldom-seen white lynx of Alterr and hare of Kitar. More litters were brought up for the Sanctum members, these painted black, with the same designs in gold.

"And our horses?" he asked

The old woman gestured and more soldiers trotted up to collect the reins of each. "Only the Black Swords may ride within Vanach Settlement," she explained. "Your horses will be stabled at their barracks nearby."

And if you want to escape, you'll be slower than our soldiers, Isak finished in his mind, but his only response was a curt nod.

With a click of the tongue he brought Hulf to his side. He didn't want the dog to follow, so he let a sliver of magic race over his skin as he crouched down to pull the dog close. He pushed his fingers deep into the hound's fur and breathed in his warm scent.

"Stay," he whispered into Hulf's thick ruff of grey-black fur. "Wait in the woods for me."

He felt the rune on his chest warm as the magic slithered out with his words, installing the command deep into Hulf's animal mind. The dog whined in response, but Isak repeated his words and ran a palm over Hulf's muzzle before nudging him away again. The dog sat as ordered, his ears down, his eyes on Isak as the white-eye took his seat in the litter. He knew Hulf would stay there until they were out of sight, but then he would run off as soon as any of the locals tried to go near him. He would be safer than the rest of them, most likely, away from danger and hidden by his tattoos.

Isak watched his comrades, far from surprised when Daken took the crow of Larat and Vesna the dragon of Karkarn—one unconsciously scratching at the Aspect tattoos on his chest as he did so, the other very deliberately touching the ruby tear on his face. To Isak's surprise, Zhia headed straight for the Goddess of Fertility's chair, running her fingers over the hare design almost as though testing her bathwater before she got in.

Doranei made for Nartis' snake, while Shinir, appropriately in Isak's mind, took Amavoq's wolf and sat glaring at those taking note. The battle-mage Fei Ebarn, Leshi and Veil did not appear to care about which they chose, leaving Legana, Mihn and Tiniq all staring reluctantly at the remaining choices. When at last they too mounted their chairs, the horns sounded again and Isak's bearers started off, leading the party through the great arch and onto a wide, deserted highway that led directly to the Grand Ziggurat ahead.

Isak looked up at the arch as they passed through. There were arrow-slit windows all the way up the huge stone arch, he realised, though it was so narrow he doubted there would be space within to draw a Farlan longbow.

Large, grand buildings, most several storeys high, lined the highway. Many had colonnaded open walks around the lower floors; the upper floors were supported by pillars, but they looked precarious to Isak as he passed. He noted again that the population was being kept well clear of the foreign visitors, warned to stay away by the constant blaring of the trumpets, perhaps. What Isak found notable about this elegant old city was the lack of life: those few people he had seen wore plain clothes, and only the Blessed were wearing any sort of adornment, while the houses and streets were almost dead, without the chaotic air of any city Isak had seen before. No clothes hung out to dry, no carts, or piles of wood or rubbish lay in the alleys between houses. There were market stalls of a sort around one block of building, but there didn't look to be much for sale, and there was none of the accumulated everyday clutter a normal market would attract. These buildings might be offices or merchants' stores, but it was remarkable how abandoned they looked.

"So that's the ziggurat," Daken commented from behind him. "Big bugger, all right."

Isak looked ahead to the rising shape in the distance. Part of Vanach was built on the water of the lake itself, extending out from the shore towards the two islands that formed the heart of the city. None of Chief Steward Lesarl's agents had ever returned from Vanach Settlement itself, but Prefect Darass had been more than happy to fill in some of the blanks for Isak.

More than half of the nearer island was covered by the Grand Ziggurat itself, on each of the stepped levels of which were shrines to many Gods, each one as large as the temple of any lesser God in Tirah.

The larger, fortified island behind housed the twelve High Temples, which rivalled any in the Land, according to the Overseer of Toristern.

And furthermore, there were shrines to a hundred more Gods and Aspects scattered throughout the city, each one obliging every passing citizen to speak a prayer there before moving on.

Isak looked away. The ziggurat was a nagging burr at the back of his mind, but the strange state of the city nagged at him even more; it was so unnatural it was almost otherworldly. Though he could see hundreds of the silent, watching citizens of Vanach, they could have been ghosts for all he could touch them, ask their names or understand their lives.

Is this the presence of Termin Mystt? Has it seeped into the city and turned everything awry, or is it just my own fears haunting me still?

"What's fucking wrong with all of them?" Daken wondered aloud, voicing Isak's own question.

Beyond the streets they caught a trace of the more normal sounds of a city, but the horns continued to blare, and everywhere within sight remained still and quiet. Squads of Black Swords stood at every street entrance; their presence alone was enough to instil a tense, sullen silence in the citizens.

"They're frightened," Zhia replied. "Most people are wary of change and these, well, they no doubt fear change as much as they do life staying the same."

"Sounds gutless to me," Daken said, turning to stare at the nearest party of armed Black Swords. They were all young, aside from a sergeant who'd likely not seen anyone more scarred than himself until Isak was carried past. "Livin' like frightened rabbits their whole lives."

"You think they should choose death instead?" Zhia asked contemptuously. "They have no leaders, no weapons, no safe means of contact with others who might feel the same."

"Don't even look like they're tryin'," Daken grumbled. "No kind o' life if you ask me."

"It wouldn't be your life," Shinir said. "White-eyes are given immediate advancement in the Black Swords—you'd be one of the oppressors."

Daken laughed loudly. "Aye, sounds more likely. Tough shit fer the rest, then!"

As the sky darkened, Isak tasted magic on the air and turned quickly to see bright flaring lights appear in the centre of several units of Black Swords. They had encountered no mages throughout their journey, and Zhia had confirmed that none had been watching them from afar, but the exact status of mages there was unclear, despite the construction of the ziggurats and the arch they had just passed under.

"That answers one question," Zhia commented, looking the same way.

Isak nodded. "I'd expected Vanach's Commissar Brigade to be like the Knights of the Temples, to ban magery whenever they can." He didn't have to open his senses to know the hissing torches now carried by each Black Swords squad had been made by mages—the energies leaked out of them like dirty trails of smoke, tasting bitter and ashy at the back of his throat.

"The Devoted are a blind and stubborn lot, so proud of how the rest of the Land sees them. Here, where the Sanctum and councils rule absolutely, necessity perhaps trumps such lofty ideas. Those torches are not made to last.

And look around us." Zhia gestured to the city at large, and Isak saw the spitting white lights at every street corner, and forming the perimeter of a circular patch of open ground ahead.

"There must be hundreds of them—and the ziggurat is similarly lit; I can taste their sparks throughout the city. Somewhere there are dozens of mages hard at work. And considering we've not met one in any position of authority . . ." She didn't bother to finish her sentence.

"Do you mean the Commissars'll hold any magery against us? A bad example for their slaves?" Isak asked.

"I mean nothing as yet," she replied. "There would be too much speculation involved. But I doubt we're in danger because of it. Vesna and Legana most obviously look like Raylin mercenaries to the untrained eye, yet they've not caused us a problem thus far. You are already keeping a check on your powers. All I can suggest is we continue not to provide anyone with a reason to turn on us. Some contradictions of dogma can be ignored by absolute rulers, but it's never sensible to push the matter."

"So let's just be thankful we're not being escorted by a cadre of slave battle-mages," Vesna added.

Isak didn't reply as they came close enough to the open ground ahead to realise it wasn't entirely empty. There was a large oval table set in the very middle, with six chairs around it. At a reverential distance, hands clasped and heads bowed, were five commissars of varying ages, dressed in the formal black coats that Prefect Darass and his deputy had worn. It was an incongruous sight.

"Looks like it's time for the fourth sign," Zhia said brightly. This was the one part of this trip she had been looking forward to, whatever the stakes: a challenge for her fearsome mind, and one no doubt designed especially for her.

"What's that again?" Daken asked. "Mastery o' tactics?"

"Indeed, and given Xeliache is the most widely played game of strategy in the Land, I'm sure Vanach will have assembled some especially skilled players to test our Lord Sebe."

Isak glanced around at her and saw she was smiling as much as he'd feared. He'd played the game only a handful of times, just enough to know breaking the board over his opponent's head didn't count as a win. He hadn't the patience for games that took a lifetime to master, so he would have to allow a more skilled person to guide his hands here.

Even before the Last Battle and their curse, Vorizh's little sister had been a master of the game, and Xeliache—Heartland, in the Farlan dialect—had led to her and Aryn Bwr, the last King of the Elves, becoming lovers. To fulfil this sign, Isak would have to allow the immortal vampire into his mind.

"Let's get this over with," he growled, and got up from his chair.

Two commissars shuffled forward to meet them at the edge of the circle of ground. The crowd spread around the paved circle were largely Black Swords—but not all of them. Isak realised this was as close to the common folk of Vanach as he was likely to get. There was a dull uniformity to their clothing that was echoed in their wary expressions, but he did notice the women were all careful to cover their throats with a scarf.

A vampire's joke about religious humility? Isak couldn't help but wonder.

Only the officers of the Black Swords and commissars wore any form of decoration; even devices of the Gods seemed to be restricted to the Blessed. The closest thing to jewellery appeared to be the coloured thread several women had used to tie their hair.

"My Lord," said the leader of the approaching commissars in the Narkang dialect. He was a man of middle years with a prominent wart on his nose. He walked with a stick, half-dragging his left leg, like a soldier carrying an old injury. Isak noticed the younger commissar on his left was keeping his hands free, just in case the older man needed help.

"I am Sepesian Farray, representative of the Silent Council, here to oversee fulfilment of the fourth sign. I welcome you to this arena of study."

Isak glanced around. The litters carrying the Sanctum moved alongside him, obviously heading into the circle to witness events but to take no part themselves.

"Silent Council eh? Must be powerful if the Sanctum defer to you."

The man smiled politely. "My Lord is kind to joke."

"That was a joke, was it?"

Now he looked faintly stricken. "Forgive me, Lord; I did not know how much of our ways you knew. The Silent Council is solely devoted to this moment, the provision of an opponent for the fourth sign. This is our only field of responsibility."

"And not one that's been so useful up to now," Isak murmured. "Let's not delay your big moment, then. Where's this opponent?"

Sepesian Farray bowed as low as he could and gestured expansively behind him. "He awaits you, my Lord. Please, take your seat at the table and he will approach."

Isak tugged his patchwork cloak tighter around his body and stooped further, as if only now aware of the crowd watching him. Zhia followed him, catching Legana's eye to ensure that she joined them too. The Lady's Mortal-Aspect was as much a Xeliache player as Isak, but Zhia apparently thought her worth the third chair.

Isak's opponent was a young man only a handful of summers older than Isak himself, with scrappy stubble and eyes only for the board. Sepesian Farray took the first of the spare seats, unsurprisingly, while a member of the Sanctum, a tall man with a widow's peak and jutting chin wearing the white clasp of the Night Council, eventually joined them to take the last.

Isak realised the sense in bringing Legana to the table: not only was she stunningly beautiful, with arresting emerald eyes that glowed in the darkness, but her divine blood would be an added distraction to the religious fanatics.

He copied his opponent and stared down at the boards between them. Heartland was played on two hexagonal boards, with lines marking rows of triangles on each. The smaller was called the heavens and stood on a frame above the main board—that was where the Gods fought, each piece moving from one intersection to the next or descending to the main board. The majority of pieces were called soldiers, a handful of those were the Chosen. This was a plain set of old oak and polished stones rather than the ornate figurines the Farlan preferred, but it was elegant in its simplicity.

Instead of reaching for the pieces, Isak folded his hands in his lap and closed his eyes. This close to Zhia he could taste her presence in the air: the iron tang of blood, the sparkle of magic, the sour antipathy of someone cursed by the Gods. He could sense Legana on the other side of him too; it was a strange balance of Gods and monsters.

Between these two Gods-touched women he felt secure and alive, but all the more aware of the call of the grave. One was bearing the last spark of a dead Goddess, the other had been denied death again and again, and around them both he sensed a storm of torn threads—the loose strands of history's tapestry, surging wildly.

And here I sit, ready to tie another thread off—to bind it to me and those already bound to me.

He felt the delicate, probing touch of spider-feet on his hands, picking their way with the greatest care over the twists of his scars, then skittered down to the tips of his fingers and bit with obsidian-sharp teeth into the flesh of his wrists. Though they pushed into his body he could barely feel them, and he knew he would see nothing if he opened his eyes.

Zhia's magic was running over his body; it carried the scent of a tomb, but it also washed away the stink of the Dark Place at the back of his mind and he found himself relaxing into the sensation. Just the idea of giving up control made the white-eye in him scream for blood, but Zhia's touch was as deft as a lover's, her mantle of centuries a salve to his wounded soul.

Before long his right hand was numb, as if absent from the rest of his body, while his left was a mere echo of presence.

At last Isak opened his eyes to find his hands moving with deft assurance, gathering up a dozen pieces to set them on the board in a starting position that seemed oddly unbalanced to Isak. The set of the starting pieces was up to the individual player; his opponent showed just a flicker of interest in his eyes before he returned to his own pieces.

Isak returned the man's nod of respect when the last piece was set and said with a frown, "How do the little pieces move again?"

Only Sapesian Farray smiled while the spider feet dug a little deeper into Isak's hand. That time he did feel them properly.

CHAPTER 17

ISAK CONCENTRATED ON THE BOARD and tried not to smirk. The young man opposite him slumped in his seat, hugging himself as he stared down in disbelief. Most likely he hadn't been expecting that—though the sign was for Isak to show a mastery of tactics, to demonstrate understanding and insight.

Zhia had done just that with a slow, measured game for almost half an hour, and then upped the pace of every move. Attacking from three directions, she had started to annihilate her opponent—moving her pieces as soon as he'd set his down, as though his moves were unimportant and carelessly discarding his losses.

And now he had stopped, unwilling to touch his pieces again in case it prompted the immediate loss of another. With a despairing look at an equally shocked Sapesian Farray, he wilted. Hand trembling, he reached out and made a gesture over the board to indicate he submitted. Isak smiled as he stood and felt sensation rush back into his hand.

"My congratulations, Lord Sebe," Farray croaked as he struggled up. "That was—ah—remarkable!"

"What can I say? It's a gift," Isak said with a ghoulish grin. "Your man played a good game, though, he did you proud. I don't often lose more than a handful of pieces."

Farray's eyes widened and it took him a moment before he remembered himself enough to translate the words for his protégée's benefit. It seemed to lift the youth and he shakily pushed himself upright to take Isak's offered hand.

"*Time to go, I think,*" Zhia said into his mind, "*before you do a victory lap?*" Isak nodded and glanced at the member of the Sanctum overseeing the game, but he was too busy glowering at the defeated man to annoy further. He headed back to his litter instead, offering his companions a small, theatrical bow that made both Daken and Doranei briefly laugh and applaud like noble ladies at a summer fair.

"The ziggurat," he announced as he took his seat again and gestured for his bearers to move off.

This time the Sanctum members were quick to get ahead, not even waiting for their colleague to retake his litter before the first of them moved off down the road. The last traces of light had faded from all but a sliver of the eastern sky and only now did Isak properly notice the frost in the air: the announcement of autumn that, in the lee of the Spiderweb Mountains, would turn swiftly to winter.

The procession came to a fork in the road as they neared the lakeshore. Ahead was a small grove of aspen, beneath which standing stones were set in two distinct circles. Under a gentle breeze that skipped off the lake, the trembling leaves seemed to whisper a warning to Isak. He found himself transfixed by the half-hidden ancient stones they shaded; a flavour of reverence was hanging in the air that reminded him of the Ivy Rings in Llehden.

Bearing right, they reached a large intersection, at the centre of which stood a statue of Alterr in stylised armour with her head piously bowed. Beyond that was a wide bridge that crossed to the ziggurat island. By now their route was lined solely by Black Swords soldiers, all standing silently to attention. Every fifth man was holding a torch to light their way. The bridge was almost thirty paces wide, with an ornate stone parapet down each side and arches composed of Aspects of Alterr touching spear-tips at either end. Compared to the Grand Ziggurat on the far side however, it was insignificant.

The ziggurat of Toristern Settlement was imposing for certain, standing perhaps eighty feet high. But the upper level of the fifth of Grand Ziggurat of Vanach Settlement's enormous tiers was close to three hundred feet off the ground. The ziggurat's lowest level was accessed by a long, stepped ramp that reached almost to the island shore. Smaller stairways led up to the other tiers.

On either side of the ramp were massive large stone statues—not religious figures this time, but a pair of wyverns with wings furled, looking up to the sky above. Isak faltered when he stepped between them, feeling an echo of pain in his gut as he remembered the sight of just such a creature on the battlefield outside Byora.

At the very top were three small structures that proved to be the entrance to the interior of the ziggurat, flanked by shrines to Alterr and Death. With night fully descended Isak looked out over Vanach, picked out by faint lights below. The breeze whipped at his cloak and threw back his hood to expose his frayed ear and torn throat to the Sanctum. He didn't feel any urge to cover the marks of daemonic torment, and it was with a renewed sense of purpose that he turned to face the assembled members of the Sanctum.

A sparkle of life in the breeze and the heavy presence of magic in the stones beneath his feet filled Isak's limbs with a strength he rarely felt outside battle. He touched two fingers to the Crystal Skull now bound to the bare skin of his stomach then approached Priesan Sorolis, who stood before a closed door no taller than Isak. "Shall we proceed?" he asked.

Sorolis agreed with a bow and raised her hands to the attending eye of her Goddess as though begging her to bear witness.

"The last of the signs, the final Ziggurat Mystery: the one who comes to claim our secrets may only do so with the blessing of the Gods." Her voice was sincere, her conviction absolute. It was enough to stop Isak feeling scornful. The Sanctum were compelled by Vorizh's magic, but they were not loyal servants of a heretic. Their secrets were hidden by layer upon layer of dogma and devotion—a devotion perverted by the unseen truth and a hunger for power, perhaps, but no weaker for it.

"The mysteries tell us the one who comes shall walk with the Gods and command them," Sorolis intoned, her face a practised mask.

Isak nodded. No doubt they had assumed it would turn out differently—and no doubt Vorizh Vukotic had, too. Vorizh had realised that to be worthy of Death's own weapon, the claimant would need to know the link bonding Crystal Skulls and God—particularly the connection between Death and the Skull of Ruling that Isak had exploited at the battle of Moorview. Without that understanding, they might wreak devastation, but they could not undo the curse of his family—and that, Zhia had assured him, was her brother's goal, even more than revenge.

At his signal Vesna and Legana walked to his side. This wasn't what the commissars would be expecting, he knew, but it was far less perilous. Whether or not it was the demonstration they wanted, to challenge the divine spirit within the War God's most favoured would be foolish.

He turned to each in turn. Vesna did not hesitate to kneel to Isak, while Legana's obvious reluctance to kneel to any man only reinforced the point to the Sanctum. This was no bargain: this was Isak commanding their obedience, and while he saw frustration and anger on the faces of many before him, he knew they could not deny the compulsion laid upon them.

There was a long moment of quiet before Priesan Sorolis bowed to him and stepped aside, motioning for the gates to be unbarred and held open. Mihn stepped forward alongside Vesna, but the youngest member of the

Sanctum, a burly man with tight curly hair, immediately stepped in front of him.

"The one who claims our secrets must enter alone."

Isak reached out with one nailless finger to prod the man in the chest. "The rest will stay," he said, almost in a whisper, "but in dark places, my shadow walks by my side."

The man shook his head and stepped around Isak's finger, reaching out himself to grip Mihn by the shoulder. He opened his mouth to speak, but Mihn had intervened before he could, deftly twisting away the man's hand with a sharp click. The Priesan staggered back in pain, cradling his hand, and Isak tasted a swift burst of magic from Zhia that wrapped its way around his throat and silenced any cries from the man.

Isak barely noticed as the rest of the Sanctum melted silently from their path. He advanced on the near-black entrance ahead, where he could see a narrow spiral stair leading down, but nothing else. The closer he got, the more he felt his hands start to tremble. As though sensing his fear and welling memories, daemon voices sang out in the distance, faint, but unmistakable. A gust of wind swirled forward and gathered a trail of dust up from the stone floor, then fell away.

For a moment all was still around him as if Vanach itself were holding its breath. Isak glanced around. Zhia had sensed them too, that much was clear, drawn by portentous events, perhaps, or the presence of power unveiling, daemons walked the Land beyond Vanach's walls. Keeping back from the light, snuffling gently at the scents of blood and life, they attended patiently as Isak descended into darkness.

Isak felt a hand on his arm, looked down to see Mihn's steady expression. For a moment he could taste the Dark Place again—the infernal stink of his jailer, the tang of his own blood and the cold of the void below. Mihn took a step forward and the slight grip he exerted was enough to lead Isak right to the entrance. Once there Mihn made to go first.

Isak reached out and stop him. "My duty," he said. "This is no grave." And he descended, ducking to fit his enormous frame down the stair. Once out of sight of the Sanctum he paused and loosed the wrappings around Eolis. With Mihn following close behind, they soon found themselves on the bare upper floor of the ziggurat's interior. Isak looked around and almost laughed at how mundane the room was. The lowest rank of the commissars were all initiated here—thousands of men and women, far too many for any real secrets to be revealed. All the same, something akin to a schoolroom wasn't quite what he'd expected. It was empty now, but a dozen short benches stood on the far side of the room, just beyond a second stone stairway that led further down into the ziggurat. A pale green light emanated from the walls, illuminating tablets bearing a carved stone script Isak couldn't read.

"Their holy mission," Mihn supplied when Isak shot him a questioning look. "The nameless stranger who showed them they were blessed by the Gods."

Before he could say any more a sound came from the upper entrance. Isak turned to see the faint scrap of starlight on the stair's wall disappear as the door was closed behind them.

"No going back, I suppose."

"Was there ever?"

Isak didn't reply. He did a quick circuit of the room, briefly inspecting each tablet before starting down the central stair to a similar sort of room, this one partitioned by wooden panels. Icons of the Gods took centre stage on the panels, while the outer walls again bore more of Vorizh's mysteries—the coming of a saviour whose appearance would overturn the ungodly ways of the Seven Tribes, and more of the regime's founding and the duties of the commissars.

The pattern was repeated on the next two floors, where stone pillars and walls increasingly divided up the space into multiple rooms, and within each there were more of the mysteries, each coming closer to truth. Mention was made of the Great War and the curses laid down by the Gods on their enemies, of the crimes enacted by both sides.

"Strange," Isak commented as Mihn reported excerpts for his benefit. "I forget how much I know of the Land now, the secrets and lies that frame our lives. A few summers ago, half of this would have astonished me."

"And it has taken a toll," Mihn warned. "Your insight has not come without cost. The more I think on what you have endured, the more I fear where it will lead you."

Isak turned to face his friend. "Lead *me*? You mean *us*—you're coming along for the ride, remember?"

Mihn bowed his head to acknowledge the point.

"It's too late anyway," Isak continued, one hand resting on the Crystal Skull at his waist. "We're well beyond consequences now and you know it. All we've got left is success or failure." He moved off before Mihn could reply, turning his back quickly as though hoping he could avoid whatever the failed Harlequin might say. The last stairway stood before them, this one more ornate than the rest, with wyvern heads in bas-relief on the large central pillars standing on either side of the open entrance.

"The labyrinth."

Isak drew Eolis. The blade shone bright white in the dim interior of the labyrinth. Green trails of magic danced in the darkness, reminding Isak of the first time he'd gone to the dragon's lair underneath Tirah. The artefacts stored there under Genedel's guardianship had been mere toys compared to what he sought now, but still their presence had set his mind aflame. Now it was different; now he was more accustomed to magic in all its forms, the presence of the divine and daemonic as much as the wild, raging energies of battlefield magic.

But he found something new as well. Like a man who had withstood the torrent and now beheld the ocean, Isak hesitated before the entrance of the labyrinth. It was muted, hidden from view, but inescapable all the same. He knew there could be no mages within the Commissar Brigade; they would ask too many questions, as unable to resist investigating as an addict who smelled something akin to opium.

"Isak," Mihn whispered, "are you okay?"

Isak found himself biting his lip as he nodded, the torn flesh of his lips moulding around the broken teeth left to him by Ghenna's inhabitants.

"I don't know what it'll do to me," he said eventually, "what'll be left of me when I take it."

"It is that powerful?"

Isak almost laughed. "Can you not feel it?"

"The air makes my skin crawl, I know that."

"It is the sword—the black sword of Death."

Again Mihn made to go first, seeing Isak's reticence, and again it stirred the white-eye into movement. "We are beyond concerns now," he said firmly as Isak pulled him back. "There are no consequences, no tomorrows—only the deed to follow this moment."

"Another dusty quotation?"

Mihn shook his head. "You have had enough of those from me; all I have left are my own words."

Isak forced a grin in the strange half-light. "Learning your place in things at last? So no more relying on the words of others; your own carry far greater weight, my friend."

They went down into the darkness of the labyrinth. Before he'd left the last step Isak's head was ringing with the latent power resting uneasily somewhere below their feet. He tightened his grip on Eolis, holding the sword ready as he walked forward to the first turning. The base of the ziggurat was several hundred yards across, while the stone-walled passage they stood in was barely one yard wide.

At the end of the corridor he used his sword to score the wall, inscribing the "heart" rune there rather than a single notch. It seemed appropriate, given the protection Xeliath had given him in Ghenna, but it proved to be unnecessary as a voice rang out from further down the corridor.

"No breathless commissar are you," called a woman, "you come bearing power like a mantle, but you are in our domain now."

Isak exchanged a look with Mihn, then stepped forward and turned right, barely able to make out the figure ahead amidst the shadows swirling angrily around her. The woman had pale, delicate features half-obscured by her loose raven-black hair. She wore a cuirass of beautiful workmanship, and greaves and vambraces, but her sword remained sheathed on her back.

"Only fools enter the labyrinth," she warned. "It is only by my hand that you will ever leave this place."

Isak turned back the way they had come and saw the entrance had vanished, the passage ending in a dead end only a few yards behind Mihn. He didn't bother going to investigate; something told him this was more than mere illusion.

"Been called that often enough," Isak said, raising his sword for the woman to see clearly, "but in this case, you might want to think again, Araia."

The woman's eyes blazed suddenly, twin sapphires shining out through the darkness. The shadows around her started to whip more frenziedly around the narrow passageway, but Isak made no further move towards her. He put a precautionary hand on the Skull and continued.

"Your sister's at the top of the ziggurat," he said carefully. "We're here to end this."

"End it?" Araia gasped, reeling from his words as though physically struck. "There is no end, not even in death!"

"Zhia doesn't believe that."

Her voice softened. "Zhia— It's been so long . . . No, I am bound still."

"What is that?" Mihn asked, using Araia's own dialect. "What duty binds you?"

"I—I am bound to this place, bound to drink of those who come here, bound to protect our secrets." She spoke as though in a daze and Isak realised she was indeed bound—with sorcery, not oaths. The lesser two of the Vukotic children, ever in the shadows of their three remarkable siblings, were even now in the thrall of their family. Vorizh had turned them to his own purpose, using them to maintain this horrific masquerade.

Isak felt a chill of uncertainty. *Is Vorizh even here? Is this some madman's ruse, or just the next step on a far longer path?*

"Come," Araia said hoarsely, "I will show you the way through."

She beckoned them forward and watched as Isak cautiously approached. He studied her as he went: a good hand taller than her sister, and less terrifyingly beautiful, but no less arresting for it.

"Your brother is here?"

"You will meet him soon enough," Araia warned.

When Isak was just two paces away she turned abruptly, affording him a glimpse of the long-handled sword on her back, and set off. There was a bitter scent left in her wake as Isak followed, magic unknown to him, and wrought in a way he couldn't begin to guess at. All along the walls were inscribed tablets: more secrets and mysteries, no doubt, leading to the sudden shock of coming face to face with a vampire in the darkness.

Araia led them silently through the labyrinth, moving without hesitation despite Isak's certainty the passages were changing around them, that they must have crossed back over their own path more than once, through once-solid walls. The vampire moved as though led by a chain in the darkness, resigned and defeated by it.

How long has he kept her here? His own sibling! Isak shook the questions away. Vorizh was a vampire twisted into madness by Death's own weapon. He could expect no reason in Vorizh's actions, whether or not there was purpose.

After ten minutes or more Araia jerked to a halt. A new light spilled out over the walls, a constant pale blue. "My brother is within," she said quietly.

Isak waited for her to move off, but she didn't; she remained still, almost like a mechanical toy run down. There was space to pass her, however, so Isak waited a few heartbeats longer before moving through the entrance, which took them down another short flight of steps, below ground-level now, to a wide chamber covered in ornate carvings and runic script. Roughly cut shards of blue glass were set into the walls, apparently at random, each producing a faint glow that illuminated the room.

The room was empty beyond a statue in the very centre: an obsidian figure standing on a dais. His right hand, held at waist-height, was empty; in his left was a long, straight-edged sword, its snub tip resting on the ground. The sword itself was a good five feet long, and as black as the statue. It didn't reflect any light from the room; instead it drank in the blue glow, and Isak found himself dragged forward a step or two before he even realised he had moved.

The black sword had a short, plain cross-hilt, and a pearl encased in twists of metal was set in the pommel. It looked finely made, but without ostentation, for it needed no frippery; the stink of magic in the room was choking and the presence of raw, wild power fizzed through Isak's veins. The very air around it twisted away, folding back on itself as it touched magic in its most pure and warping form.

Two small doors were set into the far wall. Both were made of some pale wood and bore Elvish runes incorporated into a single geometric pattern. Isak advanced towards the statue, watching the doors as he moved. Mihn followed close behind him, but Araia stopped just inside the door.

"I'm sorry," she whispered.

Isak moved left as the shadows in the room suddenly danced into life; in a blur of jagged movement the darkest coalesced into a figure, a tall man, who drove straight for Isak, thrusting at his heart with one of a pair of swords. The white-eye twisted aside and brought Eolis up, deflecting the lunge in a burst of white lights.

On his right, Araia drew her own weapon and surged forward, the sword carving dark arcs through the air. Mihn lashed out with his staff, swiping across her hands, then spinning to kick at her knee. He blunted the vampire's advance, but Araia recovered her balance swiftly and chopped down at him. The blow never reached Mihn, for he dodged away, dancing backwards and swinging blind at the other as he went.

Her brother faded right to avoid the blow, checking for just long enough to allow Isak time to move. He clashed against the vampire's lead blade and kicked forward, connecting with his thigh and shoving him closer to Mihn. The two vampires nearly collided as Araia charged behind her brother, slashing wildly at Mihn, who turned each blow, intent on keeping at the edge of her range.

Isak felt the magic-suffused air crackle on his skin as his bloodlust sparked to life. White threads began to race over his skin and Eolis started glowing with un-summoned power, tracing blistering curves of light as he struck out. The vampire fell back from the onslaught, wielding both swords frantically to ward off Isak's swift blows. Beside him Araia was trying to corner Mihn, but the small man just kicked up and off the nearest wall, vaulting her slashing blade and putting himself back in the centre of the room again.

Even as Isak caught one of his opponent's swords and sheared right through it, Mihn dropped to a crouch and swung his staff up in the same movement, catching Araia's fingers with the steel-capped end before her descending sword could reach him. The crisp blow jerked the sword from her grip.

In the next moment Isak had battered away her brother's other sword. He chopped deep into the vampire's neck and blood sprayed over his ragged cloak as he continued drawing the sword-blade down and through. The vampire fell away as the tip of Eolis cleared the wound and punched forward again to pierce Araia's cuirass with a sharp crack.

The sister jerked to an abrupt halt, frozen in the act of reaching for Mihn's throat. The smaller man rolled backwards and back to his feet, out of range, while Isak ran Araia through to the hilt before whipping the blade back out again and leaving her to collapse to the ground.

He stared down at the vampires at his feet as their last moments of life spilled away, and suddenly sensed Mihn's eyes on him. The failed Harlequin brought his staff back to its usual upright position and looked Isak up and down, and he realised with something akin to a laugh that the gifted duellist was assessing his form, his poise after the blow.

An immortal vampire nearly ripped your gullet out, Isak thought with a sense of wonder, *and still you notice such things.*

Mihn gave him a small nod of thanks. "In another age," he began with no trace of exertion in his voice, "you would have become a great lord of the Farlan. With Bahl to teach you, you would have forged a human nation such as the Land has never seen."

Isak looked down at the ripped tunic he wore, the frayed edges of his cloak. "We're made by the trials life gives us," he replied, adding with a smile, "but I was never meant to rule—I was never built for it." He shrugged. "I find the beggar lord a more natural role for me."

Around their ankles a thin mist began to appear, swirling up over the body of one, then both fallen vampires.

"Feneyaz?" Mihn asked, gesturing to the brother.

"I would think," Isak said, though he'd never met any of Zhia's three brothers. No matter how skilled a swordsman, against a white-eye wielding Eolis the result had never been in doubt, he realised, which made it likely they were both the lesser siblings.

"What about him?" Mihn said, looking at the statue. "He makes them his protectors while he sleeps?"

"A prison of his own making—it was done to the dragon in the Library of Seasons. He's under the weight of madness and his family's curse, so why not sleep until change comes?"

"And now?"

Isak stepped up to the statue to inspect it. It portrayed a man of middle years, lean of face and build, in armour similar to the plate Zhia wore under her clothes. He reached up and rapped his knuckles on the statue's forehead. It seemed solid enough, and cold to the touch. He wiped Eolis on his cloak and sheathed it, then took hold of the Crystal Skull at his waist before he dared touch the statue's black sword.

Nothing happened. Isak withdrew his fingers, rubbing them together. The scars faintly tingled in the proximity of such power. This was Termin Mystt, he was sure of it, but it was firmly lodged where it was, despite only resting in the statue's hand rather than being grasped—part of the same spell that kept Vorizh a statue, he guessed. He looked at the statue's hands: they were in exactly the same pose, but one was empty.

"How about a swap?" he said, drawing Eolis and resting it in the statue's hand in the same way as Termin Mystt, its tip resting on the ground. He felt a shudder run through the rock and, pressing his hand back against the Skull of Ruling, he attempted to take the black sword again.

A great gust of wind swept up from the dusty floor, but Isak barely noticed. This time as his fingers touched the black sword it flared, searing-hot, even as light burst from the Crystal Skull. Isak gasped and staggered back, his hand now firmly wrapped around the black sword's long grip—it was the only thing he could see through the white light, a midnight force that not even the power of the Skull could eclipse. Power surged up his arm with such ferocity he felt his bones creak and judder. Magic flooded his body and invaded his mind with shards of ice before the presence of the Skull balanced it.

He dropped to one knee, his great shoulders shaking with the effort of holding the weapon as dark stars burst before his eyes. Suns wheeled through his mind, scorching a path across the holes torn in his memory. Voices clamoured in his ears, hundreds, thousands of beseeching voices, and as he moaned under the pressure, his own voice felt like the vengeance of the heavens, crashing through his mind.

Distantly he felt a hand under his shoulder. He tried to scream a warning for Mihn, but his voice was not his own. His heart boomed in his chest, his ribs shrieked in pain and the rune on his chest burned once more, the stink of charred flesh filling his nose.

And then the hands holding him felt blessedly cold against the surging heat of magic, a foundation stone upon which Isak braced himself. The heartbeat of more than one man pulsed in those hands, it was dozens, *hundreds*. Through the rune on his chest he could feel them, with Mihn a second conduit to those who had bound themselves to him. The soldiers of the Ghosts, their brute strength a force of its own in his veins, marched alongside the cold, remarkable men of the Brotherhood, and leading them all, the iron-hard will of Legana's sisterhood.

Blood trickled from his nose as Isak embraced his Skull's power and drove back against the monstrous, remorseless flow of power from Termin Mystt. Air returned to his lungs and he gasped furiously to clear the swirl in his mind. He felt Mihn urge him up and at last his strength returned, allowing him to rise once more and face the obsidian statue.

Shards of black glass were sloughing off it, flaking away with increasing speed. The wind continued unabated, whipping up great gusts of air and tearing clouds of dust from the statue. More and more disintegrated until, in a matter of heartbeats, just an armoured man was left, his sapphire eyes staring down at them through the breeze that threw his long hair across his face.

With jerky movements, the man—Vorizh Vukotic himself—looked at the sword now in his hand. The emerald pommel of Eolis shone in the weak light as he stiffly raised the weapon hilt-first up to inspect. His eyes widened as he recognised the weapon.

"So it begins," the man rasped.

Isak echoed his movement, struggling for a moment to bring up the black weapon to inspect. His hand shook, the raw power of Termin Mystt barely shackled by the Skull. It was perfectly, flawlessly black. Only its outline was visible; although Isak could feel some form of decoration on the guard against his wrist, he could see nothing. His left hand he kept pressed against the Skull at his waist.

An otherworldly echo surrounded him, filling his lungs and mind. Isak realised it was the presence of the divine, some part of Lord Death bound to the sword. The memories of Ghenna returned to him; those awful sights and agonising sensations, but he had endured them somehow, and thus prepared, Isak refused to submit to the terror welling inside him.

Vorizh turned to look at the bodies of his siblings as they faded beneath ever-increasing mist. Isak tensed, ready to raise the black sword, though a dull ache ran through his bones and magic prickled on his skin, but there was no outrage on the vampire's face; there was barely even curiosity.

"You had help in the tests?"

"Your last test was killing your brother and sister—don't fucking dare take exception to how I've gone about it," Isak gasped. "I've travelled most of the way across this country you've torn apart and I'll gladly kill you now."

His voice sounded hollow, distant, as if altered by the presence of the sword. Behind him, Isak sensed Mihn flinch, and her remembered the small man's account of being in Death's throne room.

The vampire's face twitched, muscles moving uncertainly into the configuration of a smile. "You bear the burden with great resilience; your Gods made you well, white-eye," Vorizh rasped. "Now I will help you become their equal."

Isak spat on the ground and turned away. His face was taut as he fought to control the raging forces inside him, but that was nothing new to the savage-tempered white-eye.

"Spare me. You'll help me how I say because you know what I can give you." He paused. "Or relieve you of, mebbe. Either way, shut up and follow me. I think your sister wants a word."

CHAPTER 18

EVERY STEP BACK UP THROUGH THE ZIGGURAT was an effort. Isak's limbs were heavy and sluggish, as though he wore armour of lead. The sword itself weighed nothing, but Vorizh had been right to call it a burden: it dragged at his mind and sapped his strength, filling his head with the buzz of wild energies and amplifying the voices of daemons carried on a breeze his cheek couldn't feel.

Behind him Isak could hear the soft, neat pad of Mihn's bare feet and sensed the man keeping as close as he could. Of Vorizh there was no sound, and more than once Isak turned to check the vampire was still with them. The sight was far from encouraging. Behind Mihn was a shifting, restless mass of shadows; only the vague outline of a human form remained—that and two darkly gleaming sapphire eyes.

A lambent glow on the stairs ahead told Isak it was the last flight to go. He almost groaned with relief as he struggled up them and onto the night-shrouded upper floor of the Grand Ziggurat. A dozen Black Swords were there now, each man holding one of the spluttering mage-torches to cast white light over the proceedings. With Termin Mystt in his hand Isak could no longer taste the magic leaking from the torches, only a sense of a great twisting cloud of magic centred on him.

He looked past the people waiting and realised each level of the ziggurat was similarly lit, as was the shoreline of the island on which it stood, and the wide bridge they had crossed to reach it. For a moment he entertained the hope that the sensation was just that, the concentric rings of torches surrounding him, but a part of him recognised the deeper resonance in the air, like looming storm-clouds, when even the Gods held their breath.

"Lord Sebe," intoned Priesan Sorolis, "you have walked the labyrinth and hold the mysteries of Vanach in your hand. The signs are fulfilled, the mysteries revealed."

The old woman's face was solemn, but she glanced momentarily at the third figure that left the ziggurat, and when she did, her hand started to shake in the folds of her robe.

She raised her arm to indicate the brightly lit bridge leading to the shore. "A place has awaited you in the Hall of the Sanctum since our founding; come."

Isak didn't respond, but he looked at his companions, feeling light-headed in the breeze washing over them. Doranei and Veil smiled, relieved by his obvious success, while those more sensitive to magic stared aghast at the black sword in his right hand. He glanced down at it and tried to flex his fingers. A flicker of worry ran through him as his numb fingers failed to respond, then at last his muscles became his own again, though his fingers moved only fractionally.

"Lead on," Isak croaked, still staring at the sword apparently fused point-down to his hand.

The Priesan obeyed and headed back down the levels with the rest of the Sanctum, but Isak made no move to follow. He was too concerned by the fact that he could not remove his hand from the grip of Termin Mystt. There was no pain, but it felt as though he were the one being gripped, not the other way around.

"Isak?" Vesna said cautiously as he approached his friend. "Is all well?"

Isak looked up warily, until he realised Vesna hadn't spoken loud enough for the Black Swords to hear above the hiss of their torches. That he had spoken at all told Isak he was betraying too much.

"It is," he replied. "We have what we came for."

"More than that, it appears," Legana commented, the divine light inside her waxing stronger the closer she came to the sword. Then she focused her attention on Vorizh as the vampire went to the edge and surveyed the city beyond. "We are thirteen now?"

Zhia stepped forward, watching her brother as intently as one might a cobra. "Brother," she said without affection.

"Sister of mine," Vorizh replied with a small smile. "See this city I built? This monument to the curses of Gods?"

"You never told me what you were planning."

He turned with shocking, blurring speed. "*Tell you?*" Vorizh hissed. "Of course not! You are too rash, for all your plotting. You always lacked vision; remember the lover you took all those years ago, the chaos it caused? You only ever see how to further your own ends in the game, never how to end it. Better you than our noble Prince Koezh, of course; our solemn heir of suffering could never resist an added burden, but both were found lacking."

"And now you have found one worthy?"

Vorish turned, unblinking, towards Isak. "Perhaps. There is change on the wind, of that I am sure."

"Daemons too," Daken growled. "Don't mean shit, though."

Vorizh cocked his head at the white-eye as Daken advanced slowly towards him. "You have a pet? One that smells of the Gods?"

Zhia shook her head as Vesna stepped in front of Daken to halt the man's advance. "Just a white-eye whose goal is glorious battle; do not indulge him."

"Another day then, lapdog," Vorizh called to Daken. "Enough battle even for your thirsty heart is at hand, I think."

The crackle of tension in the air awakened Isak from the distraction of Termin Mystt. "Is this permanent?" he demanded of Vorizh, looking at his hand. He was holding the long weapon in a reverse grip that was completely impractical if it came to fighting.

The vampire bestowed upon him a reptilian smile. "Unless you can remove your own hand, dead man," he said with a flourish of black-iron-clad fingers. "I smell the marks of daemons upon you, the endless torments of the pit. What did they do to you in the Dark Place? Perhaps your hands grew back more than once down there, before some God plucked you out and back into the light."

Isak staggered, struck by a sudden weight of memories; flashes of light burst before his eyes as lines of hurt flared across his body. Again it was Mihn who reached his side and supported the huge white-eye with a strength beyond that of his small stature.

"Aha, it was a thief, not a God!" Vorizh crowed. "Would you venture that way a second time, I wonder, little man? One day my soul may follow a similar path; what price would you ask of me for such foolish devotion, thief?"

Mihn matched the vampire's gaze unafraid. "After the cruelties you have caused Vanach's people, the anguish dealt by your own hand? Could you make amends for such a thing?"

"If your price is an apology, I would be a madman to refuse it," Vorizh said, his eyes glittering in the dark.

"You are a madman," Mihn said, turning his back on Vorizh as Isak started for the stair to follow the members of the Sanctum, "and so I offer you nothing."

When they reached the entrance, Isak paused to summon his strength. The ziggurat was the highest point for miles around, and he felt like one missed step and he would tumble, crashing into madness or death.

"So it looks like life did have a plan for me, after all," he muttered to Mihn, who was still struggling to bear as much of Isak's weight as possible. "The balance of forces, controlling something inhuman inside."

"Could the Gods even have planned such a thing?" Mihn asked sceptically.

The relief on his face was plain when Isak responded with a laugh, "No, but it'd be nice to have someone to blame. Not even Azaer forced me into these choices. This life's my own."

"But you can control the forces?"

Isak nodded. "It looks like I've made myself into the tool required for the job." He made a show of prodding Mihn in the chest as he straightened, taking his weight off him. "Never say I don't plan ahead, eh?" He took a deep breath and surveyed the illuminated road. There had to be hundreds of soldiers out there, thousands, even. Faint movement in the streets beyond told him the troops were not alone, that the people of Vanach were creeping closer to see their long-awaited saviour. The Gods' plan was not for most to know, but some things would inevitably have escaped the Commissar Brigade. What it meant for the faithful servants of the Gods, only time would tell.

The question is, have they learned to fear any change, or are they desperate for release?

"My Lord?" called a trailing member of the Sanctum, the tall one from the Night Council who looked like a eunuch, Priesan Horotain. "Do you need assistance?"

"Just a moment's peace'd do," Isak muttered. He started off down the stairs, his companions following closely behind, Zhia and her brother bringing up the rear.

Should I tell her what I found down there? Isak wondered, a glance back showing him the distance between the two vampires. *Does she already know? They'll recover, maybe even find their eldest brother waiting, but she's a cold one. From all I hear Koezh wouldn't stand for enslaving their weaker siblings, but Zhia? There's no way to tell; she feels the suffering of others but she's still a politician.*

He returned to the task of descending the stairs, trying to stop his uncertain legs pitching him forward into the night, but as he descended the great ramp that led from the lowest level to the island shore, he turned towards a strange scent on the air. It was hard to discern against the overpowering presence of Termin Mystt, but he was certain something had changed; some new presence lingered nearby.

"Anyone else sense that?" he murmured.

Fei Ebarn shook her head when Isak turned to her, but Vesna and Legana nodded, their attention focused on the unknown.

"*More than one thing*," Legana said into Isak's mind, "*a presence in the streets—a presence in the lake.*"

As though in answer to his question, a figure loomed up from the lake surface ahead of them, startling the nearby soldiers, who scrambled out of the way. The figure standing waist-deep in the water was joined by another, then a third and a fourth; lean, grey faces all silently watched Isak. Heavy, discoloured armour was bound to their filthy bodies by belts and straps, baldrics and fraying leathers. Massive two-handed swords and axes were stowed on their backs and each stared at him through a curtain of dripping, bedraggled hair.

Shock froze Isak to the spot as he saw a gaping, bloodless wound on the neck of one, a mangled arm hanging useless from another. Their pallor was not because of cold or injury; these men were already dead. Doranei had called them the Legion of the Damned.

"Zhia," Isak called softly as the panicking Black Swords fell back in disarray, abandoning Isak's party as they scattered, "is this your doing?"

"The Legion do not obey me," she replied, advancing to join him, "only my eldest brother and their own leaders."

The four sodden figures offered perfunctory bows to Zhia, but Isak could see their attention was focused on him. Dead, milky eyes observed his every movement, but only when Isak raised his black sword in anticipation of an attack did the closest advance another few steps, stopping just at the water's edge.

Vesna was immediately in front of Isak, his own sword drawn, sparks crackling from his black-iron arm, but the undead soldier appeared not to notice him. The muted scent of decay reached Isak's party: not rotting flesh, but some mouldering odour mingling with the smell of mud on the shore.

Without warning the four dead soldiers dropped to one knee and bowed their heads. Their leader spoke a brief sentence in a grating, ruined voice, then raised his head to look Isak in the eye.

"They greet you," Mihn translated hesitantly. "You bear the sword that can free them from their curse. They pledge themselves to you, in the hope that you will do so once they have proved worthy."

"Free them? How?"

"Their souls were sold," Vorizh provided, walking forward until he was face to face with the leader of the legion. The undead warrior stared at him as though desperate to draw his greatsword and attack, but whatever his wishes, he did nothing beyond facing Vorizh down.

"The necromancer who made them this way tricked them into selling their souls. Those who fall in battle are damned."

"And you can't undo it?"

Vorizh cocked his head at Isak. "Why would I wish to? They would have all returned to dust by now, had they lived mortal lives."

"You call that life?" Isak demanded in disbelief.

Before Vorizh could reply an arrow had flashed out from the darkness to strike the nearest of the undead in the side. A second shot dropped between them, then a third caught one in the shoulder.

The leader snarled and drew his weapon, growling some order, and a dozen more damned rose from the lake, weapons ready, as the first four turned to face the knot of soldiers at the bridge-mouth aiming crossbows at them. They advanced with unnatural swiftness, ignoring the hasty shots that danced between them.

Two more were caught, one high in his chest, but they snapped the shafts and continued on regardless.

"No, wait!" Isak called after them.

The warriors stopped dead, their leader turning to regard Isak once more.

Whether they understood his words or not, the command was clear enough, but before Isak could work out what to say next Mihn broke the tense silence. "My Lord, look at the bridge."

There were more sputtering lights appearing on the bridge as squad upon squad of Black Swords rushed towards them. The crossbowmen at the front were frantically reloading as a commissar bellowed orders, gesturing furiously in Isak's direction.

"I can hear them shouting," Mihn said quickly. "An army of daemons kneeling to you—Isak, they're saying you have tricked them: they think you are Aryn Bwr reborn. They have ordered the attack!"

Isak looked around. The Black Swords still on the ziggurat were staring down at them in horror, too bewildered to act, but judging from the numbers massed on the far shore the Night Council had come prepared for any excuse to turn on them. He'd already noticed the massing Black Swords; he didn't want to find out if that was enough to fight perhaps the most lethal group of individuals ever gathered.

"Something tells me they're not going to care about casualties," Vesna said, again placing his body between Isak and danger. "Do we really want to burn a path through thousands of men just following orders here?"

"Why not?" Vorizh asked, his eyes bright with delight. "You hold the power of the Gods in your hand—shatter them with a word! Be as Death, walking the battlefield once more."

Isak didn't bother replying as he scanned the island for options. There were other bridges, one leading to the far shore, another to the temple island further out on the lake. "Anyone see any boats?" he asked.

"Not here," Vesna replied, "and we're not getting across either bridge without a bloodbath."

"You want to defend a temple again? Remember Scree?" Isak demanded, but he didn't wait for an answer. Vorizh had silently withdrawn to the great stone ramp and Isak pursued him, determined not to let the vampire from his sight if he could help it.

Meanwhile Zhia had waved back the Legion of the Damned and taken their place facing the Black Swords. She reached out one hand and a nimbus of white light began to circle her. The dark surface of the lake below the bridge seemed to twitch and jump with every intoned word before rising like a leviathan and swallowing the massive bridge. Darkness enveloped it, extinguishing the torches on the nearer half and prompting terrified cries as the men were suddenly struck blind and soaked through.

"Where are you going?" Isak called after Vorizh.

The vampire ignored him and went to the statues flanking the ramp, the huge stone wyvern statues that looked so out of place there. He placed a hand on one and began to intone his own spell, but as Isak watched he realised it was not a spell being cast but one being unravelled.

Cracks started appearing on the hind leg of the first wyvern, accompanied by a great creak and the groan of stone under stress. Isak faltered, his left hand pressed against his belly as he remembered another wyvern and another time, but his memories were swept away by a more immediate shock: the grey skin of the statues had started to crumble and fall away, revealing crimson-hued scales underneath. The monster looming over Vorizh shuddered and stone cascaded off its flanks like a disintegrating clay mould. Its wings jerked ponderously and stretched up towards the heavens.

Isak turned back to his astonished comrades staring up at the emerging wyverns, except for Zhia, too busy with her delaying spells, and Mihn, whose attention was focused on the dark mass of soldiers on the bridge.

"To the temple island," Isak ordered, forcing himself to turn his back on the wyverns. Vorizh clearly had his own plans, whether or not it included the rest of them. "All of you, go!"

He shoved Doranei, the nearest, towards a paved path that led around the island to the ornate covered bridge that led to the temple island. There would be guards, of that he had no doubt, but it looked like it might be the least bloody path away from here. The Night Council had clearly been biding their time and looking for any excuse to erase the threat to their control. They would push forward as hard as they could rather than waiting for cooler heads to prevail.

"My Lord," Vorizh called, and Isak turned to see the two wyverns nearly free of the stone that had encased them. One was stepping down from the pedestal where it had stood for so long; the other was struggling to pry the remaining pieces of stone from the leathery membranes of its wings.

"It is time for us to leave," Vorizh said, indicating that Isak should take the second of the beasts.

The monster raised its blade-like muzzle to the heavens and screeched deafeningly, then shook its body and snapped its jaws with ravenous intent as it peered at the figures below. Its head started weaving from side to side as it tried to make out what was happening below it.

"You think I'll abandon my comrades?"

"What choice do you have?" the vampire laughed. "To swim with a sword fused to your palm? And you balk at killing Black Swords—men who are nothing to you, men who have abused and murdered their own, for reasons of twisted nonsense. The cruelty and horror they have inflicted—each one should be punished for their crimes, for joining the oppressors out of cowardice or malice at least. Yet you refuse to make that judgment, you who have killed many times before, no doubt. So if you will not fight, here is your alternative!"

"I'll find another choice," Isak said, and Vorizh looked contemptuous before he offered Isak a florid bow and barked a command at the wyvern. With one beat of its enormous wings the creature steadied itself, then leapt into the air, closely followed by its fellow.

Isak went to follow the rest of his companions. Mihn was yet to move; the black-clad man still standing beside Zhia and staring out at the confusion on the bridge.

"Mihn? What are you doing?"

"I—I thought I saw . . ." He looked up at Isak. "It does not matter. I am coming."

They ran together as fast as Isak could manage, Zhia close behind. A squad of Black Swords blocked the way, but Vesna was already leading the charge; his sword cut a scarlet trail through the night. As the air filled with

Daken's roars and the whip-crack of lashing energies, the ten soldiers simply vanished from their path.

The few other Black Swords remaining on the island fled in the face of such effortless slaughter and they found themselves unimpeded until they reached the bridge. It was half the width of the other, and supported by half a dozen arches.

A reinforced gatehouse stood at either end, blocking the way, but Isak stabbed down onto the gate's hinges with the tip of Termin Mystt. He missed the edge, instead driving the black sword against the wall, but Death's own weapon tore through the weathered grey stone as if through butter.

Fei Ebarn sent darting arrows of flame to dissuade anyone within the guardhouse from attacking while Isak chopped artlessly with his reversed sword at the listing gate until the way was clear. He led the rest out onto the bridge, ignoring the heavy beat of wings behind them, and attacked the few soldiers still standing their ground. To no one's surprise, Termin Mystt parted armour, weapons and flesh with as much ease as it had the stone, killing men with brutal sweeping strokes.

The bridge was covered with arches and small, interconnected buildings, which turned out to be small shrines running the length of the bridge. The moonlight illuminated curved letters inscribed into the parapet running the length; Isak guessed it was an extended prayer rather than some incantation of protection. Beyond the torches fixed at set intervals along the walls adjoining the gatehouse he could see little.

They were alone now, Isak realised; the Legion of the Damned had not followed them around the ziggurat, though Mihn continued to glance back as though watching for them. Without meaning to Isak conjured the image of hundreds of dead men tramping stolidly through the midnight waters beneath them.

All following Death's own weapon, Isak reminded himself. *The dead march in my wake.*

He shivered and pushed the thought from his mind. It was not something to dwell on; just that fleeting moment was almost enough to overwhelm Isak with the consequences of what he was doing.

"We punch through the gate and look for boats," Isak declared, pointing to the only other exit from the temple island. They could all see the hundreds of soldiers crossing the bridge to the nearer mainland.

"And if there aren't boats?" Zhia asked.

Isak scowled and looked down at the black sword he carried. "Then we may have no choice."

At the gate Isak sensed a vast gathering of power on either side of him. Fei Ebarn and Zhia both reached out to flay the defensive walls with arcs of flame while Vesna drew on his own Skull and punched the closed gate with raw power. Howls came from inside as stars burst along its length and the gate was smashed inwards, leaving nothing but blood and mangled flesh beyond it.

A great half-dome, the Temple of Alterr, rose behind the guardhouse. It was lit fitfully by ornate silver braziers. A square block stood to the right of that, the open peaked doorway declaring it to be the Temple of Death.

"That way," Isak said, pointing to a break in the walls where a pebbled slope led down to the water, but as they approached Isak realised the wooden posts flanking the slope were clear of boats.

"Looks like we'll just have to fucking kill 'em all," Daken announced as Isak looked around in vain.

"There's got to be another way," Isak muttered. "Any ideas?"

"Heretics! Servants of the damned!" shrieked a voice in the lee of the wall, startling Isak, until he realised he wasn't being attacked. He peered into the shadows and saw a man sitting in the mud, half hidden by a supporting timber. Hugging his knees to his chest, he stared at them all, his eyes wide with blind terror, and his voice descended into a low, wordless gibber.

"Perfect," Zhia declared and reached out towards the man, who didn't even have time to cry out as he was dragged through the air. Deftly Zhia grabbed the man by the throat, handling him as if he was as light as a rag-doll, and brought the keening figure up to her mouth to bite hard into his jugular. The man flailed and spasmed in her grip, but the small woman stood as still as a statue while she drank, and then held him up to inspect her handiwork. Trails of blood, black in the moonlight, ran down her chin, and the wound in his neck pulsed darkly down onto the scarf that marked him as a commissar.

With a brush of her finger Zhia sealed up the man's wound. The man fell limp and she tossed him aside to fall like a dead thing on the moonlit ground.

"He'll bring us our horses tomorrow," she announced to her companions. "I'm sure the city will be in too much chaos for anyone to notice their absence straight away."

"Since when did you care about horses?" Doranei demanded.

She smiled. "A girl with skin as fair as mine needs to be prepared. Some of us don't like to travel light." She wiped the blood from her face and licked her fingers clean while Isak skirted further around the temple of Death until he had a better view of the bridge they now had to cross. Thanks to the torches he could see the soldiers had stopped near the centre: the nearer half of the bridge was in darkness. Most importantly, there weren't Black Swords charging towards them.

"What's going on?" he wondered aloud, and magic burst into life around him as the mages drew on their Crystal Skulls to investigate.

"Fighting," Ebarn reported after a moment. "Different factions of commissars?"

Even as she said it they caught the clash of steel rising above the lap of water, punctuated by the sound of distant shouting.

Isak closed his eyes and let his senses rise up through the cool air, borne by the churn of magic inside him. High above the city he felt the invisible dart of bats come to greet him, drawn by their master's sword. Isak ignored Death's winged attendants, leaving them to swoop and spiral around his mind while he looked further still. There were daemons out there, keeping to the dark places beyond the light on the city walls, but he feared that might not last if the blood of hundreds was shed and the threat of Termin Mystt left.

"They're not soldiers," Zhia added, opening her eyes again, "that's a mob. I think the people of Vanach have worked out what the Night Council intend for their saviour."

"They're going to be sorely disappointed with me," Isak muttered. He looked back at the bridge they had just crossed. There was movement on it already: the first few pursuers were summoning their bravery. "More importantly, where do we go now? It won't be long before we're cornered here."

No one had any answer at first, then Veil ran down the tiny pebble beach to the water's edge. "Zhia," he called, "just how powerful is the sword?"

She laughed. "'How powerful'? What sort of an idiot asks that?"

"Okay, so I'm an idiot: let me ask instead, how much of its power can Isak safely use?" he snapped back. "The Menin attack on a Narkang border town—I heard they used magic to freeze the moat."

"You want to freeze the entire lake? Are you mad? I can't even see the far end from here!" Isak exclaimed.

"Not the whole lake, just enough for us to walk on," Veil persisted, pointing with his twin spikes. "Rivers and lakes freeze in winter, don't they, but not completely: we just need a foot or so on the top, just enough to cross on, surely."

"Ice?" Isak said thoughtfully, joining Veil. "Why not?"

He touched Termin Myst to the lapping water and closed his eyes. He had never learned how to do such things in the past, but with such astonishing power at his command he guessed finesse wouldn't matter that much. By focusing the earth-shattering power through the image in his mind, it should be done easily enough.

The wind immediately picked up and someone behind him gasped as the temperature immediately plummeted. Isak felt the cold on his skin: a sheen of moisture on scars that still remembered the heat of the Dark Place. The crisp smell of frost appeared on his clothes as magic began to pour through the black sword and into the water below. Opening his eyes, Isak watched the black surface of the lake grow cloudy, then whiteness spread as quickly as flames through straw, a menacing crackle cutting the tense silence around them. Before long a white path had spread before him, driving like a spear-thrust out across the water towards the far shore.

Vesna came to Isak's side. "That's a long way," he commented, watching the strain on Isak's face.

"No choice," Isak said breathlessly, his attention never leaving the water. "Soldiers on this shore."

Vesna stepped back as Isak redoubled his efforts. A dull pain appeared in the back of his mind and the Skull of Ruling was hot against his skin, but he knew he couldn't stop. The ice road continued to surge forward, then he tasted a more familiar flavour on the air and broke off momentarily to look around him. Zhia stood a little way back, her Skull held out before her, her lips moving silently.

Isak didn't need to ask about this spell; it spoke to the very heart of him: Zhia was calling a storm. Above their heads, clouds started to form, blotting out the light of the stars and moons while weaving a skein of shadows over the island and Isak's ice road. The longer they had to escape the better, Isak realised, and the thought prompted him to look over to the two bridges where the commissars would be pursuing them.

He narrowed his eyes, momentarily forgetting the task at hand. "They're no closer," he commented. "Why's that?" Unless others were moving ahead of the white torch-lights, the pursuers from the ziggurat island had stalled just beyond halfway across. Just when they were cornered, the pursuit had faltered, but there couldn't have been enough citizens there to face down the soldiers.

Isak turned to his companions, looking from one to the next. "Where's Mihn?" he said quietly, and when the small man didn't speak up or step out from behind someone Isak's voice became thunderous. "Where the fuck is he?"

Legana pointed towards the bridge they had just crossed, and a leaden ball of dread appeared in Isak's stomach.

"*A chance taken*," she said into his mind. "*That's what he said before he stopped.*"

"What sort of fucking chance?" he demanded, moving towards her with murder in his eyes. Vesna put his body between them, but he too looked like a man needing answers.

Legana's expression didn't change. If Isak's sudden advance had alarmed her, the Mortal-Aspect gave no sign. She raised her slate so she could explain to all of them, not just Isak.

—*Recognised someone.*

"Who?"

A shrug.—*Buying time.*

Vesna turned back and gripped Isak's forearm. "She's right, Isak: it doesn't matter now. Mihn's made his choice, and we need to move."

Isak snarled and grabbed the Farlan hero by his throat. "Doesn't *matter?*" he rasped, lifting Karkarn's Mortal-Aspect clean off the ground. "It fucking *does* matter to me."

Vesna hung limply in Isak's one-handed grip—he knew the young man's temper well enough—but before either could say anything Legana moved around Vesna and gently rested her fingers on Isak's shaking arm.

"*Mihn decided to delay them. Do not waste the opportunity he has given you.*"

"Sounds easy coming from a heartless bitch like you," the white-eye snapped.

"*One who has also tied herself to both of you*," she replied calmly. "*One who knows he's not dead yet, and if we get clear, wears no armour. He might still be able to swim to safety.*"

Isak's face tightened as he fought the urge to lash out. Just the idea of Mihn sacrificing himself again sent his memory back to the floorless prison in Ghenna's lowest pit; where the pain he remembered in his bones had been allayed only by the sound of Mihn's voice cutting through the clouds of terror.

"I have to go back for him," he gasped, releasing Vesna and tottering backwards.

"No," Vesna croaked, "it's too late for that." He physically pushed Isak towards the ice, and the white-eye was unable to resist for the first few steps. Then he found himself staring dazedly at the white ice beneath his feet. He opened his mouth to argue, but at that moment Doranei and Veil both kissed the knuckles of their sword-hands and saluted, even as they turned and faced the ice road.

"See you when the killing's done, brother," the two men muttered together.

They joined Isak, the rest close behind, and Isak closed his mouth and put one hand to his sternum where Xeliath's scar was, the link Mihn bore. Legana was right: Mihn would be able to jump from the bridge—but he would be trying to hold off an entire army. Even with his skill, it was asking too much to see the man alive again, but the least Isak could do was not spend his life in vain.

"I'll see you again, my friend," he whispered to the night, "even if I have to reach into the Dark Place itself and drag you back out."

With that he turned and strode out across the blackness of the lake.

Mihn slipped around the pillar and pinned the spear against it, stepped in and drove an elbow into the soldier's face. The man released his weapon and staggered back as a straight kick to his sternum knocked him flying into a colleague and they both collapsed in a heap.

Before anyone could bring a crossbow to bear Mihn had ducked back behind the shrine, a set of three trees no taller than Isak with their branches intertwined. Instead of arrows a voice came from the other side, speaking the local dialect in crisp, precise tones.

"Stop, all of you—withdraw."

Mihn waited a moment, checking the figures on the ground nearby. Two were unconscious; a third was pawing at his throat as his crushed throat slowly asphyxiated him. There were more just around the shrine. Three he knew were all dead, and the reason the Black Swords in the front hadn't rushed around the shrine en masse.

"Will you not come out, brother?"

Mihn closed his eyes a moment. The voice evoked memories of crisp snow on the ground and incense in braziers, priests chanting slowly and the calm voices of the blademasters who'd trained him. He stepped out from behind the shrine, half-expecting to be killed immediately, but the soldiers had all stepped back.

There were five left waiting for him: a balding and bedraggled Menin wearing dirty mage's robes of blue and yellow loitered at the back, while Priesan Horotain of the Sanctum was flanked by a pair of Harlequins, a man and a woman. The one who'd spoken stood in front of them all. Like Mihn, the man had once been a Harlequin but was now something more. Both were dressed in black, a colour no Harlequin would wear; both were tattooed to signify new allegiances.

"We are not brothers," Mihn said at last.

Venn cocked his head. "True: you were cast out, I believe."

"And you abandoned your people," Mihn countered. "The greater shame is yours."

Venn laughed and took a step forward. Priesan Horotain looked confused by the exchange, which was being conducted in a language he would never have heard before, but one look from the white-masked Harlequins kept him silent.

"'Shame belongs to he who beholds it; child of one's own envy and malice.'"

Mihn rested the butt of his staff on the ground, ready at a moment's notice to bring it back up, but right now his counterpart was keen to talk; if that bought Isak more time to escape, he was happy to listen to whatever the black Harlequin might have to say.

"In my years of wandering I have learned a few things," he said to Venn. "One is that there is a quotation for every instance, words to fit whatever action one might need to justify. Increasingly, I find the solace of others' words diminishing."

"I justify nothing," Venn corrected him, "but shame has always been the most foolish of notions. When the Land is being reshaped and the Gods themselves quake, what meaning does shame hold?"

There was a slight smile on the man's face, perceptible in this light only to another student of expression and stance, but one Mihn recognised easily enough. "Tell me," he asked conversationally, "how long have you been thinking about this eventual meeting? How long has pride pricked at your side, wondering when we might cross swords?"

"Oh, I admit it readily," the other said, giving a small bow. "I have looked forward to this day ever since I heard Lord Isak had taken a manservant with a Harlequin name—Mihn ab Netren ab Felith, I believe you were known as?"

Mihn inclined his head. "I know you only as Venn."

"If we were kings, you would confess I had you at a disadvantage perhaps," Venn ventured, "but such niceties are as foolish as shame. Venn ab Teier ab Pirc is the lineage my father bestowed upon me."

"I recognise the name. The blademasters mentioned you in passing."

"In passing?" Venn scoffed. "I was *their* master long before they ever realised it."

Mihn smiled. "Your pride was mentioned, yes. It is one of the ways in which I am your better."

"No one is my better," he spat, "a fact I will gladly prove." He turned to one of his colleagues. "Marn, give him your swords."

There was a moment's hesitation; Mihn could imagine the shock hidden behind her mask: a Harlequin's blades should never be wielded by another. It was a testament to the thrall she was under that the woman paused for only a moment before reaching for the blades sheathed on her back.

Mihn raise a hand to stop her. "There is no need," he said. "I will not use another's swords."

"It will be no test of my skills if you are not properly armed," Venn declared. "It must be a fair fight."

"No fight is truly fair—it would be no more so if I took her swords."

"I suppose so," Venn agreed after a moment. "How long is it since you used the blades? You have walked the wilderness for many years now; that dulls any edge."

"My apologies, you misunderstand," Mihn said. "It would be unfair on you."

The anger was clear in Venn's eyes as the former Harlequin took in Mihn's boast, even if his voice remained level. "You make a bold claim—you think yourself the King of the Dancers?"

"Others did," Mihn replied, inclining his head in acknowledgement. "The masters who taught me, many elders of the clans. I have long since realised they were mistaken."

"Even before you met me—how perceptive of you."

Mihn shook his head. "No, there was no King of the Dancers; no prophecy of our own to warm hearts while we watched the Land and those who truly lived in it. It was just a fairytale to bind the clans together; to give them hope of what might one day be. Whether or not you make the claim, it is this hope alone that gives you sway over the rest."

"Defiant to the end. I am glad," Venn announced, "I had thought to honour the failed hopes of the clans by allowing you to die blades in hand, but if you prefer your staff, so be it."

"Wait," Mihn interjected before Venn could draw his swords, "I will take a knife, if you permit it."

The black Harlequin paused, wary of a ruse, then gestured for someone to toss Mihn a dagger. Marn did so, pulling one from the belt of a nearby soldier and throwing it for Mihn to pluck from the air. He inclined his head in thanks and swiftly cut the laces of his boots to slip his feet out of them.

"If we are to honour our past when we fight," he announced, feeling the slight warmth of his tattoos trying to wrap him in the jagged shadows of the bridge, "then I would fight as the man this life has made me."

Next he sliced open his sleeves to expose the tattoos running down his arms, ripping the cloth away until he was sleeveless. The rowan and hazel leaves echoed on the skin of every man of the Ghosts and Brotherhood looked stark in the glare of the torchlight, and highlighted how lean Mihn's arms were.

"No advantage, these," he explained, gesturing at the tattoos even as he brought his staff to a ready position, "but they show the man I am for all to witness."

"As do mine," Venn replied, touching a finger to the teardrops set under his right eye.

"A pale imitation, but nothing more," Mihn declared. "One I am proud to call my friend bears Karkarn's true mark, a ruby tear granted to him by the God of War himself. And you? Admit now why you are so eager for this fight—to prove yourself against me."

"History has placed us here," Venn declared, "and it is fitting such circles are closed in a manner of the myths we both learned."

Mihn shook his head. "As my lord would put it: bugger the myths. You want to prove yourself because you are my replacement." He moved his staff through a lazy circle, but Venn ignored it.

"I see it in your eyes. It is a question I have also asked: what purpose was intended for my life? Was there a plan that drove it all? I failed my people, broke under the weight of expectation, perhaps, but perhaps not without help. A failure of memory from a Harlequin, that is rare enough, but one who was expected to be the King of the Dancers? The one hoped to lead the clans out of history's servitude fails at the last moment? The coincidence is more than unlikely."

Venn drew his swords and advanced a step, but Mihn could see in his eyes that the man was transfixed. They began to circle warily. Mihn knew he was safe turning his back on the rest—Venn would cut any man or woman to pieces if they dared intervene.

"What being loves to play with words, to rewrite history or interrupt what is in a man's mind; to send a man down a new path, one that leads to a decade of wandering the meaner, more desperate parts of this Land? Such a path might make him embittered, making him hold a grudge against the life he never had, and desperate to prove himself. There were times I almost succumbed, almost listened to the anger in my heart, almost opened myself to a shadow's whisper—but I passed, in the end, and so another was found."

Mihn gestured expansively towards himself. "So come and get me. Test yourself against the one you replaced."

Venn didn't wait to refute the claim; he leaped forward with both blades zipping through the air. He moved with astonishing speed, slashing with each step of the dance, each recovery movement turning into a lethal lunge. Mihn gave ground steadily, turning and deflecting blows with calm precision before he thrust forward unexpectedly, stopping Venn's advance dead as the end of his staff thumped against the black Harlequin's chest.

Mihn's blow was at the fullest extent of his reach and too weak to cause the man injury, but it was enough to momentarily halt the fight. Venn's surprise at the other fighter making first contact was clear, but it shook him from his anger and Mihn saw a cold resolve take over. The Harlequin looked around at where they were fighting. The dead bodies on the ground were as much obstacles as much as the shrines and arches.

Venn pointed to the open stretch of the bridge where the Vanach soldiers were standing and ordered, "Back up, all of you." He spoke in the local dialect, and several hundred men jumped to obey, forcing their comrades back until they had cleared the best part of fifteen yards. Venn turned his back on Mihn and headed for the open ground, only to have his opponent seize upon the opening; he barely managed to bring his swords up in time, only just blocking one steel-capped end from cracking his skull. Venn found himself scrambling back as Mihn directed blow after punishing blow with each end of his staff, using every last scrap of his remarkable speed to prevent the Harlequin from recovering.

Venn twisted aside as he saw one strike coming, letting the blow glance off his shoulder as he cut brutally up in response.

Mihn caught the blow and danced back out of range.

"A coward's attack," Venn spat in the moment of stillness that followed.

"As you wish," Mihn replied, attacking again before Venn could reply, using the longer reach of his staff and striking overhead like an axe, forcing Venn to cross his slender swords to catch the blow. Mihn stepped inside the man's guard and kicked at Venn's knee, then drove hard into the pinned swords, attempting to push the lethal edges back into Venn's face.

Venn didn't wait for the next attack. Swords tangled above his head, he leaned closer and smashed a knee into Mihn's ribs. Turning, he tried to wrench the staff from Mihn's hands and flick it aside, following that with a powerful reverse kick at Mihn's head. Mihn ducked out of the way and launched up to kick at Venn's chin. His foot glanced off the man's shoulder and Mihn carried the movement on, throwing himself into a backflip, his staff above his head.

Venn's swords crashed down on it, just inches from Mihn's fingers, and he used the momentum to push one side of the staff down and kick at the side of Mihn's head. The impact rocked Mihn back, but he had dropped to a crouch even before Venn's sword came around for the kill. Thrusting his staff like a spear, Mihn caught Venn's lead arm, but in the next moment was forced to roll away as the second blade followed its arc around.

Bracing his staff on the ground, Mihn jumped up and retreated as his opponent drove forward, his sword-tips weaving intricate paths through the air. Mihn watched them come, one high, one low, and darted left at the last moment, battering down at the nearer blade with his staff. Again he tried to come inside Venn's guard, but the Harlequin was expecting it; he twisted and dropped to a crouch as Mihn drove an elbow at his arm, them surged up with one sword pushing the staff aside and the other heading for Mihn's throat.

Only Mihn's extreme athleticism saved him this time: he arched his back and wrenched his staff in a circle. He struck upwards and caught the lunging sword before it could be withdrawn, aiming diagonal blows down on Venn in furious succession. The speed at which he recovered his balance caught Venn by surprise. Now, mixing short, fast swings and jabs with longer strokes, he started pushing Venn back, herding him towards the parapet running down the side of the bridge.

Venn brought his swords close to his body, abandoning the killing lunges for tighter jostling work, edging up to Mihn's body, but Mihn matched his gambit, his feet feinting to kick as he pressed in on Venn's right side. He threw himself forward, driving Venn back and forcing his arm to bend at an unnatural angle as he absorbed the pressure.

Losing one hand from his staff, Mihn grabbed Venn's wrist and smashed his shoulder into the former Harlequin's, twisting the man's hand savagely as he did so. As he bent Venn's hand down, forcing the wrist back against his throat, he used the staff to push the other sword away. Venn tried to resist the pressure and keep hold of his sword, but Mihn kept forcing it until his fingers curled in on themselves and the wrist broke with a crisp snap.

Venn's fingers went limp, his grip broken, but the sword was still pinned against his body. The pair slammed back into the parapet together, Mihn shoving Venn's back against the stone edge. As he forced the black Harlequin to bend backwards over the edge, the sword's razor-sharp edge sliced the cloth of his tunic and traced a red line towards Venn's throat.

The sight of blood made Mihn freeze and Venn's eyes widened as he felt the cut of his skin. There was a moment of perfect stillness as both men realised the kill was there. Venn was able to watch his demise in his enemy's face.

But Mihn didn't press any further. His attention was focused solely on the faint glitter of light playing on the edge of Venn's sword.

"No," he whispered, and released the pressure against Venn's arm.

The sword fell, and the two men stood as close as lovers until Venn wrenched his body upright and brought his other hand up to bear. Dragging his remaining blade behind, Venn drew its edge across Mihn's belly and felt the steel bite deep, even as the man gripped his hand.

Mihn gasped and shuddered, his hands tightly clasped around Venn's broken wrist, even as he felt the sword tear up to his ribs.

The movement spun him against the parapet and Venn felt Mihn's breath on his face as a last gasp escaped his lips, but Mihn could not maintain the pressure and released his enemy. He sagged, one shoulder over the parapet while blood spilled down his legs. He looked up, fighting back the pain to stare Venn straight in the eye. "You will always know," he whispered, "that only my vow saved your life."

Venn didn't wait to hear any more. His ruined wrist clamped to his chest, the black Harlequin spun neatly around and smashed a foot across Mihn's face. His head snapped backwards in a spray of blood and then he was falling over the edge. Mihn fell, as limp as a dead thing, and disappeared.

Venn ran to the parapet and watched the dying man hit the lake with a dull splash. The black waters swallowed Mihn and closed above his body, the ripples of his impact lasting just a few seconds before the waves washed over them and erased any sign.

He stayed there a long half-minute, watching the inky surface below. It betrayed no sign of the man he had killed.

Eventually Venn nodded to himself. No man could survive that injury, he knew that with certainty. Even without the cold water and the exertion of swimming, Mihn would be dead in minutes from such a cut. Satisfied, he turned away.

No man of such skill deserves an audience when he dies, Venn thought to himself. *It is best I did not see the light extinguished from his eyes.*

"*A sentimentalist still?*" Rojak said in the recesses of Venn's mind. The minstrel laughed softly as Venn caught the faint scent of peach blossom on the wind. "*I did not appreciate the honour when King Emin left me to burn.*"

Venn tasted sour contempt in his throat. Rojak had been the first of Azaer's most remarkable followers, but the minstrel had never understood true warriors, men like Ilumene or Mihn. There was a commonality that could not be explained to others; that went beyond the act of one killing another. Rojak had always been contemptuous of fighting men, thinking all those who killed on command were the same.

He had hunted you for years, and still he could not bear to watch that last spark fade, minstrel.

"*Let us hope the creatures of Ghenna honour your friend so. I can hear their voices call out in the night. They sense a hunt is on.*"

Venn sighed and looked down at his right arm as the pain continued to build, one final reminder of the King of the Dancers. The break was bad; it might be a lasting legacy.

"Go," he croaked to the hushed crowd behind him. "Get after the rest."

CHAPTER 19

THEY ARRIVED WITH THE LAST RAYS OF EVENING bestowing an orange halo on the great oak that spread its protective branches over the heart of the village. The village was quiet, but not deserted. Faces peered at them from several windows and a handful of children stopped their play at the stream to stare at the newcomers. Nearby a clutch of splay-toed geese waddled towards them, honking, which in turn prompted barks from somewhere out of sight, but instead of dogs racing out to circle the party of horses, they were swiftly quietened.

Child Istelian nodded approvingly and gestured for the riders to halt. He was a man of middle years who'd been a labourer all his life until the First Disciple had plucked him from the crowd and handed him a white robe. Istelian's heart still soared at the memory: the approbation in Child Luerce's eyes and that fleeting, electrifying smile on the face of the sacred one himself.

"Captain," Istelian said softly. The soldier hurried to his side and Istelian granted him a benevolent smile. "You will wait for us here."

"Wait?" Captain Tachan repeated in surprise. He was a burly, bearded Chetse, but there was no doubting his loyalty to the Knights of the Temples. "Sure about that? This is Narkang territory now; best my men check the village out first."

Istelian frowned, the expression enough to halt Tachan's protests. Twenty soldiers to command, the proud warrior heritage of the Chetse tribe, years of wearing a Devoted uniform—yet he found himself taking orders from a commoner. He chafed at the change, but Istelian was pleased to see him recognise his place.

We are remaking the Land, Captain, Istelian said to himself, *and your noble lineage means little now. It is the pure spirits who lead, those without might or riches, and Ghenna shall welcome those who oppose our will.*

"These are poor folk, and pious, cherished by the Gods. They will welcome the message of our saviour."

"Certainly," Tachan agreed hurriedly. "I meant only that King Emin's men might be hiding among them. Our enemies will seek to harm one as blessed as you."

"The Gods will see me safe," Ilstelian replied, dismounting. The remainder of the white-robed preachers, seven in all, followed suit, and fell in behind their leader.

"As Ruhen walked out to face the army of daemons, so I shall face our enemies without fear. The Child's grace shall carry me through."

"But in case—" The soldier didn't get any further.

Istelian raised a hand and cut him off. "Come, Children of Ruhen," he said, holding his oak staff high, "let us visit peace upon these tormented lands." And with the rest trailing along behind he headed down the dirt track that led into the heart of the village. A long wicker fence served as the village perimeter, encircling the two dozen houses, while cultivated hedgerows penned several tracts of land beyond.

"These are honest, Gods-fearing folk," Istelian announced to his followers. "Their only loyalty to the distant king will be born of fear." He passed through an open gate, crossed the bridge and walked onto the common land, where a cluster of villagers were already awaiting him. Istelian walked up to them, observing the apprehension on their faces with a slight satisfaction. His stature was clear to these people, his purpose obvious in every step he took.

"Good folk, may I ask the name of this village?" Istelian asked them loudly.

The villagers glanced at each other like nervous sheep, before one found the courage to speak up. "Tarafain," said the youngest man, a broad-shouldered individual with a rolling local accent. "How can we help you, sir?"

"Sir. "—these people know their place.

"I seek the village elders. I would speak to you all of peace."

The farmer's eyes widened and he pointed mutely towards a stone-fronted building, clearly a tavern, on the far side of the green. There were a handful of people sitting outside and watching life in the village pass by.

With a curt nod to his guide, Istelian continued on.

The tavern was the only two-storey building in the village; blackened beams protruded out from lime-wash walls and smoke rose from a chimney at each end of the building. A youth lounged at the stable door, watching them with an insolent expression on his face.

"You are the village elders?" Istelian enquired of the four lounging outside the tavern door.

A middle-aged couple were sitting furthest from him, with an old crone on their right and a greying man opposite her. The elder two seemed to be scowling at him; the woman through poor eyesight, the man perhaps due to the mug of beer he gripped.

"I'm the headman," the younger man said in a deep voice. At last he did stand, and offered a bow of sorts. His wife jumped up beside him, but the other two made no such effort. "Hesher Vres at your service."

"I am Child Istelian," he said, inclining his head to return the greeting. "The Gods have favoured me to number among the ranks of Ruhen's Children. I would speak to you and your village of peace."

"Got enough o' that already," the old woman croaked. "Don't need no more; be off with you."

Istelian turned to regard the crone. She lacked the tattoos or charms he'd expect of a witch, but he knew in rural places those too stubborn to die were permitted much freedom to speak.

"And you are?"

"A woman who's seen enough o' this Land ta know we don't want nothing from the east."

Istelian sniffed. "You have no wish for peace? You would prefer King Emin steals your sons for his army of daemons? Are you a heretic?"

The old woman hissed and rapped her knuckles on the table-top. "My sons died in the king's service," she screeched, "and I'll have no false priest diminish their sacrifice!"

"I am no priest," Istelian replied smoothly, "and I know your sons served their king faithfully, but it is this king who now betrays those he should protect."

The older man growled and drained his beer. "Better watch your tongue, boy—some folk round here won't take kindly to you bad-mouthing the king."

"I know the thrall you are under, the fear of his armies you all feel." Istelian threw out an arm to gesture back the way he had come. "But I bring peace in my wake—the word of Ruhen to set you free, his servants to stand beside you against the tyranny of the great heretic."

"Great heretic?" the man echoed, rising from his seat to glare at Istelian eye to eye. "That's the twist o' your dogma now, is it? Make him out to be Aryn Bwr?"

"Ruhen's peace will free you all," Istelian insisted. He stepped back and raised his voice so those inside the tavern, no doubt listening intently, could clearly hear him. "Ruhen will free you from the cares of this Land, free you from the tyranny of war that has so plagued us, and drive off the daemons that continue to torment us."

"Hah!" spat the old woman, jabbing a thumb at her fellow doubter, "he's already seen those buggers off."

"You have faced down daemons?" Istelian asked, astonished by the outrageous claim.

"A few," the old man confirmed with a deepening scowl. "So what's this peace you offer then? Might it be the rule of the Knights of the Temples rather than Narkang? Tribunals and inquisitors? Religious law and counter-insurgency? How many'll die while you enforce your peace?"

"How dare you make such claims?" Istelian spat. "Ruhen is the emissary of the Gods and I am his mouthpiece. To question me is to question the blessed child, and that is heresy of the foulest kind."

"Not allowed questions under your peace, eh?"

"Honest devotion to the Gods is Ruhen's way. To accuse and undermine, to whisper and lie, that is the work of daemons and all such heresy must be rooted out."

The old man scratched his white-stubbled chin. "Aye, thought as much."

Istelian felt the fury erupt within himself; it was all he could do not to strike the man down where he stood. "Henceforth this village is under the protection of the Knights of the Temples!" he declared loudly, "and you are all now subject to the laws of the Gods. Rejoice, people of Tarafain, you are free from the tyrant of Narkang and protected by the peace of Ruhen!"

He spun around and snapped at the nearest of the Children behind. "You, summon Captain Tachan; inform him there are heretics in his village!"

"Heretics?" the old man mused as the Child ran back the way they had come. "Well, I must admit, Lord Death weren't so happy to see me last time He did."

"Silence!" Istelian bellowed and backhanded the old man across the mouth. "You dare speak of the Chief of the Gods in such irreverent tones? Headman Vres, this man is a poison thorn within your community. Assemble the village. His re-education must be witnessed by every man, woman and child."

The old man slowly spat a gobbet of bloody spit onto the ground at his feet. "Now that weren't so peaceful."

"You are a heretic!" Istelian hissed, grabbing him by the arm. "There can be no leniency shown to the enemies of the Gods—the daemon within you must be scourged from your body!"

The old man gave him a blood-tinted grin. "Daemon? Not quite." His weathered face twitched strangely, his cheeks shuddering as though something was fighting to escape from within. A white patina appeared on his skin, the lines around his eyes smoothing away as his brow softened and become narrower.

Istelian staggered back into his remaining attendants, one hand raised protectively. "What magic is this?" he screeched. "You are damned! Sold to some creature of the Dark Place!"

"It's more of a loan," the old man said, his voice higher now, almost feminine, "and I believe 'Goddess' is the appropriate term."

The man's pale, ghostly colour increased with every word and as he stepped forward, the fading light seemed all the more pronounced. "You claim to speak in the name o' the Gods, but you know nothing of them," the man said in a voice that cut the air like the crash of thunder. "The shadows in Ruhen's eyes are born of Ghenna's darkness, and I'll not leave this village to fall under the rule of a shadow. We don't submit to shadows here."

Istelian gaped, looking left and right in his astonishment. Faces had appeared at doors and windows, the ignorant rustics all staring at him without any of the respect due to him.

"You will *hang*," he croaked through the deepening gloom of evening. "It's a crime against the Gods to speak such things. Your tongue will be torn from your mouth and fed to the dogs—your eyes will be put out, your body driven onto a stake. All these torments await you in the next life, and so they will be visited upon you in this one too."

The sound of running feet seemed to spur him into movement and Istelian straightened up. "Captain . . ." The words faded in his throat as he saw only one figure approaching.

"Child Istelian!" the man called, sleeves flapping as he made up the ground. "They're gone—the soldiers, all gone!"

The old man stepped forward, a knife appearing from nowhere. Quick as a snake he slashed open Istelian's cheek, and the preacher fell back with a cry—

But the old man didn't follow up his assault; he just stood before the table with a satisfied look on his face, his knife still at the ready.

"Looks like your soldiers have learned to fear the ghosts of dusk," the old man said evilly, "but I think that'd be too easy for you. So let's find out how strong your faith really is, how much this peace of the shadow's really protects."

He grabbed Istelian in a surprisingly powerful grip.

Despite his desperate efforts, he couldn't break free, and when a second man, barefoot and dressed all in black, took his other arm, Istelian felt the strength drain out of his body. He was dragged back to the gate, and beyond it he saw the horses they had arrived on, those of the preachers and the Devoted soldiers too, all riderless and whickering nervously. The old man and his fellow daemon-worshipper took him past the horses and tossed him down into the dirt beside the road.

"See the trees?" the evil old man rasped, his face shining with what looked to Istelian to be a terrible delight. "The light's fading now. Might be you start to see eyes, appearing in the shadows below them." He grabbed Istelian's hand and slapped the bloodied dagger in it, closing it around the grip.

"There's your path, back through the trees. Lead your preachers that way and protect them with the peace you offered these folk today. Best you run, though—see if you can outrun 'em—for I swear on my tarnished soul you'll suffer if you ever come back here." He gave Istelian a shove with his boot and sent him sprawling in the dirt.

"Go!" the old man roared. "Run back to your shadow and tell him we're coming for him next!"

Vesna watched his friend slump against a tree and sink to the ground, his weight pushing the tip of the black sword a foot into the earth. Their makeshift camp was quiet, a full night and day of travel enough to drain them all. Hulf crept up to his master's thigh, instinctively wary of the terrible weapon Isak held.

"Isak," Vesna began before tailing off. He squatted down in front of the scarred man and tried to make Isak look at him, but the white-eye stared forward at nothing, while his left hand idly stroked Hulf's back. The dog's ears were flat against his head; his whole manner had changed, for he felt the loss of Mihn as deeply as the rest of them.

"You've hardly spoken since we left Vanach," Vesna said at last.

In the failing light Isak's right hand looked excessively shadowed. Perhaps it was just the comparison with his bone-white left, but to Vesna the skin looked darkened beyond the shadows of deep scars. The Mortal-Aspect's eyes were constantly drawn back to the black sword in Isak's hand. Nartis' lightning had burned the colour from Isak's left arm, imbued the skin with its own colour. Who could say what effect the Key of Magic, Death's own weapon, might have?

"There's nothing to say," Isak said, at last looking up at him. "He's gone."

The sun had gone down and the broad canopy of the fir trees under which they sat advanced the gloom further. Fei Ebarn was in the process of setting a fire while Zhia teased forth the shadows of the forest to hide its light. Isak's face was blank, drained of anger or any form of animation; that was what Vesna feared more than anything in a white-eye: dull, passive acceptance.

"You don't know that," Vesna tried, but Isak didn't even bother responding.

He did know; anyone could just by looking at Hulf, but Isak's soul had been tied to Mihn, and now the white-eye looked as though it had been cut out. Anger, even violence, Vesna could understand; that was how a white-eye reacted to loss, but not this: quiet surrender was reserved for those last moments of death, when all was done and all that remained was the spark in their eyes to fade. To see Isak so defeated troubled the Iron General side of Vesna as much as Mihn's loss wounded the mortal side of him.

"He had his reasons," Vesna persisted.

"Oh good. *Reasons*."

Vesna felt his hand start to shake. His grief at Isak's death had barely started to wane when Tila's murder gutted him entirely. Only the spirit of Karkarn had kept him moving, driving him to march west with the Ghosts, but the more he numbly obeyed his duty the more he had felt a part of himself wither.

As I hide from the pain, Vesna realised, *and put it aside in favour of duty, less of a man is left. I can feel the God inside me swallowing the loss, but it's an indiscriminate beast. Tila would never forgive me if I let the man she loved slip away. I have to endure this pain somehow, and so must Isak.*

"You had reasons too," Vesna said hoarsely, "reasons you didn't share with me. You left me to mourn your loss, to be the one Carel blamed for your death."

"I know."

"That's all you have to say?" Vesna asked after a long pause.

"What else is there? This is a war, people die. It'll claim more before it ends." Isak raised the black sword. "I hold death in my hand; can it be much surprise when those close to me are lost?"

"And you can just accept them?"

"We're close to the end now. I'll have time to mourn when I'm dead." He tugged his cloak a little more over himself and Hulf and the dog settled down at Isak's side to share in the white-eye's body heat.

"I'm so tired. Please, just let me sleep."

A part of Vesna wanted to smash his iron fist into Isak's face, to wake the monster inside him—anything to dispel this meek, empty shell of a man. But the general at the back of his mind told him it was time to retreat and fight another day; there was no point forcing the issue, not so soon after Mihn's loss.

Feeling like an old man, Vesna rose and left Isak to his sleep. At the fireside Veil and Doranei huddled together on a fallen tree and warmed themselves. They had watched the exchange without comment.

"Not what you expected, eh?" Doranei asked.

Vesna glanced back. "What I feared, maybe. Mihn was an anchor for him, just as Tila was for me." Even speaking her name twisted like a knife in his gut, but the pain was no stranger to Vesna these days and he wouldn't hide from it, not any more. "And Carel too. Without them, he's adrift."

"If he don't look dead, he's angry," Veil commented, "that's what we always said about Coran, the king's former bodyguard, when someone asked his mood. True enough for lots o' white-eyes—but Isak ain't like most of 'em."

"He don't look either," Doranei said, "and that makes me worry. We might have the means to kill Azaer, but without the will, that could mean nothing. There's a lot of death ahead of us yet—a whole lot of death, if what those Byoran soldiers said is true. The shadow won't care how many die to defend it; whole cities could fall and it'd just make us look like the Reapers or daemons it claims we are."

Veil clapped his remaining hand on his Brother's shoulder. "Aye and Isak can't follow your example. There are no wine cellars round here for him to crawl into for a month."

Doranei shrugged the man off, but he made no retort. He wasn't proud of how he'd dealt with his own mourning, Vesna knew that, but the look on the faces of both King's Men showed he wasn't living in shame either. It had happened, then Doranei had found a way through and not let his comrades down. Everything else was just pride.

An object lesson for the rest of us, Vesna thought, seeing once more the last flutter of pain on Tila's eyelids. *Face it all, and overcome.* His stomach felt hollow and a sour taste filled his mouth. He fought the urge to bend and retch, to empty a stomach that had barely been able to manage breakfast. The

War God's chosen looked away, hiding the tears that threatened in his eyes as Tila's voice echoed through his mind.

"Let's find some other way then," Vesna said in a choked voice, "lest the end in sight isn't the one we're hoping for."

Doranei reached into his tunic and pulled out his pack of cigars. He shook out the last one and lit it from the fire. "Give him time," he said at last. "The fire running through him from that damn sword, the shock of mourning—the man needs time. He came back from the Dark Place, that's a punch none of us could ride so easily. I'll never bet against him."

"In time to win this war? Azaer's forewarned, and everything you've told us says it's not one for a single, simple plan but has contingencies built into every scheme."

"You want to know one reason why we're so effective? The King's Men?" Veil asked abruptly. "Sure, we're good in a fight, and some of us ain't got a soul, but that's not the only reason. We live in a different Land to that of ordinary folk, soldiers too: everything we've seen and done sets us apart from the people we protect."

"We think different," Doranei continued. "The job makes you think different, and that's often the edge that counts. We do the unexpected, tackle problems in a way most wouldn't, and catch 'em unawares."

Veil pointed towards Isak. "Now just imagine how *he* thinks now, after all he's gone through. He saw the holes in his own mind and knew them as a weapon to cripple a man he couldn't beat in combat—a man none of us could, by design of the Gods themselves. Not even Azaer's seen that. Not even Azaer'll see him coming."

Vesna gaped. "And that's where your faith lies: in the fact that his mind's been damaged by horrors that might easily have destroyed him entirely? Isak's my friend, but—"

"Isak sees the Land different," Veil insisted, "and King Emin's genius ain't for politics, not really. He knows how to use others, how to direct their minds, develop their skills, nudge research or uncover strength they never knew they had. Doranei here, Coran, even Morghien and Ilumene too—we've all been refined by the man, all made better and more useful to him. Isak can change the entire Land, and with King Emin's guiding hand he'll finish the job."

"I'll never bet against him," Doranei repeated firmly, "and nor will you, whether you realise it or not."

Grisat eased his way around the corner table and sat with a view of the door. The evening trade was paltry, just half a dozen others in, along with the landlady. He scowled down at his beer—maybe it was just the stale-smelling piss they served here. The mercenary gingerly sniffed it. Certainly not something to shout about. He took a mouthful and grimaced as he swallowed: piss was just about right.

So much for Narkang folk knowing how to make a decent beer, he thought sourly. *I could have stayed in Byora for this sort o' crap.*

Without meaning to, Grisat's fingers went to the coin hung around his neck. It was still there, lurking under his jacket—a hard presence against the skin over his heart. The First Disciple, Luerce himself, had handed it to him, watched him put it on. It had been some sort of test, Grisat realised now—not of him, but of the coins.

All so eager for the honour now. He took another swig of the beer and shuddered, both at the taste and the memory of the fervent faces within Ruhen's Children. Their desperate and savage embracing of Ruhen's message frightened Grisat as much as Ilumene did. He'd not been a willing convert, just a mercenary looking to earn some coin who'd been forced into something more by Aracnan. When that black-eyed Raylin mercenary had died, Grisat had gone into hiding, hoping they would forget about him and the part he'd played in encouraging the Byoran cults' doomed uprising. The coin he'd taken off, but not daring to throw it away, he'd hidden it in the chimney of the room he'd taken—until Ilumene had tracked him down again.

Should've thrown the damn thing away, he thought miserably, prodding again at his chest. *Too late now.* The leather it was strung on was still around his neck, but it was unnecessary; now the coin stayed where it was, half-embedded in his skin. If Grisat put his finger on the metal surface he could feel the beat of his heart underneath. But some instinct told him to leave it well alone. He had left the leather loop on too, refusing to cut it away out of some desperate hope that he'd wake and find the coin was not slowly being drawn inside him.

If this is a dream, though, what does that make my nightmares?

He swallowed another foul mouthful. In his memory the shadows twitched and moved silently at the corner of his vision—never when he looked directly at them, but he could sense them always behind him. At first he'd thought the shadows some sort of salvation. *I suppose in some ways they were.*

Aracnan's mind had been decaying, slowly collapsing in on itself, and the fire of the Demi-God's increasing madness had been agony when he'd reached out to Grisat's mind. In his dreams the shadows had muted that touch, dampened the pain of Aracnan's lingering presence. It was only later the terror had seeped into his bones as a figure of shadow with eyes of emptiness stared through his soul.

The door opened and a woman stood in the doorway. She wasn't dressed for this part of town; her voluminous dress was of fine green cloth, and it reached the top of high, well-polished boots. Grisat blinked at her as the woman inspected the room, a slight curl of distaste on her lips. A plain grey cloak hung from her shoulders, open enough to see a matched pair of daggers belted to her waist and a fat necklace he guessed was a push dagger.

Mebbe she knows this part of town well enough after all.

Grisat gulped down half of the remaining beer and scowled at it again. The taste wasn't improving with familiarity. Without looking at the woman he slid two silver coins to the far side of the table. She made no sign of noticing, but went to the bar and ordered herself a drink, casually inspecting the other drinkers there while she waited for it.

Satisfied there was nothing unusual, the woman headed towards a free table, changing direction at the last minute to sit on his left, a seat that gave her the best view possible of the rest of the room. As an idle gesture she flipped one of the coins over so the king's head was face-down and slipped the second in her pocket.

From that she produced a blank coin like the one tormenting Grisat—ground down and scored with a knife so a circle was scratched on one side and a cross on the other. She didn't place it on the table, just turned it around in her fingers to show him both sides and returned it to her pocket.

"I was expecting someone else," she said coolly, one hand resting on a dagger grip. "Who're you?"

"Someone sent to pave the way. He'll be following soon enough."

"When I least expect it?"

Grisat grimaced. This woman was far too like Ilumene for his liking; he recognised the calculating eyes of a professional killer, the fondness for knives.

She picked up the small glass of cloudy liquor she'd ordered and knocked it back in one. "Orders for me?"

"Package for me?" he countered.

She looked at him appraisingly for a long time. Grisat did his best to ignore her scrutiny and knocked back the last of his beer. Seeing his shudder the woman flashed him a predatory smile. "Next time, ask for something stronger."

"Next time it'll be him sittin' here."

She nodded and reached into a pocket in the inside of her cloak. "Good." She drew out a flat leather pouch two hand-spans across and put it on the bench beside him. Grisat heard the clink of metal links within. "It was expensive," she said, touching the package with one finger. "Silver isn't cheap these days, nor are mages. Remind him that when you see him."

"You get paid for this?"

She smiled. "Handsomely. You one of those who found themselves in too deep before they knew they were even *in* anything?"

Grisat didn't reply. The fact that he wasn't the first, or likely the last, did nothing to cheer him. "Your orders," he began gruffly. "Alert your agents to be ready; get them to join up to a useful part of the army or something, if they aren't there already. How many knives can you muster?"

"Depends how good they need to be."

"Endgame quality."

A flicker of surprise crossed her face. "I hadn't realised. If we're that deep in I've maybe five besides me good enough for our friend with the beautiful scars."

"Use the best four."

She nodded. "Simple kills?"

"Each is carrying something the master wants. Securing it is the highest importance, but it'll never leave their sides, so most likely they'll need to kill to take it. They'll need to have time to escape or hand off the prizes."

"The targets?"

Grisat counted off on his fingers. "The Mortal-Aspect of Karkarn, Count Vesna. An illusionist, Camba Firnin. Some friend o' the king called Morghien. General Lahk of the Farlan Ghosts. A Brotherhood battle-mage called Fei Ebarn. High Mage Tomal Endine. You also need to surveil High Mage Ashain and the scryer, Tasseran Holtai—both likely to be somewhere near Moorview—for when your friend joins you."

"That's a bastard of a list."

"If it was easy, you wouldn't have been brought into play. You and yours have been kept back exactly for this sort of job. For each success you can name your price."

She raised an eyebrow at that. "Don't think you know our friend so well after all. He doesn't tend to take kindly to that sort of thing."

Grisat shrugged. "Special case, this one. He knows the value—"less they ask for something stupid, he'll be good for it."

"That should prove an incentive. I'll get to work," the woman said, smiling. "Do I tell them as soon as possible, or a particular day?"

"They take the opportunities they find." With that Grisat rose to leave, the package slipped under his own coat. Before he walked away he hesitated. The woman looked up warily, her hand again on her dagger.

"Those who get in too deep without noticing—you ever seen one get out alive?" he asked in a quiet voice.

She gave a cough of surprise, pity and wonder mingling on her face. "The reluctant ones? No. That might change with the end in sight, but my advice is to accept it. You look like a mercenary, right? Well embrace the cause and enjoy your pay—there's no quitting and our *friend* prefers an agent who needs him, not just fears him. Expensive whores, drugs, jewels—doesn't matter what, if you're his all the way and you lose the hangdog face, he'll not piss you away so easily."

She looked down and flicked her empty glass with her fingernail. "Send the barman over on your way out."

Chapter 20

Lord Fernal sat alone in a dim study, picking at the plate of cold meat and cheese sitting on a table beside him. The window shutters were open and he watched the last of the daylight recede in the east, slivers of light gleaming on the drifting river that cut across his view. The fields and hedgerows were already dark, but his predator's eyes caught the small movements of rabbits on the fringes of the human domain. He watched them moving warily, ears twitching at each shout and laugh from the banquet hall nearby, but not driven from their grazing by the clamour.

A knock came on the door. Fernal sighed and called for them to enter. A liveried guardsman announced Duke Lomin, but the nobleman was already inside the room before Fernal nodded his assent.

"My Lord," Duke Lomin said, "your absence has been noticed at the banquet."

Fernal turned in his seat to face the bearded soldier. "Noticed? I would hope so; I am their lord after all."

"The new arrivals were all keen to toast your health."

"Really?" Fernal asked wearily, "and after that I'm sure they'd be commending your lineage, Duke Lomin." The man coloured and Fernal held up a hand. "I'm sorry. The insult was not aimed at you but your peers."

"Whatever their feelings, you should come down. You have called them here, after all, and have given little reason for so many to assemble."

"Is their lord's will not enough?"

"Not for long," Lomin said. "My Lord, why *are* we all here? There's no insurrection to put down, no threat of invasion from the south—if anything, the army should be heading north to the coast to face down the Yeetatchen raids."

"The fact that you don't believe Ruhen is a threat does not alter my policy, Duke Lomin," Fernal said with a growl.

"Yes, my Lord, and we are bound to follow you to war—this we know, but some of us have been beyond the Farlan borders for months now. If there is no enemy to fight, well—it is testing the limits of obedience."

"Chief Steward Lesarl has more than a few things to say about Farlan obedience," Fernal said with a gesture of one taloned hand to the letters on another table, "but call it what you will, I realise they are chafing under my authority."

"My Lord, you've gathered the rulers of fourteen Farlan domains, along with their troops, here in this pitiful little border town, with no enemy to fight and many concerned they will have to refuse you outright if you press to take the fight to the child, Ruhen."

Fernal rose and went to face Duke Lomin; the massive, midnight-blue Demi-God loomed over him. "Do they send you as their emissary?"

"I am the highest-ranked among them, it is my place to speak to you. They seek assurances that you will not drag the Farlan into another nation's war."

"You mean a war that concerns us just as much as it does our ally fighting it?" Fernal shook his head sadly. "I will never understand your people, Duke Lomin. However, I understand there are formalities to adhere to. Lead on to the banquet."

As they went out into the torch-lit street and headed for the banquet hall Fernal's liveried guards fell in around them. A pair of Lomin's own hurscals kept to the fringes. Before they reached the hall, however, Duke Lomin stopped and pointed ahead.

"Suzerains Amah and Danva were the most anxious to speak to you themselves, rather than be represented by me."

"Both recently come into their titles, no? Their fathers lying among the dead on the Chir Plains?"

"Danva's father was suzerain-in-regent for his infant nephew, now dead of scarlet fever, but Amah was uncle to the previous suzerain."

Fernal nodded and moved forward to greet the two recently arrived noblemen. Both knelt and offered him their swords as tradition demanded.

"My Lords," Fernal said in his deep, rumbling voice, "I am glad to see you both here."

"Thank you, your Grace," Amah replied quickly, a burly man with greying hair and cheeks scarred by some childhood illness. "Might we now know why we are here?"

"Because I command it," Fernal said.

"The situation here requires so many soldiers?" he countered, barely keeping the anger from his voice. "Is the concern rebellion or invasion?"

"Rebellion is always a concern of mine," Fernal said pointedly. "I am newer to my title than even you both. However, the greater threat remains in the Circle City."

"The child, Ruhen? My Lord, have I missed some piece of intelligence? All I hear is that he preaches a message of peace and denounces the corruption of the priesthoods." Amah frowned. "Correct me if I'm wrong, but did not the Farlan nobility mobilise specifically to face down the cults and prevent civil war?"

"For which you have my gratitude. But it does not override other matters."

Amah shared a look with Danva. "My Lord, the child's threat is surely to the cults? Since we have broken their power and now formally limit it, why are we not allied with Ruhen? Our goals coincide; the enemy is a common one, yet I'm told we have slaughtered two parties of missionaries and turned back others. Why do you seek war, my Lord?"

"They have had their warnings; they refuse to heed them. As for the missionaries slaughtered, they came with several regiments of Devoted as escort and preferred to fight rather than return to their own lands. You would prefer foreign powers be allowed to march troops into Farlan territory?"

"Of course not—but I still do not understand your antipathy, the preference of provoking war over building links with our new neighbours."

"You would have me welcome messengers of *peace* who come accompanied by *hundreds* of fighting men?" Fernal asked, taking a step towards the suzerain.

Unlike Duke Lomin, the suzerain could not help but edge back from the Demi-God's size and brutal appearance. He didn't even notice Fernal's guards putting their hands on their weapons.

"There is a specific agreement between myself and the suzerains of the Farlan. You have received a copy of it?"

Suzerain Amah nodded.

"Good, so you know the terms already then. Nowhere does it say I must explain myself to you, only that I will not lead you into a war on foreign soil without recognised justification. I choose not to dwell on reasons or explanations; otherwise I might require a few of my own, and point out our finest are already fighting in such a war."

"My Lord," Lomin interceded, stepping forward, "we are all aware of the terms, and we shall abide by them. The question remains: what threat exists on our border? The expense of maintaining such a large force here is significant, and we all have matters to attend to at home, in addition to the new lands we are now administering here in Helrect and Scree."

"You are telling me I must release the nobility to be about their own affairs?"

Lomin bowed. "It would seem time for that, my Lord. All intelligence suggests the Devoted troops are heading for the Narkang border—they pose us no threat. The purpose of this show of strength is achieved, to my mind."

And there you have it, Fernal thought as he looked around at the faces watching him, emotion showing even on the faces of Lomin's hurscals, hovering behind their lord. *They offer me a way out, a way to save face and move on. The question is—do I take it? Where does my duty lie? I gave my oath to serve the Farlan, to ensure they do not fall into civil war, but what of the Land itself, the friendships I bear and the war they are engaged in?*

He lingered a moment on the elder of the two hurscals, a man whose much-broken nose and weathered face told its own story. He was balding and had cropped short what little of his hair remained, making it easy for Fernal to see the tattoos of knighthood on his neck. The blue markings showed he had been ennobled on the battlefield, and Fernal could see in his grey-brown eyes what he thought of not marching to support the Ghosts, the tribe's proudest legions.

"My duty is clear," Fernal said, staring straight into the hurscal's eyes, "and this show of strength is indeed done. The nobility are released to return home. Duke Lomin, please convey my words to those attending the banquet."

"I will do so," the duke replied, sweeping up the suzerains as he moved past—his powerful arms taking them by the shoulders before they could object and dragging them both with him. The hurscal however didn't move.

"My duty is clear," Fernal repeated.

"Is it just me," Suzerain Torl asked quietly, "or do they prefer to preach at dusk, when the shadows are longest?" He indicated the white-robed Children of Ruhen holding court in the town square. They were less than twenty miles from Byora now, deep in the heartland of Ruhen's powerbase.

Count Macove nodded, careful not to stare at the group of preachers. There were only four of them, but a score of wide-eyed followers lingered at a reverent distance and at least one squad of Devoted soldiers kept a close eye on events. From what Torl could see, that was unnecessary; there were no dissenting voices, no expressions of disapproval. Most of the people here were converts already, accepting Ruhen's promised peace with the fervour of those scared of living in uncertain times.

"They can't all be touched by the shadow," Macove muttered in response, "there's too many of them now—unless the shadow's power has grown vastly. Theatricality perhaps?"

Cedei, the Brotherhood veteran, hawked and spat on the cobbled ground. "Sounds about right. Bastard's always loved a show."

Cedei was typical of the Brotherhood in Torl's eyes: an unremarkable man with a weathered face, speckled grey hair and cold, intense eyes. *A born streetfighter, that one,* Torl thought. *Macove's the nobleman, the knight with height and muscle on his side, but I'd never bet against Emin's bloody hands of history if it came to a fight.*

"Tell the others to hang back," he said out loud. "We're not looking for a fight here, just getting the lie of the Land."

Cedei nodded and fished out a pipe and tobacco pouch. He filled the bowl and made a show of casting around for a light, checking for their escort of Dark Monks, the religious order both Torl and Macove belonged to. He caught no one's eye and made no additional gestures, but once the pipe was lit he looked satisfied enough.

"Shall we then?"

The three men edged a little closer to the preachers, careful to act as they looked: interested merchants who posed no threat to order or the safety of the preachers. Only Torl wore a cloak, and that was pushed back off his shoulders despite the chilly weather and heavy grey clouds—all the better for the Devoted to see they carried only knives for their own protection. His three gold earrings of rank had been removed now they were in enemy territory, as had Macove's two, though both men found themselves touching a finger to their ear from time to time, then checking the cords around their necks from which the family relics hung.

"Brothers!" exclaimed a voice from their left, and Torl almost jumped as a man appeared from the crowd, not dressed as a preacher, but with the exact same expression as those in white. He'd been tasked with rooting out potential dissent in the crowd, Torl realised, meeting the naysayers head on before the white-clad preachers could be dragged into a shouting match.

"Do you come to hear the peace of Ruhen?"

Cedei nodded enthusiastically, immediately deferential. "We do, sir. Passed a good few preachers on the road—and more'n enough signs o' what war's done to this Land besides."

The man inclined his head benevolently and Torl forced himself to respond in respectful kind, Macove following his lead. The ageing suzerain felt his fists tighten as he bent his back to the man; he was unused to considering any commoner his equal, let alone his superior.

"You are come from Narkang lands?" he asked with a studied expression of guileless interest.

"That I am, sir," Cedei agreed with a bob of the head, "my friends from the north."

"Scree," Torl said hoarsely, "what once was, anyway."

"So you have all suffered by the cruelty of avaricious men," he intoned. "Yours is a common story, brothers."

"We've seen enough fighting, aye, ta know the horrors of it," Cedei said. He looked askance at Torl. "Some witnessing more'n others."

"Your family?"

Torl bowed his head, trusting Cedei's instincts for spinning a plausible story. "My wife and children," he confirmed, "we were separated in the rush to escape the firestorm."

"And they were murdered by men claiming divine inspiration," the man finished for him. "The King of Narkang let his army run riot on the defenceless refugees."

"Bastard did nothing when the Menin came either," Cedei added with venom. "Could've used some righteous fury when my town was burning."

"But he saw no profit in it," the other man said sadly, "such is the way of men of power. Only Ruhen's peace will free us of this—only Ruhen is not so clouded by the cares and fears of our mortal life, not corrupted by desires for power or magic only Gods should be able to wield."

Cedei nodded obsequiously and it was all Torl could do not to gawp at the man's superb acting. "Hoping ta hear a better way, sir. We've all heard rumours that King Emin commands monsters, but no matter what, the priests would only sing his praises."

"The cults are wedded to their own love of power, the thrall they hold the people in with empty promises of the afterlife." The man lurched forward and unexpectedly embraced Cedei, causing several more in the crowd to turn and watch the exchange.

"Open your heart, brother! Come, let us get closer and hear our saviour's message of peace!" Torl saw smiles and approval on the faces of the crowd, and more than one echoing the man's exhortations.

Torl and Macove held their ground as the man led a beaming Cedei away, one arm draped over his shoulders to guide him to the front of the crowd. Torl could sense the envy radiating out from those around them as Cedei was brought to the front of the crowd, the people parting easily before them, but closing up just as quickly afterwards.

The main group of preachers were assembled on a small platform in the centre of the square, next to a large well. The lighter marks on the stone indicated something had recently been removed from there—Torl guessed a shrine to an Aspect of Vasle inhabiting the well—though how the preachers had justified demolishing it he couldn't fathom. Perhaps the local priests charged for any water drawn; perhaps it was destroyed under cover of dark and King's Men blamed for the desecration.

"Brothers," began a burly preacher, slipping his white hood from his head, "Sisters, blessed children! May the peace of Ruhen embrace you all and cast the fear from your hearts."

There were muttered responses from the crowd, no one wanting to stand out by speaking up too loudly, but the preacher basked in their attention nonetheless. He fell silent for a few heartbeats and then his expression turned grave. "The peace of the child is a blessed thing. We, his children in spirit, were born with purity in our hearts and minds. We too were once free of fear and our hearts yearn for that time of peace, but this Land is one assailed and it cannot be. Only the child, our Lord Ruhen, possesses a purity of spirit that cannot be diminished by the works of daemons and evil men—for his is the quintessence of that first, perfect gift we are each given by the Gods."

Torl nodded along with the rest of the crowd, though it sickened him to his stomach to hear such words go unchallenged. The Brethren of the Sacred Teachings, called by most the Dark Monks, were an Order dedicated to the preservation of the Pantheon's majesty. He had spent his life studying religious texts and defending the innocent from all sorts of threats. That he could not draw a sword and strike this man down pained him physically, but he forced down the feelings and continued to listen.

"In these dark times," the preacher continued after the crowd had hushed again, "we find ourselves assailed. The Land itself and the Gods that rule us are assailed, estranged from their children by the wickedness of priests in love with power. We choose peace for our hearts, we choose a path of purity for our lives, but it is not always enough."

He gestured towards the liveried Knights of the Temples standing at the mouth of an alley. "Some are forced to take up arms in defence of peace, to fight those who cannot stand to see it flourish in this once-beautiful Land.

Place your trust in these guardians and place your faith in the child: his peace is a shield against the cares of this life.

"And still they come, and still the devoted servants of peace are beset. This is the dusk of the Land, brothers and sisters, and a great darkness shall soon be upon us."

The preacher bowed his head a moment, as though struggling physically with the strain of the darkness, and Torl saw the crowd surge forward as if to support him with all they had. Many of those watching were the poorest of this town, but not all; Cedei's account of the assault on the Ruby Tower had described a small army of beggars camped outside the gates, waiting for a glimpse of their saviour. Now, it was not only the mad and the desperate finding solace in Ruhen's promises. He recognised how they would be swayed to Ruhen's service even as his horror deepened.

"The darkness will come in many forms: in the faces of men and on the wings of daemons—but do not fear it; it is fear they crave, terror they seek to inspire. Without oppression and fear, the King of Narkang is nothing but a man ruled by his own vices. Darkness walks this Land, as you have all borne witness. Daemons walk this Land—the voices in the night, the shapes beyond the boundary lines, given freedom to hunt by those enemies of peace, eager for the blood of innocent men."

The preacher took a step forward, staring directly at the faces of those nearest him, Cedei included. "But should we fear them, my siblings under Ruhen?"

"No!" screamed several, howling the words back at him and prompting the preacher to incline his head with stern approbation.

"No, we should not: their power comes from your fear; that is how they become strong over us. When the daemons came to Byora, the child did not fear them. An army of daemons, loosed from Ghenna's dark pit and sent to kill the child by King Emin himself—but Ruhen did not fear them. He marched out with one disciple at his side, one man walking in the footsteps of a child!

"The daemons were weakened by his resolve and they could not harm him, for peace is anathema to them. A great victory was won that day—not by armies, not by lords or mages, but by common folk like you and me. The people of Byora cast off their fear; they saw the child unafraid and knew they had no need of it. Fear weakens us, but without it no force in the Land can prevail over us!"

The crowd began to cheer and shout, stamping their feet and drowning out the preacher's next words so he was forced to stop and quieten them before he could continue: "Be as the child, in all things. If darkness assails you, stand tall and meet it without fear. As children of a greater cause we shall face them, side by side and armoured by the child's perfect peace." His voice lowered to almost a prayer, and the crowd went suddenly silent, rapt, as he finished, "With the blessing of the child, my brethren, we will march out and show them the resolve children of peace possess. Against that no spears can prevail."

The crowd found their voices again, but now there were no wild calls or shouts; many had sunk to their knees and begun to keen wordlessly. Torl could not bring himself to follow their example. Instead, with his head bowed and hands clasped, he spoke the words of a prayer in his mind, first to Lord Death, then a grace to the Aspects of Vasle. From all sides the voices joined and slowly built into a chorus, a lament and entreaty that was primal. Torl felt it deep inside him.

When the mood finally broke and people started to move from where they stood, some returning to their labours, others to approach the preachers directly, Torl felt Macove put a hand on his arm and lean close in. "What was all that about?" he asked quietly, the words almost lost in the resuming hubbub of daily life. "Is the child building an army?"

Torl shook his head and gestured for them to leave. He needed a drink after witnessing that. "No, my friend, it's something more basic than an army." He glanced back at the centre of the square, where Cedei was now embroiled in conversation with one of the white-cloaked preachers. He decided to leave the man to it; infiltration was one of his skills, and he would be safe enough on his own. At the last town Cedei had spent an entire evening in the company of one such preacher, acting the convert and ever-keen to hear more of the child's great works.

They had all left the town by the time the preacher was found dead in a whore's bed with an opium pipe in his hand. Subtlety, it seemed to Torl, was the one thing not taught to the King's Men, but the more he watched Ruhen's preachers the more he wondered what outrageousness would be too much for the credulous, fearful masses.

"A sacrifice," he said with a heavy heart. "Ruhen expects an invasion. He does not believe the Devoted can face us in the field, so he portrays King Emin as a monster and godless conqueror."

"And still he asks people to face us down?" Macove's breath caught as he realised the truth of it. "Oh Gods!"

"Exactly," Torl said. "To meet Ruhen, the king's armies will have to march through a river of innocent blood, cutting a path through unarmed fanatics as well as Devoted armies. Ruhen does not care how many we kill; his audience is the people beyond these parts. If we slaughter a hundred thousand of his followers, he will only laugh for we will be playing into his hands. We must hope the king puts a careful man in command of the army he is preparing." He sighed, feeling a chill of age and foreboding in his bones. "To reach our enemy we will have to confirm these people's worst fears."

CHAPTER 21

KING EMIN LEANED FORWARD and looked into Amber's eyes. The Menin's eyelids twitched as he came within grasping distance, but his hatred had been dimmed by the king's return to Kamfer's Ford. Emin might have commanded the army, but he hadn't been in control of the one who'd torn Amber's birthname away; that one had been working a revenge all of his own, and Amber didn't know what to do about that.

The only one with reason enough to do what he'd done, Amber reflected. *That why I don't feel the same hate for him, or have I just used up all I had left?*

"You've been quiet a long time, Major," the king commented at last. "Do I need to repeat my offer?"

Amber slowly shook his head. They sat in a private room in the tavern Amber had been quartered in—well, private once that scowling lump Forrow had cleared the other drinkers from it. Nai, Carel and Ardela were with them at the table, the necromancer scrutinising the floor for reasons Amber couldn't find the strength to be interested in. "You'll use your influence with the Chetse to secure us passage home if I persuade the legions holed up in Farrister to fight for you," Amber said. "Don't see how I can persuade them if their commanders couldn't."

"You are a man of renown, Major Amber—your word carries weight, I suspect. In any case, it isn't all the troops in Farrister you need to persuade. My mages tell me many of the rank and file would like to take my offer."

"Your problem's General Arek," Amber confirmed. "Man's from the outer lands, as I recall; his family died years back."

"It seems he is resistant to any form of compromise. He would prefer to fight to the death, and take as many of us with him as he can."

Amber sighed. "That surprises you? There's nothing you can offer him."

"I was hoping sense might prevail. I had thought the Menin officers might feel a duty to their soldiers."

"You destroyed his life, his reason to live!" Amber snapped. Forrow reached forward immediately, but the big Menin soldier ignored the hand on his shoulder. "What did you think was going to happen?"

"That he wouldn't be ruled by personal feelings," Emin retorted angrily. "If he wants his men to live, he'll agree."

"And you think I can persuade him? I've barely met the man—and he's got half a dozen officers who outrank me. Or are you hoping I'll kill him and take command of the army?"

"I hope you will sway him," King Emin said, standing. "You leave in the morning under escort. Their supplies are almost out, so if you care about saving any of them you should hurry."

He marched out, not waiting for a response, and Forrow followed. The king's bodyguard slammed the door behind him hard enough to shake the room, but once they were gone silence reigned. Amber stared at the vacant seat in front of him, exhausted by the idea of rejoining a Menin army again. He found it unreal to be even thinking of fitting into that structure again, however much he craved a return of order to his life.

"Well?" Carel said eventually. "You going to let them all die?"

"War's over—if they don't see that, what can I do?"

"That ain't what I asked. Are you going to do your damnedest, or just pass on the message and pick up a shield?"

Amber glared at Nai.

The necromancer was unusually still and quiet; his hand twitched and Amber spied the edge of a tattoo under his sleeve.

Ah, that explains it then. Even the necromancer's chosen a side in this war—we really must be coming to the end of things. Nai of the Brotherhood, eh? Whole Land's gone over to madness.

"I don't get a choice there, do I, Nai?"

The man didn't answer, but Amber continued anyway, scratching his cheek where Nai had marked him, "See, our friend with the odd feet there, he's still got a hold over me—not just that dead man's bag to keep me from killing him; he can do worse than that if I don't come back as ordered. The rune he scratched on my cheek might have healed, but once a necromancer's got his hooks in you there's no escape."

"Oh stop fucking whining, boy," Carel snapped. He rapped the butt of his stick on the floor in irritation. "Your war ain't done, whatever the king says."

"You think?" Amber said with a snort. "Maybe Arek's right then."

"Piss on Arek. The man's a fool looking for a glorious death and he don't care who he takes with him. One way or another you got to persuade him to take the king's offer. You think you ain't a part of this fight? That's not what I heard from the last days of Scree."

Amber frowned. "Dragged there on some fool's errand, used as bait for King Emin and left to die by that damn vampire? You drunk again, old man?"

"Pah, I heard it a different way: you worked as hard as any to save those refugees, the ones not taken by Azaer's madness. You fought and bled on the barricade, leading from the front rather than looking to save your own skin."

"Someone had to take charge or we'd all have died. You think that means I'm at war with the shadow too?"

"It means you used to give a shit about folk, and I reckon you still do. You're no friend of Azaer and you don't like seeing innocents die. Look at me; I'm old and crippled—Death Himself only knows what I got left to give to this life, but I ain't giving up yet. You've got a whole lot more strength left in that arm o' yours, and if you've given up on life, just tell me now and I'll end it for you—stop you wasting what little drink we got left."

Amber didn't speak for a while. He looked from Carel to Ardela, recognising the impatience on the faces of both. The young assassin had proved to be good company on the journey here, keeping her thoughts to herself while Nai chattered away enough for the three of them.

Once back in Kamfer's Ford Ardela had rejoined her sisters. They had all been marked with tattoos by their priestesses, but she was still an outsider among the nascent Sisterhood, as the soldiers there were quietly calling it. If that bothered Ardela, she wasn't showing it, but she'd sought out his quiet company most days since.

He'd not asked about the Harlequin's sword she carried, except to inspect it. It was a beautiful weapon, so balanced and swift through the air he could see why Ardela had taken it, but even so, it was like she was inviting the hatred and contempt of others with such a clear admission that she had been part of that night of murder.

"That why you're here?" Amber asked eventually. "To find a death you can be proud of?"

"I ain't afraid to die, but I ain't hunting it either."

"And you know why I'm here," Ardela added, rubbing her palms together as the tattoos on them continued to itch. "My sisters need everyone they can get if we're not to just fade away."

"Nai brought me here to sell me to the king; to use the link they made between me and Ilumene, and that's not likely to prove useful unless Ruhen leaves the protection of his armies. The only thing that kept me walking was the thought of killing King Emin and now it turns out he wasn't even responsible.

"Sure your dead boy would've told him, but I know that someone offers you a victory, you don't get to choose. So now if I've got anyone to hate, it's your boy, Carel, and to hear the King's Men tell it, he's more broken than I am." Amber sighed wearily. Part of him wanted to lash out at anyone within reach, but mostly he just wanted to sleep for a hundred years and wake when all this was over. Right now when he slept he dreamed of ravens croaking urgently at him.

"When—" He winced and rubbed his brow with greasy fingers. "When my lord was grieving, I made it my duty to bring him back—nearly broke my neck, he did, but I waited out his rage. Right now I can't think why I'd ever do something so stupid."

"Because you're not one to abandon your men," Carel said. "What if your lord was here now—if Nai conjured up his spirit from the Herald's Hall to ask his orders, what would he say?"

"How should I know? Never could predict him."

"Guess."

Amber rose and walked to the window, staring out at the street below while jumbled, senseless thoughts clashed in his mind. He tried to recall his lord's face, but that was lost, like everything else to do with the man. A now-familiar yoke of fatigue settled about his shoulders and wormed its way into his bones, the same insidious wriggle as when the Gods' spell had entered his mind, leaving him just as hollow. At last he said, "He'd say— Ah, he'd tell me not to waste their lives. If we fight on, the only winner is Azaer. The Gods only know what's happened back home. Azaer's working towards Godhood, and I saw enough in Byora not to want that. If my duty to my tribe helps prevent that, then all the better."

He straightened and turned to face them. "Nai, tell your new master I'll do what he asks. Don't expect them to fight alongside Narkang troops, but they will fight—I promise him that."

Doranei wriggled through the yew's branches, doing his best not to shake the spread of branches supporting his body. It was not long after dawn and the ground beyond his vantage point remained blurred by mist, but below him there were signs of a campfire; clearly Doranei wasn't the first traveller to think this a good spot for the night. He slipped his pack free from the branch and dropped to the ground, covering the fifty yards to their main camp as silently as he could.

The others had woken with the dawn and Daken, Ebarn and Legana were all bent over bowls of porridge as Doranei trotted in. He checked his pace a little to avoid startling the horses, they'd only got them back a few days previously and half of the beasts were still spooked at being led through the wilds by a newly converted vampire. As soon as their belongings had been delivered, Zhia had sent the scowling, snarling former commissar west, not even bothering to discover her reluctant servant's name before she ordered him to spy on the border and warn her if the Black Swords left Vanach lands.

"We'll have visitors soon," he announced to the party at large, looking round to check they were all there. Veil and Vesna both were reaching for their weapons when Doranei motioned for them to stop. "They're moving too quick for Black Swords. I reckon it's the Legion."

"Of course it's the Legion," Zhia said from the shadow of her small tent. "They've been covering our retreat since we left Vanach, but we'll be crossing the hills today."

A grunt came from Zhia's left and they all turned to watch Isak flailing weakly at the blanket covering his head. After a few false starts, he managed to free both his arms and head enough to sit up. He stared bleary-eyed at his companions for a long while before he spied the porridge and started to struggle his way to his feet.

"Piss and daemons!" Vesna drew his sword and cast around as though someone was charging through the trees towards them. "Isak, where is it?" he cried urgently.

"Eh? What?" Isak said, still groggy with sleep.

"The sword!"

"It's in my bloody— Oh." Isak blinked down at his right hand and flexed his fingers. "Well, that's weird."

"What do you mean?"

"I can still feel it." Isak looked between Vesna and Zhia with a puzzled expression. "It feels like I've still got it in my hand."

Zhia covered herself in her thick shawl and walked over to him. She frowned as Doranei went to her side, and the air around her fingers shimmered briefly. "It's still there," she announced, looking as surprised as Isak. "It's in the stain somehow, Isak; it's becoming part of you."

He pushed back the loose sleeves of his shirt and raised his hands. The shadowy stain on his right arm had deepened; the skin there was near-black now. Just as lightning had burned the colour from his left arm, so his right hand and arm appeared to have been washed in soot and left as dark as a charred branch. The scars on his skin remained visible, each ridge and swirl obvious in the dull morning light, but the contrast between his hands couldn't have been more visible.

"Take your shirt off," Vesna asked, sheathing his weapon. He helped Isak pull his shirt over his head, revealing the man's brutalised torso. Isak had lost some of his bulk while in Ghenna, but he remained a starkly muscled white-eye on whose skin the old injuries were mere decoration. The black stain on his skin balanced his white arm almost perfectly, reaching to just beyond the shoulder, but instead of stopping abruptly it tapered away.

"Looks like a rash o' some sort," Daken commented.

Doranei shot him a look, but then realised the other white-eye hadn't been making a tasteless joke. He realised what Daken meant: it wasn't like gangrene taking hold of a limb, but it was too close for comfort, and the idea that it might spread further worried him.

"Can you make the sword manifest?" Zhia said.

Isak frowned down at his hand, his fingers twitching. For a while nothing happened, then Doranei saw the air start to tremble. He blinked and winced as dark stars began to burst around Isak's fingers; it was hard to keep his gaze on the soot-stained limb, but he was not faring as badly as the lesser mages among them.

Both Ebarn and Legana had reeled away, assailed by what Isak was doing, while Tiniq's face tightened with strain and he turned his shoulder towards the white-eye as though facing a gale. Doranei was watching the man so intently he only realised Isak had succeeded from the shock on the ranger's face.

As Isak stood, Doranei felt Zhia lean back against him, the presence of Death's weapon a constant discomfort for her. Termin Mystt had reappeared in Isak's fist, point-down, its black surface absorbing the morning light. Isak retrieved the sheath he'd once used for Eolis and carefully slipped Termin Mystt inside. The clips that normally attached it to a belt he hooked around his wrist to hold the sheath in place and keep it from inadvertently touching anyone.

"The shadow's retreated," Vesna pointed out, moving carefully around Termin Mystt to point at Isak's shoulder. The fading edge of the mark had moved away from Isak's neck, leaving the top of his shoulder only a slight shade darker than the rest of his pale Farlan skin.

"Stain," Doranei broke in, prompting a puzzled look from the Mortal-Aspect. "Call it a stain, not a shadow—not when Azaer's our enemy."

Vesna nodded his assent. "Stain it is: your skin's still darker, though, Isak—manifesting the sword's only limited the hold it's taken on you."

"I never expected to master the damn thing, I suppose," Isak said at last, "even with the Skull this was never going to be long-term."

"What happens when it takes over entirely?" Vesna asked. "Do you die? Or become Death's Mortal-Aspect?"

"It won't come to that," Isak said firmly.

"No? Look how far it's gone already!"

"Not much a surprise, is it? I'm balancing the scales in my head; the sword in one hand, the Skull of Ruling in my other. One arm's white—it's only fair the other balances it out."

"Fair?"

Isak waved his free hand dismissively. "Not fair then, but fitting, maybe. If you're worried, we can stop by Llehden on the way back and ask the witch, but I don't reckon she'll be surprised. Legana?"

The green-eyed woman observed him for a long while. Her face was as still as a porcelain doll's and Isak could read nothing in her expression. Eventually she nodded. "*You strive for balance*," Legana said into his mind." *We can't be surprised if balance is what we get.*"

"Exactly: so we'll only start worrying if it goes past that. Now, you said something about visitors, Doranei?"

Before the King's Man could reply, a guttural voice called out. They all turned, reaching for their weapons.

There were six figures, no more than twenty yards away, each one bearing enormous weapons as pitted and battered as they were themselves. Their leathers were tattered, their mail torn to reveal mortal wounds. What few scraps of plate armour they wore—mismatched pauldrons and vambraces, and one had a holed cuirass—were similarly rusted and ancient.

"Lord of the Black Sword," Zhia said, translating the words for Isak before he could remind himself Mihn was now dead, "we honour you."

Only the colour of their eyes, deep-blue, rusty-brown and amber, stood out against their pale dead skin and mouldering clothes. The colours reminded Doranei that they had been mercenaries somewhere out east, most likely of Menin and Vukotic blood.

Isak advanced to meet the undead mercenaries, Vesna close at his side. If the warriors of the Legion noticed anyone beyond Isak and Zhia, however, they made no sign of it. "I thank you for your greeting," Isak replied through Zhia, "and for hindering the pursuit."

"We have pledged ourselves to you," one of the mercenaries at the centre of their small group said. "We will serve you."

Doranei gave a start when he realised he recognised the face from Scree: one side of his emaciated face had been mangled by a blow to the head, and his jaw hung loose as though in a mocking grin. The Legion had appeared just before King Emin claimed the Skull of Ruling and left Vorizh's journal behind, not knowing its value.

Strange, Doranei thought as he, glanced around at the rest of their party, *if I'd gone with him into the cellar that night—if I hadn't been so dazed after we left Rojak to burn—maybe I'd have found the journal and Mihn would still be alive. No way of knowing, but I'm sure there's a lesson in there somewhere.*

"Will you obey me now?"

"We will."

Isak nodded, his movements as heavy as if he was still asleep and dreaming. "Go south then, go to the King of Narkang at Camatayl Castle, and obey his orders as you would mine."

"And then you will break our curse?"

"Your service is required," Isak growled. "Once our war is over, we will break your curse. Perhaps we will even find a way to pull your fallen comrades from the Dark Place."

"Isak," Vesna said in a warning voice, "don't."

"Don't what?"

The Iron General turned his back on the undead mercenaries so he was almost face-to-face with his stooping friend. "Don't start thinking that way," he hissed. "Don't let yourself get distracted. You barely made it out of Ghenna after careful planning and the loss of Xeliath. Don't start thinking you can mount a raid on the Dark Place to rescue his soul. Don't waste what Mihn sacrificed."

Isak leaned a little closer to the Farlan hero. "And *you* don't pretend you know what I'm thinking," he said angrily. "I haven't forgotten the stakes in this game, but those we can save we're going to. Their souls are linked by this curse, so might be they can all be saved. But don't you worry; I'll see this to the end. Mihn's sitting on Maram's bank and I ain't going in to fetch him."

He pushed past Vesna and again directed his attention to the undead soldiers. "What is your name?" he asked the one who was speaking for them.

"Ozhern."

Isak inclined his head to them, and was rewarded with a stiff, wary bow from the soldiers of the Legion.

"I am Isak Stormcaller, and I require your swords for half a year. Go ahead of us to the King of Narkang, Ozhern, and tell him I come in your wake. We will cross the Crag Hills by mirror-magic and continue south, but you can travel faster and without rest; you will reach the king first."

"It is agreed, but mark this," Zhia reported back, "before six months are out, the Lord of the Silent Castle will return to the west. If you betray us, he will lead our vengeance."

"I understand."

The undead mercenaries turned without further comment and ran back the way they had come, moving in near-silence and with a speed that belied their unhurried movements. The grass was barely disturbed by their passage and the six figures looked like ghosts as they headed back towards their comrades and quickly disappeared from view.

"Will the king thank me for that?" Isak wondered aloud.

"He will," Doranei assured him. "If the Devoted mobilise against Narkang, he'll need every soldier he can get—he'll find a use for them all, even those without their humanity."

Isak nodded and went to gather up his possessions, any thoughts of breakfast vanished on the wind. Doranei left him to it, knowing Isak wouldn't want anyone taking Mihn's place and fussing over him. Instead he went to help his Brother, for Veil was similarly encumbered and unable to tie his belongings to his saddle. As he did so Doranei caught sight of Legana, stepping in to help Isak; he saw the conflict on his face as she did so.

Legana was unsteady at times, unreal and ethereal all the time, and so dramatically changed from the tough young woman he'd first met that Doranei found it hard to remember the two were the same person sometimes. She had been beautiful; she was even more so now, in a terrifying way, and she carried the same weight of centuries that Zhia did. He secured the last of Veil's saddlebags as Legana ignored Isak's hesitation and inexpertly gathered his belongings. They were a strange pair together, each marked by the events they were caught up in.

They were all marked, by Mihn's tattoos and Xeliath's rune.

Legana didn't quite treat Isak with reverence, but her manner had once been of veiled and indiscriminate contempt towards everyone. Now there was a patient acceptance that the old Legana had never known: they were family now, bound by the magic that had marked them.

You don't have to be friends too, Doranei thought as Hulf came bounding up to Isak, returned from his regular dawn wanderings. *Some things you do for family and it's a tie that'll live with you for ever.* He looked down at the owl tattoo on the palm of his hand. *And this makes us family, maybe with Legana playing mother to us all.* He laughed out loud at the thought, receiving a slap round the head a moment later.

It was Veil, peering at him strangely. "You still asleep there?"

"Eh?"

"Your mistress calls," Veil explained with a nasty grin, "but you were daydreamin' about Legana by the looks of it."

Doranei turned to where Zhia was standing looking impatient. "Just as well we're family," he grumbled as he rubbed the back of his head and headed over.

"Climb this branch for me," Zhia commanded before he'd even reached her. "I want you to loop a rope around the end."

"Eh?" Doranei looked up at the small tree, an elderberry with long, slender branches.

"Was that too complicated a request?" Zhia said sharply. "Climb, tie, try not to fall on your head."

"Not sure it'll take my weight so well." He turned away from her stern expression and fetched Isak's massive horse instead. The branch was higher than a man could reach, but from Megenn's back he found it a simple enough task to tie the rope on as ordered. Slipping down, he offered her the rope.

"Put a stake in the ground and tie it down," she said, ignoring the proffered rope. "We need an archway big enough to allow horses through."

Doranei didn't bother asking why, but summoned Daken to help haul over what was left of the fallen tree they'd burned overnight. With a bit of levering it was moved into place and the rope tightened around it so that Zhia had the arch she required, weighed down by a log the size of a man.

Without bothering to thank them, Zhia came around the straining branch and knelt under the arch, one hand pressed to the Crystal Skull at her waist. Doranei exchanged a look with Veil as he retreated out of her way; his Brother was overly amused at Zhia's displeasure.

The vampire reached out a gloved hand with her palm vertical, as though pressed flat against a door rather than in mid-air.

Doranei could see nothing of her face, but he had spent enough time in her company to recognise the taste of magic in the air as she drew on the Skull. The smell of her perfume seemed to wash over him on the wind and Doranei instinctively tilted his head up like a dog catching a scent.

"Down, boy," Veil muttered from beside him, "mind on the job."

The King's Man scowled and pursed his lips.

Faint trails of light began to swirl through the air around Zhia, slow and languorous. The wisps were barely more than suggestions in the air, but they traced a pattern that almost looked like runes before fading and being replaced by others. The trails continued to move outwards, spreading up to the edges of the branch and tree trunk until there was a silvery-white glimmer on the inner edge of the arch.

"Thought mirror-magic had to be worked from the destination," Veil whispered in Doranei's ear.

"It does," he confirmed, "but we're going further than anyone's capable of by themselves—she's adding her strength to the link, or we'll never reach the mirror."

Behind them the rest of the party had gathered the horses and were preparing to lead them through the archway. The light around the edge of the arch continued to brighten while the air within grew dark and shadowy, reflecting the shadow of the courtyard Mage Ashain would be using, Doranei guessed.

He disliked trusting a man who'd been so vocal an opponent of the king's for so many years, but there was no denying the man's skill.

The shadowy air seemed to coalesce with a snap, almost as tangible as a curtain that trembled under Zhia's fingers. The vampire stood and gestured for Vesna to go ahead. "The link is secure, but we should not waste time."

Vesna nodded and briskly walked his horse through, vanishing into thin air as the dark curtain billowed around him. They had agreed he would go first, in case there was any form of treachery—it was unlikely any enemy mage would be able to hold a link open if the Mortal-Aspect of Karkarn attacked him, but as it was, the curtain settled with unnatural speed and was still long before the next person went through.

"Move yourselves," Zhia snapped at those lingering behind. "Ashain is only mortal and his strength will be quickly sapped."

Veil's earlier mirth vanished and he jumped to obey with the rest. Doranei sent the horses through one by one, then it was his turn to step through. He couldn't help but glance at Zhia before he did so, and she gave him a slight smile, her irritation melting away. The King's Man took a deep breath and let his fingers settle around the hilt of his brutal broadsword before stepping forward.

With the sensation of a trickle of water dancing over his entire body at once, he pushed through the grey curtain and out into the courtyard of Leppir Manor, many miles to the south. He shivered and almost stumbled as the Land around him seemed to reform in a bright flash of light, grey pillars and flagstones replacing the trees and leaf-strewn ground. His stomach lurched and black stars burst before his eyes, fading only slowly when he tried to blink them away. The touch of the curtain had left a chill on his skin that raised every hair and set goosebumps on his body. A wave of dizziness passed over him and an ache blossomed in his head.

"Stop gawping and move!" snapped a voice he didn't recognise, and he turned to see Mage Ashain, his bearded face contorted with effort. He moved to the side of the enormous mirror he'd just stepped out of, where Daken was waiting, ready to grab at the reins of the next horse to come through.

"Only way to travel eh?" the white-eye laughed, apparently unaffected by the strange sensation.

Doranei shivered again as Hulf scampered through, followed quickly by Isak. "Prefer my hangovers to follow a drink or two," he croaked, pinching between his eyes as the ache continued.

Daken cackled. "Let's see what we can do about that, then!"

Chapter 22

At dusk, after a day of rest and recovery at Leppir Manor, Isak began to grow restless. The manor was owned by King Emin and maintained by a steward as a useful waystation on the border; the region had been fractious for years. After long weeks of travelling their horses were in need of rest; they all needed to replenish their supplies, repair clothes, tend weapons and spend at least one day not fleeing from search parties of Black Swords.

The haunted look was still on Isak's face when he headed through the long hall. Without speaking Vesna followed his friend outside to the courtyard, where Hulf lay watching the steward's geese from a safe distance. The dog gave a happy bark at the sight of Isak and ran to him.

It had been a warm day and neither man had bothered with anything thicker than a tunic. Isak's brown sleeves were rolled up to the elbow, displaying the strange balance of light and dark on his scarred forearms. The Skull of Ruling was a bulge at his waist, kept secure by a thick strip of cloth worn under his shirt. His right hand was empty again, the skin as dark as charcoal.

Hulf kept clear of it, Vesna saw, though he couldn't begin to guess whether that was wariness of the black sword's return or fear of touching Isak's stained skin.

"Isak," Vesna began hesitantly, "what does it feel like?"

"The sword?" He raised his hand to inspect his skin. The look on his face was one of wonder and disbelief, as though even Isak couldn't believe the strange turns his life had taken. "Like a cloud's crossed the sun, that sudden chill—but the rest of my body is still hot, warmed by Ghenna's echo in my bones."

Vesna flexed the black-iron clad fingers of his own God-touched limb. "Do you feel Death's presence?"

Isak laughed softly. "I've felt that for a while, my friend. No, I know you didn't mean it that way: you mean can I feel Death's spirit as you feel Karkarn's?"

"I suppose I do, yes."

"No, and for that I'm glad. He's not so much a part of me as that—maybe it's because the Gods are weakened, but all I can feel of Death Himself is an echo in my bones. It's not so different to when I had the Reapers caught in my shadow. Maybe it's better to say I'm walking with one foot in the lands beyond this one. Part of me is still there, and Termin Mystt's the key to reaching it. I actually feel more complete this way, can you believe that? My soul's caught between realms, but with Termin Mystt in my hand I feel like I'm on the border between them. It's not enjoyable, but at least it feels like I can reach both parts of me from here."

"Will you be able to step back from it?"

"Step back?"

Vesna caught his friend's arm, careful to touch the cloth of his sleeve only. "Isak, you can't live this way for long, remember? You might walk the border between lands, but you're still flesh and bone, a mortal man. Even using Ruling to balance the power of Termin Mystt it isn't something you'll be able to endure for long. You remember why you did this, right?"

"You're fussing like an old woman," Isak growled. "I've forgotten nothing."

"So you remember you will have to give this up?" Vesna persisted.

Isak shrugged. "Soon this will all be over, one way or another. It might not be quite the Age of Fulfilment some hoped for, but there'll be a resolution between us, Azaer and I have ensured that."

"And we will win," Vesna said firmly, "never doubt it. Azaer has nothing to match our power and—" His voice wavered, but he finished, "and I refuse to allow Tila's death to be in vain."

Isak winced at the mention of her name. "I feel her death on my shoulders," he whispered, "and Mihn's too. How many others do I bear? What chains of responsibility will I have to drag after my Final Judgement?"

"You'll not bear them alone," Vesna declared fiercely. "There's an army of us behind you, all those marked Ghosts and Hands of Fate: they've embraced your fate and your burdens too. The ivory gates will shake as we march up Ghain's slope, but it'll not be for long years yet, my friend."

"Think so? What place in this life will I have afterwards? On that day, victory or no, the Land'll be done with me." He raised a hand to stop Vesna as the Mortal-Aspect began to argue. "You think you can change what I am? I was born for this Age, and this Age alone. Once the Land's remade, my purpose is done—*I'm* done. But I've lived long enough with Death's hand on my shoulder and Death's Aspects in my shadow, and my friend, I don't fear it. Part of me craves some form of relief from all this. I'll give up the sword easily enough, my friend, or it will give me up."

They came to a stream running merrily through the moorland that ran east from Leppir Manor. The ground was studded with clumps of purple heather, rejuvenated by recent rain. Twenty yards beyond the stream, half-concealed by the grass, was a lichen-clad stone circle the height of a man's knee. Isak didn't enter, but placed his left hand on one of the stones and bowed his head as though in prayer. That done, he turned to face Vesna and sat without reverence on the stone.

"Calming the local Aspect?"

Isak nodded. "Two, actually—a lord and lady, for want of better words. The circle's dedicated to some Aspect of Nyphal, a safe rest for travellers unwelcome at the manor."

"And the other?"

"The river-spirit—a son of Vasle." Isak smiled in his crooked way. "Both are weak, they were even before the Gods drew on their Aspects at Moorview. The union's probably all that's keeping them from being hunted by daemons each night."

"I'm sure Tila would have found great romance in a union of competing Gods," Vesna said.

"No doubt, but my mind's on other things right now."

Vesna squinted, trying to see Isak's expression.

"We're about to have a visitor," he said by way of explanation, looking up at the sunset sky past Vesna's head. "I wanted to have this conversation away from the others."

As Vesna looked up, he saw a dark shape in the sky that soon resolved into two shapes with outstretched wings. With his divine-touched senses he reached out and tasted magic on the wind, the scent of large creatures and a dry, ancient odour that he recognised all too easily.

"What do you want with him?" Vesna demanded before the pair of wyverns reached them. "You surely can't plan on trusting a madman?"

"It's not a question of trust," Isak replied, still watching the wyverns. "He carries a Crystal Skull, so he'll be involved before the end, one way or another."

Hulf crept to Isak's side, pressing up against the white-eye as his natural boldness faded in the face of those enormous predators. The wyverns shone blood-red in the evening light as they wheeled around the stone circle and dropped lightly to the grass beyond. Golden eyes peered rapaciously at them as the beasts folded their wings and settled themselves.

Vorizh Vukotic slipped to the ground and shrugged off the oversized cape that hid his pale skin from the sun. Despite his efforts, the skin across his eyes and nose was as dark as Isak's arm; they'd seen that streak on Zhia's face often enough. Underneath the cape was the familiar black whorled armour Aryn Bwr had forged for each of the Vukotic family, contrasting with Eolis' white grip, visible over Vorizh's right shoulder.

"Lord Isak," Vorizh called, bowing with all ceremony to them, "do you now accept my gift?" He gestured to the second wyvern, which was weaving its head from right to left. At first it watched Isak as if he were a rabbit coming into striking distance, but under Isak's scrutiny the wyvern furrowed the ground with its claws and ducked its head low.

Vesna realised the creature was nervous in Isak's presence—or the sword's, at any rate.

"I've enough to do without learning to handle such a creature," Isak said eventually.

"Then what is it you want of me? My sister is already your servant, and she is skilled in most disciplines."

"I have something I need you to do." Isak gestured to the stone circle and stepped inside it, Hulf still at his heel. "Come inside. I've seen to it the local God won't object."

Vorizh cocked his head at the white-eye, intrigued at last. "If you want a vampire bound," he commented with a trace of contempt, "I believe my sister's tastes run more that way than mine."

Isak ignored the comment; she'd have heard worse from saner men over the millennia. "It's dusk," he explained. "The shadows are at their longest now, and I'd prefer not to be overheard." A spark of magic left his blackened fingers and danced around the circle, leaping from stone to stone until a haze filled the air between each one. "Circles can be used for protection as well as binding."

Vorizh inclined his head and joined Isak inside, and Vesna followed a moment later. As he passed through the barrier Isak had created Vesna felt a frisson of energy run over his skin and a sudden whisper of wind through grass filled his ears until he was on the other side and then there was calm again: a magic-dulled stillness.

"And now," Vorizh said, "what service can I render to one who commands Gods and frees daemons?"

In the depths of a thicket a hundred yards from the stone circle, someone watched, a shadow on their shoulder that brushed the figure's pale skin with spidery claws. "What bargain with Vorizh must be kept even from his companions?" the figure wondered, eyes fixed on the stone circle. "After all we've seen at his side?"

"One the boy would be a fool to trust in," the shadow replied, *"but he can feel the end drawing near. I so prefer desperation in my enemies—all the better to let them seize their undoing."*

The two men faced each other, neither speaking. A space had been cleared in the town square, and soldiers crammed every side-street, watching the silent meeting of two weary but unbowed men. The elder looked small in his armour, the wrinkles on his face more apparent when viewed opposite the scars of the younger man. He was more heavily armoured, his banded pauldrons and solid breastplate bearing a fanged skull device. His younger opponent wore leather armour stiffened by grooved steel rods. They both carried Menin steel half-helms.

A cold wind drove down from the north, stretching out the banners that flew proudly from the town's tallest buildings, fluttering madly in their reach for freedom, though beyond these walls they would be burned or trampled into the dirt. Here was their last bastion.

"You come as his envoy?" General Arek asked at last. All around him, hands tightened on grips as they awaited the reply.

Amber shook his head, slowly, regretfully. "I come as a Menin."

"You come to join our stand?"

"No."

"Then what?" There was no rancour in the general's voice, none of the antagonism Amber had expected, no interest nor passion; the man was playing his part. Beyond the fatigue in his eyes, Amber saw relief, and the promise of a longed-for end.

There is no such promise for me.

"I come to save the lives of these warriors. I come to lead them back across the Elven Waste and return them to their homes," Amber declared, loud enough for all to hear.

"You will lead them against our enemy?"

"They are no longer the enemy; they are the victors in our war. All that remains is the long march home, to follow in the footsteps of our ancestors."

Amber could tell from the tense silence that the significance was not lost on anyone there: the Long March had been instigated by the most infamous of Menin lords, the man who had nearly obliterated the Litse tribe before a mysterious change of heart. Amber alone among his people knew the truth of this mystery, but they all knew that Lord Grast, instead of completing his scouring of the Land, had marched his tribe across the Waste to a new home, letting the weakest fall by the wayside until only the strongest survived. The Long March had meant rebirth for the Menin, but it had meant terrible loss too, and it revealed the callousness of rulers.

"You would play Deverk Grast's role?" General Arek asked. "I do not think you strong enough to follow the dark dragon's lead."

"I am no dark dragon, and I make no such claims, but I will do what must be done."

"You are of noble birth? What emblem would take the dragon's place?"

The question caught Amber unawares and he reeled from the bursting stars of pain and loss in his mind. "I . . ." Amber closed his mouth, the air sucked from his lungs. To answer the question he tugged the gauntlet from one hand and unfastened the vambrace from his left arm. On his forearm was a dark rusty-red tattoo, a bird in flight.

"A red merlin? You are from the west slopes?"

Amber nodded. "But of late I'm accompanied by ravens; the red merlins of my home are just a faint memory."

The comment deflated the general. "I would have preferred a dragon to that dark omen," he said, "yet you come to us speaking of ravens and a long march. I think you bring us nothing but pain, all for a faint promise of home."

"That is all I have."

"You would accept King Emin's offer? You would become a mercenary under his banner?"

"I would do what I must," Amber said. "I have nothing else."

"I cannot," the general replied after a long pause. "I cannot ask that of my army."

"I know." Amber looked around at the assembled faces. Most were hidden behind thick black beards, but he was Menin; he knew the anger contained within each man. "We are Menin," he started, "we are the finest soldiers this Land knows. We have seen much since crossing the waste—the squabbling of the Farlan, the foolish obedience of the Chetse, the resolve of

Narkang. We have seen weakness and strength, but what do they see? Battle-thirsty monsters? Warriors who cannot comprehend defeat? The place of a general is to make the choices that must be made. Your men will not like the decision, but they are not Farlan—they will not whine, nor argue and plot in secret. They will know the right of what must be done. A sour taste in the mouth is not enough to sway Menin."

"I cannot," Arek said, almost in a whisper. "They have stolen all we are . . . they have cut out my heart."

"You must," Amber declared. "There is no other choice."

With sudden passion Arek tore the helm from his head and threw it on the ground before them. "*You* do not order *me*! *I* am the commander of this army—there is nothing I *must* do! Our lord is lost, our generals and noblemen are lost; there is no other but me."

"And so the decision is yours."

Arek straightened, composing himself. "And mine alone," he added for emphasis. "Of the Menin this side of the waste, I hold the rank—I am the lord who holds life and death in my hand."

He took a step closer to Amber and stared straight in his eye.

"Do you understand me, *Major?* I am lord here; I acknowledge no authority beyond the God of War himself!"

Amber bowed his head. "I understand," he said quietly. *And so it comes to this: you ask this of me because you do not have the strength. You cannot bring yourself even to save the men who would die at your command.*

"I invoke the right of challenge," he declared, and saw the relief in Arek's eyes as he spoke. "We are the chosen tribe of Karkarn and a warrior must lead us. It is my right as Menin—does any here deny it?"

He cast right and left towards the closest men, the colonels and majors who flanked General Arek, watching for their reaction, but Arek saw no reason to wait. The ageing general stepped back and drew his broadsword, waving over a man with his shield without ever taking his eyes off Amber.

"I acknowledge your right," Arek replied with a renewed vigour, "and I call no champion. Draw your swords."

Amber did so, sliding his scimitars out of their scabbards, the soft whisper of steel on leather a deadly promise. He settled into the stance beaten into him over years in the training Temple of Haysh the Steel Dancer, hands at mid-chest and tips directed to Arek's eyes—and advanced slowly.

Arek attacked wildly, slashing at Amber's hands, but never coming near his target, then changed tactic, bringing his shield and sword close together as he advanced. Amber gave him ground, his swords still at a long guard, to give him time to manoeuvre. When Arek lunged forward over his shield, Amber danced to the limit of the general's range. He was watching to gauge how he intended to fight.

The general obliged him by not making him wait; he charged forward and aimed a savage cut down at Amber's knee. Amber twisted left and parried, hunching his shoulder to deflect the inevitable blow from Arek's shield away from his neck, stabbing across his body as he did so. His left scimitar punctured the mail on Arek's arm—it wasn't a killing blow, but Amber was faster than the older man and now he pushed up from his knees, sweeping the parrying blade up to slash over Arek's armour and shield-arm.

Amber followed with a lunge that glanced up off Arek's cheek-guard, but by that point the general was reeling. He retreated on instinct, retreating behind his shield, and Amber hacked down onto it with such force that his right scimitar bit and caught. He immediately turned and pivoted around the shield as Arek thrust forward and cut at the general's leg. Amber twisted back the way he'd come, the movement pulling Arek off-balance. His sword was barely raised against Amber's return blow; somehow it caught it, but in the next movement Amber stepped forward and drove his pommel into his opponent's neck.

He had freed his other sword by that twist and now Amber wasted no time in chopping down over the shield. His blow caught Arek perfectly and the general fell, his neck broken and half-severed, and dead before he hit the ground.

Amber stared down at the blood that sprayed out over his boots, looking shockingly bright on the chalky ground. He took a breath, and felt a small puff of wind stroke over his face: the Land suddenly returning to focus again. The corpse lay quite still, legs not even twitching as blood continued to leak out. The hard-packed pale ground greedily drank it down, but Amber knew Arek was already gone, his soul carried away.

Was that just a breeze or the passing of a soul? he wondered distantly. *The wings of ravens, bearing him to his Last Judgement?* "Lord Death," Amber cried, "judge him fairly—and remember the part you played in his death today. This blood is on your blade too."

He looked up at the colonels of the legions, seeing approval on the faces of several. None spoke now to refute the claim he had made in the blood of another.

"Burn the body," Amber said, "gather his ashes and bring them with us. They will be the burden we bear on our long march. Once we return home I will carry them to his people and tell them of his bravery." He paused and raised his voice. "Gather your weapons—the Menin march once more to war!"

Chapter 23

A white falcon soared above Byora, far from the voices and clamour of the city below. Lord Gesh watched it with envious eyes; his own great wings provided him with no such freedom now that tradition and politics dragged at his heels. The touch of the thin autumn sunlight on his body failed to warm him, and the soft kiss of magic that had carried him this high was no longer the sheer indulgent pleasure it had once been.

He was not entirely alone up here, of course, but his guards maintained their distance. Their lord's fatigue was obvious, even to other white-eyes. *The burdens of leadership, or something more?* Gesh was not sure he knew himself. Restful sleep had eluded him ever since he had ascended to Lord of the Litse.

Perhaps it's guilt?—no, hardly; Celao had been an insult to their God, and the people of Ismess had suffered for it. Now they cheered Gesh with a passion: a lord who truly embodied their God.

And Ismess welcomed Ruhen's Children with open arms, their enthusiasm the greatest of any quarter of the Circle City. The preachers had been careful to speak out only against the priests of the city, not the God who was their patron. The cults of Ismess had seen the clerics' rebellion in Byora and the Devoted's own power struggle in Akell. They had seen sense and chosen survival over principle. The Gods were weakened and Ilit would not intercede, even for his own priests, so they had quietly closed their temples and gone to ground or left the city, leaving no opposition to Ruhen's Children, no dissenting voices to his message—and no refusal of the food appearing in their markets.

And yet I barely sleep, and a shadow covers the sun and bars me from its warmth. Lord Gesh banked away from the breeze and let it carry him in a wide, lazy spiral towards the high towers of Byora. The red sash across his chest fluttered madly as the air rushed past—Lord Ilit trying to tear off the mark of his place on the Devoted's ruling council? He guessed not, no matter how frantic a movement it was. So long as the Devoted did not force their laws on the Litse, their patron God could have no complaint that his people were shielded in their hour of weakness.

From where he was he could see little of Blackfang's tabletop surface. The broken mountain was high enough that it was an effort to climb that far in the thin air, but the Ruby Tower's peak was still below him as he descended. Gesh heard the beat of wings as his two guards followed him, but he was more intent on the city below. He was above Breakale district now, and he could see a crowd massed around the Stepped Gardens there. Many wore the mismatched, poorly dyed white clothes prevalent among Ruhen's supporters. As he moved closer he saw neat lines of figures, not in white, formed up like soldiers but without any obvious livery.

New pilgrims? Or does Ruhen now have soldiers of his own to carry this message of peace? But they weren't the only crowds in Byora, Gesh saw. Just as in Ismess—and Akell and Fortinn quarters, no doubt—he saw large gatherings at street corners and Ruhen's burgeoning army of followers praying or singing wordless hymns at the Walls of Intercession that most of the Circle City now saw as the key to their salvation. Ruhen's followers had dismantled many of the quarter's temples and put up hundreds of shanties in their places, temporary structures in the main, but enough to house the pilgrims flocking daily to Byora in search of this child the preachers all spoke of.

Lord Gesh descended slowly, letting his great wings be seen by all long before he touched his toes to the ground. Ruhen stood on the highest of the garden's three tiers, in the centre of the top step, so that everyone in the area could see him. The ground sloped away dramatically, with a dozen steep steps leading between each fifty-yard-wide tier. Alongside the child was Mage Peness, wearing scarlet robes, the three remaining Jesters, and Luerce, the First Disciple. Behind them were five masked Harlequins, Ruhen's own bodyguard, put in place after an assassination attempt had narrowly failed.

Of Duchess Escral there was no sign, but Gesh was not surprised. She was alive, he had heard, but afflicted with some illness that left her enfeebled. Her place as ruler of Byora had been taken by Ruhen, a wordless and bloodless coup that none objected to. Even the Knights of the Temples acknowledged his primacy.

"Lord Gesh," Ruhen sang out as the slender white-eye dropped lightly to the ground, his bodyguards following suit a moment later. The child, Byora's saviour, as many called him now, wore a long grey tunic, caught at the waist by a plain belt. His dress was understated for the adopted son of a duchess, functional and neat rather than elegant. He wore only a single pearl at his throat for ornamentation.

"Lord Ruhen," Gesh acknowledged, bowing low. "Koteer, Mage Peness," he added as he straightened, "a fair wind guide you all."

He gestured to the soldiers he had seen earlier and was about to ask who they were when he realised he knew. They were formed into ten blocks of fifty: too many to be Harlequins, but their steel helms had white-painted faces or white leather masks underneath.

"Your people, Lord Koteer?"

"The warriors of our clan," the white-masked son of Death confirmed. "Our blood and kin."

There were no large towns or cities in the Elven Waste, so five hundred warriors on top of those who had been working as mercenaries with the Jesters must have left the clan's home villages poorly defended at best. It appeared the Jesters did not care if there was a home to return to once their business with Ruhen was done. Perhaps these Demi-Gods had a new one in mind, and not one where their mortal followers could accompany them.

Ruhen advanced to Gesh's side and looked up at the Litse lord with his intense, shadow-laden eyes. Under that scrutiny Gesh felt the fatigue of earlier recede, and a warmth seep into his bones that the sun couldn't provide.

"Your people thrive without the shackles of their priests," Ruhen said. "Already I can feel the strength of the Litse returning."

Gesh inclined his head. "Optimism returns," he countered, "and that has been rare among my people for decades. It is the only start I could wish for, now our ancient enemy has been defeated."

"We have a new enemy, one just as terrible as the Menin, only their hatred is for all who look to the future." As the little boy stepped forward to the edge of the upper terrace there was a collective intake of breath from his followers. They moved forward eagerly onto the lawns where the most devoted of Ruhen's Children sat or knelt in small groups. The soldiers stayed where they were on the lower tier, but the Harlequin bodyguards advanced to crouch on the lowest steps in front of Ruhen, wary of letting even white-cloaked devotees within striking distance.

Gesh found himself standing like an attendant with Luerce and Koteer. All of them were stilled by the upwelling of emotion that broke like a wave and filled the air around them; a great thermal reverence that made Gesh want to open his wings and catch it and draw their wordless prayers into him as a God might.

Gesh kept his eyes on the child. Ruhen looked too small to contain such a force of personality, but he had the immediate attention of every person there. His neat little hands were clasped together as though he was about to begin praying, but he did nothing of the sort as he looked around the gardens. A tiny zephyr danced across the grass between them and swirled around the child to twitch the long hem of his tunic and ruffle his wavy brown hair.

Ruhen half-turned at the touch, a ghost of a smile appearing on his lips.

Just that small expression was a soothing touch to Gesh's heart. He touched his fingers to the pocket where he kept Ruhen's coin, the one given to him as Lord Celao slowly expired. Though Ismess now lacked priests to complain, Gesh would still not wear it around his neck. His new allies did not appear to care; it was enough that he had accepted it in friendship. Ruhen understood that the Litse were a proud race. They wanted no master but one of their own, and so he did not force one on them.

But here I stand anyway, Gesh realised, *finding strength in a child's reflected glory.* He smiled as Ruhen started to speak to the crowds below. *But through him the Litse will be great again. In these dark times, his very frailty makes us all strong.*

"We live in years of hardship, my siblings," Ruhen said, and as the people pressed forward to hear better Gesh tasted magic in the air. Mage Peness had his eyes closed and his lips were moving silently. Ruhen repeated his words and this time Gesh heard them as though the child was speaking directly to him, as if they were alone in the cool autumn afternoon.

"War has drained us all," Ruhen continued, "and fear in its purest form walks the lonely places of this Land while our Gods lie weak and injured. There is much to fear in this Land—enemies mass on our borders and even together, even united, our armies might not prove strong enough to defeat them."

Gesh felt a chill at Ruhen's words, remembering the preachers in his quarter who spoke of an army of daemons attending the enemy. He was not afraid of battle or foolish peasant rumours—no Chosen white-eye would be so weak—but with all that had happened recently, from the collapse of Scree to the waking of a dragon in the Library of Seasons, he wondered what other terrors might accompany this Age. One army of daemons had been faced; how unlikely was it that the King of Narkang had bound another to his service?

Ruhen's voice comforted him, and Gesh let it wash through his mind. The very fear he mentioned was diminished by a little boy who could speak of it so simply, so honestly.

"We are servants of peace, all of us, but we must give thanks to those who march out to defend this peace, those who have overcome the fear in their hearts and gone beyond the city walls to face the oncoming threat."

There was a great murmur at that, many no doubt remembering the day Ruhen faced down the daemons outside Byora, but Gesh was thinking of more practical details. His few remaining troops garrisoned the southern towns and villages ruled by Ismess; the only recruitment there was a legion raised to fight under a Devoted banner. Most of the Litse white-eyes had gone with the Devoted armies; their gift of flight was invaluable for coordinating movements and watching for invaders.

General Afasin's Mustet troops had taken recruits from Akell and marched to the Narkang border to meet the threat head-on. A modest force of Byoran and Imess soldiers had accompanied them, enough to escort the half-dozen mages who were unwelcome within the Devoted ranks.

"This army of the devoted has fought the fear that clouds hearts. In the service of peace, of the Gods themselves, they drive fear from their minds and think only of serving the innocent and weak."

Ruhen's voice remained calm, Gesh realised; he never displayed the grand passion an orator would normally use. He spoke to each person individually, leaving righteous fury for those who sought to manipulate their audience. Instead Ruhen's words were personal, a conversation where one side need only listen, and recognise the wisdom of what they were hearing.

"This service of peace is a calling none can deny. Those of us blessed by the Gods with wisdom must guide others; those with health must minister to the sick; those blessed with strength must support and protect their brethren."

Gesh nodded absentmindedly. His own forces might be weak, but an army from Embere was now camped outside the Circle City, ready to defend it. He felt the truth of Ruhen's words in his bones, cementing in his heart his decision; he had taken the right path by allying the Litse with the child. All the while something tugged inside at him, some deep compulsion that he was not doing enough for his people.

Gesh's thoughts turned to the bow Ilit had gifted him with, the good it could do to the armies protecting them. He was strong—the greatest warrior of his people. Though he knew his place was in Ismess, the urge to leave and follow the Devoted army momentarily took his breath away.

He opened his eyes with a slight gasp—he hadn't even realised he'd closed them—as the desire washed over him. Looking around him he saw others doing the same, nodding heads and faces awakened to action.

A massive force from Raland—fully thirty thousand battle-ready troops, Knights of the Temples wearing Telith Vener's device as well as the Runesword emblem of their Order—had been not far behind the Embere Army, and they were now headed to Tor Salan to recruit the city's ruling Mosaic Council. The entire Order of the Knights of the Temples had answered the call, and Gesh's heart swelled to be numbered among such men.

Duke Chaist, Telith Vener's hated neighbour, had not felt the same; he had broken out in quite a sweat at the sight of so many battle-ready Raland troops appearing at short notice, apparently—but the pressure had in the end forced them to put aside their petty arguments. These bickering children, who switched the focus of their bullying and slyness as easily as breathing, were now united under a more noble banner than the Runeswords they carried.

All around the Stepped Gardens Gesh saw movement. The Harlequin guards crouched, hands on sword-hilts, but the people struggling to their feet were not advancing on Ruhen—it was quite the opposite. As Gesh fought the sensation to move himself, white-cloaked disciples and common folk alike began to turn towards the gates of the city.

"Against faith," Ruhen was declaring, "fear can have no sway. Those who face the darkness are the most blessed of the Gods—they walk without fear, shielded by the faith of those they protect."

From the assembled crowds came cries of urgency and desperation as more and more people left, some even picking up loose stones that they might carry as weapons to smite the Narkang heretics. Gesh shuddered and shook himself, trying to fight the mad mood crawling over him, until he was forced to embrace the magic inside him again and open his wings. The reminder of his own strength, the power and will of Ilit that flowed through his bones, cast aside the fervour or spell—he could not tell which—and he saw with fresh eyes the effect on those assembled.

Several of the nearest disciples were lying on the ground, frothing at the mouth or convulsing with apoplexy; many more knelt with arms outstretched, reaching out as though Ruhen truly stood just before them, speaking to them alone, and they could embrace his words. Gesh took a step back as the little boy looked down at the arrayed people, savouring the effect he had had upon them.

"Face them down, my brothers and sisters," Ruhen said softly, almost tenderly, to renewed howls. "Let faith sustain you, let faith protect you. Face them with the strength of peace in your hearts—face the heretics and sweep them from this holy Land of Gods and peace."

As the screaming intensified, Gesh could stand it no more. He leapt into the air, as desperate as the rest to leave that place.

Amber rode towards the castle with no regard for the soldiers attempting to block his path. Behind him was a troop of twenty Menin soldiers, in full armour and caked in dust from the long ride. A cold wind blew from the south and stretched out the banner carried by the man behind him. The black flag had the Menin rune at its centre, with their former lord's Fanged Skull on one side, on the other a golden bee to signify their new master.

Amber could see the confusion on the faces of Kingsguard; probably the only reason why blood hadn't yet been drawn. He had marched the remaining Menin legions hard all the way from Farrister, not giving anyone, least of all himself, time to pause. There was dissent still, he could hear the whispers abruptly cut off when he came into view, but the king's choice had been no real choice at all.

"Major," shouted a voice over those of the young soldiers demanding he stop, and Nai trotted out into the road. The necromancer—perhaps *former* necromancer, Amber reflected, thinking the king would likely not stand for that continuing—was dressed in functional black like a proper member of the Brotherhood now, and carried an edged mace slung over one shoulder.

"He's even got you wearing boots, Nai," Amber replied, raising a hand for his troops to halt. "What's the Land coming to? What would your former master say?"

Nai glanced down at the army boots he'd been issued with. He had never worn footwear, not crossing Byoran or Narkang lands, in the whole time Amber had known him. "That the king's a genius?" Nai muttered. He gave a sniff. "Apparently bare feet detract from the mystique the Brotherhood's aiming for."

Before Amber could reply he was forced to jerk the reins of his horse out of a young officer's grip. "Hey, try and take them again and you'll lose your head," he growled.

"Whoa!" shouted Nai, running between the two men as weapons were drawn, "step back, Captain!"

"He can't take an armed troop into the castle!" the captain yelled, struggling fruitlessly against the arm Nai had wrapped around his bicep.

"That's not your decision!" Nai said, loud enough for the captain's troops to hear too. They all had their weapons out and the only thing now keeping them from the Menin was the bee device on Nai's collar. He gave the captain a shove and sent him reeling backwards into his troops. Before the man had recovered his balance Nai was already drawing magic into himself.

The Kingsguard were drifting closer from all directions, hands reaching for weapons. The Menin showed no sign of backing down. Nai held his hand out to the captain as though warning him to stop, but instead of speaking he made a sweeping motion with his hand that cast a trail of spitting sparks towards the faces of those about to attack. The soldiers reeled, hands raised to cover their eyes and swat the sparks away from hair and clothes.

By the time the magic had faded to nothing, Nai had made up the ground and grabbed the captain by the collar and hoisted him up one-handed for all to see. Coils of green and black light raced around his hand, growing faster and more intense with every passing moment. The black light left a smoky, sulphurous trace in the air, and Amber realised Nai's past had to be common knowledge now: he was playing on the fear others felt at the word *necromancer*. It had the desired effect as the eager troops scrambled back.

"All of you, sheathe your weapons!" Nai roared, turning to make it clear he included the Menin in that order. Amber gave a small gesture and his men obeyed, spurring compliance from the Narkang troops.

"Now, get back to your duties. You, Captain—you and your men see to Major Amber's horses, you hear me? Amber, please dismount and follow me—just a few officers, please; the rest can wait here or return to your troops, I really don't care."

Amber cocked his head at the man. Nai wasn't really suited to giving orders, but he appeared to be learning the Brotherhood way, expecting commoners and generals alike to jump on command.

"Since you asked so nicely," Amber said before continuing in Menin, knowing the necromancer was the only other able to speak the dialect, "Dorom, Kesax, with me. The rest of you wait here and try to not to kill any of the king's precious troops. Apparently they don't have many to spare these days."

With the two colonels as his side, Amber followed Nai to Camatayl Castle. Kamfer's Ford had grown in the days he'd been absent; now corrals, barracks, tents and warehouses were dotting the plain around the town. There were wagon-trains approaching, laden with food to maintain the army King Emin was building, and beyond he could pick out troops practising manoeuvres.

The Kingsguard inspecting the faces of everyone entering the castle said quietly to Nai, "If they're going in armed, you keep 'em clear of Forrow, eh?"

Nai nodded at the sense of that and waved Amber and the colonels through and across the cluttered courtyard. Amber could see a large feathered hat at the centre of a knot of soldiers. Men instinctively parted for them before King Emin had even noticed their arrival. Nai placed himself square in front of the king's bodyguard to block his path.

"Ah, Major," Emin said cheerily, "I wasn't expecting you back so soon."

"It's General now," Amber replied, feeling his hand tighten instinctively into a fist before he could catch himself.

"General? Ah, the Menin right of challenge? I hadn't realised that worked in the military too."

"It doesn't—but General Arek could think of no man higher ranked than he now our lord was dead."

"Hardly a fair fight," Emin said with an appraising look. Arek had been a fighting man, but few reached the rank of general while still in the prime of their life, and Amber was powerful, even for a Menin.

"He realised that," Amber said, his tone of voice making it clear he didn't want to discuss the matter further. Arek had died like a warrior, in a manner of his own choosing.

"As you say, General Amber." Emin gestured to the men around him. "Since you are here, please report on the state of your men for my advisors."

Amber recognised several faces: Dashain of the Brotherhood, General Bessarei of the Kingsguard and Suzerain Derenin among them, but only the Farlan veteran Carel had given him any sort of proper acknowledgement.

"I command ten battle-ready legions—five heavy infantry, two medium and one of archers—plus one of skirmishers and a legion of cavalry support, if I can secure fresh horses for most of them."

"And they will fight under my banner?"

"They'll fight for me," Amber said stiffly. "I have promised them your assistance with supplies and in crossing hostile ground and in return they will fight any troops who try to block their path. But they'll not fight under your flag any time soon."

Emin hesitated a moment, most likely picturing a map of the route Amber was planning for his army. It would cut through the heart of Ruhen's lands and past Thotel to the great high plain that interrupted the mountain line there. It would give him everything he needed.

"That is acceptable. I thank you, General. Will you permit troops to be attached to your command? The Devoted have many Farlan in their ranks, and I believe their cavalry surpasses your own. I offer a few legions of my own best, the Green Scarves, and mages too, since you are assuming the lead on a dangerous journey."

Amber turned to the men who'd accompanied him. "Green Scarves," he muttered to them in Menin. "Will you fight with them if they provide support?"

The pair exchanged a look. "We heard of them in dispatches," Dorom replied, "but neither of us have personally encountered these legions. I believe they were a major irritant for our lord's armies during the advance: brave soldiers led by a God-marked daemon."

"Led by a daemon?" Amber asked King Emin.

The king smiled indulgently. "He does get a bit over-excited at times—I believe they're referring to General Daken. The Green Scarves are currently commanded by Colonel Dassai, but Daken will be rejoining them soon."

Amber straightened a little. "Your mission was a success?"

"It was. And that leads me to this: Isak Stormcaller will be arriving here soon. You and your men had best keep clear of him."

"Clear?" Amber growled.

"Well clear. If you need a reason, it's this: he went to find an object of great power, Death's own weapon. None of us know the damage he'll wreak if he's attacked. You know his mind is damaged; the Gods alone know what toll Termin Mystt is taking, so he may prove indiscriminate."

"I shall instruct my men accordingly."

"You do that." Carel spoke up, ignoring the shocked looks from some of the king's advisors. "All you'll get is a bad death, and you better believe I'll be leading the massacre o' the rest o' your boys before anyone gets a chance to stop me. Don't reckon many o' these boys here will care who's giving the order if it's to kill Menin."

Amber bit down on his lip, fighting the anger that blossomed hot in his stomach. "I hear you, Carel," he said after a moment. "You have my word."

Emin looked from one man to the other. "I think we all understand each other, so let us move on. General Amber, what condition are your troops in?"

Amber kept his eyes on Carel a moment longer before returning his attention to the matter at hand. "Their condition?" he said, "tired mostly. Being holed up in a town on short rations hasn't done any of them much good. I could do with a week to get them back into proper order before they're ready to fight a drilled army."

"You have it: a mile or so north of here there's a stretch of heath you can camp on. Plenty of water there too." He thought for a minute then said, "General, the bulk of your troops are heavy infantry. You will not fight alongside my armies—what about an élite force not of either of our tribes?"

"Got one up your sleeve, have you?"

King Emin inclined his head, smiling slightly as he tugged one braided cuff then the other in the manner of a travelling conjurer. "My mage assisting Lord Isak's swift return tells me we have had an offer of assistance from an unexpected source. I suspect your battle tactics will be to push through anyone arrayed against you and break their order. These troops could provide a breach of the lines on command."

Amber narrowed his eyes at the king. "Just who're you talking about here?"

"The Legion of the Damned—I believe you saw them at work in Scree?"

"Not up close, just from the city walls, but I didn't much like what I saw. They slaughtered more'n a thousand at the gate itself, gave 'em nowhere to run and never listened for quarter."

"I am told they've pledged their loyalty, though obedience might be yours to persuade. Mage Ashain informs me they will arrive soon. They are travelling faster than Lord Isak's party."

The big officer scowled. "Don't sound an easy task, but I'll use 'em, sure. Bastards'll be worth the trouble."

"Good. The bulk of my troops are spread out in an attempt to restore some order to the eastern parts of Narkang. If I need not recall them to support your army I am thankful."

"The bulk of your troops?" Amber asked, gesturing towards the thousands of soldiers encamped beyond the castle walls.

"The men you see here are largely raw recruits and those mostly inexperienced troops who survived Moorview. I've had to divert much of the Canar Thrit reinforcements to the Vanach border to dissuade any expansion of boundaries there, and the legions from Canar Fell are untested in battle. General Bessarei here tells me he needs another month before sending them into battle. We will be marching, I assure you, but it will be in your wake, once the enemy are forced to react to your efforts."

Amber gave the king a brief bow of acknowledgement. Tense and tentative allies they might be, but still Amber felt the warrior spirit inside him cry out to obey this ruler. Loyalty and duty were beaten into the minds of every Menin warrior. For generations they had had a lord without equal, one worthy of reverence and sacrifice. Though pride and anger kept Amber aloof and disrespectful, in that moment he realised he would always be a soldier in need of a master.

The king's ice-blue eyes glittered knowingly as Amber met his gaze and a chill ran down his spine—did the king realise that too? Had he been counting on it when he sent away the best of his army?

"Thank you, General," said Emin. "I'm sure you are keen to see to your men. Gentlemen, we shall reconvene in the morning."

After King Emin's meeting with his newest general, both Menin and Narkang commanders swiftly moved on to the many tasks screaming for their immediate attention. Carel found himself alone in the lee of the castle wall while life continued around him. Gusts of wind swirled across the courtyard, invisible but for the leaves and dust they picked up, but they were all Carel could see. Sweeping over men as though they weren't there, the twists of wind possessed a strange life of their own that perfectly matched the high, urgent calls of the swifts that Carel normally heard only in the northern summer. There was no God here, not even those spirits too weak to be called Aspects; maybe because of that, Carel was entranced. For months the old warrior had felt himself little more than a puff of wind amidst this great storm.

It wasn't just those who'd died. Mihn had been a source of quiet strength, and not just to Isak; Vesna was a friend he'd relied on. He'd been set adrift from his life on the wagon-train and he couldn't imagine how he could ever go back, even after Isak's death. He'd belonged in Tirah Palace, but with the Ghosts marched away and all his friends dead, Carel had found no real place for him there now. The Chief Steward would always have work for trusted veterans, but he had felt like a ghost, walking corridors that echoed with voices of the departed.

"Is this place any different?" Carel asked himself. "It's no more of a home for me—or is home just chasing after that surly brat the rest o' my life?" He pulled his jacket a little tighter around his body and glanced down at his left sleeve where his arm had once been. The back of his damn hand was itching again, the hand that'd been tossed into a fire, so Mihn had said.

"Sure someone told me somethin' about that," he muttered as he stepped back to make way for two porters carrying a crate; the men were careful not to notice him talking to himself—there were many around without livery or uniform who'd take exception to being disturbed by a servant. "Was it your mother, Isak?" he asked himself.

He shrugged and forced himself to start off across the courtyard and back to Kamfer's Ford. "Think it might've been, superstitious lot, those caravan folk. First time I met her, too—Horman brought her along when I was still in the guard. Man was so alive then, walking well and made taller by love."

He stopped by the gate and looked around at the bustling inhabitants—soldiers and clerks for the main, little more than boys, wearing the green-and-gold of the Kingsguard.

"That's how I remember your father," Carel whispered to the small gusts of wind that followed him across the courtyard, "so young he still had fluff on his cheeks, but on his arm was this dark-eyed beauty—she was a wild and wilful one, was Larassa. You got more from her than Horman ever let you know."

He headed outside, letting the breeze cool his eyes where tears where threatening to form. "No memories of your ma; that always hurt you. Now they say you don't remember me either?" His thoughts dissolved into memory, the day King Emin had returned to Kamfer's Ford, not so long after Carel had arrived himself, and met in Major Amber a soul as damaged as his own. When the king returned, Carel had been the first person he'd summoned. He'd hardly expected to meet the man again, but a pair of Kingsguard had hustled him all the way to a private meeting.

Surprise had melted into shock and sick disbelief when he was presented to the King of Narkang. The man had been full of worry, the stink of it filling the room, leaving Carel fearful for his few remaining friends. But to learn that Isak was alive— The king's words had robbed him of the ability to stand; the king's new bodyguard had had to half-carry him to a chair.

But the grief at Isak's death, still eating at Carel's guts, was doubled at what he heard then: his boy, dragged out of Ghenna, scarred and scared and traumatised—Carel's head had already been reeling when the final punch came, driving the wind from his lungs, emptying his stomach and leaving black stars of pain bursting before his eyes. Remembering that moment even now forced him to stop by the road and drop to his knees, retching, as his heart threatened to burst.

"*Carel, I'm sorry, but there's more,*" the king had said. "*He—*" For a moment even the King of Narkang had been lost for words. "*His mind was hurt, Carel. The pain of Ghenna was too much for him. The witch of Llehden had to take memories from his mind to save what was left. He—Isak—he doesn't remember you. He will not know you if he sees you again. Carel, I'm sorry, but you are lost to him.*"

It wasn't far, but it took Carel a long time to reach the town, lost as he was in his memories. He found himself resting on the swordstick he used to support himself more often these days. He only caught himself at the river, when the click of the stick's metal tip on the bridge woke him from his thoughts. Carel stared at the stick, struck by a sudden urge to throw it into the river.

"You'll have to do better than that," a woman called.

Carel turned and peered through the low light at the speaker. "Ardela?"

"If you're going to pitch yourself off, best find somewhere higher," the former Hand of Fate advised, stepping lightly over to him. She was dressed in men's clothing as usual, but judging by her battered brigandine and black breeches worn over high boots, this time she'd looted the tent of some Brotherhood man. Short, unruly curls of dark black hair poked out from beneath an ancient wide-brimmed hat that Carel guessed would make the king laugh.

He looked down at the river, some twelve feet down below. "You could be right, but I was more thinking of takin' my life back from this damn thing."

"Your swordstick?"

"I keep finding myself putting my weight on it," he admitted. "It's turning me into an old man."

"That ain't the stick, old man—anyways, not as if you're one o' those wrecks shuffling around with their white collar stained so bad by wine, folk won't believe they were ever in the Ghosts."

Carel straightened up automatically. He was certainly more grey-haired than in his army days, but it had been the loss of his arm that ended his fighting career, not his age. "I'm not so old as that."

"True," Ardela conceded, "but any fool can see the weight on your shoulders, so maybe the stick's not so bad an idea."

"Since when did you find such wisdom? Come with the tattoos, did it?"

Ardela automatically looked down at the circles on her palms. They were recently done, and the slow way, as she'd not been present after the battle. "I think that's experience, not wisdom. There are times I've needed a stick too."

Carel looked the muscular young woman up and down. "Somehow I find that hard to picture."

"Aye, well, I'd have said the same about Legana. First time I met her I thought she was just some mad blind woman out in the forest—a long way from the Hand of Fate I'd heard was the best of us," Ardela said with fierce pride. "She walks with a stick now; that's not so much a ruse as the blindfold she uses to shade her eyes, but it doesn't mean she's so weak as all that. Any man here'll come off worst against her, I promise you that."

"I'll not be the one to test her," he said, forcing a smile, "but I like the thought o' not being entirely useless. So how does it feel, to walk as silently as the Grave Thief?"

"No different yet, not till Legana's back. The magic to link us comes from her; these tattoos are mostly to make the job easier for her; at least that's what Nai says. Doing it all from scratch, she'd need Mihn there every time and that ain't so practical for a sisterhood. With the tattoos done and a brand ready, the God part of her can put in the magic easy enough."

"Brand?"

Ardela grinned, reminding Carel more than a little of Isak. White-eyes didn't enjoy pain, he knew that, but the prospect was enough to animate the savage fighter within them and Ardela looked no different there.

"Aye, that 'heart' rune they all got on their chests—came from Lord Isak, I'm told, but it's the pain of the tattoos and the branding that opens the path for the magic. Don't understand it much myself, but given some of the shit I've seen mages do it makes sense."

Carel hesitated. "So it's a link to Isak too? To Mihn, to Legana, to Xeliath too, if she'd still been alive?"

"Guess so, why?"

"Come on." And without bothering to explain, Carel set off to the small compound on the eastern edge of the original town, the large stone house and a pair of barns which had been appropriated by those priestesses and Hands of Fate who'd answered Legana's call in search of a new purpose. The original owner had died in the Menin advance; King Emin had been glad to offer his new allies the space to make their own. Carel guessed it housed a hundred or more of the sisterhood, a good dozen of whom had been priestesses of the Lady.

The compound was surrounded by a wicker fence the height of a man, and armed women stood on guard at each of the gates. The guard stepped in front of Carel well before he reached it, her spear lowered enough to force him to stop or be impaled upon it. The Farlan veteran didn't break stride but struck with surprising speed, battering the spear aside with his stick, then stepping inside her guard, he turned into her blow as she struck at him with the butt of the spear, getting too close for there to be any real force in it.

"Stay your weapon!" Ardela called from behind him. "He's with me."

The guard scowled at Carel, her face only inches from his, before growling, "Doesn't mean he'll be welcome, heretic."

"Watch your tongue, bitch," Ardela snapped back. "Now step aside or I'll put you down."

"What do you want, heretic's friend?" the guard said, flushing with anger, but directing her antagonism at Carel. She knew full-well Ardela was one of their best killers.

"You to get out my way," Carel said quietly. "I ain't going to ask again."

The guard blinked and found the handle of his swordstick pressed against her throat. The rounded pommel was solid brass and he could see she knew how little effort it would take to crush her windpipe, one-armed or not.

Carel eased himself to one side, allowing the guard to do the same and edge out of his way so he could slip through. He wasn't surprised when Ardela stayed outside while he continued on.

The enclosed area was a hive of activity. The doors of the nearer of the barns were wide open, and Carel could see the small forge inside. Before it were several tables where all sorts of work was being done, but none that interested him. He ploughed on to the other side where he could see a gate leading to the stone-walled courtyard of the main house, and his gamble paid off: the priestesses were taking advantage of the daylight.

"Who are you? What are you doing here?" the nearest woman spluttered in outrage. Judging by the wrinkles on her face, Carel guessed she was older than he was, despite the bright copper hair tied back in a plait.

"Your new recruit," he declared, stepping past her. One young woman was stripped to the waist, with just a scarf wrapped crossways over her breasts to cover them. Three copper-haired priestesses were gathered around her, tattoo needles poised. He nodded companionably at the young woman and found himself a stool opposite her, shrugging off his coat as he sat.

"And to think Cedei told me I'd not get so much as an eyeful round here," he commented as he fumbled one-handed with the toggles on his doublet.

"What in the name of the Dark Place do you think you're doing?" hissed the oldest of the priestesses, brandishing a long bone needle tipped with black ink.

"I want you to tattoo me; I need it done before your Mortal-Aspect arrives."

"You're not one of us—why?"

Carel winced as he tugged his doublet over his maimed arm. The stump underneath looked pale and withered in the dull light of day. It had been a clean cut, made by Eolis when Isak realised the arm couldn't be saved, but still the swirls of scarring from where he'd cauterised the wound looked horrific to Carel.

"I've got my reasons."

"Not good enough," the priestess snapped. "I'm not wasting hours of work on some ancient veteran just because he wants to rejoin the Ghosts."

"Do it," Ardela called from the open gate. The priestesses turned in surprise, more than one tensing at the sight of her. "You can't deny Carel—he's more right to this mark than any of us."

The priestess shook her head firmly. "Our sisters are the only ones who have a right to it. He is no one."

"He's more than you know. The tattoos belong to Mihn and the witch who made them; the Ghosts and our sisterhood are only borrowing that power. Mihn did it out of devotion to his lord, and Carel's got more claim to that than we do."

"Then he can wait for Legana to return—if she sees the right of it, she will decide."

Ardela moved in and shut the courtyard door behind her. One hand rested casually on the hilt of her plundered Harlequin sword. "Man's clearly got a reason for wanting it now. I've spent enough time around those at the forefront of this war to recognise that look in his eye. It's a reason that goes to the bone."

"I do," Carel said, a quaver entering his voice as King Emin's words echoed in his mind, "one that's my own. Your Mortal-Aspect don't think that's a good reason, she can take the damn tattoos back."

The priestess's expression became pointed. "She might yet do that—the spirit of our Goddess flows through our sister's veins. Neither cares much for the pain of the undeserving."

"She can take 'em back with a rusty knife," Carel growled, sitting forward to look the priestess straight in the eye, "my oath on it, if she don't think I'm worthy."

The priestess sighed and glanced at the young woman whose tattoos were unfinished. The woman nodded and reached for her shirt.

"As you wish. Carel, is it? Well Carel, let's start with your hands. I'm going nowhere near the soles of your feet till you've washed."

CHAPTER 24

CAREL EDGED FORWARD, his steps uncertain, the tip of his sword pointed at the Kingsguard's face. The scuff of his boots on the ground and the chink of chainmail were the only sounds he made. The soldier watched his approach from behind a large round shield and waited for an opportunity; his sword he kept close to his body, half-hidden behind the shield. Only his eyes moved, glancing constantly between Carel's sword-tip and his shuffling feet.

The veteran feinted but was ignored except for a twitch of the shield, then his opponent suddenly moved, trying to swat Carel's sword away with his own. The former Ghost only just managed to avoid it; once he would have caught the blade and ridden any buffeting, but he had no shield of his own, and that affected the way he now fought. He took a step closer, crowding his opponent and trying to batter down on his arm.

The man responded by turning behind his shield again and driving forward. Carel was forced backwards, his sword-arm caught by the shield, and he heard the ominous scrape of steel over mail across his belly.

"You're dead, old man," laughed a soldier on the sidelines. "Thought you Ghosts were meant to have some skills?"

Carel stepped back, scowling. "Been a while since I used one o' these."

"Stop trying to fence with it, then!" called a voice from somewhere behind him. "Fast way to get dead that looks."

The Kingsguard soldiers all tensed and several had started reaching for their weapons before they caught themselves.

"Easy boys," Carel said, "man's an ally now, remember?"

General Amber was standing behind the dozen young Narkang warriors, all of them in full armour, their faces flushed from sparring. He didn't bother to confirm Carel's words; the look on his face was stony and he was also dressed for war. "Take your hands off your weapons, *boys*," he said at last, "less you don't fancy reaching manhood."

The Menin looked to his left, in case the Kingsguard hadn't noticed the bodyguards who followed him everywhere. They carried long axes, using them as unwieldy walking sticks so they were constantly to hand.

"How's about everyone here remembers their orders?" Carel demanded loudly, then turned to the big Menin. "Amber, what're you doing here? Thought you were marching out today."

He inclined his head. "Until I saw your efforts just then, anyway. You keen on getting yourself killed, old man?"

"Just rusty is all."

"Prancing around with a swordstick will do that for a soldier," Amber agreed. He held out his hand and Carel, after barely hesitating, handed over his sword. It was a one-handed weapon, naturally, with a thin double-edged blade that tapered to a long point.

"It's light," Amber commented, "but you're not going to put out anyone's eye with it." He gave Carel an assessing look, stepped to his left side and prodded him in the ribs then shoulder. He shook his head. "Just mail? Most soldiers won't bother slashing at you, especially if you're as close as you just were. Get some steel bands to cover your ribs—you're open to sticking there."

Carel's eyes went to Amber's twin scimitars. The general had a long reach with them, but it was a curiously elegant style of fighting that belied the man's size and strength. They were heavy, slashing weapons and few had the skill to thrust with such swords. "You would."

"But most likely I'm not who you'll be facing: I need to stand back and cut faster than my enemy lunges, and so do you." He waved a finger in the vague direction of the Kingsguard Carel had been sparring with. "Ask any of them: they'd try to close and pin you, then jam something in your ribs just as you got there."

"So I need a scimitar? Maybe if I had my old one, but that's best in General Lahk's hands. I'm too old to learn with a full-weight sword."

"You're too old to learn," he agreed, "so stick to what you know—and don't move like you're fencing. You've not got the speed to lunge any more, so don't bother; stand off and use your experience." He turned to Carel's sparring partner. "You, advance on me like before."

At a nod from Carel the man did so, again coming low behind his shield. In one smooth movement Amber drew a scimitar and stood ready, left arm tucked behind his back to mimic Carel's lost limb. He stood more square-on than Carel had, and he moved his sword moving constantly, all the while watching his opponent advance. Carel felt his hand tighten around the grip of his own sword as the two came within striking distance, then smiled as Amber took a pace back and out of range.

The Kingsguard hesitated a moment, then hurried to make up the ground again, but in that moment Amber moved right and slashed high, right to left. On instinct the Kingsguard pushed his shield forward to block the blow, but Amber tilted his body and let the blade skip lightly off the shield before flicking it back around and underneath to touch against the arm. By the time the soldier's own sword had come up to strike, Amber was further around and the soldier's blow barely reached the Menin's pauldron while Amber went for a second strike to the back of the man's neck.

The scimitar hovered six inches from a lethal blow and the soldier froze. Even as Amber stepped neatly away, the man's face showed he was imagining the blow falling on a part only knights could afford to protect properly.

"Steal a knight's pauldron; pad and protect that shoulder," Amber said as he sheathed his weapon. "You cut from range, then they'll do the same. You *will* take blows, but most'll be looking to bring the fight to you. If they do get in close, surprise them and meet it—put your weight on the shield and thrust over."

Carel nodded and sheathed his weapon.

His movement reminded his Kingsguard opponent that his was still drawn, and he lowered his weapon.

"You got time to spar?"

"Sorry," Amber said, "we're marching out today. The army's just waiting for me to return. I want to get a good distance under my belt before evening."

"So why're you here?"

Amber opened his mouth to speak, then hesitated. Carel recognised the flicker of pain in his eyes from several evenings of hard drinking together. It was easy for Amber's mind to slip to subjects that physically pained him; Nai used his name regularly to reinforce the man's defences against it, but there was no healing the wound completely.

At a look from Carel the Kingsguard backed off to give them privacy; Amber's bodyguards did the same once the Kingsguard had moved away from their commander.

That's a sad sign right there: I'm just an old cripple in their eyes, no threat to anyone.

"Lord Isak will return here soon," Amber began hesitantly. "I'll be gone by then, but we will meet—before we reach Byora. I do not know—" He stopped.

"How you'll act?" Carel prompted at last, looking at him. The Menin's face was an open book now, his thoughts writ clear.

Amber ducked his head as though Carel had swung at it. "How I'll act, yes. He—he broke my mind. He tore out a part of me."

"None of us are whole, friend," Carel said softly. To emphasise his point the veteran raised his good arm and the stump of his left. "That's what war does to us. That's what we do to each other."

"For a time, all that kept me alive was the hatred I felt. Nai gave me a—" He cast around for the right word in Farlan. His command of the dialect was impressive, reinforced by magery, no doubt, but Carel could see his thoughts were still a jumble. "The necromancer gave me point of reference," he went on, "but it was either pain or hatred. I chose the one that would keep me alive."

"I understand." Now it was Carel's turn to feel the hurt of memories, but his were as much shame as grief. "I blamed a friend for Isak's death. The boy was a white-eye, for pity's sake—he was supposed to outlive the grandchildren of anyone I knew, not die before an old wreck like me. I couldn't deal with the loss, I realise that now, so I heaped it on another. I'm just glad Vesna was strong enough to survive it—though he wouldn't even return the favour when he lost his betrothed, just took it all on his own shoulders."

"Vesna? The Mortal-Aspect?"

Carel nodded sadly. "Cruel blessing, that, I think. He's the sort to take on the burdens of the whole Land, thinking it's his duty, but the Gods' strength can't do much for a man's soul. He'll feel it all in a way no God was supposed to."

"That's what we do to each other," Amber echoed with a haunted expression. "I can't be sure what I will do when I meet your lord. I can't be sure how strong the hatred is—so I ask you to be there when it happens. We are . . . we have come to understand each other, I think. Seeing you beside him may keep my mind clear."

"I'll be there," Carel said fervently, "for more sakes than yours. He's as damaged as you, King Emin says, and carrying a burden that dwarfs anything we could imagine. The boy'll need me, even if he don't know me."

Amber bowed his head in understanding. "Good. After all this loss, we cannot afford to waste what remains."

He turned to head back to his troops, the Menin bodyguards surrounding him. Carel watched the man leave with sadness in his heart. *All this loss, aye. What will be left even in victory? Will we envy the dead?*

When Ardela found him, Carel was taking a beating from a woman half his size. When Dashain stepped back abruptly and lowered the training stick, it took him a while to work out it wasn't a ruse. Gasping for breath, he touched his fingers to the welt on his cheek and winced. The sticks were lighter than swords, of course, but they still hurt when swung with force.

"I knew punishments were different in the Brotherhood," Ardela called, laughing, "but it seems silly to give them a stick of their own!"

Dashain bowed to the newcomer. "It makes them more willing," she countered. "They think it's foreplay more often than not."

"Eh?" Carel huffed, trying to catch his breath long enough to join in with the banter. "I'd be trying harder if that was the case. I ain't that old!"

In response Dashain hopped forward and cracked her stick across the veteran's buttocks before he could move to defend himself. "At least your brain's not as slow as your feet, old man—but don't pretend you could keep up anyways."

Carel raised his hand in surrender and let the stick fall to the ground. He grabbed the cloth lying next to his sword and brigandine to wipe the sweat from his face. By contrast Dashain looked barely ruffled, with little more than an attractive flush on her dimpled cheeks and a rogue strand of hair that was quickly pushed back.

"So how goes you today?" Carel said once he'd dried his face. "Busy with Daughters business?"

Ardela shook her head. "Don't call us that—the Lady's dead."

He noted the change in her demeanour. "As you wish," he said, "but no one knows what to call you now, 'less you'd want 'Sisterhood' to catch on."

"That's Legana's decision." She shifted uncomfortably. "And it's why I came to find you."

"She wants me to come up with a name?" Carel asked before his brain caught up with his mouth. "Legana? She's here?"

"At the compound," Ardela confirmed. She indicated her torso with a slight look of discomfort. "Got my scar and everything—and no, you can't see it."

The attempt at humour didn't diminish Carel's tension; he'd been waiting too long for this moment. "They're all here?" he asked, his voice strained.

She shook her head. "I was waiting for them at a village I thought they'd have to pass. We came on ahead, but the rest are only an hour out."

Carel grabbed his possessions, sheathed the sword and started off towards the compound where the former Hands of Fate lived, then stopped abruptly.

"You met them at the village?" "Gods, Dashain really did beat the sense out of you, didn't she? That's what I said." "I'm tired, is all," Carel growled. He caught his breath, then asked, "So how'd he look?" "Isak?" Ardela's lips tightened. "Tsatach's balls, Carel, he's a sight. You'd best prepare yourself." "How?" he demanded, then shook his head. "Sorry, not meaning to be angry with you." They set off again and he asked, "So

how do I prepare myself for seeing him? I know his body's a mess, that he's less pretty than me these days—but that's not what scares me. I got used to that snow-white arm of his, and I stopped noticing much else about him—it was like Lord Bahl: you didn't see the face so much as the presence."

"Well, he's balanced out the arm, for a start," Ardela muttered. "His right's as black as a charred log now." She couldn't keep the tinge of horror from her voice. "I didn't hear why, but that dog o' his was keeping well away from that side of him."

Despite everything, Carel smiled. "Little bugger always did want a dog," he said sadly. "His father never let him, though; I'll bet Horman was scared it'd go for him when he smacked Isak about."

"Looking at the size of Hulf the man might've had a point."

The veteran didn't speak again until they reached the compound and came face to face with Legana—and found words failed him. Carel had always been told that she was as beautiful as she was savage, and he'd still been expecting someone a little like Dashain or Ardela. But Legana the Mortal-Aspect was neither: her beauty was far from the knowing elegance of Dashain or Ardela's lithe athleticism. Legana was divinely exquisite; not merely enticing but heart-stopping, with a glamour that surpassed physical attraction. From beneath a shawl that shaded her face, Legana's emerald eyes shone, and the strange image of a beautiful young woman resting on a walking stick served only to enhance her arresting presence somehow.

—*Carel?* Legana scribbled on the piece of slate hanging from her neck.

"I— Aye, that's me." He found himself ducking his head to her.

—*Your hand?*

He showed her his palm. "I didn't give 'em much of a choice," he said, feeling the need to explain himself in the face of Legana's unblinking scrutiny.

The Mortal-Aspect cocked her head at Ardela, who had come to stand between them. She touched a finger to the former devotee's arm and nodded.

"Legana says the choice is hers. The tattoos are nothing alone."

"I know that, but I had to hope I could persuade you."

"Then do so," Ardela repeated, her face tight with conflicted emotion. "You're not Brotherhood, nor serving Ghost who'll need every edge behind enemy lines. After the ritual on Tairen Moor, she'd not planned on sharing the power with anyone but those sisters who accompany her."

"Call me a sister if you like," Carel said dismissively. "My link to Isak got severed by something that witch did—now, I ain't blaming her, but the boy's pretty much all I got in this life. I want that connection back, and I want to be at his side, come whatever may."

"He does not remember you," Ardela continued as if he hadn't spoken, "and meeting you might cause him more hurt—you're not the only one he's forgotten, but you're the most important. Seeing you might only make things worse."

Carel said angrily, "If it got cut from his mind, he remembers nothing, but we were like family once and he learned to trust me. I ain't going to abandon the boy. There's no man nor woman alive knows him as well as me. I'll be there to clip his ear 'til the day I die."

His shoulders sagged. "All I'm asking for is for him to feel *something* when he sees me again. I know he won't know me, I ain't kidding myself about that, but this link you've got might make me something less than a stranger and you know I'd die for him before any o' your sisters."

Legana was perfectly still as she observed Carel, who lowered his own gaze, unable to bear the weight of her scrutiny; he could feel it as the warmth of a fire on his cheeks. The moment stretched out: half-a-dozen heartbeats, a dozen, and Carel felt helplessness wash over him. He looked up, preparing to say something he knew he'd regret, when Legana moved with blinding speed: he caught the glint of a knife, his shirt was slashed open and she slammed her palm against his sternum with enough force that he should have been knocked from his feet.

Carel rocked backwards, but he was anchored by a sudden surge of magic that wrapped tendrils of fire around his ribcage. Black stars burst before his eyes as the energies raced out over his body and sparks crackled from his fingertips. The hand on his chest became searing hot. Distantly he heard himself cry out in pain and smelled the sizzle and stink of burning flesh. He watched dark shapes writhe over his raised hand, frozen in the act of reaching for Legana's, the inked skin of his palm reshaped by her magic. Dancing faster than he could follow, black worms of magic slipped down his arm, leaving behind a wet-looking trail of thinner rowan leaves twisted around the original ragged hazel. On his palm the magic writhed in a tight circle until suddenly all that was left behind were the circles and owl's head tattoo, now alive and bright with magic.

Carel sagged as the energies flowing through him broke off, unable to bear his own weight. Without Ardela slipping her arm around him, he'd have dropped to his knees. For a while all he could do was pant like an exhausted dog.

"*It is done,*" said Legana's voice in his mind. "*You are one of us, bound to us.*"

"Thank you," Carel gasped.

"*It is not a gift. There will be a price,*" she warned.

"I understand," he whispered. "I'm here to help Isak in whatever way I can."

"*Even if that is by leaving his side and never returning.*"

Carel found the strength to stand again. *Gods, maybe Commander Jachen was right: she's a pitiless bitch to the end.*

"I told you," he repeated angrily, "I'm here for Isak. If he needs me to go, I'll go."

At last she smiled at him. "*Then I'll call you brother,*" she said, "*or perhaps sister, since you were so insistent about that.*"

Carel was too drained even to smile. He nodded vaguely. "My thanks," he managed. "Time to go and see what Isak thinks now." He wobbled a moment before righting himself, waving off Ardela's assistance and heading back towards the gate.

Legana put her hand on Ardela's arm and squeezed it. "*Go with him. He might need a friend. There are still some novices who require the ritual; our reunion would have had to wait, even without Marshal Carelfolden's urgent need.*"

Ardela caught up with Carel just outside the gate. "Easy there," she told him. "Take a moment, Carel."

"Wait?" he demanded.

She planted herself in front of him. "Yes, wait—and breathe, will you? You look about ready to pitch on your face."

"I can catch my breath on the way," he huffed, but when he tried to push past her, Ardela easily held him back.

"Do it for me, then," she said. She pointed to his tattooed palm. "That might be just be a means to an end for you, but it's more than that to the rest of us. Take a moment and really look at what she's done. You're linked to us for ever, but you've not even bloody looked at the scar on your chest!"

Carel scowled. "Seen it before," he mumbled, but he stopped and lifted his shirt to see the raised scar. The shape was familiar enough, a circle bearing the heart rune, just as Isak and Mihn had borne. "Strange though," he murmured, "I barely knew Xeliath, and now her name's on my chest."

"I never even met the girl," Ardela said with surprising gentleness, "but Legana still told me to think of her once the ritual was done." She touched her fingers to the stump of his left arm and moved the pinned-up sleeve covering it. Underneath, though distorted by the uneven scar tissue, was another tattoo, still identifiable as the concentric circles on Carel's palm despite looking as though viewed through a sheet of ice. Ardela didn't appear surprised at the sight, but Carel gaped, for the priestess hadn't put a tattoo on his hand-less arm.

"The magic is all about balance," she explained, seeing his face. "These tattoos are what we are now. The course of the rest of our lives is mapped out in these lines, whether they're but few short days or decades from now. There's a purpose to the link between us all. It might be you're destined for different things, but it's all I'm likely to have, so don't go treating it lightly, hear me?"

Carel sighed. "Aye, you're right, Ardela. I'm sorry—can't help but rush, these days, it's either that or stop and think about things I don't want to." He smiled weakly. "Come on, you can tell me about this purpose we share on the way."

Like a pair of mismatched lovers, the two walked through the muddy streets of Kamfer's Ford until they reached the edge of town, the boundary marked by rune-carved stones set there by the king's mages. Beyond that was a forest of tents set in ordered lines, the pale autumn sunlight glinting from a thousand metal objects, almost like a river at sunset.

And working its way through that river they could see a knot of soldiers wearing the green-and-gold of the Kingsguard, and the slow confusion of the troops in its path parting neatly before it.

"Looks like the king has gone to meet them too," Ardela said. "You want to wait?"

"We can follow on behind. Isak won't want a grand welcome and the king's got work to do. He'll be leaving them to rest soon enough."

They wound through the army camp into a field of well-trampled grass that ran alongside the stony highway leading north. Carel felt a jolt in his gut as he saw a stooping figure wearing a ragged cloak, taller than those around him and unmistakeable as a white-eye, facing King Emin and his scarlet-coated bodyguard.

"Gods," he whispered, "it really is him." He squinted to try and make out more, but the distance was too great for his ageing eyes.

"Seems so," Ardela said.

Carel glanced down at the scar on his chest again. "To come out of Ghenna—for Mihn to creep in there in the first place . . . the man was a Harlequin, I know, but merciful Gods, I'd have thought that beyond even him." At his side Ardela tensed unexpectedly, and he looked at her. "What? What is it?" he demanded.

"Ah—bad news. Isak'll need you at his side more'n ever now."

He shivered. "Something to do with Mihn?"

She said gravely, "Legana told me he died—in Vanach. They didn't say much about it, not in front of Isak, just that he died to cover their escape."

Carel gaped. That was the last thing he'd expected to hear. Even as he struggled to find words, it felt ridiculous to even consider such a thing. At last he stammered, "*Mihn* covered their escape? Not the Mortal-Aspect of Karkarn? Not the Mad Axe? A small man with a wooden staff decided to take on the entire Vanach Army to let the rest escape? What sort of sense does that make?"

Ardela raised a hand; the other hovered over the hilt of her knife and Carel realised he'd taken a step towards her. He deliberately moved backwards a pace.

"You don't need to tell me that," she explained patiently. "All Legana told me was that he saw something that made him stay behind, and they don't know what. She thinks it was a Harlequin—which makes sense, I guess, but either way, that's all I know. Best you ask Count Vesna for the rest of the story."

Carel fumbled silently for his tobacco pouch. When he pulled it out Ardela took it from his hands, also without saying a word, filled the bowl of his pipe and struck an alchemist's match to light it.

"Thanks," he muttered, pointing with the pipe towards the meeting up ahead. "Looks like we've got time for a smoke before I get my turn." He offered her the pipe, but she waved it away.

At last they saw the reception breaking up. King Emin headed back to the castle, leaving half of his Kingsguard behind to clear a path for Isak. Carel realised he needed only to stay where he was, for Isak's party was being led across the field towards him. As soon as he caught sight of Carel, Vesna went ahead, waving away the soldiers who'd been about to drive the veteran out of the way.

Carel watched the emotions flicker on Vesna's ruby-studded face: the pleasure of friendship replaced swiftly by the pain of grief, then hope mixed with wariness. "No greeting for an old friend?" Carel asked at last, approaching the Mortal-Aspect.

"Given I failed to find fitting words of parting," Vesna said, "that's probably no great surprise. It is good to see you though, Carel—and you're not so old as that."

That broke the tension between them, and Carel reached out to embrace the Farlan hero. Vesna wrapped his arms around Carel with a fierce relief, almost squeezing the breath from him.

"Careful, boy—I'd expect that from him, not you!" Carel gasped.

Vesna looked behind, and saw Isak was watching them with a frown on his face, and said carefully, "Carel, you do know it's not simply—?"

"Aye, I do," Carel said sadly, "but it's an improvement on never seeing him again, so I'll take it." He stepped back to inspect Vesna. "You look well, my friend."

"As do you." Vesna pointed to the sword at Carel's hip. "Particularly now you've finally realised a swordstick is a little girl's weapon." He hesitated, and then said gruffly, "I'm sorry for leaving Tirah so abruptly. A friend shouldn't have acted that way."

"None of us are so attractive in grief," he said, forgiving him instantly, "not even you." He plucked at the Mortal-Aspect's shirt. "Godhood clearly suits some better'n others." Vesna'd always that uncanny knack of looking ruggedly dishevelled where others were filthy and exhausted, even before he'd been filled with divine power. "Anyways, time's come to forget our failings and go back to what we know."

"An old friend?" Isak called from behind Vesna. "From the Ghosts?"

Carel went to face the white-eye he now barely recognised, but before he could get there, the dog lurking at Isak's heel had leaped forward to place itself between the two of them. Then the dog caught Carel's scent, and after a moment's hesitation it began to wag its tail, sniffing at the hand Carel offered.

"I was in the Ghosts, but you introduced us, lad," Carel croaked, buffeted by his emotions. It was all he could do to stay upright as he stared at the damaged man. With his knees buckling underneath him, the dog's fawning almost pushed him over until Vesna clicked his fingers and drew it away, leaving the two men to their strange reunion.

Isak tilted his head, searching his tattered memory. "I—I don't . . ."

Carel raised a hand. "I know, lad. There are holes in your mind. Don't try and remember." He gazed at his boy: every visible part of Isak was marked somehow—even the lightning-kissed hand was now a mess of scars, some haphazard, some runic, and the end joint was missing entirely from two fingers. The very lines of Isak's face, once as familiar a sight as any in the Land to Carel, were altered, his jaw uneven, furrows of deep scar, and frayed edges to lip and ears.

"Damn, but it's good to see you, boy," Carel croaked.

Isak's face twitched and his stoop became a little more pronounced, his left shoulder dipping forward as though the weight of everything had grown too much. Then he touched his white fingers to the bulge at his hip, and that steadied him. Now Carel could see Isak's right hand was oddly clenched, not quite in a fist, but his fingers were curled as though he was holding something.

Grey scars showed up plainly against his blackened skin, and his thumb turned inwards at a strange angle. Carel wondered how well he could grip a sword, but then he realised Isak wasn't wearing a weapon. For the first time since he'd seen Isak return from his first battle, Eolis was nowhere in sight.

"Not a distinguished list, that," Isak said at last, "folk who're pleased to see me."

"Aye, well, more distinguished round here, I'm guessing. Anyways, less you've changed as much as it looks, you won't care how distinguished a man is if he'll let you take his tobacco." He held up his pipe. "Never had any money of your own; years back I decided lettin' you help yourself was better'n watching you steal it from others."

Isak looked blank, but he took the pipe from Carel's unresisting hand and as he inspected it briefly, some shadow of recognition passed across his eyes before he raised it to his mouth and began to smoke. In a handful of white-eye-sized inhalations the pipe was finished.

Isak tossed the pipe back to Carel. "Vesna says my sense of humour's returning," he said with a tentative, crooked smile.

Carel stared at the spent pipe. "Don't throw a parade just yet," he muttered, "it was never up to much, you little bugger."

Isak's face froze. "Mihn was your friend too?"

"He was," Carel said, "and I'm waiting for an explanation better'n the one Ardela just gave me. Covering your retreat? Remember what happened last time some bloody fool decided to do that?" Without even intending to Carel found himself poised to prod Isak in his scarred chest as he made his point, but his expression of alarm and dismay stopped him in time, reminding him that former closeness between them no longer existed.

"Do I remember that?" Isak said in a hollow voice, "yes, all too well." His face tightened and became resolved. "Just remember: I had reason for doing what I did."

"And Mihn shouldn've known better than to take a second crack at the other lands," Carel snapped. "Dyin' in a fight ain't the same as lettin' some witch half-drown you—and there's no one ready to go in after him that I can see."

"Mihn made his choice," Isak said stonily. "He thought the risk worth taking."

"For what, eh? You can't tell me that, you can only guess!" Carel shook his head. "Ah, lad, I'm sorry; it ain't your fault your recklessness is rubbin' off on others. Only to be expected from the Chosen, I guess."

"You've got the scar," Isak said abruptly, staring at his ripped shirt. "You've linked yourself to me."

Carel nodded. "Whatever foolishness you've got planned, I'll be right behind you from now on."

"You want to restrain me?" Isak sounded incredulous.

"No, lad, just clip you round the head from time to time, make sure you've really thought through whatever you're planning to do next. Never was able to stop you from doing what you wanted, but I could make you think again sometimes. The more you stand there lookin' like some tortured God, the more that might be in the interests o' the whole Land."

Isak looked down at his strange, mismatched hands. "God? No God ever looked like this."

"No mortal's got skin that colour either, Isak," Carel said. "Vesna looks normal in comparison now."

"Maybe we need new Gods," Isak replied, abruptly crouching, and the dog immediately broke from Vesna's grip and leaped forward to tuck itself under his white arm. Isak hugged the animal close with that one arm and rested his chin on its head. Carel noticed he kept his black arm well clear.

"Maybe it's time to change this old order a little," Isak murmured, "make Vesna and Legana our Gods instead."

"And that would be better? Vesna's just a man, touched by Karkarn or not."

Isak nodded distantly, his eyes still averted. "Maybe our Gods just need to do better, then."

Carel forced himself to laugh. "Aye, well, if any man could chastise 'em, it'd be you."

A ghastly smile crept onto Isak's lips. "There's another, but he's feeling a bit ragged these days." He stood again, apparently having found strength in the dog's presence. "So is this how our friendship worked?"

"How'd you mean?"

"I steal your tobacco; you lecture me about life."

Carel hesitated, then smiled. "More or less, come to think of it. Oftentimes there's beer involved somewhere too."

The white-eye grinned, the gaps in his teeth adding to an already macabre expression. "Let's do that then."

CHAPTER 25

"SO THIS IS THE PRICE OF COMMAND?" Amber asked.

Nai gave him a puzzled look. "Price?"

"To hide at the back like a damned coward," the general clarified. His face was mostly hidden by his steel helm, but his stance was telling: taut, ready to charge.

Nai made a point of checking all around. "Nope, we don't seem to have moved by mistake. Exactly what part of this is cowardly, General Amber?"

Amber loomed towards him, his hands in fists. "We're at the back of an army, you fool!" He looked at the ranks ahead of them. "The enemy's the other side of that lot."

"But we're still on foot, right?" Nai looked down mournfully at the heavy boots he wore. "This might be my first battle, but I'm pretty sure cowardly would be to have horses so we could run away if it went bad—Ghenna's teeth, in any other company I'd call that sensible!"

"Any other company?" asked Sergeant Menax at Amber's side, a man nearly as tall as the general himself, if rather less inspiring. "Just what're you sayin' about us?"

Sergeant Menax had been given the job of leading Amber's troop of bodyguards because the general had asked for the ugliest, evilest bastard sergeant in the whole army. For reasons Nai didn't understand, sergeants who'd got away with every sort of vicious criminality ended up as highly valued in Menin armies—those failing to make the grade were generally hanged somewhere along the way.

"You people are the most insanely death-obsessed madmen I've ever met," the former necromancer said. "Your interest in surviving any battle seems transitory at best, and at worst a secret shame you're determined to make amends for."

"Eh?"

"You're all fucking idiots is what I'm saying."

Amber raised a hand before Menax tried something stupid. "I'm a front-line officer. That's where I should be when the fighting comes."

"You're a general now," Nai countered, "which means you need to stay alive more than lead the charge. I'm guessing the king'll use sarcasm at me if my first report says you died fighting in the line." The newest King's Man pointed off to their left, where the small knot of undead soldiers stood unnaturally still and quiet. "Anyways, once they get stuck in, I'm pretty certain you'll not keep clear."

Amber turned to follow Nai's gesture. The Legion of the Damned were less than a legion now; it was hard to count them accurately when they were standing in a formless mass, but he estimated some six hundred of the undead mercenaries remained. He could only communicate properly with them though Nai; the mage had some way of planting directions in their leader's mind. Without that he'd be forced to resort to hand gestures—as if battlefield communication wasn't hard enough at the best of times.

"Having a horse is still cowardly," Menax repeated. "It ain't the Menin way."

"Your armies have cavalry," Nai protested. "They're over there!"

Menax sniffed. "And a bunch of fucking cowards the lot of 'em, chinless noble-born brats with no spine, savin' yer presence, General, o' course. Useless, the whole crew."

"What about Colonel Dassai's troops? Our supporting legions are led by Narkang noblemen, but I hear they give good account of themselves."

"That's easy when you're trying to cause trouble, distract an army from its purpose. Might have t'let a wasp sting you before you c'n swat it."

General Amber let out a heavy breath and the pointless conversation fell dead. They were waiting on a floodplain where a Devoted army had established camp thirty miles in from the Narkang border. Colonel Dassai was making a nuisance of himself as best he could, with half his Green Scarves occupying the high ground to the left while the rest busied themselves raiding the Devoted line. The cavalry had sparked a near-revolt within the Menin ranks, until wiser heads had prevailed. Amber had been careful to keep the Menin-hating colonel and the blue-tattooed élite cavalry away from his Menin infantry. Under General Daken, the Green Scarves had seen more fighting than any other legions during the Menin invasion, and neither side were showing much interest in forgiveness.

The bulk of Amber's army was spread out ahead of them: his five heavy infantry legions were formed up in two lines, with a third of medium infantry. On the left flank the useless Menin cavalry waited; the Menin archers were on the right, where they could support the infantry, but would be able to withdraw easily without being massacred or disrupting the spear-wall.

In the sky wisps of thin cloud stretched like lace in the gusty wind. A flock of black birds turned above the plain, delighting in the surging wind as they readied for the feast Amber intended to provide. He could feel the wind on the back of his neck, bearing a promise of autumn.

Everywhere I see black birds, he said in the privacy of his mind. *The call of crows wake me at dawn, ravens attend me at dusk. Are they the souls of those we've killed?* A colder prickle went down his neck. *Am I drawing them in my wake like I'm already marching up Ghain's slope, the chains of sin around my neck? Or is Nai right and they're the souls of those we've lost, come to guide us?*

"Does this general have no pride?" Amber wondered aloud. "We've been here all morning, making him look like a coward in front of his men."

"Cautious, perhaps?" Nai ventured. "They might not know you're a bunch of madmen eager to die in battle. He might be wondering what an army half the size of his is doing here."

"His Litse white-eyes have had plenty of time to scout for surprises," Amber said. "There are none—none that they'll be able to find anyway."

"My point exactly," Nai said darkly. "Might be they're not fools."

"You wouldn't understand, Narkang man," Menax said scornfully.

"I'm from Embere," Nai protested.

"Same place as this lot, no?"

"Dassai said their banners're from Mustet, southwest—Embere is east. That's hundreds of miles' difference."

Amber nodded. "And Nai's not a man for patriotism anyway. His allegiance is to his art, right, Nai?"

The King's Man looked shocked. "Quoting the mage Verliq to me now? I'm impressed."

His lack of response showed how much Amber cared about that and they fell silent again while the breezes danced around them and black birds circled overhead.

Bringers of the Slain maybe, Amber mused. *Guess if any Gods have the strength to be abroad these days, it'd be them.* "Anyone seen the Bringers of the Slain before?" he asked, surprising himself almost as much as those around him.

"You don't see 'em," Menax said, "not without gettin' your eyes plucked out."

"Only on a fresco," Nai added, "seeing them before you're dead would be . . . well, as portents go, it's like pissing into the face of the Reapers."

"What did the fresco look like?"

Nai frowned. "A figure of sorts, made up of a flock of crows: it had a face, I think, but mostly it was wings and beaks."

Very deliberately Amber angled his head up and the others followed suit. The rooks or whatever they were darted momentarily closer as a gust of wind buffeted them, then they climbed and spiralled towards the river.

What would Horsemistress Kirl think as she saw me now? What message would her raven speak for me?

"Where's our scryer?" Amber asked. "I want an update."

Colonel Dassai swore and wrenched back on his reins, one arm raised high to halt the unit. The captain beside him bellowed the order and they clattered to an untidy halt, the companies strung behind them following suit like surly offspring.

"Ready bows," Dassai yelled, waiting a heartbeat as the captain repeated the order. "Bugler, order all the others except Second Company back to high ground." He stood up in his stirrups: the enemy camp was stirring, a sudden mass of movement that made him think of a nest of snakes, long coils unfolding and preparing to strike. Troops were running for the defensive ditches—and then Devoted cavalry burst from the left flank, driving hard to cut them off.

Dassai checked behind him. The other companies were still wheeling and preparing to withdraw. He could see their officers bellowing orders; most had followed his example and were not yet wearing their helms, displaying the sweeps of blue-stained skin on their faces left there by Litania, the Trickster Aspect.

"First Company advance!" he ordered, and as one they turned. Every man there knew his job; the Green Scarves had been at the forefront in the war against the Menin, raiding and punishing at every opportunity. Then, they had been the bold and the arrogant, as eager for battle as their commander, General Daken. Those who remained were disciplined veterans now, but still bold, their arrogance now earned.

The horses drove forward unchecked as their riders nocked arrows and prepared for slaughter. The Devoted cavalry had poured from their camp with little regard for order, each man intent only on getting clear of his comrades so he could manoeuvre; though two companies numbered only a hundred men, their sudden advance and the volley of arrows as soon as they were in range took the Devoted unawares.

With horsemen still pouring into the fray, those in the lead turned away from the attack, heading back to the safety of their camp.

"Two more volleys," Dassai called, firing himself even as he called out the order. The wind was behind them for the moment and their arrows carried well, most striking home.

The cavalry ahead of them broke into two halves, one group wheeling aside while the other charged straight for Dassai's archers. He looked back to ensure the rest of his men were clear; they were already at the foot of the sloping high ground where he'd left the second legion. Their passage stirred up a clamour of rooks that had been feasting on the ungrazed ground. With indignant caws and lazy strokes of their wings, the birds made for an ancient oak to the north that dominated the horizon.

"Find yourselves a good view," Dassai laughed as he watched the rooks. "There'll be food enough for all of you soon!"

A rogue gust of air thumped down onto his back and whipped a stalk of grass across his face. Dassai watched the grass dance away through the air, carried high by the wind.

"Lord Ilit doesn't approve," the captain commented with a smile that crinkled the long pair of blue lines running from forehead to throat.

Dassai reached over and roughly patted the man's stained cheek. "Tough shit for Ilit then!" he replied. "We're Litania's now. If Ilit don't like it, he can argue it out with the Mad Axe."

He looked at the Devoted camp, where more cavalry were emerging, accompanied by heavy infantry, judging by their broad oval shields.

"Fall back," Dassai called, and the captain repeated with a bellow. "Back to the high ground so they can bravely drive us from it. Looks like General Afasin's found his spine after all!"

The captain bared his teeth in anticipation. "Reckon the Mad Axe will want it as a souvenir?"

Dassai laughed as he turned with the rest of the unit and they started back to the high ground the other legion was holding. He cocked his head in thought.

"You know, Captain? He might just."

"They come." The scryer was a hairless woman with delicate features, one of only a hundred or so women still supporting the army; most had been left behind at the camp with the supply wagons and a few hundred cavalry as escort.

"As planned?" Amber asked.

The scryer closed her eyes to focus her magical sight and Amber realised with a start that there were thin white scars on her eyelids. He'd heard of some who intentionally put out one eye to better channel their abilities, but he'd never seen magical runes cut into the eyelids. The symbols reminded him of when he'd been in the Library of Seasons at the Circle City, and a black pain throbbed at the front of his head as the memory blossomed in his mind: the Fearen House with its hundreds of magical books, Nai at his side and his lord at the desk. The man's face was a blank, a featureless mask of flesh without expression or animation. Amber shuddered, involuntarily bowing his head and drawing his hands to his chest.

A cold and hollow sensation blossomed in his chest: he heard his mother's voice in his mind, distant and garbled—an old memory, his mother calling his name from the verandah at home, but it had been a powerful one. Now it was barely within reach, eroded by the magic of the Gods as they erased his lord's name. He had been at his training temple, still several years off his army commission, when his mother had died giving birth to a baby girl. The child had died too, but Amber had named her Marsay in private, despite Menin tradition not to name stillborns. He still thought of her in his quieter moments. The pain in his chest intensified. Marsay's life had ended before it had even begun; now her family name had been torn from history too.

"Amber?"

He became aware of a hand on his elbow and he looked up at Nai's anxious face.

"No time for memories," the King's Man said. "You hear me, Amber?"

Hearing his name repeated dulled the chill seeping into his bones. He forced himself to take a breath, to fill his lungs with the surging energy that filled the air above them.

"No memories," he said in a hoarse voice. "Scryer, where are their infantry?"

"Advancing from the camp," the scryer replied. "Heavy infantry, coming to match ours."

"Nai, do they have mages?"

He nodded, his fingers closing around a silver charm hanging from his neck that shone brightly in the dull light. "Two, but neither surpass me, I'm certain. You've no need to worry about them."

"Will they discover our plan, though?"

Nai's eyes flicked towards the Legion of the Damned, tramping in silence behind the left flank. "Only if they investigate closely, and there's nothing to attract their attention. They're not strong enough to bother wasting their energy."

"Good." The black birds swooped and danced over the ground between the armies and for a moment he imagined they were tracing letters in the sky: a distant, desperate attempt to restore the name that had been stolen from him.

"Cavalry pushing ahead," the scryer reported, her eyes closed once more. "Four legions-worth on the slopes of the high ground, more getting into position behind."

"Sound the drums, close for charge," he ordered, and the deep, heavy boom of Menin wardrums rolled like thunder over the plain. The drums confirmed the orders every officer had been given. In normal circumstances they might be alarmed at being told to present a flank to cavalry, but they all knew the plan of attack.

Amber gestured for his guards to start towards the left, heading for the gap between the undead mercenaries and the rear of his infantry lines.

"I need to be closer," he said aloud, though not even Nai had questioned his movement. "We cannot rely on the Legion alone."

The sound of hooves grew louder, then there were shouts of panic from the flank they were heading for. The Menin cavalry were scouts and skirmishers, not troops of the line. Amber knew he could rely on them to follow their orders: to visibly and noisily panic when the enemy closed on them.

He'd wondered if Colonel Dassai would argue, but he had accepted his orders and Amber knew he'd follow them to the letter. Not even the famous fighting spirit of the Green Scarves would stop him letting Menin and undead mercenaries take the brunt of the enemy attack.

"Dassai's men are running from the field," Nai commented, "and the flank's crumbling, just as you commanded. So this is what battle looks like, eh?"

Sergeant Menax hawked and spat noisily. "Battle's worse," he said with contempt. "Whole fucking lot worse. This is just folks running away."

"But still, for my first battle—even knowing the plan, it's a little alarming to watch our flank crumble like that."

Menax grinned. "They raise conscripts to fight us and you'll see what fucking crumbling looks like! I saw the Cheme Third face down fifteen thousand savages from the waste once. All fighters, true enough, but no order: field looked like a slaughterhouse once the Third had finished chopping their way across half a mile o' ground."

Amber loosened the ties on his scimitars. "Lost both my swords that day," he commented. "The earth was stained red by the end, blood soaked everything." His voice hardened. "But the Third's gone now. I'm the last of them, because they never learned how

to retreat."

"Buggered if you're learnin' today, sir," Menax said with feeling.

"No, there's no retreat for us," Amber agreed, his eyes on the stirring crowd of undead right in front of them. The Legion of the Damned had seen their enemy. "Nai, they ready?"

"They know."

"Good. This is the first step home. Every one's going to be stained with blood."

A torrent of cavalry swept away from in front of the Legion—his Menin cavalry, eagerly following orders. Amber would have used this same tactic against the Farlan too, so proud were they of their élite—that battle would never be fought now, but before they reached the Waste and started the long, dangerous journey home, Amber was determined Menin prowess would be remembered across the West.

He drew his scimitars as the Legion of the Damned advanced into the attack. This close he could smell them. Nothing living smelled that way, mouldering and ancient. The thunder of hooves intensified—

Then it faltered, and Amber felt his hands tighten around the grips of his swords as the scream of horses rang out and rooks cawed derisively overhead.

Dust and movement obscured his view, but Amber knew the horses had caught the scent of the Legion and started panicking. He started to run forward, suddenly desperate to be in the midst of the fighting himself, and from the maelstrom emerged a rider in the blue and red of the Knights of the Temples, at full pelt. Amber stepped away from his men to meet him before any of them could stop him, but the rider was clinging frantically to his steed and barely aware of anything else. Amber swung a scimitar as the Devoted soldier passed, cleaving up into his ribs and tipping the man from his saddle.

Before Amber could finish the man off, one of the Legion had spotted the enemy on the ground. The injured soldier shrieked in terror at the sight of the undead mercenary, but his cries were short-lived. Wielding a spiked axe with little effort, the mercenary grabbed his prey with one emaciated hand and drove the spike into his gut.

Discarding the corpse, the mercenary took a step towards Amber, a look of dark malevolence on its desiccated face. It wore a skullcap helm, one large steel pauldron on its left shoulder and a leather cuirass that sat at an uncomfortable angle on its hips. The big Menin faced it down, scimitars at the ready, but in the next moment the mercenary refocused its attention and it stalked jerkily back to the fighting.

Amber looked back at Nai. The King's Man was far smaller than the Menin around him, but a black flame flickered lazily on the edge of his mace. For all his apprehension, Nai's magery made him more deadly than the rest.

Amber led the way. They ploughed into the flank of the cavalry, where one regiment had broken off to protect their rear. A javelin glanced off his helm and fell between him and Nai, but the Menin didn't even flinch as he slashed up at his attacker's legs. The Devoted soldier caught the blow on his red-painted shield, but before the man had a chance to draw his own sword he was thrown unceremoniously to the ground. As Amber watched, a dark figure dropped down onto the soldier and pinned him down with one knee on his chest as it pounded at his head.

Amber looked around; he could sense the tide of movement falling away from the assault. At the back the Devoted were still pressing forward, unaware of what awaited them, but the Damned were surging through the kicking mess of cavalry with unnatural purpose, chopping through limbs and dragging men from their horses. Someone shrieked for the retreat, rendered incoherent by terror and drowned out by the clamour and screaming, before he too was savagely cut down.

The undead were killing whatever they could; even the horses were not immune, and Amber was powerless to stop them. He saw one axe-wielding warrior near-decapitate three in as many swift strokes. Distantly he heard more hooves, and he realised the slaughter would not end there: either Colonel Dassai was coming to cut off the Devoted's retreat, or the Devoted reinforcements were arriving—only to find themselves collapsing into confusion when their horses shied away from the unnatural assault.

However, the Damned were not immune from harm. Amber watched one Devoted soldier stab his spear into the face of a mercenary, the weight of the blow snapping its withered neck.

The mercenary dropped like a stone—but the victory was short-lived as another came from behind a horse to open the soldier's ribs and behead him in the blink of an eye.

Amber let his scimitars sink to the ground. The cavalry were in total disarray. Some would probably escape, but the Damned were swarming through them so quickly that many could not even see the danger as they died.

"Sound the drums," he croaked, "ready the charge."

Somewhere nearby the alarm was being sounded. General Afasin wanted to turn and curse at whoever it was—their efforts were only increasing panic in the camp—but he found himself transfixed by the sight before him. The bulk of his army, more than twenty thousand men, were spread out across the floodplain—and they were crumbling. The battle had been raging for an hour, and the infantry were now heavily engaged, but barely any of his cavalry were still fighting—somehow their first assault had been routed entirely, even the reserve driven back.

"Captain Kosotern," he said quietly, "where is that mage?"

The captain appeared, dragging a bearded figure after him. "Mage Bissen, sir."

Afasin stepped forward and though Bissen stopped struggling, Kosotern had to hold the man up as he sagged under the white-eye general's gaze.

"I made no—" Bissen started, breaking off as Afasin raised a hand.

The general bent down and with his face inches from Bissen's, he said softly, "Light cavalry, horse-archers, and scouts protecting the flanks. That was your report."

"Your scouts confirmed it," the mage protested. "You saw them raiding our lines yourself!"

"I saw some of them," Afasin agreed. He straightened and rearranged the red sash of his order, which had snagged on a link of armour. "And yet somehow two legions of heavy cavalry have been routed and slaughtered."

Bissen opened his mouth to reply, but Afasin never gave him the chance. In one swift movement he drew his sword and ran the mage through.

Mage Bissen staggered back and crumpled to his knees, reaching one hand out to the captain in a desperate, dying plea for help. Misinterpreting the action, Kosotern snarled, drew his own weapon and stabbed Bissen in the chest to finish him off.

Afasin watched the blood drip from his sword a moment then raised his eyes to watch the battle. Even at this distance he could see the line buckling, the right-hand legions disintegrating as they were outflanked.

"The day is lost," he commented, quelling the roiling anger in his belly. "Send out the remaining cavalry to cover our retreat."

"General!" came a shout from further down the line, and he and Kosotern turned, swords still drawn, to see a man on horseback racing towards them. "A message from Colonel Gittin!"

Without waiting for a response the rider reached them, dropped from his saddle and lurched the remaining steps to fall at Afasin's feet. The horse was lathered and caked in dust, the soldier himself filthy and exhausted. "General, it's all true!" he wailed, drawing himself up to his knees.

"What is?" Afasin snapped, reaching out and dragging the man upright.

"What the preachers said—the warnings!"

Afasin glanced back at the knot of white-cloaked followers of Ruhen who stood at the head of a rabble of civilians. He'd barely been able to prevent them from marching out with his troops; the zealots had been quite certain Ruhen's divine presence would protect them from any harm.

"Warnings?"

"The army of daemons," the soldier gasped, "they march with *daemons*! Our cavalry are slaughtered, broken entirely."

"By daemons? The bloody sun's shining!"

"The colonel's words, I swear it!" he pleaded. "I saw the cavalry charge. They never reached the enemy flank—and in the next moment they were overrun. No humans could move or kill so quickly."

Afasin threw the man down. "Kosotern, sound Full Retreat—we go as we are. Belay my last; they're on their own. No idea what that fool Gitten's talking about, but we're too few to protect the camp once they've cover of night on their side."

"Full Retreat? What of Ruhen's Children?" the captain asked in dismay, glancing back at the preachers. "They'll fall behind, and we're not positioned to escort them. They're barely armed, sir!"

Afasin's lip curled into some form of smile. "They want to fight so badly, let the bastards cover our withdrawal. Someone fetch my horse. We don't have long."

CHAPTER 26

DARKNESS CAME QUICKLY TO THE FOREST. They waited in silence as the shadows descended, watching the light of an ill-omened moon play over the distant grass. The creatures of the forest were wary of what walked the Land after sunset.

When a cloud briefly masked Alterr's yellow eye, Grisat noticed a pale light far out on the moor and shivered. It moved steadily, keeping well clear of Moorview's ordered boundaries, yet unafraid to be seen. It was well away from the moor road, he knew; nowhere any sane traveller would be at night.

Daemons, Grisat thought to himself, his fingers pressed against the coin charm half-embedded in his skin. He had been finding that coin less of a threatening presence the closer they came to Moorview, seeing what creatures were being drawn to such a place of slaughter. Now the cold shadow settling over his shoulders felt like a greater protection than the steel plates sewn into his jacket.

Most villages he had passed had been draped in mourning cloths, black banners hanging from the gates and long ribbons of cloth fixed to the branches of prominent trees. It was hard to tell if war or daemon predation had started the mourning, but many of the ribbons looked recent, not yet touched by the elements.

The countryside was still and empty for the main part. Even during the day few went too far from home without company. There were a few ancient, vague stories of the Age of Darkness, but now folk'd be scouring their memories for everything they had ever heard of that time, when the Gods had weakened themselves as gravely as now. He'd left a package by the highway leading north from the moor, pretty sure no one other than the intended recipient would stumble across it—but if any did, they'd mutter a charm against Finntrail and their deadly gifts and hurry on.

"Our friend is coming," whispered a voice in his ear.

Grisat bit down onto his lip. He'd not heard Ilumene creep so close; the man had got right up to him without disturbing the forest undergrowth.

"Where?" Saranay, the third of their party asked. She was dressed little differently to when Grisat had first met her in that Narkang bar.

Ilumene pointed back into the forest and they both turned to look. The ground undulated for miles up to this ridge abutting Tairen Moor, providing ample cover for anyone approaching. Grisat could see nothing except a mass of black overlaying the chaotic tangle of trees behind them, and he could hear as little as he saw.

"Who is it," Saranay muttered, "some bloody Harlequin?"

Grisat flinched and fought the urge to giggle hysterically. He could well guess who it was, and idle comments like that in the company of cruel men often proved to have consequences.

It was a few minutes more before three ghostly faces loomed out of nowhere. Even though he was expecting them, Grisat had to muffle a whimper when he saw the Harlequin masks and Venn's tattooed face. They wore dark woollen cloaks over their regular clothes, as much for concealment as warmth, Grisat guessed.

They really mean to do this. We're to steal past hundreds of soldiers—into the castle to murder men who could turn us inside out with a word.

"Shall we go?" Venn asked curtly without greeting them.

Grisat's eyes widened: the black Harlequin had his right arm in a sling, his wrist in a splint. Though he'd never seen the man fight himself, he had heard of him from Ilumene. That someone had injured Venn was as remarkable as Venn betraying no apprehension at assaulting a castle left-handed. He'd heard Venn was a powerful mage, though when he'd asked Ilumene back in Byora he'd just laughed and said, "One of 'em is anyway," without deigning to explain further.

"You've found them?" Ilumene asked, and Grisat turned his attention back.

"No. They would notice my efforts to scry the castle," Venn admitted.

"As much as I'd like to kill every soldier here, I don't think we've got time," Ilumene said.

"What do you suggest, then?"

"I've been here more'n once, and I know the ones we seek. They'll be in the state rooms: Holtai at the top of the tower, most likely, since he's the scryer, and Ashain in the king's chamber since he's an arsehole with a chip on his shoulder. We use the forest gate—there'll be guards there, but not many. You can't get troops through this forest without utter chaos, so the road's the only path to watch on that approach. Holtai'll no doubt have a web across that and the ground moor-side, leaving the walls and guards to dissuade any coming through the forest."

"Easy, when you think about it," Saranay scoffed. "I don't know why you even needed us to come along."

Ah, some sense at last, Grisat thought. *Ilumene and Venn might breeze through this mission—we mere mortals won't fi nd it so simple.*

"Glad you think so," Ilumene said, his eyes fixed on the castle wall just visible through the trees. "We wait for that cloudbank to cover the moon, then move."

The forest gate was on the right where the road cut through the trees and a hundred yards of cleared ground between forest and walls. From where they lurked Grisat couldn't see the guards on the walls, but he knew they were there, so a straight run would be lunacy.

"Won't we be seen?" Grisat hissed as Ilumene began to edge his way into a position where he could see the moon clearly. "You said they'd detect any magic."

"We best not use any then."

Grisat hesitated, looking to Saranay for support, but she was focused on the castle walls. He followed her gaze and caught a wink of light from atop the battlements, then a second.

"A signal?" he breathed, feeling the heat of Ilumene's scorn as soon as the words left his mouth.

"You think?" he asked. "But who would be signalling from the castle wall? Don't tell me there's a traitor in their midst, Grisat—say it ain't so!"

The mercenary bit down on his lip and looked away. Ilumene was always at his most antagonistic and animated before a fight. Keeping his mouth shut was the only sensible choice from here on.

The signal repeated a few minutes later, and intermittently after that, but they had to wait in the shadows for almost half an hour before slow-drifting cloud covered the moon. Ilumene wrapped a black scarf around his head with slow, deliberate movements, then slipped silently onto the open ground, Saranay and Venn at his heel.

Grisat followed as silently as he could, wincing at every twig breaking underfoot. The shield he'd looted from the battlefield felt ungainly, slung over his back, but he'd seen men spitted for questioning Ilumene's orders, so he kept silent.

The castle wall ahead bulged out in front of them, protecting the ballista behind, and a square barbican enclosed the forest gate. The dense forest, steep slope and cleared land, not to mention the swift rivers running behind, meant the castle wasn't as vulnerable as it might look at first sight.

The group stopped when they reached the wall and pressed themselves flat against the stone to hide from those above, but there was hardly time for them to check their bearings before the signal came: a husk of corn dropped from the battlements above, flashing down past Grisat's face. Venn plucked it from the air and held it up to Ilumene, a quizzical expression on his face, but Ilumene only beamed in response and headed off along the wall towards the gate.

In less than a minute the group had reached the near side of the forest gate, where they found a rope hanging down the shadowed corner of the barbican. The squat little building had just the gate below and a small room above, which no doubt housed a couple of soldiers. A ditch in front was deep enough to need a bridge to cross it and made breaking down the iron-banded gate difficult for any attacker.

Ilumene scrambled up the rope with an agility that belied his size and pulled himself over the lowest part of the battlement. Grisat held his breath, aware how exposed the man was, but there were no shouts of alarm or warning. Within minutes, a tiny scraping sound came from the gate as the bolts were drawn back and it opened, just enough for them to slip through. Ilumene closed it after them again, a wide grin on his face. In the gloom Grisat could make out a spray of black droplets on the man's ash-grey brigandine.

"Saranay, up those stairs," Ilumene whispered, pointing to a narrow flight set into the wall. "Deal with any curious guards that come your way and keep the gate clear for us."

She scowled at being left behind, but didn't argue. She spared Grisat an ambiguous look as she trotted up the stairs, one long knife free from its sheath.

Ilumene was already focused on the next step of his plan. He kept lookout—for what, Grisat had no idea—but after a long wait he finally gestured, and without a word started off around the walled yard. His group followed noiselessly. Grisat had been shoved into the middle by one of the nameless Harlequins; he was forced to follow Venn so closely he was terrified of tripping him and causing a commotion. Ilumene led them through the stable and into a cobbled courtyard, then past the large main door to the castle to a smaller one set in the stone wall. While his companions crouched in the shadow of a massive creeper, Ilumene turned his attention to the door.

He had it open in a matter of seconds—their agent had managed to leave the great bolts open, Grisat guessed. Once inside, Ilumene allowed them to pause, and Grisat found his heart was pounding so furiously against his chest that he could feel the coin's pinch on his skin.

"Servants' quarters," Ilumene whispered, pointing ahead where a short corridor was faintly illuminated by moonlight from the room on the left. As he led the way, Grisat caught a glimpse of a long hallway with an enormous map painted on one wall. Once past the moonlit room it was almost pitch-black in the servants' corridor, but there were no obstacles, so Grisat copied Ilumene's lead and walked with one hand following the line of the wall, the other on his knife.

It took a time to traverse the castle at such a cautious pace, but eventually they came through a curtained arch into the tower. Ilumene glanced back at his comrades and nodded to Venn before drawing his other long knife and trotted up the stairway, one of the nameless Harlequins close on his heel. Grisat followed as fast as he could, but he didn't even see the guard until Ilumene's knife was sliding out of the man. Beside him a second Narkang man was gaping in horror at the sword piercing his mailed chest; the Harlequin had lunged and his sword, arm and outstretched leg describing a near-perfect straight line.

Both guards had died without a sound, and they continued up the staircase. Grisat could taste the fear in his own mouth, peppery and sour, as his heart thumped madly. One small mistake, one tiny sound and they would all be dead. *Well, maybe not* all, Grisat thought bitterly, *but I'll be first to bite it, so screw the rest of 'em. This is their cause, not mine. I just don't want to die.*

At a grander door than any they'd seen thus far, Ilumene gestured for Grisat and one of the Harlequins to wait. Grisat had worked some jobs in Narkang; he recognised the king's bee emblem worked into the carved door panels. Venn and the second Harlequin disappeared up the stairs towards the upper chambers, where the scryer was most likely quartered.

Ilumene caught Grisat's eye and gestured to his back, and Grisat nodded and sheathed his knife before slipping the narrow cavalry shield off his back, his eyes still on the door in case it opened unexpectedly. Ilumene took hold of the shield and inspected the runes he'd scratched into it a few hours before. The marks were very like the coins they all wore as a mark of their allegiance; Grisat hadn't asked questions, but the fact Ilumene had checked the runes cheered him.

Got to be some sort of protection, Grisat had told himself, *something temporary, before Ilumene gets his knife into the man.*

Ilumene gestured that he and Grisat would go through together, then split up to draw the mage's attention while the Harlequin came in close behind. Grisat drew his sword and hunched low behind the shield, waiting for the signal. When Ilumene rapped smartly on the door with his knuckles, Grisat almost dropped his sword in surprise.

There came a grunt from within, the surprised sounds of a man waking suddenly. "What is it?"

"Tea, sir," Ilumene called, affecting a breathy wheedle to his voice. "Found some juniper berries in the kitchen; thought you might want some."

"But how—?" The man's voice tailed off and Grisat heard footsteps in the room beyond that stopped short before they reached the door. "Come," the man ordered eventually, unbolting the door with a sharp clack.

Grisat flinched as he stood poised to burst through the door.

Ilumene turned the latch-ring smartly and opened the door part-way, not enough to afford the mage within a view, but sufficient to provoke any pre-emptive attack, should one be coming, but nothing happened, so Ilumene grinned fiercely and elbowed Grisat, prompting them rush in side by side.

Huddled behind his shield, the mercenary caught only a glimpse of the room beyond: a large fireplace was in front of him, the orange glow of flames casting a soft light across the rich red rug and slender chairs set before it. Dark wooden furniture blended into the shadows around the walls. There was a narrow spiral staircase on the right, at the foot of which stood a man, his face illuminated by a lamp on the wall above him. White traces of light were frozen in motion around his lowered fingers as Grisat started to charge forward, his feet suddenly leaden.

Ilumene was already a step ahead of him, driving forward with his knives held low. The mage's mouth was open, an O of surprise, before a flash of light danced in his grey eyes. Grisat watched the change as he continued to flounder forward.

Bright stabs of light blinded him, crashing through the room with the fury of lightning, and Grisat felt the impacts against his shield, a double-punch that smashed him aside like a rag-doll. As he fell, more stuttering light tore through the air and in the after-light he saw figures captured in movement: red droplets of blood flying up, hanging in the air, while the Harlequin wove a path through them.

A cry of pain and Ilumene's deep bellow shocked him back to his senses, and the clatter of steel and crashing magics assailed his ears. Grisat heard himself moan before his voice was drowned out by the wet slap of meat and the gasp of a dying man. He felt a body fall on his legs, limp in death, as a flash of energies scorched the beams overhead and winked out.

Then there was nothing. All was still. Grisat blinked and tried to sit up, but his body would not obey. Fear echoed from deep inside him; somewhere distant there was pain, but though he could sense its presence, he could not feel it. A cough broke the quiet, then there were muttered curses and the scrape of boots across the floor.

He heard a knife clatter on the bare wood of the staircase and he tried again to look up, but he couldn't manage more than to stare at the scorched plaster, gaping like a fish drowning. For a moment he thought there might be words of some half-remembered language, but the effort of trying to fathom their meaning exhausted him.

A face appeared above him: Ilumene, bloodied and battered. His mouth hung open in a savage grin as red-tinted saliva dribbled out.

"Still with us?" Ilumene rasped.

Grisat tried to reply, but only a whisper of air escaped his lungs. The big soldier mouthed something in reply, but it was increasingly distant and garbled, as though his ears were submerged in water. He tried again, and failed, but Ilumene nodded as though he had understood the mercenary's words all the same.

Ilumene brandished a glassy object above Grisat's head and he tried to focus on it, but it caught the light and dazzled him. Ilumene grinned again and crouched to wipe his stained dagger on Grisat's jacket. The mercenary flinched as the slender tip danced past his eyes, but Ilumene didn't appear to notice.

"Sorry 'bout the shield pretence," Ilumene said, sheathing his dagger. "You looked like you needed a bit of encouragement before you went through that door with me. A Bloodrose only works for the wearer, though, so false runes is all I had for you."

Grisat had to strain to understand his words; that effort drained his strength and dimmed the room around him.

Ilumene patted his shoulder and stood. "You just lie there now," he said gently. "Get a good long sleep. Don't worry about the rest o' the guards." He slipped the glassy sphere into a cloth bag and tied it at his waist.

Grisat's chest was tight. He didn't try to speak again, or rise; he felt completely drained. Ilumene's mention of sleep grasped him like a loving embrace.

"Don't worry 'bout the guards," Ilumene repeated with a wolfish grin. "Venn's finished upstairs so mebbe we do have time t'kill 'em all. Emin does enjoy these little surprises."

As the room darkened, Grisat watched Ilumene draw his knives again and turn towards the door. A blanket of peace settled over him, warm and comforting. The shadows crept closer, but now he didn't fear them. It was time.

CHAPTER 27

"GET OUT OF MY WAY!" Doranei snapped as he shoved the soldier aside, raising his fist at the man's comrade. The soldier reached for his weapon on instinct, then thought better of it and fell back.

"Doranei, I'm not a damned child," Mage Endine insisted as Doranei dragged him through the milling troops. "Get your hands off me—that's enough!"

Doranei growled something unintelligible and continued. Beneath Camatayl Castle it was utter chaos; barging was the only way of getting through the crowds.

"Doranei, damn you, stop," Endine squeaked, struggling to keep up with the big King's Man. "I'm warning you—"

From nowhere a bright white light enveloped Doranei. He heard shouts as men reeled from the blinding trails darting through the air and his own voice joined them as coils of light wrapped around his limbs and wrenched him from his feet. The Land spun around him and Doranei felt his feet dragged into the air.

"Next time," Endine warned from somewhere below his head, "listen a bit more carefully."

Doranei looked at the scrawny little shit standing a few feet below him, one hand extended and wreathed in jagged bands of light. There was a smug smile on the man's unshaven face.

"Let me down!" Doranei demanded uselessly.

"Not until you compose yourself," Endine said. He cocked his head at the King's Man and twisted his hand slightly; the Land lurched around Doranei again and the sour taste of black tea filled his throat as he was righted, but he was still held captive in the mage's grip.

"Now, you are one of the finer killers in this army," Endine began, as if he were lecturing, "quite skilled, and armed with a Demi-God's sword. I realise you are assiduous in the execution of your duties—indeed, devoted to a fault, and for that I commend you." Endine paused and the dancing trails of light around his hand trembled and turned red and green, adding a sickly shade to the mage's pallid skin.

"But," he continued in a voice that shook Doranei's bones, "do not forget the power I now wield dwarfs anything you could ever hope to control!"

Doranei gaped in astonishment, but the feeble-looking mage hadn't finished yet.

"After all," he said in a more normal voice, "as my famous colleague was wont to say: what's the point of all this power if I can't bend the very fabric of the Land to my will?"

"Ah, okay," Doranei croaked, "point taken."

"Good," Endine said with a smile, and released the magic.

Doranei fell in a heap at the man's feet. For a moment he lay there, then he pulled himself onto his knees. He glared up at the mage. "Was that really necessary?"

"I believe so," Endine replied primly. "You appeared to be labouring under the misconception that I am too feeble to protect myself."

Doranei shook his head to get the dirt out of his hair and groaned. "Ashain was no weakling either," he said, "and you just told me he's dead!"

"I didn't say there was no danger, just that you couldn't do much about it. Next time you decide to drag me through the fields, perhaps you would bear in mind that I'm most vulnerable when distracted?"

Doranei struggled up and brushed himself down. He caught the eye of a passing company of soldiers who'd slowed to stare at them. "What the fuck're you looking at?" he roared, taking a step towards the newly recruited troops. "Get back to your divisions!"

They jumped to comply, and he felt his irritation drain away as he watched them march off untidily, a lieutenant with down on his cheeks barking nervous orders. Most of the army were new recruits, hastily armed and barely drilled. Narkang had been recruiting for almost a year now in preparation for war, but Doranei feared for these children.

"Gods, when did I get old?" he breathed as more soldiers clattered past in ill-fitting armour.

"You were probably drunk at the time," Endine replied acidly. "Now you know how I feel, forced to spend months on end around you cocky Brotherhood wretches."

Doranei grimaced. At least reinforcements had arrived from Canar Fell. They were a brash and unruly lot—it was no surprise that General Daken hailed from those parts—but for all their youth, the warrior spirit in that coastal corner of the nation did not appear to have been diminished by peace. They came bearing spears and shields, but every man also carried the axe he'd been trained to wield since childhood. They were inexperienced, but at least they had the hunger for battle King Emin so desperately needed.

"Come on," he muttered, waving Endine forward. "Your news can't wait." As they started up the slope towards the castle Endine's charm-studded robe was enough to ensure the steady stream of troops on the road made way for them.

They found the king up on the battlements, surveying his troops with his two remaining generals, Bessarei and Lopir. Dashain and Forrow lurked behind.

"Your Majesty," Doranei called to announce himself, "Endine's got news you need to hear."

The king turned with a frown. The lack of sleep was clear on his handsome face, greying hair more obvious for the lack of his customary ostentatious hat. "Doranei. Should General Bessarei hear this? He was about to march the Kingsguard out."

"Ashain and Holtai are dead," Doranei said bluntly. "Endine's just had word from Moorview."

His words were met with a stony silence, though he could tell this was truly news to them all. But there were no gasps, no oaths or promises of retribution. We *all know the enemy we face;* we *know how ruthless and inventive Azaer is. Our king expects setbacks already, and we've not even crossed the border!*

"It seems two regiments were not enough," the king muttered angrily. "I should have been more forceful with them."

"Your Majesty," Endine interrupted, "you and Ashain kept your distance for a reason, to preserve the truce between you. That he was too proud to accept a greater escort—"

"Is my fault," Emin finished. "I should have given him no choice! To prevent a spat between supporters I allowed one to make a choice I knew was dangerous—and as a result that we have lost two of the Crystal Skulls. The damage those could do to our armies . . ." His voice tailed off as he glanced down at the thousands of eager young men who might be about to bear the brunt of such a decision.

"The Devoted have no mages to use them," General Bessarei reminded him, "and Dashain reported there are few in the Circle City to match ours—Tor Salan too, thanks to the Menin."

"And we still hold the majority," Emin said, seeming to rally from his despondency. "Dash, that's your priority: bodyguards for each of the Skull Bearers, trusted men only. Not all of them have Endine's skill or Vesna's martial prowess."

"Morghien and Lahk are deployed well behind enemy lines; it may be weeks before even a mage could track them down—"

"Then get started immediately—Doranei, take the news personally to those we need to protect. Tell them to gather together and consolidate their strength—though I doubt even Ilumene would try to kill them right under our noses."

"What about you, Sire?"

"Me?" Emin shook his head. "I'm in no danger from him."

"Are you sure?"

The king's face hardened. "Azaer wants me there at the end, Ilumene too. This is personal for all of us; it has been for years now."

"Tactically it makes no sense either," Dashain added. At a look from both men she explained, "You make the greater command decisions, Sire; you are a known entity to them. To kill you when you are no Chosen makes no difference to the skill of armies, but it forces a new leader. It hardens the resolve of your people and most likely Count Vesna would take your place as supreme commander, aided by more experienced generals like Suzerain Torl and General Lahk. They might be foreigners, but they're allies the legions will trust."

"It weakens the child's claim to act as intercessory for the Gods too," Emin agreed, "if it's the Mortal-Aspect of Karkarn whose banner flies over the army." He paused and looked out over the fluttering standards arrayed across the town and fields around it.

"In fact, Dash, make that happen."

"I will."

"Ah, Sire, there was something else: most of the garrison was killed. Some managed to flee, and the civilians weren't harmed, but the attackers stayed to fight anyone who'd face them. When the guards returned, they—ah, they found one of their own on the gate."

"On the gate?" Emin stiffened. "Pinned to it? Impaled to the wood?"

Dornanei ducked his head. That was how Ilumene had left one of the king's closest supporters on the night of his bloody defection to Azaer.

"You bitter little child," King Emin whispered to the wind, "always the braggart and bully." He straightened and looked at Dashain. "Organise greater protection for the queen and my son as well. Dragoon all retired Brotherhood for the job. He'll be keen to return to Ruhen's side, but we take no chances."

Dashain left immediately, almost running in her haste to get to the restricted chambers of the castle, where their more unconventional methods of communication were kept.

The king turned back to his view. He was silent for a long time.

"All these recruits," King Emin said at last, "all these men we have gathered in haste . . . who knows how many Ilumene has seeded among them?"

"That's always the way," Doranei said. "In an army there are always strangers, men with unknown pasts."

"General Bessarei, lead them out; make all haste to support the advance army. We've already decided our plan. The worst we can do now is allow Azaer to distract us from the course at hand. This war must be won by swift action."

Doranei looked at the tens of thousands beyond the castle walls. Their armies now were larger than the fifty thousand who'd faced the Menin at Moorview. Mercenaries from the Western Isles and the Denei Peninsula, battle-clans from Canar Fell and recruits from up and down the coast, men grown tall and strong over decades of plenty in the kingdom, bolstered by the finest of the Farlan and Amber's hardened veterans. "It will be," he declared with certainty.

Emin nodded. "We've seen to that, Isak and I. We have escalated and hurried this conflict to disrupt the patient plans of an immortal. The lives lost by consequence are on us, chains we will drag up Ghain's slope. The pace of war quickens. These are the final days, my friend. Soon the Land will be remade and Death's Judgment against us all will be set in stone."

Morghien watched the shadows lengthen from a marker-stone at the side of the road, pipe in hand but barely remembered as he waited. Tsatach's eye was bright in a clear sky, casting warm yellow light over the young oaks lining the road. The air was cool, but his jacket was thick and covered in metal scales, so the journey here had been enough to warm an old man's bones.

"Too much of my life's been spent waiting at a roadside," he muttered to the empty air.

"*It is who you are*," said a voice in his mind, feminine and as delicate as a wisp of smoke. "*A choice you made a century ago.*"

He drew on the pipe, just about managing to coax the last embers back into life. "I thought it was because I welcomed a Finntrail into my soul. Don't think I ever felt the urge before."

"*What, then, are the treacherous gifts it compels you to leave for travellers at the roadside?*"

Morghien smiled. The origins of the Finntrail were a mystery even to him, but it was common knowledge that when a desperate traveller found food or drink by the roadside around twilight, they had likely been left by a Finntrail. Once the gift was consumed, the Finntrail would haunt their prey for days, slowing draining the life from them.

"Wisdom," he decided. "Wisdom's a treacherous thing in the hands of most."

"*Only its application.*"

Morghien shrugged. "And yet I pass on wisdom to all those I meet, Seliasei, irrespective of the brains they might have to apply it. Look at Lord Isak now, I opened his eyes to the unnnatural side of this Land and see how he plans to use that knowledge?"

The Aspect laughed, the trickle of water in a stream. She had been with Morghien longer than any of the others inhabiting his soul and knew his humour well. "*So you did—perhaps all this can be blamed on you. Without you I'm certain this fulcrum of history, this instrument of the Gods, would never have found his own way to destiny.*"

"Bah, you've been consorting with the Brotherhood too much, my lady," Morghien said with mock displeasure. "Starting to pick up their bad manners."

"*The company I keep . . .*"

"Includes ghosts, Finntrail, unaligned spirits and other lost voices," Morghien reminded her. "I'm a civilising influence on the lot of you."

He felt the Crystal Skull at his waist pulse as Seliasei drew briefly on its power, his eyesight suddenly sharpening to a hawk's piercing clarity. "*Seekers of wisdom approach.*"

Morghien scowled. "There's only one sort of wisdom they recognise."

"*The sort you intend to grant,*" she replied, her voice fading on the wind as the minor Aspect receded to the back of his mind, waiting to be called upon.

He waited for the travellers to come closer before bothering to move. When they spotted him two soldiers were sent on ahead, the scarlet sashes bearing the Runesword of the Devoted their only insignia. The men looked local, stocky, with tanned skin, quite unlike the Raland men who'd been brought here, which meant their efforts to recruit had not been in vain.

"Who're you?" one of them called from a dozen yards away. Neither carried crossbows, Morghien was pleased to see, but their spears still had the reach over his own weapons, and several of their comrades behind had arrows nocked. They both wore stiffened leather armour and ill-fitting helmets and had shields slung over their backs—not regulation Devoted kit either; it made Morghien wonder how disciplined these recent recruits were likely to be.

"Name's Morghien," he replied with a wide, welcoming smile—an expression many had commented looked sinister and unnerving on his weatherbeaten face. "I'm hear t'speak to your preachers."

"The village is only a couple hundred yards away," one pointed out.

"Hear 'em preach with the rest."

"Oh, I think I should do so before that happens."

"Why?"

"I might not like what they say," Morghien replied cheerily.

"The debate's half the fun, I reckon, but not everyone agrees."

The soldiers both levelled their spears immediately, and glanced around at the trees on either side as though expecting an ambush to be sprung. Morghien waited patiently while exactly nothing happened.

"You're a rare breed of fool," advised one of the men while his comrade beckoned their officer over.

"You don't know the half of it, friend," Morghien said, "but I'm one brings wisdom with him."

"Wisdom?"

"A little knowledge—that dangerous thing your preachers seem to fear."

The soldier frowned, bemused by what he was hearing, but a few moments later his superior arrived and he gladly stepped aside, though he kept his spear levelled, clearly expecting the order to run Morghien through at any moment.

"Troublemaker?" asked the man with a captain's insignia badly stitched to his sash.

"Madman," was the response. "One who don't like Ruhen's Children much."

The captain looked around Morghien towards the village. "Damn. They've been watching out for us. Well, friend, looks like you're screwed. I was going to kill you quick, but now the villagers have come out to play it looks like you get the public execution—not so quick."

"I do like an audience," Morghien replied, gesturing down the road to where the villagers were watching nervously at the boundary stone. "Shall we?"

He set off without waiting for a reply, not wanting the captain to remember prisoners should be disarmed before they came quietly.

"Hey, you! Wait there."

Morghien turned, but kept walking backwards, a quizzical look on his face. One soldier hurried forward to catch him up, but in his haste he didn't keep a proper eye on the ageing wanderer. Morghien lurched forward unexpectedly and grabbed the shaft of the man's spear, pulling it past him as he aimed a heavy kick at the soldier's leg.

The soldier fell, dropping his spear in surprise and Morghien hammered down with it onto his chest, hearing a rib crack before he reversed the weapon and hurled it at the second soldier. He tried to dodge, but succeeded only in letting the spear scrape across his breastplate and slice into the unprotected inside of his arm.

"To arms!" the captain yelled over his shoulder, affording Morghien plenty of time to draw his weapons and advance. The second soldier was still clutching the gash in his arm, when Morghien reached the captain and deflected a wild swing before burying his axe in the man's knee. He finished him off with a thrust to the throat and let the body fall between him and the remaining soldier, who was half-beheaded as he lurched around the corpse.

Morghien stepped behind a tree to afford himself some protection from any rash crossbow bolts that might come his way. The villagers coming down the road had clattered to a halt at the sudden violence, but now they stared aghast at the felled bodies. Two of them dropped to their knees at the sight.

Not the usual reaction, Morghien thought to himself as the soldiers behind started to shout in panic. *I'd have thought they'd scatter from any sort of fighting.*

"Murderer!" shrieked one of the lead villagers, "heretic!"

Great, one of those.

His attention was soon caught by screams from the main group of soldiers. He peered around the tree in time to watch the last of the crossbowmen shot.

"About bloody time," he muttered, walking forward without haste while Farlan Ghosts rose from their leafy hiding-places to attack.

A flash of copper caught the light as Shanas, former devotee of Fate, joined the fight, the tattoos on her bare arms blurring as she slashed the nearest Devoted's thigh. They were outnumbered two to one at least, looking at the fifty-odd soldiers in the column, but a dozen fell to the glaives of the Ghosts in their first charge.

Morghien ran forward and released the power of the Crystal Skull at his waist. The misty form of Seliasei swooped out from his body, buoyed by the sudden rush of power, and reached for the nearest terrified soldier, while three more insubstantial figures followed.

The black jagged shape of the Finntrail ran jerkily along the road, and hooked the leg of one Devoted, dragging him to the ground. A slender wolf-shape darted past it, leaping at another but passing straight through the alarmed soldier, while a grey hawk clawed at the eyes of the next. Though too weak to hurt the man directly, the wolf spirit's flowing mane of fur filled his eyes for long enough for a Ghost to take the soldier down; he followed the wolf's path and battered aside the next man's spear before chopping across his face. Blood sprayed high as the man fell backwards, just as a spear thumped into the Ghost and downed him.

The Ghost flopped back, keening with pain as the spear jerked clear and blood poured from his side. His nearest comrades responded by calling out their battle hymn. Seliasei caught his killer's spear-shaft and tossed it aside as the words were taken up by the remaining Ghosts. The Devoted soldier was dragged from his feet amidst a roaring invocation of Nartis' rage, then the dark Finntrail spirit pounced again.

Morghien caught up to the fighting, stepping into Shanas' lee as the athletic young woman danced past less nimble opponents, never stopping, never getting into a test of strength with the men she faced. Shanas slashed at arms and legs with cruel accuracy, and when they turned to follow her path, Morghien chopped and stabbed in her wake, magic flooding through his limbs to add force to each blow.

The Devoted were boxed in: the Farlan Ghosts pressing in on both sides and a pair of black-clad King's Men blocked the road behind. Splinters flew as the brutal glaives shattered their shields, men howled and whimpered as they sought to run but were given no quarter. Morghien saw the cowering preachers ahead, one shouting an incoherent prayer as Seilasei rose up before them on a column of flowing mist.

Faced by a minor Goddess rising radiant in the dappled light, the leader of the preachers broke off his beseechings and stared open-mouthed. She looked down at him pityingly, smoky trails of hair moving in a breeze he could not feel, and stepped forward. With the power of the Skull within her, Seliasei's face now possessed a light and texture Morghien had rarely seen before. The curve of her breasts was more than a suggestion in the dim light, the smooth lines of her belly opaque and alluring.

"Daemon," the preacher gasped as though it were his dying breath.

"No," Seliasei said in a voice like running water, "I am a daughter of Vasle, born of the divine. And you: you are my enemy." With a movement so elegant it seemed like a caress, the Aspect cupped his face in her hands and looked deep into his eyes for a long moment—then she snapped the man's neck with barely a twitch of exertion.

The Ghosts cut down the last of the soldiers and put the remaining preachers out of their misery with brutal efficiency. When all the enemy were still, they saw to their own, dispatching those too injured to help, then moved on to search for valuables, supplies and any weapons worth taking.

Morghien watched them with a chill on his neck. No matter how many times he had done the same—food or arrows were always important to an inveterate wanderer—he still lacked the seamless transition between warrior and scavenger that veteran soldiers possessed.

"Brothers," Morghien whispered, a tiny spark of magic crackling on his tongue.

The Finntrail, hawk and wolf-spirit both turned to regard him, revelling in the strength they drew from Morghien's Crystal Skull. They returned of their own accord, and he shivered as each entered his body: the wolf a delicate brush of chilly fur on his skin, the Finntrail coming as an ache in his bones and a bitter taste lingering on his tongue.

He did not withdraw Seliasei; she was the strongest of them and would do more good speaking to the villagers than he could ever hope to. But as he turned towards them he hesitated. The villagers had closed on them, creeping forward while they chopped down fifty men, and that disconcerted Morghien.

He tugged on the invisible thread of magic linking him to Seliasei and the Aspect came forward without question, gliding along the road until she was at his side and watching the advancing villagers with him.

"*I see a Wall of Intercession, or what serves as one outside the cities,*" she said, looking past them and into the village. "*A hedge of some sort, it is covered in strips of cloth—each one a prayer. I—*"

The Goddess broke off and Morghien felt a wave of revulsion wash through her. His concern deepened: Seliasei was always so assured and calm, and her reaction was profoundly worrying.

"What is it?" he urged.

"*Devotion,*" she said in a horrified whisper, "*worship I cannot touch. It hangs in the air, a festering cloud of prayer surrounds this place.*"

"Shanas," Morghien called quietly, "get the men ready to move out." He took a few paces forward, then stopped as he saw the leading villagers flinch and tense like fighting dogs going on guard.

"'We come in peace' might not be the best opening here," Morghien muttered to himself, roughly wiping the blood from his weapons and sheathing them. He saw now that several of the villagers were carrying weapons, hatchets or knives for the main. They might not be a soldier's weapons, but they were enough to kill. There were a few-score of them now, and more were trickling out from the village behind. Now Morghien could smell the anger in the air.

"Invaders, tattooed daemons!" shrieked one man.

Before he could continue his tirade a tall woman with long, greying hair raised her voice above the mutters. "Leave our lands," she called. "We want none of your savage ways here."

"You would prefer the iron fist of the Devoted?" Morghien called, "religious zealots writing your laws, fanatics torturing anyone who disagrees with you?"

"Priests have ever ruled us," the man spat. "Now we are free of them, but assailed by your king's heresy!"

"There was no heresy."

The woman shook her head. "Your king weakened the Gods; your king opened the gates of Ghenna! This plague we suffer, it comes from the hand of your lord."

Morghien shook his head despite the sourness in his gut. He knew the king had done that—Morghien himself had threatened the Chief of the Gods not so many months ago, but the blame was not so simple as one isolated act.

"It is Ruhen who has weakened the Gods. Ruhen is the heretic!"

"Lies!" hissed the man beside her, his face contorted with rage. He was smaller, and dressed in some sort of bleached cloak that Morghien realised was intended to echo those worn by Ruhen's Children. "Your king brings an army of daemons to kill us all—your king brings the end of all in his wake!"

"Ruhen has murdered priests of the Gods," Morghien continued, returning his gaze to the woman who looked to be a village elder. "Ruhen has weakened the Gods by killing and driving out their servants. He seeks himself to be made a God."

"Go, leave this place!" the woman shouted, her gaze darting to those edging forward on either side of her, weapons in hand. "Your king is not welcome here; your cause is not welcome here."

"You prefer this peace promised by the Devoted?" Morghien replied, aware he had little time before they ran for him and his men were forced to slaughter civilians too. "You tell *me*, who stands here with a Goddess at my side, that my enemy is an emissary of the Gods and my cause is a heretic's?"

The woman stepped forward in front of her more hate-filled neighbours. "The Devoted promised us peace. Ruhen promises protection to those who follow him." Her tone turned bitter. "And you? You offer nothing but the slaughter of our protectors—whatever they might preach, daemons walk these woods at night. We've lost several of our children already—livestock have died and the chickens will not lay, the goats do not give milk any more. Will your Goddess fight for us tonight, if the daemons come?"

"She will!" Morghien declared, but the woman just shook her head sadly.

"But tomorrow you'll be gone. You have your war to fight; you're not here to protect us, and the beasts of the Dark Place are legion. Either you go, or you stay and kill us too, but don't pretend you haven't condemned many to death already."

Morghien hesitated. His relationship with Emin Thonal had always been rocky: two wilful men with certainty in their hearts, but of late Morghien had been increasingly nervous of the path they trod. He could see no other that led to victory, but he knew his friend well.

The King of Narkang and the Three Cities was a bold strategist. He had risked much during his conquest, and grown confident after decades of success. That he had only a half-mad white-eye and remorseless Mortal-Aspect of a dead Goddess to temper his plans was little comfort to a man who could sense just how great the upheaval in the Land was.

"We leave," he said with a troubled heart, seeing even the clear-thinking people of these parts were against them now. Folk needed to survive the days and weeks, and only his enemy could ensure that at present.

"Are we still on the side of right?" he whispered to himself, though he knew Seliasei could hear him still. "Or has this Land been so turned upside down it's now Azaer who's right?"

Seliasei touched his arm and urged him to turn away. The Ghosts were formed up, ready to defend him if necessary. Shanas, at their centre, had a worried expression on her young face.

"*Azaer forces you to do this,*" the Aspect said softly. "*The shadow wounds you wherever it can, and this cuts both you and the king to the quick. The stakes have been raised by both sides. This must end one way or another, else both sides fall and chaos reigns.*"

"And that is what I fear," Morghien said. "We've both done so much damage in the name of victory—can either of us win now? Can this hurt be undone, stemmed even? Azaer would let it all fall to ruin rather than lose—but if Emin has the choice, what will he prefer?"

By way of reply Seliasei drifted inside him, embracing his soul and surrendering herself to him, as she had for decades now. The act wasn't submission; he didn't need to dominate the Goddess they way he did the Finntrail.

But can I trust Emin still? he wondered privately as he headed to their camp. *Fate's eyes, do we even know what we've done? Are we all damned?*

Chapter 28

THE COLUMN WOUND ITS WAY SLOWLY towards the border, through lands scoured clean by the Menin invasion. Villages and towns were half-flattened or burned by foraging parties, the skulls of the slain piled high alongside the road by their newfound allies in honour of their lord.

The silence in the ranks of the Narkang Army was palpable. Emin felt it like a sickness in his gut. He was glad Amber had insisted his troops marched separately—how any general would be able to restrain his men after witnessing this, he didn't know. The eastern flank of the nation had become a wasteland, a memorial of empty fields and settlements slowly returning to nature's embrace.

The Menin lord had wanted his enemies to know the devastation he inflicted was as much the price of refusing battle as wanting his own troops to know there was no retreat. He had given them only one stark option: victory was the only way for them to survive.

From his saddle King Emin watched buzzards circling lazily over the fields. "The scavenging will have been good this summer," he commented sadly to his bodyguard, Forrow, then asked, "How many more days of this, Dash?"

"Before we reach the border?" Dashain said. "Not many—another week and we'll be into Circle City territory."

"And another week on from there before we sight Byora?"

"Or an army marching out to defend it."

"You think they would face us?" Emin looked back down the long column of soldiers behind them: nearly twenty thousand heavily armed men, Narkang recruits mainly, in this army alone, with Denei mercenaries adding a swift and savage edge.

"Azaer does not care about losses, only to blunt our advance. It has all the Knights of the Temples at its disposal, so why not throw some in our path to drain our strength? But I for one do not look forward to laying siege to Byora. We can't encircle the whole of Blackfang and now the Circle City's unified behind the shadow, we'll be attacked on all sides as we try to break the Byoran walls."

The king sighed, hearing the truth in her words. "We are the invaders," he agreed, "and whatever slaughter we inflict will only cement the impression Azaer wishes the Land to hold."

"That he's the beleaguered emissary of the Gods, besieged while his followers are slaughtered across the Land. More and more will flock to his banner until he has enough followers to become a God. Would the shadow usurp Death Himself?"

Emin gave a bitter snort. "I'm sure it would love to—but we will not allow it. It cannot, not without Termin Mystt and the Skulls."

"What about—?"

Emin shot Dashain a furious look. "Not another word—don't be such a fool!"

She ducked her head in apology. "Not a cheering thought, though, is it?"

"No," Emin said, frowning, "but it only adds to my resolve. We must finish this now. Isak must use Death's own weapon to end this finally. If we fail in this, it is only a matter of time—"

Captain," Dashain called suddenly, barking the word loud enough to make the general's aide flinch in his saddle, "pick up the pace. The bastards can rest when we're all dead—until then, march them harder."

General Amber turned and felt the spear crash into his breastplate and bounce away. Following decades-old training he cut down without seeing, following his own momentum to twist and bring his other scimitar around into the neck of his attacker. The man fell and Amber pushed past, his right hand held close to his body as he stepped behind the next soldier's spear and shield and drove his scimitar down into the man's arm. The Devoted yelled in pain, trying to fall back, but before he could, Amber reversed the sword and punched upwards, shattering his jaw with the guard.

Another party of Menin appeared from behind some trees and charged straight into the Devoted flank. Nai was at their fore, and Amber's attention was caught by the poorly-fitting square-edged helm on his head. He tore his eyes from the mage—distraction here could get him killed—but even as he did so the Devoted troops crumpled under the pressure. Some turned to run, but few made it more than a step or two before Menin spears and swords pierced their backs.

He stumbled over a fallen man and had to catch himself on the nearest soldier, a squat brute who stood over a downed enemy, huffing with restrained bloodlust.

The soldier flinched at his touch, then noticed Amber's Menin armour. "Hurt, General?"

Amber grinned, though his shoulder was aching badly where an axe had dented his pauldron. "By these little fucks?"

The soldier laughed at that—he was perhaps the only Menin there who couldn't look down on these short westerners. "And the pay for killing 'em ain't bad."

Amber grunted as he sheathed one scimitar and transferred the other to his right hand. His injured arm was starting to go numb—not broken, he guessed, but it wouldn't be in any shape to swing a scimitar for much longer: his were savage chopping blades which required strength as well as skill. With an effort he stooped and tugged a shield free from a corpse. It wouldn't be much fun taking a hit on his bad arm, but the fight was far from over.

"Nai," Amber called, waving the necromancer over, "where's the Legion?"

"Not far." He limped over, and Amber noted blood running down the leg he was favouring. "About half a mile that way." He pointed towards the trees on the other side of the clearing. Little more than deer paths ran through the heavily wooded ground south of the Evemist Hills and the army was split into companies and regiments, fighting a hundred individual battles in this place where there were no clearings or fields to fight in. "Bastards are dug in like ticks," Nai added. "They've got scouting parties and support groups in all directions."

"Lancers!" someone shouted, and Amber's regiment immediately contracted, like a spider drawing its legs in close. Leaving their injured, the infantrymen ran for the cover of their comrades and raised a wall of shields against the threat.

Nai abandoned Amber without a further word as he returned to his unit.

The crash of horses through the undergrowth was coming from two directions. Amber craned his head around to see if anyone was left out in the open, but he couldn't see anyone. Clearly the lancers had come to the same conclusion; urgent shouts rang through the trees, calling off their charge.

Amber could just about make them out as they wheeled about: the soldiers wore dark blue tabards, and red caparisons protected the horses.

"Must be Vener's army," Nai called from twenty yards away, answering Amber's unvoiced question. "That's full uniform they're wearing."

"So these are the men they've sent ahead," Amber realised at last. "Thought there were too many left to be the Akell troops." He looked up at the sky, squinting for a moment through the yellowed autumn leaves, but the sun was hidden behind thick cloud. "Someone find me west," he growled, glancing at his wrist where there was a tear in the sleeve under his vambrace.

A lieutenant shouldered his way over and pulled a lodestone from his own sleeve—it was a traditional gift for Menin receiving their commission. The mage-forged thin iron bar was hammered to a dull tip at each end, with a hole punched through it so it would hang free on a thread. It pointed west, towards the Palace of the Gods, the Land's greatest concentration of power, unless skewed by something nearby.

"That way," the officer said once the bar had settled on a direction. Both he and Amber looked east, following the other black-painted tip.

"We can't wait for those lancers to come back," Amber announced. "We'll push through the trees there, move on another couple hundred yards, then settle down."

The lieutenant repeated the order as he tucked his lodestone away, but the troops were already moving off, and Nai's regiment followed suit a few moments later. The path was clear enough that they made good time, heading towards the same place the Legion were bound.

Amber caught the distant sound of fighting on the air, and looked around for a suitable place to defend if necessary. After some minutes he found a rise and positioned the two regiments up and around it. Once he was happy the men were properly deployed, he tried to get a better idea of the source of the sound: there were screams and shouts and the clash of weapons, but Amber was beginning to recognise the difference between normal troops in battle and the Legion.

"Captain, hold this position until we return," he ordered, then turned to the necromancer. "Nai, you're with me," he said, and pushed his way through his men. Two tall infantrymen fell in behind him; he was a general now, and the pair had been ordered not to leave his side without reason.

It didn't take them long to find the source of the noise: a large encampment beside a river, surrounded on three sides by an earthen mound studded with stakes. It was filled with Devoted troops and a contingent from Tor Salan—Amber recognised the city-state's standard—but the majority were not soldiers of any army. With a creeping sense of dread, Amber realised they were civilians, and they were being butchered.

"Nai, order the Legion to withdraw," he hissed.

"I've already tried," Nai said anxiously. "They're ignoring me, or blocking me in some way. We can't stop them."

There had to be a thousand people in and around the camp, Amber thought. He could see some had weapons and were frantically trying to fight back, but the dead merceneries were savagely chopping through them.

"Ruhen's Children," he muttered, watching as two figures in long white robes went down under a flurry of axe blows. "They've brought their supporters here—are they supposed to be fighting with the army?"

"I don't call that fighting," Nai said darkly.

"No," Amber agreed, "that's just dying early. You can't stop this?"

"They're ignoring me. I know Ozhern can hear me, but his head's full of bloodlust, nothing more. Amber, don't risk going out there. I don't know they'd even recognise you."

"I ain't going," Amber said, rising. "Let's get back to our own men. Those lancers may be watching this too. There's nothing we can do here and evening's coming on. I want to be in a camp by sundown—with this much blood there'll be an army of daemons round here, true enough."

Nai scowled and glanced back towards the Legion of the Damned. "Just at nightfall, eh?"

Amber opened his eyes and scowled. "Could have sworn you were someone bringing me brandy there."

The priest of Shotir gave him an anxious smile and looked around as though expecting to see someone doing just that. Then he advanced cautiously on the blood-spattered general, his hands held out before him as though Amber were a growling dog. "Just coming to see to your arm, sir," the Menin healer said, his voice apologetic. "I do not touch liquor myself."

"Gods, you're serious?" Amber forced himself to sit a little straighter. "All the blood and death you people see and you don't drink? You've been seeing to the worst-wounded first, right—I've seen enough of them today to need a drink, and you get in much closer than me."

"Drink is a mocker," the priest intoned solemnly as he knelt by Amber. He was a young man, little more than twenty summers, with a thin face, unusual for his calling, for the work provoked a fierce hunger. This was a man of iron-hard will, Amber surmised.

"It brought my father low, and his father before him," the priest continued as he unfastened Amber's armour and helped the general get his cuirass off.

Amber grunted in pain as the healer levered his arm up enough to unhitch the pauldron. "Brings us all low," he said through gritted teeth, "but after a day like this, that's the whole idea."

The darkness was punctuated by the lights of cooking fires and torches lining the freshly dug rampart. If he stood on the top of the rampart, Amber knew he might just about be able to make out the fires of another camp on either side: the Menin straddled the makeshift road, with the ground in between patrolled by those half-mad Narkang Green Scarves.

"I find other diversions," the priest replied as he finally freed the general's arm. He gently probed the injured shoulder, observing Amber's discomfort until he found the spot where the pain was worse, at the very top of his arm. He put his fingers flat against the flesh and closed his eyes, and a slight warmth permeated Amber's skin as he probed the damage.

"The bone is cracked," the priest pronounced after a moment. "You're lucky; I can make it useable for the morning."

"Do it," Amber said with a nod. He knew it'd hurt like a bastard, and it'd still be fragile in battle, but it was better than nothing, and any improvement, no matter how slight, might just keep him alive. He tried to smile, but he was so exhausted all he could manage was a twitch of the cheeks.

Strange: it's been a while since I cared much for surviving. But it looks like my body still does, no matter what my mind might think. Training only gets a man so far—I've seen even the best soldiers give up—but for whatever reason, it looks like some of me ain't ready to go.

"General!" someone called, and Amber was reaching for a weapon before he managed to catch himself. Three figures were marching towards him, and his one remaining bodyguard immediately placed himself in front of Amber.

"General, you have a visitor," the voice continued, and now Amber placed it: Colonel Dorom, one of the commanders for the legions in this camp.

"You done?" Amber asked the priest, starting to struggle to his feet.

"Done? I haven't even started yet."

"Well, go see to someone else for now," Amber said, "or get yourself some food. You make me cry in front of that bastard, someone here'll gut you."

The priest, taken aback, stared at Amber for a moment before turning to see who the newcomer was. He could make out a broad man, taller than average for the West, with a bald head and the handle of some large weapon sticking out from behind his back. He was flanked by two Menin in heavy armour. Meeting the healer's gaze, the newcomer bared his teeth and growled like a dog, startling the man.

The priest retreated to the sound of the newcomer's laughter, melting away into the dark towards the hospital tent.

"You must be General Daken," Amber said wearily in Narkang, not bothering to rise.

"Fame precedes me, eh?"

The big soldier looked up at the white-eye's grinning face. "Something like that, Mad Axe. Can't think of many with your reputation willing to walk into the camp of men who'd like to see you dead."

"Always had a forgiving nature, me." Daken pulled something from his belt and swung it towards Amber. "Brought you a present, too. Renowned for kissing up to my commanding officer, I am."

Amber heard liquid slosh inside a flask and snatched it from the air. Using his damaged arm to pin the flask against his body, he opened it up and took a sniff. It wasn't anything he recognised, but strong spirits needed no introduction. He took a swig and started coughing hard enough to sent fresh jagged pain shooting down his arm.

Daken laughed, the sound disconcerting amongst the battle-weary troops. "Aye, kills a cold stone dead too!"

"Feels like my throat's been coated in lime plaster," Amber spluttered, waving the flask back at Daken.

"Take another. Goes down easier the second time."

Amber did so, and admitted, "True enough, but most things probably taste smooth once half your mouth's been burned out. Drink with me."

The white-eye took two long pulls on the flask himself and squatted down before his new commander. "Now we're all friends, hey?"

"Far from friends," Amber said with a spark of anger in his eyes, "just on the same side for the time being. Forget that and we'll kill you, orders or no."

"Don't you worry about me; I'm loveable enough until I get some booze inside me."

Amber couldn't help but smile. This one was obviously as mad as his nickname suggested. He would cheerfully go through the Ivory Gates of Ghenna, just to have a look round, and then saunter back out again.

"The priest says strong drink is a mocker," he said.

"Fucking priests, eh?"

"Indeed." Amber slowly levered himself up. "Well, General Daken, what can I do for you?"

"Oh, nothing, just reporting in," Daken said. "Got me some catching up to do, looks like—we passed a whole lot of bodies on the way here."

"We're making a name for ourselves," Amber agreed. "The Devoted aren't so keen to face us in open battle now."

"Ah, what's in a name, eh?" asked the Mad Axe. "Send 'em King Emin's way—he must be over the border now, and following in your bloody wake. Sends orders that you're to hold position and let them make up ground; there's forty legions just itching to get at these Devoted knights."

"We'll hold," Amber said. "It'll take us time to clear the rats from this run anyways."

"Good, then." Daken looked Amber up and down. "So: killed one of the Chosen, they say. Lord Tsatach?"

"I did."

"Had to settle for your Duke Vrill myself," Daken said. "Don't suppose I'll get one like Tsatach in this lifetime now, more's the pity."

"No one liked Vrill anyway," Amber said, in case Daken was looking to needle him—being a white-eye, he might not even have intended on it. "Man was a bastard, and only a half-decent soldier, for all he was a white-eye."

"Aye, pisses me off, that does—but you can only kill what's in front of you, I s'pose."

"Is that why you're in this? To cement your reputation? Or to eclipse older legends who gave you your nickname?"

Daken grinned widely and bowed with surprising grace. "We all have our reasons. I'll leave you to your healing now, General Amber." And with that he turned and sauntered away, drinking from his flask and meeting the eye of every glaring soldier he passed.

"Ravens sit on that man's shoulder," Amber muttered to himself. "Marked by the Trickster? Creatures below, Litania's a fool if she thinks she owns that one."

He eased himself back down to where he'd been sitting, groaning with fatigue and the pain in his shoulder. "Wake me when the healer returns," he told his bodyguard.

CHAPTER 29

"GETTING A BIT FAR FROM THE CAMP, AREN'T WE?"

Isak looked at Carel and shrugged. "Wanted some space to breathe, away from all that."

"Without guards?"

The stooping white-eye smiled crookedly and walked on to a jutting stone, from where he had a good view of the day's last light. Carel checked around and, seeing no one, found a seat near Isak. Guessing he wanted to talk, Carel fished out his tobacco pouch and tossed it over.

How many times did I tell that boy he was hard of thinking? Now it's near enough true, I reckon. The effort it takes him demands more of a run up. He fetched out his hip-flask and took a long pull. The evenings were getting colder now—it wasn't just his old bones that felt it. In enemy territory Carel wore a hauberk whenever he was awake, getting himself ready for when he might need to fight in it again. Isak had on a long, shapeless shirt and his usual ragged-sleeved cape. He refused to wear armour now—he seemed to loathe the weight of metal on his body.

"Ain't you cold, lad?"

Isak shook his head. "Never cold," he said in a hollow voice. "The Dark Place is always with me—the stink of it in my nose, the dust and dirt ground into my skin. The fires there—they keep me warm."

Carel shivered and fell silent again. Being in the Dark Place was bad enough, but bringing a part of it back out with you, that just compounded the horror.

And still he turns it to his own advantage, Carel realised, *I taught him that—to take the bad parts of his soul and make them work for him.*

I'd just meant to channel his aggression, not give him a means to carry Death's own weapon!

"What happened to my father?" Isak asked abruptly. "Did I kill him?"

"To my eternal surprise, no," Carel said with a cough. "You gave it a good go, but he'd been possessed by a daemon at the time, so on balance it was fair enough."

"I don't remember my mother, but I wouldn't, would I?"

"No, lad, but you never minded hearing about her."

"Larassa, that was her name . . ."

Carel smiled and swapped one of the lit pipes for the hip-flask. "That was her. She was a wild one, your ma was." He looked up as a sudden movement caught his eye: black shapes darting through the night, accompanied by excited clicks on the edge of perception. "Calling bats to you again?" he murmured.

Isak shook his head sadly. "I don't need to call them now. They can hear the sword's call."

"Can anything else?" Carel asked more seriously, "daemons, maybe?"

"Maybe," Isak admitted, "but they're no threat."

"Really? Fate's eyes, boy, you sure about that?"

The white-eye looked up with a mournful look. "You've no idea of the power in my hands—none at all."

"So tell me, share the burden."

"The burden would flay the flesh from your bones," Isak said. "When I say you've no idea, I mean just that: you can't understand the sheer power; most mages wouldn't be able to. I can feel the Land under my skin, the slow reach of mountains, the pounding rivers, the clouds darting above them in the dark."

Carel fixed his eyes on Isak. At last he asked, "Why're we out here, Isak?"

Isak was silent for a while, then he said, "To find some peace. I—*we*—were once friends, you say. I don't remember you, but I do remember something—some*one*—I trusted, and that memory calms the storm in my mind."

"How much longer can you stand it?" Carel asked with dismay. "How long before Termin Mystt tears out your mind, rips your soul apart? I can see the toll it takes on you—half the army can."

"My soul's already torn," Isak whispered. "There's no stitching these strips back together again; they're only good to hang on the trees at midsummer. All I have are pieces—the white-eye, the mortal, the dead man . . ."

"The Gods-blessed champion," Carel added firmly, "the Lord of the Farlan, the Chosen of Nartis and conqueror of Aryn Bwr. Don't make you any less of a man. Look at all of us—Vesna, Emin, Doranei, me as well. We're all in pieces one way or another. That's what fighting men are." He hesitated, bowed under by the weight of thoughts and feelings a soldier normally tried so hard to ignore.

Then he shook himself and went on, "Isak, we fight as a unit because together we're stronger. Together we can do what alone we'd never manage. All us soldiers, we're dragging the ghosts of fallen friends and chains of sin as only killers can. It steals a part of you—"less there's nothing worth stealing; those're the most broken of the lot of us. One-legged men, all helping each other to the bar—that's a soldier's joke, ain't it: drinking together and falling as one."

Carel scratched his chin. "Anyways, point is this: you'll not find a bigger crowd of misfits and madmen than in an army, and war only makes us worse. War takes the best of us and cuts out their best, so the only way any of us survives is with the help of his friends.

"But it only works if you trust the man beside you, trust his shield at your side. We draw our strength from each other, Isak—it's when we step away from the line and move on our own that we're at our weakest."

Isak smiled wryly. "That's one lesson I've learned—one of yours, maybe, that I did take to heart: I remember not to be just the colour of my eyes, and I remember that without others I'm nothing."

Carel heard the fatigue in Isak's voice. He gave the massive young man a nudge to shake him out of his maudlin thoughts. "You realise half of what I said was just to shut you up? You always were a mouthy little bastard—I needed to give you something to chew over so you weren't picking fights all the time."

Isak laughed briefly and the tension visibly drained from his hunched shoulders. "I think you don't realise how much you taught me," he said, sounding far more like the youth Carel had once known. "I hope the Land appreciates it one day."

"Hah! Aye, a bloody statue would be nice, yes—but I won't hold my breath. Right now I reckon I'd settle for one sufficiently appreciative woman."

"Do you trust me?" Isak asked unexpectedly.

Carel narrowed his eyes. "Aye, I do," he said firmly, "but if you've got anything nasty planned, I'd like to hear about it first."

"Sorry—"

—and a loud thwack broke the peace of evening and Isak was driven forward. He staggered a few steps and then dropped to his knees, a crossbow quarrel protruding from his back. Carel howled with rage and jumped to his feet, tugging his sword from its sheath as he looked for their attackers.

He didn't have long to wait: two men broke from the cover of a tree, one discarding a crossbow as they ran, their swords drawn.

"Back off, old man," the taller of the two called, "or we kill you too."

"No other way it's going to happen," Carel growled. He spared Isak a glance: he was still on his knees, but his abused face was contorted with pain.

The two men didn't respond as they charged forward with swords and daggers drawn. Both wore army leathers and hauberks; most likely they'd just slipped off the tabards which indicated their unit.

Carel backed around Isak, not wanting to leave the white-eye, but aware he stood little chance, a one-armed man against two trained fighters. As they reached Isak, both men glanced down to check on him, obviously well aware of a white-eye's resilience. They shared a grin at the expression of pain on his face and his clawed, empty hands.

"Looks like that stuff was worth the price," the leader commented, then gestured at Carel. "Keep him back."

"Name your price. We'll double it," Carel shouted.

"Sorry, friend. Ilumene don't like traitors—he takes it personal like."

Without warning Isak swung around, as though taking a wild swipe at the man advancing on him.

Carel blinked as black stars burst before his eyes. A blurring sense of darkness streaked across his vision and a wet clap echoed around them. He reeled, head suddenly aching as though the air pressure had dropped in a heartbeat. It seemed that Isak had drawn a curtain through the air in front of him, a dark haze that melted to nothing as the taller attacker collapsed sideways, his entire body chopped in two. The second man grunted in shock and pain, staggering back with his dagger-hand pressed to his temple, and Carel seized the advantage.

He slashed up at the underside of the man's hand, slicing through the soft flesh before stabbing him in the kidney. The man howled and fell to his knees, dropping his weapons.

Carel worked his sword savagely in the wound as the man screamed at the top of his lungs.

"Who's working with you?" he yelled in the man's ear. "Tell me, and I'll drag you to a healer!"

The soldier's eyes were wide with pain. "I don't—" he gasped, and then managed, "The coin—"

"Coin?" Carel demanded, but as he did so he saw a chain under the man's collar. He tugged hard on it and the necklace came away in his hand. The soldier shuddered as the sword slid out of his back.

Carel held it up—it was just a scratched coin on a chain—and tossed it aside, and for a moment he thought he saw something akin to hope in the man's eyes, but then Isak stabbed forward like a mantis and impaled him on the black sword.

In the blink of an eye the weapon had vanished from sight and Isak was left flexing his crabbed fingers as the corpse flopped to the ground.

"Isak!" Carel shouted, suddenly remembering the bolt in his back. He discarded the sword and ran over, but before he could touch the bolt, Isak raised a hand to stop him.

"It's not bad," he said, "really—"

"Not bad? There's a bloody arrow in your back!"

Isak grinned weakly and rapped his knuckles on his chest.

"Armour?" Carel gasped, tearing at Isak's shirt until he could see the leather cuirass underneath. "You little bastard, why didn't you tell me?"

"Wanted it to be convincing," Isak said. He made a small gesture and looked all around as he pushed himself back to his feet, then he returned his attention to Carel, apparently satisfied with what he saw or didn't see. "There's still metal in my flesh, though. Help me off with this, will you?"

"We're safe now?" And when Isak nodded he unsheathed his knife to cut away the shirt. The bolt had penetrated his armour, the plate of stiffened leather absorbing most of the blow, so no more than the tip had gone into Isak's flesh.

"You still got lucky," Carel growled. "Reckless bastard—what did he mean about it being worth the price?"

Isak winced at the sting in his back. "They wanted my skin broken—the bolt was tipped."

"Poison?"

"No, something Emin told me Ilumene was skilled at making: it dulls magic, so it would make any energies I tried to gather slip through my fingers."

"Didn't you use magic just now?" Carel asked, bewildered.

Isak flexed his fingers and smiled. "Of course—but they were just hired agents. All they saw was an unarmed white-eye and a one-armed old man. They weren't to know nothing they cooked up could match Termin Mystt."

"What about me—was I just bloody bait for you? What protection did I have?" Carel shouted, suddenly furious at Isak's risk-taking.

"Why would they have shot you? You're not the threat; the white-eye mage was."

"They might have had two bloody crossbows!"

The white-eye just shrugged. "True—they didn't, though."

"Oh well, thank you very much," Carel snapped. "Glad I could be of use."

"You were," Isak said firmly. "We knew there'd be agents in the army—how many is anyone's guess. But I knew they wouldn't pass up the opportunity to take me when I looked most defenceless. Better they try me, than go for one of the weaker ones carrying a Crystal Skull. You said it yourself: trust the man beside you. Well, I did, and we both survived."

Carel stopped dead, hearing his own words turned against him. The anger remained undiminished, but he'd long since learned anger was no use when arguing with Isak. No one could compete with a white-eye there.

"You could have told me," he mumbled, retrieving his sword and turning his back on Isak. "Trust me enough to tell me, too."

"Sorry, my memory—you know? Not what it used to be—"

"Eh?" His anger faded in the face of Isak's unashamed lies. "You brazen little bugger—at least pretend to be repentant!"

Isak turned his head to watch the grey blur of Hulf, bounding through the darkness towards them. "Don't think you taught me that one. Anyways, doubt it'd be much use to a soldier, eh?"

She watched it scuttle through the darkness, six-legged and wrapped in shadows. From tree to clump of grass, stalk-eyes forever turned her way. A bisected tail curved over its humped back, fat pincers tucked down over its mandibles. Uneven plates covered its body, upraised and cracked, like flagstones assailed by tree roots. To most eyes it would be near-invisible, but to Zhia those folded shadows shone like a lamp.

Not a typical suitor, Zhia thought to herself, *but I smell the same apprehension from this creature.*

The daemon made its way closer: forty yards, thirty, never moving directly, slowing as it came until it was creeping with the delicate, fearful steps of a deer watching the wolf.

Zhia sighed. She could only imagine it had been sent with some message for her, but by whom or what, she couldn't decide. It was smaller than Isak's oversized puppy, so hardly much of a messenger—unless that was the intention?

She watched it wriggle into a long-abandoned fire-pit and pause there as though contemplating the last few yards of ground, but before it could decide the path was safe, a circle of light appeared around the edge of the pit.

The daemon drew its limbs closer to its body, moving instinctively away from the light, and turned to seek a way out. Finding none, it started to dig frantically, scraping at the muddy ash with all its limbs at once, desperate to hide as the light steadily brightened.

Threads broke from the ring, writhing worms reaching up into the air only to find nothing and fall inwards, where they scorched the dark armour of the daemon. The creature hissed and scrabbled for purchase, snapping at the threads with its pincers, only to get one set snagged and caught, which increased the daemon's panic. The threads of light closed inwards on it like a carnivorous plant, snaring its prey in a sizzling, shuddering bundle of scorched chitin.

"Instructive, is it not?"

Zhia turned to find her brother standing just a few yards off. She hadn't sensed his approach, but he was the only one who could take her unawares. He was unarmoured, dressed in fine silks procured from the Gods alone only knew where, embroidered all in black to serve as contrast to the plain white scabbard that held Eolis.

"Instructive?"

"The creature is ruled by its baser instinct to hide from the light and pain," Vorizh explained. "It cannot bring itself to burst through its cage of light until it is too late. It is hard to pity something that cannot comprehend sacrifice."

The vampire's face was a picture of ghastly fascination, and Zhia was struck by the strangeness of the sight. Vorizh was a mad recluse, both animated and restless, and in normal times she would see him perhaps every few centuries. Koezh, their elder brother, was very different. He was driven by his duty as leader of the Vukotic tribe, one of the Seven Tribes of Man; he was a man used to stillness and calm, his emotions well-hidden behind a mask of duty. And yet the two looked very much alike.

Sometimes she wondered if Vorizh served to remind Koezh that the alternative to that duty was to break under the strain of their curse, to become a monster fascinated with the death of daemons.

"Why did you kill it?" she asked.

"Perhaps it was coming to kill you, dear sister. Did you never consider that?"

Vorizh's moods were rarely predictable, but after centuries they followed well-trodden paths. "Did you send it to kill me?" she asked in weary irritation.

"That would be madness," Vorizh countered, a sly smile on his face. "It barely merited the name of daemon; it was little more than a scavenger on the shore of this Land. It could never pose a threat to one such as you."

"That's no answer."

"Yet answer enough," he spat. "What do you care for them anyway? They are not mortal; you do not feel their deaths in your gut—leave the loss of immortals to your betters, to those of us elevated to a higher station."

"A higher station now, is it?" Zhia asked. "Does that make your damnation less than mine, or greater?"

"Greater in all ways!" he cried. "You cannot begin to understand my suffering; you cannot hear the death-song of this Land and its Gods."

"That was a tune we both played once. Are you not bored of it?"

"Me?" Vorizh exclaimed. "You ask that of *me*? Your hands drip with the blood of mortals as yet unshed—I know your part in this, the games you continue to play!"

"Ah, outrage and condemnation, the tyrant's call down through the ages. What future for Vanach, dear brother? You think our deeds comparable?"

Vorizh stopped, his face changing to a picture of calm with such speed Zhia felt her skin crawl. "Comparable—yes, sweet sister, and complementary too. You play your games with mortals and I with immortals; that is the difference between us."

"I'm immortal."

"And you too are caught in my web. The roots run deep, dear sister, most especially within the blood we share. You obey your blood, the instinct within."

Zhia bit back her response. Fantasy and reality blurred into one with her brother, she knew that, but she was certain he did not guide her actions. He could not even know of some of her deeds. She had learned millennia back that to believe all he said was to forget his madness and the tint it cast on all things.

"What of King Emin, Isak—do they obey your machinations?"

"The mortals I leave to you," Vorizh scoffed, "and in their failures I see your weakness."

"Failures?"

"This land you pass though, these villages and towns that worship your enemy. Your king fears to encourage the tales being spread about him, and so he spares his enemy's worshippers: the very power-base of a God left untouched."

"He has his reasons," Zhia said firmly, "and I do not control him. The Walls of Intercession are torn down, but only a monster slaughters tens of thousands just to undermine a weaker enemy. The Legion of the Damned has slaughtered enough to expunge their comrades' thirst for it."

"An irrelevance; those battles determine nothing. They are not the true test of power."

"Is there a point to all this?" Zhia demanded, her patience running out.

He gave a sly smile. "The more a fly struggles, the more it's lost to the web."

"A lesson for me? Oh thank you."

Vorizh suddenly peered suspiciously at her, staring so closely he almost seemed to be hunting for her soul through the windows of her eyes. "Have you made your move?"

"Move?"

"Don't pretend you're content to simply allow this to play out. They are less than cattle compared to us. What power do you wield over events?"

"Why would I tell you?

"Our goals are the same; together, none of them can oppose us."

Zhia shook her head and started to walk away, but Vorizh darted around her with unnatural speed and grabbed her arm. "Tell me, sister! Events move apace—are your games with the mortals complete? You claim not to control this king, and that's a risk we cannot afford."

"Our goals may be the same," Zhia said slowly, her eyes fixed on the hand gripping her, "but that does not mean you can give me orders or lay your hands on me." Vorizh's fingers were as pale and slender as any woman's, and even after all these years he still wore a signet ring. Once it had been made of gold, but now it was some greyish-black metal she couldn't identify. The pressure on her arm increased a touch, then Vorizh stepped back, satisfied he'd asserted his dominance.

"You will know the plans I've laid as they play out," Zhia said, "but not before. As for you, the damage you've done to the Land is severe enough. If you wish to be involved, take your orders from Isak or King Emin. This is the time for mortals, their decisions and deeds."

She started towards the Narkang camp, but paused after a few steps. "And brother dearest, next time you lay your hands on me, you'll die. Do you understand?"

Vorizh's sapphire eyes gleamed at that, but he said nothing. Zhia turned her back on him and walked away, leaving her brother to the shadows.

"Shouldn't we tell him?"

King Emin looked up, momentary surprise on his face. The tent was dark, and smelled of mud and cold soup.

Vesna looked between the faces of his companions: Emin, weary-eyed and thin, showing his fifth decade at last. Isak, all expression lost to the scars and abuses of the Dark Place. Legana, all the more breathtakingly beautiful in the gloom of a single lamp, her green eyes shining with inner fire, as predatory and terrible as a Goddess's should, while the sinister handprint on her throat was pitch-black against her pale skin.

And what about me? Vesna asked himself. *Do I look the part of a God? To soldiers who're desperate for a warrior, perhaps, but to the rest? Hah! Only the Gods alone know. I don't carry it like Legana, marked by injury though she is. Maybe it was then she found her wisdom; I still have to find mine.* He touched the ruby on his cheek, the sign of Karkarn's covenant with his Mortal-Aspect. *No, the Lady chose well—I guess she had better folk to choose from. We soldiers, we turn on ourselves too easily, but we're all Karkarn has.*

"Tell him?" Emin asked at last. "Why?"

"You don't think he has the right to know?"

"When do rights come into it?" Isak asked.

"He's my friend," Vesna insisted. "He has been for a long time now. How am I meant to hide that from someone, knowing it's a secret that's likely to kill him?"

"*What if we do tell him?*" Legana said into their minds. "*A general cannot be loyal just to his friends.*"

Vesna stared down at his hands, the one covered in black-iron twice the size of his normal one. "I don't know what'd happen," he admitted.

"So can we risk it?" Emin said, his tone making clear his opinion.

Vesna shook his head. "It feels like a betrayal."

"There'll be enough of those to go round," Isak said.

Vesna glanced at the white-eye, unable to tell if that was a callous joke or not, but Isak's face gave nothing away. He lowered his gaze again. "More than enough," he muttered. "Too much for all of us to bear. You really want to add to it?"

CHAPTER 30

DORANEI LOOKED UP AT THE THICK CLOUDS AND SCOWLED, unable to gauge the position of the sun behind that uniform covering. Past midday, but beyond that it was a difficult call. The army snaked along what passed for a road in these parts: traders' routes to the Circle City had seen little traffic of late, so tolls had been poor and repairs non-existent.

"Copper for your thoughts," Veil said from beside him, nudging Doranei's elbow as he spoke.

"Just a copper?"

Veil smiled. "Never heard one of yours worth more'n that."

Doranei didn't reply; he was in no mood for banter. The closer they got to Byora, the more he felt the pressure like a great weight on his shoulders. The king had taken him aside a week back to reveal Doranei's next mission, and the dread had been growing ever since.

"Thinking about Byora?" Veil asked. "Sebe, mebbe?"

The two men rode, mounts that'd been left without owners after the last skirmish. Veil wore his spike-tipped vambrace most all the day, now the threat of infiltrators was ever-present.

Gods, I wasn't, Doranei thought guiltily. *Thanks for reminding me.* "Just trying to work all this out, what'll be coming next."

"A fight, if we're lucky."

"But then what? Ruhen's no warrior—he'll let the Devoted fight for him, but the shadow won't be in the thick of it. Does he run? Let it all burn around him? Draw us into a trap?"

"He'll run," Veil said confidently. "He'll let us inflict the horrors o' war on his expendable followers, and that'll do the job of recruiting thousands more for him."

"Where does it end?"

Veil shrugged. His long hair was tied back and covered with a scarf to keep the worst of the road's dust out. "It ends when we catch him. And when it's over, we start living again."

"Living?" Doranei echoed. "What in Ghenna's name is that? This war's all either of us have ever known. You going to retire, go into trade?"

"Hah! We're killers, my friend, there's no retiring for us. But there'll always be enemies, never fear—just not ones of Azaer's calibre—and I for one won't be complaining about that."

"So that's all my life will ever be?"

Veil looked askance at him. "You? Probably not. You"n' Dash'll be running the Brotherhood one day soon. Sir Creyl's got no fire left in him, not really. I ain't pissing on the man's name, but his edge went with his title and he's not complaining. Got himself a family now, a legacy, and life better'n the Brotherhood could ever offer—while we get a commander pushing the paper who knows what it's like down at the sharp end, which ain't nothing neither. Meantimes, Dash makes the decisions and she's the one with a heart o' cold steel; they both know that so it'll all keep working and we get the hope of something better—that's if we survive to retire."

"Why me?"

"You're the favourite son Ilumene could never be. You don't want to be king, simple as that. Let's face it—we all love that spark of fear in the eyes of folk at court. They see the bees on our collars, they know the reputation of the King's Men, and we're Gods—and daemons—in their eyes. That feeling of being above the law, that's the rush for all of us, but Ilumene, he wanted adulation too: the glory as well as the power."

Doranei raised his eyebrows. "Been thinking about this much?"

"Hah, mebbe a little, aye."

Doranei was silent for a long while. Eventually he said, "Veil, you'd say we're about as loyal as it gets, right?"

"Eh? What sort of dumbshit question is that? Remember Canar Fell—that old bugger from the Three Cities conquest who'd pissed off the duke? The king sent us there to protect him and you never hesitated—you took a crossbow bolt and threw yourself out a damn window to save the man, all 'cos the king felt he owed a debt."

"Aye, I remember," Doranei said with a wince, working the shoulder he'd broken in the fall. He had only survived because he'd taken the assassin with him and had landed on the man. "I was just making a point: we're loyal—but why? What for exactly? Why'd we do it?"

"Piss and daemons, what's the king asked you to do?"

He shook his head. "Just thinking about what's to come."

"If you say so— Ah, *shit*!" Veil gasped as he scratched his cheek with the wrong hand while he thought—*again*. He let go of his reins and used his right hand to wipe the blood away, wincing at the pain. He scowled at Doranei as though it was his fault, but Doranei hadn't even broken a smile this time.

"Sure as shit ain't the adornments we get," Veil muttered. "Why'd we do it? Too dumb to know any better, I guess. Man needs something t'believe in. At least we don't have to pretend some waddling inbred fool is a king we owe our lives to."

"And look what it costs us," Doranei said, pointing to Veil's spikes. "Are we really so desperate for purpose, for something bigger than ourselves to believe in?"

"'course! Only a bloody fool thinks otherwise too. Life's not pretty or nice most o' the time; you don't buy into the lie a little, you're always going to be waiting for things to fail. Take marriage—even someone like Zhia, who's not exactly normal. Does any man really think his wife's always going to be beautiful, always going to be happy to see him and full o' joy? Don't make me laugh! You do your best to ignore the bad bits or soon enough they're all you'll see—and then the good is wasted."

"I guess so," Doranei said. "Who're the heroes of the nation? It's us—madmen like Coran and Daken who're as bad as they are good, or someone like Beyn who was a bastard, no two ways about it, but a fucking hero all the same. Bad bits are easy to see if you want."

"Or moody shits like yourself," Veil added, "who falls into a bottle whenever he's angry, upset, sleepy or horny, far's I can tell."

"Least I got two hands, fucker."

Veil was too quick for him, clouting him across the mouth with his remaining hand moving before Doranei had even finished speaking. The bigger man growled and swung a punch that would have taken Veil off the back of his horse, but he dodged and brought his reinforced vambrace crashing down onto Doranei's head.

Stars burst before his eyes, but Doranei instinctively reached out and grabbed Veil's brigandine. He dragged Veil towards him and headbutted him and he heard a crunch as he caught Veil right on the nose.

Veil fell backwards off his horse, his single hand flailing for a grip.

"Ah, fuck!" Doranei gasped, moving drunkenly as he tried to keep his balance.

"Fuck's sake, Doranei," Veil yelled from the road below. "What the fuck's wrong with you?"

Without even meaning to, Doranei dropped from his horse and advanced around the beasts towards Veil. "You took the first swing, don't bitch about what you get!"

"Like that, is it?" Veil demanded as he struggled up, spiked vambrace pointing at Doranei. "I could've rammed this in your fucking neck without even thinking. Next time maybe I won't bother holding back."

"Oh fucking try it," Doranei snarled, his hand settling about the grip of his enchanted broadsword.

"Ahem," said a voice behind them. "Children, is there a problem here?"

Doranei let his hand fall away from his sword and turned to face King Emin, sitting on his caparisoned horse, his head cocked to one side. Beside him, Dashain looked furious. Lord Isak was blinking as though dazzled by the muted daylight.

"No problem, Sire," Doranei mumbled, unable to meet the king's piercing ice-blue gaze for long.

"Excellent news. In which case there's no need to trouble the healers, is there? Given there's not been a problem, no one can have been hurt."

Doranei touched a finger to the right-hand side of his head. He winced as his fingers came away bloody. "No, Sire," he said, "no need to trouble them."

"No, Sire," Veil added in a muffled voice, "all good here."

"If I may, your Majesty?" Dashain broke in. "I appear to have a discipline problem with my men."

"Of course." Emin waved graciously. "It is your prerogative."

"Thank you." She glared at the two Brothers. "Now, who started it?"

There was a pause, then both men said, "I did," in the same breath.

"Good. Consider it at an end. Kiss and make up."

Another pause in which the pair inspected the ground at their feet before mumbling apologies.

Dashain growled, "Did I not make myself clear? Did I fucking stutter? Do I look like I was joking? Bloody well kiss and make up, or I'll flog the pair of you."

There was silence, quickly broken by a cough of laughter from Isak. Doranei stared at the daemon-scarred man for a heartbeat, then back at Dashain. A few carefully muted sniggers came from the column of soldiers which had ground to a halt to watch the fight.

Doranei blinked, then a growl of annoyance from Veil turned into a laugh and he turned, grabbed Doranei by the tunic and pulled him closer before planting a big kiss on his lips, to the whoops of laughter from the onlooking soldiers.

Veil stepped back with a loud, theatrical smack of the lips and turned to bow to the applauding troopers. "Not so bad as I'd expected!" he declared over the catcalls and lewd shouts. "Oh don't kid yourself, soldier," he added, pointing to one of the louder soldiers, "you ain't that pretty."

"Aye, well, glad I shaved now," Doranei replied, blowing Veil a kiss as he mounted his horse again. "Got a reputation to maintain."

"If we've quite finished, children?" the king enquired idly, but in a tone of voice that quickly hushed the soldiers. "Back to the war, I think."

"Aye, Sire," Doranei said and gathered the reins of his horse before remounting. "Back to the war."

"So go back to the part where you and Veil kissed," Zhia purred as she dabbed at the cut on Doranei's head.

"Think I've told that enough already today," Doranei replied grumpily. Without meaning to he took a deep breath, inhaling her faint perfume as the vampire stood over him, her clothed belly barely three inches from his lips. "You only get it the once."

"Now that's something a girl always likes to hear," Zhia sighed, looking down at him and affectionately stroking his cheek. "And we're not even married. How quickly the romance fades."

"Aye, well, you didn't pick the best prospect there: no home of my own, no assets beyond my sword, no prospects beyond a sharp and pointy end the day I'm not quick enough."

"You really need to work on your proposals, sweetness."

"If we were married and you died, would that mean I'd be free to chase other women?" Doranei countered. "Them's the rules, after all."

"Chase all you like," Zhia said, prodding his wound a little harder than strictly necessary, 'but if you catch them, you'll find out what they truly mean by 'a woman scorned.'"

He snorted. "I don't doubt that."

"So was that all I get?" Zhia persisted, setting down the bloodied cloth and tilting his head so she could look down on the wound. She licked her finger and ran it along the length of the shallow cut and Doranei felt a tingle on his skin as it healed. "By way of proposals, I mean."

"You truly want to marry me?" Doranei gasped, failing to conceal the astonishment from his voice.

"It's nice to be wanted," she said with a coquettish smile.

He winced. "Bit of a mismatch, though."

"Don't worry, sweetness. I'd not actually make you marry me." Zhia shook her head and her long, lustrous hair fell loose about her shoulders. "We are set on too different paths for that. The proposal would do."

"Well," Doranei said cautiously, "might be I could do better'n that, if I really had to."

"Trust me; you really would have to do better. I'm a rather unique woman."

He pursed his lips in thought. "I always thought you'd be the one doing the proposing, though. It's not as if you'll ever be the little wife on some man's arm."

"I'm old-fashioned, remember? Some traditions I don't mind."

Doranei took her hand in his and kissed the back of it delicately. Zhia smiled expectantly down at him, but before he could say anything he felt her tense and the smile become frozen. White trails of light danced inside the dark blue of her eyes, a gust of wind dancing around their close-walled tent as she drew deep on the magic in the air.

"What's wrong?"

She looked around, her hand slipping out of his. "I don't know. Something." In the blink of an eye her sword was in her hand, though there was barely room for a drawn weapon inside the tent. Doranei scrambled for his own sword-belt and hurriedly buckled it on. He was pulling on his pauldrons and helm when he saw Zhia hadn't yet moved.

He drew his sword and stared at the black, light-pricked surface for a moment. The weapon was older even than Zhia, and incredibly powerful; Doranei had taken it from Aracnan, Death's bastard son. He found himself checking his palm for darkening skin whenever he sheathed it.

"Something comes," Zhia declared, and stepped outside the tent, Doranei following on her heels.

Half the remaining Brotherhood were still sitting around their supper fires; they looked worriedly at Zhia. Veil made a small gesture, but Doranei shook his head, dismissing the offer: whatever was coming, it clearly wasn't a normal attack.

The tents were quivering under a strengthening wind. Twenty yards away the king's standard was stretched out by the wind to display to the whole Land the bee emblem, Death's own.

Zhia continued to look around, focusing on nothing, while more faces appeared.

Tiniq's nose rose to a scent on the wind that Doranei couldn't detect, then he ran to fetch his own weapons. Others stood and started scouting around, but Zhia ignored them all and set off down the path that ran down the centre of the camp.

Doranei kept on in her shadow, his apprehension growing with every step. The wind strengthened and a log on a Kingsguard fire sent a sudden spray of embers dancing across their path. Zhia's sword was up before Doranei could move, but there was nothing there and she quickly continued on her way.

"What can you sense?" he whispered.

"I'm not sure." The tone of her voice made it clear she had no intention of saying any more.

At the edge of the camp a unit of Daken's Green Scarves were on duty. Their lieutenant, a young man with blue spirals visible behind the cheek-guards of his helm, stepped forward smartly to greet Zhia, but she went straight past him without a word and stopped just behind the picket, staring out into the late evening gloom beyond.

At first Doranei, standing beside her, could see nothing in the darkness. Then he detected movement, and an intake of breath from the sentries behind showed they too had seen it. Zhia raised a hand and they readied their bows.

"Is that a man?" Doranei asked quietly as the movement began to resolve itself into a shuffling figure, moving by fits and starts.

"Once perhaps," Zhia said. "Now—? Is this one of my brother's games?"

The figure came closer and Doranei could see its right leg was badly gashed and it was limping. A chainmail shirt hung open at the front, but he could make out little beyond a bloody mess running from chest to groin. A long wisp of hair hung down on one side of its head. The figure was staring emptily at the ground as it trudged on until it was barely a dozen yards away from Zhia.

Then it stopped and looked up, and the sentries started to curse under their breath. Even Doranei took a step back as he looked at the figure's face.

Its eyes were burning: bright yellow flames leaked like tears from eye-holes that were empty pits of fire. Its jaw hung slack and Doranei could see more fire within there, boiling and rushing up its gullet into its head. It took another step forward and raised its arms almost beseechingly towards Zhia.

That was enough for the sentries. Two fired; one arrow caught it in the arm, the other hit just left of where a man's heart would be, rocking the figure back on its heels, but it just stared dumbly at the shafts for a moment before struggling forward a few more paces.

A third arrow caught it in the throat, snapping its head back up, and a spray of fire poured down its chest. From its upturned eyes, twin spurts of flame shot a foot up in the air. But it was the wound to its neck that had Doranei captivated: the fire burned bright as it cascaded down the front of the figure, illuminating fat metal staples running all the way down its body.

"Lords of Ghenna," Doranei breathed, "what is that?"

"That," Zhia replied slowly, "is my brother's madness." She took a step forward and the figure reacted as though shocked by her presence.

Doranei tore his gaze away from it and looked at Zhia, who now had eddies of crimson light flowing off her body and sword and streaming away in all directions as she drew deep on her magic. He could feel the presence of her power on his exposed cheek: the prickling heat of a bonfire and a shock of ice-cold air hitting him together.

"A Chalebrat," Zhia said, "a fire elemental—stitched by magery into a corpse." She held out her left hand and the whirling magic tightened around her, lighting up the bones of her hand against her skin before the corona of light became too intense for Doranei to watch any more.

She took another step closer and the figure, leaking fire from its various wounds, staggered back, but not quickly enough to avoid Zhia's sword, which flicked out and sheared through the crude staples holding its front together. The corpse burst apart and collapsed to the ground like a discarded coat while a ten-foot figure of flame unfolded against the night.

Zhia punched forward with an open palm and the Chalebrat was thrown backwards a dozen yards, flames streaming in its wake. The fires of its insubstantial body guttered under the blow.

Doranei readied his sword, but the Chalebrat was making no move to attack; instead, it looked up at the night sky before vanishing, leaving only a trail of light in Doranei's eyes.

"Was that another lesson for me?" Zhia shouted up at the sky.

Doranei followed her gaze and at last he made out the shape of a wyvern, lazily hovering above where the Chalebrat had been. As his eyes adjusted to the loss of light, Vorizh's pale face became clear against the black clouds above.

"A distraction!" Vorizh called with a laugh as a sword entered Zhia's back. "And now I leave you to your loving embrace."

Doranei held her close and blinked back the tears. He had one arm around her, just below her throat, the dark green embroidery of her dress bunched in his fist. The scent of flowers filled his head as Zhia shuddered, a tiny gasp of air escaping her lungs. His hand shook, unable to let go of the weapon it held. The hilt pressed right against her back, but still he drove it forward as his guts turned to ice. Zhia tilted her head down to stare at the tip of the weapon now protruding from just below her ribs and gave a cough that could have been surprise.

She dropped her sword and Doranei felt her fingers reach up to clutch his hand, her usual strength absent, her hand closing about his like a lover's might. Doranei closed his eyes and pressed his face against her neck, still holding her tight, and Zhia leaned her own head into his for a moment. Doranei could hear nothing but the rush of blood in his ears and the terrible pounding of his heart.

He felt her legs begin to sag, his grip the only thing holding her up, and gently he lowered her to the ground, sliding his black broadsword out and lying her on her back. She trembled only slightly as he withdrew the weapon and cast it aside. He cupped her face in his hands.

"I will," Zhia whispered. A flicker of pain crossed her eyes, and then she was gone.

Doranei gave a strangled howl as the woman went limp. From nowhere a black mist rose from the ground, stealing up out of the scrubby grass to curl around the edges of her body. Horrified, Doranei fell back; he couldn't take his eyes off Zhia's corpse as the mist swarmed up and over her body, licking at Doranei's discarded sword and his boots until he stumbled back a pace.

"She will what?" the Goddess-marked lieutenant said in a hushed voice.

Doranei's stomach lurched. "Before . . . this . . ." he began, choking on his own words, "she knew . . ."

He sank to his knees, grief filling his vision. "I wanted to ask her a question."

CHAPTER 31

RUHEN OPENED HIS EYES. "She's dead."

"Good," Ilumene said, "I never trusted the bitch, never mind her little gift to you."

The boy looked at his muscular bodyguard, just returned from his hunt in Narkang lands. Ilumene was dressed for battle, in white-bleached leather armour stiffened with painted steel strips. Beside him, Venn's normal black was covered with a white cape. His ruined wrist was encased in a bright, milky crystal. He might carry only one sword now, but he had lost none of his Harlequin dexterity, and he carried a Crystal Skull. Venn was far from vulnerable.

"What about the element of surprise?"

Ilumene shrugged, his grin wolfish. "Fine when you're using it, but some never do. They just hold their surprise in reserve, waiting—always bloody waiting. You've been carrying that sword Zhia gave you for months. I know you've been wary of revealing that she'd sided with us. Now we know they've found out about Aenaris, there's no reason not to use it."

Ruhen blinked, and the shadows danced in his eyes. "I had best not disappoint you, then," he said at last and gestured towards the ornate doors of the Duke's Chamber. "Shall we?"

The fine wall hangings of the lower chamber of the Ruby Tower had been covered by strips of cloth, collected by the white-cloaked devotees of Ruhen from all over Byora. The Knights of the Temples had spread far, and the response had been great. Even those states as yet unscathed by war had heard of the horrors inflicted—the obliteration of Scree and Aroth were all too easy to imagine when daemons roamed the lonely roads and woodlands, providing fertile ground for a message of peace.

The preachers had brought back prayers back from every village, town and city, and Ruhen could *smell* the power in them, growing drip by drip. Currently that power was out of reach—daemons and Gods alike were shaped as well as sustained by the worship of their followers, while Azaer had refused to become dependent on mortal followers. This was a time of transformation however: the Land would be remade, and he would too.

"I still don't like this," Ilumene said at last, not moving from where he stood. "We're wasting a lot o' men."

"Learning compassion, Ilumene?" Venn inquired, a look of sour scorn on his face. "I hadn't thought old dogs of the Brotherhood capable of such tricks."

Ilumene gave him an unfriendly look. "Aye, and I can juggle too. I'd teach you how, but there ain't much fucking point, is there?" He turned away from Venn and squatted down to look Ruhen in the face. "You gave me command of the armies, remember? Making sure they deliver is my responsibility."

"And thus far their job is to be defeated," Venn continued. "Success isn't admirable until you're asked to do something difficult."

Ilumene ignored him, waiting for Ruhen's response.

The boy showed no emotion at the squabbling of his underlings. "You are concerned we might lose the support of the Devoted?"

"They ain't happy about Emin's armies cutting through 'em, but backing out at this stage ain't an option, not with the losses they've taken. Continuing to take my orders, though—that might be harder if we've done nothing but lose 'em men. You provide the Devoted with legitimacy for their expansion, but Telith Vener and Afasin still see you as just a figurehead, one to be used and dropped if it costs them too much. We can disabuse the buggers of that, but it'll stall us at a time we really don't need."

"Afasin speaks with no voice now his army is broken," Ruhen said in a voice so soft it was almost a whisper. "The others know that."

"He still speaks within the council and that's enough." Ilumene straightened. "The Knight-Cardinal's yours, body and soul, but he's the only one of 'em. Lord Gesh too, perhaps, but on military matters his opinion ain't worth much. If you show your power now, folk might start to ask why we're retreating away from the Circle City in the first place—and certainly why we're doing so while sacrificing ten legions or more, whether or not they're our weakest troops. It's a half-arsed commitment to battle, a sop to Karkarn's will that will convince no one and loses too many in the process."

"What does my general advise, then?" Ruhen asked, one hand raised to stop Venn's objections.

"Either send most of your forces, or beat the retreat for them all. What else is there? Defeats paint a picture that serves our purposes, I know, and every report of savage sorcery and inhuman combat brings more followers to the cause, but we ain't following the old plan very closely any more."

Ruhen nodded slowly. "This mortal vestment remains something I wear, and you do well to remind me of mortal concerns. But this defeat would serve us."

"So we make it a defeat, but one we're truly escaping from, rather than leaving in our wake. Provoke a response to truly flee from. We're at the point where we need to take risks—to show them as a real danger, they actually need to *be* a real danger to us. We're leaving the Circle City anyway, but your followers don't know that. They need to feel there's no choice before they flee."

"You suggest a flawed battle-order?" Ruhen asked. "One that will go wrong quickly enough to require a retreat for all forces?"

"For starters, but we need to sacrifice more than that. Our surprise is gone, you know that. So we can't hold back the power you wield or Emin won't buy what we're selling. He'll know using Aenaris will come at a cost for you, but he'll be just as suspicious if you refuse to use it when you're finally faced with your enemy."

"And we then pray for controlled disaster?"

Ilumene shook his head. "Leave the prayers to the Devoted. I'd prefer to trust our enemy: give them something on which to concentrate their ferocity, a sign of your power that the whole Land'll take note of. It forces them to meet power with power, and in the sight of the Land yours is the more palatable."

"You're suggesting we stay here?" Venn demanded, advancing on them to force himself into the decision. "How long—days? A week? Are you *so* certain of our scrying that any delay does not risk us being trapped?"

"March the Embere troops out with everything the Circle City has to offer," Ilumene urged. "Keep Certinse's four legions from the West in reserve. Send the army beyond the fens to meet King Emin head-on. The faithful masses will follow them, and they'll take grave losses, but the survivors will scatter, taking word of what happened far and wide. We lose what we lose and accept that. They're recruiting hard in Embere, Raland and Tor Salan, and after this loss they'll bring together every soldier they can."

"Who will lead this disaster?" Ruhen asked.

Ilumene smiled. "Express your confidence in General Afasin—white-eyes are born for war, after all. He'll be cautious, unwilling to commit, and Emin will break him. Telith Vener will support Afasin over Chaist, and Certinse won't oppose if I tell him not to."

"We get word of the defeat and flee with the remaining troops, carrying word of their ungodly crimes in battle. Perhaps plague and ruin marches alongside our enemy? Rojak, does your bride-in-chains think she could manage that?"

Venn's lips became a tight little smile as the dead minstrel came forward in his mind. He gestured with his crystal-bandaged hand and a flash of dark light burst onto the tiled floor at his side. Ilumene blinked, and then there was a ragged figure kneeling on the floor, her head bowed. Slowly the Wither Queen looked up, staring with undisguised hatred through her matted grey hair.

"My queen would be delighted to aid your holy mission," Rojak said, savouring every word.

The former Reaper and Aspect of Death spat on the floor between them, and the spittle became a pale maggot wriggling on the ground, until Ilumene stamped on it. The action caused her to flinch, but the hatred in her dead eyes remained.

"I am your slave," she hissed at last, "as I knew you would always make me."

Ruhen shook his head. "Lord Isak made you this way; it was he who made you dependent on Venn's power. But if you continue to serve, your price will still be paid: you will still have your place in the Pantheon, and before we are done you will see the truth of my words."

"I see only lies and false hope." She bared her broken, decayed teeth. "But still I have no choice."

With that, she was dismissed and Rojak receded once more, leaving Venn in control of the body they shared. "The decision is made," Ruhen said after a long silence. "Let us go to the Devoted council and offer our wisdom."

He reached behind his head and touched the weapon wrapped entirely in leather that was strapped to his back. The sword was enormous and unwieldy, but he bore it as though it weighed nothing.

"Perhaps it is time we gave their sceptical souls a little encouragement."

"Your Majesty," the scryer croaked, looking up from where he knelt at the roadside, ignoring the splattering rain and the ground churned into mud by the soldiers. "The enemy has halted and taken position on the plain to the northeast."

"Scouts confirm it," Dashain said. "Looks like they're all together, and actually offering battle for once. Can they think choosing the ground will win it for them?"

King Emin shook his head and scowled. Neither Vesna nor Isak commented. They were surrounded by a full regiment of both Kingsguard and Tirah Palace Guard, providing personal escorts to the two men, and the sight of the Ghosts' distinctive black and white tabards had added fire to the bellies of their untested recruits.

"How many?"

"Your Majesty, I lack Master Holtai's skill," the scryer said, a quaver in his voice. He tried to summon the image clearly enough to estimate the Devoted numbers. "Soldiers? Perhaps twenty thousand? Fifteen of infantry, five of cavalry, I'd guess."

"But?"

"There are others—or *something*, at least. Civilians, or barbarians from the Waste—"

"How many?" the king demanded.

"I have no idea," the scryer admitted. "I cannot even guess—several thousand, at least, but they are just a formless crowd. I have no means of comparison."

"An army of the devoted," Vesna commented sourly. "They've found their saviour. The people of the Circle City have come to fight for their new lord."

"The shadow would throw away its worshippers so easily?" Dashain asked, but her voice was more hopeful than aghast. She had seen enough of Azaer's work to know compassion was never a factor.

"It doesn't need so many now," Isak explained, his great shoulders more stooped than normal. "My actions have seen to that. Those it would overthrow are weakened. The shadow doesn't need the power it had planned for."

"Not just your actions," Vesna said pointedly, "Zhia's too—and handing Aenaris to Ruhen was deliberate, not the consequence of something else."

"We can save the blame for another day," Emin muttered, casting a quick glance towards the huddled figure of Doranei, still mounted and waiting on the edges of the king's guards.

Whether or not Doranei deliberately had placed soldiers between himself and the man who had ordered him to murder his lover was unclear. No one, not even the king's bodyguard, wanted to explore that question, but it hung in the air all the same. Zhia had betrayed them when she handed Aenaris to their enemy—Ardela had seen her attempt to poison Ruhen frustrated by the touch of the shining sword they had all been at such pains to hide.

Though they had no actual evidence it had been her, Zhia had always been one to play both sides, and her unswervingly principled brother Koezh was the only other one who'd known where it was hidden in the Byoran Marshes. Doranei had agreed to his king's request—he had *asked* Doranei, rather than ordered—but none of that eased his hurt now.

"This is almost the entire Devoted force this side of the Evermist Hills. They must have a plan beyond letting us slaughter them before the eyes of the Land," Emin said at last.

"Is that not enough?" Vesna asked.

Emin shook his head. "It's a damn waste, and Ilumene's too clever to throw away so many soldiers. For a start, we believe they're looking for a reason to march east, towards Thotel and beyond. That's a long way to travel, even if he can convince the Chetse to let them pass without a fight, and he'll want troops to spend on that journey, not here."

"So they have a surprise waiting for us?"

"No," Isak said suddenly. He wasn't looking at Emin; his attention was also fixed on Doranei. For once Isak's head was uncovered. His hair had grown long enough to hide the uneven shape of his skull, but the rain was falling like tears down the carved channels of his face.

"No?" Vesna prompted, black-iron fingers flexing; the spirit of Karkarn within him sensed impending battle.

"What surprise could they hide?" At last he looked at the rest of them and pointed with one charcoal-black finger at the scryer. "They don't want the final confrontation here. We still control the greater number of Skulls. They're not so stupid as to think they could hide another army from Endine or Vorizh—so what surprise could there be?"

"That's what worries me," Emin said, "but we have no choice. General Bessarei, make camp. Tomorrow, we march on the enemy."

Ruhen stood before the thousands who had answered the call to accompany their armies. He closed his eyes and breathed in the faint honey scent of snowflowers, carried on the swirling breeze that grew steadily colder as the morning progressed. The flowers filled the southern end of the Stepped Gardens where an old wall stood. Above them fluttered tiny, five-pointed winter stars, which dotted the uneven top and colonised every nook and cranny of the wall itself.

The wind carried more than just the scent of flowers. He tasted the hopes and fears of all those assembled and felt the fervour of their belief like unexpected sunshine on his cheek. On his back he wore the wrapped sword—Ilumene had adapted a cross-chest baldric and incorporated it into Ruhen's tunic. He was small enough that the sword still threatened to catch on the ground, but Ruhen was determined to keep it with him, especially now Zhia was dead and her secrets revealed.

This was his temple, even more than the prayer-festooned Duke's Chamber, with its walls of unassailable conviction built by desperation and longing.

He wore a pearl-detailed tunic, open at the front to display a scored coin hanging on a chain around his neck. His preachers had carried the symbol far and wide; people spread across hundreds of miles now wore one just like it as an expression of their devotion. Most had not been touched by Ruhen's shadow-spirit, of course; they were simple objects of faith, but there were dozens that did carry some trace of him, and Ruhen could feel his presence reach out like the folds of night.

Behind him he sensed Ilumene and Venn moving up to stand close as Luerce appeared on Ruhen's left. The pale-skinned Litse was known by the whole crowd and the murmurs increased as they saw him. He was the First Disciple in their eyes, the shepherd of their flock of children, their link to Ruhen himself.

Strangely it was not Ilumene but Venn who would remind Luerce of his true position—the one he occupied in Azaer's eyes. Or perhaps it was the spirit of Rojak in Venn's shadow that was jealous of the reverence they showed Luerce, reverence that should rightly belong to Rojak as Azaer's most favoured.

My twilight herald has a human soul still, Ruhen reflected, smiling inwardly. *He fears the slow dissipation that Jackdaw has succumbed to, forgetting he is not one to be burned at the wick but a far greater part of me.*

The end comes soon; they can all sense it. And in their human ways they bicker and squabble, for the waiting is suddenly too much for them to bear.

"Brothers and sisters of peace," Ruhen called out in his solemn, child's voice. "War has come for us." He bowed his head, his eyes closing for a moment as he savoured the new flavours bursting on the air: the earthy tang of fear blossoming, nectar-sweet anticipation, and hope, too, their faith in their saviour remaining unshakable. Against such flavours, how could flowers ever compare?

"War has come, with its many faces, but with one purpose." Ruhen spoke in his usual soft voice, but Rojak was on hand to carry those words to the faithful. "The king and conqueror, ever keen to expand his reach; the heroic knight, eager to kill for his lord and further his own legend; the white-eye butcher, hungry for blood and pretending slaughter is glory rather than a monster's basest desire. They come, and this day the Knights of the Temples shall face them.

"I am just a child, too weak to march, too small to fight. They go to defend us, those of us who cannot defend ourselves, but they are outnumbered by an enemy more terrible than any the Land has seen."

He hesitated, showing rare apprehension on his face to those close enough to see and appreciate the frailties of their saviour.

"Our defenders face a terrible enemy, but it is not the Knights of the Temples that Narkang's daemons seek to kill: no, they are coming for *me*—it is *my* blood they seek, and if our protectors fail, this plague of daemons will come to the Circle City."

He shook his head sadly. "I cannot allow this horror to befall you, you are all innocent in this, but as long as they fear my message of peace they will hunt me. It is clear to me now that I must leave Byora, leave this protecting home and step out into the Land to walk alongside the preachers who carry my words."

He stopped, the conviction on his sombre face enough to dampen the dismay and alarm that rushed around the gardens. There were gasps, the spice of panic waxing strong on the wind, but no shouts or cries this time. He didn't want them to feel outrage, not now. The horror of what he was about to provoke would do that.

Until then, let them have hope. Let them see the saviour they desire.

"This path has opened before me. The Gods have shown me the way."—he smiled—"and all without the help of priests to interpret their wisdom."

The comment lightened the mood a shade and Ruhen saw many of his white-cloaked followers sit up a little straighter at their saviour making a small joke in the face of such impending terror.

"I will travel east," he announced. "I will journey into the Waste, letting the will of the Gods guide my feet. I will travel into the lands scarred by the excesses of war and hatred, over poisoned earth and across fouled water, to seek the answers I know are out there. But before I go, I wish to share with you a gift, to protect the brave defenders of peace and this city, all I have ever known."

He turned, and Ilumene hurried forward.

"I ask for three of you to carry this gift," he continued as Ilumene untied the bindings around the sword on his back, then he gestured at the Litse. "Luerce, bring forward three whose faith is strong enough to bear this burden."

There was no lack of volunteers, but the stern, silent Harlequins at the base of the steps prevented a sudden rush forward. Luerce picked his way down the steps with an almost fussy precision, revelling in the reverential air, uncaring whether the awe was reflected or not.

This one is the perfect servant, content in his place and faithful to his word, Ruhen reflected as he watched the shaven-headed disciple survey his eager flock. *He is a rare man within my coterie of flawed traitors, trusting in his rewards to come and careful not to dream too grandly. Ilumene did well there.*

"Venn, shield your senses," Ruhen called behind him, and a hurried flare of power told him his order had been obeyed.

Three white-clad disciples came stumbling up the steps behind their shepherd: a burly, bearded man with odd-coloured eyes and the mien of a soldier fallen on hard times; an older woman, grey-haired but with a proud bearing and strong, handsome features, and a slim, black-haired youth following close behind.

Ruhen bowed to the three when the tallest came level with him and they stopped, hesitantly sinking to their knees. The Stepped Gardens grew quieter still, a congregation at prayer, as Ruhen looked down and, without ceremony, slipped off the cloth wrapped around the hilt of his sword.

The air filled with sparkling light, each mote of dust on the breeze glittering like a cloud of ice crystals. Gasps ran around the crowd and the wide-eyed youth kneeling before Ruhen gave a moan of shock. Ruhen slipped his small fingers around the shining sword grip and drew it from the scabbard. The blade sang in the daylight, casting a corona of dancing, dazzling light around him, and his followers sighed and whimpered, their hands raised to shade their eyes from the burst of white light that was as bright as the sun.

Ruhen was unable to look at the weapon held high above his head, but he felt his hand tremble at its touch. Without looking he could feel the pure, bright light shining through his skin, seeping into his bones and forcing his shadow-soul away. He gritted his teeth, unused to the discomfort slowly building towards pain, but determined.

Aenaris—the Key of Life, had been buried far from the sight of others in the Library of Seasons until the Menin lord broke the spell hiding it. Aenaris, wielded by the Queen of the Gods, Death's equal, until the last days of the Great War. Azaer had kept its distance during those terrible days of earthquake and flame, of which only confused memories remained.

Many said the Queen of the Gods had sided with her beloved creations and fought at their side. Her name was considered accursed by all followers of the Chief of the Gods; it was recorded only in works of heresy, invoked fruitlessly by the foolish or the mad.

Did Zhia know her gift would pain me? Ruhen wondered as his skin crawled and the palm of his hand shrieked in pain, *or does the Land seek balance for the white-eye's burdens?*

With an effort he lowered the weapon, feeling the shadows in his eyes recoil as light filled his mind. He took a step forward, then one more, and sensed the three disciples were within reach.

"My gift I give to each of you," Ruhen croaked, "and so I charge you: bear my blessing in the name of peace."

It was a long blade, wider than Ruhen's palm, with a short tip like a crystal formation and a large forward-slanted guard. Each of the grip's eight smooth faces was engraved with a phoenix, flanked by leaf-laden branches. Ruhen forced himself to face down its breathtaking presence and stare directly at the weapon more potent and powerful than anything in existence except its mate, Termin Mystt.

With his eyes closed and a single image in his mind, Ruhen touched the tip to the chest of each of the three terrified disciples. "Bear my blessing," he whispered tenderly to each as the vast magic surged out of Aenaris.

The youth was knocked backwards by its force and caught by Luerce, standing behind him, while the woman cried out in something between agony and ecstasy. The bearded man shuddered as though impaled and dropped flat on his face. The air shimmered white around him and rampant magics hissed in his bones.

Ruhen staggered back, visibly struggling with the power until Ilumene came forward to steady him. With Ilumene's big hand carefully holding his own, Ruhen managed to return Aenaris to its sheath. Ilumene wasted no time in rewrapping the hilt until the crystal sword was again entirely hidden from view, then he stepped back, blinking away the ghost-trails of light.

Dazed by the power of the weapon, Ruhen stared dumbly at his hand as the pain receded. Everything was blurred after Aenaris' bright light. Slowly focus returned and he looked down at the small hand of the body he'd stolen before its mother even realised she was pregnant, blinking at what he saw.

Aenaris had left its mark on him, Ruhen realised gradually. The pain in his eyes and reeling shadows under his skin diminished, but a white mark remained on his hand. His palm and the inside of his fingers were scorched white where he had touched the crystal sword. He flexed his hand, testing the sore, taut flesh for signs of greater damage, but if he had really been burned, the Key of Life had healed him, just as it had when an assassin had shot him the day the Harlequins arrived.

His attention was dragged towards the three disciples by a sudden howl from the youth, who was convulsing in Luerce's arms. His eyes was staring unseeing up at the sky, his back was arched in pain. The alarmed First Disciple eased the youth onto the flagstones at the top of the stairs just as pinpricks of light appeared over the surface of his body. The same thing was happening to the other two, though the woman had somehow stayed upright, but as the flowering stars intensified, she moaned and bent forward as though in prayer.

Each of the three curled up as the light started weaving a skein of shining threads over them. The spider-silk slowly enveloped them and Ruhen found himself taking a step back as his immortal senses felt the rush of magic around them continuing to expand until it had become an unseen torrent of power in the air.

Venn sensed it too, and distantly Ruhen heard the former Harlequin gasp and fall to his knees, nearly overwhelmed despite the shield he'd had raised.

The woman shuddered as though struck by two great blows and writhed left and right under the cocoon of power. Where she touched the shining threads they stuck to her clothes, then her hair and hands too, searing her skin just as Aenaris had marked Ruhen. One hand pushed out, reaching towards him, an awkward movement, jerking forward and back, and when she moved, a lattice of white threads remained.

Beside her the young man kicked wildly, his silence disconcerting, as though he was suffering an agony that could not be expressed with a scream.

The three figures became increasingly blurred, hands and feet thrusting out under the webs of magic, all unnatural angles and movements that expanded the cocoons and all-too-soon stopped corresponding to anything human. Behind them Ruhen saw a scramble of figures, Harlequins and disciples alike, drawing back—all fearful of touching those glittering threads that seared the pale daylight.

The younger man's cocoon tumbled down the slope onto a lower tier, momentarily out of sight until an arm or something drove upwards and expanded its form higher than a man. The two remaining came together with a hiss and crackle of competing energies, burning the air between them and creating some sort of barrier against which both pressed as they continued their astonishing growth. By fits and starts their progress went in opposite directions, blackening the grass as they reached it and scoring trails over flagstones.

Another spasm brought one, then the others, up even higher, as though a horse were rearing up within the cocoon. Shapes pressed against the inner surface, curved and alien in form, but against the intense light Ruhen's eyes could not make out anything definite. Again the boy was forced to retreat, now shielding his shadow-lidded eyes from the light.

Something arched and held its position, working up into the air with sharp, jagged movements. The shapeless masses were growing larger with every passing moment and at last the cocoons were starting to weaken, sagging and tearing in places. The light-bound shapes rose again, this time driving up from the ground and huge grey talons ripped through the membrane. The frayed edges curled away as they were torn, flapping in a breeze Ruhen could not feel, until they caught against the talons and feet above them and melted onto the flesh and bone.

The nearer shape lurched forward and almost toppled as a long limb pressed against the inside of the membrane and ripped it open with a savage jerk. Shreds of burning white light burst out and lashed across Ruhen and his most loyal. He heard Ilumene cry out in alarm, but he had no time to turn as light suddenly exploded across his eyes. Ruhen reeled, hands clasped to his face as searing pain more intense than the burning touch of Aenaris blanked out his vision.

Ruhen cried out for the first time in his life, shock and pain mingling to cause the Land to lurch underneath him. Only unseen hands stopped him from falling to the ground—hands he realised were Venn's after crystal wiped across his face and hauled the pain away.

Ruhen shuddered, half-cradled in Venn's trembling arms, and tried to blink away the blur in his eyes. He felt his left eye obey and gasped as he suddenly made out the shape ahead of him: a near-translucent outstretched wing the size of a ship's sail. His right eye saw nothing though, just a uniform white nothingness, as though thick fog had suddenly descended.

He touched his fingers to the skin there and hissed as he discovered a long, raw wound curving up from his cheek to his ear. His eye was too numb for him to be able to tell whether the lid was even open or not, but questing fingers found it was, though covering his eye with his hand made no difference to the dull white blur he saw.

"Master, can you see?" Venn demanded hoarsely, tilting Ruhen's head to inspect the burned flesh. "Your eye, it's gone entirely white," he croaked, lowering his voice as he added, "the shadows are gone from it."

Ruhen struggled up, disorientated by the unfamiliar sensations, but more horrified by his childish frailty and weakness. "It is blind," he gasped. "I see nothing."

The wing above was suddenly retracted and a long claw protruding from the wing's knuckle was driven hard against the ground seeking purchase. It caught the edge of a paving stone and stuck fast while the struggling creature heaved against the smoking remnants of membrane around it.

"The sword," Venn suggested, watching the beast like Ruhen, mindful that only swift action could properly repair injuries.

Venn's wrist had set as it was, pressed agonisingly back into the semblance of position, but then it had healed that way. To undo that was beyond any healer's skill. Though the Key of Life might have that power, the pain it would cause was too great; Venn's breathtaking skill was gone forever, at least in mortal terms.

"No," Ruhen croaked, pushing away Venn's hands and steadying himself, his attention fixed on the monsters as shrieks of panic rang out across the Stepped Gardens.

The nearest tore away the last of the membrane and lifted its head to the sun, oblivious to the aghast faces watching. A thin blanket of autumn cloud covered the sky, but the dragon shone with an inner light that lovingly illuminated every scale. Huge muscles bunched under the shimmering reptilian armour, while a needle-tipped tail wove with a cobra's promise. Its broad head was grey, seamed in black below its spiral-horn-studded brow, while the top was almost perfectly white, echoing the hooded cloaks all three had worn. The man's disconcerting eyes—one had been brown, one green—were now pale and luminescent.

The dragon stretched its wings out wide and roared a challenge to the heavens that Ruhen felt like a blow to his ears.

Beside it, the second beast rose up and regarded its sibling with unblinking eyes; this one was more slender, with a sharp beak and a spear-like head where once an ageing woman's face had been. It was even whiter than the first, carved from ice, with eyes a paler blue than any Litse's, but when it opened its mouth to add its voice the tongue and flesh were unnaturally black.

The last, the young man, was darker than the others. The only white on its body was a streak that ran down its spiked spine; the rest was shadowed grey. Great claws tightened and furrowed the earth as the dragons' birth-cries split the sky and tears fell from the heavens to splatter on the heads of those fleeing the gardens. Ruhen didn't move, unafraid of the enormous monsters, enraptured by the sinuous, lethal shapes crafted by his mind.

"The power of the Gods," he whispered, savouring the thrill of creation that was only intensified by the pain that remained in his ruined eye. He touched his white-marked fingers to his face. "And this I sacrifice."

Hunger. Prey.

The words echoed out from their minds, barely formed thoughts and emotions. Azaer heard them, just as he had heard the silent calls of men like Venn or Witchfinder Shanatin: an echo beyond human ears, a need of basic and primal origins.

"*One must stay and watch over this city until you are called,*" Ruhen ordered, and the three heads swung down to face the boy who commanded them.

Behind him, Ruhen felt Venn tense at the scrutiny of these inhuman, terrifying beasts.

"*I am marked by your rebirth, just as you are marked by the devotion of your former selves. One will stay; the others will fly west and fight in my name.*"

The largest of the three drew back at that, whether affronted or angered, it was impossible to tell, but Ruhen stared it down. With each passing heartbeat he sensed the latent feelings of the three devotees returning as they remembered their blind obedience, their desperation to serve, their sense of purpose in his presence. He was so much smaller than they, but that resonated deep inside their hearts: the protection of the weak, the service of innocence. They would follow the child to a new form of glory.

Obey.

The dragons leapt into the air one after the other, driving up with their powerful hind legs before sweeping out their huge wings and battering the air down. Ruhen was driven to his knees by the force of their strokes, but once aloft they circled low over Byora with little effort needed.

"*One to stay, two to go,*" Ruhen repeated, and the third dragon, the greyest, broke away from its siblings and turned into a long circle that encompassed much of Byora before turning and heading up to Blackfang's jagged mountaintop. The remaining two beasts watched it go, then they too began to climb high into the sky, until they were indistinct shapes against the distant clouds. There they drifted on the far winds for a time until they caught the scent of those they sought and darted away on long, powerful wing-beats, cutting through the air like the arrows of Nartis.

"Venn, Rojak," Ruhen said to his black-clad disciple, "now it is your turn. That Skull of Song you hold: sing a song of fair winds and summer skies. The Stormcaller knows how to ward against dragons. Remove that option from him."

"See my power, white-eye," Ruhen whispered to the wind as flakes of snow began to sweep past. "Match it if you dare. Unleash the horrors of the Dark Place against me—declare yourself the monster the whole Land secretly believes you to be."

CHAPTER 32

THE FIRST WINDS OF WINTER scoured through the Narkang army, dragging at their raised spears and trying to wrench banners from the grips of their bearers. Tiny snowflakes drifted on the breeze, only rarely falling to the ground. Isak watched the white specks and shivered at a cold he could not feel.

While all those around him were bundled up in coats and furs, Isak wore his usual shirt and cloak only. For him the chill in the air was one of the soul, not of the body; the snow looked like blossom gliding across a dead place. *Death's own blossom: and soon the dead fruit will fall.* It was a dismal sight, promising an unnatural harvest.

Now he stood and watched the troops gradually moving into position on the plain in front of him. Orders were shouted, horsemen were thundering in all directions, horns and drums sounded. For once he was surrounded by people, and yet totally ignored. He had no place here, and no rank or unit to impose purpose on him.

In the distance he could see the enemy, already assembled and waiting on the higher ground. Soldiers stood in neat rows half-way up the shallow slope, with staggered knots of cavalry and archers wearing red sashes spread across the plain. In complete contrast, the left flank was a disordered mass of people, thousands of clamouring white-clothed faithful, only held back by the presence of the Devoted cavalry.

"Isak!" cried a voice over the chaos, and he turned to see a rider pulling up beside him. The black shield hanging from the saddle had a small bee painted in one corner, and beneath it was a long-handled sword. Isak couldn't see more than the plain grip and brass scabbard tip, but he knew there would be bluebells on the scabbard, as incongruous as blossom in late autumn.

"What the fuck are you doing?" Doranei called.

Isak gestured at all that was going on. "Everyone has orders but me."

"My lord—"

The white-eye cut him off. "I'm not a lord, no longer even a soldier."

"Aye, well, I still thought you'd be with the rest of the Farlan." He pointed to the division of Palace Guard in the black and white of the Ghosts assembled on their right flank. Each man was in heavy armour, their horses in full barding. Isak was already picturing what would happen when they rode into that undefended mass of Ruhen's followers.

"Most likely I'll spook the other horses," Isak said. "Turns out I'm just a danger to those around me."

"Hah, could've told you that for free," Doranei replied with a scowl. "Where's the rest of your bodyguard? Carel can't ride with the Ghosts, and Tiniq had a bad enough time riding back from Vanach; horses dislike his scent as much as they did Zhia's—he'd be thrown before he reached the enemy."

Isak made a show of looking around at the ground nearby. "Seem to have lost them somewhere," he concluded.

Doranei frowned. "Great, one of those days," he muttered to himself. "Man was bad enough before the sword scrambled his brains."

"Don't worry," Isak said, slipping his hand around the Crystal Skull at his waist, "I'm here, with the rest of you. Might be I'm not enjoying being on a battlefield again, though. It brings up bad memories."

"Aye, well, we all got things we can't afford to think about right now," Doranei growled. "You ain't special in every way, so focus on your job, soldier."

"Good advice from a man who carries a reminder of his pain on his saddle."

Doranei's face tightened. "That's my business, I still know my duty. Stay where you are and stick with the reserve. General Lopir's over there with Legana—probably Carel and Tiniq too, just giving you some space." He pointed to a group of horsemen a hundred yards off. "If we need you and your black sword, we'll come and find you."

"If you need Termin Mystt," Isak suggested, "when you have wyverns, Crystal Skulls and Mortal-Aspects at your disposal, might be I'll not need an invite."

Doranei gave him an angry look. "As you say. See you when the killing's done." He didn't wait for a response, but headed back the way he'd come.

The main line had started their advance: two blocks of eight thousand spearmen apiece flanking the central bulwark of halberd-wielding Kingsguard. There was no manoeuvring such large units of men; they could only advance and attack whatever was in front of them. But with cavalry protecting their flanks, there would be no stopping them, either.

Isak watched them go, and his keen ears detected the clatter of the first cavalry skirmish not long after. He turned to head towards General Lopir's staff, but took only a step before something brought him up short: a sensation unlike any he'd felt before, skittering down his spine as though an icicle had rolled over it. His mouth fell open, about to speak, until he remembered he was alone, with not even Hulf at his side. He took a deep breath and straightened up, ignoring the familiar tug of his abused muscles, and cast his senses out across the Land.

The tramp of boots echoed through his chest, the rush of wind in his lungs. Isak closed his eyes and felt a song ring out across the copse-studded plain and touch his mind with its silent, soaring cadence. Rising high through the clouded sky were crisp, lingering notes of beauty. His eyes jerked open unbidden as the sense grew stronger, keener, like the piercing cry of a hawk where once there had been only birdsong.

"Something comes," he muttered to the empty ground around him. "The bastard's wasted no time in using it, not now Zhia's secret is out."

The magic ringing through the air became more insistent and Isak heard a cry from Lopir's group: Ardela was calling his name. He turned unsteadily and saw her waving him over.

"*Isak, what is it?*" Legana asked as soon as she was close enough to speak into his mind.

Isak turned and looked up into the sky. The note peaked and began to fade almost immediately and he realised now it was just an echo, the ripple of vast magic done, but no threat in itself.

What he feared was the results of such a thing.

"*Is it Ruhen? What has he done?*"

"What has he done?" Isak said to the wind, "he's used Aenaris for something—and so the Land slips further out of balance."

"*Not even the shadow would wield it in battle, not now, with the Gods so weakened. To tear the heart of the Land out like that—it serves no purpose.*"

Isak scowled. "An immortal destroys carelessly," he said at last. "They can pick up the pieces of civilisation at their leisure."

They both knew how far Azaer was prepared to go. He invited slaughter to claim authority; he tore apart cities and fuelled the fires of fanaticism. They were right to assume the worst.

He started for Emin's command post, his senses open to the Land. Something was approaching, though still miles off.

"You said he wouldn't use it!" King Emin shouted as soon as Isak was close enough. "You assured me this wouldn't happen!"

"We don't know what's happened," Isak replied as he reached them. "Ruhen isn't with their army."

"Endine?" Emin snapped, but the mage nodded in confirmation.

He was looking even paler than normal. He pushed away Forrow's supporting arm, only to sag again. "Ruhen's still in Byora," Endine gasped. "That was miles away—it hit me so hard because I was scrying the plain."

"But it is Aenaris," the king said flatly. "And you look ready to collapse, not to work some great magic in response."

"It is Aenaris," Endine confirmed, wincing. He shook his head as if trying to clear it of something.

"Isak, we didn't plan for this—we all agreed the shadow would be wary of using a weapon containing purest light! So what now? My money's on the rest of our mages being hit at least as hard as Endine. You're the only one who uses your Skull as a buffer."

"Something comes," Isak said again, looking up but seeing nothing in the eastern sky. "Let's save the guessing about *why* for later—it's the *what* I'm worried about."

"And if he's trying to force your hand? The toll Termin Mystt is taking on you just by holding it . . . how long will you survive if you're made to use it in battle?" Emin sounded desperate.

Isak glanced down at his black hand, resting as always as though around the grip of a sword. "If I fall, someone else will pick up the burden. If he thinks to win that way, he underestimates our resolve."

"Vesna? Legana? They might survive for a time, but for long enough? And what of you? You're the very heart of our plans—the fulcrum for it all. But everything hinges on Ruhen believing the same, that you'll be there at the end: the Gods' own agent of change."

"Life gets in the way," Isak said impassively. His eyes returned to the sky, and this time he saw two dark shapes against the high clouds. "But before all the crying and manly embraces, we've got a pair of dragons coming our way. Any thoughts?"

The king's face tightened. "Only that you might be on your own for the time being."

The dragons flew in tandem, scrutinising the ground below. The armies were obvious even from such a height. They did not communicate, but instinct drew them to the further army, to the sparkling needles of power they could sense within it: mages holding their power close to hand, Crystal Skulls, throbbing with latent power.

The mages did nothing in response, even as the dragons closed and descended. There was no call to the clouds above, no surge of warning energies to threaten them. The dragons dropped with shocking speed, all wariness gone as they dived towards the soldiers below. Within the ranks were the mages, the dragons could taste them on the breeze, but the stink of men and horses were just as tantalising. Thousands lay below them: enemies to kill . . . enemies to feast upon . . .

Isak watched the dragons drop like hunting falcons, tilting their wings only at the last moment to avoid crashing to ground. Their talons splayed, they swooped over the Narkang legions, gouging a path through the ranks before spitting a lance of flame into the heart of the troops and climbing again.

From someone within the ranks of the Kingsguard came streaks of green fire. The first cut between the dragons as they neared, but the second caught the larger across its white belly. The dragon was kicked back through the air, momentarily halted, but otherwise unharmed. It spat another gout of fire into the soldiers below, but the mage appeared to be unhurt; a third bolt flew up and struck it full on the wing, bursting like a firework and scattering in all directions. It provoked a furious roar of pain and anger, but it caused no damage that Isak could see; although the dragon retreated hurriedly, the wing was still whole, its movements unhampered.

"Born of magic," Isak said to himself, realising why the battlemage with the Kingsguard—Fei Ebarn, he guessed—had not managed to wound it. "It's more resistant to her spells." He turned to the king and pointed. "Ruhen's created dragons of his own. The Gods alone know what that must have cost him."

"Ebarn can't hurt it?"

He shook his head. "She can: the power's there, but not the instrument. She's scared of drawing deeply on the Skull; she doesn't have the strength to control it. It's not she can't kill it—the Skulls can kill Gods. But she'll burn her mind out in the process."

"So what then?" Emin turned to follow the dragons as they wheeled for a second pass. "Can you bring down a storm and drive them off?"

"No—not without tearing holes in the army. The storm loves me a bit much, and I've got more power than just a Skull to control. Endine?"

"Perhaps." The mage's face was screwed up on concentration. "Can you shield me?" He sank to his knees, both hands wrapped around the Crystal Skull entrusted to him. Isak went to stand behind him. As he stretched out his arms, his sleeves slipped back to reveal the unnatural white and black skin. In his left hand he held the Skull of Ruling, while the black sword of Death appeared in his right. A spinning skein of black and white started to turn in the air above them while Endine muttered and chanted below him.

He tasted the eager strains of magic reaching up to the heavens and had to force himself not to add his own spirit to that familiar flavour. It spoke to something deep inside him, resonating with the kernel of fury in his soul. The shackles on his white-eye nature were strong, chains of pitted iron in his mind, but he would for ever be a Chosen of Nartis, and the spirit of the Storm God raged within him, undeniable, and unextinguished, even by death.

The dragons above turned towards them, then parted and raced out over the flanks of the army, wary of Isak's power and Endine's spell. Isak looked up to the clouds and saw the swirl above as the air lazily responded to the mage's call, but it was short-lived as light suddenly parted the clouds in the east, diffuse and white against the pale blue sky beyond.

He checked behind him. The sun was still covered, but even as more clouds were drawn near, the new light was undoing Endine's spell like a sword cutting through a weaver's work.

"I can't," Endine moaned from below him, "I'm being countered."

Isak growled and lowered his arms, his shoulders sagging as he released the power he'd been holding. "We're running out of options."

A great crash echoed out across the plain, followed by distant screams, and they turned to see the smaller dragon scattering their cavalry on the left flank, tearing at men and horses with impunity. Another mage on that flank gathered his wits enough to attack it, hurling up slender bolts of grey magic, then a murky grey shape followed, huge wings beating as it dragged a heavy body up into the air.

"No!" Isak exclaimed, "don't waste your strength!"

But his warning was unheard, and a third monstrous shape appeared above the army and drove towards the white dragon. It assumed a sentinel post above that flank of the army, daring the dragon to attack. The white dragon broke off its slaughter and wheeled away, then turned back and flew hard and fast, directly at the newcomer, which climbed higher, seeking some advantage over its enemy, but the white dragon didn't care about positioning, only about closing the distance between them.

It picked up speed and flew hard up towards the grey monster, head stretched forward to meet its foe—but when they came together there was no impact, no snapping of jaws and tearing of flesh; the grey beast simply winked out of existence and with an exultant roar the white dragon turned and arrowed down towards the army again, careless of the bolts that burst on its scaled hide and tore thin streams of blood from its tail. It flamed at the illusionist below with terrible accuracy and the dragon rose again, armour-clad figures tumbling from claws as sudden detonations of magic and light burst from the ranks below it.

"Piss and daemons," King Emin moaned, "that was Camba Firnin."

"Pretending to fight fire with fire," Isak said, a brief, black spark of grief in his belly as he recalled her smiling, scarred face. She was one of those who'd brought a much-needed touch of compassion to the Brotherhood, for all that her strength of will matched the rest of them. "But dragons aren't so easily fooled."

He hesitated, then grabbed Endine by the shoulder. "Keep them occupied, watching and wary," he shouted, then pushed out through King Emin's bodyguard and hurried towards the thin corridor between the Kingsguard and the regular legions. The space had been left for messengers and mages; it was wide enough for a single white-eye, even with Doranei trailing wordlessly in his wake.

He emerged the other side to the cold smell of fear and blood. The faces behind the helms were frightened, and the sight of a scar-covered white-eye carrying a long sword that hurt to look at didn't help. Inside him Isak let the magic slowly build, a wellspring bubbling up through his heart, and the ache grew inside him and sank deep into his belly. Isak stumbled as the scars on his stomach flared with pain and memory, black stars burst before his eyes and an overwhelming loneliness washed over him, images of the dead appearing before his eyes: Camba Firnin joining Mihn and Tila, ahead of a host of other faces. The wind whipped around him, gathering in a spiral of snowflakes in response to the building magic. Whether the dragons noticed, he couldn't say, nor did he care; he simply walked on, getting clear of the army's lines while filling his tired bones with rage and fire.

"After all this," he said aloud, "you think I'm *frightened*? All this loss and you think I've got anything more to fear?" His voice became breathy and constrained as the anger inside him was fanned by magic.

"All I've done—all those I've killed? Nothing's going to stop me; nothing's going to slow me. I'm coming for you, Azaer, and when I catch you, I will chain you like a dog."

He looked up at the sky and saw the dragons high above, circling and watching, not sure whether to attack or flee. He smelled their animal nature, the blind and unthinking obedience filling their minds. But these were not true dragons: they had no will or sense of their own. They would not be driven off; they would kill or be killed, they could not comprehend anything more. On the plain ahead of him he saw the crowd of Ruhen's worshippers closing alongside the Devoted cavalry. He ignored them. They were too far to stop him, and too close to run now.

"Is this what you wanted?" he cried to the eastern horizon. "To have your followers see the darkness inside me? To reaffirm their faith? To have the Land bear witness to your pathetic claims of purpose?"

He lowered his head and looked at Termin Mystt, the black sword reversed in his hand.

"So be it," he said, and stabbed the sword into the ground at his feet. A great crack of thunder split the air and the dragons rocked as though struck by lightning. "I don't fear the darkness any more. Fear can't stop me now."

The ground trembled, deep, distant rumbles welling up through the earth. Anchored by the sword, Isak dropped to one knee and stayed steady, as though about to fulfil some ancient prophecy. All around him the Land shook and the magic pervading it rushed up to meet Termin Mystt. The sound built, booming underground, growing loudly and more violent the closer it came, as the plain shuddered beneath them.

Distantly he sensed the charging enemy falter, and in their hundreds men fell and were trampled, horses screamed and reared, turning desperately, looking for some avenue of escape, but the whole plain reverberated with the building power of Termin Mystt and they could see no way out. Isak closed his eyes and let his senses sink into the ground, carried deep below by the raging force of magic emanating from Death's black sword.

His ears rang with the jangling clamour of rampant forces—the numbing, pounding, shifting earth, the blistering energies that tore the ground and seared the sky. Down he went, unaware of his own body beyond the frantic hammer of his heart. The magic ripped a jagged path and dragged his mind with it. He knew what it would seek; he had done nothing more than send it down. To try and command such power would rip his soul away. No mortal would survive such an attempt, even to try would mean being torn from the Land and the Gods that ruled it, to be destroyed beyond even Death's compassion or judgment. The magic plunged onwards, guided by something more basic than a mage's skill. Isak felt the heat on his cheek and though he felt no fear, something deeper and more primal gripped him.

He opened his eyes, rocked back by the buffeting winds, but still held steady by the sword. His shoulder screaming, his clothes billowing, Isak added his own voice, howling his pain up to an unhearing sky. The clouds roiled and the sun was driven off as even the air was ripped open by the dead-light of Termin Mystt.

Isak forced his head down and tried to make out the plain through the swirling magic surrounding him. Great rifts appeared in the ground, and as he watched, half-blinded by pain, the rents were savagely pulled open. The wild magic shook the ground and worried its wounds with a frantic fury. Ear-splitting crashes detonated as the plain opened up and three, then four enormous cracks in the ground started racing towards the enemy, a hundred yards long, then two hundred, swallowing the nearest of the cavalry, covering others in dust before the fissures finally stopped.

The cliff-edges of each rift shuddered all the while, the ground crumbling further with every passing moment. Isak watched them fall, while from below clouds of stinking smoke were expelled by the force of their collapse, and faint trails of red light tinted the sheer earth walls on either side.

Soon a huge wedge of ground ahead had fallen away completely, spreading out from where Isak knelt. The entire centre was broken up: a barrier to both forces if they still intended to fight.

For a time only red-lit clouds of dust were visible, but then he heard a sound, one he knew only too well: the heave of pained breath, the scrape and rasp of a body dragged over rock, the clank of huge chains.

Something moved below him and forced its way up the jagged slope he had created. He could see little, but he turned his head up to the sky and watched the distant dragons peer down from their far positions. The magic spent, they came closer once more. He could see their necks craned forward, their wings outstretched to steady themselves as they stared down.

"I'll see your dragons," Isak croaked, his throat dry and aching, "and I'll raise you."

The white dragons swooped closer, scenting power within the wedge-shaped crater, but unsure what they faced. They flew with the staggered creep of hunting animals, their growing hunger driving each other forward. It wasn't the scent of prey on the air; even these mindless creations would know that, but they had been created to kill and now the scent of death hung thick around him.

They obeyed their compulsion, ignoring Isak as they came to the edge of the crater, hissing with savage desire. In the dimmed light they looked ghostly, but their claws and teeth were obsidian-black and more terrible than ever. The larger dropped to all fours, wings held high above its back, ready to take flight once more as it quested and snapped at the air.

A roar greeted it, an ear-splitting challenge that had purple stars bursting before Isak's eyes even as he cringed from the sound. Through the smoke he watched the white dragon tense and crouch, ready to move, either in attack or escape—while from the darkness another winged shape slowly emerged. It roared again, wings also raised, but forever held crooked and stiff above its back. It was soot-black and massive, with a brutal horned snout and mad red eyes. The ragged, smoky wings cast an unnatural shadow over its awkward body. It was hampered both by the great chains that tethered it and the savage, unhealed wounds gouged from its rotting flesh, but still the Jailer of the Dark advanced on its smaller cousin, roaring.

Now Isak could see the terrible slashes oozing black-red ichor that Xeliath had inflicted as she fought it on the slopes of Ghain; only its unnatural strength allowed it to move with such injuries. Once again he felt the hot ache of loss for the fearless woman who'd died at this dragon's claws.

The white dragon wove its head left and right, still hesitant, but its companion had no such uncertainties: it screamed an answer to the challenge and leaped forward, throwing itself down from the edge of the crater to strike across the newcomer's back. Its claws tore into the larger dragon's wings, tearing ribbons from the membrane as bones snapped under the weight. The Jailer rode the assault and lashed forward with its blade-tipped tail, punching a hole in the smaller dragon's wing before stabbing its side and causing shocking scarlet blood to fly.

The other hurled itself forward, claws extended, and the Jailer wrenched itself around, half-dodging to one side despite the weight on its back, and its teeth caught the dragon's left foot, snagged it and dragged it off-balance. The white dragon's claws were scrabbling for purchase on the rocks while its wings slapped at the smoke-laden air, trying to regain its balance. The tattered black dragon didn't give it time to recover but shot its head out with shocking speed and caught it by the wing.

It dragged its prey closer, and both beasts reared with their claws extended, but the Jailer was by far the bigger and with ease it pushed past the white dragon's defences and caught its arm. The white dragon twisted to bite its captor, but the Jailer pinned its other forelimb and raked a claw down its scale-armoured neck before continuing its assault, rocking from side to side to dislodge the one on its back.

It snapped and bit down on the white dragon's wing, crushing it, before releasing and wrenching itself around to deal with the one half-perched on its back. It used its tail to tangle the other, which was quick to try and escape, but the combination of tail and huge iron chains snagged it and it found itself writhing and twisting to try and work its way free. Then the Jailer brought its huge claws to bear. One rear foot pinned the shoulder and it raked its claws horribly along the belly before gripping its enemy's forelimb with its mouth. As it tore at the shoulder with its free claws, ripping open the scaled skin, the Jailer heaved backwards with all its Gods-cursed strength.

Isak heard an enormous crunch as the joint distended. The white dragon's desperate clawing broke off as it screeched in pain, but the Jailer was remorseless and worked the ruined limb back and forwards. Bones snapped, flesh tore, and at last it heaved its prize free as the white dragon screeched and shuddered, bright blood pumping furiously from the wound.

The Jailer, seeing the other scrabbling back up the slope in an effort to escape, left its stricken prey. With its undamaged wing flailing frantically, the white dragon limped forward like an injured bird, pushed off-balance by its own efforts. The Jailer of the Dark was hampered by its own injuries and chains, and the white dragon reached the top of the crater and started to creep back towards the Devoted lines, but before it could go far, the larger beast caught hold of its tail.

The Jailer used its hold to haul its own brutalised body forward, viscous ichor oozing sluggishly from its wounds. In full view of the Devoted army, the Jailer bit down and tore free a great chunk of flesh, wrenching its head back as it did so and casting an arc of blood through the air above them. The scarlet-splattered white dragon tried to turn and fight, but it was pinned by the Jailer, which crushed the smaller beast's forelimbs in its huge jaws while the crescent-blade of the Jailer's tail chopped away at its flanks.

With savage exultation the Jailer of the Dark ripped at the dying thing in its claws. One forelimb had been torn clean away; the other had been chopped in two. The Jailer broke one thick hind leg before moving on to the dying dragon's throat, tearing it open, then dipping its horned snout again and again into the bloody wound until the neck was half-severed and it could bite the head off entirely.

The huge black dragon stared out towards the Devoted army, blood pouring from the dead thing in its jaws. It tossed the head aside and bellowed a challenge to any still brave enough to meet it. Isak watched the Jailer and remembered the stories he'd heard about it: the all-consuming pride that led it to defy the Gods—and the strength to somehow resist even Death, forcing the Gods to chain it instead.

He looked down at the sword in his hand. His fingers were numb with the power shaking through Termin Mystt, and the raised scars on his blackened hand were bright in the half-light as magic surged through them. With an effort he forced himself upright, resting all his weight on the sword until he could arrange his trembling legs beneath him.

In the crater, the dragon was straining at its great chains. Isak gritted his teeth and heaved at the sword, but at first, barely able to feel his arm, he could not move it, unable to bring his strength to bear. He resisted the temptation to wrap his other hand around the grip. Instead, he stood over the black sword and tried again, crying out in private agony as the magic fought him and his ruined body disobeyed.

But then it moved—Isak felt the slight give, and so did the dragon, sensing the drag back to Ghain. It turned to face this new threat, but Isak ignored it, closing his eyes and focusing on the task at hand. The dragon started towards him, but the sword gave another inch and the huge chains jerked hard at the Jailer. It strained to fight, but Isak heaved with everything he had, and every inch he drew the sword out of the ground, the dragon was hauled back another dozen yards until it disappeared behind the hanging curtain of smoke and Isak felt the resistance give. With a great roar he pulled Termin Mystt free of the earth and sensed the ground close up over the Jailer of the Dark. The great, accursed dragon was once more sealed in its place of torment.

Isak staggered backwards and fell. He heard voices, shouting behind him, but he could not make out the words. Fatigue struck him like a blow. The Land turned to black and then he felt nothing at all.

CHAPTER 33

DORANEI FELT SOMETHING NUDGE HIS ELBOW. When he bothered to look up, High Mage Endine was offering him a bottle. The King's Man grunted and took it, not even bothering to sniff the contents before taking a long swig.

"Easy," Endine said, patting him on the shoulder, "that's the good stuff." He walked around Doranei and sat opposite him, staring at him over the fitful flames of a cooking fire. It was late and most had turned in for the night, ready to be up at dawn, but Doranei had wanted some time alone and that was in scant supply on the march.

"Apricot brandy?"

Endine beamed. "Indeed!"

Doranei took another gulp. "Goes down well enough—smooth as a virgin's tit." He paused and inspected the bottle. "Where'd you get this from? There's a bitter almonds flavour at the back of it."

"I tested it for poison first." Endine laughed. "You think I'm such a fool I'd just accept the finest spirits in the kingdom turning up free without a little suspicion?"

"Why in the name of the Dark Place did it turn up at all?"

"A small part of the resupply consignment—some merchant from Canar Fell, one of those old pirates the king befriended during the wars of conquest and made rich after. The man rode into camp a few hours back, at the head of a wagon-train, food, weapons—even bloody horses."

"Free?" Doranei asked between gulps.

"Well, not quite free. I asked Dashain about it. It appears our friend Count Antern has been busy these last few months back in Narkang, making deals, selling concessions or assets—Antern's mortgaged half the nation, as far as I can tell, and the credit extended to the Crown has been—well, I doubt even the Brotherhood could have bullied such terms out of the nobility and merchant houses."

Doranei gave a snort and shifted to a more comfortable position.

"Antern's mortgaged the nation? Aye, the king's a man of forward thinking, no doubt about that."

"What do you mean?"

The King's Man gave him a sour smile. As much as he'd drunk since they'd eaten, his brain was still working all too well. "The prosperity of Narkang—you think that was a selfless act?"

"It's a fine legacy for any king."

"Aye, well, sure it is. You're a member of the Di Senego Club, right? Where the king collects intellectuals and the like? There're a lot of merchants on the membership rolls too: all men who owe the king more than a few favours. They got help over the years, and now they're all figures of note in their particular trades. But haven't you ever noticed the common thread in those trades?"

Endine frowned. "Perhaps—but what king wouldn't involve himself in such things? He's long admired Farlan horse-breeding, and the population's increased in the last few decades, so food production has to be able to keep up."

"Iron ore and leatherworkers, too," Doranei said. "Our responsible king, putting these merchants in the same room as inventors and mages of all types; no other reason for it, I'm sure."

"What are you saying?"

The King's Man pushed himself to his feet. "This nation he built, these men he surrounded himself with: now these merchants are falling over themselves to support his war effort, all ready at a few weeks' notice to lead supply-trains into a lawless warzone." He spat into the fire. "It's almost like he knew one day he'd want to wage a war of some sort and built a nation to service it."

"What? That was his motivation?"

"Pah, who don't like power too? It's not been a hard life for a man like him, being king—when you're that clever it's always good to make sure the whole Land knows it. And the richer Narkang became, the better he could fight his secret war. Before his sister died, screaming about shadows with claws, he was just some nobleman drinking and whoring his way through life, forever looking for a use for that big brain o' his."

"And that's all the nation is to him?"

Doranei shrugged and belched. "Maybe, maybe not. Who's to say? You ever thought you knew his mind, truly?"

"Narkang and the Three Cities is just a machine for this war, one built over two decades?" Endine gasped. "No, there must be more to it than that—

one loss doesn't define a man like that. He's not Vorizh—he's not so cold that he'd see us just as tools—"

"Sure, if you say so. He's not one for being ruthless, our king, that's for sure. All gentle smiles and gracious waving at the commoners; no surrounding himself with murderers and madmen who drag fucking great dragons out o' Ghenna itself." Doranei made a show of looking down at himself, prodding the brigandine he wore and pretending surprise at the sword hanging from his hip. His point made, the King's Man swung around and stared out at the dark camp beyond.

"Question is, does that make you proud or angry?" he asked over his shoulder. "Me, I got a touch of both." He slapped his belly and wandered off into the dark. "And a whole lot o' piss besides," he muttered as he went, a shadowy figure already. "Where the fuck'd we put the latrine?"

Isak opened his eyes to a dead Land, scoured grey by the hot wind so that even the grasses underfoot were lifeless and withered. He saw buildings in the distance, a tiered city wall and great square towers. Even from afar he could see they were in ruins, their people long since killed: the bones of a city, broken, jutting from its corpse.

"Where am I?" he said aloud. The wind snatched his words away like a jealous child.

"An ending," came a deep voice behind him.

Isak turned and regarded the figure that had appeared from nowhere: gaunt and insubstantial, and far taller than any man. The face was hidden beneath a black cowl, one bone-white hand bearing a double-headed spear. It was said the Harlequins and Jesters both wore white masks to echo Death's own emotionless, featureless face, but even weakened, the God showed Isak nothing of His self.

"Not my ending," Isak declared, fighting the bone-deep compulsion to kneel. "So why here?"

Death did not speak for a long while. Instead, He surveyed the wasteland they stood in, the destruction done there. Isak realised that beneath the dust and grey grass there were stones laid in some semblance of order. Few were visible, but there were enough to imagine the shape of the building that once stood there. There was no sun, just the dull grey sky of a permanent twilight.

"Why here?" Death said at last. "To show you the consequences of power."

"This is the City of Ghosts?"

The Chief of the Gods didn't reply, but He didn't have to. The dust clouds swirling all around contained shapes, Isak realised, figures and movement—snapshots of life, burned forever into the place they were erased. Long sinuous bodies, tall figures on horseback, a woman who stood over them all, sword raised high. Isak caught glimpses only before the wind shifted and then they were gone, only for other broken souls to momentarily appear elsewhere.

Pale lights, mournful faces and the lonely cry of the wind; that was all they were. This was no judgment of the Gods; this was damage so profound even Gods could not affect it.

"This was a place of beauty once," Death said, "and in our rage we tore it apart—tore it from the Land." He raised His spear and pointed to a rounded plateau. "There we cursed Aryn Bwr and his allies, unmindful of what it would cost us."

"What you stole from yourselves," Isak finished. "You lessened what you were in the name of revenge—you who call yourselves Gods."

"And now you lessen us further. By your actions, we are forever diminished and the shadow will take domain over the Pantheon."

"You don't know that."

"All you have done—you opened the way for Azaer, a being of no power, only words."

Isak took a step towards the God and looked up into the depthless black of its cowl. "You think the shadow's words weren't power? That it wouldn't have slowly crept into position after years, decades of whispers in the dark eroding the whole Pantheon? I've cleared the path some, not opened the way. I've made my enemy hurry and adapt carefully laid plans rather than allow it to choose its own time and place for the battle to come."

"Azaer was just a voice on the wind, a spirit, like countless others. Azaer was nothing—until you made it so."

The white-eye turned away and watched the shifting shapes on the wind. Behind them an unearthly light danced around the far ruins of a broken spire, half buried by the dust and sand that was all that remained of the ground here.

"You made Azaer, not I. You brought reason into the minds of mortals. You blessed them with fear and envy, the power to create and dream—all in your need for worship." "Azaer is no daemon, feeding off the fear of mortals. The shadow lacks even that."

Isak nodded. "A shadow's between the light of worship and the dark of dread. Those private thoughts and cruelties, the unspoken, unformed prayers that are mortal thoughts—that's what shaped Azaer. The petty desires and spite; greed in forms as numerous as the creatures you gave mortals dominion over."

"You try to absolve yourself?" Death asked, stalking stiffly forward. "You hide now from what you have done? Azaer will soon challenge us because of what you've done—Azaer is *a challenge* because *of your actions."*

"No," Isak said simply. "I know what I've done, the price I might yet have to pay. But you sowed the seeds of your own destruction, and I might yet be able to redress the balance of the Land. For good or for ill, I intend to try."

"Even if the entire Land burns in your wake?" Isak's smile was sad. "I am what you made me. Now you *live with the consequences."*

They broke from nowhere, rushing up like a flock of flushed game but with murder in their hearts. Daken barely turned in time as the lead attacker hurtled towards him with mad abandon. The notched edge of the rusted sword he held above his head was already coming down towards the white-eye's face. Daken spun to one side, his great axe following him round and catching the man so hard in the ribs he was thrown from his feet.

General Amber stepped in to protect Daken's flank, his scimitars slicing the air towards the next attacker. Behind them Amber's Menin bodyguards surged forward, hunched low behind their shields, taking the impacts in their stride, moving steadily forward, chopping and stabbing at the frantic, unprotected attackers.

Daken drove ahead again, battering a bloody path through the fanatics with great sweeps of his axe, and Amber followed him, embracing the rush of battle: no time to think, no use in it. A man drove on, carried by the tide of his comrades and fought until he could not move. That was the Menin way; that was what had been drilled into him, year after year. The strokes he performed without thought; his arm knew the movements as his heart knew to beat, and he let it subsume him into those blessed, empty moments when the loss in his mind was distant and forgotten.

And then the Land snapped back into focus. The enemy were gone, taken down in a blinding slaughter, none fleeing, all lying there dead or dying. Only a few-score men and woman in rags for armour, but they had fought to the end against veterans. Amber blinked down at the squirming figure at his feet.

It was a young man of no more than fifteen summers, barely an adult, thin-limbed and pale. Old scabs had formed around his mouth, and the white scars of ringworm were clear on his neck. His collarbone had been cleaved through and Amber's scimitar had chopped into the ribcage below as well. Blood poured from the wound, bubbling up like oil from the ground. The youth stared in shock at the sky above, his mouth working feebly as he tried to scream his last pain. Before Amber could end it, he saw the light fade in the young man's eyes; his body sagged and the flow of blood tapered off.

"Guess that answers one question," Daken commented as he kicked a corpse out of his way.

Amber looked up with a frown.

"What the reception would be like for us," Daken explained, pointing towards the city walls a few hundred yards off. "No Devoted, but plenty more o' these fuckers."

"None of them ran," Amber muttered, wiping his scimitars and sheathing them again. As he reached up his pauldron snagged again and he was forced to tug it back into place. The straps holding it had been sheared through in the last skirmish. "Not even when they realised they would be slaughtered."

He looked around at his troops. They all bore the scars of the running war they were fighting: half-healed cuts and deep bruises, mismatched armour where some piece had been irreparable. Every skirmish now ended in a flurry of scavenging, belts and boots as valuable as weapons and food. With every day they looked less like a Menin army; more barbarian warriors than hardened, drilled infantry.

Every day Amber felt their eyes on him, the unspoken thoughts that he was the one doing this to them—he was the one asking for this relentless battle, and he could promise only leagues more of it to come.

"Aye, I heard folk were dumb in these parts," Daken said.

"That's what surprises me—not that they're dumb, that they were so fanatical. Tor Salan was as secular a city as I've ever seen, founded on magic and science, not devotion to the Gods. Not the most fertile grounds for tales of a saviour."

Daken made a face and went back to surveying the haphazard shapes before them, the mounds of steel, brass and stone resting where they'd fallen. The Giants' Hands—Tor Salan's famed defences—were now lying useless.

"Oh I don't know. Your lot cut the heart out o' this city, remember? You killed every mage here, so those defences don't work and their way o' life collapsed around them. Might have made them a little desperate, a little more open to persuasion."

Amber nodded. For all his bloodthirsty bluster, Daken had travelled far across the Land and seen enough to know how life worked for most folk. His counsel, or the kernel of it, at least, tended to be useful more often than not.

"At least the Devoted couldn't use the Giants' Hands on us," Nai said, joining them. The necromancer used his mace as a walking stick, the odd-sized boots he was wearing making him lurch even more than normal.

"Your king said they would retreat, that they don't want to fight here," Amber pointed out. "They never intended to defend Tor Salan, only recruit here."

"Well they did that," Nai said. "The scryer says forty thousand have dug in around the road to Thotel. Too many for us to break through, I'd guess, what with another army marching down from the north."

"North? Where did you hear that? The scryers didn't tell me that," Amber said.

Nai shifted uncomfortably. "Ah, a different source, that one."

"Fucking daemons?" Daken exclaimed. "Tsatach's fiery balls, you just don't learn, do you? Bloody necromancers."

"I didn't invoke anything," Nai protested, "but some covenants still hold true."

"So what now? Do we dig in and wait to be attacked?"

"The army needs a rest," Amber said. "The king said supplies would follow us once the way was clear. I don't think we're welcome in Tor Salan now, and we've killed enough civilians for the time being. We advance as far as we can without getting caught in a battle and dig in, but we won't be attacked. Daken, your Green Scarves can raid the Devoted as much as you like, but the way home is blocked to us, so until King Emin's army reaches us, we wait."

He looked east towards the Devoted army, many miles away now. His skin felt cold. Even the realisation that they would have to fight through Ruhen's armies to find the way home did nothing for him. The first milestone on that journey had been crossing the border, such as it was. The second had been reaching Tor Salan and ridding it of Devoted troops.

Perhaps by the third, I'll start to feel something again. He scowled and looked up at the sky. Crows wheeled high above.

Isak blinked and uneasily opened his eyes. Slowly his surroundings came into focus: curved wicker struts arched over his body. His feet pressed against wooden boards. Underneath him was a sticky bedroll; above him, a ripped canvas was lashed over the struts, admitting a little light through the various tears. He could just make out a pale grey sky through them, and dark patches on the canvas showed where spots of rain had fallen.

The bed rumbled and jolted beneath him; igniting a dull ache in his skull that made him groan and put his hands to his head—

—or one hand, at least. Isak blinked at his white palm in confusion until he realised his right arm had been loosely bound to the nearest strut. The dusty black palm was empty, as it usually was when he woke, but clearly someone had decided not to take the chance.

He fumbled with the leather ties, eventually getting free. He inspected himself, and discovered someone had changed his clothes, put him in breeches and left a shirt and boots to one side. The blanket had slipped off, and he stared down at his body. The indentation in his belly was most obvious: a wide mess of scarring the size of his flattened hand, followed by the raised circle of the rune burned into his chest. That seemed so long ago, his first night in Tirah Palace, but unlike his other injuries he remembered that searing pain with fondness.

"Still not so pretty," Isak croaked and patted the cloth strip that bound the Skull of Ruling to his waist.

He'd not been without the Crystal Skull since taking Termin Mystt. Without it his mind, assailed by the raging power of Death's black sword, would be torn apart completely.

The faint smell of mud drifted through the hanging canvas flaps at the rear of the wagon, evoking fragmented memories of his life with the wagon-train before the day he was Chosen by Nartis. He flexed the fingers of his right hand. "If that's my father driving," he muttered, "I'm gonna punch the bastard."

"If I were your da," laughed Carel from the driver's seat just behind Isak's head, "I'd have whipped you out of that bed at dawn and told you to set the traces!"

Isak struggled around until he was kneeling on the grimy mattress. Bowing his head to avoid the struts above, he shoved the canvas open to see Carel's grinning face looking back while another man held the reins. Carel held out a filled pipe to him while the hooded driver turned to acknowledge Isak: Tiniq, General Lahk's brother. He was one of the few bodyguards who hadn't been returned to the ranks of the Ghosts—as he disliked riding almost as much as horses hated to be ridden by him, he'd doubtless volunteered to drive the wagon.

"Thought you'd lost that habit," Carel commented mildly. "Passing out like some girl on the battlefield? I dunno, smacks o' cowardice to me." He laughed.

The white-eye tried to find the words to respond to Carel's banter, but his mind was blank.

Carel thumped him on the shoulder and smiled fondly. "Don't worry; I know what you're like when you're just woken up. Here, make yourself useful, lazy bugger."

Isak frowned, but he took the pipe and pressed his thumb into the bowl, lighting it with a spark of magic before handing it back. "I thought for a moment I was back on the wagon-train," he said as Carel puffed away at the pipe.

"Relieved, then?"

Isak sighed and scratched the patchy stubble on his cheek. "I don't know, to be honest."

"Fate's eyes!" Carel exclaimed, "I never thought you'd miss that lot! Don't tell me you're looking back fondly on life there?"

"Nah—they're still a bunch of bastards; the ones I can remember, at least," Isak said. "I think I've lost a few in my head; I can't remember enough names and faces for all the caravans." He shrugged. "But life was simpler then. I might not have liked it much, but at least I wasn't coming apart at the seams."

"Ah, well, life ain't fair. At least people care about your opinion now, eh? All those wagon-folk would pretend you'd never even spoken; now a whole army's marching on your word alone."

"Not my word, the king's."

"Hah! Sure, he gave the order, but he's following your lead—yours and Legana's." Carel paused. "They're an odd couple those two, but thick as thieves nowadays. You reckon they, ah—?"

"Reckon what? That they're—?" Isak laughed. "Bloody soldiers, only one thing on your minds."

"Well, he's a king, ain't they expected to shag everything in sight? Anyone who gets married for political reasons won't stay faithful."

"Any man tries that with Legana, he'll find out the hard way how quick she can draw a knife. They're friends, nothing more. They both—they can see each other as a person, not just a Goddess or king. Brings them close, means they can trust each other, and so can I."

"Plus Ardela looks the jealous type," Carel added.

Isak looked past the veteran at the column of men, horses and wagons and recognised the broad road they were slowly trundling down: the trader route to Tor Salan. "So how long was I asleep?" he asked.

"Passed out like a big girl, you mean?" Tiniq quipped, attempting to join the banter.

"Fuck off and drive the wagon," Isak snapped.

After a moment of uncomfortable silence Carel waved the pipe in Isak's face and the white-eye took it, happy to have the distraction.

"You were out three days," Carel said. "The king went after the Devoted troops when they retreated, but they were in better shape to march and they're well ahead. He left you with a rearguard, but after a day I decided there was no telling when you were going to wake up, so we loaded you into this and went to catch 'em up. We reached the army mid-morning today—they keep having to stop and probe ahead because the Devoted have left divisions of troops staggered behind them—they're not waiting for a fight, just looking to strafe any ragged edges, but it all needs a proper response."

"We'll make good time on the road," Isak said after a moment. "Is anyone cutting cross-country?"

"Aye, Vesna and Lahk have taken five divisions to harry their flanks, but given the ground this road'll be the fastest route for as many infantry as we got."

"So now we chase them," Isak said wearily, "all the way to the Waste. Let's hope the Chetse take exception to them, slow them up enough for us to force battle."

"Reckon they will? Where's Ruhen going, anyway?"

"Keriabral, Aryn Bwr's fortress—where this all started, near enough."

"Why? What's out there?"

Isak took a long draw on the pipe before replying, as though reluctant to voice the answer. "Why? Because I weakened the Gods, and now's the time to challenge them, when they can't defend themselves."

"And he can really do it?"

"That and more," Isak said with a grim expression. "He's got thousands of devoted worshippers, near-limitless power and half the opposition he expected."

Carel fell silent.

"And you can stop him?" Tiniq asked in a quiet voice.

"If I can catch him, I can kill him—not just his mortal body, Azaer too. And we still hold the majority of Crystal Skulls; without them he can't make the Gods of the Upper Circle kneel, so he can't avoid us forever." He sighed. "Unless he's mad enough to kill them all. There's always that."

CHAPTER 34

ILUMENE LIT HIS CIGAR FROM A BURNING STICK, puffed appreciatively at it and continued on. There were wary faces around the campfire; Devoted soldiers watching him like mice watching the cat. He ignored them; he enjoyed their fear, but he had better things on his mind.

Venn walked silently ahead through the regimented rows of tents, the white leather grip of his sword almost the only thing visible in the dark. Ilumene caught him up again before they had reached their destination, the tents of the Jesters and their acolytes at the edge of the main army camp.

"Any guesses what this's about?"

Venn shook his head.

The former King's Man blew a lungful of smoke across Venn's face. "Not even a guess?"

"I suspect they will offer us a drink," Venn said at last, realising Ilumene was going to keep talking until he got a response.

"Well, I won't complain there. Doesn't sound like 'em though, unsociable lot, our Jesters."

"It is an unusual sort of drink."

"Seen it before, then?"

Venn nodded. "In my years of bondage," he said solemnly, "I travelled the Waste for a time. The Jester clans welcomed me as befitting one bearing a holy charge."

"Too bad most others thought of you as the entertainment, eh?"

Venn stopped and looked Ilumene in the face. "Our reasons for being here are not so different."

"Never said they were." Ilumene looked Venn up and down. "Someone's got prickly now he ain't the fighter he used to be."

"I remain skilled beyond most others in this camp."

"Never said you weren't," Ilumene said with a grin. He puffed away at his cigar and then continued, "Come on. If it's some quaint barbarian custom we're invited to, Rojak will complain if he misses it. Won't bother me o' course, but I reckon he'd keep you up the rest of the night singing all manner o' filth. Minstrels are all the same, after all, just entertainment for the low masses."

If Rojak responded to that in the privacy of Venn's mind, the former Harlequin made no sign; he gracefully matched the taller man's pace without appearing to hurry. They were admitted to the Jesters' camp without a word by the white-masked guards and escorted by curt hand gestures to the tall tents where their Demi-God lords awaited them.

The small camp was strangely silent, even quieter than the subdued Devoted on three sides of them. The warriors were all loitering on the edges of a central square around which were the Jesters' own tents. Over the last few weeks he had discovered there was a clear division within their ranks, though little difference in the way they dressed. The Harlequins wore their porcelain faces to ensure all roles and moods were conveyed solely by gesture, but Venn had suggested it had started as an echo of the serene faces of the divine, unencumbered by emotion. Whatever the truth, the only way to tell white-masked Acolytes and Hearth-Spears apart were the weapons they carried. The Acolytes, the élite, carried long, two-handed swords; they worked as mercenaries alongside their lords. The Hearth-Spears, the men and woman of the clans, defended their homes with javelins or spears and oval shields.

Ilumene looked around. Most of the hundred élite Acolytes were assembled here, so whatever was going on, it looked like they were involved.

"Lord Koteer, Blessed Sons of Death," Venn called as he approached the seated Demi-Gods, "I thank you for your invitation to attend this ritual."

Koteer, the eldest of the Jesters who spoke for them all, looked up. His grey skin faded into the night's darkness, leaving his white mask even more stark and ghostly. "We intend to raid the enemy—with your permission, Ilumene, as the voice of the Child," he announced. His voice was accented with age, but his words remained precise and clear. "We invite the Harlequins to join us."

"Just the Harlequins?" Ilumene asked. "What if the rest of us want to join in the fun?"

Koteer regarded him. "It will be a night raid, tomorrow, when the moon is darkest. The Harlequins can move silently at night. Any others will betray us."

"Your Acolytes can see in the dark?"

Koteer gestured and the two disciples of Ruhen edged forward to get a better view. Smoky braziers flanked the entrance of each large tent; the flavour of incense was heavy on the air. Ilumene could make out a blackened bowl, some dark liquid bubbling gently within it, sitting upon a small iron brazier. Koteer unbuckled the vambrace from his left arm and pushed up his sleeve. Accepting a knife from the nearest Acolyte, the Demi-God started intoning something, then slit open his wrist, letting a stream of darkly glowing blood pour down into the bowl. Then he stirred the contents with the blade of the knife and handed it back.

With blood still dribbling from his wrist, he ran his fingers over the wound and spoke more arcane words in Elvish, the language of magic, and the wound sealed. An Acolyte came forward with a fresh piece of linen to wrap around the wrist and Koteer held that in place while his vambrace was buckled back on.

Another Acolyte stepped forward with a silver jug, poured something that looked like water into the bowl and stirred it again with a naked blade, then small flasks were passed forward by all the watching Acolytes and carefully filled by Koteer's attendants.

"The clans share our blood, one and all; many of the Acolytes are our sons, but they remain human," Koteer said. "This ritual temporarily brings out the divine in their blood. Mortals cannot endure that too often, but in times of war, the risks are worth taking."

Venn said, "I will send thirty Harlequins to join you—I can spare no more; the risk of assassins remains too great."

"Acceptable," Koteer confirmed. "We will double back while the army moves on; the enemy are close enough that we can cover the distance in the day and strike their camp in the darkest part of night."

"And when you reach them?" Ilumene asked. "You'll never get near Emin or the Farlan boy; they're too well guarded."

"We go to kill their élite," Koteer said with a sudden hunger in his voice, "to prove ourselves the greater warriors and weaken them for the battle to come. We do not go to win the war."

Ilumene nodded in approval. "It'll slow their pursuit up; give us time to negotiate the Chetse border if they're watching for ambushes every night. You have Ruhen's permission, send them my best."

"I have seen your best," Koteer replied without humour, "and it is a savage thing. That is what we shall give them."

As the last of the sky turned to black, Doranei and Fei Ebarn headed out into the hushed army camp, where quiet snores mingled with the song of cicadas on the cool night air. Both were armed in their own way: Doranei in blackened armour, Ebarn in silver chains and crystal shards attached to a snug coat. There was not a breath of wind, Doranei noticed; after the blustery morning where the wind had been at their backs like Ilit's hand urging them on, it had steadily faded to nothing, the God's strength spent. Now the hushed Land waited, adding to the tense quiet of the army camp.

"So, you and Veil then," Doranei said at last, when they had moved beyond the last tent.

Ebarn gave him a suspicious look. "What about us?" The battle-mage was a strong woman, and well able to use both the stave she carried and the long-knives on her belt. Magic might be her greatest weapon, but in a mêlée the stave was an effective way to keep soldiers at arm's length until she could burn them.

"Just making conversation." He stopped and turned to face her. "I didn't mean anything by it—just that you seem good together."

"And there's you, the expert in relationships?"

Doranei gave a wry smile. "Screwed up a few in my time, right enough. That must have taught me something!"

Ebarn nodded to acknowledge his point and they continued their patrol. King Emin's more obvious élite now walked the camps at night, mostly just to be visible to the many untested soldiers. No amount of training could prepare a youth far from home for the true chaos of battle—or the sight of dragons being hauled out of the Dark Place, for that matter. Emin wanted his mages and skilled killers closer to his men in a way a king could not be.

"So. Me and Veil," Ebarn said after they had passed the first sentry post, seeing the soldiers stand a little taller in their presence, "you give your blessing then?"

"I ain't the boy's father; he don't need me to hold his hand."

The mage smiled. "Just as well. He hasn't got many to spare."

"Aye, so long as he takes off those damn spikes before he slips in your bed! Probably the first mistake I'd manage."

"Way I hear it, you'd have managed more'n a few by the time you get to the bed." Her eyes twinkled with amusement

"Aye, could be true," he admitted.

"How's he dealing with it? Losing his hand, I mean."

"Like the rest of you would, I'd guess: he's pretty pissed off—he's always trying to scratch his little finger and he's about ready to punch holes in the ground when he forgets and finds it gone all over again. Man's about as hard to ruffle as any of you, though. He'll be fine—he's more worried about you!"

"He's in good company there," Doranei said darkly, "but I ain't been drunk in days; that's got to count for something, no?"

"For you, aye—Veil told me you'd be good. I've got to admit I wasn't so certain, but it looks like he knows you better."

"Simple and obvious, that's one reason Zhia liked me in the first place," Doranei agreed. "When your days are full of lies and games, I guess not having to deal with that shit at night is a blessing. And yeah, Veil knows me well enough. I'm Brotherhood to the bone; ain't one who'd survive retiring, not like him or Sebe. When duty's all I got, it's enough to keep me moving." He sighed. "It's pathetic really. I'm like Isak's dog Hulf, lost without a master."

"At least you realise that. Most wouldn't."

Doranei snorted "Most haven't spent so much time asking why in the name o' the Dark Place they're doing what they're doing. You know, I just realised something about all I've done, all that bad shit in the name of the king—it's not that I'm kidding myself here, when I die, me and Lord Death are going to have a long old chat. Old Bones might have a few comments at my Last Judgment, and Ghain's slope is going to be one long bloody walk."

"I sense a 'but' creeping in."

"Aye, there's a 'but'—seems to me, the deciding vote ain't going to be Death's. Either we stop Azaer or we don't. The final judgment about me might depend on success, not the *right* or otherwise of what I've done. Either the Gods owe all of us one bastard of a favour, or an Upper Circle God's going to have it in for us. Azaer's not a forgiving type, even in victory."

Ebarn was silent for a long while. "So now you've depressed the shit out of me," she said eventually. "And this is you dealing with things better?"

"Gives us a prize to aim for, you've got to admit."

"Incentive like that I didn't need," she muttered, running a hand over her short hair as though trying to brush off her mood. "Now I know why Endine doesn't want to talk to you anymore."

"Pah! The scrawny bugger should know better than to have a serious conversation with me when I've had a few—the man knows I'm a mean-spirited drunk."

"That all it was?"

Doranei looked away into the dark of the countryside. This was a sparsely populated part of the Land, most of the towns nestled close to the cities they were bound to for fear of the regular wars between states. Most of the smaller settlements were now abandoned, according to the Narkang scouts.

"Mostly," he admitted at last. "Neither of us has been an idealist, not for years; what truth I spoke he knows anyway, he just doesn't like to think about it. With Cetarn dead he's feeling lost. He wants his faith to be a shield against the Land the way Cetarn's bulk was."

"Lost without his friend, eh?" Ebarn said pointedly. "There might be more than one man feeling that way. So maybe you'll go a bit easy on him?"

"I see what you mean." Doranei picked up his pace. Now wasn't the time to talk about their own frailties. He'd got the golden bee on his collar and the sword of a dead Demi-God on his hip: he was a King's Man. He didn't want to know what men might say behind his back, though he guessed it would be as much hero-worship as distrust—conquered a vampire princess, ear of the king, cold-hearted bastard who murdered his lover, a hundred different things. Best he didn't hear any of them.

I might be a bastard in their eyes, Doranei realised, *but they want killers on their side, ones they can't imagine falling in battle. Few of us liked Coran—maybe none of us, to tell the truth—but you were still glad to hear him snarl at your side when the Soldier beckoned.*

They headed to one of the advance pickets, fifty yards out from the camp, near enough for voices to carry if it was attacked. All ten faces turned their way, then the squad's sergeant saluted gravely before returning his gaze to the darkness beyond.

The sergeant was a few winters older than Doranei, but the rest were frighteningly young—but the recruiters didn't care much about *actual* age so long as they were strong enough to use a spear.

"Evening, boys. All quiet out?"

"Yes, sir," squeaked the private he was looking at, the youngest of the lot. "Nothing more than a bat."

"Did it give the password?" Doranei meant to joke, but his weariness and lingering grief made the words sound angry and the boy's face paled. "Never mind, son; just a joke. See any daemons?"

The boy shook his head violently. "Nothing, sir. Corporal Rabb, in third squad, he said he did last night, thing like a dog, shining silver in the moonlight."

"And his sergeant said it was a damn rabbit," said the squad sergeant, glancing back. "Sergeant Garelden, sir. Sorry, foolish talk is all. Until they see their first fight, they're always jumpy at the unknown."

Doranei remembered the fears of his first mission well enough. "Sure it wasn't actually a dog?" he asked the private.

The soldier shook his head, eyes wide. "It ran without a sound, the corp said, and big as a wolf, and then it just vanished."

"Aye. His name's Hulf." Doranei raised one palm to show the whole squad. "You seen these tattoos on the Ghosts and my lot? The Mad Axe decided the dog should get 'em too, give him a fighting chance if he's going to run with the army. In darkness he'll run like a ghost and likely sneak up on any daemons out there, just to give 'em a fright. He's got his master's sense of humour, that pup, but he's with us. You've nothing to fear from him."

"Yes, sir."

"Enough of the 'sir' crap. I'm no officer."

"Well, *sir*," Sergeant Garelden drawled, turning back to look at Doranei, "you're a King's Man and no infantry private, that's for sure. Rank or no, think it's best we use a bit o' respect for anyone on first-name terms with the king."

Doranei hesitated, then said, "I suppose you've got a point there. Fair enough."

"Thank you, sir."

Ebarn watched Doranei with a smile on her face while the rest of the squad, under the stern eye of their sergeant, turned back to the darkness beyond, wanting to show how alert to their duty they were, especially while the eyes of the king were upon them.

"Question, sir?" Garelden asked quietly, never taking his eyes from the darkness.

"Sure—what is it?"

"The enemy, sir," he said slowly, as if not quite sure how to ask what he wanted. "I was hoping you could tell us a bit more about 'em—the child, I mean. All we've heard is rumour, and not much of that's made a lot of sense."

Doranei shared a look with Ebarn. "So your question is, 'what're we doing out here?,' right?"

"No, sir; I know my duty, my boys too. We're with the king to the end and it ain't our place to question what we're doing. We're all loyal to the bone."

Doranei realised some of the younger men were looking alarmed at the very idea of a King's Man thinking them disloyal. "Right, so the question is "why're we out *here*,' mebbe? Why here and why now?"

"Just hoping to understand a little better," the sergeant said carefully, not wanting to make a point of contradicting Doranei. "We're marching into foreign lands to fight for our king, fight for our country, and none of us got a problem with that; it's why we joined. But when I ask my boys to kill another man for a cause, I'd—well—"

"Want to know the cause?" Ebarn supplied, then, added, "It's a reasonable request. I think we all forget most of the nation hasn't been in this war as long as we have—most don't know it's been going almost as long as the king's reign."

"It ain't the time for a history lesson," Doranei growled, "nor for telling two decades o' secrets."

"Don't worry; we all know our duty here, right, Sergeant Garelden? So you get the quick version; most likely you heard it already, but rumour messes up most stories. There's a shadow, as old as mortal life—it's not a God and not a daemon, just claws and a voice that can whisper inside a man's head, persuade him to do stuff he sometimes thought of in the quiet of night, but never really meant. We all got a bad side. Some of us let it out, and some of us get it forced out by others—life ain't fair, and sometimes the shit gets too much. But for some, a shadow talks and talks at you until you let out that dark bit of your soul that you wouldn't want your loved ones to see. With me so far?"

"Aye, I think so."

"Well the shadow loves this power, but for centuries that was all it had—one or two folk here and there, a few whispers and fearful stories. Then the shadow found the Last King of the Elves, and it found the key to unlock that dark part, the hunger for more than we've got: *ambition*. A lot else happened and the Elves and Gods made their own mistakes, and the Great War was the result."

Doranei cleared his throat, but Ebarn didn't object when he took up the explanation. "All that was a long time ago, but it's still important. When our king was a young man, the shadow made an enemy of him because the king's a man who brings out the best in others—that's his genius, really. The shadow knew it had found its opposite—its mirror-match. As the king's power grew, the shadow's did too, and it finally had a chance to take advantage of all the things it'd learned over the years.

"You can't hide from a shadow. Whatever strong-room you put your secrets in, shadows creep in as you shut that door. And this shadow's learned as much as the Gods about the balance of the Land. Daemons did its bidding, furthering its legend in return for the souls they covet, and the Last King, Aryn Bwr himself, gave his soul over to the shadow before he died. Then when Aryn Bwr tried to be reborn, the shadow played the Last King for its own purpose. It knew the Gods would fear their old enemy—and all those with the sort of power Bwr'd wielded—but none of them cared about something as weak as a shadow.

"It had seen how the Great War weakened the Gods, and now it knew it could bring about the same: it could stop the prayers that sustain the Gods; it could make folk turn against the priests who carry those prayers to the Gods. And now it intends to use the weapons Aryn Bwr himself forged—the Crystal Skulls—to unbalance the Land so it can force itself into the Pantheon of the Gods."

"So that's why the child of Byora has sent preachers out across the Land?" Sergeant Garelden asked, as rapt as his young soldiers. "He's gathering worshippers for when the shadow becomes a God, stealing them away from the other Gods to weaken them?"

"Exactly. Now there's more to the story, and some things I won't tell you, but that's the heart of it. That child, Ruhen, has an immortal soul, and it hopes to become a God. We have to stop that happening and we've got a weapon to do just that."

"So that's what we're fighting for—to stop a shadow killing the Gods?" one young soldier breathed, wonder mingling with terror in his voice. "We're fighting for the fate of the whole Land?"

Doranei shook his head and forced a smile, clapping his hand on the youth's shoulder. "No, lad, you're in the infantry. Let folk like Ebarn and me do that; you just remember what you learned your very first day of training."

"What—? Sarge?"

"Come on, Private, you've heard it so many times it should be carved into your heart!" Garelden replied.

"Oh, that." He swallowed. "You fight for the man beside you; you fight for your friends around you so you don't let them down."

"Aye, that's it," Doranei said. "Don't think about where the war's going or what the king's thinking; you're here to be strong. Victory only comes if men like you stay strong. Look after the man beside you and he'll look after you. Kill the enemy before they get you or the man at your side—that's the only way any of us are going to make it home."

"Yes sir," the soldier said. He looked down at the ground, another question clearly on his lips.

"Go on," Doranei encouraged, "ask it, even if you're afraid to. There's no shame in fear, only in letting it rule you. Fear is a shadow," he added, amending the Brotherhood's long-standing mantra about grief, "and we don't submit to shadows."

"Yes, sir. I just—I don't know what it'll be like, when we do have to fight."

"Fucking terrifying," Doranei said with a rough laugh. "It looks like the Land's exploded around you, and everything's moving too fast for anything to make sense. That's why you stick to the man at your shoulder. You're safer when you're together, and once you realise you're not alone, the chaos will fade."

"What about killing, sir? I'm a soldier and we're going to fight—but what's it like, to kill a man? I've never done more'n split a lip before and—well, you're a— you're a King's Man." The soldier hung his head, fearing he'd insulted Doranei.

"I'm a King's Man, aye, and I've killed more'n a few in his name: it's part of what we do. Don't mean I've enjoyed it, but I was trained to kill, sure enough, better than any soldier." He looked around. "Gods, now you've made me feel old, lad. So what's it like? Don't know I can tell you rightly; it's different for everyone, far's I can tell. First man I killed, I couldn't stop my hand shaking afterwards. Knife went in so easy and smooth I couldn't believe it. It frightened me, how easy it was, in truth."

He sighed and looked away, trying to work out how to explain it in a way that wouldn't break the boy's spirit and mean he didn't last longer than his first battle. Those who feared the killing were the ones who hesitated. At last he said, "It's easy t'kill a man. I'm serious, killing a man's so easy you'll be scared too. See that spear you got?" He took hold of the shaft and lowered the weapon so he could tap the slim blade on the end. "This is sharp and hard—people ain't. You put your shoulder into it, not just prod like a girl, and this'll go through flesh and bone and out the other side, right through a man. We ain't made to be hard to kill, and the first time you put a man down you'll feel the weight of that like a punch to the gut.

"Afterwards comes the screams and the stink of spilled guts, blood, shit and mud all mixed and filling your nose. Then the chaos of battle comes back and grabs you in its teeth and you're more scared than ever before—but that's what battle is: more noise and movement than any mind can keep up with, so keep your mind on the job and don't let all that distract you." He released the spear.

"Killing a man's easy," Doranei repeated sadly, "forgetting the next day that he was just like your brother—that his mother'll be weeping when she hears, or something'll break inside his father, never to be fixed—that's the hard part. Come see me after your first battle, lad, and we'll drink until we forget those we've killed.

"You don't get a choice about killing sometime, and not in war, that's for sure. Just remember to share the burden or it'll eat you up inside. There's no shame in sharing; and any man who thinks so can explain himself to me or the Mad Axe—we'll both—ah, *respond*—the same. Understanding consequences is what makes us men. Sometimes you got to accept consequences, sometimes you got to know when they're too great. Without understanding that choice you're nothing."

Doranei and Ebarn walked away in silence, leaving a stunned silence in their wake. After fifty paces Ebarn draped a sisterly arm around Doranei's waist. "Fine speech. Inspiring. Really roused them for the fight ahead."

Doranei sighed. "Sorry. Took myself down some unexpected path."

"Aye, sounded like it. Dark down there, is it?" She raised her free hand, showing faint trails of light dancing and swirling. "Need some light to show you—" She stopped, so suddenly that she dragged Doranei to a halt. "What's that?" she muttered to herself, swinging around.

"Something wrong?"

"I, ah—I don't know."

"What the fuck does that mean?"

She looked up at him, eyes wide. "It means yes; it has to be!" She dropped her right hand to the Crystal Skull hanging from her belt and cupped it, reaching her left hand up into the sky. Doranei reeled away just in time, covering his eyes just as a stream of light surged up into the inky night sky.

"*Ware! To arms!*" Ebarn roared, sending the column of light a hundred feet in the air before running forward, half-dragging Doranei with her.

The light continued to drive up and forwards, arching out beyond the pickets, where it cast a faint starlight over the ground below. He shook himself free as small sparks of magic began to race over his fingers, Ebarn's chains and shards coming alive with power, and followed blindly, trusting her skill to lead him.

Halfway back to the picket Doranei saw them: small squads advancing on the sentries stationed all around the army. The nearest were closing on the post they'd just been standing at and there was no time: the sergeant didn't even have time shout as his soldiers instinctively huddled close and levelled their spears.

The men on either end died almost in the same instant. Masked figures with flowing grey hair and double-handed swords danced around the clumsy spears before cutting each down. Ebarn snarled and punched forward with her open palm and a burst of crimson fire smashed into the nearer figure's chest.

The other white-masked figure ran for them and Doranei moved to intercept, belatedly recognising the figure as an Acolyte. "It's the Jesters!" he yelled to Ebarn as he aimed a sweeping strike at the swordsman.

The Acolyte stepped to one side, intent on catching Doranei's blade and deflecting it down, not realising the midnight-black blade was speckled with unnatural light until too late. Doranei's sword sheared right through the Acolyte's weapon and he followed it with an upward flick that chopped up into the fighter's throat.

To his left he heard Ebarn shout; the harsh syllables lit up the night and tore into grey-skinned Acolytes with ease. Doranei pushed on to try and reach the beleaguered squad, but before he could, someone shrieking in agony was driven out of the squad's line by a tall figure, also white-masked, but the height of a white-eye.

"Our brother's sword," the figure said in a cold, ancient voice. "Are you worthy of it, warrior?" The Jester raised its sword. The acid-etched blade shone weirdly as it reflected the light of Ebarn's battle-magics as it saluted him in some formal manner. "We shall see."

Doranei made no response but he fumbled at his belt and ran to meet the Demi-God, tossing a pouch of sparkle-dust in front of him as he went. The Jester dodged with alarming agility, and the pouch passed its head. It didn't touch the Jester, but some of the dust leaked out and a white-glittering path was traced through the dark just past its eyes. Realising that would do no more than make the Jester hesitate for a moment, Doranei pulled his short axe and went on the attack. Sensing him come the Demi-God wheeled right, keeping its long sword between it and Doranei. He caught it with his axe and yanked down, but the Jester dropped the tip and let the axe slid harmlessly off, deflecting Doranei's follow-up slashes as it planted its feet.

Lashing out with unnatural speed, the Jester directed a flurry of cuts at Doranei. The King's Man barely blocked the first in time, only his training saving him as the next slashed down at his knee. He caught the third and chopped at the Demi-God's arm, his axe glancing off the scales of its armour. He stepped forward into the fight and tried to rip his sword across the Jester's wrist, but it was already moving back.

He kept on, knowing attack was his best option. With the sword he'd taken from Aracnan Doranei could strike as quickly as his enemy, though his reactions remained mortal. The light-speckled sword cut through the air so swiftly it felt like it had a mind of its own. The Jester tried to batter it from his hand, but Doranei rode the heavy blows, deflecting the last upwards with the axe following close behind. Again the edge was turned by the Jester's armour, but Doranei pressed in behind it.

With his sword he engaged the Demi-God's weapon, then hooked his axe into the back of the Jester's knee, hauling back and slamming his head into the Jester's midriff. The Demi-God fell onto his back; Doranei stumbled himself, but caught himself in time and swung down at the Jester's feet. The scale-armour couldn't resist his sword and he chopped right through the Jester's ankle, swinging up almost blindly to deflect the inevitable swipe of an injured warrior.

The Jester was lying supine, and the strike was weakened by panic and pain, and Doranei was able to batter away the weak blow. He threw himself forward and hacked his axe at the Jester's face, and as he felt it bite he followed up with a stab to the armpit that drove deep inside the Jester's body, which suddenly went rigid.

Doranei rolled back to his feet and looked around wildly for the next threat, but none of the attackers were going for him.

The remains of the squad were cringing in a small knot behind their shields, back to back, spear-heads wavering. Surrounding them were five Acolytes, identically dressed, each with blood on their long blades. But none were bothering to look at the infantrymen; their eyes were all on Doranei and the corpse at his feet.

"Reckon I'm worthy, then?" Doranei shouted at them, not caring whether they could understand him or not. "This good enough for you—a dead God at my feet?"

Any response was precluded by a burst of magic from Ebarn, long slivers of white that flew like daggers at the nearest of the Acolytes, tearing bloody ribbons across its chest and slicing through the sword arm as the Acolyte tried to parry.

The Acolyte dropped, dead before it hit the ground, and the others broke and sprinted off into the darkness. Doranei looked at the corpses on the ground. Only one looked to have been killed by the soldiers. He'd taken down two; that left five Ebarn had dispatched.

"Oh Gods," Doranei breathed as the sergeant threw down his spear and started to check on the fallen. One youth's frantic, pained breaths told Doranei the dismal news; another howled as soon as the sergeant touched him. The rest were already dead, among them the youngest of their squad, his neck sliced clean open. Blood no longer flowed from the wound; too much had already run out down his studded jacket into the dry earth beneath.

"There's no time, Brother!" Ebarn warned, running to his side and pointing towards the next picket. "It's a coordinated attack."

"I know," Doranei muttered, unable to tear his eyes from the boy's sightless eyes. "I just—"

"Shift yourself!" Ebarn yelled, giving the King's Man a rough shove, and when that didn't work she hauled him around and made him look her in the eye. "It was a quick death and you can't ask for more. He's in Death's hands now, and we need to see to the living!"

Doranei sheathed his weapon and started to run towards the next post where, without a mage, they most likely hadn't been faring so well. "We see to the living," he repeated.

Chapter 35

THE HOURS PASSED SLOWLY as the weight of his burden grew heavier, eroding his strength with every moment passing, in the saddle, on foot or by the fire while Carel forced him to eat. Isak could feel it happen, and he could do nothing about it.

Though the hours of each day dragged, the days were somehow racing past. News of skirmishes and blood spilled washed over him: riders from the Menin force brought word of bloody battles fought; dutiful updates came from the king, conveyed by the battered remnants of his Brotherhood, though Isak guessed they were mostly sent to monitor his sanity, or what remained of it.

On occasion he made jokes, little moments of foolishness Carel would scrutinise for meaning. Sometimes the conclusions were good, and the veteran would nod, satisfied, and continue; at others a sadness would take him and he would sit and stare into the fire next to his young charge, an old man hunched against the autumn winds.

Magnificent views went unremarked-upon. Great clouds of green and blue birds filled the sky as they approached the deep lakes that dotted the plain. The fading sun cast gold and copper light over the rusty flanks of the mountains in the distance. One morning he'd awakened surrounded by ghosts in the pale dawn, which slowly revealed themselves to be towering termite mounds twice the height of a man, covering the grasslands for miles: silent, still monuments stretching off into the distance. Isak felt they were oddly fitting as they trudged on, mile after mile, in pursuit of a battle where there would be no retreat from either side.

Isak watched himself just as carefully as Carel, wondering at the damage done. From time to time he would see the monstrous white-eye he had become, shuffling from one day to the next, and it brought a tear to Isak's eye, but the threatening flood never arrived. The ache in his heart swelled, but never broke. Something inside wouldn't let him submit, something inside was too broken to submit.

The power suffusing Isak's body meant his senses were rarely closed to the Land around him. He felt the brief moments of grief Vesna permitted himself, the fatigue that threatened to consume King Emin; it all drifted on the wind and settled like snow on his shoulders, adding to the burden of the black sword.

And yet—

And yet he had realised it was not his sanity that was failing. The kernel of self within his broken and brutalised body remained.

The Skull of Ruling kept him balanced, he knew that, and he held it close as hungrily as an addict. The arm of the scales creaked and groaned, but the balance remained. His mind drifted with the tides of the wind, carried by the clouds above and fogged by the heavy depths of soil below, but something remained apart from it all.

My hunger for the end? A white-eye's need for victory? The daemons left little of me and the witch of Llehden took more, so how much is left of the boy I once was, the boy Carel loved? Did he die in the Dark Place, or when his memories were torn out? Or was he only ever an imagining—a false echo in my mind?

"Isak," Carel called from his side, slapping the white-eye's boot as he spoke, "you going to sit there all afternoon?" He took the reins from Isak's hands. More gently he said, "The halt's been called. Time for lunch."

"I'm not hungry." The massive charger stood patiently while Isak disentangled himself and slid to the ground.

"That don't matter. You'll eat something while I take Toramin to drink." Carel slapped a bruised apple in Isak's hand along with a lump of bread, then took the reins and tugged on them to urge Isak's horse into a walk. "If Hulf gets more'n the core, you'll both feel the back o' my hand."

Isak looked at Carel, a frayed smile on his face. "You realise that hurts you more than me?"

"Aye, I know—you bloody Chosen and your Gods-granted strength." Carel spat and loosened the saddle-strap. "Still, it hurts me, and it'll hurt your dog—so why do that to us, eh?"

Isak didn't answer, but he sat on the flattened grass at the side of the road, ignoring the soldiers around him, and bit into the apple. Out from the muddle of horses and men Hulf bounded, barrelled into Isak and fought his way into his lap with enough force that he would have knocked over a normal man. Isak took another big bite of the apple and offered the remains to the dog, who snapped it eagerly up.

As he ate the bread, Isak ran his fingers through Hulf's thickening fur and stared blankly down at the dirt road. The dog's coat had become noticeably thicker in the last month as autumn advanced. The dog's warm, playful presence was a great comfort, a reminder that Isak was more than ephemeral; it was Hulf as much as anything that kept him in the weary flesh of his body. Lurking at the back of his mind was the sense that he no longer belonged in the Land of the living; the lure of the wind was strong, like he could simply let go and drift away.

Carel fought that with every joke and insult, with his gripes and awkward words of pride and praise, but it was the physical that worked best: Carel's thumps on the shoulder, Hulf's feet kicking delightedly in Isak's lap, the burning muscles when he hacked down a tree for firewood or lifted stones to build a firepit.

"Isak?" Vesna was standing over him with his usual look of concern. The ruby teardrop embedded in his cheek seemed to tinge that with an air of despondency, but Isak knew the Farlan hero well enough to dismiss that thought.

"My friend," Isak replied as brightly as he could manage, "how are you?"

The question seemed to startle Karkarn's Mortal-Aspect. "Me? I'm fine—I won't pretend it's not annoying to have my God root through my mind, but having the bastard's blood in my veins means I don't tire easily." He gestured at the soldiers all around, men and women from the Kingsguard and Palace Guard. "We're pressing them hard, as fast a pace as the baggage can manage, and it's taking its toll."

"I thought the enemy were getting further away?"

"They are." Vesna crouched at Isak's side to let Hulf lick his fingers. "They're getting supplied as they travel—for a retreat, someone's planned it bloody well."

"Ruhen always planned on heading this way, his preachers must have struck quiet deals over the last few months. The battle becomes irrelevant if he gets Aenaris to Aryn Bwr's fortress, to the barrow where Aryn Bwr first discovered the Crystal Skulls."

"So do we need to push harder, or get the Menin to delay them?"

"We have time," Isak said. "They'll slow down once they're out of lands Ruhen controls."

"It's a shame the Chetse won't try to stop them, but if anyone's going to have a problem there, it'll be us."

"Aye—what fool invited a Menin army along?"

Vesna smiled. "I'm sure he had his reasons, whoever he was." He hesitated, as if wary of asking what was on his mind, then said, "Isak, do you know what it will take to kill Ruhen? Zhia gave him Aenaris, correct? The Key of Life? If it has the power to create dragons—if it's the match to Termin Mystt—how can you be sure you can kill Ruhen with it?"

"Termin Mystt's more than enough to kill a shadow, a child too," Isak said with a frown, "more than enough to kill a God."

"But he'll unleash all his power to stop you—power beyond imagination, beyond control—so how does that confrontation happen without tearing the Land itself apart? What will be left? Karkarn has told me something of the Great War, of the Last Battle that ended it all. The City of Ghosts is a place where the balance was broken, where the border between this Land and the place of Gods and daemons was fractured by the magic unleashed. Crystal Skulls alone didn't manage that; it was the Keys of Life and Magic, wielded by *opposing* sides!"

"Ifarana was her name," Isak said, as though in a trance. "She was Life herself. Death too bore a name once, when He was not Chief of the Gods alone but ruler in tandem."

"And they killed her for betraying her own kind!" Vesna hissed, red light flickering in his eyes.

"Was it betrayal, or compassion? Are you so certain of Karkarn's memories? Do you believe the other Gods were blameless in a war that saw the creation and obliteration of entire species? Think of the fall of Scree, the fanaticism that swept the Land this past year—the rage of Gods is a blind and savage thing, and only fools trust in it. When I stripped the Menin lord of his name I discovered something I hadn't expected: the Gods themselves *feared* what I was doing, and what it might mean. And it wasn't just the drain of their strength they were afraid of. History has taught them the folly of their own rage, my friend; they know that's a force as uncontrollable as any." He leaned forward and gripped Vesna's arm with his black hand.

The Mortal-Aspect stared down in horror at it, aghast at the hurricane of power he could sense, on the cusp of manifesting.

"Gods and mortals: we're no different when rage takes us," Isak continued urgently. "We can't be trusted, and we can't be reasoned with. Our worst comes out and no amount of guilt afterwards can make up for what's done. History is written by the victors because facing the full horror of such shame tears one's heart apart.

"You're a man of conscience and compassion, my friend. Are you sure you want a part in this, and all it entails? More important, maybe: I may not have much humanity left, but how can I share this with those I love so dearly?"

"Anyone else still find those buggers creepy?" General Daken stared towards the knot of undead soldiers twenty yards away, just beyond the perimeter marked out by Amber's bodyguards.

"Aside from the fact they're not much more than preserved corpses?" Nai asked. "Not especially."

The six figures were dressed in mismatched pieces of armour and ragged clothing as faded as their own grey skin. Nai had taken a closer look that morning, before anyone but the sentries had risen. Though the drifting song of daemons and spirits was strongest around dusk, most mornings Nai awoke to the sound of distant voices, his senses long since attuned to the daemons he and his former master had treated with.

Up close to the Legion of the Damned, Nai had seen nothing but withered limbs and jutting bones, skin turned to leather, emptiness in their cold eyes. Only when he embraced his magic did Nai find much more than a dead body inexplicably standing; only then did the warrior notice him, shifting the pitted, rusted axe a fraction.

Daken ran a hand over his shaved head. "Aye, well, you're used to shit like that, necromancer. Us normal folk, we prefer our dead things to stay still."

"In their defence," Amber said in a rumbling voice that took Nai by surprise, "they've not moved all night."

"And that's also more'n a bit weird. They ain't moved an inch; they're in the exact same damn position since I turned in for the night."

"Hold on a moment," Nai interjected, "since when have you been considered part of 'normal folk,' Daken?"

The broad white-eye smirked. "Since I started to keep bad company," he said, looking at Nai and Amber in turn. He pulled out a flatbread, smeared it in oil and as he proceeded to eat it, turned his attention back to the Legion of the Damned.

Daken had ridden in to the Menin camp just as the sun went down, bringing Amber news of the enemy's progress before tackling what little beer remained to them.

The Devoted armies had met and merged not far from where the Menin now camped; the unwieldy mass tens of thousands strong had barely stopped as it entered Chetse lands. They guessed there'd been no confrontation; the

Chetse had lost many of its best in the past year, and the Devoted troops alone numbered seventy thousand, and they were backed by a protective curtain of perhaps twenty thousand of Ruhen's ragged, exhausted followers, whose burning faith would not let them turn back.

It had been too late last night for Daken to return to his own men, camped several miles ahead near the Chetse border, but Nai had been glad of the ebullient white-eye's company; Even Amber reacted to his natural charisma.

The enemy avoided even skirmishes now, except when Daken's cavalry could force a fight on them, and the lack of violence was taking a toll on Amber. Without the savage struggle of battle to energise him, he was almost as lifeless as the Legion, who stood close at hand and watched over their ally.

"They don't interfere with your appetite then," Amber commented after Daken had lapped the last of the pale oil from his fingers.

"Takes more'n creepy for that," Daken declared. "I've got a reputation to maintain after all."

"What's being a mad axeman got to do with breakfast?" Nai wondered aloud.

Daken waved an admonishing finger towards him. "An empty stomach's good enough reason t' kill, best there is—but so's interrupting me when I've got a face-full of anything sweet!" The white-eye laughed coarsely. "I'm a man o' many reputations, as many as Morghien's got spirits buzzing round his head. If I fell today, it wouldn't be just mercenary captains who'd doff their caps and mourn. Whores and chefs alike would grieve my passing!"

"A fool and his money, eh?"

"A connoisseur!" Daken protested, "a man of appetites and enthusiasm—show folk with taste some quality to appreciate and we're faster'n any fool to hand over our money. Difference being, fools never learn and I make damn sure I'm paying attention while I'm enjoying myself."

"No likely the courtesans of Narkang will celebrate one fewer rival while your whores and chefs weep."

Daken hauled himself up and began to brush down his horse, readying the beast for the day to come. His clothes were torn and dirty; the shadow of a bruise was still visible on his cheek, but he tended to his horse rather than himself. "Fucking necromancers," he said with a smile, "always missing the point."

"Which is?" Nai asked as he readied his own meagre possessions. Amber remained where he was, watching the two of them with a faintly curious expression; Nai thought he looked like a man trying to remember what it was to have friends and comrades.

"Simple: life ain't that they cheer or weep for you, it's that they notice you passing and you had yourself a damn good time on the way! You lot sneak through the shadows, gathering power and money too, and most importantly, prolonging the inevitable, but you forget to spend all you've gathered. Power's fun enough, but it ain't nothing compared to an immoral woman in your bed and fine food in your belly. Where's the use in your long life if it ain't fun?"

"So speaks a man who's never held true power in his hand," Nai countered, slender spindles of light erupting from the fingers of his upturned hand. "You've never tasted that fire on your tongue, never learned the secrets of the Land while magic echoes through your bones."

"Pah, fire on the tongue? Prefer the taste o' some girl's sweat misself. Once this is all over, I'll introduce you to some ladies I know—they'll show you there's something better than magic t' have echo through your bones."

"I'll take that offer," Amber joined, his words hesitant and awkward. "Got to be better than the aches I've got right now." There were dark rings of fatigue around his eyes, rings that had been there for many days now.

"Be a pleasure, General," Daken said, smiling. "The girls like a man with scars too, which makes it easier." He nodded towards Nai. "And this one's funny-looking—best there's more'n just my beauty t' distract 'em from his weird feet." He heaved his saddle up onto his horse's back and secured it, slid his long-axe into a hook, offered Amber a sloppy salute and mounted.

"Time to go greet my king," he announced. "He'll probably need my help with the diplomacy t' come. Messages for him?"

Amber stared at the white-eye for a long while, long enough for Nai to be about to reach out and touch the Menin on the arm when he finally spoke. "Messages? No, I have none."

"So just your humble greetings and request for further orders? Or shall I just ask what took 'em so long?"

"Ask what you like," Amber said, at last seeming to focus on Daken and stand a little straighter. "He is my ally, not my king. My price was that he got my troops through Chetse land and supplies on the other side. How he does that is his concern."

"Aye, guess it is." Daken leaned forward on his saddle, noting the eyes of Amber's bodyguard as they all fixed upon him. Behind their curling beards and steel helms he could see little, but the white-eye appeared to find enough to confirm what he was thinking.

"It's what happens on the other side I'm more interested in," Daken said lazily. "So may be time you asked your men which way they want to march."

"My men are Menin," Amber said, "and they follow their commander—or they kill him. There is no asking."

"Aye, well, ask yourself then: there's a fight coming, either in Chetse lands or out the other side. If it's the one, you'll be with us, but the Devoted have a start on us, so I'm guessing it'll be the other and then—" He jerked his reins and wheeled around. "Well, ask yourself, is all I'm saying. You here for glory or safe passage?"

"You don't think we've earned both?"

Daken grinned. "Anyone who walks away from the fight to come, they ain't likely t' be remembered. The rest of us'll be so shining with glory Tsatach hisself won't need to lift his eye over the horizon for years to come!"

"Or you'll be dead," Amber called, "dead, forgotten and cursed for all eternity."

The white-eye laughed and pulled up his shirt, revealing the tattoo of Litania covering much of his chest. The tattoo there was still, the Trickster Goddess still weak, as all her kin were, but Daken's point was made.

"Nah, must have a few favours saved up—I've done some dirty work for this immoral bitch over the years. The rest o' you bastards might be fucked though, aye!"

Two days later the Narkang army arrived at the Chetse border. King Emin rode with General Lahk and Vesna ahead of a legion of Kingsguard heavy cavalry, each in full armour. Emin and Vesna were resplendent in their ornate plate; Lahk, in his usual austere battle-dress, Lord Bahl's black-and-white tabard, was as famous a sight as the extravagant lion's head helm hanging from Vesna's saddle. King Emin's armour echoed that of the Kingsguard, but was suitably finer in every aspect, surpassing even Vesna's for artistry; mage-engraved runes incorporated into a design of bees and oak leaves.

Behind them, nestled within a screen of Kingsguard, rode the less prepossessing: Isak in his tattered leathers, Legana with a shawl covering her face from the weak sun and Daken in plain armour and a stained green scarf.

Carel's cream uniform was emblazoned with Isak's crowned dragon crest, but weeks of travelling meant it was far from pristine.

"King Emin," called the ageing Chetse at the head of the receiving delegation, "I am General Dev. I command the armies of the Chetse until a new Lord of the Chetse is Chosen."

Dev's thick arms were uncovered despite the cool air and steady drizzle, and gold and copper torcs framed the ritual scars on his biceps. He wore a warrior's kilt, but carried no weapon. He stepped forward to bow low. Those behind him followed suit. Their clothing indicated they were ruling landowners and the remaining Tachrenn of the Ten Thousand, but they held back to make it clear the general spoke for all of them.

The Chetse borders were aggressively defended; their slow-burning war with the Siblis ensured that every man grew up a warrior and any Chetse would feel naked when unarmed. Emin knew it was a deliberate gesture of friendship, that Dev had met them without his axe in hand.

"General Dev," King Emin replied in surprisingly good Chetse, "your reputation precedes you. I am glad to finally meet you."

"Yet you do so with an army at your back," Dev pointed out. "Not an auspicious start, would you say?"

King Emin inclined his head and dismounted, Lahk and Vesna doing likewise. "It remains my hope that I can prove Narkang's friendship to your tribe," he said as he advanced a little way on foot, "if you would agree to hear my offer?"

"I'm a soldier, not a politician. Friendship is something that is earned, not bought with gifts."

"A soldier's friendship perhaps," King Emin replied, unruffled by Dev's gruff words, "but a nation is a different beast. The business of a nation is improving the lot of its people, and the gifts I intend are to the Chetse tribe as a whole."

"It isn't my tribe you need to persuade, it's me," Dev said.

Emin nodded. "And if your reputation were that of a greedy man, I'm sure your friendship would be far more cheaply bought."

Some of the Chetse gave an angry start at that, and more than one hand tightened around an axe-shaft until General Dev raised a hand without looking back.

"I might not be greedy, but the Menin left our armies badly depleted and our capital city in turmoil. The expense of invasion is considerable." He ran a hand through his thinning grey hair and spent a while regarding the

Narkang force stretching out for miles behind King Emin, no doubt looking for the Menin.

"I'm not here to fleece you," Dev continued at last. "Well, not entirely. You want to take an army through Chetse lands, almost past the Gate of Three Suns itself, and you'll pay, and you know that—so not a surprise to you, that one."

He sighed. "But that's not the problem. Money and concessions don't buy off the blood-oaths many under my command have sworn."

"The Menin," Emin stated gravely. "Is your hatred really so great that it defies reason?"

General Dev gaped at him. "You of all men can ask that? They *obliterated* Aroth! They slaughtered most of the population, civilians and soldiers alike, all wiped out without mercy. How can you ally your people with such monsters?"

King Emin turned back towards his troops and looked at the faces of his soldiers before replying to the general's question. "How? Because I must. Do you think it was easy? Do you think my people are sheep, to be led unthinking whatever I decide? This war *must* be fought, and I am outnumbered. My choice was to kill them all and accept grave losses, or bring them to the fold and use their strength for something greater. You are a reluctant ruler of your people, but a king must make such choices."

"Why is this war so important to you?"

"Because the child Ruhen will overturn the Pantheon of the Gods if we do not stop him. Because *all* of the Gods are threatened by his actions—your own patron included."

"Tsatach?" General Dev said with sudden venom. "Then why does our God not warn us, or act? Do you claim greater knowledge than the Gods, or is he so weakened he cannot even find the dreams of his chosen people, his priests? Or does he not care? Are all the promises of the cults so empty our God himself will not stir to warn us?"

Emin looked into the ageing warrior's eyes and saw the terrible strain Dev was under, and his heart softened at the sight. Here was a man struggling to hold his people together, alone, and no doubt challenged at every turn. The priests would prove little use, that powerful élite more of a hindrance than anything.

Have you prayed—is that the source of your anger? Does your God not answer you—now in your time of need, are you abandoned?

"The Gods do not fully comprehend the threat," Emin started to explain. "Right now they are at their weakest; they fear any confrontation where artefacts powerful enough to kill them are used."

"So you do claim you know more than our God." There was contempt in Dev's voice there, but it was weak; his heart was not in the scorn, Emin could see that. His political skill told him the Chetse leader was hoping for some way out, some ray of light, or sign from a power greater than himself.

"The Gods know," he said softly, "but it is in the hands of mortals now."

His words struck Dev like a punch to the gut. "What can mortals do where Gods dare not?" he said hoarsely.

"We—" For a moment Emin's words failed him, then he said, "We can match this threat. My allies are more than just Menin, and upon them I gamble the future of my nation. The future of the Land itself lies in our hands, and now we have the strength to win this war."

"The Devoted army is greater than yours," Dev warned. "They outnumber you comfortably."

"But they have only numbers on their side. We have Gods, and others besides. The Legion of the Damned march with the Menin; Karkarn's Iron General and Fate's Mortal-Aspect sit but a few yards from you, and then—and then there is another stronger than any of them.

"General Dev, I urge you: allow us passage, our Menin allies too. I have given them assurances; they have fought and died for my cause. I would make the Chetse Narkang's greatest allies in trade rather than make threats, but I cannot stand aside, and I cannot allow the enemy to escape."

The general's shoulders slumped. "My people will not accept it," he said, almost apologetic now. "Our honour demands blood."

King Emin turned again, this time seeking out two sets of eyes among the crowd. They were simple enough to pick out; even hunched over, Isak was far taller than those around him, while Legana's eyes shone in the shadow of her shawl. The white-eye slipped from his saddle and made his way forward, his cropped sleeves revealing the black and white skin of his arms.

The king's guards opened a path before them.

"General Dev," Isak said with a bob of the head, his Chetse rough, learned during his days on the wagon-train, "my name is Isak."

Already staring aghast at the mass of scars and unnatural lines visible on the white-eye's hands, face and neck, Dev staggered back a step when he heard Isak's name. His own men breathed curses or gasped in alarm, many making warding signs against daemons, but Isak did not react, not even when the boldest pulled their weapons. He stared into the old man's eyes, watching the shock play out.

"But you— It cannot—" Dev glanced back at his own men and realised some were on the point of attacking. With a feeble gesture he stopped them, wonder and horror blossoming all over again when he turned back to Isak. "How is this possible?"

"Not easily," King Emin suggested before Isak could reply, "but perhaps it goes some way to showing the power we possess?"

As he spoke Isak raised his right hand and a burst of black light exploded from it. General Dev and King Emin both recoiled from the sudden flare of darkness that had struck with painful speed; when they opened their eyes again Isak's fingers were wrapped around the grip of Termin Mystt. In the light of day its deep, unnatural blackness absorbed the sun's rays so completely it looked like a tear in the fabric of the Land.

"I hold Death's weapon in my hand," Isak announced to all those watching. "The Dark Place could not hold me; the Menin lord could not stop me. Do you want me as your enemy?"

"General Dev," Emin interjected hurriedly, "my army outnumbers any you could field, I am certain; we possess many Crystal Skulls and Death's own weapon. You must see reason."

"I've told you," Dev said with a helpless gesture, "my people have sworn blood oaths! The honour of the tribe demands blood be spilled, forcing trade agreements on us as alternative to unleashing Ghenna upon us does not satisfy honour."

—*You want blood?* Legana wrote on her slate in Chetse, holding it up for Emin and Dev to see while she spoke the words into Isak's mind.

"My people will *have* blood; they will fight the Menin, no matter what threats you make."

Legana looked from the general to King Emin and back. "*You men and your honour—look what it does to you,*" she said into the minds of Isak and Emin. She used her sleeve to erase the first message and quickly wrote a second.

—*A duel. Amber against a Chetse. You will have blood.*

"A duel of champions?" Emin echoed, thoughts racing. "A formal resolution to satisfy your honour? Even your more bloodthirsty warriors must realise the Chetse can ill-afford the huge loss and battle would mean, General Dev. This practice is ancient; the Gods themselves endorsed it before the Great War."

"This is some sort of trick," Dev muttered. "You planned all of this."

"I didn't," Isak said with a crooked grin. "I only planned threats."

"This is no trick, General Dev," Emin said, shooting Isak a warning look, "but it might serve your purposes. You do not want to fight, I assume? Might your people accept such a thing? The terms would be simple enough—if your champion wins, our Menin allies turn back and we go on without them. If their champion wins, we are all granted passage. The trade terms I'm prepared to offer would not be contingent on either outcome, but the formal contract would serve to satisfy the dignity of your tribe?

"The Chetse consider combat a noble trial, do you not? One that rests in the skill of the warriors and the will of their Gods? General Amber is a skilled fighter for certain, but he is no mage nor white-eye, just a veteran soldier. Surely you have a man to match him, so we can put it to the will of the Gods?"

General Dev was silent a long while, scrutinising the faces of all three but gleaning little from a Goddess, politician and mangled white-eye.

"Perhaps," he admitted at last. "I must speak to my people to see if they will honour any such outcome."

He bowed and turned away, walking back to his advisers with heavy footsteps. From somewhere high above came the mocking caw of a crow.

Amber marched out to the battle-ground as soon as dawn came. A circle was marked in the earth between the Narkang army and the far smaller Chetse force, twenty yards in diameter. Spears had been thrust into the ground at regular points around the furrowed circle and already there were soldiers standing at them, keen to get a good view of the duel to come.

"General Amber," King Emin called from his right.

The Menin soldier stopped and turned to face his ally. "King

Emin." He stood tall, not bowing—and realising he didn't even feel the urge to bow. *Strange. In— In my lord's presence I always felt unworthy, blessed to be there. Now I feel nothing. The whole sham of formalities sickens me.*

"Thank you for agreeing to this," the king continued. "This is not what I wanted, but I thank you for the risk you're taking for my cause."

"For your cause?" Amber said. "You think that's why I'm doing it?"

King Emin inclined his head. "I think you are serving your army and honouring the agreement we have made. Your motives are your own; my gratitude remains."

Amber looked up at the sky where thick bands of cloud reached up from the eastern horizon. "Hope it doesn't rain. I hate fighting in the wet."

"Kill 'im quickly then!" Daken suggested with a laugh, trotting over to join the two men. He had a mug of beer in his hand and offered it to Amber, who shook his head. "No? Might be your last chance—I hear they've got a big bastard for you!"

Amber looked at the Chetse soldiers. They were all broad men, with wild sandy-brown hair; their barrel chests and thick arms made it clear how easily they could swing the long-axes each man had on his back.

"Big, eh? Well that's not much of a surprise."

"Aye, could be right there. Either way, the odds on you were lengthening all bloody night."

"You're running a book?" King Emin demanded. "We're supposed to be maintaining the dignity of the situation—preserving the honour of the Chetse and the nobility of this ancient practice."

Daken grinned. "Never been one for honour, didn't you know? And this nobility thing's harder than I realised—you might have made me a marshal of some place I've not managed to visit yet, but nobility? That escapes me." He raised a finger. "Soldiers, though, I get them well enough. Gossipy, money-grabbing bastards, no matter what tribe they come from, and bugger me, do they like to gamble. So yeah, I've been running a book. I spent half the night in the Chetse camp, gauging their mood, finding out who their champion's likely to be . . . There's a whole mixed bag of feelings about this and our hero Amber here, but when you're offering brandy and good odds you get to make friends quick in an army camp."

"And what have you found out?" Amber asked.

"That he's a big bugger."

"That's all? It was my brandy you took there, wasn't it?"

The white-eye's grin widened. "Once I heard he was a big bugger, didn't seem like you'd need it."

"By which time you'd already stolen it."

"Aye well, I've got a nose for this sort of thing."

Amber shifted the baldric loosely slung over his shoulder so his scimitars were in a more comfortable position. "Did you find out anything else?"

"Aye. Them buggers like good odds. If you lose, I might need t' sell that marshalsy you gave me, your Majesty."

The king regarded Daken for a long moment. "Maybe I'll just let them cut bits off you instead for payment." He turned away from the white-eye and offered his hand to Amber. "I'll leave you now; I'm sure you want to prepare alone. If you need anything, let me know. Otherwise—good luck, General."

Amber took the man's hand stiffly, not trusting himself to speak, but the king just turned and moved towards Doranei and Endine.

"Any more words of advice?" he asked Daken as he watched the king walk away.

The white-eye shrugged. "Pointy end goes in the other bastard. Aside from that, wouldn't surprise me if the king had a trick up his sleeve, but don't count on it." He ushered Amber to the circle, where Carel joined them and gruffly wished him luck too. Trailing along behind were Amber's Menin guards, each of them looking about to explode as they matched glares with the Chetse, but it never went beyond that. General Dev had assured the king that his men were bound by the honour of the duel not to spill blood outside it, while Amber had threatened to execute every man in the squad of any Menin starting a fight.

Once inside the circle, Amber handed his weapons to Carel and rolled his shoulders in slow circles to loosen them up. Thanks to the efforts of Narkang's healers, his various injuries had all healed, but still he felt stiff and old—too old to be fighting this close to dawn, whether or not he'd managed much sleep.

"Reckon they've found a white-eye?" Carel asked, conversationally. "Can't have many to pick from, what with their best marching with your lot."

"I've fought white-eyes before," Amber said.

"If they do, likely you're in luck," Daken decided. "The best'll have been in the battle at Moorview and most likely killed. If they drag out any old white-eye he'll be quicker'n you, but still most likely dumber. All strength and no skill."

Amber glanced up at the empty sky again and made his way out into the centre. More soldiers had arrived at the circle now, both Narkang and Menin. A few of the younger recruits attempted a cheer as their army's champion reached the centre, but Amber scowled at them and the sound withered.

The recruits were part of the cavalry scout groups—most of the infantry were formed up in their companies, ready either to march or assault. For the main it was officers and élites here, those who weren't bound by orders from dawn to dusk. The Menin contingent was near-silent, far more typical of Menin soldiers than Amber's own quarrelsome Cheme legions had been.

"Thank you, Carel," Amber said, glancing back. His face was set like stone, the hard lines of a veteran soldier about to fight once more. "I'm glad you're here. There is a distance between my men and me; though they are loyal they fear me. Death omens follow me and my namesake's defeat lingers in my shadow. If I am to die, it will be in the company of a friend."

He turned to Daken, the white-eye's easy grin absent for now. "As for you—well, keep your bastard hands off my brandy."

Before either man could reply, the Chetse soldiers on the far side of the circle parted suddenly, allowing General Dev and a second man through into the circle. A murmur went up on all sides: there could be no doubt that this was Amber's opponent. Half a head taller than the general he accompanied, the soldier could have easily been mistaken for a wildman from the Waste, but for the fine detailing on his axe and pauldrons.

His long, tangled mass of sandy-brown hair was kept out of his pale blue eyes by red bands, until he put on a shallow bowl-helm. His clothes and mail shirt looked like they had been patched repeatedly; they were festooned with fetishes. From the man's dark skin Amber could see he was an easterner, probably from the desert clans on the edge of the Waste, where the Chetse fought a near-constant war against the Siblis who lived beneath the desert. Any veteran of those savage skirmishes would doubtless be a dangerous opponent.

"General Amber, Chosenslayer and last survivor of the Cheme legions, your opponent, Dechem of the Wyvern Clan, champion of the Agoste field." General Dev's voice was loud enough to drown out the whispers racing through the onlookers.

In response to Dechem's introduction the Chetse soldiers gave a single, sudden shout. Amber didn't catch the word, but it prompted Dechem to turn and salute those behind him with his long-axe. On his back Dechem wore an oval shield, but looking at the length of his axe, Amber guessed it would be staying there.

Just as Amber decided no man could use the weapon one-handed, Dechem turned around and did just that: he flourished the weapon, using long diagonal strokes, first in one hand, then the other, all performed adeptly before he saluted Amber. The Menin reached back with both hands and Carel put the hilts of his scimitars in them, allowing Amber to draw the weapons and bow in one movement. He rolled each wrist in turn, moving the brutal weapons through slow strokes to loosen his hands without showing Dechem how fast he could strike, and with that the others retired to the circle's edge.

Neither fighter moved. Though the duel had officially begun, Amber had been told it was Chetse custom to stand a while and size up an opponent. After titles had been announced, insults thrown or respect offered, all bluster was put aside and it was just two warriors ready to do battle.

Amber was significantly taller than his opponent, but the long-axe lent a greater reach and could both chop and hook. Dechem was a champion of the

Agoste field, the Chetse veterans' forum, but it was likely he'd never have faced twin swords like Amber's before, which gave the Menin an advantage. Temple training in the Menin homeland required them to face warriors carrying all weapons, and Amber had duelled against the long-axe many times before.

Dechem decided the moment had ended. He raised his axe and cautiously advanced, while Amber stood his ground, his swords held out before him. The Chetse made some exploratory passes, circling as he cut, poised to leap backwards should Amber try to rush him.

The Menin kept his own movement to a minimum, edging beyond Dechem's range when necessary, mostly just watching the axeman move. The strokes were superbly dextrous, neat and swift without unnecessary backswing.

At last Amber advanced, stepping forward and lashing up at Dechem's knuckles with his left scimitar. The right he readied to chop down with, but the Chetse twirled backwards with a grace that belied his bulk and swung around behind his body as he moved. Amber held back, realising in time he'd be caught in the leg before he could strike a blow of his own, then leaping forward in behind the stroke.

His first blade scraped harmlessly down the Chetse's shield; the second bit the rim and scored his chainmail. Dechem hammered at Amber's forearm with the butt of his axe then brought the head around to chop at his head. Amber caught the axe shaft on his scimitar and tried to push it down and away, but the Chetse wrenched his weapon back, quick as a snake, and struck high.

Amber twisted and dodged the cut, slashing up at the shaft. Dechem saw the danger and backed off, instinctively aiming another cut in his wake, but Amber held. When he advanced again he had one sword high, the other at chest height. Dechem responded by probing forward with the long-axe, twisting it one way then the next as he sought to snag something with the head's hook. He feinted at the lower weapon, then went left suddenly and flicked the axe down at Amber's knee, even as Amber slashed across his face. Neither weapon scored as Dechem's movement took him away.

Amber didn't wait this time, but struck down at the axe and followed it past his knee, all the while slashing at Dechem's head with his second sword. His scimitar was turned by the Chetse's helm and pauldron and he took a hurried blow on his shoulder as the powerful warrior heaved his axe back.

Dechem drove Amber a step to the side, but the Menin was able to hook the axe again and chop from left to right down into his opponent's forearm. The scimitar caught Dechem between wrist and elbow, tearing open the chainmail. A spray of blood leapt up and Dechem lost his grip on the long-axe and fell backwards. Amber was already moving in for the killing blow before he realised the fight was won: Dechem's arm was half-severed, the bone exposed, and blood spurted over his legs.

Amber stayed his thrust half a foot from the downed man's throat. "Yield!" he commanded. "Enough have died—yield!"

Dechem croaked something unintelligible, cradling his ruined arm without a thought to continuing the fight.

Amber looked up and scanned the watching soldiers. "Nai, get here!" He checked the main concentration of Chetse, but none were moving, not even as the former necromancer ran forward to the injured man. Amber discarded one weapon to make his point clear, but still none of them took a step to help.

Bastards probably think his life's mine to spend as I see fit. Great Gods and little fishes, I've had enough of honour. Any more and I'll choke.

Nai dropped to his knees at Dechem's side then slid one foot under the man's shoulder's to support him. Blood leaked everywhere, running through the soldier's fingers like it was being poured from a jug. Without speaking Nai jammed his fingers into the wound, and Dechem howled.

The Chetse would have punched Nai in the head had Amber not caught his arm, but just the attempt was enough to pale his face and after a moment of feeble struggle he submitted to Nai's ministrations. Amber, checking the wound, realised it was too grave to save the arm. He'd seen the results of enough cuts like that, even with a priest of Shotir to hand, and after a quick exploration Nai came to the same conclusion.

He wrapped his blood-slick hands around the cut and closed his eyes. A bright light emanated from between his fingers, flaring red, then fading to pink that burned to white. Dechem roared like a wounded lion and fought against at Amber's grip, but in the next moment he fell limp and the Menin general released him as the wound began to hiss and crackle. There was no smell of burnt flesh, but Amber backed away all the same. He'd seen enough of surgeon's work; magical or not it was still enough to turn a sane man's stomach.

"Happy now?" Amber muttered, looking from General Dev to King Emin. "Or would you've preferred I killed him?"

Of Isak Stormcaller there was no sign, but Amber couldn't tell whether that meant the scarred white-eye was just as sickened of honour, or that he didn't care about anything any more. Rumour said that General Lahk had been rejected by Nartis and had all emotion burned out of him. Certainly the man bore lightning scars down his neck, but Amber hadn't spoken to the man enough to be able to tell. With Isak . . . well, it was hard to tell there too. One moment he wasn't much different to any other young man, but it took only a heartbeat to switch to either traumatised recluse or blank, empty shell.

I guess the same could be said about me, though, Amber reflected as Carel approached him, his scabbards and baldrics in hand. They each cleaned and sheathed a scimitar in silence, the weapons sliding home with a whisper before Amber pulled the baldrics on and tightened the straps.

"Man was good," Carel muttered.

"Aye. Seems like a waste now, doesn't it?"

Carel caught Amber's arm. "It wasn't, and you've got my thanks. Without that duel we'd have had to threaten and probably fight our way through. I don't want Isak unleashing that sword's power any more'n he has to. Little bastard's never known when to stop."

"When to stop?" Amber said in a hollow voice, looking back at the man he'd spared. "Then let's hope he learns one day."

He raised his voice, turning to the handful of bearded Menin watching him intently. "What are you waiting for? Sound the advance!"

CHAPTER 36

GENERAL LAHK SLOWLY UNFASTENED the embossed buckles of his jacket and eased it off. The stink of rancid wool and unwashed skin filled the sleeping half of his tent, but he'd long since grown used to that. His linen undershirt was greasy to the touch and he pulled it up over his head and discarded it on the bed. Slumping down in his campaign chair, he began to unbuckle his greaves and unlace the high cavalry boots before wearily tugging them from his legs.

He sat for a moment with his feet on the edge of the bed, looking up at the peaked roof of the tent. It took him a while, but eventually the white-eye general heaved himself up again and stripped off his leggings so he was naked. It was chilly in there, but even the northern parts of the Chetse lands were far further south than back home, where snow would be coming soon—these plains and valleys had never been covered overnight by a white blanket. Outside was dusty scrubland dotted with patchy clumps of brown grass. What little rain fell vanished almost immediately into the parched ground.

Lahk ran his fingers over his body in his nightly inspection. Once he'd finished checking his body for the ticks and infections that plagued every soldier, he opened the small box beside his chair. Inside was a mirror, several rolled pieces of cloth and a clay pot. He raised the mirror briefly and stared at the face reflected in it: white eyes, weathered cheeks and uneven eyebrows; the lump of his nose and broad, muscular jawline common to his kind; the scar on his cheek that most white-eyes had in one form or another.

He picked up the candle illuminating the inside of the tent and brought it closer, staring into his own eyes, following the circle of his white irises and the small black dot at its heart.

Not so different to any other man's eye, Lahk thought to himself, *and yet it means so much.*

He touched the gold ring in his ear, an ornament he'd not cared for until recently. As a white-eye his skin healed quickly and earrings were an annoyance, but despite all that, Lahk had taken to wearing the single ring of rank normally left packed and forgotten in his belongings. It was a reminder of home, of the tribe he'd left behind—though most of those he knew and respected were with him now.

He unclipped the ring and set it on the table, wiping away the slight trace of blood on his earlobe. It would be half healed by the time he woke up, but this was as long as he'd ever been away from the tribe that was his entire life. Lord Bahl had not been one for conquest, and his faithful general had been kept largely within Farlan borders.

He'd been made a marshal for reasons of political etiquette as much as anything, and he felt little affection for the manor or the lands he owned. It was the grey streets of Tirah he missed, the cloud-wreathed spires and besieging forest beyond. He had his orders still, but the cause was a remote one for a man so used to the certainty and strength of Lord Bahl.

He picked up the mirror again and inspected the scars on his neck. The skin was red-raw where his cuirass, dented by a halberd a week back, was rubbing. He was loath to ask the smiths to beat it out again; that it rubbed against his tender scar tissue was not a good enough reason to distract them from their more vital work.

With the mirror he followed the line of jagged scars, running from his neck, branching around his shoulder, then spreading down over his chest and stomach in a long fern pattern. Another scar, two fingers thick, ran down his shoulder and back before it merged again with the other at his hip and ran down the buttock, with more strange fern-spreads, then tapering until it reached his calf, where it ended.

The scar was old, darker than his flesh, with whitened cracks crossing it where the skin was dry. It had been years since Nartis had so savagely rejected him as Lord Bahl's Krann, but he could still remember the white-hot pain, as if a strip of his skin had been ripped off his body and discarded. And then he'd smelled the burnt flesh . . .

With the patience of many years' practice, Lahk began to daub wool-grease onto the worst parts, centred on his neck and hip, moving in turn to the other scars on his body, feeling an echo of each one as he reached it: the chunk of flesh gouged from his thigh in the Great Forest beyond Lomin; the small scar on his bicep which was the only trace of an axe blow that had broken his arm and pained him to this day.

The litany of injuries continued: his cheek, pierced by the steel-shod butt of a spear that had broken two teeth. White-eye bones healed—some had been forcibly mended a dozen times or more—but teeth didn't grow back. Sword-cut to his forearm, here; a knife-wound up his ribs, there, that had notched two of them. The dark circle above his hip was an arrow-wound, innocuous in size, but it had caused terrible damage within and the healers had only just managed to save his life that time. His kneecap, spilt neatly across the middle; his ankle, shattered by a lance; another arrow-wound to his thigh . . . Even the fingers he was using to massage in the ointment had suffered. His little fingers had been broken four times between them—the one on the left hand had fared worst and now barely moved; nowadays it was usually splinted to its neighbour. Even his knuckles were scarred and ugly with use.

His kind didn't age as quickly as normal humans, yet as each day ended, General Lahk felt the years more heavily: the slow, stiff ache in his shoulders, the dull clunk from his shoulder socket whenever he drew his left arm right back, the gnarled and twisted toes, with every nail ridged and bruised.

Everything hurts, Lahk concluded, easing back into his chair and ignoring the cold that raised goose bumps on his flesh. *Am I lucky or foolish? I've served longer than almost any other—as long as Suzerain Torl, and I don't envy him his body. I've seen the discomfort, and even shitting pains him.*

The thought made Lahk look down at his crotch. *The one I always forget.*

He took a little more ointment and pushed his penis aside. Even that was scarred, the faint white line down its side marking where a sword had sliced, missing the groin artery, but tearing away one ball, leaving his sack looking even uglier than most: a small, misshapen lump half-covered in hair.

He stopped as the weight of damage drained the strength from him. He'd only once seen disgust on a whore's face, but the hurt of it remained with him still. The woman he kept in Tirah was cheerfully unbothered by any sort of disfigurement, but it was her presence in the dark of night that made him pay her house bills, not the sex.

Gods, he thought, *I've never even met a white-eye female—and my brother's been as useless as me when it comes to bringing new life into the Land.* "Are we only good for killing?" he said aloud, though the empty tent never gave him any answer.

My body's a record of service—sometimes I think it belongs to the army. Maybe one day Quartermaster-General Kervar will ask for it back. Would I complain? No other man can be this damaged. Each time they patch me up and send me back out, because I'm the fool who does not say no, who does not complain or argue. For thirty-five years I've been first to be tended by the healers. Any other soldier would have lost his arm or leg and been pensioned out—or be dead of his wounds, more likely—yet here I am, still fighting.

He sat back and reached into the box once again, this time withdrawing a cloth roll. Fumbling a little, he fitted a small porcelain pipe and ivory stem together, then withdrew a tiny black lump from a pouch, placed it in the bowl of the pipe and used the candle to heat it. Finally breathing in the thick smoke, Lahk closed his eyes and waited for the dull aches in his body to fade. He used the drug rarely, only when he knew the pain of old injuries would keep him from sleeping, but they had been riding hard for a week now, through these inhospitable Chetse lands, and his ankle and knee in particular pained him enough that his brother had not been the only one to notice. Others had asked, King Emin and Carel most pointedly.

Lahk bowed his head. *I am not my lord. I do not have his strength.*

Memories of Lord Bahl filled his mind. As Lahk had been the bedrock of the Ghosts, the unmovable heart of that entire legion, so Bahl had been for Lahk: his strength and power surpassed the general's understanding.

Had I known him, had I fought beside him before that day at the temple, I would have never offered myself so readily. He bore the weight of the nation on his shoulders; he suffered the whispers and lies while he served them all. Without him—without a ruler of his ilk—I am lost. Isak wears greatness like a mantle, but see how that incandescence has burned him. I follow him out of habit as much as loyalty. Truth and justice are just words to me. All I ask for is purpose.

The lingering note of pain in his limbs began to dim and his head fogged as the drug started to take effect. He spat on the ground, revolted by the bitter taste—in truth, everything about it revolted him, not least the days when he felt the need for it growing further apart from the catalogue of injuries, seen and unseen, he had accumulated.

He capped the pipe, dismantled it and put it away in the box before slipping his leggings back on again. His movements were slow and ponderous, but that was as he wanted: the smoke drove away the pain and the doubts and allowed a few hours of emptiness in his mind. The lumps were deliberately small, limited by the strength of will some saw as an iron soul. Some things were necessary and therefore they were done. He could make no sense of how others could lie and betray themselves out of doing what they needed to.

The chill in the room was gone now. As he went about the motions of stowing his armour and boots, unable to let himself sleep while it lay in disorder, he muttered the words of prayer he'd been taught so long ago. He couldn't pray to Nartis, not since that day he was so gravely scarred, but the words of reverence his father had taught him returned without effort. As a boy, Tiniq had always scowled as he mumbled them at their bedside, trusting in his brother's strong voice to hide his own reluctance. Now Lahk always pictured Lord Bahl as he spoke the words taught to all Farlan under his breath:

"Give me strength, lord, for all I must do. Give me strength, lord, for the fear I must face. Give me strength, lord—"

He broke off, suddenly aware there was someone else in the tent. His battle-instincts had been dulled, but even as he realised they were there, he felt no panic. It was simply awareness, not fear. The long-knife entered his back cleanly: a quick, professional strike that pierced his great heart and sent the general rigid. He tried to turn, but the person had a firm grip on his arm. As Lahk moved, the knife twisted in the wound and the sharp blossom of agony spread around his ribcage, flowering hot over his skin though the blade was as cold as ice.

He felt his heart stutter, then a flicker of fear as he realised he was dead, but that faded almost immediately. Lahk remained standing even as the knife was removed and driven in again. The first blow had killed him; Lahk knew that with utter certainty, and his life's blood spilled from his back, but he had seen too much death to fear it now. Battle had been his life, not his pleasure; he had no dreams of glory to follow, no heroic death to seek. He was beyond pain.

Lahk stared at the faded tent cloth, and at last his immovability ended. His killer eased him forward, just a step, to reach the bed and then down he went—sprawled across it, his face perched on the edge looking at the tent wall just a foot away. The light dimmed, the tent grew dark around him and Lahk found himself sinking into darkness. But the darkness was not empty, he felt power there—strength beyond mortal bounds. Something waited patiently for him, and Lahk would face it without regrets.

I come, my lord. I come to serve you once more.

"Give me strength, lord," his killer finished, "for the man I must be." He withdrew the knife and wiped it on the bed. Once the weapon was sheathed he stood for a while looking down at the body.

"I'm sorry. You deserved better," the killer whispered.

He collected the Crystal Skull from Lahk's armour and held it up to the weak light for a moment. The shadows in the room swarmed and danced around him, swirling up to meet him even before the killer bent to blow out the candle. Then he left, wreathed in shadow, as unseen by the guards as when he had entered.

Isak sat, unmoving, as Suzerain Torl spilled the news, tears shining wetly in the ageing warrior's eyes, his grey and lined face crumpled by grief.

"Dead?" he asked dumbly.

"Found by his guards this morning," Torl choked. "Stabbed in the night, his Crystal Skull taken."

"How?"

"They claim they don't know. They swear no one entered or left all night." Torl's face hardened. "Shinir will find the truth of it, but I've known Lahk's hurscals for years . . ." His voice tailed off. He looked shaken to his core. Even after all the death and battle he had seen, for his implacable friend to be murdered without putting up a fight tore at the man's heart.

"It must be done—it's better Shinir questions them than Tiniq getting his hands on them. Speaking of Tiniq, has he been told?"

A strangled howl answered his question, and Isak rose and saw the hooded figure of Tiniq, staggering down the pathway between the Palace Guard's tents. He had a messenger by the throat and was dragging the man in his wake, apparently unaware he still had the man in his grip.

"Tiniq!" Isak shouted, and the ranger stopped dead, hesitating for a moment before swinging around to face his lord. Isak and Torl headed out past their guards to meet him. The man's eyes were red-rimmed with grief.

"Let him go, Tiniq," Torl ordered. "He's not the one to blame."

The ranger looked down to find the young messenger in his hand still. The man hung from Tiniq's grip, his knees dragging on the ground, both hands wrapped fruitlessly around the man's fist. With an effort, the shaking ranger released him and the messenger flopped onto his back, gasping for air.

"Go with him, Torl," Isak said. "Lahk was your friend; you should help prepare his body."

"Prepare his body?" Tiniq echoed hoarsely.

"Funeral rites—he was our greatest general, and we will honour him as such."

Tiniq shook his head. "We wrap the body and bring him with us."

"Bring him?" Suzerain Torl said, horrified. "Damn it, man, he was your brother!"

Tiniq advanced on the suzerain, for a moment looking like he was going to attack him, then he started fighting for control. "He was my brother, yes," he said, "and we *will* honour him—he wouldn't care about a eulogy or memorial. We honour him by following the example he set." He looked around wildly at the soldiers drawing closer, hearing the whispers already running through the crowds. "You hear me?" he shouted, "you want to honour my brother, you'll bloody march for him! You think he'd want to lose hours of daylight when there's an enemy to catch? You think he'll give a shit about pretty words being spoken over him? There's the job at hand, nothing more, and your job is to catch and kill the enemy. If you want to honour him, you'll give him fifty miles this day to make up the ground we've lost!"

He voice wavered. With one final glare at Torl and Isak, Tiniq started off again towards his brother's command tent.

"You heard him," Isak said quietly. "We march for General Lahk; we'll honour him tonight. Go and make sure he doesn't kill anyone, Torl. I'll get them ready to march; no man'll need telling twice today."

"The final test?" Ilumene asked, hurrying forward.

Ruhen turned and smiled. "The final test," the child in white confirmed as Ilumene joined him. He still towered over the boy, though Ruhen was taller than natural for his years. His composed stillness or smooth, restrained purpose set him apart from normal children—that and the shadows in his remaining eye.

"It all went as you intended?"

"All involved passed the test," Ruhen replied, "and that is all I ever plan for."

Ilumene nodded in approval. "At least some things about that damn white-eye are predictable."

"You think him incapable of restraining himself?"

"All the time? No, but you catch that boy off-guard and his first reaction'll be to call the storm inside. Don't give a man time to think and he'll act on instinct—that's when you know his true heart, and it tells you he doesn't suspect our agent."

Ruhen pursed his lips. "Let us not make too many assumptions; they have surprised us in the past."

"Aye, well, they're running out of cards to play. Once our agent performs his task, they'll be left reeling and unable to stop us."

"And then the game will be ours," Ruhen finished, savouring the words on his tongue with the ghost of a smile. "But until then, it remains at risk."

It was morning and the Devoted army was ready to march again. Seeded through their ranks were ragged figures in greys and whites, the wild-eyed, exhausted and half-starved preachers and followers who called themselves Ruhen's Children. Some knelt and muttered prayers, watched by Chetse farmhands and villagers. They all faced Ruhen as they droned devotionals of Venn's and Luerce's devising, or keened wordlessly, arms linked with their fellow devout, or gripping the shoulders of the person in front.

"It is a lesson for us both," Ruhen said after a while, gesturing to the masses around them.

"In what?"

"In the unexpected. Look at these soldiers, professional, obedient, but unremarkable in many ways. They have no proud pedigree, no great nation to inspire their pride, nothing more than a basic level of devotion and the regimen of training."

Ilumene followed Ruhen's gaze. "Unexpected, aye," he commented as he watched the white-clad worshippers slowly clump together.

They had no tents or supplies with them—they were beggars, the mad and the lost, who either had nothing, or had not understood what they might need on their journey. All the way through the central states they had been in lands sworn to Ruhen and the Knights of the Temples, and the local preachers at every village and town had provided basic provisions. The followers who had accompanied them from the Circle City hadn't fallen away as some had expected; instead, they had swelled in number, and for every one who found the going too hard, or who fell to sickness, a dozen more joined the cause, driven by a consuming zeal.

Advance scouts had negotiated supplies for the army once they'd entered Chetse lands, but the haphazard organisation of Ruhen's Children fell away. Ilumene had predicted a vicious but necessary culling as only the strongest among them survived, but something entirely different had happened, and now the man and boy watched in silent wonder as men, women and children crawled from the tents of the Devoted, ready to resume their march.

Without orders, the men of the army had taken them in, sheltering and feeding them without complaint. There was enough to go around, they estimated, but it was the care and effort expended that surprised all who saw it.

"I underestimated them," Ruhen said. "I had not thought soldiers would embrace my message too."

Ilumene laughed softly. "They didn't, not really," he said when Ruhen turned enquiringly towards him. "It's not that you underestimated them, you just don't know 'em."

"I have watched humans for long enough, I think," Ruhen replied coldly.

"Watched, yes, but you ain't one." Ilumene prodded the boy on his thin shoulder, ignoring the dark look he received.

"This bag o' bones you're wearing," Ilumene said, grinning, "this doesn't tell you what it's like to be human. Those scar-hearted troops of the Devoted haven't embraced your message, not so much as you think. They're simple men; all soldiers are when they're on the march. The Devoted's weakness has always been its disparate roots: competing cultures and peoples, all wearing the Runesword. It's always much harder to get strangers to fight side-by-side for a cause that matters to neither. This army doesn't understand its purpose here, so it's made one up."

"They embrace the spirit of the message without paying attention to the words?" Ruhen said hesitantly.

Ilumene nodded. "This ain't devotion or fanaticism, it's humanity, grubby and uneasy maybe, but it's naked humanity for all the Land to see. They see the weak and broken and they care for 'em. They see others driven by devotion and they honour them. They hear talk about protecting the innocent—and sure, it seeps into some, but it's really two more basic instincts converging. Soldiers are always looking for a cause. It takes a heartless man to watch some poor fool to die at the side of the road."

"They have made frailty their banner," Ruhen mused. "That it matches my message of innocence is mere confirmation in their hearts, a justification for what they all feel is right."

"And now we've got an army," Ilumene added. "Your followers are the common thread for all these troops, some of whom faced each other on the battlefield last year. They're bound together now, and they'll fight together because they're all fighting for the same thing. The Knight-Cardinal knows he's just a figurehead; his soul's bound to you and that's shackled him as surely as a pet dog. Soon the rest'll realise just how empty their authority is too, and on that day, any of 'em with a backbone left will most likely be cut down by his own men." He shrugged. "If not, I'll do it myself."

CHAPTER 37

UNDER AN EVENING MOON the men of the Ghosts assembled around a small rise, on top of which stood a broken standing stone which had been struck by a lightning bolt and split open to reveal a white fissure down its centre, following the path of the strike. Vesna had deemed this small shrine to Nartis an appropriate place for the general's funeral.

The Ghosts formed up around the hillock in division blocks, five hundred men apiece, standing silently, even as the sun went down and a cold wind picked up. The officers prayed around the stone as the body was prepared. Isak stood back, leaving the preparation to those who wore the black and white.

Tiniq stood alongside him, his hood low over his face, and he said nothing as they watched the ceremonies. Legion Chaplain Cerrat, the young man appointed in Lord Bahl's last degree, led the observances with Suzerains Torl and Saroc at his side, while Vesna, Swordmaster Pettir and Sir Cerse, Colonel of the Palace Guard, knelt opposite them. Stretched out on the flat strip of grass before the shrine-stone was the linen-wrapped body of General Lahk. Only the face was visible. His eyes were closed and his skin drained of colour. His hands had been set around the longsword he'd carried for years, its plain pommel and notched blade catching the last of the daylight. Once they had cremated his body, the fire-scorched sword would be thrown into the first lake they could find. Farlan legend said that a warrior's weapon would follow its master into the afterlife, to be in his hand on the slopes of Ghain.

Carel appeared at Isak's side, wearing a Palace Guard tabard. His expression was grim.

The sight sent a cold shiver down Isak's spine for a reason he couldn't quite place. "I forgot you'd said were in the Ghosts," he said softly. "Uniform suits you, old man."

Carel turned and looked Isak up and down. The white-eye had no such thing to wear; even the dragon-emblazoned uniform of personal guards was lost to him.

Carel shifted uncomfortably. "Can't say I ever thought I'd wear it again, not until the day I was the one wrapped up in linen."

"You kept it for your own funeral?"

Carel frowned at him. "Gods, makes my head hurt to think you've forgotten that! Can't remember the times you asked me to show it to you—the uniform you'd one day serve in, and most likely die in, being a white-eye. I looked damn good—the ladies of Tirah appreciated it, I can tell you."

"But I never did," Isak said, a little uncertainly.

"No," Carel confirmed, "the Gods had a different plan for you. You got your own uniform."

Isak nodded and returned his attention to the shrine ahead. "We'll gather his ashes and take them home?"

"It's what he'd have wanted," Tiniq broke in from Isak's other side. "Eternity with his comrades was always his wish. Me, I'd want to be set free on the winds, but we always were different."

Carel grunted in response. "Not sure I give a damn," he said eventually. "As long as a cup's raised in my memory, I'll be happy. Don't reckon I'll be there to care, after all, but I'd like to be remembered well. Isak?"

The white-eye flinched. "Just as long as it's not like last time," he said in a small voice.

"Aye," Carel said, putting a hand on Isak's arm. "Sorry, lad, didn't think there."

Isak lifted his hands up so his long sleeves fell back and revealed the bent and scarred fingers. "The memory's always there, whether you bring it up or not. As for what happens after, I don't care—it's the *way* I die that interests me."

"Sounds like you've got a plan," Carel said suspiciously.

"More peaceful than last time, that's all I'm asking. General Daken's taken his cavalry on ahead. He's forced a few skirmishes with their rearguard, but that's all; their pace is fast enough that we can't catch them, and the bastards aren't interested in fighting."

"Your point?"

"That this is building to one last battle. Daken's snarling like a frustrated dog, so I hear." He flexed the black fingers of his right hand. "When they get to where they're going, they'll give us the battle we want and not before. We're not far off matched, so how far I'm prepared to go might swing it for us."

"You're going to sacrifice yourself?" Carel said in horror. "You can't!"

Isak pursed his uneven lips. "I'm not saying that, just that it might get desperate. I don't know what I'd do—I don't know what I'm *able* to do, but there's more power in this sword than in any Crystal Skull. If I use it to win a battle, I doubt there'll even be anything left to cremate." He sniffed. "I never much liked prayers or temple anyway, so maybe it's fitting I dodge one last boring service."

Out of the corner of his eye he saw the glint of a tear in the veteran's eyes. "What is it?"

Carel shook his head, but Isak persisted. If it hadn't been for the solemnity of the occasion, he realised Carel might have even shouted at him, but as it was he saw a shocking and profound sadness in the man's face.

"You don't get it, do you?" Carel croaked at last, tears spilling down his cheek. "You have the power to change the Land around, the strength to command the Gods, and yet you never really understood people half the time, did you?" He was quiet for a dozen heartbeats as he studied Isak's brutalised face. Eventually he sighed, looking deflated in his borrowed tabard.

"Funerals aren't for the one who've died," he started, "they're for the rest of us, to remember. Gods, boy, I stood in the Temple of Nartis at *your* funeral, then just a few weeks later I was standing there again, mourning Tila—but it wasn't just her memory in my mind that day. I loved that girl, but you were the son I never had. I stood there all alone; I couldn't leave, not even after the High Cardinal had finished the rituals. It felt like my damn heart was ripping open, the pain worse than when I lost my bloody arm." He looked at Legion Chaplain Cerrat, standing at the head of the body, his white robes billowing in the cold evening wind, then at the man kneeling next to him.

"Look at Vesna," he hissed, jabbing a finger towards the man, clad in his famous black and gold armour. "Lahk was a friend of his, a man he served with for more'n a decade. Look at him."

Isak did so, and realised that the hero of the Farlan was weeping, his hands shaking as his tears flowed over them. His head was bowed, as if he couldn't lift it for the weight of grief. His normally pristine black hair fell in disarray about his face and though he was not making a sound, every Ghost was aware of his grief. Swordmaster Pettir put his hand on Vesna's shoulder as Chaplain Cerrat continued, but the gesture seemed to increase the burden Vesna felt, and he bowed lower under its weight.

"He's grieving Tila as well," Isak said when he found the strength to speak again.

"Pain like that doesn't just go away," Carel said in a small voice, "not when it cuts to the heart of you. It's grief for you too," he added after a moment.

"Me?"

"The Gods only know why, but you do have friends, Isak. Your death hit more'n me hard, and we had long enough thinking of you as dead to let the pain go in deep. That you were—all that you had to—" He gestured helplessly at the scars on Isak's hands and neck.

"Your worst fears were confirmed?"

"Gods, boy, you're really no good at this, are you?" Carel said, wiping his sleeve over his face. The tears still flowed, but he ignored them. "It's hard enough to lose a friend; near breaks a man to lose one he loved. The guilt and shame we feel at letting you do what you did, end up where you did—that opens up another tear in an already broken heart."

"And if we leave the best of us in our wake," Tiniq added in a choked voice, "what then for the Land we march on into?"

At the shrine, Vesna stood to face the crowds. It took him a while to find the words, but once he started they tumbled out with ease: the battles Lahk had won, the defeats he had salvaged, the unswerving devotion to their tribe's cause—and the legion surrounding him now.

Before he had even finished recounting the most notable of General Lahk's deeds, a low murmur arose from the ranks all around him: the battle hymn of the Ghosts, three lines, repeated again and again, while Vesna spoke his last and set the fires burning. The song rose with each heaving breath of the Farlan's finest as they honoured the best of them, and it continued as the flames rose higher and the officers retreated away from the burning body, until it was echoing around like a storm, rumbling through the hills where they stood and crashing out across the Land for allies and enemies alike to hear.

And still the tears flowed, but pride shone in every face.

King Emin turned in his saddle and surveyed the mud-stained ranks trudging along in weary, sour silence. The rain had been falling for a week, a near-constant drizzle that never quite cleared up but never grew strong enough to rain itself out. The rivers they forded grew steadily deeper and swifter, leaving the troops soaked from head to foot.

The undulating, fertile foothills around Thotel had gradually levelled off as they marched beyond the Chetse's capital city and further into the break in the mountains that led to the unknown reaches of the Waste. Now they were on vast open plains with barely a handful of trees visible. Away from the rivers, the ground was brown, covered in scrub, few crops able to survive in the open, exposed earth.

This countryside was the province of sheep and goat-herders. There were a few communities, clustered around the rivers, while the bulk of the population were closer to the mountains, north and south of the army's path, affording them a clear route. The few Chetse warbands that shadowed them kept their distance—the Menin troops were sandwiched by a legion of light cavalry, more than enough to stop any hotheads who might have disagreed with the honour settlement.

"They're quiet again, Doranei," King Emin commented.

"It's a strange march we're on," Doranei replied, his eyes on the road. "They've all got things on their mind, and no outlet."

The coldness between Emin and his King's Man was visible to the whole army, but neither let it interfere with the task at hand and the army's officers and men of the Brotherhood steered well clear of mentioning it. Forrow kept a suspicious eye on his Brother—his job was to mistrust all of them—but they all knew neither was to blame.

"I'd expected Ruhen to leave a force in his wake by now, to sacrifice some troops in order to slow us down, but aside from a few raids, there's been nothing; they're all marching with him. Why?"

"Azaer doesn't have much interest in battle, so might not have thought so hard about tactics."

"But Ilumene?"

Doranei shrugged. "The man's no general, whatever he thinks. He might have more of an instinct for battle than Azaer, but Ilumene's never led an army. I can't say for certain if I'd want to lose a third of my forces—and my numerical advantage—in an attempt to gain a few days' breathing space. Those Devoted generals will have realised they're not in command now, so they won't be keen to volunteer their experience, not when it's likely to get them sacrificed."

"Or perhaps they have a vested interest in keeping us close? How many Skulls do they have? Five, at least one of which could still be hidden in some soldier's pack in our own ranks."

"Want to order another surprise search?"

Emin shook his head. "No, it'll be well hidden, I'm sure. Magic had to have been used to gain entry to the general's tent, and we don't have enough mages to search so many thousands. And anyway, I don't trust all the mages."

Doranei looked over at the collection of juddering carriages and brightly caparisoned horses at the heart of the army. Magic was their one major advantage over the Devoted, so King Emin had gathered as many battle-mages as he could bully into service. They might not be able to match Tomal Endine for power or skill, or even Fei Ebarn, but more than a dozen extra magic-users would add bite to any assault.

"Me neither," Doranei said eventually. "Bunch o' whining children, the lot of 'em. It's amazing how many different delays they found that prevented them reaching Moorview in time. Most of them'll just shit themselves when the battle starts."

"Your Majesty!" a small man perched on a powerful horse called, and with some difficulty, High Mage Endine negotiated his way past a regiment of infantry in Canar Fell colours to reach the two men.

"Endine, you're well? Not too drained?" King Emin enquired. "I know you've taken on the bulk of the scrying and warding each evening."

"Pah! Most of those fools can't be trusted with it," Endine huffed, almost overbalancing in his saddle as he cast a dismissive look over his shoulder.

"Gods, man, you're still crap on a horse, even after all these weeks," Doranei exclaimed.

"I have had little practice," Endine replied tartly. "I've spent half the days sleeping in the carriage, but those bickering idiots who flatter themselves my peers have driven me to refresh my riding skills again."

"It's good to see you getting some exercise," the king said with a small smile. "It lifts the spirits of the whole army. We do need you rested, however, and preferably not catching a chill in this damn rain."

Endine scowled. "Your Majesty, you'll not get rid of me quite so easily, I'm afraid."

"My dear—"

"Emin," the mage broke in sharply, "you are my friend as well as my king, and I've known you long enough to know when you're being politely evasive. You've been avoiding me for weeks now, and we both know why."

The king took a breath, about to retort just as sharply, but instead he sighed. "Doranei, would you mind?" he asked.

The King's Man saluted and rode away to a suitable distance, giving the two some privacy but remaining close at hand.

"Endine, my friend," Emin began, suddenly at a loss for what to say. Even as he faltered he realised that was sufficiently telling already, if the mage hadn't already worked out what was wrong.

"Were you not going to bother to say goodbye?" Endine asked quietly. "We've been friends for more than ten years—I've known you since you founded that damn club of academics. You were the one who paired my skills with Cetarn, for pity's sake!"

"And as such," Emin replied slowly, "I don't want to acknowledge the end of what I built there."

"I'm not your pet, your Majesty."

"I know that—but I am your king, and you are my subject, and I am responsible for my subjects. If I must ask them to do something foolish and dangerous, the responsibility remains mine."

"All the more reason why you should spend some time with your friend," Endine said, "remembering better times, before he volunteers to do something stupid."

"You will not volunteer, my friend."

"No?" Endine sat tall in the saddle. The thin, sickly man was shorter than his king, but with a Crystal Skull in his possession he had a grander presence these days. "King you may be, my friend, but some things you cannot dictate!"

"No, that wasn't what I meant," Emin said, trying to placate him. "I won't have any man volunteer for something I know must be done. I am the king. I know why you would do so, but I will not allow you to absolve me from responsibility. My duty to my subjects is this—that I must look them in the face and *ask* them. Cetarn's sacrifice at Moorview—he realised it just as I did, and Legana with me, but I asked him all the same. I would not have the burden of cowardice added to my guilt."

Emin lowered his head. The recent years had taken their toll: there was more than a little grey in hair that looked thin and wispy under his rain-sodden hat. His cheeks were gaunt and greying. Though the king had never been a large man, there was less fat on his body than ever before. Though he might be strong for his age still, worry had slowly eroded what bulk he had possessed.

"There is a war to win, your Majesty. You cannot distract yourself with feelings of guilt."

"And yet I do," Emin said sadly. "I have lost many friends, and I will lose many more in the weeks to come. I know I must ask you to push yourself far beyond a sensible limit, that Ebarn and Wentersorn stand almost no chance of surviving what I must ask of them, and so I am reluctant to ask—"

"Then don't!" Endine cried. "Make that one fewer burden to carry. We're not the only ones who'll go to our deaths when it comes to battle—far from it. Wentersorn's a mercenary—you recruited him just for the attack on the Ruby Tower and he's had plenty of opportunities to escape if he wanted.

"These soldiers here—they're the ones who must fear, they're the ones in the jaws of uncertainty. We mages, we have a single, noble purpose that we embraced a long time ago."

"One fewer burden?" Emin managed a smile. "The fate of the entire Land rests on our shoulders. The blood spilled in the Waste will be the ink used to write the future of all peoples."

He broke off and watched the ordered lines of Legana's Sisters as they followed close behind the mages. There were more than a hundred of them now, a dozen priestesses with at least a regiment of spear-wielding former acolytes. Legana had named them the Sisters of Dusk, though she declined to explain why, even to those few brave enough to ask Fate's Mortal-Aspect directly.

The women wore leather armour reinforced with steel bands and, perhaps in echo of their leader, each carried a pair of long-knives on her belt. Legana was at the heart of them, a thin shawl hiding her face. Though she limped, as always, the pace of the group never faltered. As evening fell, she would walk through the camp, her face uncovered and her green eyes shining bright. She looked taller in the ghost-hour, edged in light as the shadows lengthened, while her bodyguards, blessed and augmented by the touch of the divine, faded into the background as they pulled off their boots to reveal Mihn's owl tattoos.

Emin could feel her green eyes on him now, and thought he saw Legana's head dip in greeting. Her knives were hidden by the folds of her cloak, but everyone in the army knew they would be there when she needed them. There were rumours in the camp that she could call them to her hand, the same way Isak could produce Termin Mystt in an instant, but Emin knew it was just the speed of a skilled woman enhanced by her divine blood.

"There are too many I've failed to spend the time I should with, these past few weeks," he said at last. "Too many I may not see again."

As one the Sisters turned to face them, a hundred faces looking their way, making Endine flinch. Emin smiled, knowing that was Legana, talking into the minds of her followers. The Mortal-Aspect had been Emin's closest advisor leading up to the battle of Moorview, becoming friends as she'd helped him to plan a war that involved Gods, magic and belief. That disconcerting, otherworldly reaction had been a private joke between the two of them—a salute from a friend.

"Legana? I think she'll be the last of us to fall," Endine grumbled, "her and Daken, soaked in blood and standing back to back most likely."

"You may be right there." Emin squinted up at the angry grey sky, ignoring the rain falling onto his face. There were birds circling high above, despite the poor weather. "Let us hope they won't be the only ones left."

Chapter 38

Light snow fell unnoticed as Morghien stood at the hill's peak. His attention was focused solely on the plain, a featureless expanse scoured by centuries of storms. In the distance a fat column of soldiers advanced towards them, a creeping stain of shadow over the grey earth. They were miles off yet, their scouts not yet in threatening range, but fear still fluttered in Morghien's stomach.

"So many years ago," Morghien mused, breaking the tense hush, "all these years, and what have I learned?"

"Learned?" asked Shanas, the tattooed young woman at his side. "Old man, don't start on that rubbish—you can go senile and catch up with your true age later. For the next few weeks I need you sharp."

"*Need* me?" Morghien echoed. "I'm not sure what good I'll be doing here. I'm not a soldier; I'm nothing to what's coming."

Shanas flashed a smile. "Maybe not, but until we meet up with the army your spirits and magic'll keep us safe at night. I'm buggered if I'm witnessing all this only to get eaten by some bastard daemon in the night."

Morghien turned to look at the attractive young woman. She had changed in the few months he'd known her, hardened from a meek, wary girl into a more elegant version of Ardela. He didn't much approve of that, knowing Ardela's dark history, but when he reflected on it, it was more sadness that he felt. She was better educated than either Legana or Ardela, and capable of far more gentleness. In another age, Morghien thought, she would have been a truly great Temple Mistress, tempering their youth and guiding her order wisely. Instead, she had developed hard edges and a brittle strength, and reminded Morghien more and more of Doranei, a good man damaged by brutal times.

"As you wish," he said eventually. "Just promise me you'll see the other side of it. Witnessing such things loses its shine, I find. Remember to enjoy the life that comes after it too."

"Aye, sure, whatever you say, old man." She frowned at him. "You realise you ask for a lot of promises when you're maudlin?"

"I do?"

"You've twice asked me never to start drinking—what's that all about?"

He lowered his eyes. "It's the easiest way to ruin a fine future," he muttered, thinking again of Doranei.

"Let's make sure we have a future first, eh?"

Morghien returned his attention to the army in the distance. "I dreamed last night of just that."

"Our future? Settle down, grandfather!"

"No," he said, "that we didn't have a future."

"Sounds like you're in need of a drink, then."

"Aye, mebbe I am. I found myself in Death's throne room: I was dead and awaiting the Last Judgement."

"Old Bones was a bit annoyed with you then?" Shanas laughed, elbowing him. "I could've told you threatening the Chief of the Gods was a bloody stupid thing to do."

"If only that was the problem," Morghien said, shivering slightly at the memory. "Problem was, it wasn't Lord Death on the throne, it was a shadow—Azaer, wearing a crown of gold and carrying Death's sceptre."

"Bloody hell," Shanas exclaimed, all trace of humour gone. "No wonder you're looking like someone walked over your grave today. So what happened?"

"I don't really remember—we spoke, Azaer said something, then I was dragged away in chains towards a great fire. That's when the morning sun woke me."

"Good thing too. That's not a dream you want to finish."

"But ever since, I've not felt like I'm truly awake," Morghien said. "All this day, ever since we sighted Keriabral, it's felt like I'm trapped in a dream of my past."

Shanas turned to face east, away from the army. There in the distance, just a vague shape on the horizon, was Castle Keriabral, the ancient ruins of Aryn Bwr's own fortress. The Last King had built the fortress within a huge crater several miles across, using the near-sheer outer slopes as part of the defences. The castle stood on the highest part of the plain, and the land around it was desolate, except for a shadowed area to the south, where there was an oasis.

"And that's where your bad dreams came from," Shanas breathed.

Morghien turned to look. "A hundred years on, near enough, and that's where I find myself in my nightmares. We had a division of Knights of the Temples to escort us—more'n enough, given the locals are malnourished savages."

"We?"

"Mages and historians for the main. I'd become an apprentice of sorts to a brilliant old man by the name of Cheliss Malich. His son, Cordein, wasn't so impressed with my presence, but anyone who knows their Farlan history shouldn't be so surprised by that."

"Cordein Malich, aye," Shanas said. "And three of you survived: you, Malich and the minstrel Rojak too—"

Morghien scowled. "Malich and I survived. Azaer brought madness down upon us, infecting one man as he was digging up artefacts on the inner slopes, then slowly moving through us all. The shadow was interested in Malich and me and it spared us because of his talent and my unusual nature. And merciful Gods, that boy was talented—arrogant and spiteful at times, at others brilliant and noble.

"The crazed ones turned on me when I refused Azaer, trailed me for miles once I escaped that place. But Rojak? I'm not sure I'd say he survived it, it was just that his body kept on going. He'd been a sweet lad. He wrote some fine songs about the castle our first week there. I don't honestly know what happened to him; I only remember him gorging on the wild peaches that grew in the oasis—fruit the locals wouldn't touch."

"And now you're back."

Morghien nodded slowly. "I'm the only one left from that folly," he drawled, "but I can't say I'm much interested in returning."

"You expect me to come all this way and not see bloody Castle Keriabral?" Shanas demanded.

"Save it for later," Morghien said soberly. "The damn thing's been there for seven thousand years. What's left is impressive, but it ain't likely to change. The remaining towers are a sight, that's for sure, and so's the Glass Bridge and the tiered gardens, even run wild. Ever heard of a water-falcon?"

Shanas shook her head, pushing back an errant trail of copper hair.

"Most people think it's a myth, as rare as a phoenix and harder to spot. That's worth seeking out; you won't find many more beautiful sights than that. But after last time I ain't going without a high mage in tow, not until the shadow's dead. Don't reckon you should either, fancy tattoos or no."

The wind suddenly raced down over them, howling mournfully as it swept icy fingers across their faces. Tiny snowflakes danced before Morghien's eyes as his fur-lined hood whipped forward and long straggly hair fell across his eyes. The wanderer cursed and pushed the hood back again, though he didn't mind the cold, instead recalling the searing sun of high summer.

"We're not going to Keriabral?" Shanas asked, shivering slightly. "You said that was where we were headed."

"The vicinity," Morghien clarified. "I don't think Ruhen's heading there either. Some stories say Aryn Bwr forged the Crystal Skulls in his great forge at Keriabral, where its fires were fed by the River Maram itself, but I reckon that's so much horseshit. Who'd live in a castle where a Devil's Stair was open—whether or not daemons could get through, it wouldn't be much fun to live anywhere near that. No, there's nothing in Keriabral or even the crater that Ruhen wants. He's got somewhere else in mind."

"Planning on playing the mysterious old bastard any longer?" Shanas asked impatiently.

At last a small smile crept onto Morghien's face. "All the days I got left. There's only one other thing around here, and it's the reason Aryn Bwr built his fortress here, in a place that was never populous, nor of any strategic value during the Wars of the Houses."

"Well, what is it—where do we find it?"

Morghien scratched his cheek, found a louse in his lengthening beard and crushed it between his fingers. "What is it?" he echoed, "I don't rightly know. Best you ask Legana about that. As for how we find it? We don't, not us feeble mortals, anyway. It's the heart of the Land, so Mage Verliq wrote, but it ain't for the likes of us. Azaer knows it though; the shadow led Aryn Bwr there in the first place, and where an army of seventy-odd thousand men, women and children marches, I reckon we'll be able to follow."

He kicked at a rock and headed back down the slope to where their small troupe was waiting. Their numbers were much reduced after travelling through this unknown, dangerous wilderness. Just before he reached his horse, Morghien looked up again at the faint lump of Keriabral's crater walls and the blur that would resolve into three enormous towers as they neared. Closer still, and the two fallen towers would be visible, the rubble crushing the small city that had comprised Keriabral's lower reaches.

It was all a ruin now, though tribespeople from the Waste had colonised parts, but the crown of towers had been intended to be the Last King's enduring monument and the magic was still strong, even millennia later. From those towers you could see the shattered remains of Aryn Bwr's impregnable dream. Isak himself had seen it, in his own dreams, for the bitter memory had lingered long in Aryn Bwr's mind.

"You know, the bastard even bragged about it in Scree, so Emin told me," he said, rounding on Shanas, who stopped dead.

"Who, Azaer?"

"And Rojak," Morghien said. "A scene of slaughter painted on the theatre door—Emin recognised it from what I'd told him: four towers standing, one fallen, and flames getting ready to take another, the towers so tall even Tirah Palace looks like a child's toy in comparison. Those towers burned the day Keriabral was taken, the day the Gods threw their armies at its walls and didn't care that in the process they extinguished entire races they'd created for the war. That's pretty much when Aryn Bwr became the shadow's pawn. The more I think about it, the more I reckon that painting was Azaer announcing the slaughter to come, the destruction he'd profit from once again."

Shanas looked at him a long while then said, "So it's agreed, then. We don't want him sitting on Death's throne when our times come?"

"No." "Then get on your bloody horse, old man, there's still work to be done."

Ruhen walked ahead of his disciples, his remaining eye fixed on nothing that Ilumene could discern. The white-cloaked soldier followed at a distance, behind him trailing Larim, the Menin mage, Koteer of the Jesters and the black Harlequin, Venn. They watched Ruhen in silence, waiting for a sign from the child that they were finally at their destination.

Ilumene knew they were being watched; though he'd yet to find the observers, his senses prickled. The army had settled at the base of a long rise, while their small party continued on another mile to this hill. The ground was mostly rock and dust; stunted bushes and creeping roses were the only growing plants. The hill itself was as high as anything within sight, studded with enormous boulders and surrounded by more. It reminded him of a childhood story he'd once heard, of two giants arguing and hurling rocks the size of houses at each other.

A shallow slope ran north for miles, following the contours of a distant river, hidden by a narrow band of woods. It was the only visible boundary; in all other directions the undulating scrubland simply faded into the horizon.

He glanced back at Venn and the black Harlequin nodded, gesturing to the waiting soldiers behind. Two squads each of Harlequins and Acolytes of the Jesters spread out at Venn's command, trotting at a brisk pace around the lower slope of the hill, heading towards the rear. The horse scouts had already swept the vicinity, but Ilumene saw no reason to trust them; he knew Morghien had not yet met up with the main force.

The old bastard's got more sense than to take us on, Ilumene reflected, *but that doesn't stop him leaving a surprise in our path—a barbed gift like that damn Finntrail spirit in his head.* But boredom set in and at last he called, "I only see broken stones and a whole lot o' nothing."

The boy turned to face him. With the low sun behind him, Ruhen's face was even more shadowed than usual. Aenaris remained wrapped on his back, its light still hidden from view.

"The sun has not yet set," Ruhen said in response. "There is nothing to see."

"Some sort o' spell?"

Ruhen shook his head. "What we search for lies at the heart of the Gods' power, hidden from all until dusk, when they recede a fraction from the Land."

"I thought they were weak enough already? Surely we should be able to find it when there's still light to do something about it?"

"Some conventions remain," Ruhen said plainly. "It is part of the balance of the Land: this place is revealed at dusk to those who know it's here."

"Sounds like a load of mystical shit to me," Ilumene grumbled.

The boy with shadows in his eyes smiled at his bodyguard's irreverence. "The very heart of religion," he said with what might have been agreement, "but when one plays the game of Gods, one must respect most of the rules. It makes breaking the others far easier."

Ilumene looked at the sun. "Not long to wait then," he muttered as Ruhen returned to his slow walk up the hill. The sky was more open here, Ilumene thought, and far preferable to the cramped atmosphere of the Circle City, where Blackfang Mountain intruded on most every sight. To the Byorans the Waste was huge and empty, even more than his home in Narkang, which looked out over the ocean. The Waste was too big a space for humans to live in; the horizons were too far away.

A man could get lost here; he could go mad while his soul wandered the miles of emptiness in all directions. Ilumene grinned. *Except horizons won't mean much to me soon. Precious little will limit me soon.*

He turned back towards Keriabral, trying to pick out the crater wall in the distance, but it was out of sight now. Clouds massed on the horizon, blurring everything beyond the rabble making their way into the Devoted camp. There had been hundreds of deaths among Ruhen's white-clad followers in the last few weeks, but no one stopped. No one cared. There were always thousands more, even some Chetse, following as dumbly and patiently as the rest, stepping over the dead and dying, who were blessed by the Wither Queen's rat-spirits under cover of night and left for the Narkang troops. Each night the survivors would crawl into the tents of the weary, red-eyed Devoted soldiers, following some unvoiced command Ilumene never gave.

He had heard no word of rape or theft, or of violence done by the soldiers to their pathetic charges; that as much as anything surprised Ilumene. The camp was close to silent at night, the soldiers showing little interest in gambling, whoring or anything else. Instead, they huddled in small groups and spoke in hushed tones, as though they believed the holy mission their leaders had proclaimed.

Even Certinse, Vener and all the rest're silent now, Ilumene reminded himself. *They were so sure of their control, of their strength—and now they've found it runs like dust through their fingers.*

"Ilumene, Venn," Ruhen called from thirty yards up the slope, and the two scrambled in his wake, Venn easily outstripping the heavier man, moving with nimble, economical steps.

"It's time," Venn breathed as he arrived at Ruhen's side.

The boy was walking without hurry as the last rays of the sun faded and withdrew from the Land. Shadows deepened, stealing forward from rocks and crevices to swarm up the hillside. As the dark rose it flickered uncertainly, and Ilumene found his eyes watering at the sight. He blinked furiously, and saw Venn was similarly afflicted as they staggered after Ruhen, but the boy was unaffected by the wavering, shifting curtain of air around the peak of the hill. He pointed, and Ilumene saw the underside of his finger was still bleached white by Aenaris' touch.

Gradually shapes began to form at the peak of the hill: silhouettes of things on the cusp of this Land and the next, drifting uncertainly between here and the Other Lands of Gods and daemons. Ilumene found himself pushing against a barrier of air that unexpectedly gave way, and as he stumbled forward, he almost collided with Venn.

A pair of standing stones loomed ahead of them, rising up from a raised area at the centre of the hill's flattened peak, and now they could see others all around them, rough-hewn and weather-worn, but power hummed through them. Some had toppled over, others were broken-topped, but many of the ancient rune-engraved monuments still stood like sentinels. In the very centre was a rough circle of irregular paving stones spreading for thirty yards in all directions, surrounding the two tallest stones. Beyond the rise, Ilumene could see the strange rocks continuing across the tabletop hill, spreading like roots through the dusty ground as they merged back into the hill itself.

"What is this?" Ilumene gasped. "A temple? Out here?" He looked around. "Must have been a damn big one—but where's the rubble? And how have these engravings survived?" He went up to one and traced the curves and lines cut into its surface, looking for words he recognised.

"Think of it as the first temple," Ruhen said solemnly, "or maybe the soul of every temple. The boundaries of the Land are thin here."

"So not a temple then?" Ilumene asked, frowning. "What about the stones, and this floor?"

Ruhen continued towards the tallest pair of menhir, where Ilumene could see a humped arch and a steep set of worn stairs. "Echoes of other temples, a place carved by the force of reverence itself." He stopped at the top of the stairs and turned to face them both. "And here is the entrance. Here is the heart of the Land and all its Gods."

"Here we become Gods," Venn added, the pleasure of that thought driving the wonder from his face. "I can feel the power here; it's in everything—the air, the earth . . . all around us."

"And here we will become Gods," Ruhen agreed, "but first there is much we need to do."

"We're not going in?"

"No. We are not yet ready. Venn, you will stay with your Harlequins—keep these standing stones within waking sight at all times. Have the Acolytes guard the other side of the hill. No one must be allowed up here without my express order. Ilumene, we will return to the army. They must prepare defences for when King Emin and the white-eye come."

"They'll be digging ditches and sorting ramparts, at first light," Ilumene confirmed before hesitating slightly. "What about your Children, do you want them stacking stones too?"

"I have a greater burden for them." As Ruhen spoke a gust of wind surged up the hillside from the direction of the troops, and all three turned to face it. It carried the usual stinks of an army, sweat and animal musk, festering wounds, shit and urine—only now it was intermingled with something else, something stranger.

Ilumene heard a chuckle on the wind as he recognised the sickly sweet smell of overripe peaches. They had gathered cartloads of rotten fruit at the oasis outside Keriabral's crater wall. They were withered and well past their season; the wind had dried them on the trees, and insects had burrowed into those that had fallen, eating the goodness from within, but still Ruhen had insisted the remains be collected.

Ilumene heard the voice on the wind again, and this time he made out Rojak's unmistakable laugh. The dead minstrel was not quite so confined to Venn's mind here, it appeared. The smell of peaches lingered, and Ilumene realised that the fruits were no longer inedible husks, though there was no way they could smell like that naturally.

"Aenaris?" he asked.

"It is the breath of life," the boy answered. "Its gifts I shall share with my faithful servants."

"To the same effect as it had on Rojak?"

"I still have my herald," Ruhen said, "I have no need of twenty thousand more. No, this gift is a burden too, a covenant with my chosen few. Gods are anointed in the blood of the innocent—but who says the innocent can't put up a fight first?"

As Ruhen walked back through the camp heads lifted at his passing. Devoted troops saluted their leader, while the preachers and white-clad followers knelt, heads bowed in prayer. Ruhen's smile lifted the fatigue from their faces, provoking gladness from all he passed. Luerce, first among Ruhen's Children, fell in behind his lord and the rest followed without any order needed, the ragged column swelling with every step.

The campfires that lit the way were small, limited by the paucity of wood on the parched plain, but enough to define the boundary of the camp. Through the lines of tents, past the watching soldiers and generals of the Devoted, Ruhen went with a train of attendants. Those spread further out sensed something on the wind, and answering some unspoken command, men and woman crawled from the tents to join the burgeoning crowd. Soon it became clear Ruhen was heading to the furthest part of the camp, where the supply wagons were drawn up. The pickets set around the supplies parted like evening mist as they approached. Cauldrons of rice-heavy stew bubbled slowly over cooking fires, and as he continued to the wagons at the back, the men tending the food stepped aside and watched the mass, now numbering in their thousands, as they followed in reverential silence. The crowd surrounded the wagons, kept separate and under guard by the Hearth-Spears, the grey-skinned warriors from the Jesters' loyal clans.

Ruhen climbed up onto one of the two wagons piled with fruit. He looked around at his assembling followers: people were still coming out of the camp, but there were enough present for him to start. He slipped the wrapped sword from his back and a collective sigh raced around the crowd. Under their white cloaks and ragged clothes he saw they were emaciated and dull-eyed with fatigue. Most had been painfully thin before the journey had started; they were barely standing now, driven on by fervour and desperation to the very limits of their life.

"Brothers and sisters of peace, our time draws near," he started, his clear voice carrying. "This Land is a wounded beast, weakened and fearful. The Gods themselves tremble at what must come to pass, at the betrayal of their priests and the heretic King of Narkang."

Ruhen held up the sword for them all to see. Even with its light covered, there was a palpable air of power around it. The coin hanging from Ruhen's neck glinted in the fading light, displaying the rough cross scored on its surface.

Slowly, solemnly, Ruhen slipped the covering from Aenaris and pure white light blazed out like a beacon across the camp. The boy's skin looked unnaturally pale in its light as he held up to for them all to see. As one the masses fell to their knees, crying out blessings and wordless sounds of devotion. Ruhen turned in a full circle, allowing all of his assembled worshippers to see his face, not trying to hide the burden Aenaris was as his blind right eye shone in the gloaming.

The massive sword was as light as a feather, but it ate at the shadows inside him, making it feel as though it was made of lead rather than pure, flawless crystal. He was forced to squint against its light, the camp beyond growing darker to his one remaining eye as the Key of Life eclipsed his shadow soul, but even in the darkness he spied a shape moving, circling beyond Ruhen's Children like a wolf on the hunt, her cold blue eyes bright in the darkness. Ruhen nodded respectfully and the Wither Queen faltered, matching his gaze for a moment before taking two last steps and fading into nothing.

He looked down at the peaches, which had been restored to ripeness by Aenaris. He lowered the sword and whispered lovingly to the unnatural crop. Power flowed out of the weapon and the sickly-sweet stink of fruit almost past their best grew, filling the air with their odour while the skin of his fingers hissed and crackled.

Wincing at the sensation, Ruhen completed the spell and went to do the same with the other wagon. He transferred Aenaris to his other hand and staring down at the palm of his right, which was burned as white as bone by the sword's power. As he repeated his workings, Ruhen faltered slightly, his legs wobbling underneath him to moans of fear from the onlookers, but then he caught himself and stood straight again, forcing himself to look up at them and meet their eyes before he rewrapped the sword and hid its searing light.

"These fruit are my gift to you, most faithful of siblings," he said hoarsely, struggling to find the strength to raise his voice momentarily. "Share them amongst yourselves, ensure all of your brothers and sisters are permitted a bite.

"Soon we will be forced to defend this holy site. This is the place of our rebirth, of the Land's rebirth. Here we will defend our Land, our Gods and our future."

With stiff limbs he returned Aenaris to its sheath and took a slow breath before continuing, "During the Great War the Gods blessed many of their followers as they headed into battle. Battle is soon coming to this place. The Knights of the Temples are steadfast and brave, and they will do their duty to the Land, I know. But no one will escape the savagery, and the Gods have granted me this boon for you: we stand in service of innocence, defenders of the weak—you have all followed me here out of that ideal, but now you are the innocents to be protected.

"The Knights of the Temples have sheltered you, fed you with their own rations, and done so without complaint, for they see our holy mission. And now it is my turn: so eat of this fruit, share it amongst your enfeebled and exhausted brethren, and receive my blessing.

"The path before us is hard; the covenant I offer is as much a burden, for it is one of strength. As I have taught you these past months, the defence of innocence is no easy duty—but do not fear this burden, do not fear the heavy blessing of the Gods, for I will care for you. Come the dawn light, you will be reborn, and then we will lead the Land itself to rebirth!"

A fervent roar rose up from all around him, shaking the ground with its upwelling of passion. Arms raised to the heavens, some prayed, some shouted and howled and many wept. Luerce and his senior preachers stepped forward, climbing up into the wagons to renewed calls and wordless paeans echoing out across the dark sky.

With the greatest reverence Luerce picked up a peach. Juice ran down his fingers as he bit into its flesh. He tore a chunk away and passed the peach to the eager hands of the next man, then swallowed the sacrament with his eyes closed, his face turned to the sky above. All around them the supplicants reached forward, desperate for their lord's blessing, and soon the preachers were handing out the peaches as fast as they could.

Copying the First Disciple, those nearest tasted the flesh and passed the rest back, moaning with ecstatic pleasure at the sickly, half-gone peaches as they handed more and more to the crowd beyond. Many grabbed handfuls and started pushing back into the crowd beyond, holding the fruit aloft as they made for those who could not get close to the wagons.

Ruhen stood on the wagon and watched them approvingly, dark shadows dancing in his eyes. He turned back at the hilltop almost a mile away. "The twilight reign is here," he whispered, the words sweeter on the tongue than any fruit. "My reign is come."

Chapter 39

General Daken reined in and raised his hand to call a halt. Almost as one, the Green Scarves stopped to survey the enemy. The white-eye glanced around at his men, élite among the Narkang army. The officers had all been marked with flowing blue tattoos by Litania, the Trickster Goddess inhabiting Daken's skin, and they were almost as irregular as the savage men they led.

Many wore Menin armour and helms, mismatched pieces scavenged from the dead, which were now augmented by the banded armour of the Knights of the Temples. There were now five complete legions wearing green scarves—King Emin had expanded their numbers with reinforcements from Canar Thrit, troops experienced at fighting Black Swords from Vanach and their Carastar mercenary allies—and they had been entrusted with the job of leading the way towards the Devoted.

"Looks like all of 'em," Daken said at last, scanning the plain ahead. "Anyone else suspicious about that?"

"Aren't we expecting sort of mage's surprise?" Colonel Dassai asked.

"Aye, but it would still be nice if they pretended otherwise. Makes it a bit bloody obvious when they're all lined up like this." He gestured towards the Devoted army, stationed at the base of the hill ahead and a shallower rise on the left flank. He couldn't make out the earthworks around the hill, but he knew they were there from the positioning of the enemy soldiers. Angled lines of troops marked stark lines of defence, static positions around which their cavalry could move. More than a legion of cavalry patrolled the open ground between them and there were clear channels for more to descend from the high ground in response to any threat.

"And the scouts say this is the best approach?" Daken said with a scowl.

"Aye, sir, given the size of our army. The ground's more broken on the east flank of the hill, a defender's dream. There're ridges to defend and stick your enemy full of arrows from, while you've got nothing more than a tired mob coming up towards you, all leading to a slope too steep to climb."

Daken grunted. The Devoted had divided their infantry broadly equally between the hill and the neighbouring rise, unwilling to concede high ground so close to the part they had to hold at all costs. King Emin hadn't given him the full picture about what Ruhen would be doing there, but he'd made it clear they needed to punch right in and give a small force under Isak's command the chance to end the war.

"Dassai, send a rider to the king," Daken said after a long, silent look at the defences ahead of them. "He should send the Denei cavalry to the east and south flanks—might not be we can attack there, but we can still rule 'em. The Devoted's got nothing to touch Denei horsewarriors—two legions will be a right thorn in their side. Skirmishers too—in close formation, if Endine don't think much of their scryers; might make 'em think the Legion o' the Damned's about to crawl up their arseholes."

The colonel repeated the instructions to a messenger as a respectful suggestion to their liege and sent him off, then turned back to the white-eye. "And now?"

Daken spat on the ground ahead of him. "Now we secure this plain." He turned in the saddle, watching the rider race back the way they had come. They were several miles ahead of the main army, which was heaving forward like an aged and weary monster. The king would be ordering a halt soon; it was well into the afternoon and getting any closer would be foolish. Better to set camp and rest for the coming day, then march unencumbered the few miles.

"There'll be no fighting today, not unless we provoke it." The white-eye forced a grin. "What do you say, Dassai? Want to pick a fight?"

"First blood for the Green Scarves, aye," Dassai agreed. "We've got a reputation to maintain after all."

Isak sat outside his tent and watched the orange flames flicker and glow. Hulf had burrowed under his legs, teeth bared at faint sounds the humans were trying to ignore. It was well past the ghost-hour, but many hadn't yet retired in the Narkang camp. King Emin and Legana shared the fire with him in a tense silence. The culmination of their plans was at hand, and they all feared the coming day.

Snow fell fitfully, adding to the shroud of quiet over the camp. On the edge of hearing, daemons howled like unholy wolves anticipating the morrow's feast. Hulf growled softly again and Isak put his white hand on the dog's back, trying to calm him, but it did no good; Hulf would not be soothed.

It's hard to reassure him when I can't forget, Isak thought sadly. *We're an army in mourning already—how many of us believe we'll see dusk again?*

He looked at King Emin, and recognised the glitter of tears in his eyes. Emin's grey hair had been roughly cut back and with his hat discarded, revealed even more clearly the lines of his ageing face.

"What was your son's name again?" Isak asked softly.

Emin jumped as though stung, then said quietly, "Sebetin. Oterness chose it—Sebe died in Byora just before the naming day and she always had a soft spot for him. She said he had a gentle soul compared to the rest of the Brotherhood. I don't think I could ask for Sebetin to grow up better than that."

Isak didn't say anything else; he had nothing that could alleviate Emin's own guilt and fear. There were thousands—tens of thousands, in opposing camps, but united in that moment—all thinking of those they might never see again. Vesna had gone off to watch the sun set and be alone with his thoughts of Tila; Doranei sat a little way from his king, staring down at the black star-speckled blade he'd used to kill his lover. It wasn't clear the King's Man had even heard Sebe's name spoken, though Isak knew he felt guilt for both deaths.

And what about me? he wondered. *Is this fear I'm feeling, grief for those who're lost, or something else? I wish you were here, Mihn; that I do wish, but my guilt's unchanged. There've been too many deaths on my account already, so perhaps one more makes no difference to the weight of my chains. Or maybe I'm just too broken to feel anything more.*

His hands tightened and he felt a slight resistance in the palm of his right where the black sword still resided between one Land and the next.

You deserved better, but I know you'd say they all did—all those I killed, all those who died alongside me. Is it cowardly of me to want a way out of all this? I fear the chains I'll be dragging up Ghain's slope, but I'm so tired of this fight.

"*Look*," Legana said unexpectedly into their minds, brushing the grey-seamed copper hair away from her face as she tilted her head up to the sky.

High above them the dark clouds of night were cut through by flame, a thin trail of light that faded only slowly, then a second bright path streaked alongside where the first had passed.

"What is it?" Isak whispered, watching the strange sight with fascination. "A shooting star?"

Legana shook her head and pointed as another blade of light tore through the dark, this one an arc, curving gracefully around. The air was perfectly still and silent, no deep and savage cry of dragons breaking the calm.

"*They're hunting*," Legana said at last, wonder and delight in her voice. "*If only you could see it with my eyes.*"

Isak frowned, still not understanding, but a gasp from Emin told him the king had realised what they were looking at.

"The phoenix dance," he croaked in astonishment. "I've heard the stories but not even Morghien has seen this!"

"Phoenix?" Isak asked. "Are you sure?"

"Birds of flaming plumage, who scorch the air as they dive on their prey," Emin said softy, and Isak gaped at the sight as two trailing paths like fire-arrows raced through the night above them, faster than any falcon could swoop. Distantly he heard the click and chatter of bats in the night sky, Death's messengers fleeing the talons of the phoenix: the chosen creature and symbol of the Queen of the Gods.

"Is it an omen?" King Emin wondered aloud. "Do they herald the rebirth of the Land?"

Legana shook her head. "*Some will see them that way perhaps, but I've had enough of omens. The future shall be as we make it. The phoenix tell us something far more important.*"

"Which is?"

She smiled and rose to leave, unsteady on her feet until Ardela appeared at her side to steady her. Legana put her hand on Ardela's, letting her support her with loving care. "*They remind us that there is still beauty in the Land.*"

Isak stepped out of his tent and looked up at the sky. A brisk wind threw the drizzle down onto his face, but while his guards scowled at the cold, unwelcome dawn, Isak savoured it. His bones carried a memory of Ghenna's close, oppressive air and unnatural warmth so for him, the chill winter rain slapping his cheek was a pleasure, the surging wind and open ground around him a moment of release from the memories that bound him.

All around him men and woman were waking, and several Sisters of Dusk emerged from Palace Guard tents, dragging their coppery hair back into braids and ponytails for the day's battle. Isak watched one, a tall woman in a studded jerkin at least a decade older than the grim-faced Ghost at the entrance of the tent she'd just left. With a deft hand she buckled on her spaulders and vambraces before collecting her long-knives and spear from the tent.

She paused a moment to run an affectionate finger down the soldier's cheek, then headed out without a backwards glance. The soldier watched her go, then caught Isak's eye and ducked his head with a sheepish expression. The white-eye's laughter echoed around the camp.

"Morning, lad," Carel called, rising from beside the dull fire embers. "Get any sleep?" He looked stiff in the chill morning air, and had dark rings around his eyes, but once he'd taken a few steps there was a renewed purpose to the ageing warrior's gait. He was already dressed for battle and carried a peaked helm looted from some Devoted corpse in his hand. Carel had blackened the helm's surface in the fire, Isak saw, burning off the painted insignia and ensuring he wouldn't look like an enemy in the chaos of battle.

"As little as you," Isak admitted. "As little of any of us." He'd slept in his breeches and long boots like the rest, but his chest was exposed to the faint daylight and he saw Carel's eyes drawn to the scars on his body. Most prominent among them was the fat band around his throat and the distinct white mark of Xeliath's rune.

Around his waist was the cloth band that kept the Skull of Ruling pressed against his skin. It was faded and stained by many weeks of constant use—but then, nothing about him was pristine, Isak reflected. He reached up towards the sky and stretched out his white and black arms, still thickly muscled, despite the damage done to them.

"You shouldn't come," Isak said once he'd finished stretching out the familiar discomfort of a night on hard ground. "I know you want to be at my side, but the best of the Ghosts'll be hardpressed. It's too dangerous for you."

"Don't worry, I'll stick with the women and the cripples," Carel said with a fierce grin.

"The Sisters of Dusk are with me, Legana too."

"Well, that's tough shit for you then, ain't it? Can't tie me up like you have Hulf."

A whimper came from Isak's tent as the dog heard his name. Isak had tethered him to a stake to keep him away from the battle, but Hulf was used to freedom and Isak had to hope the rope he'd used would last long enough.

Isak sighed. Though his memories of the man were fractured and broken, Carel's presence remained soothing for him; he calmed the burr of fear and fatigue at the back of his mind, just as Mihn had. And then Mihn had died, trying to protect him.

"Then you keep with them, you hear me? Stay with Ardela—I can't be watching over you, I can't be at your side."

"Don't worry, lad," Carel said, nodding, "I was a Ghost, remember? Sometimes the white-eyes or Lord Bahl himself had to be left exposed in the teeth of battle. Don't feel right, but that's the way it is; a normal like me can't always be in the worst of it. There's places I can't follow you and weapons I can't stop. I'll do my part and give you the space you need."

"Good—you just remember that. Even if you don't understand what I'm doing, you leave me to it. I'm not part of the battle; I've got my own mission."

"Aye, my Lord," Carel confirmed.

"I'm no lord, not any more."

The veteran scowled. "Piss on that. You're the lord I follow, the one I'm proud to obey. If this old man only has one fight left in him, it'll be in your name and there's nothing you can do about that."

Isak smiled. "As you wish."

"My Lord!" a voice called from beyond the ring of tents: Tiniq, returning from his nightly patrols. The Ascetite ranger's nightvision was far better than any normal man's, so he spent the night roaming between sentry positions and slept in the wagons during the day. Now he trotted forward, holding out something coiled and silvery in his hands for Isak to see.

"I found this in a pack last night," Tiniq explained as he reached Isak and deposited a hinged cuff attached to a chain in Isak's open palms.

Isak frowned down at it, sensing some latent magic in the metal. "I don't understand," he started.

Without warning Tiniq slashed forward at Isak's belly with a short knife, and Isak gasped, the silver chain spilling from his hands—but before he could react, a surge of power roared up from inside him and he screamed with pain.

Tiniq dropped to a crouch as Isak howled and the Crystal Skull tumbled from the slashed strip of cloth across his belly. Quick as a snake the ranger scooped up the Skull, dropping his knife in the same movement and catching up the falling chain in his free hand. Isak dropped to his knees as the air turned black around him, his hands rising as though to shield his face from the suddenly-unchecked magic coursing through his body.

With one deft movement Tiniq brought the chain up and snapped the cuff around Isak's black wrist. Without waiting to see if the stricken white-eye had reacted, he kicked backwards at Carel, knocking him sprawling. As the nearest Ghosts came forward, Tiniq ran behind Isak with blinding speed, dragging the chain after him so Isak's right arm was pinned against his chest.

Strands of black light filled the grainy morning air and Isak screamed again, falling to his knees as sparks burst from his eyes and the magic of Termin Mystt ran rampant through his mind. The daemon-scars on his body flared red and as his cries intensified, lightning snapped out through the air all around him. The Ghosts faltered in the whip-crack of light that lashed past them and Tiniq took the opportunity to throw the chain around Isak's body again, looping it under his right elbow and back over his left shoulder.

That done the ranger glanced around, checking he wasn't about to be gutted by any of the startled soldiers, and yanked a shard of glass encasing a black feather from his tunic. He dropped it, and a storm of black wings erupted from the magic-saturated air around them. The cloud of wings hammered furiously for a brief second, beating back the stunned guards, and then melted into nothingness, leaving behind only the glass shard on the ground where Isak had been.

Carel dragged himself upright and stumbled forward a few steps before falling to his knees in disbelief. Isak was gone. Tiniq was gone—had betrayed them after all this time. The weapon they had hoped might win this war was now in their enemy's hands.

"Sound the alarm," he croaked, his voice initially too hoarse to the guards nearby to make out. "Alarm!" Carel cried, grabbing the nearest dumbstruck soldier and dragging him around to face him. "Search the camp, fetch Vesna! They can't have gone far—find him, damn you!"

The Ghost gave some sort of garbled reply, but Carel was already heading for the king's tent, until the beating of wings in the still morning air stopped him dead. With a mounting sense of horror he saw Vorizh Vukotic's wyverns rising into the sky, a few hundred yards away. The vampire was astride the leading beast, but he turned towards the second, with the great bulk of a white-eye draped across its back and Tiniq's smaller frame perched just behind.

The Land seemed to squirm around him as the wyverns beat the air with their wings and climbed steadily, rising in the sky and heading towards the Devoted army. Shouts rang out from all around, but Carel didn't hear them. He tried to run, but his legs betrayed him and only the arrival of some soldiers at his side stopped him from falling to the ground.

"Archers," Carel tried to shout, but the strength had drained from his body, the air driven from his lungs, and the command came out only as a gasp, the cut-off exhalation of a man run through. He felt it as a pain in his gut, an upwelling of horror that enveloped him as Isak was carried off into the distance.

Chapter 40

Vensa watched the soldier yelling himself hoarse as he wove through a mass of startled soldiers. Men were running in all directions, most with their weapons drawn, a cacophony of voices, panic and confusion breaking out in the heart of the camp.

"Soldier!" he roared as the man reached him, still gabbling frantically, "take a breath and tell me what's happened."

In that shout came the full force of Vesna's divine presence and it rocked the man like a punch to the chest. He gasped and stopped dead, wide-eyed for a moment, before returning to his senses. "Lord Isak, my lord—he's gone!"

Vesna grabbed him by the shoulder. "Gone? What do you mean?"

The soldier swallowed hurriedly, feeling the Mortal-Aspect's impatience like the heat of a fire. He wore the black and white of the Ghosts; he was old enough to be a veteran, but right now he was as flustered and frightened as a raw recruit. "He's been taken—Tiniq's taken him, with that bloody vampire's help!"

"*Tiniq the ranger?* He's the bloody traitor?" Vesna demanded, shaking the soldier, who went white with terror. Vesna realised he'd dented the man's steel pauldron and he quickly released the Ghost. "How? That's why those wyverns were flying towards the enemy?"

The man bobbed his head, too frightened to speak. "He took the Skull from Lord Isak and used some glass feather to disappear, so Carel said."

Vesna broke into a run, heading towards Isak's tent. Even before he reached it he could sense the panic and confusion emanating from the throng around it, but they stilled as he arrived as though calmed by his presence.

"Carel! What happened?"

Carel lurched forward, his face pale. "The bastard took him," he croaked. "He cut away the Skull and let the bloody sword cripple him with pain."

"He's alive?"

"Screaming," he moaned, "howling like the whole damn Dark Place was tearing his skin apart." He held up a shard of glass. Small fractures ran down one side of it, marring the clear view of a raven's feather encased inside. "He used this to disappear."

Vesna took the glass shard from him and inspected it. "Tiniq must have stolen this from the witch before we left Moorview," he muttered. "He's been planning it all this time?"

"But why?"

He shook his head. "I don't know. He always was a strange one—I just thought he was as mad as any other Ascetite. Could he really have been an agent of Azaer's all this time?"

As he spoke a second figure sprinted up, and the Ghosts were turning with weapons half-raised before they realised who it was.

"Is it true?" Doranei demanded, gasping for breath. "He's been taken?"

Vesna offered the glass shard. "He used this to reach the vampire—Vorizh's also betrayed us."

"Karkarn's horn," Doranei breathed, "we've lost Termin Mystt, the Skull of Ruling, two wyverns and a vampire all in one go?"

"Eolis too," Vesna reminded him. "Vorizh took it when Isak claimed Termin Mystt."

"And none of you had a fucking clue?" Doranei shouted, wheeling round at the Farlan soldiers, who bristled. "A traitor in your midst this whole fucking time?"

More than one would have stepped forward if Vesna hadn't raised a hand to stop the argument from developing. "There's no time for that," he said. "We've lost our greatest weapon—we can't delay any longer."

Doranei grabbed the shard from his hand. "You're right: Azaer's got all the power it needs now. I'll see if Endine can do anything with this. You get the army moving."

"What chance do we stand now?" Carel yelled at the King's Man. "The two greatest weapons in creation are in our enemy's hands!"

Slowly and deliberately Doranei put a hand to Carel's chest and pushed him back. "Yes, Azaer's got all the cards, but that changes the game."

"Meaning?"

"Meaning," Doranei replied calmly, fully composed again now, "the shadow doesn't give a shit about this battle. It's got bigger plans than beating us on the field, and for those plans it needs the swords and Skulls in use, not out here tearing us apart."

"Why wouldn't it wait?"

"You saw the toll Termin Mystt took on Isak; these weapons are not to be used lightly—and do you think it trusts its allies so completely it'd risk being vulnerable in their presence? Azaer's goal is to become a God, not a conqueror! Why wait before doing that? Why wait for any possible surprises we might pull to win the battle? All those soldiers have to do is defend the hilltop until Azaer's a God, and then we're all fucked anyway. But to make that happen the shadow needs to be within the barrow, deep underground and away from anyone its mages could use the Skulls on!"

"How long?"

"How in the name of the fucking Dark Place should I know?" Doranei shouted. "Do I look like a bloody mage? Vesna, you've got more chance of knowing—what does your God say?"

The Mortal-Aspect of Karkarn blinked, but if his God had answers, he was not sharing them. "I don't know, but how long can a ritual take when you've that much power?"

He looked around and raised his voice so that the ground shook with divine authority. "Arm yourselves! Leave everything else—we march right now!" Lowering his voice he looked hard at Doranei. "What happens even if we punch through? Isak was going to kill Azaer—how do we win without that option?"

"I don't know, but rituals can go awry—maybe Legana or Endine can find a way to disrupt it. You're leading the strike now; there's no one else. Who's commanding the Ghosts?"

"Colonel Cerse!" Vesna bellowed, and the commander of the Ghosts ran up, still pulling on his heavy armour. In his wake came Suzerain Torl, dressed in the lighter armour of the Dark Monks.

"Here, Vesna," Cerse replied. "Your orders?"

"The battle order remains the same, but you're leading the Ghosts," Vesna said. "Make General Lahk proud of his men. Torl, you have command of the Farlan forces."

He started back towards his tent to put on the rest of his own armour, but hesitated when he realised the soldiers were all still staring at him in awed silence.

"Move yourselves!" he roared, jerking them into action. "May Karkarn's blessing shield you all. The Farlan ride to war!"

"At last we meet," came a distant voice through the darkness, "my most useful of playthings."

Isak raised his head and muzzily made out a small figure standing a few feet in front of him. A small, slender boy, looking barely fourteen summers, but with the presence of a king. He was dressed simply, with a wrapped sword bound on his back, and he dominated a view containing Harlequins, mages and Demi-Gods. Even the one blind eye and scar on his face served only to enhance his unearthly air.

Isak recognised Ilumene standing close to Ruhen's side, while on the boy's other side he saw a black figure with teardrops tattooed on his face: the black Harlequin, Venn. Ilumene grinned malevolently at Isak, but the best he could manage in response was to look straight through the man, as though he wasn't worth noticing.

"But as you see," Ruhen continued with a small, secret smile, spreading his hands to indicate himself, "I am growing up. The time has come to put aside my childish things and you, beloved toy, have almost served your purpose."

"Fuck off," Isak croaked.

Ruhen's smile widened. "Ah, you do not disappoint. Always the white-eye, even after all I've put you through."

Isak took stock of himself. He was on his side, his right hand pulled tight against his chest and a chain of silver looped diagonally around his torso. The sky was oppressive, sullen grey clouds with a taste of rain on the wind. He could see a perimeter of cut stones, both standing and fallen, and fractured paving slabs underneath him. It appeared that they were standing on the remains of an obliterated temple. His senses told him he was on the bare hill their scouts had spoken of; Aryn Bwr had described it as a barrow. The air hummed with power and the stones beneath him trembled at the artefacts gathered in one place.

He pushed himself up with his left hand until he was kneeling, then hunched forward and retched until the waves of pain and dizziness passed. His hands were trembling and his head swam; even the simplest of movements was exhausting. It was a huge effort just to turn his head enough to see Tiniq's hooded head behind him, a grim expression on the ranger's face. The end of the chain that bound him was in one hand, the Skull of Ruling in the other.

"Traitor," Isak managed, but even as he said that a shocking pulse of energy ran up through his arm, setting the nerves aflame and his bones creaking until Tiniq quietened the flow.

"I think you should be more civil," Ruhen warned. "It's only the link he holds that is keeping Termin Mystt from shredding what's left of your mind."

Despite the boy's words, anger and hatred continued to growl unabated in Isak's gut. "Stabbed your own damn brother in the back?" Isak hissed, blinking away the stars that burst before his eyes. "Did you let him see the face of his killer—or were you too much of a coward to let him know what his brother was before he died?"

This time the pain was worse, and Isak's vision went white as power ran rampant through his body and his ears filled with his own screams. Eventually Tiniq relented and cut the flow again, leaving Isak panting and sobbing in a heap.

"My brother needed no such burden," Tiniq hissed. "He died clean and quick. You all used him like a dog and you think to condemn me? Piss on you all, the whole damn tribe of the Farlan who'd have hung me in an instant had they learned what I am."

Isak grunted and rolled over so he could again see Tiniq through his blurred and wavering eyes. "What's that, then?"

Tiniq's face became stony. "There's no name for what I am: twin of a white-eye," he spat, "an impossible birth. I shouldn't have survived; your kind don't share, except my soon-to-be dead mother was infected by something almost as strong as white-eye's blood."

"You're a *vampire?*" Isak croaked in disbelief.

Tiniq sneered, "And to think the Gods placed you above my brother. There's no name for what I am. I was infected by the vampire blood, but sharing a womb with one touched by the Gods. For years I fought the thirst, knowing my own people would kill me if they ever discovered the truth."

"Until the shadows spoke to him," Ruhen added, delight in his voice as he savoured the words and his own triumph. "Until I gave him the strength to survive its growing call—to become more than a man in hiding from his own nature."

"What are you going to offer me, then?" Isak said, weakly pushing himself back to his knees.

"Offer?" Ruhen cocked his head to one side. "Why should I do that?"

Isak tried to smile as he gestured to the black hand bound tight to his chest. "Got anyone else who can hold this? You reckon your pet Jester could stand it?"

Ruhen turned and looked around Ilumene at the tall, grey-skinned Demi-God not far behind. "Koteer? I think he might, yes: a son of Death with Ruling in his hand and Aenaris nearby—yes, if you forced my hand, I think he would."

"But would you trust the bastard to follow orders?"

If Isak stirred anything up, he couldn't see it. Koteer remained impassive, and Ruhen was more amused than anything else.

"Trust? Koteer's brothers have died for the cause. Loyalty like that buys everything they were promised and more." Ruhen looked past Isak. "But I don't think you will press the matter. Your friends might yet break through to meet you. It would be a shame if Ilumene had already taken your head before Emin managed to conjure something."

"We wouldn't want them to be disheartened now," Ilumene agreed. "They might give up and leave us to it."

"You don't want that?" Isak coughed.

"Of course not," said Ruhen. "The greatest magic is always consecrated by blood, after all, and the presence of power is almost as important. I don't need your cooperation, you see, just your presence. With a majority of Skulls and the rest nearby, magnifying the presence of Demi-Gods and Mortal-Aspects . . ." The boy laughed. "It will be more than enough; you overestimate any resistance the Gods are likely to mount."

Isak had nothing to say. Under the assault from Termin Mystt and Ruhen's carelessly spoken words, he felt enfeebled. He found himself unable to move from his position of subjugation, kneeling, head bowed, before the shadow eye of Ruhen.

"Ilumene, set your pieces," Ruhen said to the former King's Man, and Ilumene nodded and beckoned forward a white-eye in bright robes and a Farlan man Isak hadn't noticed before. The former had to be Lord Larim, the Menin mage who was Larat's Chosen—they hadn't found his body at Moorview, and no one had dared to hope the man would be dead. The sickly-looking Farlan had dark circles around his eyes and gaunt cheeks. The armour he wore was that of a general of the Knights of the Temples and Isak realised belatedly this had to be Knight-Cardinal Certinse, the last living member of that troublesome family.

"Definitely going to make sure I kill you," Isak declared in a heavy, slurring voice. "Get myself the full family set."

If the Knight-Cardinal reacted, Isak didn't see, for Tiniq struck him on the back of the head and sent him sprawling to the ground, pink and black stars bursting before his eyes.

"Close order infantry on both hills, archers behind and space for the cavalry to descend. Give them leave to range around the rear of the hill. I doubt an attack'll come there, but we still need to watch for troops like the Legion. What we can offer Emin is the lower rise—this flank's the best one to attack but it leaves them badly open. Larim, you're the heart of the defence," Ilumene began in a business-like voice. "Yours will be the only Skull outside the barrow."

"What? The rest are going in with you?" Certinse blurted out.

Ilumene nodded. "Six Skulls and Aenaris are what the master needs, so you'll make do with what you've got: seventy thousand troops to stop them taking one fucking hill, so don't whine."

"Seventy thousand closely packed soldiers facing five Crystal Skulls amongst Narkang and Tirah's élite?" the man protested. "It'll be a slaughter—how long do you expect us to last?"

"Long enough. Don't worry; we've a few cards still to play."

"Those damned fanatics? Last I heard you'd poisoned them all; they're just lying on the hillside like they're bloody dead."

"They're resting—conserving their strength," Ilumene assured him as Larim gave the Farlan a reptilian smile. "Most of 'em any

ways. Probably."

"Unarmed and too ill to move, if they're not already dead!"

Ilumene draped a comradely arm around Certinse's shoulders and the slender man shrank under the touch. "Haven't you learned to trust me by now? They'll give a good account o' themselves, and they're not the only tricks our friend has up those big sleeves of his."

Larim who bowed his head to acknowledge Ilumene's words; a strange gesture of deference given the reputation of the Chosen of Larat, Isak thought. But then he remembered what Doranei and King Emin had told him about Ilumene—if anyone was to command the respect of savage and callous men, it was him.

"Don't bring them in too early," Ilumene added for Larim's benefit. "Feel free to tire their mages first. Blood must be spilled this day, the blood of thousands—our ritual demands it."

"And if they do manage a breach?"

"Then they'll be vulnerable to your surprises, but don't let it get to that. Our positions are fortified, our troops disciplined. The Knight-Cardinal and his generals know their trade well enough; soften them up as they approach, outflank them with cavalry and let them exhaust themselves on the shield-wall."

"It's the Legion of the Damned I'm more concerned with," Certinse said in a subdued voice. "They can break the line and open us up."

"So you find 'em, Larim, and you break 'em," Ilumene declared. "They're not invulnerable and they'll be at the heart of Emin's assault. The Knight-Cardinal's right, the Legion is their greatest weapon—but how many do they number now? Five hundred? They can't recruit, and every skirmish with General Vener's troops has reduced their numbers. You direct your magic there and use Vorizh—his presence with those wyverns will counter their impact."

"Questions?" Ruhen asked, prompting all three men to turn and shake their heads. "Excellent, then we will delay no longer. Venn, Koteer: summon your troops. It's not that I lack faith in the Knight-Cardinal's abilities, but if King Emin does break through we will be fighting in near darkness."

Ilumene came towards Isak and before the white-eye had managed to focus on him properly, the man had slipped a leather noose around his neck and yanked it tight.

"Come my little pet," Ruhen said with delight as Ilumene dragged Isak stumbling forward on hand and knees. "It is time we went to meet our Gods."

Standing high in his stirrups, King Emin cast around to check the army was ready. It was an impressive sight by most standards, but nagging doubts still lingered. The bulk of the army was infantry, arrayed in two lines on each side of him and angled like a flattened V, since they would be charging an enemy set at an angle. At the centre of the army was an arrowhead of heavy cavalry, serving as the hinge between their forces, Kingsguard and Palace Guard, with the remaining Ghosts on foot behind, alongside the Legion of the Damned.

Between the three sets of troops were gaps of fifty yards, space enough for the cavalry to manoeuvre or the advance units of skirmishers and light cavalry to retreat. They had already engaged with the Devoted's ranging cavalry, but neither side was keen to get embroiled in a standing fight and it had been short-lived.

On his right were the four heavy infantry legions of the Kingsguard and the same number of Menin, while the left flank was headed by the mercenary legions and the battle-clans of Canar Fell. Behind both were the Narkang regular spearmen, and cavalry and archers ranged on both flanks. Emin had ordered there be no reserve at all, unable to contemplate retreat or even a protracted battle.

"Endine, is Nai ready to provide our decoy?"

"He is, your Majesty. The battle-mages know to wait for him to act first. Wentersorn and Morghien are ready too."

The king took one last look around at the men and woman riding at his side. Count Vesna shone darkly at the head of the Ghosts; Legana was a gleaming emerald thorn amidst her spear-bearing sisters. Doranei and Veil clapped each other on the shoulder and Daken snarled with barely restrained blood-rage, already sinking into the white-eye battle-fury. Carel, a still, silent figure behind him with his face hidden by his helm, was steeling himself for the slaughter to come.

"Brothers!" King Emin called, drawing his sword and holding it high for as many as possible to see. "Our time has come—our place in history is at hand!"

There was a roar from the soldiers around him, one that was taken up by the savage battle-clans before the rest joined in. Soon even the fanatical Menin added their voices and the air shook with murderous intent.

With Endine's assistance Emin continued, this time with a voice that echoed like thunder down the assembled ranks. "My brothers: the enemy lies before us, the enemy of the Gods themselves! There can be no retreat, no respite or surrender. Here is our moment. This day we determine the future of the Land itself! The songs of heroes will bear your names, each and every one of you fêted by the Gods themselves.

"We go to fight, we go to die. This nameless place shall forever be remembered by those who speak of glory. Your names, your legions, will be whispered with reverence by all peoples to come. This is our war—this is our purpose. Come, my brothers—the Gods await us!"

To remind them of Moorview, he removed his feathered hat and tossed it forward to resounding cheers up and down the line. In its place went an engraved golden helm, a band of black-iron lattice-like bee wings covering his eyes and nose. A second cheer rose up as the symbol of their king and greatest of the Gods shone in the pale light.

Emin lowered his sword and there was a renewed bellow from the thousands at his side as they started off towards the enemy, legion after legion marching in unison, the glaives of the Ghosts and halberds of the Kingsguard ready to chop a path through the Devoted. The word had been spread through the officers and sergeants; every man knew his place that day. Not a step backwards would be considered.

Alongside allies whose legend spanned the West, alongside the hated Menin who would never show weakness, the soldiers of Narkang and the Three Kingdoms roared their defiance.

"Thank you, my friends," the king said to those around him, the clamour almost drowning out his words. "It has been an honour."

Before anyone could respond Count Vesna roared out the first line of the Farlan battle-hymn and the sky erupted into sound once more.

Ruhen led his small party to the entrance to the barrow—the place of power to where his shadow soul had once led Aryn Bwr. There the Crystal Skulls had been unearthed, their place in the Land's fabric revealed and subverted. Isak managed one brief glance back at the Narkang army advancing over the plain and felt a shudder of fear for them. There were thousands of Devoted massed on the hill's slopes, divisions of archers perched in inaccessible parts, and lines of heavy infantry blocking all the routes to the summit.

The lower rise was similarly covered in troops, serried ranks of infantry on its lower slopes, with channels for the cavalry to surge down. He couldn't see the fanatical mob of Ruhen's Children, but something told him the talk of a blood sacrifice was not just some idle reference to battle.

As devoted as they might be, Ruhen's Children were unarmed and sickly, from what their scryers could discern. Their lord might simply have them driven into a cavalry charge to be obliterated, and the attackers would have no option, no matter how horrific the act.

"Come on, puppy," Ilumene said, yanking Isak's leash and dragging him to his knees once more. "Heel."

Tiniq gave him no time to rest, kicking Isak's buttocks and causing the white-eye to cry out in pain, but somehow the survival instinct inside him drove him onwards. The chain binding his chest grew heavier with every step. A whimper of fear crept through Isak's lips as he took the first step down the wide entrance, set between the two enormous carved stones each more than sixty feet high. His skin crawled under the chain's touch, and as memories of the Dark Place gripped his mind, suddenly it burned and tore at his skin. It was only the pressure Tiniq maintained on the chain that kept the shuddering white-eye from pitching forward down the steps.

As the darkness surrounded him Isak's stomach heaved and he bent over; puke dribbling over his lips and piss darkening his trousers.

"Don't bring back good memories, eh?" Ilumene cackled, dragging Isak forward once more.

Isak slipped and fell, moaning and shaking uncontrollably as the scars on his body burned as they had in Ghenna itself. Again he was beaten upright; again his deep instincts drove him onwards. He heaved desperately at the silver chain, but it was imbued with magic stronger than even one of the Chosen. He wrenched round, trying to dislodge it, but more violence brought him back to his knees and he realised the links were bound together behind his shoulder.

Ilumene stopped and smashed a steel-covered knee up into Isak's face, breaking his misshapen nose again and snapping his head backwards in a burst of pain and blood. "Do what you're fucking told," he growled at Isak, and when Isak tried to reach out with his free hand, he punched it away, then whipped out a dagger and sliced deep into the muscle of Isak's forearm as punishment.

"Listen to me, white-eye," he continued, "you remember this pain? You remember what the daemons did to you? Aye, you feel it in your bones: you're crippled by the memories. Well, here's your one chance; keep quiet and don't cause us trouble and you'll not go back there. Hear me? A free pass, like all the Chosen—but don't you dare fucking cross me! Any trouble, any delaying tactics, any attempts on any of us, and you'll not even see the slope of Ghain.

"You've fallen that way once before and it'll be damn easy to send you straight into Ghenna a second time. There'll be no escaping again. This place is halfway to the other lands. The flames of Maram light its heart, so Ruhen tells me, and I'll gladly toss you in if you cause any trouble, so here's your last chance: behave, or burn until the end o' days in the darkest place."

Isak was too sickened to reply, but his face told Ilumene that he understood the words. The former King's Man straightened and looked up at Tiniq. "Keep a tight rein," he said, and started back down the dim, red-tinted darkness of the tunnel. At last Isak found the strength to follow, wheezing and whimpering and stumbling on the stony floor as it sloped forever forward. Somewhere in the recesses of his mind, Aryn Bwr's words returned to him and he cringed in terror.

Down into darkness, into the bowels of the Land . . . Deep, so deep I feared going further would bring me to the six ivory gates of Ghenna itself.

Ahead, Ruhen walked on, unafraid and perfectly at home in the dark. From the rock all around distant voices emanated: the voices of the damned, calling him home.

Chapter 41

Vesna watched the Narkang cavalry approaching the enemy, the skirmishers between them falling quickly back. Up above, the sky refused to brighten as thick clouds came rolling in on a stiff southerly wind. He checked around him, careful to keep the mounted Ghosts in line with the marching infantry. The left flank were looking ragged already, the battle-clans eager to close with the enemy as the first flights of arrows darted up into the sky.

Ahead, the Green Scarves increased the distance between them and Vesna, looking to entice the Devoted to stand and fight. In their centre were skirmishers, firing thin volleys of arrows, while their tattooed comrades jumped forward into the attack. As he watched, the bait was taken, one legion of Devoted cavalry thinking to drive back the irritant, followed slowly by two further down the line.

The Green Scarves had enhanced their reputation on the advance to Thotel with an eagerness to fight that none of the Devoted cavalry could match. Their banner was a tattooed man holding a green noose, but crucially, those were only being carried by legions harrying the right flank. Thinking they faced lighter opposition, the Devoted drove straight for the heart of them, looking to punish their impetuousness.

Even from his position in the line Vesna heard the answering roar of the Green Scarves, and before the eyes of their savage commander, kept at the king's side, two legions charged to meet them and the crash of impact echoed out across the plain. The archers sprinted up behind, making up the ground quickly to bring their own swords to bear.

The clash of steel was distant to Vesna's ears, but the divine spirit in his blood quickened at the faint clamour. With the archers swarming around the left flank, the Devoted were taken by surprise, and when their supporting troops moved to assist, the remaining Green Scarves charged.

"Colonel Dassai's giving them a bloody nose," Swordmaster Pettir commented. "Weren't expecting a punch right down the centre."

"Let's hope it doesn't backfire then," Sir Cerse, commander of the Ghosts, replied. "Dassai's young and eager to fight, but he'll get swamped if he stays there too long."

Vesna watched the fight continue. The legions had dissolved into a senseless mass as Dassai's men hacked a path into the panicked Devoted, but the enemy had more skirmishers, and cavalry not far away. He checked left, waiting for any activity on the rise to the left, but for the moment there was nothing—no response from the reserve cavalry stationed there.

The centre of the Devoted broke, fleeing back towards their lines, while those on the right peeled back away, seeking the protection of their infantry stationed on the hill. Almost in the same moment the cavalry on the rise started to move, heading down the shallow slope towards the left where there was still fighting. The skirmishers had already turned to join that battle, but they faltered as they saw two fresh legions heading towards them, while the Green Scarves were in chaos still after the fighting.

"Come on, Dassai," Vesna found himself muttering, "get your men away."

The fresh troops charged towards the fighting, swarming around the rear and pressing in on the beleaguered Narkang men. That spurred the rest of the Green Scarves into action, but it wasn't to withdraw; instead of leaving their comrades to flee as best they could, they charged in a disordered mass towards the fighting, first one legion absorbed into the fighting, then a second, and the skirmishers followed fast on their heels.

"Fate's eyes," Vesna breathed as the centre of the plain became a broiling storm of steel and screaming horses.

He knew the main body of the army were too far away to be able to help them—their pace was already slow to avoid exhausting the men before the fighting itself. With an effort he tore his gaze away, knowing he had his own work to do, and instead inspected the enemy lines as they came closer.

The rise on the left had two lines of troops, a thick band of spearmen and a thinner one of archers behind, while more cavalry remained at the peak—no doubt waiting to outflank the Narkang troops and attack their rear. The hill had a double tier, the accessible slopes too constrained for so many soldiers, so before they even started up the hill they would have had to break through a shield-wall. It was a daunting prospect, one made more alarming if the best of their cavalry was in the process of being slaughtered.

"Are they being driven back?" Sir Cerse asked, sounding hopeful as he peered forward.

Vesna looked around the fighting for any reference points. *There, the first engagement,* he thought with a flicker of gladness.

There was a stretch of debris-strewn ground leading to the current fighting, surely an indication that the savage Green Scarves were still driving into the enemy. The conflict abruptly collapsed in on itself, the Devoted cavalry fleeing and the Green Scarves holding their ground, content to let them go.

"Now get out of the way, you bastards," called Pettir, sparking cheers and shouts from the Ghosts all around. "Clear the way for the real soldiers!"

Vesna nodded. They were closing on the enemy lines; already the first arrows were arching towards their left flank and more would be coming soon. The Green Scarves quickly retreated, bloodied and under sporadic fire from both enemy positions, but their point had been made. Vesna knew Daken would be snarling with a white-eye's fervour at the display of aggression, but the worst was yet to come for all of them.

"Two hundred yards," he commented, pulling on his helm and lifting his shield to prop the bottom on his thigh.

All around him men were doing the same as they came into range of the enemy bows. Most likely they wouldn't be targeted, being the furthest from each enemy line and the most heavily armoured, but Vesna knew this would be a day of terrible surprises. There was quite enough to kill him out here without adding complacency to the list.

"May Nartis be with us," he said aloud, a common commander's blessing among the Farlan.

Pettir cackled at his side. "Don't need 'im!" the Swordmaster called out to all those within earshot, "we got our God o' War right here beside me—today, boys, we fight like Gods!"

The air became hot in Isak's throat, each breath a rasping struggle as he staggered on down the tunnel. The slope was shallow, the tunnel wide enough for four Harlequins to comfortably walk abreast, and very high—even had he been able to stand upright and stretch up his arms, Isak wouldn't have been able to reach the irregular roof of the tunnel. All of a sudden the tunnel opened up and those leading spread out into some sort of cavern without a word. Ruhen walked on into the centre of a space thirty yards across, all dark stone and looming stalagmites. The dull, lambent red glow was stronger in here, but it was still so dark Isak could see only the flow of rock and the barest details of those ahead of him. Stalactites above shone wetly in the faint light. Beyond them the glint of a crystal seam crossed the roof.

"Are we there yet?" Ilumene asked, unimpressed with the bare rock chamber.

"Less than halfway," Ruhen replied, facing away from them.

Isak looked past the boy and saw more tunnels leading off into darkness. Which path was the right one, he couldn't tell, but he felt a flicker of hope as he looked around the room. There still was time for the army to break through; he just had to hope they would do so in time, and that someone like Legana could follow the link between them through these tunnels quicker than Isak was moving.

The room swiftly filled behind him, the Harlequins and Acolytes forming neat squads while they waited for their saviour's directions.

"Koteer, leave some Acolytes here," Ruhen said suddenly, turning to face the dozens filing briskly in.

As the boy spoke Venn began gesturing with his Crystal Skull, and trails of darkness followed his movements; the magic gave the curling gestures an elusive life of their own as they spread out and lingered faintly on the walls and rocky formations. Koteer spoke a few words in his own dialect and a group of five Acolytes bowed in acknowledgement, followed by a pair of Harlequins who did the same at a gesture from Ruhen.

"Let them blunder in the dark, led a merry dance," Venn intoned, his Crystal Skull pulsing with red-tinted light.

Isak heard a dry whisper race around the edges of the cavern; he wasn't the only one there to look for the source. The black Harlequin laughed as he saw the surprise on the faces of those around him, but instead of explaining he gave a theatrical flourish and bowed to the assembled figures.

"What was that, an invocation?" Tiniq asked from behind Isak.

Venn inclined his head to the man just as a sudden stink of decay filled the cavern. Isak's stomach lurched again and he dry-retched as the stench betrayed a presence he recognised only too well. A gust of wind rushed up from nowhere, sliding greasy fingers across his brow, and as Isak recoiled at the touch, a cold cruel voice whispered, "*Now I see you bound and kneeling, a slave as you tried to make me, white-eye.*"

Her presence momentarily surrounded him, but before Isak could attempt to respond the Wither Queen was dragged away again. He shuddered as the stink of plague washed over him in her wake, but he forced his head up to see the Aspect of Death manifest at Venn's side. In the magic-suffused air Isak could sense enough to see he was not the only one shackled by Ruhen's disciples: the power Venn held contained her just as effectively—and without it she would be almost as stricken as he was.

"My Queen," Venn said, the echoing voice not quite his own, "you will haunt these tunnels too, distract any who follow us, lead them astray as you play your games."

The Wither Queen's dead eyes flashed with hatred. "I will do as you command," she croaked in the rasping voice Isak remembered only too well from his own dealings with her.

At a tug on his leash Isak forced himself on again as Ruhen started off down a tunnel set just behind a stalagmite. Venn turned to follow without a further word, secure in his hold over the Goddess, and an escort of Harlequins padded along behind.

Through the rock and dirt underfoot Isak thought he felt some distant shudder—the roar of daemons, or the heave of great beasts fighting. Again he tested the silver chain, but with magic running through it, its strength far exceeded his own. His thoughts on the friends no doubt fighting and dying on the surface, Isak stumbled on as slowly as he dared through the dark towards his enemy's final victory.

"*Now.*"

The command went out as the sky filled with noise. Vesna heard no response, he just had to hope Nai and the other mages had heard him as the Farlan heavy cavalry charged. Behind, ahead, left and right: the voices rang out with hatred and fury, the soldiers screaming down their fear as the shuddering impact neared.

He didn't look; there was no time, and the God in him already knew. With near-perfect timing the centre hit their enemy positions almost as one, the Menin and Ghosts making up ground with a mad, reckless burst of speed, the left flank not far behind.

The Devoted infantry stood behind a shield-wall at the foot of the hill. The irregular slope and narrow front meant their packed thousands could not all fit, so the first line of defence was set at its base. Arrows hammered down from the slopes, regiments of archers perched on every precarious ledge on the rocky hill, while more legions of spearmen waited in a second line on the slope.

Behind him, Vesna sensed a powerful pulse of magic break like a storm-cloud over the charging cavalry. A shockwave raced through the ground, causing his own hunter to check its stride mid-charge, but the magic flashed forward ahead of them in a heartbeat. Without looking back, he knew Legana's Crystal Skull was blazing with power, the magic gathering up stones and dirt around the defensive trench dug by the Devoted. In his mind Vesna heard her scream with pain at the power she wielded, but ahead the loose ground jolted and writhed before rising up across a hundred yards of ground.

The line rushed up to meet them in those final yards, and Vesna tightened his grip on his sword and roared. His horse leaped in that final moment, and the whole leading line followed suit, the horses' minds soothed by magic to be unafraid of the solid wall ahead of them. His head down, Vesna felt the impact on the beast's barding, bodies and shields smashing against it, a spear punching into its belly and snapping under its momentum. All around him the tidal wave of cavalry smashed forward, crushing the ranks of Devoted infantry in an explosive impact.

The black, bitter taste of incarnating daemons blossomed in his mind and he tasted their unholy scent away on the right flank. He bellowed with renewed strength, colours and flashes of light dancing before his eyes, the Land moving too fast even for his God-blessed vision. Impacts rocked him one way then the other and his horse writhed and screamed beneath him as the stink of blood and bowels filled the air and added to the chaos and clamour.

His feet slipped from his stirrups and he threw himself forward, not waiting for his horse to fall. The golden lion helm blazed with unnatural light as Vesna unleashed his Skull's power and before his feet touched the ground, one Devoted was dead on his sword. Vesna charged on with terrifying speed, driving his shield at a standard bearer, and as the man's helm crumpled under the impact, his sword sheared through the shield and breastplate of another, spraying blood high into the air. He moved on through the reeling ranks, chopping and battering so fast they could do nothing but watch their deaths come.

All around him Vesna sensed his brothers driving forward, killing and bludgeoning, falling from dying horses or impaled upon the spears of their victims. Many of the first charge had died, and Vesna sensed their deaths with sudden intensity as the God of War honoured their falling, but their loss had been accompanied by hundreds of the Devoted, rank after rank killed in one swift burst; three legions broken so quickly many of their number did not yet even know it.

Behind came more mounted Ghosts, driving into the last remaining space with slaughter on their minds. Vesna felt the blood spatter and gush over his black armour while the roar all around only got louder.

Larim, Lord of the Hidden Tower, looked around in confusion. The charge had been astonishing, driven by a desperation he could not understand. They had advanced under a hail of arrows, tramping forward while they died in their hundreds, but never wavering. When the charge had come a white corona had surrounded Larim and the mage gloried in his new power, while waiting for a magical assault.

On his right, black shadows blossomed, daemons raging out across the weakened boundaries and leaping for the first line of the defenders. Larim sent a dozen golden arrows to answer them, each shining dart the length of a man, but he gave no order; it was a feint, he knew it. Within the Menin ranks, men were ripped apart, golden light enveloping their bodies and charring their flesh before they even fell to the ground, but Larim held back the full force now at his command.

The daemons had been only half-summoned into the daylight; they were easily driven off. Larim laughed, realising it was that fool Nai who'd dragged them forward. Even without the Skull he was a far more powerful mage, his necromancy far more refined than that shoeless worm's.

There.

Larim found his gaze dragged right, where the attackers had yet to close on the rise. Thirty yards left to go, and deadly rain was hammering through shields and armour, when a burst of magic rippled the ground between them. From nowhere dark figures appeared; tall, ragged barbarians rushed forward, outstripping their allies in the last yards of the charge. Magic flashed out from the ranks, cutting forward into the defenders with red and white light, and fire erupted around one legion standard just as the unnatural barbarians reached the Devoted spear-points.

At last he unleashed the power of his Skull; churning the earth across the defending ranks as he threw wave after wave of golden arrows at the Legion of the Damned. In his mind he shouted up to Vorizh, circling up above, never slowing his assault, even as the air screamed around him under the force of bucking energies. Man and undead alike were torn apart, the nearer flank shattered by his furious assault, even before the dark shapes of the crimson wyverns dropped down from the heavy clouds above. A larger one followed—Ruhen's grey dragon, called from Byora—and landed awkwardly on the furthest edge of the attacking Legion.

The pale white-eye giggled as he saw, amidst the cloud of dust and further, the dragon had crushed a whole section of Devoted defenders. As though inspired by its careless abandon, he redoubled his efforts at the attacking force, though they had closed with the Devoted now, and his magic incinerated attacker and defender alike.

From the broiling maelstrom of fighting, coils of black smoke reached up and whipped across the dragon's flank. The two wyverns recoiled at the attack, realising the power behind it was beyond them; and they flew up into the air until they were hovering above the fighting. Larim laughed more, and directed his assault on the source of that magic. A white shield formed above the troops and his arrows burst upon it, cutting short his laughter. There were two Skull-bearers there, one deflecting his attack and the other tearing strips from the dragon's wings while the beast writhed and bellowed in pain.

"I don't need to kill you," Larim muttered. "Enjoy this while it lasts. You cannot afford your attack to be blunted, and even now it falters."

As he spoke, a figure dropped from the lower wyvern, spiralling down towards the mage attacking the dragon. Magic lashed up to meet him, but Vorizh reached the ground with blade slashing down. The black-armoured vampire disappeared into the press and Larim flinched in shock, sensing a sudden cut-off of energies—but not through a mage's death; it was the casual abandoning of a spell.

The surging mass of undead troops enveloping the Devoted line vanished in the blink of an eye, and though the dragon and wyverns dipped again to attack, Larim felt it like a punch to the gut.

Mage Endine struggled to keep his seat, one hand wrapped tightly around the saddle horn, the other was outstretched towards the Devoted lines. At his side Emin looked around, craning his neck to try and make out what he could of the left flank.

"The illusion's gone," Endine reported, sensing the break in Morghien's spell.

"Is he dead?" Emin demanded, watching the three monsters renew their assault. He smacked a gauntlet on Doranei's shoulder and the King's Man yelled an order. The foot legion of the Ghosts bellowed and charged forward with the Legion of the Damned, towards their hero, Vesna, raging at the heart of the slaughter.

Endine didn't reply; he couldn't tell, and he had only one thing on his mind right now. It wasn't hard for him to make out the brightly coloured figure of Lord Larim on the hillside, huge golden arrows erupting from the shuddering air around his hands. The small mage narrowed his eyes and felt the Skull respond, momentarily glowing hot before a bolt of crackling white light flashed forward towards Larim.

The white-eye saw it coming and a grey shield briefly obscured him from view, but then the bolt struck—not the shield, as Larim had expected, but at the ground, further down the slope from him.

"Got the bastard!" Endine screeched, his lined face suddenly filling with animation. "He's drunk with blood-lust—he's not thinking properly!"

As he cried out, the ground at Larim's feet tore open, a jagged wound ten or twenty yards long, and the white-eye was thrown down, together with the mages and soldiers around him. Stones the size of men tumbled down the slope, cutting a path through the second line of defenders waiting below, but it was the sight of Larim falling forward that made King Emin catch his breath. All around him energies corkscrewed up into the sky as the abandoned magic dissipated. The white-eye lurched drunkenly before toppling over, only just catching himself as his head and shoulders went over the edge into the fissure.

"Close it up on him," Doranei demanded from the king's other side.

"I don't have that sort of power," Endine snapped.

"Not even with the Skull?"

"You've been spending too much time around white-eyes," Endine said. "The rest of us need a little more elegance if we're to avoid our hearts exploding out of our chests!" He closed his eyes and with the Skull of Knowledge held in both hands, he began to whisper arcane words under his breath. A bluish aura appeared around him, whipping up from stillness to a sudden fury in seconds. With a grunt of effort Endine pulled his hands apart again and cast the magic forward. It arched through the air towards Larim, tearing through the desperate defences of the lesser mages and plunging directly down onto the white-eye. Larim somehow managed to wrench himself around, and Endine rocked backwards as the white-eye dragged himself from the fissure's edge. Enveloped in a blue-tinted cloud, Larim's own Skull winked and sputtered with light while Endine moaned with effort, his exhausted muscles suddenly straining to close his hands again.

"Emin!" he croaked, his hands shaking wildly, and the king looked at him, wild-eyed for a moment until he realised what he needed to do.

"Daken!" he shouted to the tattooed white-eye on Endine's other side, "grab his hands!"

Emin took one, Daken the other, and together they forced Endine's palms back onto the Crystal Skull. The mage cried out with pain as they did so, but suddenly they heard a crack and a crunch of bone and the pressure vanished. The mage's hands crashed against the Skull with force enough that Emin feared he might have broken them, but Endine was already straining to see the figure on the hillside.

Figures fluttered around where Larim had been, but there was no sign of the white-eye, or the magic he'd been struggling to re-gather.

"Dead," Endine confirmed hoarsely after a moment, almost slumping forward in his seat until Daken jerked him back.

"Then the time's come," Emin announced. He pulled Endine around to look the scrawny mage in the eye again. "You have command of the army, my friend."

Endine nodded weakly as Ebarn forced her way up to his side, the crystal shards on the battle-mage's jacket shining as she prepared to unleash her power while Endine gathered his strength.

"I want a defensive square of those spearmen," Emin added, directing his words to Dashain as well as Endine. "We need this hinge to hold, or we'll be split apart and butchered."

"We know our duty, your Majesty," Dashain yelled, "now move!"

The king didn't wait for a response but spurred his horse forward, the King's Men and Legana's Sisters close behind. Ahead the ground was stained rusty-red with blood and churned to a muddy mire, but they all knew that was only the beginning.

CHAPTER 42

THEY WALKED FOR WHAT FELT LIKE AN AGE. Isak dragged down the pace as far as he could, but whenever Ruhen got too far ahead, Tiniq or Ilumene would hammer at Isak's broad back with the pommels of their knives—never hard enough to break his bones, but the pain of the blows lingered long after he had dragged himself up again.

The tunnels twisted and turned, forever descending into the bowels of the Land. The oppressive warmth of the tunnels grew and the mixture of sweat and blood dried stickily across his back while the silver chain remained a hot presence against his skin. They passed through another chamber, then a third and fourth, and each time another squad of soldiers was left to hide in the side tunnels, ready to ambush anyone passing through. Twice Ruhen turned back from the path he had taken, doubling back without haste to take another instead. No one questioned his decisions; Ilumene and Venn were the only people even to speak to the child, and it was clear from the brief responses that Ruhen was not interested in conversation. He was too close to his goal; from time to time his serene face flowered briefly into moments of rare animation and expectation before he caught himself.

Isak kept his eyes down, exhausted and pained by the burden of Termin Mystt, enfeebled by the proximity of Ghenna and the ache it sparked deep in his bones. As they descended he felt the silver chain as Death's final judgement, the weight of his sins bearing down on him as he came ever closer to the Dark Place of Torment. At last he realised they were in a wider tunnel than before, one that was slowly broadening until it suddenly opened out into a vast cavern that made even Ruhen stop in wonder. Isak heard Ilumene breath an oath at the sight, stopping as he stared up and all around.

Isak took the opportunity to sink to his knees.

The cavern was barely brighter than the chambers they had passed through, but magic filled the air with such intensity that Isak felt a stab of pain in his gut. Behind the great twisted scar on his stomach a fire burned, reminding him of the agonising wound that had killed him. He screwed up his eyes in pain, moaning piteously, but Ilumene kicked him in the ribs and sent him sprawling. His eyes flashed open and he stared up at the roof far above.

The cavern was several hundred feet high, with dozens of natural pillars all studded with crystal formations that glinted with orange-red light. As Isak hauled himself upright he realised the light was coming from the centre of the cavern, fifty yards off, and obscured by pillars wider than a man's outstretched arms. Through them he glimpsed movement, flickering orange flames reflecting off the stone surfaces. Ahead were carved columns marked with ancient runes and angular images.

"Come," Ruhen called to those behind him, "the sacrifice has begun. Soon we will be ready."

Under Ilumene's urging Isak shuffled forward, trying to make more sense of the cavern before he slipped and crashed face-first to the floor again. His jailers wasted no time in beating the white-eye brutally until he cried out in agony.

Then Ruhen's voice stopped them short. "Enough. Let him rise."

Isak stayed on the ground a little longer, curled protectively as best he could, expecting the violence to return, until he looked up tentatively and saw the boy with one white eye staring at him. "I promised you peace if you do not interfere," Ruhen said, the swirl of shadows in his eyes never more obvious than in the cavern's half-light, "and torment if you defy me. But trust is not easily won; faith is never your first instinct."

Isak grunted in response, unable to form a coherent reply, but Ruhen said, "Let this be a gesture to you. They will not harm you unless you break my faith. I am to be a God this day, so let mercy be my first act."

Isak stared at Ruhen, momentarily forgetting the pain as the unexpected words slowly fitted into place in his mind. "Mercy?" he croaked in disbelief.

The shadow-eyed boy smiled. "You think I do not know what mercy is? King Emin might not believe it, but he has long been my enemy. When you are at war your enemy sees you just as a monster, you understand? A creature incapable of reason, abhorrent in all ways. How else could you fight them?"

"What about the rest, my friends? Mercy for them too?"

"Most will die," Ruhen said, "but such is the nature of war. You fear eternal retribution? I admit I do not know what Godhood is like, but I choose to believe petty revenge would stain my victory. Those who oppose me must be dealt with, but to cast them all into Ghenna out of spite?" He turned away and headed for the centre of the vast cavern.

"We have time yet, Isak," Ruhen called back as Harlequins began to make their way between the stone pillars. "Rest a while, then join me with your Gods. We stand at the heart of the Land, on the cusp of a new age. History is born anew this day; the fulcrum of this moment can be permitted a few breaths to savour a purpose fulfilled."

Vesna snatched up a sword that stood in his path, buried in the chest of a dead soldier. He ducked a blow and brought his own longsword up under the movement, dragging it across the Devoted's chest with Gods-granted strength, opening the man up. The next attack he caught on his new weapon, shoving the soldier back and slashing at his face. The man stumbled and fell before the blow could connect, toppling backwards over the corpse of a comrade.

The Ghosts on either side of Vesna continued forward, their glaives swinging and falling in terrible rhythm. The fallen man was trampled, unnoticed, by the Farlan élite who squeezed the breath from his lungs before a heavy boot landed on his neck.

Vesna was the heart of their relentless march, shouting himself hoarse in between savage assaults on the Devoted. The remains of the first line were butchered and they drove on into the second, faltering on the slope as the effort sapped their limbs and arrows smacked down on all sides. But a renewed surge came behind Vesna, silent and swift, and it drained the resolve from the faces ahead of him. He didn't need to turn to see the Legion of the Damned behind him, just charged on ahead of them, casting terrible flashes of light into their ranks to disrupt them before the wave struck.

Shields dropped, spear-heads lowered as yellow flames danced over tabards and tunics. Vesna ran forward with a half-scalped man at his side, grey, desiccated skin flapping loose as the undead mercenary chopped down with his enormous axe and almost split the first defender in two. Vesna took the one beside him, but blinded by spraying blood, the man never saw his own death as Vesna impaled him, shoving him bodily into those behind.

The ranks were deep enough for most assaults, but Vesna's veins sparkled with war's own lifeblood and he punched through them with ease. In his wake came the undead, spreading like rot in a wound, dragging the fractured line apart with every batter and swipe. An arrow smashed into Vesna's back as he turned to survey the breach, momentarily unable to reach any defenders.

The force smacked him forward and he staggered, half-falling against a dead man, who grinned up at him with a broken, hanging jaw.

An arrow protruded from that man's gullet, but he had no use for talk anyway; the undead soldier shoved Vesna aside and drove on, ruined face no hindrance as he surged down behind the line, chopping with abandon at the rear ranks. Vesna recovered his balance and flexed his shoulders. Feeling no wound, he waved forward the remaining Ghosts at the base of the hill. As he did so, more of the undead jumped past him and Vesna turned to see a counter-attack barrelling down the hillside, several regiments of the reserve charging to seal the breach.

The God-spirit inside him whispered words Vesna didn't know and an arc of blood-tinted fire whipped across the advancing Devoted as arrows dropped like hunting falcons. The front rank collapsed, cut in two as blood sprayed high and shockingly bright against the threatening sky. Vesna ran to meet those remaining, battering one fear-crazed soldier aside and parrying the spear of another before smashing his vambrace into his chest. The soldier was thrown back as Vesna chopped through the legs of the next, both men savagely finished off by the eager undead.

Behind him came the remaining Ghosts, the foot legion who'd arrived in the wake of his insane direct charge. They swarmed forward after the Legion, almost a thousand men in heavy armour bursting their hearts to ascend the slope, swinging their short-handled glaives. The second line crumpled, split apart and descended into chaos. The archers and remaining reserves behind them raced to stem the tide, but with Vesna holding his ground and the Legion chopping through all who faced them, they could do nothing.

Gasping for air, the Farlan nobleman drove onward; King Emin and his black-clad attendants were close behind as he headed upslope. There would be more at the crest, of that he had no doubt, but the breach was won.

There's still time.

"Form square!" Endine yelled hoarsely, his reedy voice echoing like thunder across the battlefield. The Narkang spearmen ran to obey, the first legion forming a shield-wall in the centre of the dip between rise and hill. On their right the Farlan Ghosts tore into the defending lines, but the Narkang men knew they were not there to help them. Arrows dropped from both sides, the Devoted on the nearside of the rise barely involved in the battle, but also aware they needed to hold their position.

Ahead of the shield-wall, on the open ground past the gap between rise and hill, stood a great huddled mass of white-cloaked figures. It was unclear whether they were armed—or whether Ruhen's Children posed any threat at all. Although they massively outnumbered the three legions of spearmen, it didn't look likely that the fanatics would be able to do much at all.

Endine turned to the left flank, where the battle clans were embroiled in savage fighting. The mercenaries were less enthusiastic in their assault, but holding position and tying up the Devoted forces as required. They didn't need a breach there, despite the efforts of Wentersorn and Morghien, trying to draw Vorizh into the fighting. So as long as the left held their ground and prevented the remaining cavalry from encircling the centre, their job would be done.

For a moment he stood still, overwhelmed by the cacophony that surrounded him. The breach on the hill was clearly marked by a great stain of churned bloody mud. The High Mage felt a sudden, powerful sense of dismay at the sight of the desperate, savage struggles going on all across the field, the piled corpses, the screams of hundreds of injured men and women. The dead, already in their thousands, reminded him of the emptiness of that victory at Moorview.

Then a memory of his great friend, the oversized mage Shile Cetarn, filled his mind. They had been colleagues and rivals for years. Cetarn had always been cheerful and ebullient, even as they parted and he walked to his death. The man had been imperfect and arrogant, blinkered and stubborn—and he had been a hero.

When Death's winged attendants called to him, Cetarn had not blinked or faltered. What more could a man ask for but be remembered like that? *I'll see you soon, my friend,* Endine thought, drawing once more on the Skull he carried. Above him the air erupted into flame. *Soon, but not yet. I'll keep you waiting a while longer now.*

Amidst the chaos, Amber found a moment of peace. As he moved through the ranks, cutting, hacking, battering his way through, his mind receded into calm. The pain of memory was gone, the fear and exhaustion of daily life had faded into the background. No black birds lingered on the edges of his vision, no ache of their presence drained the strength from his limbs.

He saw only the enemy ahead of him—the splintered shields and spear-studded bodies, the terror on their faces, the shocking scarlet of blood on the pale ground—as the Menin drove steadily forward. They were almost silent, lost in the slaughter as their God had taught them, unaware and disinterested in what happened beyond this fight. The Land could have burned around them and the Menin heavy infantry would not care; until the enemy were all dead or the last frantic defender fell, they would keep to their task.

Amber lunged, his right-hand scimitar scraping across a Devoted's shield as his left-hand blade hacked into the man's neck and he fell. Another took his place, only to be smashed from his feet by the infantryman on Amber's right. Another volley of arrows flashed down and his comrade was caught in the shoulder. He reeled and hissed with rage, but continued to push forward. Another glanced off Amber's pauldron and clattered against the man behind him even as a ricochet skewed wildly past his face and struck someone else.

The line was fragmented, their order barely holding as more soldiers pushed past Amber, eager to be in the thick of the fighting. The first of those died in a heartbeat as an arrow pierced his neck; the man died standing in the spot his general had been about to take.

Amber felt the blood spatter against his helm, but this was not the time to hesitate. He shoved the corpse forward and as it toppled it tangled the legs of a Devoted officer for long enough to let Amber stab him in the face. The man fell shrieking, his mouth a butchered ruin. Amber, numb, trod on the officer's head and used him as a platform to attack the next.

"Reform!" came the shout behind him, the cry taken up by the sergeants up and down the blood-soaked band of ground, and he looked around, momentarily confused, until he realised the enemy were all dead. Arrows still crashed down on all sides, and he watched a Menin raise his sword with a victorious yell, only to have one thwack straight into the eye-hole of his helm. His head snapped back, his limbs twitching as the arrow drove deep into his brain, then he dropped to his knees, pitched face-down into the mud and was still.

As the rear ranks moved up past Amber, he watched the hail of arrows clatter onto their upraised shields. Still nothing could stir him until the sight of Nai running towards him, blood running from a cut down his cheek, awakened something else inside him, reminding him of their purpose there.

He looked up the slope. It would be a hard tramp, one few commanders would want to assault had there been only a legion of defenders ahead; as it was, there were at least five: five thousand men there, bracing themselves. He raised his sword as the new front rank locked shields and the disordered remnants of his own moved in behind them.

"No surrender!" he roared, and his shout taken up by the thousands all around him. "We are Menin—we will show these cowards how true warriors fight!"

They started up the slope with steady, careful steps. Arrows smacked down, but the soldiers didn't even flinch at the impacts. Amber pushed his way back to the front, ready to enter the fray again when there was space. If he was fatigued, he couldn't feel it. If he was wounded, the pain was another part of him that had receded into the shadows. He would kill, and kill again: no retreat, no rest.

Over the battlefield came the rumble of thunder; the quick bright stab of lightning cut across the sky. Amber felt his lips draw back in a ghastly grin as the air prickled around them. He could feel Karkarn now—the hand of Death on his shoulder had been replaced with the War God's.

"Our God is with us!" one man shouted nearby. "His blessings fall upon us!"

"Karkarn bear witness!" Amber cried in response, a refrain from an ancient saga of the Menin. "The blood we spill, the death we wield—we are war! *We are Menin!*"

As they closed on the second line of Devoted defenders, he could see the fear in their faces.

From horseback, Endine watched the beggars, Ruhen's Children, approach. It was foolish—it was *madness*—but they were coming. He couldn't begin to guess how many, but there were thousands, their torn white clothing flapping in the breeze, their voices joined in some low moaning paean. Above their heads he could see the shimmer and dance of unrestrained magic, a vast power unveiled. The grey dust had coated their skin, lending an inhuman, unnatural paleness to the faces slowly edging towards them.

Endine looked around, trying to fathom the ruse of an unarmed mob advancing on formed-up infantry lines. On his right, the Legion of the

Damned and the Ghosts had punched like a lance through the enemy lines, taking the king and Legana to their target on the hill, while beyond them the Menin were steadily butchering those opposing them, uncaring of the toll on their own numbers.

The left hadn't fared as well; Morghien and Wentersorn had exhausted themselves driving off the grey dragon and Vorizh's wyverns. Even with the Skulls in their hands, neither was mage enough to inflict the damage needed to gain the rise, and the mercenaries were slowly being forced back. Behind the crowd of Ruhen's Children he could see the cavalry, the battles swift and savage, but nothing that looked conclusive to him.

"They're coming, sir!" yelled an officer, and he and Ebarn drew once more on their Crystal Skulls. Pain screamed down his neck and he almost blacked out at the furious surge of magic running through his body, but he drove it back. Spitting cords of light erupted from his up-stretched arm, wrenched unwillingly back on themselves, until a roiling ball of energy spun above him.

He hurled it towards the mob just before Ebarn scattered dozens of twisting black shapes into the air. The ball of light struck first, exploding like a siege-weapon in the heart of the mob and tossing bodies high. The bright cords flung out in all directions, suddenly released from the magic containing them, crashing out through the mob to set light to dozens more.

The mob faltered just as Ebarn's magical arrows darted down with the angry zip of hornets, tearing into unprotected flesh with terrible ease, but neither spell stopped them; the dead fell unnoticed and were trampled in the mob's eagerness to reach the army. The voices grew in intensity and volume, building to an uncontrolled rage as they quickened their advance.

"Ready!" called an officer from somewhere through the haze of burnt air surrounding Endine, "take the impact!"

And the mob smashed into the shield-wall with a crash that made the ground shake. Endine felt the blow in his bones, and for a moment his control of the magic wavered, fading into nothing as tiny claws of pain dug into his scalp. He saw the enemy clearly now, and heard the panicked shouts from his soldiers, for they didn't look human: deathly white and hairless, they were more like daemons of the daytime.

They hurled themselves forward with terrible speed, talons raking at armour and bursting through iron-bound shields. Endine saw one spearman drive his weapon into a man's shoulder. The point slammed home—then glanced up and away, leaving only a grey groove along the white bony plate that covered his chest.

"They're swamping us," Ebarn shouted, her face frantic as she watched the shield-wall buckle.

The Brotherhood mage was hurling bundles of darting arrows and they were killing their targets, but Ruhen's Children ignored the deaths and spilled around the shield-wall facing them, desperate to throw themselves at the spearmen. The two mages sat on horseback at the heart of the square, but suddenly Endine felt very alone. Ebarn was right: they would soon be encircled by the white monsters. Even as he recovered himself and cast more burning energies, he saw figures scrambling over the shield-wall itself. The reserve squads ran to meet them, enveloping their furious charges with impaling spears, but it took a hail of blows to fell each one.

Ebarn shrieked with rage as she drew deeper on the Skull and Endine felt a jolt in his stomach as he realised she couldn't possibly survive such power, but then he followed suit. The Land went white around them as bolts of lightning split the air, scorching men and monsters alike as the two opened themselves completely. Then the shield-wall collapsed under the weight of the fanatics and a great animal howl went up. Endine could barely see what was happening; fire licked the edges of his robes and the horse beneath him screamed in fear.

A group of the monsters ran for him and Endine picked them up and tore open their limbs in a spray of greyish blood. More came, and he watched the flailing figures grappling with each other in their bloodlust. He killed dozens with consuming fire, still they came. Distantly he heard Fei Ebarn's cries cut off as a detonation of rampant energies ripped her apart, but he had no time to look, for his own gaze was dimming as he continued to lash out at the white figures advancing towards him.

Sharp fingers reached for him, tearing through the flesh on his skinny thighs as they tried to pull him down. His horse bucked and wrenched away from the attackers, and Endine continued to fight as his skin went cold and numb. He barely felt the talons digging deeper, and some fell away as he killed them, but even in the blinding storm cloud surrounding him they fought on.

At last he was done, and the Land went from white to grey to black as one final burst of pain erupted from his heart and the talons closed around his ribs. He fell, and all around him, the heart of the Narkang army died.

Daken scooped up a discarded shield and grinned at Vesna. The white-eye had blood running freely from a torn lip and his cheeks were splattered with the deaths of a dozen men. They stood at the crest of the hill with dead and dying men all around then. The rigid lines of defenders had collapsed and the hill was now a free-for-all, a thousand individual battles being fought up and down its slope.

"Waiting for those dead bastards to get all the glory?" Daken rasped, brandishing the shield wildly.

Vesna looked back at the Ghosts and Kingsguard struggling forward in their wake, hampered as much by the corpses covering the ground as by the slope. Beyond them they could see the lower line of defenders was still holding against one legion of Kingsguard, while the Menin had slaughtered those in front of them and were pressing the upper line hard. In any normal battle this would have been won; Vesna would be turning inwards to seal the victory and meet the Menin in a double envelopment, but with nowhere to go, the Devoted couldn't crumple and run. Their only option was to fight to the death, and thousands had already done so.

"Wait for the king," he commanded. "We can't do it alone."

"He'd better hurry, then!" Daken swapped his axe to his shield-hand and thumped his free fist against his chest. "Wake up, bitch! You ain't sleeping through all of this!"

For a moment nothing happened, then Vesna saw faint trails of blue light creep up from around Daken's breastplate. Four, then a half-dozen or more, the trails wavered uncertainly in the dull daylight until Daken cackled with mad delight and turned towards the standing stones at the hill's peak.

The hilltop was close to flat, but at its very centre the ground rose up in an approximate circle around the great carved monoliths. More defenders were stationed there: Ruhen's final line, protecting the entrance to the barrow. From where he stood Vesna could see they were heavily armoured, an élite troop standing with shields locked and weapons ready. There were no archers among them, and for a strange moment Vesna felt a sense of calm: the faint breath before the storm returned.

They had scattered entire divisions. King Emin and his close guard were still fighting in the wake of the Legion's dwindling but inexhaustible troops. Daken and Vesna, the point of the spear, had driven right through the enemy.

Vesna turned back the way they had come—

He gasped in horror: the disordered, unarmed mob of Ruhen's Children had swamped the legions left to protect their centre. One whole side of the square had been engulfed, and even as he watched the rest folded in on themselves.

"There is magic on them," Karkarn whispered in his ear, *"the touch of Aenaris."*

Vesna shuddered. Whatever Ruhen's Children were now, they had just overrun and crushed several legions of battle-ready soldiers. "This is Ruhen's tactic—he'll break us from the rear," he cried to Daken, then roared, "Ozhern!" his voice amplified with unnatural power, but he received no response from the commander of the Legion.

He ran towards the nearest of the Damned, the Crystal Skull he carried pulsing with warmth. He reached out a hand and grabbed at the air, the flicker of Karkarn's spirit inside him obeying his unspoken command. The undead mercenary jerked around as he was yanked bodily through the air and hurled towards Vesna, driving his spear into the ground to catch his balance as he hit the earth. Tattered hair fell across the dead man's face as the weapon was tugged out of the ground.

"Look!" Vesna yelled, feeling the War God again stir inside at the mercenary's hostile poise. He pointed, and after a moment the undead warrior turned towards the rout at the base of the hill, then jerked back towards Vesna with a flash of understanding. In the next moment the entire remaining regiments of undead had broken off and were barrelling headlong down the slope.

"Emin!" Vesna yelled, "get the regulars to turn and attack them, Kingsguard too!"

The king turned too, visibly startled, by what he saw there. At his side Dashain, one arm hanging limp and useless, barked orders to a captain of the Kingsguard.

"My mage is dead," Emin shouted back. "I cannot contact them!" He cast around for a few moments, then yelled, "Legana! Order our regulars to withdraw and engage the centre!"

The Mortal-Aspect stood amidst a pile of corpses, long-knives bloody and an aura of emerald light shining about her. She glanced at the spear legions just starting up the lower slope before returning her piecing gaze to their direction and gesturing: it was done.

Vesna didn't wait; it would take them a while before anyone was able to react to the orders. Shoring up the rear would mean nothing if they couldn't break through this final defence and reach Isak in time. Daken had already set off towards the standing stones and Vesna fell in behind the white-eye, realising what the man intended. The blossoming taste of magic filled the air and he hesitated, for a moment not sure if it was Litania, Daken's own Aspect—but the power far exceeded hers. With a thought he threw out a wild, unfocused mass of energies, just as two enormous detonations crashed down on his shield.

The impact stopped him dead and he rocked back on his heels. The blistering shield above them exploded into a shower of sparks. From behind him he sensed Legana hurling something in response, and the sky turned emerald as she lashed at the standing stones. He gathered his wits and moved on, struggling to catch up with Daken, who was ploughing on regardless. With an effort he threw up another shield around them, a haze of sparks obscuring the hunkered soldiers ahead of them, but in the next moment he realised it was not necessary.

From the standing stones a figure rose up in the air, four fat crackling bands of light driving into the ground beyond the soldiers. He glimpsed a robed figure wreathed in fire, a slender man with white-blond hair, moving away from Vesna towards the rocky back slope of the hill. With Larim dead and two Mortal-Aspects advancing on him, the mage who'd grabbed the dead Menin's Crystal Skull knew he was outmatched. He was no fanatic, he had no desire to die for his master, so he withdrew, dropping behind the defending soldiers, leaving them to their fate.

Daken, half-crouched behind his shield, charged with a roar as Litania's trails of blue light reached out to the waiting spears. Vesna stopped and channelled the energy of his own shield towards Daken, throwing the force behind him just as the white-eye reached the line of defenders. Blue sparks burst on the waiting spear-heads, their shafts shattered into splinters and leaving only unarmed men in his path.

Vesna pushed forward and the white-eye was bodily thrown into them, crashing right through the overlapping shields and scattering soldiers left and right.

With Doranei and Forrow as his side, Vesna raced to the breach before the defenders had even worked out what had happened. He cut through the first man and beheaded the next. Doranei turned the other way, attacking the right-hand side of the hole with long, sweeping blows of his star-speckled sword, while Forrow went in after Daken, roaring as though possessed by the mad spirit of his predecessor.

In their wake came the Ghosts, breathing hard but far more skilled than anyone they faced, and close behind came the swift Sisters of Dusk, spreading out around the ring of soldiers while the Ghosts attacked from within. Vesna found himself on flat pavestones, beyond the main line of Devoted, and a Harlequin leaped forward, twin swords whistling through the air. He caught one on his own blade. The other hammered into his pauldron, but the God-blessed armour turned it. Before he could counterattack, the Harlequin had peeled away and was dancing towards a Ghost. He slashed down at the back of the man's knee and the Ghost faltered, crying out in pain, but he never even had the time to fall before he was spitted in the side. Vesna whipped a fistful of sparks towards the Harlequin, but the figure jinked to the side with inhuman speed. He lunged forward and was parried, but this time Vesna charged on and crashed bodily into the Harlequin. A blade scraped down his armoured side, and then he had driven it from its feet and they fell together, Vesna's greater weight driving the wind from the Harlequin's lungs as he landed on it. He head-butted it, and the white mask it wore shattered and fell away as Vesna stabbed his sword into its belly.

The Harlequin spasmed and cried out, its voice high and feminine, and Vesna felt a jolt in his gut at the sound. He looked down and saw a woman's small features, her face contorted by pain. He hesitated, even as she moved, stabbing the point of her sword into the joint of his armour and driving him off her, his sword tearing out of her gut in a great spray of blood. For a moment they lay side by side, staring into each other's eyes, and then a boot stamped down on her neck.

"Get up, you bastard!" Daken roared, turning as he shouted to swat away a spear with the butt of his axe. He brought the weapon back around and chopped down into the Devoted soldier attacking him, dropping the man with a crunch.

Vesna felt a sharp pain in his side as he fought his way unsteadily to his feet, and then he felt Karkarn invade his mind quite suddenly, and gasped as the War God turned a weapon and cut clean through a man's arm. The cold, clear soul of a God washed away the grief threatening to consume him.

Vesna staggered back as the God fled again, too weakened to take control for any longer than that, but the sight of the soldier dropping to his knees and shrieking at the wound brought him back to the fight. His side was on fire, but he found himself able to move and fight still, so he drove the pain from his mind and moved on.

All around him the Ghosts and Sisters were butchering the reeling, shattered remnants of the Devoted defenders; their spirit had been broken by their commander's retreat and Daken's mad rush. Those still alive, the few score defending the far side of the stones, were driven off and the Ghosts let them go, glad for any moment to catch their breath after the exhausting ascent through the lines.

"Emin, go!" Vesna yelled, pointing towards the black, open stairway between the two tallest stones.

"You're not coming?" the king gasped, running up to him. "We'll need you."

Vesna pointed back the way they had come, and even from this distance they could clearly see their troops falling to the crazed white monsters of Ruhen's Children. Even as they surveyed the slaughter, he gestured at a Devoted regiment advancing towards them. "You need someone watching your back here. The Ghosts need to make a stand, and me with them. You need men who can walk in the shadows down there—Legana's going with you, Daken, Doranei, Leshi, Shinir—but my place is here. You can handle that shadow's Harlequins without me."

As Emin nodded, Vesna saw a line scored down one side of his helm. The king held out a hand. "Karkarn chose his Iron General well."

The Farlan hero faltered as his mind suddenly conjured an image of Tila's last agonised expression, the remnants of a shattered Harlequin's mask surrounding her face. He took the hand. "Get it done and get out," he said gruffly. "We'll be needing a great king after."

Emin ducked his head and tore off his boots, the Brotherhood and Legana's Sisters following suit. Before Vesna could turn back to the fight, another man ran up to him, heaving for breath and covered in blood.

"Too old for this shit," he, tearing his helm from his face and sucking in great lungfuls of air. "Cut my boots for me, will you?"

"Carel, stay here," Vesna ordered, but the veteran just spat on the ground and straightened up.

"Fine, I'll do it myself."

"You'll die!" Vesna protested.

"My boy's down there!" Carel shouted, "and I'm going." He started to run the edge of his notched sword over his boots, trying to slice the laces open and get his feet free, but the weapon had blunted and wouldn't cut properly.

"Carel, listen to me."

The old man dropped his sword and grabbed Vesna with his one hand. "You listen to me, boy!" he shouted, "I'm going, an' that's the end of it! You want to part on bad terms, that's your choice."

Vesna stared into his eyes a moment longer, then bowed his head. He pulled his dagger from his belt and bent to slash Carel's boots open. He dragged them off Carel's feet and ripped open his leggings so the tattoos were exposed. "I don't want to part that way," he said, "I'd rather call you brother before the end."

Unexpectedly Carel embraced him. "Aye, brother it is. I never meant those words I said back in Tirah. You know what grief does to a man."

Vesna nodded, unable to speak.

"See you in the Herald's Hall," Carel added, breaking away from the Mortal-Aspect and retrieving his sword with a grunt. "Put in a good word for me, y'hear?"

With that he was off, half-running, half-limping towards the stairway where most of the Brotherhood had already entered.

"Goodbye, brother," Vesna whispered, filled with sudden certainty that he wouldn't see the ageing warrior again. He shook himself, then shouted, "Right you bastards! *Form line!*" The Iron General looked around at his remaining soldiers. Some three hundred Ghosts out of the two thousand who'd ridden to Moorview had reached the top with him. No doubt there were more left back on the slope, still fighting, but three hundred would have to be enough.

"Well, brothers," he called out as they started to get into position, "looks like we've found a good place to die. Let's give the bards something to sing about, eh?"

And all around him, the Farlan battle-hymn started up again.

Chapter 43

At the centre of the cavern there were more standing stones, each one as high as the pair marking the entrance, set in a circle thirty yards across. They'd not been carved or quarried, and the only markings they bore were the rune of a God, carved on their inside faces, above a small niche. Isak could feel the presence of the Gods here; this place was a lodestone for their spirits.

As he dragged himself towards the centre of the cavern Isak felt the heat on his skin, and he quailed inside, knowing the sight he would soon be faced with. When they had rounded the last of the great pillars even Ilumene had faltered, the leash falling slack for a moment, until Ruhen had gestured and the former King's Man trotted up to his side again.

A swift-flowing river of fire, ten feet wide, was swirling around the standing stones, high flames leaping like grasping hands from its surface. A single stone slab crossed it. Isak cringed at the memory of Ghenna as the heat and pain of his torments radiated out of his many scars. He dropped to one knee, his arm thrown across his face as though to protect himself, but he could not tear his gaze from those flames.

"Lit by the River Maram," Ruhen announced with delight, "holy beyond the Palace of the Gods itself. This is the heart of the Land, the very bedrock of the Gods and the worship that sustains them." The boy turned to face Isak and he saw the shadows surge and dance in the mismatched eyes. His pale skin was tainted by grey swirls as Maram's light showed Azaer's true self through its mortal vessel.

"This is the place?" Isak croaked, fighting for breath. He forced himself to his feet again, standing for a moment with the silver chain dragging at his shoulder, until he dropped heavily to his knees again and prolonged the moment a fraction more. "This is where you had Aryn Bwr forge the Skulls?"

Ruhen gestured towards the standing stones and Isak realised each of the niches set below each God's rune was were werelarge enough to take a Crystal Skull. "I merely showed him this place; his decisions were his own."

"But you gave him the idea—how to restrict the power of the Gods."

"I told him the truth of the crystals he found here, the link each one had to the Gods, how worship and magic flowed through them. How each could be limited, the Last King discovered himself. He saw them for what they were: beings of power who cared little for their creations. He made them care, he made them dependent on their followers, and for that they hated him."

Ruhen looked at Isak, his face strangely intense. "Do you remember any tales of the Age of Myths? The mountains they carelessly tore down, the moon they threw into the night sky? They acted without regard for consequences. The myths speak nothing of the mortals lost when the mountains fell or the waters rose. The Elves suffered, the Tribes of Man suffered, and so Aryn Bwr tried to limit them, to grant the Gods understanding and bring the creation of mortal life full circle."

"And for that they cursed him," Isak whispered.

"They did not see it as a gift," Ruhen said. "They could accept no hand but their own shaping their existence." He crossed the slab and entered the circle itself. "Bring him," he commanded.

Ilumene followed eagerly, half-dragging Isak after him, with Tiniq and Venn close behind. Once inside Isak felt a sudden coolness on his skin; the oppression of Maram's flames dimmed within the circle.

"Venn—the Skulls."

The black Harlequin reached into a bag at his waist and withdrew three Crystal Skulls which he placed in the alcoves under the runes of Vrest, Amavoq and Ilit. Tiniq tugged Isak towards the stone bearing Death's rune and put the Skull of Ruling there, but he kept his hand on it to maintain the link between it and on Isak's black sword. The Harlequins and Acolytes spread out, outside the ring of fire, keeping a wary eye on the entrances to the tunnels. Koteer, the grey-skinned son of Death, took up position on the bridge itself, making himself a barrier to anyone else's entry.

"It is almost time," Ruhen said in a quiet, reverential voice. "I can feel my children dying."

He nodded to Ilumene, and the big man let Isak's leash fall to the ground as he drew his sword. Ruhen followed, the strain clear on his face as he unwrapped the shining crystal hilt of Aenaris and drew it. He reversed the sword and drove it down into the rock until the blade was half-buried, then handed Ilumene the Skull he had been carrying.

Isak recognised it: Dreams had been fused to Xeliath's withered hand. Once it had been Life's, the Queen of the Gods, now it was linked to Kitar, Goddess of Fertility.

Ilumene slipped the Skull onto his sword so it fit around the blade and turned to face Ilit's rune, and Isak gasped as a burst of magic filled the room like a thunderclap, the shadows receding as Aenaris shone with a bright clear light.

"Ilit, come forth," Ruhen intoned, his small face tight with unaccustomed strain. "Ilit, I summon you."

The light intensified, the air shuddering as though under sudden assault. Isak shied away from the magic that spiralled down into the circle with a great rushing sound. There was a surge of a stormy wind, then a funnel of air appeared from nowhere, spinning tightly into a whirlwind ten feet high before melting into nothingness to reveal the white-robed figure of Ilit, staring imperiously at Ruhen.

The God's narrow face was sharp, the jutting lines of his nose and brow as solid as his hair was flowing and ever-moving. He carried a golden bow in his hand, and the shining Horn of Seasons nestled in the crook of his arm. Ilit's piercing, sky-blue eyes focused on Ruhen. His expression was one of rage. "This—"

But the God didn't get a chance to finish his words as Ilumene ran him through, the jewelled bastard sword blazing with light as it drove deep into Ilit's gut. Ichor spilled down his pristine robe and the God staggered back. He raised his hand to strike Ilumene down, but the grinning warrior twisted the sword in the wound and Ilit faltered, holding still just long enough for Venn to cleanly sever the God's head.

Isak felt Ilit's death like an explosion on his skin, a sudden battering of wild magic and life-force torn apart before they dissipated and were absorbed by the rock of the cavern. He shuddered, feeling a hollow pain in his stomach as the Land roiled beneath him, reeling from the sudden, enormous death it had suffered. He retched again as the scent of ichor filled his nose and Ilit's death-scream crashed through his mind.

"See my resolve, Gods of the Upper Circle," Ruhen intoned, eyes wide and shining bright. "See my power and despair. I can tear you all down, each and every one of you."

He turned to Venn as the black Harlequin wiped the dead God's blood from his blade. "Herald of twilight," Ruhen crooned, "attend me."

Venn stopped as though stung by a wasp, his mouth open. A wisp of black mist snaked out like a daemon's tongue, followed by more and more. Faint trails crept from his eyes and ears too, and coalesced into a shadow slipping out of Venn and becoming a kneeling figure, head bowed before his master.

Isak caught the sharp, sickly scent of rotting peaches on the air and recognised it from Doranei's accounts: Rojak, the minstrel responsible for Scree's destruction.

Isak was helpless under the weight of Termin Mystt and the silver chain. He could only watch as the shadow's lips parted and Rojak spoke silent words to his master's mortal vessel. Ruhen smiled and looked away. A sliver of white light broke away from Aenaris and dipped down to the flowing flames surrounding them.

The magic gathered up a small stream of fire and carried it up in the air, high above their heads, where it swirled with malevolent intent. Isak's ears rang with the distant howls of the souls within Maram's fire, which broke apart at a word from Ruhen and became twelve streams, each one twirling out to encircle the top of each standing stone, crowning them with flame. Isak could sense a greater spell being worked as the power of Aenaris grew stronger yet again. It momentarily blinded Isak with its light as the wreaths of fire hissed and spat on the stones they now bound.

There was another great burst of light, and when the stars in Isak's eyes cleared he saw each ring of fire break and slither like snakes towards the alcoves beneath each rune. Ilumene and Venn placed their Crystal Skulls into the appropriate niches and all six were covered by flame. Balls of fire filled the empty alcoves.

Isak couldn't see behind him, but the jolt of pain that wracked his body and filled his bones with acid told him Tiniq had released his contact with the Skull. Magic filled his body; he felt it leaking out like blood seeping from a wound, but the loss was a relief and after the first moments of agony he realised the power of Termin Mystt was joining that of Aenaris, its mate, and fuelling the ritual Ruhen was performing. He screwed up his eyes and tried to fight it, to disrupt or slow the spell, but the effort was excruciating, like claws tearing at his mind, and he had to release it, whimpering like a dying puppy.

All around him he sensed the power in the Skulls twisting and knotting, their unleashed presence like beacons in the night. Distantly he could sense the others too, Legana and Vesna both crying out as fire wrapped around their Skulls—

Close—they were close!

Hold on, Isak screamed at himself, desperate to keep his mind removed from the terrifying power surging through his body. *They're coming. Hold on!*

Vesna roared and struck again, flames from his Crystal Skull surging down the length of his blade to burst on the Devoted's shoulder. The man crumpled, but another lunged at him frantically as his comrade fell. The Mortal-Aspect felt the man's sword scrape up across his cuirass and over his bicep; he twisted and brought his left arm down like a hammer, snapping the blade against his armour. A backhand blow shattered his attacker's helm and threw him backwards, and a Ghost hacked into his hip, felling the Devoted.

He looked around and saw Ghosts and Devoted alike dying. The Farlan line had buckled under the press of greater numbers, but they were holding, fighting with the fury of daemons, and the Devoted were being repelled. Vesna levelled his sword and the magic engulfing it lanced out, lashing fire across the retreating soldiers.

"More coming!" one man yelled, and a ragged group of Devoted came charging from the left. The waiting Ghosts readied themselves for another assault. All around them a carpet of death covered the hill.

That last wave that should have swamped them, Vesna thought, but for the ferocity of the Ghosts. As he watched the Devoted fell, one by one dropping to the ground, and he suddenly realised they were not charging but fleeing.

"The Menin!" Vesna shouted with the strength of a God, "they're our *allies*!" And behind the Devoted came dark, heavily armoured men with a tall soldier at the front: General Amber, driving his men onwards. He slashed a last Devoted across the head, and the impact snapped the man's neck sideways and felled him instantly.

The line of Ghosts opened and Vesna saw a hundred or more Menin surge into the gap, some gasping, others howling warcries that no longer contained words.

General Amber staggered towards Vesna, one arm slack and trailing blood as he walked. "Iron General," Amber rasped, forcing himself to stand tall, "we stand with you."

Vesna raised his flaming sword high above his head and the Ghosts cheered raggedly. "We welcome you," he bellowed, as though his men could regain their strength from the power of his voice alone. "Karkarn stands with us."

"And daemons hunt us," Amber croaked as Nai ran to his side and grabbed the general's arm.

Amber flinched in surprise, then seemed to realise who was there. Nai carried one of Amber's own scimitars; clearly he'd picked it up when Amber had been wounded, but he dropped it now and wrapped his hands around Amber's bleeding arm. A swift burst of magic made Amber cry out with pain.

"It's sealed," Nai announced, retrieving his weapon, "but your ribs are broken. You need to hold back. They need you alive."

Amber growled a curse at the man and turned away. "They need me down there," he grunted, "but I can't help them now. Those daemons will tear the heart out of us, and once they do, I'll have no men left to need me."

Vesna turned to where he pointed; he couldn't see the slope itself from where they were standing, but he knew there was fighting all up it. Beyond the base, however, Menin and Narkang soldiers were advancing side-by-side on the boiling mass of white monsters who had ripped into the very heart of the army.

"Look—the Dark Monks," someone cried, pointing to the low ground between hill and rise. "They're moving to attack!"

Vesna felt a jolt as he saw Suzerain Torl's cavalry aiming for the rear of Ruhen's Children, though fresh Devoted cavalry stood in their way. Once he got into that strip of ground there would be little room for Torl's horsemen to manoeuvre, but the suzerain appeared to have forgotten the tactics he'd championed among the Farlan. Even at that distance Vesna could see this was not a strafing run; the Dark Monks were getting ready to charge directly for the enemy, though they had already fought several engagements and their horses had to be almost blown.

"He's trying to buy us time," Vesna realised. "He knows the pressure needs to be relieved."

"He'll die, then," Amber rasped, his arm pressed to his side as he moved up to stand beside Vesna. "They'll get pinned down by the infantry on the rise and crushed."

"He's the best of us," Vesna said to shouts of agreement from the Ghosts nearby. "Torl doesn't fear death, only failure."

Suddenly Amber dropped to one knee, gasping in pain. Vesna half-picked him up but that seemed to only hurt Amber more and the Farlan hero felt a sudden pang of fear for this man he barely knew.

"You're hurt badly—get that armour off."

"Piss on you," Amber growled. "If I'm done, I'll go fighting, not sit on my arse while my men protect me."

"Then you'll die, you fool!"

Amber scowled, straightening up for a moment and looking Vesna straight in the eye. "I'm Menin," he said angrily, making it clear that was the end of the matter.

Then he added, "Promise me one thing."

Vesna felt the words catch in his throat. They didn't have time to talk; already he could see more Devoted cresting the hill and moving to attack them.

And yet . . . and yet what other time do we have left? Might be we'd already have fallen if this man hadn't killed himself reaching us. He could have seen to his own, led his remaining troops away from this slaughter, but he chose to stay and die with us.

"What is it?" he asked.

"If any of us live," Amber panted, "lead them home."

"Home?"

The Menin general's face was now white with pain. Vesna realised in that moment the man's injuries might be greater than just broken ribs; Amber might be bleeding inside too.

"You're their general now," Amber whispered. "You're their God. Lead them home. Fulfil my promise."

Vesna bowed his head in acknowledgement and the movement seemed to instil a flicker of new life into Amber. "I'll die with my sword in my hand," the Menin declared.

"You're not dead yet," Vesna warned as the line of Ghosts parted to incorporate Amber and the handful of Menin with him. "We'll take them together."

Amber gave a brief nod, still wincing at the injury to his side, but there was no time for further words as the enemy arrived.

A spear shot towards Amber's cuirass and glanced off, but the Menin appeared not to even notice. With a roar he hurled himself into the mêlée and Vesna went with him, the two men bearing death in their wake.

They ran as fast as the dark allowed, the ground shaking underfoot, groaning like the Land itself was assailed. The upheaval spurred them on. Legana led with her Crystal Skull in one hand, the flames trailing from it lighting their path. On one side of her jogged Daken, on the other Ardela. Close behind were King Emin and his Brotherhood, Carel and the two Farlan Ascetites, with the eighty remaining Sisters of Dusk following.

After the initial shock and pain of having her clothes set alight, Legana had wrapped her hand in magic and allowed the Skull to burn there, though she was unable to stop and work out why flames licked over the Skull's glassy surface. Not long after they'd entered the tunnel a God of the Upper Circle had died; as soon as she'd told them, Legana had upped their pace, careless of her own poor balance, the injuries others carried or the chance of ambush. Whatever had been done to the Skulls must be part of Azaer's plan. Time was running out.

The tunnel widened a shade and up ahead an opening appeared, lit by a faint crimson glow from the chamber behind. Daken didn't break stride but sprinted ahead of the rest, his movements blurring as a blue shadow-image appeared in front of him. At the opening he checked himself and let Litania's shadow whip through, to be met by swords flashing out from either side—but they cut only mist. Then Daken smashed one weapon from its owner's grip while Ardela, beside him, smacked down the other, bringing her Harlequin's sword back up in one smart movement to cut into the ambusher's neck. Daken didn't bother finishing off his; he left the disarmed Acolyte to those behind him.

From the lee of a stalagmite a slender figure danced, diamond patchwork clothes suddenly bright in the light of Legana's flames. A long-knife flew through the air and caught the Harlequin in the shoulder, slowing its lethal lunge just enough for Daken to be able to parry the sword and bring his axe-blade down on the Harlequin's leg. Still the white-masked figure turned and slashed at Daken's face, and the edge scraped across his cheek-guard as Daken barged into the Harlequin's shoulder. The impact knocked it off balance and Legana moved even faster than a Harlequin to open its throat.

More Acolytes converged on Daken, trying to pick him off, but King Emin and Doranei reached his side in the same instant. The sight of Doranei's star-lit sword made them hesitate, and then the rest of the Brotherhood had come through, Veil leading the charge.

Out of the darkness on the other side of the cavern a dagger flew towards the king, who reeled away, crying out, as the air around him suddenly filled with white light. The dagger fell harmlessly to the floor and Legana stormed past the Brotherhood before any of them had found the new threat, kicking the knife away as she went.

A pair of dead blue eyes shone out from the darkness of a tunnel entrance, and as Legana advanced, a figure wearing a tarnished crown emerged into the half-light of the chamber.

"You are too late," the Wither Queen rasped, malice shining out from her face. "Ilit is dead. They dare not oppose him now."

Legana paused only to hurl a gout of flame at the Aspect of Death and the Wither Queen vanished backwards into the tunnel again, mocking laughter echoing in her wake. Legana started to head off in pursuit, until King Emin shouted after her, "She's leading us off the path! You can't follow her."

Legana's blazing emerald eyes turned back to him. "*She will dog our path. I must stop her*," she said into their minds.

"What about Isak?"

"*You are all connected to him; you can find him without me. I will meet you there.*" And with that she vanished into the darkness, her bloodied long-knives ready for the fight to come.

King Emin muttered a curse and looked around at his troops. Ardela stood poised to run after Legana, but then she realised she would only hinder her mistress.

Instead it was Leshi who moved first. The Farlan ranger was gripped by a murderous fury over Tiniq's betrayal. "This way," he said. "We're running out of time."

Swords crashed down on both sides, hammering against Vesna's black armour. The dead were piled high around the standing stones; though his men had been greatly thinned by the repeated assaults, they were refusing to be broken. White light whipped around the Mortal-Aspect as he turned aside an axe and punched the man who'd struck him. A Ghost threw himself forward and dragged down the Devoted who was trying to stab up under Vesna's guard; a Menin moved to Vesna's lee and chopped down another soldier.

The Ghost fought his way on top of the Devoted and hammered at his face with the pommel of his sword, smashing teeth and bone with repeated blows until the soldier was still. He scrambled back towards the line, his feet slipping on the blood-slicked corpses, but a spear got him first. Vesna saw his mouth fall open in shock and pain, but all he could do was behead the Ghost's killer and drag the dying man back.

Behind him Amber knelt, bleeding from half-a-dozen wounds but refusing to submit to death. The Menin general forced himself upright again, and the remaining Menin roared their approval even as Amber was forced to use his scimitar to keep himself upright.

Vesna scanned the ground, then grabbed an abandoned spear. He handed it to Amber in exchange for the blunted scimitar, which he hurled at the last knot of Devoted soldiers still fighting. It caught one in the side of the head and sent him staggering into the man beside him, the distraction enough for both to be cut down.

He looked around at the bodies lying around the circle they had defended. Some were crying out in agony; others gasped like dying fish, but all of them were aware their time had come.

"We can't face much more of this," he said, to himself as much as Amber. "There's too many of them."

"Look," Amber croaked, pointing to the foot of the hill, where the white daemons of Ruhen's Children fought on against the few remaining Kingsguard and Menin. There would be no relief, Vesna realised: what few troops left on the hill were dying by the hundreds in that horrific slaughter below.

"Cavalry," shouted someone, and Vesna saw the Dark Monks, Suzerain Torl's command, fully engaged with the enemy, outnumbered but pressing forward towards the rear of Ruhen's Children with no regard for their own lives.

"Torl's buying us time with his own life," Vesna moaned, "but for what? There's no one left—"

Further off there were other fights going on as the Devoted forced the mercenaries and battle-clans further and further away from where they were needed.

"Not them," the soldier shouted back. "Who the fuck's that?"

Even the weariest heads lifted at the surprise in his voice. Everyone turned to look where he was pointing, and there, behind the rise, were several legions of cavalry, advancing in an ordered line.

"They're not ours," Vesna realised with a sinking feel. "How in the name of the Dark Place did they hide those reserves?" A wave of helplessness washed over him and he dropped to his knees, the cold realisation that they were beaten draining his God-granted strength. They could not possibly survive this; even with Torl's sacrifice, the heavy infantry could not slow Ruhen's Children much longer. Thousands of the white monsters had died, perhaps ten thousand, but there were still enough left to wipe out the last few of King Emin's men who were left defending this peak.

"No, look! They're not Devoted banners," shouted another, the golden eagle of a Swordmaster emblazoned on his armour. He forced his way to Vesna's side. "They're fucking *Farlan*!"

Vesna pulled himself to his feet again and scanned the battlefield. *Farlan? How—?*

"It appears your people prefer to fight only at the very death," Amber grunted, his face twisted in pain. "May it prove as decisive as Moorview."

Vesna had been straining to see who it was arriving at this late point. Suddenly animated, he shouted, "Look at all the colours! Look at them—they're nobility—it's Lord Fernal! It's our fucking heavy cavalry!"

CHAPTER 44

"SOUND THE ADVANCE," Lord Fernal shouted in his deep, growling voice, "make all the noise you can: get them to turn our way!"

The buglers sounded their high repeating notes that cut through the air, the sounding order swiftly echoed by the hunting horns carried by many; after repeating the order again and again, they fell to just blaring loud and long, until the Devoted cavalry encircling Suzerain Torl's troops broke off their attack and milled about the foot of the rise in a disordered, chaotic mass.

Their commanders desperately tried to regain some control, but the Devoted began to retreat, unwilling to stay in this confined spot to face heavy cavalry.

"Now get out of the way, Torl," Duke Lomin muttered from behind his face-plate, a berserker's raging face heavily engraved with runes of Karkarn and Kao, the berserker Aspect. "Give us a run."

"He will," Suzerain Fordan predicted, checking his warhammer was secure on his saddle. "Torl shamed us all by marching when we would not—he'll see what we must do."

Lord Fernal turned to look at a black-armoured figure on his right, the only other non-Farlan among them, but behind that black-whorled decoration he could see nothing. If the other outsider felt the same bemusement at the Farlan nobility, he made no sign; he merely adjusted the white tabard bearing Fernal's crest he was wearing over his armour.

"He sees," the black-armoured knight said as the Dark Monks broke away.

The Farlan nobles continued forward at a steady pace, their anticipation almost palpable as the rearmost of Ruhen's Children came into view.

They quickly closed the gap and were starting to ready themselves for the charge when two shapes dropped from the sky, landing with heavy thumps. It felt to Fernal like the wind had been punched from his men. The horses shied away from the monsters, while the men themselves faltered in the face of the figure riding the lead monster. Three figures hovered above the wyverns, their wings outstretched: Lord Gesh and two other Litse white-eyes. Gesh brandished a golden bow that glittered with magical light.

The Litse lord's shot arched elegantly towards them, and three thousand men, nobles, hurscals and sworn swords alike, watched it fall inexorably—

—until, without warning, the air shimmered into surging eddies, twisting the arrow abruptly and sending it soaring up into the sky again. This time as it fell back down, its energy was spent and it clattered harmlessly against some distant nobleman's armour.

Vorizh Vukotic urged his wyvern forward, the beast walking awkwardly with its wings half-unfurled for balance. Behind him were several score of Ruhen's Children, peering in confusion at the wyverns, who hissed and roared their defiance at the advancing Farlan troops. Unafraid—or enchanted by their master—the monsters stood their ground as the Litse white-eyes circled above them, each readying his curved spear to slash at the knights below.

"Ready to charge," Fernal commanded, "on my signal!"

Forty yards from the wyverns, the black-armoured knight spurred his horse forward. Vorizh's laughter echoed across the battlefield as he drew Eolis with a blazing flourish, but the knight did not falter; instead, he forced his horse into a breakneck charge, couching his lance as he closed. Twenty yards, ten, five—the lance-head snapped down just as the wyvern dodged around it, moving far quicker than any normal creature could.

The lance wavered as the wyvern slipped to the knight's right—but it was enough. The steel head drove into the side of the wyvern's neck, and the crisp crunch was audible over the thunder of thousands of hooves hammering the ground. The wyvern staggered under the impact as the shaft of the lance shattered, but even as Vorizh slashed at the knight, he drew his own sword and deflected the blow up and past.

The wyvern's flailing wings caught the knight's horse and it lurched sideways, battered off-balance by the heavy blow, but the knight slipped nimbly from its back.

Vorizh too jumped from his stricken beast as the wyvern vomited blood onto the churned-up ground below, but he faltered when the knight pulled the tabard from his chest. "Koezh!" Vorizh shouted, "noble brother! Come to teach me the error of my ways?"

Koezh didn't respond as he raced towards his younger brother, the air burning around him. Vorizh flicked Eolis round to meet him, but Koezh's own weapon was already moving and the silver sword clashed against the black in a blaze of light, once, twice—

Koezh pressed forward, and Fernal felt a jolt inside him as he watched the vampire move with shocking speed and a grace the Demi-God had never before witnessed. The black sword tore through a haze of magic as Vorizh filled the air with fire to buy himself some space, his desperate defence turning Eolis into a blur of silver, but Koezh was always ahead of him, bewildering his brother as he worked his way into position. And then it was over: Koezh slashed upwards as Vorizh, dodging the previous strike, inadvertently moved into the way. His armour split with a crack and Koezh danced forward and smashed his shoulder into Vorizh's chest, unbalancing him, and in the next instant, chopped hard into his brother's neck.

Vorizh was driven to his knees by the force of the blow and Eolis spilled from his limp fingers. Koezh caught the hilt of the sword on the tip of his own and deftly flicked it up so he could pluck it from the air.

"I'm sorry," he whispered as he withdrew his sword.

Vorizh fell backwards, mist rising up from the ground to meet him.

Koezh glanced back, and saw the advancing line was almost upon him. Above them were the other wyvern and the winged white-eyes, who had retreated into the sky, stunned by Vorizh's death. He ran to his horse, and after a quick check to ensure the wyvern had not badly injured it, he mounted up.

Lord Fernal called the charge and the cavalry leaped forward, lances slowly descending as they closed on Ruhen's Children.

Koezh was out of position so he didn't wait for them; instead, he urged his horse towards the nearest of the white daemons racing forward. His swords were a strange pair, though both were made by the same Elf; Bariaeth was an ugly black blade forged in Aryn Bwr's grief and hate; silver Eolis was the last king's finest creation. For all the daemons' speed and fanatic fury, Koezh was faster, and heads tumbled in quick succession as the mismatched swords killed with equal ease. Then the Farlan were behind him, and Koezh cast an arc of light ahead of him to drive a path into the enemy.

Behind him Fernal roared with bestial bloodlust as he readied his own warhammer. As the first of the white monsters ran to meet him, Fernal tightened his grip on the reins and turned his charger to meet them head-on. First one, then a second, and a third, crashed into the steel-ridged barding covering the enormous horse's chest and were smashed from its path, falling under the hooves of those around it.

More and more of Ruhen's Children fell beneath them. Fernal swung his massive hammer and a head disintegrated under the blow. Beside him

Suzerain Fordan's voice was raised in strange delight, his laughter cutting through the screams and sounds of butchery.

As Fernal cracked skulls and shattered bones the deep, distant crack of thunder came rolling down from the sky. He heard a blessing in that thunder, a benediction from his uncaring father. He growled and struck again. The God of Storms had no place here; the company of these frail and fearless men was all the blessing he needed. Horses tripped and riders fell to the ground to be trampled by their own, or set upon by Ruhen's howling monsters. As his horse slowed to a halt, unable to get through the press of flesh, Fernal felt the claws grasp at his legs, but the storm was now surging through his veins. He swung his warhammer tirelessly as the Farlan fought on with equal fury; as the black-armoured vampire cut a swathe of scarlet death; as the thunder continued to boom up above and lightning split the sky. Some part of him, some divine flicker in his blood, told him the end had almost come. A shiver ran down his spine as he realised the entire Upper Circle of the Gods were close by, drawn forth by the power Ruhen commanded.

Still he fought and still he killed. Until the last of Ruhen's followers was dead, nothing else in the Land could matter to him.

Isak raised his head as the shadows unfolded all around him. Ruhen knelt at the centre of the circle, his small fingers around the crystal sword's grip. Aenaris pulsed with power, casting its white light over the stones and revealing the indistinct figures in front of each one. Isak could taste the magic that filled the air; he knew the Gods attended.

Behind him he sensed Lord Death, summoned by the vast power as both Aenaris and Termin Mystt responded to Ruhen's call. He tried to fight it again, to break the flow, but he was not strong enough. He could not even free himself from the silver chain that bound him, or command the weapon stuck fast in his own hand. Termin Mystt was a burning brand against his chest, the chain itself was eating at his skin.

He could only watch as the Gods themselves, so weak they could not fully manifest, bowed their heads to Ruhen. A wisp of light was dragged out of the blue shadow of Nartis, then Kitar and Karkarn, and in moments each thread was wrapped around the blazing blade of Aenaris as the Gods submitted to a power they could no longer match.

Venn stood before the one unclaimed stone, an empty space where Ilit had been killed. Then the shadows squirmed, and a shape appeared there too. Grey matted hair and dead eyes, a tarnished crown and cruel triumph on her face: the Wither Queen manifested and knelt and her soul leaped forward to join the others. The Goddess of Disease gladly claimed Ilit's place in the Upper Circle of the Pantheon of the Gods.

Once there were twelve bound to him, Ruhen smiled in the stark light of Aenaris. With his free hand, he pulled a small bottle from his tunic, thumbed off the stopper and downed the contents in one. He tossed the empty bottle into the flames surrounding them.

Before the poison could take effect, Isak heard shouts from beyond the circle, cries of warning, followed swiftly by the clash of steel. Ruhen looked up, but his smile remained in place, his plans complete. Isak tried to stand, but Tiniq struck him again, leaving the white-eye as bowed as the insubstantial God in his lee. Through the stars bursting before his eyes Isak saw men and women charging towards the bridge across the flames, but there were Harlequins and Acolytes ready to meet them.

Distantly he made out Daken's shouts above the clamour and he twisted his head to see the blurry man of the Brotherhood exchanging blows with an equally blurred Harlequin. One of the Sisters of Dusk was at his side, thrusting her spear at the white-masked warrior, but the Harlequin somehow defended itself against both attackers, its slender blades striking like snakes and catching the Brother in the shoulder, sending him reeling.

Isak looked back at Ruhen and saw the shadows under his skin turning uneasily in Aenaris' light. The boy was pale; his skin was almost translucent, like a plague victim's, and his smile was faltering as the poison began to take effect. Isak felt panic set in. The Gods had submitted; the sacrifice had been made on the slopes above them. Now Ruhen had only to die, to free Azaer of his mortal vessel, and a new God would ascend to stand above them all. The Harlequins and Acolytes were outnumbered, but they were supremely skilled. Emin wouldn't be able to break through in time.

He strained yet again at the chain, but his efforts succeeded only in causing a black burst of agony as Termin Mystt grated against his collarbone. The fire licking at his mind intensified and he felt it burning a path through his soul. Isak screamed again, unable to bear the forces raging unchecked through his body.

"Azaer!" roared a voice from beyond the circle of flame.

Isak tried to focus through the pain, but his vision blurred as every scar on his body came alive with old hurts. The attackers surrounded the circle now, though not even a Harlequin would attempt to jump these flames. Distantly he could make out Doranei as the black broadsword carved through an Acolyte's sword and body.

"Isak!" shouted someone else, "Isak, *get up*!"

Now he could see Carel, sword and face both bloodied, roaring like a drill sergeant. A Harlequin turned to strike him down, but King Emin was at his side, shouting at Azaer, his face illuminated by red sparks bursting from the edge of his axe. Doranei turned and struck the Harlequin, claiming another life as Emin continued to shout for the dying boy's attention.

Slowly Ruhen turned Emin's way, his movements dulled by the poison, but Isak could see the shadow recognised his old enemy. As soon as the boy had turned his way Emin pulled something from his belt and held it up. Isak felt a faint note of recognition as the light caught it: a cracked glass shard with a dark strand within.

Doranei grabbed the king's hand and before any of the defenders could take advantage, they dropped the shard onto the rocky ground. Black wings burst around them, sweeping from nowhere to envelop the pair in a flurry of movement before melting away an instant later.

Ilumene was already moving to Ruhen's side as the wings reappeared on the near side of the flames, between the standing stones of Nartis and Tsatach. The Gods, still bowed in obeisance, showed no sign of noticing, but as the wings vanished and the two men staggered back, Ilumene lunged forward. The king parried with a drunken swipe as he fell back against Nartis' stone.

Isak felt another jolt inside him as Doranei left the king's side and threw himself at Koteer. Emin slipped around the stone just in time to let Ilumene's sword raise sparks where his head had been, then responded with a flurry of blows with sword and axe. His former protégé laughed as he battered them away, but Ilumene kept his distance now, using the longer reach of his bastard sword to keep Emin away from the kneeling Ruhen.

On the far side of the circle Doranei was hacking madly at Koteer. The power of his sword more than made up for his opponent's size and strength, but as Koteer gave ground, his eyes flicked to the figure beside Ilit's stone, and Venn, unnoticed, drew his own sword as Doranei turned his back to him.

Isak tried to shout a warning, but Tiniq smashed the pommel of his sword down onto his head and he found himself on his hands and knees, once again barely able to see. He blinked hard, trying to focus: Doranei was a blur of furious movement ahead of him, and Venn was stepping forward, his own sword ready.

Through the darkness came another blaze of light and he saw Venn falter as fingers closed on his shoulder. He turned in surprise to see the Wither Queen holding him. Her eyes blazed blue, then faded and turned to emerald and as Isak watched the Black Harlequin shook her off and slashed at her face—but from nowhere she brought up a long-knife and caught the blow.

Then the Wither Queen reached out and took Venn by the throat, green sparks dancing across her fingers. Venn shrieked and wrenched himself around to try and escape her grip, but all he succeeded in doing was dragging the Goddess with him, her ragged cape billowing in an unnatural wind.

Then the rags and tarnished crown melted away into the darkness and suddenly it was Legana standing there instead. Venn tried again to run her through, but the Mortal-Aspect, moving with incredible speed, slapped his sword away. Her face became cold and focused and she closed her grip, her thumb driving into his throat, crushing his windpipe. Venn staggered back, his ruined hand pawing weakly at his neck, but Legana didn't wait for him fall; with one blindingly quick stroke she slashed his broken neck open and watched the blood gush out.

As Ilumene glanced up and saw his comrade fall he barely avoided an eviscerating stroke from the king. The big man snarled and threw himself forward, hammering down on the king's axe-shaft and smashing it from his grip. Emin tried to thrust his sword forward, but Ilumene barged into him and the two men became pinned together, their swords trapped between them.

Ilumene drove Emin backwards until he was standing against a standing stone. "You're too late!" the former King's Man crowed. "There's nothing you can do to stop Ruhen, and my soul's a part of him."

The king grunted under the pressure, but instead of reply he slipped his free hand down to his belt and dragged a dagger from it. Ilumene lifted him bodily so his head was pressed back against the flames in the stone's alcove and the king cried out in pain, even as he jammed the dagger into Ilumene's ribs. The big man gasped and released the king, but as he fell back, a bright ruby light burst into being from under his armour and with a shout Ilumene headbutted the king. He released his sword, then pulled out his own dagger as he bashed Emin's head into the stone.

"Surprise!" he shouted, slashing his dagger across the king's cheek. "I always was one trick ahead of you—you never could keep up, old man," and he punched Emin until the king reeled under the onslaught and fell back against the menhir.

Ilumene snarled with satisfaction, but the king beat Ilumene back a step, then he hurled himself to the ground and grabbed his discarded axe. He hooked Ilumene's leg, driving the spike into his calf, even as a second burst of light from Ilumene's bloodrose amulet absorbed the pain of his wound and the bigger man stabbed down into his shoulder.

"I don't need to," Emin croaked, dragging the axe towards him and pulling Ilumene's leg with it.

The big fighter twisted as he fell and drove his knees into Emin, then he tried to fight his way backwards, but he floundered; his leg was caught under Emin and the king was hanging on with every last scrap of strength.

And then Isak moved: with a great scream he drove himself to his feet and drew the power of Termin Mystt inside him. Black flames danced over his skin as the raging torrent of magic ripped through his frail body. The roar of power filled his ears and the Land drew back from around him. Isak could see the small boy going limp ahead of him, creeping like a thief towards Godhood.

He howled, and sent all the shrieking energies of Death's weapon into his arm. As he dragged up his hand, he felt the chain tighten about his chest, but still he hauled, barely noticing as Tiniq slammed his pommel down onto Isak's neck again. Fire engulfed him and the pain of the Dark Place welled up from his lost memories as the black sword bit into his shoulder and kept going. Higher and higher it went, and the Land became a white haze of agony before his eyes as he carved through his own collarbone and on into the shoulder. Then the edge caught the silver chain and it burst apart in an explosion of dark power that threw Isak's sword-arm back.

He let the force drive his arm around in an inexorable sweep as Termin Mystt sheared through Tiniq's descending sword and kept going. Though he was barely able to see the traitor, Isak swung with all the fury and desperation of a dying man and the black sword caught Tiniq in his belly and sliced through to his spine. If Tiniq yelled out, Isak couldn't hear it above his own cries, but he let the traitor fall dead while the white light of Aenaris filled his mind.

The Key of Life surged with fresh power in response to its mate, but Isak could barely see it through the fog of his last few breaths. His ruined shoulder was numb, but the pain was absolute and it took his last remaining strength to manage those few steps to Ruhen. The boy's fingers were loosening around Aenaris' hilt.

Isak raised the sword high, then fell to his knees, slamming it down and catching Ruhen square in the chest. The boy's eyes jerked open at the impact, but his grip on Aenaris was beyond mortal strength and the black sword only caused the shadows in Ruhen's eyes to dance with greater delight. More power flowed as his life seeped away, Azaer's apotheosis rushing forward like a tidal wave.

"A shadow you are," Isak said, slurring through the agony as blood poured from his half-severed shoulder, "and a shadow you'll remain."

He released Termin Mystt and the black sword embraced its new master, its enormous power surging into Ruhen while a hurricane of magic exploded around them. Isak reached out to the dim circle of fire behind, and the pulsing magic in the air raced to obey. The flames rose higher as the Sisters of Dusk fell to their knees all around the circle, but then the river of fire parted, surging up on both sides, and through the gap in the flames came a figure, hands pressed to his belly as blood spilled from a mortal wound. He struggled forward, obviously close to death, but somehow managing those last few steps. His face was briefly visible through the surging storm of light and blackness.

Mihn.

Dragged off the slope of Ghain by his master—still-dying of Venn's wound and clothes schorched by the flames of Maram—the Grave Thief staggered up behind Ruhen.

The pain fell away: his shoulder, his scars, the ruined fragments of his mind—Isak felt nothing, and in that last moment he smiled. Then he reached out and put his hand on Aenaris, drawing one last scrap of magic into his body. He felt it fill him and drank deep of the blazing white light.

"But a shadow must have a master."

It went racing into his bones, through arteries and veins, up over his skin, until the scars on his body began to shine with pure, blinding light. It covered his almost-severed shoulder, then surged from his mouth and his eyes.

Light filled Isak; it shone out of him like a beacon, and under the assault Ruhen's shadow soul was cast backwards, stark and black in the radiance, while man and boy were consumed by white flame. It tore the shadows from where they were tethered and burned them with the light of creation.

Death reached out and took them in His cold embrace. Isak felt his own body crumble to ash and scattered by the power of Aenaris radiating through his bones. His mind was suddenly free, set soaring on the storm.

Then the light consumed the last of him and Isak felt a final moment of balance descend. Beyond it was nothingness. Beyond it was peace.

EPILOGUE

SILVER KISSED THE RUSTLING GRASS as they rode towards the hill. A black-armoured man led the way, but there was no danger; he went out of habit, and a need to be alone with his thoughts. They had left their escort behind and ridden out from the small camp as the sun neared the horizon. It was spring and the air was warm; darting birds chased the last of the day's insects before they went to roost.

The lesser moon, Kasi, was midway to its zenith in a cloudless sky, but this was Silvernight and another ruled the heavens: the third moon, Arian, cast its silver light over the quiet plain as they continued towards a hill their scouts could not find in the daylight. There were seven of them in total. The armoured man was out front, a man and woman behind flanked a girl riding a Farlan pony who was staring with wide-eyed wonder at the silvery plain stretching out ahead of them. Behind them were three women, their white hooded capes shining in Arian's light. The sky turned a deep sapphire-blue as the sun passed below the horizon and as the shadows washed over their small group, two of the women began to softly sing.

The girl turned in her saddle to watch them, though she knew not to interrupt. Her mother had taught her these words, years back, but she'd never heard them sung with such irreverence as from the oldest of the three, a scar-faced woman with a mass of crow's feet around her missing eye. Her reedy voice made it sound more like a sea-shanty than the prayer to dusk.

As she watched, Legana, mouthing the words as she had no voice of her own, took the older woman's hand. High Priestess Shanas, on Legana's other side, sang with her eyes closed and a smile of contentment on her face, and the girl found herself whispering them too as Arian's light settled over the Land.

Soon the only colour to be seen was the mute woman's emerald eyes, shining from the dark of her hood.

"Can I ride ahead?" she asked her mother once the prayer was over.

"No," growled her father from her other side, "bad things are out there. You stick close, you hear?"

"Bad things don't come out on Silvernight!" she laughed, smiling sweetly up at the bearded man. "*Every*one knows that!"

"They do round here," he said gruffly, "so bloody listen to me for a change."

She pursed her lips and looked in silent appeal at her mother, but she shook her head. "Not this Silvernight," she said, touching her daughter's cheek. "This is a special one. You'll stay with us."

"I know it's special," she argued, "but I can meet you on the hill—that's where we're going anyway—"

"You'll be riding back across my lap if you try that," her father snapped. "I'd rather kill your horse from under you than let it happen."

"Doranei!" her mother said sharply as the girl gasped and hugged her pony's neck. "There's no need to frighten her."

"You think?" Doranei caught the look in his wife's blue eyes and turned away.

"I do. I know we've all met him before, but this is a special night for Gennay. Don't spoil that with your temper."

He grunted, but Gennay's fear was already gone; her face was alight with excitement. "The Dusk Watchman," she breathed. "That's who you mean? Am I really to be his priestess?"

"Who told you that?"

She turned and pointed. "Ardela did—isn't it true?"

"Oh for pity's sake! Why—"

"Enough," her mother snapped before softening her voice. "Yes, my dear, it's true: you're to be his priestess if you wish—but the choice is yours, Gennay, you must remember that. You'll not be getting the tattoos tonight; there's time enough in the years to come for all that. Right now you're just here to greet him—that's honour enough for one day, and one afforded to very few in this Land."

Gennay beamed at the two of them. "Manayaz will be so jealous—I'm the special one for a change, not him."

"Aye, well, it's not something to be bragging about," Doranei warned her. "The Sisters of the Dusk are a secret cult, and don't you be forgetting it. If you'd been born into a different family you might never have heard of them your entire life—and if you can't keep a secret, you don't belong."

"Yes, Father," she said with a smile.

"Good. Now you'll wait here while I go on ahead and see an old friend," he murmured, and spurred his horse on to catch up with the lead rider just as he reached the base of the hill.

They paused there together, looking around at the ground beneath their feet, then the rock-studded hillside ahead. A flicker of movement caught their eyes and both turned to watch a silver shape bound across the stony ground then pause and survey them. It was thick-furred, and larger than any deerhound, and it watched them silently, barely visible within the silver-edged gloom of twilight. After half a dozen heartbeats it broke into a run again before vanishing into thin air, only to reappear away to the west, where it skirted warily around the last members of their party.

The pair followed the ghost-dog's movements until it headed out across the open ground they had crossed and vanished completely from sight.

"Hard to picture, ain't it?" Doranei commented quietly as they found themselves staring back down the bare slope. "How this once looked."

Vesna sighed and slipped from his horse. "Sadly, all too easy," he said at last. "Doesn't matter if the bodies are buried; some of us still hear their cries a decade on."

"It's more than a decade, my friend," Doranei said, also dismounting. "It's what, sixteen winters now? We're getting old." He paused and looked the Mortal-Aspect up and down. "Well, some of us, anyways."

Together they started on up the hill, both walking with their hands on their hilts as though unable to let go the savagery done in that place. They were halfway to the top before either spoke again, lost in the memories of friends lost.

"She's a pretty little thing," Vesna said, glancing back at the riders below. "Got her mother's eyes."

Doranei laughed loudly. "Aye, well, never much chance of anything else now, was there? She's a holy terror, that girl, to her brothers and me besides. It's hard to stop her when she's got such a look of her mother about her; the Watchman might regret making that one his priestess."

"Don't be so sure," said a third voice from up ahead, "I have never been one for excessive reverence—witness at my Mortal-Aspect back there."

The two warriors stopped and stared up at the face smiling down from the top of the slope. He wore a bright white cape that swirled about him and carried a staff of perfect darkness in his hand. A silver dog darted out from behind his cape with the wariness of a wild thing, only to retreat back into the shadows a moment later.

"Gods, I'll never get used to that!" Doranei exclaimed as he rushed forward to grab the newcomer in a hug. "Another one who's not aged a damn day, but I'm glad to see you all the same."

"Well, now, a little silver in your beard gives you a distinguished air, so you have not suffered greatly on that front," said the smaller man with a laugh. "More fitting to your position in life, one might say, my Lord."

"Hah! Lord Protector of the Realm? All that means is holding General Daken's leash until King Sebetin's old enough to do it himself." Doranei stepped back and inspected the white-cloaked man. "Gods, but look at you, Mihn: better than you ever were in life—and holding that black staff in your hand like it was nothing more than a twig."

"Thank you, my friend," Mihn replied. "You are too modest, though: Lord Protector is not bad for a man of the Brotherhood, and Narkang thrives under your stewardship. The queen herself told me so. That was a kind thought, by the way, putting the shrine in the Royal Baths so I could see Emin once more before he died. If you can only stop King Sebetin marrying one of your daughters, he will have an untroubled reign, I suspect."

Doranei shook his head. "He's had a warning on that front," he said darkly. "The cocky little sod has a lot of his father in him, but he's not fool enough for that."

Vesna pushed Doranei aside and stepped forward to hug Mihn too. "It's good to see you, Mihn," he whispered.

"And you, my friend," Mihn said a broad smile. "It is always too long—but my cult is well-established now, so it will be sooner next time, I promise. And you will be pleased to know I have also visited the Ring of Fire. The Menin continue in peace—the stability you gave them remains." "I'm glad to hear it. I don't fancy walking there again any time soon—took long enough the first time."

Vesna stepped back and they all looked down the slope at the figures ascending. Without warning Doranei hopped back from where he was standing, hawked noisily and spat on the ground beside Mihn.

"Charming," called his wife. "Perhaps General Daken isn't entirely to blame for the young king's behaviour?"

"Shake his hand, spit on his shadow," Gennay piped up. "Isn't that what you always say, Father?"

"Is it?" her mother said, her eyebrow raised. "Not in my earshot he doesn't."

"It is a great pleasure to see you again, Zhia," Mihn said, bowing low to her. "You are, as ever, the rose to your husband's thorns."

"So let us hope the girl hasn't inherited her father's brains," said a voice from nowhere, "otherwise she'll not be much of a priestess. As treacherous as her mother, that I could learn to appreciate, but never a simple-minded one."

Gennay looked around in surprise for the one who'd spoken, but she only worked it out when her father stamped on the ground where he'd spat. A soft chuckle drifted through the evening air.

She looked down. While most of their shadows were dark in the light of Arian, the white-cloaked man's was as perfectly black as his staff. As she stared, the shadow reached out towards her, moving forward as it had when Mihn had bowed.

"Karkarn's—" She was cut short as Zhia tapped her smartly on the cheek.

"We're not in the Light Fingers now, young lady."

"Quite so," the shadow said smoothly, "and whatever part of Karkarn you were thinking of, you would be doing me a grave disservice. I—*we*—are the Dusk Watchman. We are the Emperor of the Gods, and Karkarn is our vassal."

"We are also still a little full of ourselves," Mihn added with a tight smile. He reached out a hand and took Gennay's, raising it delicately to his lips in formal greeting. "My Lady Gennay, it is a pleasure to meet you at last. My name is Mihn, and while my shadow rejoices in its new title, you may call it Azaer."

"*May?*" the shadow demanded. "She may *not*—I demand respect from our priesthood."

"Mihn," Doranei growled.

The small man raised a hand to cut him off. "Both of you; behave." He cocked his head at the girl. "Your father is a great man, you know that? But he dislikes my shadow; you must forgive him that, he has good reason."

"And," Doranei broke in, "the shadow's still sore your mother gave him everything it wanted, so it could taste its own medicine. You'll find it doesn't like underestimating us mortals, or the lengths we'll go to, to keep a secret."

Mihn raised a hand and Doranei fell silent again. Gennay thought for a long moment, then asked, "Why is Azaer your shadow if your friends don't like it?"

"A fair question," Mihn said, "but I fear the answer is long and complex." He gestured towards the centre of the hilltop, where she could see a circle of standing stones shining in the strange half-light.

"Your parents have friends and family to remember, so perhaps we should leave them in peace for a while?"

She looked at her mother and father. Zhia touched Doranei's arm, and the Lord Protector of Narkang and the Four Cities waved her on with gritted teeth and a scowl.

Mihn smiled and went to embrace his Mortal-Aspect as the last three arrived at the top of the hill, then took Legana's hand from Ardela. "Come with us, Gennay," he said as he walked arm-in-arm with Legana towards the stone circle.

Gennay followed them onto a piece of strangely paved ground at the very centre of the hilltop and looked around in wonder. The pale paving stones shone as the last traces of day fled the sky. She could see two enormous menhirs flanking a stairway into the hill itself, but Mihn led her to a flat tablelike rock in the very centre. There were words written on it—an epitaph, she realised—but to whom, it didn't say.

"A lot of people died to get us here today," Mihn said sadly, "but I imagine you will have heard quite enough about the wars."

She nodded; her parents both carried the scars, inside and out. "My father's a soldier," she began hesitantly, "but he doesn't like to talk about it, even when Manayaz or Sebetin ask, even though he's teaching us all how to fight."

"There is no way to describe it," Mihn said softly, "and he hopes you will never have to find out."

"Uncle Daken seems to think it's fun, but I don't think he's right."

"Daken thinks a lot of strange things are fun," Mihn agreed, "but that is who he is. You cannot hide from who you are; you can only accept it and make it work."

"Do you know him too? He's a white-eye. Everyone says he's mad, but I don't think he is."

Mihn squatted down beside her, and his strange black shadow slid like oil over the stones. "People say lots of things about white-eyes," he said gravely. "Some of them are true, others are not."

"They are stubborn and troublesome," Azaer added in a voice like the whisper of wind through the trees, "more troublesome than you can ever imagine."

Mihn ducked his head, though whether in acknowledgement or sadness, Gennay couldn't tell. "And yet capable of great things," he whispered, to himself as much as anyone, "and great sacrifice too—he gave his body and soul to drive your shadow out of Ruhen and burn it into mine. Given the plan he devised, my taking a mortal wound pales in comparison to the burden he took on himself."

"He burned your shadow?" Gennay asked, confused.

Mihn gave her a sad smile. "He consumed himself with light—how else does one cast the strongest shadows? And I was there behind it, to catch that shadow in my own and die just as a new God was born."

Gennay looked down and saw his pitch-black shadow squirm, but Azaer had nothing to add to that.

"Azaer and I were enemies," Mihn continued, "or, to be precise, Azaer and the old king were enemies, and they fought a war, as you know. That war weakened the whole Land. My friend Isak realised that victory in that war would not be enough. He saw that he had to force both sides together, so the war would never happen again."

"Some of us were less than amused by it than others," the shadow added, claws briefly appearing at the end of his black fingers.

At a look from Mihn the claws disappeared again and the shadow retreated behind him, ignoring the play of moonlight as it traced shapes over the stones.

"Many were unhappy, but it is done and the Land is healed," Mihn said. "My shadow holds the power of the Gods, and I control my shadow. It is not a choice either of us would have wished for, perhaps, but it is done—and we can hardly complain about our lot in life when we rule the Gods. You have heard about Isak?"

When she nodded, he smiled. "Good. Most of what they say about Isak is true, but he was my friend, and a very good friend he was. He gave his life to heal the damage we had all done. He died in a chamber beneath our feet while tens of thousands fell on the slopes of this hill. Your parents and Vesna have come here to remember Isak, along with all the others who died on that terrible day. The memory scars all those who survived—remember that and be gentle with your mother and father."

Mihn gestured to the flat stone beside him. "Stay here a while, think of Isak and all the others. If you want to join the Sisters of Dusk, you must always remember those who died, and protect their sacrifice. Remember them at Silvernight especially; that was his birthday."

"Did Isak . . . Did he write this?"

Mihn shook his head. "The words are mine, but I think he would be happy with how we remember him. He always wanted to be more than just a white-eye, more than the warrior he was born to be. He gave his soul to do just that, leaving nothing to pass into the lands of no time. All that is left of him is the light he burned into me, and the memories in those who loved him. You see Hulf, roaming these hills? He could not bear Isak's loss. The two shared one wild soul, so I made Hulf a part of me too, and the light is within us both now."

He gestured to the words on the stone. "This is how I remember all of those who died here, men and woman, friends and strangers. I must go and speak to the others now. Legana will stay with you."

Gennay felt the prickle of tears. It wasn't only her parents who had suffered in the wars, she knew that: Uncle Veil was missing a hand, Old Carel his whole arm, and Aunt Dash was half-crippled too. Gennay could scarcely believe the withered woman had fought here too, but none of her parents' friends would dare make an idle boast like that; she knew that for certain.

She was too young to remember much about the old king, but she knew he had been badly hurt too. In Narkang men and women bore their battle injuries with quiet pride, even now, all these years later. They had all suffered; they had watched their friends die, seen cities fall and armies slaughtered. She couldn't begin to imagine any of that, but she had seen the look on their faces when they remembered, and just thinking of that now made the tears run down her cheeks.

As Gennay slowly read the words before her, she tried to conjure an image of Isak as her parents had painted him: a Farlan white-eye, Chosen of Nartis for a time—though he'd been not many winters older than her brother, Manayaz, was now.

He was tall and brooding, her mother had said when Gennay had asked. *Reckless and quarrelsome*, her father had added, *and as scarred as the rest of us put together*, Uncle Veil had contributed, to general agreement, but they had done so with smiles on their faces, even old Carel, who didn't smile at much.

So that was what she pictured: a big, frightening man perhaps, but young and uncertain as well, with the same sort of foolish, lazy grin as King Sebetin, who won friends as easily as breathing. And one who had given his life for his friends.

Legana arrived beside Gennay and gently squeezed her shoulder, then she reached out and ran her pale fingers over the stone, touching each word in turn as though bringing them to life in her mute world. In the far distance the silver dog ran, as swift and free as the wind.

Gennay read the words aloud for all of them, for the tens of thousands who had died on the plain, and for the smiling white-eye in her mind.

In the long dusk I dream,
Of joy, of love and life.
The shape of things,
Their colours, lights and shades;
These sights eternal,
Look ye also while life lasts.

ACKNOWLEDGMENTS (PART TWO)

OK, SO I HAVE TO ADMIT that many other people have put a huge amount of work into the Twilight Reign. Without their efforts and dedication the series might never have come about and it certainly wouldn't be the thing of pride for me that it is now. I barely know where to start, but two figures stand out:

Firstly my lovely wife, Fiona, without whom I'd no doubt be a borderline psychotic and malnourished recluse. Well, more so anyway. It's easy to get drawn into the world you're writing about and forget about what's actually important. It's been a relentless effort on her part to keep me cheerful and engaged with real life while I worked through this project of a million words—and an effort for which I'm hugely grateful.

The other woman whose-word-I-must-obey-because-she's-always-going-to-be-right-and-arguing-only-makes-it-worse is Jo Fletcher; beloved editor whose portrait would no doubt hang, Lenin-like, in Death's office if He had one. She gave me my chance and made damn sure I didn't waste it, improving the books at every step and being my most vocal champion in an industry where obscurity kills most careers.

Along the way have been so many others who also deserve thanks, particularly: Louise Gould who stepped into the breach to edit this last book when all sensible advice would be to run away, my entire (and extended) family who've all been hugely supportive, and Pyr *Über*editor Lou Anders for all his work, advice and enthusiasm on the other side of the pond. Also Simon Spanton for taking up the reins at Gollancz, Gillian Redfearn, Charlie Panayiotou, Jon Weir, and all the rest at Gollancz and Pyr, plus agents John Parker and Simon Kavanagh, and website supremo Robin Morero.

Not to be forgotten are my long-suffering readers—particularly Nathaniel Davies and Richard Lloyd-Williams, but also Steve Diamond,

Simon Kavanagh and Sarah Mulryan. Additionally thanks to those writers I like to think have over the years become, well, people I've met: Joe Abercrombie, James Barclay, David Devereux, Jaine Fenn, Suzanne McLeod and the many others on the Gollancz list who combine to make it far more than a collection of competitors.

About the Author

Tom Lloyd is the author of *The Stormcaller* and *The Twilight Herald* (books one and two of the Twilight Reign). He was born in 1979 in Berkshire. After a degree in International Relations he went straight into publishing where he still works. He never received the memo about suitable jobs for writers and consequently has never been a kitchen-hand, hospital porter, pigeon hunter, or secret agent. He lives in South London, isn't one of those authors who gives a damn about the history of the font used in his books, and only believes in forms of exercise that allow him to hit something. Visit him online at www.tomlloyd.co.uk.